O F
L O V E
A N D
L I F E

OF
LOVE
AND
LIFE

Three novels selected and condensed
by Reader's Digest

CONDENSED BOOKS DIVISION

The Reader's Digest Association Limited, London

The Reader's Digest Association Limited
11 Westferry Circus, Canary Wharf, London E14 4HE

www.readersdigest.co.uk

ISBN 0-276-42654-1

For information as to ownership of copyright in the material of
this book, and acknowledgments, see last page.

CONTENTS

MARCIA WILLETT

A WEEK IN WINTER

Thirty years ago, Hector Todhunter
introduced his new bride, Maudie, to his
family, less than a year after the death of
his first wife. Ever since that moment,
Maudie has endured the bitter hatred of
Hector's daughters, especially Selina's.
Now alone and short of money, she has
no option but to sell Moorgate, Hector's
beloved family home. But in doing so
Maudie knows she will unleash Selina's
pent-up wrath as never before.

PROLOGUE

THE LONE WALKER ON THE HILL shivered a little. The sun had set long since, sinking gently, received by plump, cushiony clouds above a fiery sea. The glow was all about him, transforming these bleak moorland heights with a golden light. Far below, where lanes and tracks weaved and curled, shouts and laughter drifted up into the clear air. He paused for a moment, dragging his gloves from his pocket, watching the small figures of men as they prepared to stop work for the day.

The old house, built at the moor gate in the shadow of the hills, was being renovated. Even from this distance he could see the evidence of it in the yard: piles of timber, a bonfire still smoking, ladders and scaffolding. A schoolmaster, recently widowed, he'd walked these paths for years, during holidays, and could remember when the cream-washed walls had been bare granite and the yard full of cows. He'd heard the voices of children as they'd clambered on the swing beside the escallonia hedge and seen smoke rising from the chimney on cold autumn evenings.

Now, an agent's board leaned against the low stone wall that bordered the narrow lane, and the workmen were ready to go home. A pick-up idled in the yard while someone opened the farm gate. The truck was driven through the gateway, waiting while the gate was shut and the man safely aboard before disappearing behind the shoulder of the hill.

A sudden gust of cold wind came snaking over the moors. The walker drew his collar more closely about his throat and walked briskly onwards, his face to the west. A handful of chill rain made him blink and he began to hurry, his mind on supper, his landlady's warm kitchen, hot, strong tea and the comforting smell of cooking.

He did not see the muffled figure crossing the moor below the house, pausing within the shadow of the thorn hedge, climbing swiftly over the dry-stone wall.

The clouds gathered overhead and the rain began to fall steadily.

PART ONE
CHAPTER ONE

MAUDIE TODHUNTER poured herself some coffee, sliced the top neatly from her egg and settled herself to look at her letters. A promising selection lay beside her plate this morning: a satisfyingly bulky package from The Scotch House, a blue envelope bearing her step-granddaughter's spiky writing, and a more businesslike missive stamped with an estate agent's logo. She slit open Posy's card with the butter knife and propped it against the marmalade. Posy's writing required concentration.

Don't forget, she had written, *that you promised to think about Polonius. Pleeeze, Maudie! . . .*

Maudie plunged her spoon into the yolk of her boiled egg and shuddered. The idea of housing the boisterous Polonius, a large English mastiff rescued by Posy during the Easter holidays, filled her with horror.

'I am not a dog person,' she'd told Posy severely. 'You know that.'

'Well, you should be,' Posy had retorted. 'Taking him for walks would keep your weight down. You told me you can't get into half your clothes. Anyway, it's only for term times. Mum's promised I can have him at home for the holidays if I can find a home for him during the term. Mind you, she'll be spitting nails if she knows you've agreed to have him . . .'

Maudie chuckled as she spread marmalade on her toast. Selina had fought hard to prevent the alliance between her stepmother and Posy, but their mutual affection had been too strong for her. As soon as she was old enough to be independent, Posy had spent as much time as she could with Maudie, ignoring her mother's sulks and fielding her accusations of disloyalty. Posy was bright enough to know that Maudie might well house Polonius simply to irritate Selina.

Resisting such a temptation, Maudie opened the package. Soft squares of tartan tumbled onto the table. Distracted from her breakfast,

Maudie caressed the fine woollen samples. She examined them closely, reading the descriptions on the white labels stuck to each square: Muted Blue Douglas, Ancient Campbell, Hunting Fraser, Dress MacKenzie. They slid over her fingers and lay among the toast crumbs. Miss Grey at The Scotch House had done her proud as usual.

'Something different,' Maudie had pleaded. 'Not dull old Black Watch.'

Maudie had been a customer at The Scotch House for years, and her measurements were kept on file. Tall, with a generous bosom and long legs, Maudie remembered the good old days when clothes could be made to measure without costing the earth. She had a passion for fabric: supple tweed in earthy shades, nubbly raw silk the colour of clotted cream, crisp white cotton, cherry-red lambswool.

'You're so understated,' Hector had said once. 'Not like Hilda . . .'

No, not like Hilda, who'd loved floral prints and fussy frocks with pussycat bows; not like Hilda who held it an article of faith that a woman should make the best of herself at all times; who considered it a sacred duty to be good-tempered and forbearing at any cost. After a while, when Patricia and Selina made it painfully clear that she would never replace their dead mother, Maudie had made it almost a point of honour to be as different from Hilda as it was possible to be.

'Be patient,' Hector had pleaded. 'They're young. It's still raw for them and Hilda was such a wonderful mother.' Everyone had wanted her to know it, eager for her reaction: a wonderful mother, a wonderful wife, a wonderful friend. Even now Maudie struggled against the resentment that had festered intermittently for thirty years, corroding and insistent, clouding happiness, destroying peace—and now Hector was dead, too.

Maudie gathered up the scraps of material and thrust them back into the envelope. The rain that had swept up from the west last evening had passed to the north, and the sun was shining. From her table beside the French windows she could see cobwebs glinting in the hedges. A few leaves, golden and russet, were scattered on the lawn. The sun had not yet risen high enough to pierce the shadowy waters of the ponds, but the big square living room was bright and cheerful. Soon it would be cold enough to light the wood-burning stove, but not yet.

Maudie took up Posy's card again. The child's personality flowed out of the spiky letters, which carried the usual messages of affection, cloaked beneath sharp observations and teasing remarks. She refused to allow any concessions to Maudie's advancing years—'I'm seventy-two, child!' protestingly. 'So?' impatiently—and was now suggesting that Maudie should drive to Winchester to see her new quarters, meet her fellow students and share a pint or two at the local pub. *We're in this old Victorian house,* she wrote. *It's fab. You'll like Jude. He's doing theatre studies with me, and there's Jo, who's doing art. She's cool. I've got this big room to myself on the top floor. It's great to be out of Hall and independent. You've got to come, Maudie . . .*

She laid the card aside and looked almost indifferently at the last letter bearing a Truro postmark. Far too early, surely, for the agents to have a buyer? Moorgate still had the workmen in, although they were at the clearing-up stage in the house itself. Hector had always insisted that she should have Moorgate. The London house should be sold and the proceeds divided between Patricia and Selina; Maudie would have an annuity and Moorgate—and, of course, The Hermitage.

Here, in this colonial-style bungalow built at the end of the nine-teenth century on the edge of woodland a few miles to the northwest of Bovey Tracey, she and Hector had spent their summers ever since he'd retired from the Diplomatic Corps. Maudie's father had bought it for his own retreats from his desk in Whitehall, and Maudie had always declared that she would live in it if anything happened to Hector. Her friends had not believed her. 'Haven't you heard?' they said now to one another. 'Maudie's gone native in a wooden bungalow in the wilds of Devon . . . I know. I couldn't believe it either. Mind you, she was always a bit odd. Terrific fun, but underneath . . . Not *quite* cut out for the motherly bit and I wonder if she didn't give darling Hector a hard time.'

Maudie knew what they were saying and revelled in it. Once married to Hector she'd acquired a reputation for tactlessness, laughing at the wrong moment, a worrying lack of respect for the hierarchy, while on the domestic front she was startlingly naive. Dinner parties for twenty diplomats and their wives, bazaars, the children's Christmas party were out of her ken. The men liked her—though some feared her—despite these failings. Those years she'd spent at Bletchley Park during the war, and her subsequent appointment as assistant to a well-known physicist in America, lent her an odd glamour that some of the wives resented.

'And that's what attracted Hector,' murmured Maudie, picking up the long white envelope. 'After Hilda's perfection in the home he couldn't resist the opportunity for fun. And we did have fun when the girls weren't around to disapprove and make him feel guilty.'

There had been more disapproval—especially from Selina—when they learned that Moorgate was to be left to Maudie.

'My whole childhood is wrapped up in that place,' Selina had declared. 'We always spent the summer at Moorgate with Mummy.'

'But what would you do with it?' asked her husband, trying to suppress his embarrassment. 'It's been agreed that Maudie should sell the house in Arlington Road. What more do you want?'

Maudie had appreciated his partisanship but had no wish to be made out as a martyr. 'I wouldn't want to stay in London without Hector,' she'd said abruptly. 'But you and Patricia will get far more for that place than you would for an old farmhouse on the edge of Bodmin Moor.' She'd smiled grimly. 'Or do you feel that you should have *both* houses, Selina?'

'Of course she doesn't.' Patrick had been horrified. 'For heaven's sake! Hector is being scrupulously fair . . .'

'To me? Or to the girls?' Maudie had looked innocently enquiring.

'I meant, well, given the circumstances . . .' Patrick had grappled with his confusion until Maudie had released him from his misery.

'I shall have my father's house in Devon and an annuity. Moorgate is my insurance policy. Hector knows that neither Patricia nor Selina would ever use it or afford to keep it without a tenant in it.' Maudie had shrugged, preparing to leave. 'Shall I tell your father that you're unhappy about his plans?' She'd warded off Patrick's protestations and beamed into Selina's sulky face. At the door she'd paused. 'So *taxing*, deciding what other people should do with their belongings, isn't it?'

Remembering the scene, Maudie chuckled again, briefly, then grew sober. What would Selina say when she discovered that Moorgate was to be put on the market? The elderly tenants had died and Maudie had brooded long as to whether she should relet it or sell it. Expediency forced her hand. The bungalow needed a new roof and her car should have been replaced long since. She would sell Moorgate. It would be a comfort to have a cushion between herself and the sharp realities of life.

As she slit open the envelope and drew out the sheet of paper, Maudie wondered again what had happened to those investments of which Hector had told her years ago. She hadn't taken much notice at the time, but he had been scrupulous in showing her the extent of his portfolio. He wasn't wealthy, but she knew that even after the purchase of her annuity there should have been certain shares, which had not, after all, been mentioned in his will. Could he have changed his mind and given them to the girls much earlier? As usual she dismissed this recurring thought. Surely Selina could not have resisted displaying her triumph to her stepmother. Yet it seemed impossible to imagine Hector having financial problems that he had hidden from her. She pushed the nagging question aside and read the letter from the agents in Truro.

. . . the work inside the house is almost finished and we have erected a board to tempt passers-by. However, Moorgate being in such a remote location, we shall be relying on advertising. There is a problem about keys to the office, storeroom and cloakroom. It will be necessary to allow clients to view this area. Mr Abbot has been intending to contact you about it since he is unable to renovate this part of the house. Perhaps you would be so kind as to contact me.

Maudie frowned. Surely she'd given Rob Abbot the full set of keys, having kept one spare front-door key for herself and one for the agents? Rob wasn't the sort to mislay keys. Aged about thirty-five, tall, tough, with a keen sense of humour, he'd appealed to her at once. He'd looked over Moorgate, making notes, cracking jokes, telling her that he'd given up his engineering job in London after promotion had made him more of an administrator than an engineer.

'Boardroom politics aren't my scene,' he'd said cheerfully. 'I like getting my hands dirty. So I've come West to make my fortune.'

'Well, you won't make it at my expense,' she'd answered tartly. 'I can't afford to spend too much.'

'You'll be a fool if you don't do it properly,' he'd said. 'This old place is worth it. You'll get your money back twice over, believe me.'

She'd listened to him, making tea for them both in the huge, bare kitchen, and then they'd gone from room to room while he showed her what might be done. His ideas were simple but good and she decided, with one or two restrictions, that she'd allow him to go ahead if his price were reasonable. He'd encouraged her to visit two other properties he'd renovated and she was privately impressed.

He'd grinned at her. 'When I've finished you won't want to sell.'

'Then you won't get paid,' she'd answered. 'Send me an estimate and I'll think about it.'

That had been at the beginning of the summer. It was time to make a visit to Moorgate, to meet Rob again and to check out his work. She would drive down to Cornwall, sort out the problem of the key. She removed her spectacles, collected her post together and, rising from the breakfast table, went to make a telephone call.

The enthusiastic voice of the young agent in the office in Truro rattled on in Maudie's ear. 'It's an absolutely super property, Lady Todhunter, quite my favourite. I can't wait to start marketing it properly. It's just this thing about the keys to the office . . .'

'I quite understand, Mr . . . ?' She peered at the name typed beneath the scrawled signature on the letter. 'Mr Cruikshank, is it? . . . Oh, very well, then, Ned. I understand that keys are missing but I don't have spares for the office and side door. What does Mr Abbot say about it?'

'He can't remember ever having them.'

Maudie frowned. 'I'm certain I gave him the whole set. As I recall, there was only ever the one complete set of keys and I thought it sensible for Mr Abbot to have them until he'd finished. I kept one front-door key for myself and gave you the other. How very tiresome.'

'Couldn't there be another set somewhere?' he suggested diffidently. 'Knocking about at the back of a drawer or something?'

'I suppose there's a chance my husband had another set somewhere.'

'Perhaps you could ask him.' Ned sounded hopeful.

'Rather tricky, under the circumstances,' said Maudie drily. 'He's dead . . . No, no. Don't apologise.' She felt a stab of remorse for her abruptness. 'How could you possibly know? I'll look about for the keys but I'm not at all sanguine. Everything was sorted out when I moved down from London, you see, but I'll make absolutely certain. No, not a nuisance . . . Don't give it a thought . . . Yes, I'll be in touch.'

She replaced the receiver and returned to the table, picking up the tray and piling up the breakfast things. Pausing to watch a nuthatch on the bird table, she was distracted for a moment from the problems at Moorgate. She loved this big, sunny living room, which opened onto the verandah and the garden. An adequate-sized kitchen, a bathroom, a tiny cloakroom, two bedrooms and a box-room made up the rest of the accommodation, but it was big enough for Maudie. Each holiday Hector had chafed at its lack of space, at the impossibility of giving parties.

'For heaven's sake,' she'd cry impatiently, 'we're only here for a few weeks. Surely you can survive without them?'

He'd smile repentantly. 'Withdrawal symptoms,' he'd say. 'Give me a day or two . . .' But he'd never been able to hide his pleasure and anticipation as the day for their return to London drew near.

Maudie took the tray into the kitchen and unloaded the contents onto the draining board. Hector had always been at his best surrounded by people. Maudie was happier in a more intimate setting. Nevertheless, they'd managed pretty well, given that Maudie had never entertained more than six people at a time before she'd met Hector. Naturally, Hilda had been the perfect hostess . . .

The sudden jet of hot water, splashing against the back of a spoon, sprayed Maudie's jersey and she cursed sharply, turning off the tap. How pointless it was to feel such antagonism towards a woman who had been dead for more than thirty years. Dying young—well, forty-four was fairly young—seemed to hallow the dead with a kind of immunity. They were always ahead of the game, one point up. Maudie bashed the dishes about in the hot soapy water. Even now, with Hilda and Hector both dead, she still felt the frustration of what she called 'second-wife syndrome'. Perhaps it would have been easier to deal with if Selina had been prepared to meet her halfway. Patricia had been tolerant enough. She was simply too immersed, at sixteen, in her own growing-up to make any efforts to make Maudie feel part of the family. Selina had demanded her sister's partisanship, however, and Patricia, through loyalty or indifference, had added her weight to Selina's resistance.

Drying the dishes, Maudie struggled for rationality. It had been difficult for Hector to remain unmoved by his daughters' hostility. Patricia's attacks had been spasmodic but Selina had waged a determined, unflinching war. At twelve she'd missed her mother terribly and had no intention of sharing her father with this stranger. It was unfortunate that she'd started at boarding school in the autumn following the wedding so that, although it had been arranged for years, she could always blame Maudie for packing her off to school in true wicked-stepmother style.

'Absolute rubbish!' Hector had shouted, driven to distraction by Selina's tears and recriminations. 'You knew that you'd be going away to school next term. Patricia went at thirteen and you were perfectly happy about it until now. You know that I've been posted to Geneva and that Mummy would have wanted you to be settled with Patricia at school by the time I leave. It has absolutely nothing to do with Maudie.'

He'd slammed himself into his study leaving Selina, tear-stained and furious, outside the door.

'Look,' Maudie had said awkwardly, 'I know it's hard to understand but he feels it too, you know.'

Selina's face was stony. 'I hate you,' she'd said, quietly lest Hector should hear, 'and I wish it was you who was dead.'

'I expect you do,' Maudie had answered cheerfully. 'But while we're waiting for that happy event can't we try to be friends?'

Selina had not bothered to reply but had gone away to her room, locking herself in, refusing to come down to lunch, and the house had been wrapped in an atmosphere of gloom and ill-feeling until the term started. Oh, the joy of being alone with Hector, ghosts and guilt banished—only temporarily, however. Both would be resurrected with monotonous regularity at half terms and each holiday.

'We must be patient,' Hector had insisted—also with monotonous regularity. 'After all, at least we get the term times to ourselves.'

Hanging up the dishcloth Maudie smiled secretly to herself. What fun they'd had; careless, selfish, glorious fun.

'I have to admit,' he'd said once, 'that it's rather nice not to be worrying about the girls all the time. If Hilda had a fault it was that she used to fuss about them.'

'What's this heresy?' she'd asked, laughing. 'Can it be true? Hilda wasn't perfect, after all?' He'd descended at once into self-criticism and remorse, rehearsing a catalogue of Hilda's attributes, singing her praises, mourning her passing. She learned that it didn't do to hint, even light-heartedly, that she felt the least bit inadequate in the face of such perfection. Instead she'd done what she was good at: she'd made him laugh, made him feel young, sexy, strong. Responsibility, grief, anxiety would slide away from him and he'd respond in such a way that her own esteem would soar again and she'd feel needed, desired, witty, vital. It hadn't been easy, after all, to give up her own career, to become a diplomat's wife and stepmother to his ungrateful, tiresome daughters.

Although, at the start, it had been only too easy. She'd been on her way home to England for leave following the retirement of the physicist for whom she'd worked for fifteen years. It was Christmas, and the airport was closed by snow. Disgruntled passengers huddled together while Hector . . . 'hectored', as Maudie had said to him afterwards. 'You hectored the staff and bullied them into finding us accommodation.'

'Perfectly reasonable,' he'd said. 'You didn't refuse a nice warm bed, if I remember rightly.'

It was odd—and altogether delightful—how she and Hector had so quickly drawn together. Laughing, sharing his hip flask, making light of the difficulties—the brief episode had been romantic, unreal, yet afterwards they'd refused to be separated. Maudie had given up her career and Hector had risked the disapproval of friends and family so that he and Maudie could be married twelve months after the death of his wife.

'It might be tricky,' he'd admitted anxiously as they'd driven to meet Hilda's mother and the girls. 'It'll come as a bit of a shock. Everyone adored Hilda . . .'

It was only then that she'd realised that their life together was to be a delicate balance, a seesaw of emotions. There was the Hector that she knew, lover and companion, and the Hector who was the responsible elder son, adored father, admired friend, respected colleague.

'I feel that nobody really looks upon me as Hector's wife,' Maudie had once said to Daphne. 'It's as if there's something illicit about the whole thing; that Hilda was his official wife and I'm regarded as his mistress.'

'Sounds good to me,' Daphne had replied. 'Much more fun.'

Daphne had been the one who had done her best to make her feel at home: Daphne, who was Hilda's oldest friend and Patricia's godmother.

'You might have a problem with Daphne,' Hector had warned as they'd waited for their guests at the official cocktail party in Geneva. 'She and Hilda were at school together. They were like sisters.'

He'd been clearly uneasy at that first meeting, awkward during introductions, but Daphne had taken Maudie's hands readily, smilingly, although her gaze had been very direct, searching.

'How clever of you, Hector,' she'd murmured. 'How very clever.' And she'd leaned forward to kiss Maudie's cheek.

Even now, Maudie could remember the warmth she'd felt at Daphne's brief embrace, a warmth that had thawed her wariness.

'I like Daphne,' she'd said later, over their nightcap, and Hector had taken a deep breath, clearly relieved.

'It all went off very well,' he'd admitted. 'Very well indeed.'

Daphne had become her closest friend, her ally in the ongoing battle with Selina, her defender against the whispers of Hilda's supporters.

'After all,' Maudie had said, 'it's not as if Hector divorced the blasted woman, abandoned her for me. He was a widower, for God's sake!'

'Oh, my dear.' Daphne had looked rueful. 'Can't you see the threat you are to us old wifies? Hector's found himself a younger, attractive woman who can't cook, doesn't want children, can't tell the difference between His Excellency and the gardener and *he doesn't give a damn*. He's clearly enjoying himself enormously and looks ten years younger.'

'But why can't people just leave us alone?' Maudie had asked.

Daphne had shaken her head. 'We're all so insecure, you see. You have come amongst us and upset the apple cart. You're so confident, so sure. Some people are simply not able to cope with it.'

'I'm not nearly as confident as you imagine,' Maudie had said crossly. 'Being a second wife and a stepmother can be hell.'

'Ah, but you're not admitting it. You're not confiding in all those wives who would love to advise . . .'

'And gloat, privately together, afterwards.'

'Well, there you have it. So why do you admit it to me?'

'Because you're different,' Maudie had said. 'I trust you.' And Daphne had laughed then, laughed until Maudie had felt almost uneasy.

'I know it's odd that I should trust you,' she'd said almost defensively, 'you being Hilda's closest friend. But I do.'

'I agree that it's odd. I loved Hilda, I really did. We started at boarding school together, and I spent a great many holidays with her family while mine were abroad. But she was a serious girl, rather prim and proper, and as she grew older this developed into a complacency which, if I'm honest, could be irritating. There, how's that for disloyalty?'

'Not a bad effort for a beginner,' Maudie had answered, grinning, 'but I'm sure you could do better if you were to try harder.'

Daphne had hesitated—and then laughed. 'You are a wicked girl,' she said. 'Hector's a lucky man. He's clearly a very happy one.'

Had he been happy? Maudie took her jacket from the peg inside the door and rummaged in her bag for the car keys. What about those endless rows over Selina? Those accusations he'd hurled at her: that she was unsympathetic, cold, selfish? What about those times that he'd gone alone to see his daughter and her children because Selina complained that Maudie was so critical, so unaffectionate that the boys were frightened of her? What about the pain when she realised that Hector was beginning to take Selina's word against her own?

'Over,' Maudie said loudly, as she stepped outside and slammed the door. 'Over, over, over!'

So why, asked the small voice inside her head, why are you still angry?

'Shut up,' said Maudie. 'I will not do this. I am going to enjoy myself. Go away and leave me alone.'

She opened the door of the large shed that housed the car, drove slowly down the long drive and headed west towards Bodmin Moor.

CHAPTER TWO

THE FARMHOUSE STOOD in a small hollow beside the narrow lane. At the end of the garden, by the dry-stone wall, two granite pillars—the moor gate—leaned either side of a cattle grid, beyond which the lane climbed steeply to the moor. Maudie parked the car by the gate to the yard and climbed out. A pick-up stood next to the open-fronted barn and a bonfire smoked sulkily. It was a grey, misty day, and a brooding quiet lay over the countryside. In this land of granite and slate the cream-washed walls struck a warm note, and the old farmhouse had an air of permanency and safety, a place of refuge in an inhospitable environment.

On a hot summer's day it was an idyllic place to be, but in winter, with the wind screaming from the west, it was bleak. Left empty, the farmhouse would become damp and uninhabitable. It needed to be lived in, kept dry and warm, used as a home, not a holiday retreat.

'Mummy adored Moorgate,' Selina had been fond of repeating. 'Her family owned it when she was a little girl and she used to stay with the farmer and his wife. Then, when they retired, we kept it as a holiday home. We went there every summer, Mummy, me and Patricia. Daddy joined us when he could. We must never get rid of Moorgate.'

Even after the sale of the London house Selina kept a watching brief from a distance.

'Pure dog-in-the-manger,' Maudie had observed crossly to Daphne, after one of these sessions down memory lane with her stepdaughter. 'She hasn't been there for years. Sentimental hogwash. There was no problem when the house in Arlington Road was sold. Yet she spent much more time there with Hilda than down at Moorgate.'

'I suppose that childhood summers are always invested with a kind of glamour,' Daphne had answered thoughtfully. 'The sun was always shining. The sea was warm and adventure was always round the corner.'

'Thank you, Enid Blyton,' Maudie had said acidly.

Nevertheless, she had not yet told Selina that Moorgate was about to be put up for sale. Now, as she wandered into the yard and stood looking about her, she felt sad that the old farmhouse should pass out of the family. Posy loved it too, and for Posy's sake she wished she could keep it. Yet it would be crazy to hold on to a property that none of them could enjoy. If she kept Moorgate it must be let—so what was the point? Better to sell and be able to help Posy financially later on.

Rob Abbot came striding round the corner of the house and she gave a gasp of surprise. She could see that she'd startled him, too. He frowned a little—and then came towards her, a smile hovering on his lips.

'Come to check up on me?' he asked lightly.

Maudie grinned. 'Thought I'd catch you slacking,' she said. 'Mr Cruikshank's been wittering on about keys. I couldn't get you on your mobile so I thought I'd drive down and see if we could sort this out.'

'He's been here,' said Rob grimly. 'Poking around, rattling door handles, peering through windows. I told him that I can't break down doors without your permission. You know, I'm sure I've never had those keys.'

'It's a mystery.' Maudie shrugged. 'If they weren't on the big ring I gave you then I simply haven't a clue what I did with them. We'll have to force the locks. As I remember, there's a door from the kitchen that leads into a passage to the office. There was a small cloakroom, I think, and a kind of storeroom which had an outside door.'

'Both doors are firmly locked,' said Rob. 'And the window has a curtain pulled across it. You can't see in.'

'Can't we just break the window and get in that way?'

Rob looked doubtful. 'It's too small to climb through. Anyway, we'll have a look at it now you're here.' He hesitated. 'I shouldn't leave the car in the lane. It's very narrow there and a tractor will probably be along in a minute. Pull her into the yard.'

He opened the gate for her and went away to put the kettle on. Maudie backed carefully through the gateway and parked beside the pick-up, and by the time she arrived in the kitchen the kettle was boiling and Rob was putting tea bags into mugs. She paused inside the door. The kitchen stretched almost the width of the house, and looked out across the moor to the sea. Empty, except for some built-in cupboards, the sink and the Esse range, it looked enormous, cavernous.

'It doesn't feel as cold as I'd expected,' Maudie said, accepting her mug. 'There's a warm atmosphere.' She sniffed at the air. 'And what's that smell . . . Bacon?' She shook her head. 'I'm imagining things.'

Rob was looking at her oddly. 'It's funny you should say that. I've had the same impression once or twice. I'm on my own here now, tidying up, and the lads have moved on to the next job, but I sometimes get the feeling that I'm not alone.' He chuckled, almost embarrassed. 'No stories of ghosts or hauntings, are there?'

She watched him as he turned away, sipping his tea, staring out across the moor, and felt a twinge of uneasiness. Rob Abbot was the last person in the world to let his imagination run away with him but he seemed rather distant today, not at all his usual joking self.

'Of course not,' she said briskly. 'What nonsense. Are you certain that none of your men could have taken the keys, Rob? I have this feeling that there were several keys on a smaller ring, attached to the big one. Could you have taken them off and put them down somewhere?'

He turned back, frowning. 'It's possible. But why should anyone take them? The boys are as puzzled as I am. The house is empty, nothing to take, and it's clear that nobody's squatting in it. At the same time . . .'

'It's odd, isn't it?' She grimaced. 'Rather creepy. Come and show me the sitting room and then we'll decide what's to be done about the office. I hope you won't abandon me before it's done.'

'No, I shan't do that.' He put his mug down on the draining board. 'I wouldn't leave a job unfinished.'

'It's taken rather longer than you thought, hasn't it?' Maudie asked as they passed into the hall and she paused to look appreciatively at the restored oak staircase. 'You've done well, Rob. It looks right. Not like some tacky conversion. It's retained its dignity.'

He looked about him. 'She's like an elderly countrywoman,' he said affectionately. 'Strong, kindly, sheltering. She's not some passing fad for a townie who wants to pretend he's living the good life.'

Maudie glanced at him, touched by his warmth. 'The trouble is, now that the farmland has been sold off, Moorgate isn't really a farmhouse any more. And she's off the beaten track. I'm not certain who'd buy it.'

'No offers yet, then?' He led the way into the sitting room. The room faced southeast and the stone walls had been washed with cream paint. The oak floorboards had been stripped and polished, and the original wooden shutters were folded back on each side of the sash windows. 'Mr Cruikshank seems very keen.'

She laughed. 'He's young,' she said tolerantly. 'He'll get a lot of interest from the type of people you've just described, but it's a long way from London. Lots of people work from home these days, so maybe it'll attract a young family who can afford to ferry their children about and pay the heating bills. This warm, wet climate can do such harm.' She paused. 'Have you been lighting fires in here, Rob?'

In the inglenook fireplace were a few half-burnt logs and charred twigs in a pile of soft grey ash. Rob glanced at it indifferently.

'I had a trial run after the chimney sweep had been in, and in the other room, to make sure the fires were drawing properly. It doesn't do any harm to give the place a warm through. Actually, I was going to suggest that we light the Esse and have some background heat, if she hasn't sold in a month or two. I can pop over and keep an eye on her until you get a buyer.' He hesitated. 'If you want me to . . .'

'That would be very kind of you,' Maudie answered. 'It's not a bad idea to light the Esse. Better to pay for a bit of oil than have damp coming in. Should we have put in proper central heating, I wonder?'

'Too late now,' Rob said firmly. 'And it would have been expensive to lift these slate floors. Natural fires are best downstairs and the Esse runs two radiators upstairs and heats the kitchen. It's more than adequate with the night-storage radiators in the other bedrooms. Don't fuss.'

She grinned at him. 'Are you married?'

'No,' he answered shortly. 'What's that got to do with central heating?'

'Nothing.' She felt another twinge of uneasiness. It was unlike Rob to be so preoccupied. Perhaps he had woman trouble and her question had touched a nerve. 'Nothing at all. I'd better look at these locked doors, I suppose. Are you OK, Rob? Plenty of work coming in?'

'Too much, if anything.' He led the way back to the kitchen. 'I've fallen a bit behind schedule here, I'm afraid. The truth is, it's been an unusually dry summer and I've been giving the lads outside work on another site while I carried on inside here.'

'That's not a problem,' she said, anxious lest he should think she was criticising him. 'You've done splendidly.' She watched as he indicated the door to the office, turned the knob, put his weight against it and pushed. 'Yes, well, that's not going anywhere, is it?'

'It's a lovely old oak door and I don't want it broken,' he said. 'Come outside and see the other door. It's sturdy but not particularly worth saving. That's the one I'd go for. No point in smashing windows.'

Outside, on the path that ran along the side of the house, Maudie tried the unyielding door and attempted to peer through the grubby window. A fold of cloth obscured her view and she shook her head as she stepped back, dusting her hands.

'I take your point. What shall we do?'

'Better leave it to me,' he said. 'I'll get it opened, now I have your permission. We'll do as little damage as possible.'

'I'll tell Mr Cruikshank,' she said. 'Although if it's been locked up since the tenants left there might be things that need sorting out. You could try to break it down while I'm here.'

He frowned. 'I'd rather not leave the house with a broken door,' he said. 'Anyone would be able to get in. I wouldn't want to arrive tomorrow morning and find the house full of New Age travellers. There's a party of them up on Davidstow, so I've heard. Give me a chance to think about this. I want to be able to leave the place secure, whatever I do.'

'Sounds reasonable. Telephone me when you've done it and if you need me I'll come down.'

'I'll do that.' He looked at her, smiling a little. 'I promise not to sneak off with any treasures I find.'

She was pleased to see him relaxed again, less touchy. 'In that case,' she said, 'why don't we go down to the pub and have a pint and a sandwich before I go home?'

He laughed. 'Now there's an offer I can't refuse. I'll lock up and be right with you.'

Driving back towards Launceston, Maudie found herself rehearsing different ways of telling Selina that Moorgate was to be sold. Her fear was that, in a fit of misguided nostalgia, Selina might insist that she and Patrick should buy it. Despite the injection of cash from the sale of the London house, Maudie knew that her stepdaughter was not in a position to attempt such a quixotic act, not unless they intended to sell up and move to Cornwall. The idea of Selina living on the edge of Bodmin Moor made Maudie snort with laughter; childhood holidays were one thing, real life another. Selina's love of entertaining and being entertained demanded delicatessens, theatres, restaurants. It was unlikely that she and Patrick would make any such sacrifice. But Selina might insist that Moorgate should be kept as a place for holidays.

Looking out at the bleak moorland landscape, Maudie suddenly felt all the melancholy of the season. She knew that she was, once again, to be cast in the role of wicked stepmother. Patricia and Simon, happily settled in Australia, would receive letters and telephone calls reporting this latest calumny, and Selina's boys—Chris and Paul—would be prevailed upon to add their weight of disapproval. As she slowed to allow a sheep to meander across the road, Maudie shrugged. Patricia was too far away to lend more than token support, and the boys didn't give a damn about Moorgate and were too busy with their own lives to take action. For once, however, Posy might be on her mother's side.

Rain misted the windscreen, drifting across from the sea in thick vaporous clouds, obliterating the road ahead.

'Damn,' muttered Maudie, switching on the car's sidelights and turning the windscreen wiper to intermittent. 'Damn and blast.'

Driving carefully she cast her mind back to sunnier days: a glorious summer twenty years before, when she and Daphne had spent the holidays at Moorgate. Daphne's daughter, Emily, had been unwell and Selina, committed to assisting with the boys' school trip to Venice, had been let down by the au pair who was supposed to be looking after Posy. It was Hector who had suggested that they should all go to Moorgate: Maudie and Posy, Daphne and Emily. The sea air and walks on the moor would be good for them, he'd said, and somehow it had all been arranged. Hector and Philip, Daphne's husband, appeared at intervals— punctuation points in the long, hot days that slid seamlessly past.

Peering into the mist ahead, Maudie remembered the old wooden swing in the shade of the escallonia hedge where Emily would sit, idly pushing herself, dreaming about her forthcoming wedding, while Posy splashed about in the paddling pool. Daphne would lie on the old plaid rug, her book open across her chest, her eyes closed, as Maudie poured iced lemonade from a jug, the sunshine burning her arms. Later they would have an early supper in the huge, cool kitchen: Posy, newly scrubbed, drowsing in her highchair; Emily, bright-faced, describing her wedding gown; Daphne cutting new brown bread, placing a bowl of raspberries beside a dish of crusted, yellow clotted cream.

Darling Emily: what an enchanting bride she'd been at the end of that summer, drifting up the aisle in cloudy white, with small Posy staggering behind, the train clutched in hot, determined fists, a wreath of flowers askew over her eyes. Darling Emily, slender and fragile beside Tim's tall, broad-shouldered figure. The next summer they'd returned to Moorgate. Emily was pregnant and Tim had agreed that the country air would do her good. This time, however, Selina and the boys had been members of the party and Maudie and Daphne feared ructions. But by sheer good fortune, some of Selina's friends had taken a cottage at Rock and the boys had insisted that it was more fun to be on the golden sands with their chums than to be impeded by two old women, a young pregnant one and their small, tiresome sister. For a few years the pattern had continued, until Hector had decided that Moorgate should be let on a long lease.

Young though she'd been, Posy insisted that she could remember those summers. Her love for Moorgate was more genuine than Selina's, and Maudie dreaded breaking the news to her. Posy was her darling, the baby who had broken down her defences and made her vulnerable.

'We all have our favourites,' Daphne had said once, her eyes on Emily's sleeping, peaceful face. 'It's only natural, I suppose.'

Emily had been everyone's favourite, arriving long after Daphne and Philip had given up hope of having children. She had Daphne's short nose and small, square chin, her cornflower-blue eyes and blonde hair. She was beloved of old and young alike: sweet-tempered, merry-hearted, generous, fun. Daphne brooded over her with an odd mixture of delight, relief and gratitude that touched Maudie's heart.

'You are besotted with that child,' she'd said—and Daphne had looked almost guilty, defensive.

'She might so easily have been a boy,' she'd answered.

Maudie was surprised. 'You'd have loved him just the same.'

'Yes,' she'd replied quickly. 'Yes, of course. Only I'd always so longed for a little girl, you see.'

How anxious Daphne had been while Emily was having her babies; how relieved when it was over.

'It's a girl, Maudie,' she'd cried down the telephone. 'She looks just like Emily. Both quite well. Oh, thank God! Thank God!' She'd been quite hysterical with joy and relief.

The second time round it was another girl, just like her mother, but Daphne's reaction had been exactly the same. 'You have no idea how happy I am,' she'd said. 'Darling Emily . . .' and she'd burst into tears.

The third occasion had been quite different—but by then Tim was dead, killed in a car accident—and Emily was left with three children to support. They'd been living in Canada for ten years, and Daphne had rushed out to be with her. This baby was unplanned, the other two already in their teens, and there was no joy in Daphne's voice when she'd reported his premature birth. The long-distance call had been marred by crackles and Maudie had suspected that Daphne was crying.

'Daphne. Oh, Daphne, I'm so sorry.' She was almost shouting into the receiver. 'Oh, if only you weren't so far away.'

Hector had been standing beside her, his face creased with anxiety, and she'd shaken her head at him, indicating that she couldn't hear properly. He'd taken the receiver from her.

'Daphne,' he'd said. 'It's Hector. Don't cry, my dear. Try to be calm and tell us exactly the situation so that we can help you . . .' and Maudie had gone to pour herself a drink, comforted by his calm strength, knowing that Daphne would feel it, too, however serious the news.

Emily and baby Tim had survived, however, although Maudie had never seen him. There was no money for trips to England, but Daphne and Philip flew out to see them all every year.

'Why doesn't she come home?' Maudie had asked—but Daphne had shaken her head. The older children were settled in school and Emily was afraid that another upheaval, so soon after Tim's death, would be too much for them. Perhaps, later on . . .

Then Philip had died and Daphne had broken the news that she intended to go out to Canada, to make her home with Emily.

Now, as moorland gave way to farmland and small villages, and the clouds began to clear away, Maudie recalled the sense of desolation with which she'd listened to Daphne's plans.

'I know it's selfish of me,' she'd said later to Hector, 'but I can't imagine how I shall manage without her. We must go out and visit them.'

Not long after, however, Hector had become ill and the visit to Canada never happened. Daphne had flown home for the funeral and they had wept together, mourning not only Hector but their own pasts. Memories flooded back and they'd talked long into the night.

'Dear Hector,' Daphne had said at last. 'He was such fun. I'm so glad he had you, Maudie. You made him laugh and Hector loved to laugh.'

'We had some difficult moments over the girls,' sighed Maudie. 'I wish I had been more tolerant, but it hurt when he took Selina's side.'

'At least you've got Posy.' Daphne smiled, recalling Posy's protectiveness towards Maudie at the funeral. 'What a sweetie she is.'

'She's so like Hector. Black hair, brown eyes, not like her brothers at all; they look just like Patrick. I think Selina is irritated that none of her children looks like her. Odd things, genes.'

Afterwards, when Daphne had returned to Canada, Maudie had felt truly alone—yet, in another way, strangely relieved. During the eighteen months of Hector's illness he had become withdrawn and morose. She had struggled to remain cheerful and positive, but it had been a strain. In the last few months he had become confused, and at the end he had not known who she was. It seemed that he was reliving the years when he and Hilda were young. He became querulous, irritable, and occasionally tearful. When Selina came, he thought that she was Hilda and he'd mumbled, 'Forgive me, my dear. Forgive me,' over and over, until Maudie could bear it no longer and went to the kitchen to make tea.

Selina had come downstairs looking smug. 'Poor Daddy,' she'd said. 'Of course, Mummy was his first, true love. I think he felt guilty quite often, actually, for betraying her memory,' and Maudie, worn out with disturbed nights, frustrated and unhappy, had lost her frail hold on her temper. 'Don't be so bloody dramatic!' she'd shouted—and Selina had raised her eyebrows and gone away without her tea.

'Don't take any notice,' Daphne had pleaded, when Maudie told her. 'He's away with the fairies. It means nothing. He's too confused and sick to remember anything sensibly. You mustn't let it upset you, Maudie. Oh, if only I could be with you.'

'He talks about you,' Maudie had said, 'and Emily, too. He remembers everyone but me.'

'Oh, darling.' Daphne had sounded near to tears. 'Oh, Maudie, don't be hurt. I simply cannot bear it. Not being so far away. Please don't.'

'No, no I won't.' Maudie had tried to contain herself. 'It's just that wretched Selina enjoying every minute of it. I'm fine, honestly . . .'

What a comfort Daphne had been, even 3,000 miles away, but the fact remained that it was difficult to forget those terrible months, to remember the earlier years with Hector.

'I must not be bitter,' she muttered, turning the car onto the Moretonhampstead road. 'I must try to be balanced about it. If only I could understand his guilt. Why feel guilty about marrying again once Hilda was dead? Of course, Selina was the real problem. She kept his guilt alive. And what happened to that money? Damn! I will not do this.'

Deliberately she brought to mind the happy times before he was ill: dinner parties when Hector was at his sparkling best; holidays with Daphne and Philip; quiet days at The Hermitage. She delved further back: nights of love; snatched weekends away from the crowd; dinner for two at their favourite restaurant. It had been so easy to distract him, then, to make him laugh, to create a shared intimacy. She'd been confident that she could hold him, that his love could withstand Selina's undermining, and it wasn't until the boys were born that the cracks began to appear. With Patricia so far away, Selina held all the cards in the grandchildren game, and she was quick to take advantage.

'Darling, don't touch Maudie's skirt with those sticky fingers, you know she doesn't like it.' 'Could you hold Chris, Daddy? I know Maudie's so nervous with babies.' 'Paul couldn't help spilling his juice on the sofa, Maudie. He's only three, after all. Don't cry, Paul, Maudie's not really cross. She just doesn't understand little boys.'

If only Hector could have seen through it, realised it was simply the latest version of the feud. Maudie's lightest remarks were greeted with a cool silence, however, and the boys, growing noisy, spoilt, demanding, were encouraged to treat her as an outsider. She had few defences, no natural ease with children, no maternal instinct: not until Posy.

It was Patrick who had brought Posy over one Saturday afternoon, while Selina and the boys were at a party. He'd dumped her into Maudie's lap and gone off with Hector to look at a painting. Posy had lain contentedly, crooning to herself, staring up at Maudie with wide, honey-brown eyes: Hector's eyes. Her dark hair crisped about her head in peaks, like Hector's when he'd just come out of the shower. She made unintelligible Posy noises and smiled happily.

Sitting there, with the hot, heavy child in her arms, Maudie had felt an extraordinary sensation of warmth, wonder and longing. Carefully she'd drawn Posy closer and kissed her cheek. The child had chuckled delightfully, showing two tiny white teeth.

'Hello,' Maudie had said, feeling foolish. 'I'm Maudie. Hello, Posy. You are beautiful and I wish you were mine.'

'Any chance of tea, darling?' Hector had suddenly appeared, Patrick behind him. 'I'll look after Posy, won't I, my poppet?'

'No,' Maudie had insisted, holding on firmly. 'I'm looking after Posy. You make the tea'—and so it had started.

Maudie stretched herself, shaking off thoughts of the past, glancing at her watch: nearly half past four. She'd made good time and was looking forward to a cup of tea. It was a long drive to Moorgate, but worth the effort. Rob had made a splendid job of the old place. Settling herself more comfortably, switching on the radio, Maudie found herself wondering what could have happened to those keys.

Rob finished clearing up in the yard and looked about him. The morning had deteriorated into a dank afternoon, the mizzle settling into a steady rain. Soon it would be getting dark. He went into the house and passed through each room, pausing to look carefully about him. In the sitting room he frowned thoughtfully, then stepped across to the window and closed the heavy wooden shutters. He crossed the hall and went into the smaller living room, empty except for the wood-burning stove in the granite fireplace. Here, too, he closed the shutters before returning to the kitchen. He pottered for a while, clearing away the tea things, then locked the back door and drove away in the pick-up.

Fog rolled down upon the moor, filling the valleys, creeping among the trees. It muffled sound and covered the low-lying ground with a thick grey blanket of cloud. No one saw the figure emerge from the darker shadow of the dry-stone wall below the house, slip round to the side door and disappear inside.

Patrick Stone sat at the kitchen table, staring at a mug of cooling coffee, listening to his wife talking on the telephone in the room beyond the arch. He'd guessed at once to whom she was speaking. Only to Maudie did Selina use that brittle, cool voice. It was many years now since he'd realised that Maudie was not the cruel stepmother, the manipulative schemer, described to him by Selina. Well, he'd been young then, and passionately in love. They'd met in Winchester when she was nineteen, and at Miss Sprules's Secretarial College, and he, at twenty-four, had just embarked upon his first teaching post at a local school. He noticed her at evensong in the cathedral and a few days later at the Wykeham Arms. Selina was with a group of young people, one of whom he knew slightly, and soon he'd been integrated into the cheerful crowd. They'd paired off quickly and before long she'd begun to confide in him: how unhappy she was; the loss of her mother; the arrival of Maudie. How moved he'd been by her plight, how touched by her unhappiness.

Patrick snorted derisively and picked up his mug of coffee. How easy it had been, under the blinding influence of passion, to be shocked by her stories, to long to rescue her. How assured he'd been in convincing her that they were born for each other, how eloquent in persuading her father that he could make her happy. How long had it been before he'd learned that Selina was as vulnerable and sensitive as an armadillo? A year? Two, maybe? He shrugged, swallowing back the lukewarm liquid. What did it matter? By the time the truth had penetrated his resisting mind, the boys had been born and there was nothing for it but to carry on, working hard, concentrating on his children, hoping for promotion.

Now, he was over fifty years old and the children were grown up and gone. His responsibilities were surely at an end. Selina had lied to him and manipulated him for nearly thirty years. Now it was his turn. Now there was Mary: warm, cheerful Mary who suffered bravely, dealing with real hardship. She had an eight-year-old child who had been paralysed in an accident, whose father had abandoned them, and elderly parents who looked to her for support. She had worked for a year at Patrick's school as a supply teacher, on the days when her child was at the Care Centre, and friendship had grown up between them. As headmaster he was able to smooth her path, giving her extra hours, being as flexible as possible, and soon the friendship had become something deeper. It was she who held him in check. He talked of leaving Selina, throwing caution to the winds, but Mary refused to let him do anything he might regret.

'Let's give it a bit longer,' she'd insisted. 'You must be absolutely certain. It's such a big step and there's so much to think about. Please, Patrick, don't tell Selina about us, not yet. Wait a little longer.'

'There will never be a right time,' he'd said despairingly, putting his arms round her, and she'd held him tightly, anxiously.

Patrick raised his head as the telephone receiver went down with a click and Selina came into the kitchen.

'You'll never believe this,' she said, her jaw tight with suppressed fury and shock. 'Maudie is selling Moorgate. It's already up for sale, apparently, without a word to me. Oh, this is the end. The absolute end.'

He stirred, straightening his back. 'It's her house, after all.'

'Oh well, I'd expect you to be on her side.' She sat down suddenly at the table. 'I don't think I can bear it.'

'I expect she needs the money.' He tried to introduce some kindness into his voice, along with some reason. 'She only has an annuity, after all. Let's face it, you and Patricia got the lion's share. To be honest, I think old Hector was in the wrong there. He could have been fairer.'

She stared at him. 'We were his children. Some of the money came from Mummy's side. Why should she have it? Moorgate came from Mummy's family. What right does she have to sell my mother's house?'

'We've been through this so many times,' said Patrick wearily. 'You'd have preferred Maudie to be left with nothing, wouldn't you? After more than thirty years of marriage you'd have liked her to have been cut out of his will altogether. Good grief! What sort of man do you think your father was? He tried to be fair, despite your efforts, and you can't complain now if Maudie needs some cash. Let her do as she pleases with what's legally hers.'

'You know how I feel about Moorgate . . .'

'Do I not!' He got up abruptly. 'I'm going down the pub for a pint. Don't wait up.'

The door closed behind him but Selina remained seated, distracted for a moment from her grievance. This going down to the pub after some small scene was becoming a regular occurrence. Suspicion trickled into her mind and her eyes narrowed thoughtfully. Patrick had been touchy of late, unsympathetic, uninterested in her problems. It might simply be that he was missing Posy. She'd always been his favourite and it was odd, and certainly quiet, without her. Nevertheless . . . Suspicion, once roused, was not to be easily dismissed. Patrick had always been careful, alert to his wife's moods, anxious to placate, to soothe. Selina frowned. There had been precious little soothing this evening.

She shifted restlessly, folding her arms beneath her breasts. It was thoughtless of him to leave when he might have guessed that she'd want to talk. Patrick had once been very sympathetic, ready to try to understand what it must be like for a girl, hardly out of childhood, to lose her mother and then have her replaced by a sharp-tongued woman with no maternal qualities or sensitivity. Her face grew sullen, her thoughts with Maudie again, with Moorgate. Somehow the sale must be prevented. She would speak to Patricia, to the boys. If everyone contributed then maybe they could buy the place themselves. Selina brightened. What fun it would be to own the old house, to use it for holidays and to invite the gang for weekends. It was rather a long drive from London but it could be managed—and how impressed they'd be. It was a pity that Patrick had insisted that part of her share of the house in Arlington Road must be used to pay off their mortgage, but there was a little left, enough to put down as a deposit perhaps.

A sound of whining, a scrabbling at the back door, broke into these pleasant plans and her face grew surly again.

'Shut up,' she muttered. 'Bloody animal.' She raised her voice. 'Quiet!'

The whining ceased for a moment, to be replaced by a deep-throated bark, which rang round the courtyard and echoed up the street.

'For Christ's sake!' She hurried across and opened the door. Polonius barged past her, padding into the kitchen and through to the living room, subsiding on his rug in the corner, his mastiff's wrinkled face sad.

'You're for the chop,' Selina told him furiously. 'If Posy doesn't come up with something soon, you're going.'

At the sound of his mistress's name Polonius's ears cocked hopefully but, realising that she was not going to appear, he settled, groaning. Meanwhile, Selina had given herself an idea. Posy loved Moorgate. She, too, would be devastated to hear that Maudie was selling it. Perhaps Posy could influence Maudie, persuade her to drop the price.

Selina thought: I must be subtle. Posy loves Moorgate but she also loves Maudie. Perhaps I'll give her a buzz.

She went to the telephone, her mind busy preparing phrases, Patrick quite forgotten. She found her address book and Posy's Winchester number. Then she lifted the receiver and dialled.

Patrick was also speaking on the telephone, wedged against the coats hanging in the narrow passage that led to the men's loo, hunched so that he might be as private as possible.

'I had to speak to you.' He pressed the receiver hard against his ear to shut out the noise. 'I'm missing you. How are you? . . . I wish I could be with you . . . I know. I'm trying to be patient but I'm not certain what we're waiting for . . . OK, but I need to see you . . . No, I don't mean at school, I mean properly . . . Really? A whole weekend. Oh God, that's wonderful . . . Of course I want to, you idiot . . . Let's go away somewhere. You get so little chance with Stuart, and if he's being well looked after and having a lovely time, too, you won't feel guilty or anxious . . . I don't care much, do you? As long as we're together . . . Not too far out of London, though. We don't want to waste too much time driving . . . Oh, must you go? Is he? OK then. I love you, Mary. See you tomorrow.'

Maudie replaced the telephone receiver and went into the kitchen to pour herself a drink. She needed something a little stronger than tea or coffee after her conversation with Selina, and there was half a bottle of Chablis in the pantry. She poured a glassful, shocked to see that her hand was trembling a little.

'I'm getting old,' she muttered. 'I'm getting old when a run-in with Selina can really upset me.'

Maudie took her wine and went back to the sitting room. A series of chill, damp evenings had made up her mind to light the wood-burning stove, and the room was cosy and welcoming. She sat down and stared at the flames that flickered behind the stove's glass door. It was foolish to be upset. She'd guessed that the news would rake up Selina's grievances from the past, yet she felt unsettled. It was odd that now, when for the first time she was in a position to call the tune, there should be no pleasure in it, only this weary depression.

Her eye was caught by Posy's card, standing on the shelf above the fireplace, and she remembered the plea that she should give Polonius a home. She was filled with horror at the thought of his great form, lumbering about, but she knew that Selina would carry out her threat of rehousing him. Selina never hesitated to implement threats.

It was impossible, now, to offer Polonius a refuge without it being partly a guilt offering, a sop to her conscience. Posy cherished a dream that one day she might live at Moorgate with some gorgeous man and a brood of children, and Maudie felt sad that she must be the one to shatter it. She'd had her own dream of leaving Moorgate to Posy, but the cost of living dictated otherwise, and at least she'd be able to invest some money for Posy to help her later on. Meanwhile, she could help her out with Polonius, and if Posy detected some hidden agenda, well, there was nothing to be done about it. Anyway, she had to be told about Moorgate, and the idea of Selina getting in first with her version sent Maudie hurrying to the telephone again. A breathless Posy answered.

'Hi, babe,' she said warmly. 'Great timing. I've just this minute walked through the door. How are you? Did you get my card?'

'I did,' said Maudie, still finding it difficult to get used to the idea of being addressed as 'babe', 'and I've decided to give Polonius a try.'

Posy shrieked at the other end of the line. 'That's so great! Oh, that's really cool. Oh, Maudie, I'm just so grateful. Mum was being really mean last time we spoke. Listen. Can I bring him this weekend?'

'Well.' Maudie blinked, taken aback. 'Well, why not. But how?'

'Jude is coming down for the weekend to see friends in Exeter. I told you about Jude, didn't I? Well, he's got an old estate car for carrying props about. We'll be able to fit Polonius in the back. We can get up to London to fetch Polonius on Friday morning and be with you by about teatime. Jude can pick me up on his way back on Sunday. Is that OK?'

'That's fine.' Maudie swallowed. 'Listen, Posy, I've got some disappointing news. I'm having to put Moorgate on the market.' Silence. 'I know how you feel about it, my darling, but I simply need the money. I've done my sums and thought about it long and hard, but The Hermitage needs a new roof and there are other things . . . I'm so sorry.'

'Oh, Maudie.' Posy was struggling to come to terms with it.

'Don't think I want to do this, Posy. If there were any other way . . .'

'I know. Of course I know that, Maudie. You love it, too. Oh, hell . . . Hang on a sec. What?' Maudie could hear muffled voices in the background. 'Oh, OK . . . Look, Maudie, I've got to go. I'll see you on Friday and listen, babe, don't worry too much about Moorgate. We'll talk about it then. Bless you for Polonius. Love you lots. Bye.'

In tears Maudie sat down again by the fire.

'Oh, Posy,' she murmured. 'I love you, too.'

CHAPTER THREE

IT WAS ONLY AFTER POSY AND JUDE had left, driving away after tea on Sunday afternoon, that Maudie fully realised the true benefit of having Polonius to live with her.

'I'll get down as often as I can,' Posy promised, hugging her goodbye. 'Honestly. Oh, if *only* I had a car then I could get down midweek sometimes. I don't have any lectures on a Wednesday so I could come down on Tuesday night. Maybe Jude will lend me his car.'

Jude, a small, slight boy with a sweet smile, shook his head. 'No chance.' He winked at Maudie, jingling the car keys. 'Posy has no sympathy with mechanical things. She's broken the video, and the microwave will never be the same since she attempted to cook spaghetti in it.'

'Kill!' said Posy grimly to Polonius, pointing at Jude. 'Kill. Lunch. Go on, savage him.'

Polonius wagged his tail and Jude laughed. 'But she's great with dogs. Sorry to break up the party but we really ought to be going.'

'Are you sure you'll be OK, Maudie?' Posy looked anxiously at Polonius. 'I'm certain he'll be good.'

'Oh, he'll be good,' said Maudie cheerfully. 'Don't you worry about that. Off you go. It's been lovely to see you.'

'I'll be back very soon.' Posy was climbing in, reaching for her seat belt, winding down the window. 'No, Polonius. Stay. Good boy. Oh, Maudie, thanks so much for looking after him . . .'

Jude cut the farewells short by setting off down the drive. Waving, one hand on Polonius's collar, Maudie realised that she would see much more of Posy now. The thought made her feel more tolerant towards the mastiff with the wrinkled face who stood beside her, watching the car disappear, whining miserably.

'She'll be back soon,' Maudie told him. 'And now we're going to have a walk to take your mind off things. Just let me get my boots on . . .'

Talking comfortingly to him, she hauled him back into the house and presently they set out together. Polonius bounded ahead, overjoyed by such freedom after London streets, scattering fallen leaves. The silence of the woods was broken by the murmuring, ceaseless music of the River Bovey. The hound's lead round her neck, her hands thrust into the pockets of her jacket, Maudie strode behind him. Twenty-four hours with Posy had renewed her courage. She had been philosophical about Moorgate, sensing Maudie's distress, sympathising with her dilemma.

'Money's such a curse,' she'd said. 'I can quite see that you have to sell. Of *course* it would have been lovely to hang on to it . . .'

'I'd always hoped that you would have it eventually,' Maudie had answered wretchedly. 'Your mother is terribly upset, of course.'

'Yes, well, she would be, wouldn't she? I'm glad you'd told me before I saw her.' Posy had hesitated, embarrassed. 'The thing is, she's wondering if she can't afford to buy it herself.'

'Oh, no.' Maudie had shaken her head. 'This is what I feared.'

'I thought I'd better tell you. I didn't really want to but I think she's hoping that you might . . . well, back down a bit.'

'Back down?' She'd frowned impatiently. 'Back down how? I can't afford not to sell and I feel quite certain that Selina can't afford to buy it. Even if she could, I wouldn't encourage it. Not unless she and Patrick were prepared to sell up and live in it. They couldn't afford to run it and Selina would hate to have a tenant in. She'd want to use it for weekends and parties. Oh, it would be a disaster.'

'I know. I agree with you. And I told her so.'

Maudie had chuckled grimly. 'That must have gone down well.'

Posy had shrugged. 'We had a row. So what's new? Anyway, I thought I'd warn you. She's ringing round the family for support, but Dad thinks the whole thing's ridiculous. Try not to be upset, Maudie.'

'It's just that I'd hoped . . . I shall invest most of it for the future, and once the roof is done and the car sorted out, there might be some spare cash for you for any small thing you need. Oh, dear. I feel so—'

'Maudie!' Posy had interrupted warningly. 'You know we don't use the

G-word. It was our New Year's resolution. Remember? We were never going to feel guilty about Mum again. Or anything else.'

'How optimistic we were,' Maudie had sighed. 'It's because the house is not truly mine, I suppose. Perhaps I should move into Moorgate and sell The Hermitage. I wouldn't feel so badly then . . . No, no, Posy.' She'd felt even more remorseful as she saw the light that briefly rose and fell in Posy's eyes. 'Even for you I couldn't bury myself on Bodmin Moor. I sometimes wonder how much longer I can manage isolated here, but when I do move, it will be into Bovey.'

'I know that. Of course you will. It was just a mad moment. Let's forget about it. When are you coming to Winchester?'

As the late autumn afternoon faded into twilight Maudie felt determination and confidence returning. Selling Moorgate had opened old wounds, revived painful memories. She must strive to remember Hector without destructive doubts, refuse to allow Selina to wrongfoot her. The money from the sale would ease the financial situation, and it would be a comfort to have a sensible sum put by for her old age and for Posy.

Polonius appeared, dripping from the river, and shook himself vigorously all over her.

'Wretched animal,' she cried, wiping the cold drops from her face. 'Come on. Home, then.'

She turned back, her boots crunching over beech mast and dead leaves, Polonius loping beside her. A star twinkled high above, and tranquillity touched her anxious heart. They went together through the garden gate and into the house, and the door closed behind them.

Battling with administrative work, Patrick heard Selina's footsteps on the stairs with a now-familiar dread. It was guilt—what his daughter called the G-word—that caused the pit of his gut to contract. Part of him longed to shout the truth, have it out in the open, while the other, more cowardly, part of him feared exposure. Mary was frightened, too. What she had now—a tiny, rented ground-floor flat, her part-time job, a place for Stuart at the Care Centre three days a week—was painfully achieved, and she was terrified of losing it.

'I can't afford to mess it up,' she'd said. 'I know I sound selfish but I have to be, because of Stuart. I need to earn money and this flat is so convenient. The bus picks Stuart up at the door and I can walk to school and to see Mum and Dad. It's so difficult on public transport with a wheelchair and I can't afford to buy a car. It's not that I don't love you, Pat. I just can't see how it would work, being together.'

He'd held her hand, looking beyond her to where Stuart sat, immobile before the television set. How would the school governors react if they found out about the affair, if he announced that he was leaving his wife for one of the supply teachers? Would he or Mary be asked to leave? Perhaps they would both be dismissed.

'It's just not that easy, is it?' she'd asked, watching him—and he'd smiled quickly, attempting reassurance, convincing neither of them.

'I've been speaking to Patricia.' Selina was at the door. 'She's furious, of course. And she thinks it's a brilliant idea.'

He stared at her, puzzled. 'Thinks what's a brilliant idea?'

'Buying Moorgate,' said Selina impatiently. 'You know! My idea that we should all contribute and buy Moorgate ourselves.'

'Ah, I see.' Patrick turned on his swivel chair to look at her properly. 'And how much are they intending to contribute?'

'We didn't go into details. I just wanted to sound her out.'

'It's out of the question.' He turned back to his desk. 'Even if Patricia and Simon put a bit in, we still couldn't afford it. And what's the point? It's a long way to Cornwall. You might make an effort to get down for weekends in the summer, but it would stand empty all winter, getting damp. It's a ridiculous idea.'

'You think anything's ridiculous if it's out of the ordinary. You have no vision. No sense of adventure. You've always been afraid to take risks.'

'I married you, didn't I?' The words were out before he could prevent them. 'I'm sorry,' he muttered. 'That was unnecessary. But really, Selina, this is too much. Of course Patricia will agree with you. She's thousands of miles away. But do you seriously imagine that Patricia and Simon will sink money into an old farmhouse in Cornwall so that they can have a holiday in it once every three years? Dream on!'

Selina leaned against the door jamb, arms folded, and looked at him thoughtfully. Her instinct warned her that there were other issues involved here, and she considered carefully before she spoke.

'I realise it sounds crazy,' she said. Her voice was friendly, and he looked up at her, taken aback. 'But Moorgate really is special to me. OK,' she chuckled, holding up her hands as if warding off protest, 'I won't go over the past again. It's just that I had another idea about it. Look, I agree with you about Patricia and Simon, but I thought it was worth a phone call. No, my latest idea was that we should sell up here and move to Cornwall.' She smiled at the shock on his face, the fear in his eyes. 'It's a mind-bending thought, isn't it? But why not? You're always so tired and edgy lately, Patrick. I think your work is getting you down, and I'm worried about you. Wouldn't it be wonderful to live in the country for a change? Fresh air and peace and quiet. You could get a teaching job locally and we could be together, just the two of us. The kids could come down for weekends. They'd love it.' She watched him, her eyes cool, considering, mouth still smiling. 'I just feel that it's right. We're still young enough for the challenge of it, but old enough to be realistic.'

Silence stretched between them. She raised her eyebrows and he shook his head.

'It's . . . a bit of a shock,' he muttered, turning away, unable to meet her eyes any longer. 'I never thought I'd hear you say that you wanted to leave London. We need to think about it very carefully.'

'Do we?' She sounded amused. 'I don't think I do. Still, I can see I've surprised you. But don't think for too long, or we might miss the boat.'

She went away, closing the door gently, and Patrick continued to sit, head in hands, fear in his heart.

He thought: She's guessed that something is going on. What shall I do? Call her bluff and take a chance?

An image of Mary, singing as she fed Stuart, came to his mind. A word from Selina to the school governors and Mary might well be out of a job—and her flat, too, if she were unable to pay the rent. It hadn't been easy to persuade the landlord that Stuart would be no nuisance to the other tenants, that she could afford to pay her rent and was not dependent on benefit. Patrick clenched his fists and swore quietly; he could not put Mary at risk unless he could offer her as much or more than she had achieved for herself. On what grounds could he divorce Selina? Would he be obliged to continue to support her? Suppose he were to lose his job in the process?

Tired, frustrated, Patrick felt an overwhelming desire to weep. Mary had come into his life at a most vulnerable time. Missing his children, disillusioned with his career, bound to a wife he almost disliked, he'd been attracted by Mary's cheerful, realistic approach. He felt old and jaded as he watched her with the children, encouraging them, patient but lively. They responded to her enthusiasm and she was clearly in her element. There was no shred of self-pity or resentment when she told him about Stuart's accident, or the desertion of her husband when he learned that Stuart would be an invalid for the rest of his life.

'He simply couldn't face it,' she'd said. 'He found it horrific that Stuart would never kick a ball or swim or be normal in that way. It killed him to see Stuart in his chair. He'd weep. He just didn't come back one evening and then I got a letter. I've no idea where he is.'

'Couldn't he be traced?' Patrick had asked, horrified.

'I don't want him back,' she'd said, almost fiercely. 'He weakened me. It was like he was injured too, and I didn't have enough strength for them both. Stuart needs me, Dave doesn't.'

As the weeks passed, he'd learned of her joy when she'd been offered the teaching post, her struggle for the flat, the worries about her parents, who were very frail. Her love for her son was wholehearted, practical, vivid. Coming home to Selina was an unfortunate contrast. He'd fought to resist his disloyalty, but the temptation was too great.

Could Selina possibly have suspected his growing attachment? It was impossible to imagine her living permanently in Cornwall; nevertheless the battle was now joined and he must make some move. But what?

'Lunch!' Her voice echoed up the stair and he responded instinctively, tidying his papers, putting the top on his pen, before going downstairs.

Whistling softly to himself, Rob Abbot dipped the paintbrush into the gleaming white paint. The office was empty now and cleaned out ready to be decorated. The outside door was open to a brilliant, sparkling day, and he worked quickly in the icy, invigorating air, irritated by the thought of the imminent interruption. He glanced at his watch, pressed the lid back onto the can of paint, and crossed the small passage to wash the brush out under the cold tap in the cloakroom. Leaving it to dry, he went through to the kitchen, closing the inner door behind him. It was warm in here after the chill of the office, and he blessed Lady Todhunter for agreeing that the Esse should be lit. He made himself a mug of tea, looking about him critically, pleased with what he'd achieved.

The slamming of a car door alerted him, and he set down his mug and passed swiftly through to the sitting room. A young couple were standing in the lane, staring at the house. Keeping well back, he watched them, noting the new four-wheel-drive vehicle. They opened the gate and trod up the path to the front door. He waited for a moment, composing himself, before he opened the door to them.

'Ah, Mr . . .' The young man consulted a sheet of paper. 'Mr Abbot, is it? I think you're expecting us. Mr Cruikshank telephoned you earlier. I'm Martin Baxter. This is my wife.'

She smiled briefly, but her eyes were glancing past him.

'How do you do? Yes, I'm Rob Abbot. Come in, won't you? I often show people round to save Mr Cruikshank the drive from Truro.'

She was already in the hall, opening the door to the sitting room.

Martin Baxter shrugged, smiling. 'We'll give a shout if we need any information,' he said. 'I imagine it's pretty straightforward. Don't let us hold you up.' He followed his wife into the sitting room.

'Just look at this fireplace,' Rob heard her say. 'It must be positively ancient. Darling! Wooden shutters! Can you believe it . . . ?'

Rob retreated to the kitchen and stood by the open door, listening. He heard their footsteps cross the hall and more cries of pleasure.

'This just has to be my study.'

'Darling, have you noticed the beams . . . ?'

When they arrived in the kitchen Rob was washing out his mug at the sink, his back to the door. They stood for a moment, silenced by the sheer size of the room, before Mrs Baxter came and stood beside him.

'What an incredible view,' she said.

'Yes,' he replied. 'Even washing-up can be a pleasure here.'

She turned her back to the window, leaning against the work surface. 'I have a dishwasher,' she said briefly. 'Martin, can't you just see this with the right furniture in it? Provençal farmhouse, would you say?'

Rob stood his mug on the draining board. 'Or even English farmhouse,' he said. 'The Esse heats the water as well as being a cooker.'

'Esse?' She glanced about her. 'Oh, the range. We'd probably want an Aga, wouldn't we, darling?'

'It's probably the same sort of thing.' Martin Baxter sounded slightly embarrassed. 'Is it gas-fired, Mr . . . ah . . . Abbot?'

Rob laughed. 'There's no mains gas piped onto the moor,' he said. 'No, it's oil-fired and as good as any Aga.'

Mrs Baxter frowned. 'I think I'd prefer it to be electric.'

'Until the first power cut,' said Rob laconically. 'We get a lot of those round here. Then you'd be blessing the fact that you can cook and bath. Assuming the lorry's been able to get up here, that is. It's not always so easy in the winter. Plenty of paraffin lamps, that's what you need.'

Martin Baxter was frowning. 'Power cuts? That would be a damn nuisance when you're using a computer.'

'Oh, darling, it can't be that bad,' she said dismissively. 'Millions of people live in the country these days and work at home.'

'But you're high up here,' Rob pointed out. 'It's very exposed. Come and see it on a wet day with a southwesterly blowing. It's pretty bleak.'

Martin Baxter looked at him curiously. 'Not exactly trying to sell the place, are you?'

Rob shrugged. 'It's none of my business, either way. But I've seen people move down here to remote houses that look wonderful on a sunny day, only to sell up a year later because they can't take the long winter months. Have you any idea how much it rains here?'

Mrs Baxter looked at him angrily. 'I was born and brought up in the country. We know all about rain, thank you.'

He smiled at her. 'And where was that?' he asked sweetly.

'Hampshire.'

She turned her back on his chuckle. 'Come on, Martin. I want to look upstairs.' They went out together. 'I've never heard such nonsense,' Rob heard her say. 'Everyone knows how mild and temperate Cornwall is.'

'Well, he might have a point.' Martin Baxter sounded uneasy. 'That's more in the south, I think.' There was the rustle of paper. 'I see that there's no mains water or sewage, either. There's a septic tank somewhere and the water's pumped up from a well . . .' Their voices grew fainter and Rob listened to them walking about overhead.

When they returned downstairs, Martin Baxter put his head round the door. 'We're off,' he said. 'Thanks. We've decided to look at a place down in St Just-in-Roseland before we make up our minds.'

'Very wise.' Rob beamed at him. 'Beautiful countryside, the Roseland Peninsula. Very mild down there. And temperate, too.'

He followed them through the hall and watched them climb into the clean, new vehicle, reverse it in the yard and drive back down the lane, Mrs Baxter staring straight ahead. Rob grinned to himself, waved cheerfully and returned to his painting.

The pub dining room was full of people. Patrick raised his hand in salute to his host, but Selina was too busy scanning the crowd to wave hello. In the normal course of events she tended to avoid school gatherings, but Janet was the deputy head and it would have been churlish to refuse an invitation to her fiftieth birthday party. Anyway, Selina wanted to make a few investigations. She was certain that, if Patrick were having an affair, it would be someone connected with school.

Selina touched her cheek to Janet's and accepted a glass of wine. Patrick glanced at her anxiously. Selina was an expert at making people feel inadequate. The coolness of her embrace, a raising of the brows at the first sip of wine, the quick, patronising smile—it was a masterly performance. She was smart and well groomed, her light brown hair carefully streaked so that she appeared blonde, her clothes fashionably chic. This evening she was wearing well-cut amber-coloured velvet trousers with a matching tunic, and she'd wound a long silk scarf about her throat. She looked sexy, and she was enjoying the mild sensation she was making among this drab and dowdy group.

Sipping her wine, making no effort to mingle, she looked about her. She knew some of the people present, but Janet's personal friends and a few others were strangers. None of the women seemed likely to have attracted Patrick's serious attention, let alone made him risk starting an affair. To begin with she'd wondered once or twice if she'd imagined the whole thing, but his reaction to her test had given her cause for real suspicion. He'd often talked of moving out of London, of applying for the headship of a country school. It had always been she who had refused to consider such a move. Now, with the children grown, it was a perfect opportunity. The sale of their house in Clapham would more than cover the cost of Moorgate, with enough over to give him time to look about for a position in a local school. Personally she had no desire to live permanently at Moorgate, although she had every intention of buying it if she could. But he had clearly been horrified at the suggestion. Why?

She smiled as Richard Elton came towards her, arms outstretched. Richard was head of maths at the local comprehensive school and the only man present for whom she felt inclined to make an effort. It amused her to go along with the pretence that they were madly attracted to each other—if only because she knew it irritated his wife, a serious and rather intense woman who regarded Selina with barely disguised contempt. It irritated Patrick, too—he couldn't stand Richard—and Selina decided to play up a little to restore her confidence.

When Richard hurried away to find her another drink, Selina glanced about to see whether Patrick had been watching. She saw him near the supper tables. He was standing quite still, slightly behind a group of animated people so that his stillness was the more striking, but what made her catch her breath was the expression on his face. He was looking at someone she could not see, but his look of longing, a kind of desperate hunger, and his whole attitude of concentrated, unwary love, first frightened her, then unleashed a tide of rage. Keeping her eyes on his face she began to make her way round to where he stood. He seemed unaware of anything around him, and, as she watched, a young woman emerged from the press of people and approached him.

Selina paused, still some feet away, seeing the warmth in Patrick's eyes, noting the reluctance with which he let go of the girl's hands, which he'd held for a few moments in greeting. He glanced about quickly, nervously, but Selina had taken care to remain well screened by people and he clearly believed himself to be unobserved. Moving slowly, she edged round so that she was able to see the girl. Short, with an eager face and brown hair cut in a bob, she was neither slim nor elegant. Although that bright, intelligent look was attractive enough, and the girl was probably a good ten years younger than Selina, she was nothing special, no serious competition. Somehow this made matters worse. That Patrick might be unbalanced by some gorgeous young dolly-bird type was bad enough, but to find him behaving like a teenager over a perfectly ordinary woman was insulting.

They were talking together, but now Patrick had lost the look of intent concentration and his glance was anxious. In that brief, unguarded moment he'd betrayed himself, but now he was alive with fear and his eyes constantly scanned the crowd. It was pleasant to see him start with terror when she spoke, her eyes fixed on the girl's face.

'Hello, darling,' she said lightly. 'I wondered where you were hiding.' She arched her brows, smiling at the girl. 'I don't think we've met.'

'This is Mary Jarvis,' he stammered. 'She's one of our supply teachers. Didn't you meet at the Christmas party? I thought you had . . .'

Selina took his arm, feeling it tremble beneath her fingers.

'I didn't go to the party.' Mary's voice was calm. 'I couldn't leave Stuart. My son was paralysed in a car accident, Mrs Stone, and it's not always easy to find someone prepared to watch him. Patrick's been kind enough to arrange for me to teach when Stuart's at the Care Centre.'

Selina remained silent and it was Patrick who hurried into speech.

'He goes to school three days a week. Mary says he's coming on splendidly. It seems that he might be able to use his right hand again.'

Selina continued to smile, managing to convey an air of faint disbelief that either of them should imagine that she should be the least bit interested in the handicapped son of an undistinguished supply teacher. When the silence had stretched to embarrassing proportions, she took a deep breath, still smiling, and her grip on Patrick's arm tightened.

'Well.' It was a dismissal and Mary bit her lip. 'So nice to meet you, Margaret. Now.' She looked at Patrick. 'Shall we go and find something to eat, darling? You know I can't cope for long at these ghastly bun fights.'

She stood beside him while he mechanically piled food onto two plates, wishing that she could smash his face into the bowls and platters of food. As he turned to give her one of the plates, Janet joined them, and Selina caught a glimpse of the misery on his face before he controlled himself and began to talk to his hostess. Richard was approaching once again, and it was with some relief that she greeted him, relaxing just a little, letting him talk and joke, pretending to eat some supper while she planned a future course of action.

'Thank God that's over.' Selina flung her coat on a chair and filled the kettle. 'I need some decent coffee. Want some?'

Patrick shook his head, not trusting himself to speak. Somehow, now that he had seen his wife and mistress standing side by side, the ghastly reality of the situation was borne in upon him. Ever since they'd left the party he'd been waiting for Selina to speak. Fear quaked inside him, his gut churned and he swallowed nervously in a dry throat—but she had remained silent. He knew that she'd guessed but he did not know, yet, how to react should she accuse him. So he waited.

Making the coffee, Selina willed herself to be controlled. When she spoke again her voice was light—if brittle.

'Well, I have to say you have my sympathy. Most of your colleagues could bore for England and they were certainly in good form tonight. How do you cope with them all day long?'

Patrick remained silent. He was used to this kind of thing and had long since given up attempting to defend his colleagues. Selina was sipping her coffee now, leaning against the sink, but he would not meet her eyes. He pretended to be looking through some papers.

She laughed. 'You've got into a rut, darling. I really believe that you don't even notice it any more. I tell you what, though. This evening has convinced me that Moorgate is the place for us. It's our last chance to break away from this mediocrity. Surely you can see my point?' She paused. 'No? OK. Well, give me one good reason for staying here.'

Patrick put down the bills and letters, turning, bracing himself to look at her. It was impossible to meet her eyes. It was as if she had become a stranger—a frightening stranger—and, in that moment, he realised that he would be unable to share a bed with her. The thought of performing the familiar, intimate actions of undressing or cleaning his teeth while she padded around in close proximity, filled him with revulsion. The comfortable indifference brought about by thirty years of marriage had been stripped away, and he was seized with panic.

'I don't want to discuss it now,' he mumbled. 'To tell you the truth, I don't feel too good. I feel rather sick. Perhaps it was that salmon.'

'Perhaps.' She put her mug on the draining board and folded her arms under her breasts. 'Or perhaps it was something else altogether.'

He refused to rise to the bait. 'Possibly. There are the usual Christmas term bugs going round at school. I think I'll sleep in the spare room so that I don't disturb you if I have to get up in the night.'

'Oh, I don't mind being disturbed, you know that.' She sounded amused. 'Much better to be in your own bed if you don't feel well. The spare isn't made up and it's far too late to fiddle about finding sheets. Come on. Let's go up. The sooner you're in bed the better.'

He climbed the stairs, racked with self-disgust, emasculated by fear. He knew that resistance would be equivalent to declaring war. She followed him into the bedroom, watched him while he undressed.

'You're shivering, poor darling.'

He felt her hand on his back and shrank away from her, seizing his pyjamas, struggling into them, hearing her chuckle. He leaped beneath the bedclothes, hauling them up, rolling away to his own side of the bed while she took off her clothes. Hugging himself, eyes clenched shut, he felt her climb in beside him, felt her arm slide over him and knew with a sick shock that she was naked. So this was to be the test. Well, they'd made love since Mary, so why not tonight? If it lulled her suspicions, gave him a breathing space, why not? He knew the answer almost before his brain had formulated the question. Tonight it would be impossible to feign affection, let alone passion; tonight, he knew, his body simply would not respond. He caught her roving hand and held it fast, rolling onto his back, pretending rueful disappointment.

'Sorry, love,' he said apologetically, feeling her stiffen into immobility. 'It's simply not on, tonight. Too much of everything, I think. Damn! I need the loo. Hope I shan't be long.' He swung his legs out of bed and hurried out, leaving Selina staring into the darkness.

'The point is,' Maudie said to Polonius, as they sat in front of the fire just before bedtime, 'that you are a very large person, and very large persons do not climb onto sofas, nor do they sleep on other persons' beds.'

Polonius groaned deeply, settling himself comfortably, head on paws.

'It's no good protesting,' she said firmly. 'Your bed is in the kitchen and that's where it's staying. I want no whining tonight.'

She put several logs on the fire and wrapped herself more closely in the plaid rug. At least the arrival of Polonius had distracted her a little from her anxieties. It was impossible, surely, that Selina would persuade Patrick into buying Moorgate, and anyway it was likely now that Rob had practically finished that someone would make an offer before Selina could get her act together. Posy had been dismissive, certain that her father would prevent it, but Selina was stubborn and it would be foolish to underestimate her.

Watching the flames, Maudie remembered the campaign that Selina had waged once she'd noticed Maudie's growing affection for Posy. Though the boys had been brought to visit regularly, Posy was rarely seen. Maudie and Hector heard of outings with Patrick's parents, of parties to which they were not invited, and were shown tantalisingly delightful photographs of Posy growing up, but they were excluded as much as possible. When Hector complained, Selina made excuses: it was so difficult to find time now, with two growing boys and a baby; that Posy preferred her other grandmother. It was Patrick who had guessed what was happening and tried to put things right, to make opportunities for Posy to be with Hector and Maudie.

It was strange that maternal feelings should make themselves known so late in life. Patricia and Selina had never given her such emotions, and Maudie had been happy to remain free from the joys and anguish to which Daphne was prey. No terrors for a child's safety kept Maudie awake at night, no anxieties that he or she might fail exams, be rejected in love or become unemployed. For Hector, Maudie's lack of interest had been refreshing. She'd made no attempt to prevent him being caring and paternal, but she'd made him see that he was not *only* a father and provider, that he could be a person in his own right. She'd made it clear that she expected to have a relationship with him that was separate from the children—and for part of the time she'd succeeded. There were whole periods when they had been united, utterly together, and it was these that she strove now to remember.

Those awful scenes with Hector at the end, his begging for forgiveness, Selina's triumph, must be wiped out of her memory. Why should she believe that he'd regretted marrying her? It must be possible to concentrate on the good times, to stop torturing herself with these doubts.

Maudie stood up abruptly, disturbing Polonius, who roused himself and struggled up, yawning.

'Last outs,' she said. 'Come on. It's time for bed.'

He followed her out into the clear, cold night and ambled off while she shivered, shining the torch after him. The trees beyond the gate seemed to press closer, whispering and creaking gently, and, hearing a rustling behind her, she swung round, directing the torchlight into the recesses of the open-fronted woodshed. A feathery ball of wrens, huddling together on a high beam, was caught in the light and she turned away quickly, not wishing to disturb them.

She thought: Oh, how I wish I had someone to cuddle—and was seized with a sudden and terrible despair.

'Oh, Hector,' she cried aloud, angrily, 'if only you knew how much I miss you!'—and Polonius, thinking that she was calling him, appeared out of the darkness and led the way indoors.

CHAPTER FOUR

SELINA PUSHED HER COFFEE MUG aside and laid the newspaper flat on the kitchen table. Patrick had just left for school and she sat for a while staring sightlessly at the headlines, elbows on the table, chin in hands. She'd forgotten how big a part anger played when it came to jealousy; forgotten the overwhelming, obsessive need to possess. So it had been when Maudie arrived on the scene more than thirty years ago. She could remember quite clearly that, in replacing their mother, it had seemed that her father was rejecting her, Selina, and Patricia, too. That he could bring this stranger into their home and not be able to see it as a betrayal had been beyond belief. Patricia had been less affected by it—she'd been too preoccupied with boyfriends and parties—but she'd been shamed into a certain amount of rebellion. Even now Selina's lip curled as she thought about Patricia's feebleness, her readiness to give in.

'Daddy's still quite young,' she'd said defensively. 'He's very attractive, too. All my girlfriends say how dishy he is. You just have to face facts.'

What a shock it had been to see him in that light, as someone who wanted a relationship outside his family. With their mother gone, it should have been enough to devote himself to his daughters—his daughters and his friends. Goodness knows, he'd had enough friends! Selina had often resented the great army of people who moved through the house, distracting her parents from her own needs.

'You mustn't be selfish, dear. Your father is a popular man who likes his friends about him.' How often darling Mummy had soothed and comforted. She was never too busy to have time for her children; with Mummy, she and Patricia had always come first. How safe Mummy had been, how constant. Her dying had been a betrayal in itself.

'How could you die,' Selina had demanded, weeping bitterly, night after night, 'when you knew how much I needed you?'

Nobody had warned her about death and its terrible, unimaginable finality. How many mornings she'd woken, almost weak with relief, thinking that the whole thing was a terrible dream, only to have to live through the pain of it all over again. Yet nobody seemed to care.

'Of course they care,' Daphne had once said. 'The trouble is that Patricia and your father are attempting to cope with it too. It's very hard, Selina, but you must be brave. I'm always here if you need me.'

Oh, she'd been trying to help, but Selina hadn't wanted Daphne's help; it was Daddy she'd needed. He'd been shocked and desolate, true enough, but not for long. Barely nine months later Maudie had been with him when he'd arrived at Granny's one afternoon. Granny had been polite but cool, Daddy had been bluff and hearty in an attempt to cover his embarrassment, and Patricia had been curious about Maudie.

'You have to admit,' she'd said afterwards, 'that she's rather attractive. Quite sexy in a kind of casually indifferent sort of way. Lovely long legs.'

Selina had stared at her, baffled, frightened. 'What do you mean?'

Patricia had rolled her eyes. 'Grow up, can't you? He's going to marry her. He's in love with her. You could see it a mile off.'

Now, Selina balled her hands into fists. How well that suited Patrick and Mary. 'He's in love with her. You could see it a mile off.' Her father's expression when he had looked at Maudie, the lingering hand clasp and the reluctant parting of flesh, had been repeated that night of the party. The signs were appallingly familiar. Familiar as the upsurge of rage; the need to cling and hold; the humiliation of a man's disloyalty.

'He doesn't love you less, Selina,' Daphne had insisted. 'Love is not a finite commodity. Be generous, my dear.'

It was a concept that remained foreign to her. Even with her own children she'd needed to be first. Patrick was their father, the provider and protector, but it was to her they brought their triumphs and disasters. She must be first in their affections. The boys had always complied, but Posy's disloyalty had enraged her. Even Selina's own friends couldn't understand why she'd felt so betrayed; couldn't see how humiliating it was to discover that someone else was preferred, to imagine the victor's private triumph. And that it should be Maudie of all people . . .

Yet even the enormity of Posy's defection paled beside Patrick's. Mary's image rose in Selina's mind and she felt a suffocating fury. How the wretched woman must be laughing, enjoying the knowledge that it was for her he had betrayed his wife. Selina willed down her rage, aware that subtlety was more effective than cheap gibes or a show of contempt. This time she would win. As yet nothing had been said. Patrick had gained control of his emotions and was playing it calmly and carefully. He'd even mentioned a weekend away in Oxford, something to do with school. Later he'd talked about it in detail, describing some seminar and lectures, but she was not deceived. He hadn't looked at her, and his guilt was almost tangible, but she hadn't dared speak. She'd hardly been able to contain herself at the thought of them together. Hot, spiteful words had filled her mouth, acid as bile.

'I hate her,' she said aloud to the quiet kitchen. It was some kind of relief to say it. 'The little cow is going to be truly sorry.'

'She knows,' said Mary, her small face drawn and tired. 'Of course I realise that. But if you deny it what can she do?'

'God knows.' Patrick spoke quietly, not wanting to wake Stuart. 'But at least we'll get our weekend.'

'I'm worried, Pat. I'm not sure we should take the risk.'

He couldn't bear to forgo the weekend; it was almost the only thing sustaining him. 'Why are you worried now? Nothing's changed.'

'Oh, yes it has. I've met her now.' Mary shook her head.

'Please, darling,' he said urgently. 'Please don't give up. We want to be together properly, don't we? Not just occasional evenings and a weekend here and there. I want to look after you both. I need you.'

'I know.' She turned away from him as much as the small sofa would allow. 'But it seems so much more difficult than I first thought.'

'You're tired,' he said tenderly. 'Leave it all to me. It's just that I don't want you hurt on the way through, so I have to be careful.'

'I know.' She attempted to withdraw her hand, which he continued to hold tightly. 'Only . . . I'm not sure I've been thinking straight, Pat. It's really good, you being around and . . . well, having a man in my life again. It's almost like being on holiday. Something different and fun. But now I've met Selina it's become real.'

'I know,' he said eagerly. 'I know just what you mean. I felt exactly the same after the party. But that doesn't mean we have to give up on it, Mary. It might mean a bit of a fight, but isn't it worth it?'

'I've done fighting,' she said flatly. 'Been there, seen the film, bought the T-shirt. I'm tired of fighting.'

He stared at her, hurt and frightened. She looked away. His expression made her feel guilty and she could almost feel the weight of his love settling over her shoulders. She was very fond of him, and their brief moments of love, as well as the relief and comfort of physical passion, had been a boost during a drab, exhausting period in her life, but things were changing. She was in control again, working, independent . . .

'Look,' she said gently. 'Your wife is not going to lie down quietly so that we can walk over her, off into the sunset. I can't afford any mess, Pat. Stuart has to come first. He's settling down well at school and I think he's feeling secure for the first time since the accident. No one's going to take that away from him, Pat. No one. '

'I know that,' he said wretchedly. 'But she doesn't really want me. I'm sure of that. If I make sure she's well provided for—'

Mary laughed. 'I wouldn't count on that,' she said.

His look of despair made her feel ashamed. He had been so kind to her and she'd been too grateful, too ready to try to repay his kindness. She'd believed him to be a man who'd been neglected by his wife and was looking for comfort. She'd gone along with him, dreaming their dream, but not taking it too seriously and imagining that he was doing the same. The expression on his face showed her that she was wrong.

'Look,' she said, giving in, 'of course we'll have our weekend. We've got it planned now. We'll talk everything through then, but please leave things just as they are until afterwards. Don't rock any boats. Promise?'

He promised. Of course he did. She knew just how important the weekend was to him. After he'd gone she went into the small bedroom to look at Stuart. She kissed him lightly, moved by a fierce, protective love for him. Nothing must hurt him further; nothing and no one.

Walking home, Patrick tried to pin down his ideas. He must work through this sensibly. He wanted to protect Mary and Stuart, but if Selina spilled the beans to the school governors it was likely that he or Mary—or both—could suffer. If only he had enough money to set Mary up in her own place, where he could join her when the dust settled, then at least she would have a certain security. It would be unforgivable to damage her—yet he needed her desperately. Her little flat had become a haven for him. On these evenings, when Selina was at her bridge club and imagined him to be having supper at the pub, he and Mary were always together. They'd share a takeaway and a bottle of wine and afterwards they'd make love. The long summer holidays—no school and the bridge club closed for six weeks—had cut their opportunities considerably. It was the memory of those weeks that had made him determined to force things to a conclusion. Yet, this evening, he'd felt a drawing back on Mary's part.

He pushed the thought away. It was only natural that Mary should have moments of panic. Their lovemaking had been as good as ever, the weekend away shimmered temptingly ahead, and he felt confident again. Somehow he must make it work. As he opened the gate and felt for his key, he glanced up at the smart little terraced house. Thanks to Hector's generosity, it was a great deal better than most of his colleagues could afford, and Patrick knew that it was incumbent upon him to make certain that Selina did not suffer financially either. He must be fair to them both. But how?

A quick glance round showed him that Selina was not yet home. Relieved, Patrick hung up his coat and hurried up the stairs. With luck he might be in bed and feigning sleep before she arrived back.

Polonius sat on the verandah watching Maudie rake the leaves from the lawn. Each time she turned to look at him he sat up. his ears pricked, hopeful that she might allow him to join her. But Maudie refused to be moved by his eager expectancy. As she leaned the rake against the wooden seat and looked down into the quiet water of the pond, she allowed herself a moment of childish thrill.

Another card from Posy had arrived this morning. *How would you feel about me spending Christmas with you?* she'd scrawled, the words wedged between all her news.

It would be the final straw for Selina, of course, yet how could she resist such a delightful treat? She trod the path back to the verandah, pausing to pat Polonius, and kicked off her gumboots. She would go into Bovey Tracey to do some shopping, but a cup of coffee first would not go amiss. As she put water in the percolator and spooned coffee into the filter she was remembering Christmases with Hector. For him it was a time of parties, theatres, dinners, and he was never happier than to be dressing for some formal event, wandering between the bedroom and his dressing room, shirt-tails dangling, bending to peer into her looking glass while he tied his bow tie, frowning in concentration.

'Let's not go,' she'd say suddenly. 'Let's stay here and make love.'

He'd hesitate, shocked but delighted at such a notion. 'Honestly, darling.' He'd laugh, stooping to caress her. 'Don't think I'm not tempted but we've accepted now. Can't let people down.' He was pleased, all the same; amused and flattered to be desired so unaffectedly.

Maudie chuckled to herself. It was clear that Hilda had never been so natural with him, would never have taken the lead, and Hector found this new approach rather fun. In other respects he had been somewhat less pleased by Maudie's self-confidence.

'Poor old Hector,' Daphne had said one day, a year or so after Maudie and Hector had married. 'You're a bit of a shock for him. Hilda's beliefs were formed early by other people and she stuck to them. Fortunately, most of them were formed by Hector so there were few dissensions.'

Maudie had thought of Daphne's remarks later that day when Hector began to read aloud to her from one of the articles in the paper. After a minute or two she'd interrupted him.

'I'm reading, Hector,' she'd said, holding up her book.

He'd stared at her. 'I beg your pardon. It's just that this is a subject on which you hold quite strong views.'

'I know,' she'd answered. 'I read it this morning. I'm quite capable of assimilating facts from a newspaper article, you know. I don't have to be read to as though I were a child. I thought he put it very well, actually.'

She'd continued with her book and Hector had shaken out the pages crossly. No doubt Hilda would have listened meekly, ready to be instructed. Maudie had suddenly wanted to burst out laughing, but instead she'd got up and, pausing briefly to touch his shoulder, had poured him a drink. When she'd brought it to him he'd taken the glass but held onto her hand and kissed it. He was never one to bear a grudge.

'Oh, Hector,' she sighed now, switching off the percolator and pouring strong black coffee. 'I'd give anything to have you back. I'd even let you read the newspaper to me.'

Polonius suddenly thrust a cold nose into her hand and she started, spilling coffee, cursing under her breath. 'Wretched animal. No, we are not going for a walk. Not until later. I have to go shopping. I might take you with me, but you'll have to wait in the car.'

While she sat at the table in the living room, making her list, her glance returned to Posy's card. Might she really come to stay for Christmas? Maudie shook her head. It was best not to be too hopeful. *I shall be going home this weekend to see the Ageds and collect some stuff*, she'd written. *I'll tell them that I'd like to stay with you over Christmas and I'm sure they won't mind. The boys will be around and I'll be there for some of the hols, anyway. Fingers crossed, babe! Wouldn't it be fun? Just you, me and Polonius.*

Maudie looked at the great hound stretched before the fire, sleeping peacefully now, and felt oddly contented. She took a quick gulp of coffee and returned to her list.

Posy folded some jeans and a large black sweater and put them into her battered holdall along with some books. Slowly, she'd been moving her few belongings to Winchester, and now her small bedroom here in London had a rather desolate air. She felt more comfortable at the house in Hyde Abbey Road; more relaxed with Jude and Jo and the others than with her family.

She sat on the edge of the bed, struggling with her guilt. Surely it was more natural to want to be with friends of her own age than with two middle-aged people, especially now that the boys were rarely at home and she wasn't allowed to keep Polonius? She pushed both hands through her thick black hair, straining it back from her face in a nervous gesture she'd had from childhood. The thought of Polonius, which had automatically associated itself with Maudie and Christmas, had triggered it. Being nonchalant about spending Christmas with her step-grandmother was one thing; broaching it with her mother was another.

Posy drew up her legs and sat cross-legged, frowning. Mum was being a bit peculiar: still set on buying Moorgate but behaving like she was trying to needle Dad with it. Dad wasn't responding. He wasn't doing his placating 'of course you must have it if you want it, love' stuff which he did when he wanted some peace, but he wasn't arguing about it either. It was like he was marking time. He was absent-minded, preoccupied, although he'd been like that for a while now, even before she'd gone back to Winchester, and Mum was watchful. Anyway, she'd done the usual anti-Maudie bit and it had been difficult to just say straight out, 'Oh, by the way, I thought I'd spend Christmas with her.'

Posy climbed off the bed and went downstairs. Patrick was sitting at the kitchen table, reading. He glanced up at her, smiling, but he looked old and tired and she felt another pang of guilt.

She thought: I won't feel guilty about him. I simply won't.

'I had an idea about Christmas,' she said, sitting opposite, trying not to notice his strained expression and restless hands. 'I wondered about spending a few days with Maudie. The boys will be with you and she's all on her own. And I have to think about Polonius . . .'

Her voice trailed off and she looked away, waiting for reproaches.

'I don't see why you shouldn't,' he said. 'I guessed with Polonius down with Maudie you'd be more inclined to go there than come here.'

'Oh, don't say it like that,' she cried, 'as if I love Polonius more than you. You know I don't. It's just unfair to load him onto Maudie and leave it at that. Mum said he could come home for holidays but now she's changed her mind. I'll be here for some of the time.'

He raised his hands. 'Look,' he said gently, 'I'm not arguing. We'll miss you—of course we will—but you'll be around for a week or two, I expect. I think it's a nice idea. Maudie will be delighted.'

She watched him suspiciously, trying to detect signs of martyrdom, but he seemed genuinely undisturbed and she felt a stab of hurt pride.

'What d'you think Mum will say?' she asked.

He shrugged. 'Does it matter? If you've made up your mind, stick to it. That's my advice.'

She stared at him anxiously. This indifference was out of character and she wondered if the Moorgate business were upsetting him.

'This Moorgate thing,' she said impulsively. 'It's just a bee in Mum's bonnet. She can't really be contemplating going to Cornwall to live. She'd die without Peter Jones and stuff. Don't let it get to you.'

He smiled at her with real warmth. 'I won't,' he said. 'Stick to your guns about Christmas, mind. I'm going down to the pub. See you later.'

He went out and she sat still, puzzled. Sometimes he'd suggest she might go to the pub with him, but it was clear this evening that he had no desire for her company. Presently Selina came into the kitchen. She raised her eyebrows when she saw Posy sitting there alone.

'Where's your father?' she asked. 'He was supposed to be getting the supper this evening.'

Posy felt a familiar sense of partisanship manifesting itself. 'He's gone to the pub,' she said casually. 'He looks a bit stressed out. Why don't you give him a break about this Moorgate stuff? You don't really want to live on the edge of Bodmin Moor, do you?'

Selina looked at her coolly. 'I don't think it's any of your business. You have your own life to lead now and I suspect we shan't be seeing too much of you in the future. After all, you've always made it very clear where your loyalties lie.'

They stared at each other, all the old antagonisms rising to the surface, and Posy recklessly seized her chance.

'I suppose you're right. Actually I've decided to spend Christmas with Maudie. Not the whole holiday, but a few days. Since she's kind enough to have Polonius . . .'

Selina gave a short laugh. 'Kind! She saw her opportunity and grabbed it with both hands. Typical bloody Maudie.'

'I don't think she thought about it like that. She just knew how miserable I was at the thought of him being given away. You didn't care. You said he could come back for holidays but you've gone back on your word. And it was I who suggested going for Christmas, not Maudie. Dad seems quite happy about it.'

Selina lost her patience. 'I'm sure he does. But then he's too wrapped up in the little tart he's having an affair with to care about any of us.' She saw shock replace the indignation on her daughter's face and knew a brief moment of remorse. It was quickly smothered by a surge of self-righteousness. Hadn't she had to cope with just such a shock concerning her own father and Maudie when she was much younger than Posy? 'Perhaps I shouldn't have told you,' she said, 'but you're quite old enough to deal with it. God knows, I have to! He spends every minute he can with her but he hasn't got the guts to admit it yet.'

'No.' Posy shook her head. 'Not Dad. He just isn't like that.'

'Like what?' Selina's lips curled into her familiar sneer. 'Oh, this isn't some sex thing with a dolly-bird type. She's a fat, boring little nonentity with a crippled child. He sees himself as a knight in shining armour.'

'If he hasn't admitted it how do you know?'

'Because I do know,' Selina answered quietly. 'I've seen them together. You can take my word for it. Come on, Posy. You've seen the change in him. Admit it. You were saying as much just now.'

'So what will you do?' Posy felt oddly breathless.

Selina shrugged, eyes narrowed thoughtfully. 'I shall bide my time. She's not going to have him, I promise you that. He'll have to make a move soon, but meanwhile I wait.' She frowned and glanced at the kitchen clock. 'I suppose I'll have to get on with the supper myself.'

'I don't want anything to eat,' said Posy. 'I'm not hungry.'

She went upstairs to her bedroom. Sitting on the bed, driving her hands through her hair, she realised how important it was to have this place of security, the comforting knowledge that her parents—especially her father—were there, waiting should she need them. She felt childishly angry that this new-found love was more important to him than the company of his own daughter. It was because of this woman that he was ready to allow her, Posy, to go off to Maudie for Christmas, no longer requiring her company down at the pub. Perhaps he had lied to her; perhaps he hadn't been going to the pub at all but was with the woman now. How could she possibly face him on his return? Posy rolled over onto her side and drew up her knees, wrapping her arms about them, shivering. She began to cry.

'Where's Posy?' Patrick blinked blearily. 'She's not upstairs. Is she OK?'

'So very much OK that she's gone back to Winchester,' said Selina brightly. 'She didn't want to hang about, she said.'

Patrick looked at her disbelievingly. 'But it's barely eleven o'clock.'

Selina raised her eyebrows. 'So?'

'I've hardly seen her,' he mumbled. Selina's shiny brittleness penetrated his heavy-headed stupor and he felt the chill of caution trickling down his spine. 'I thought we might go for a walk or something.'

He turned his back on her, switching on the kettle, suddenly alert. He'd got back later than he'd intended, slipping into the spare bedroom, but he'd been unable to sleep. There had been no answer when he'd telephoned Mary from the pub. Just her voice on the machine. He'd told her that he would almost certainly telephone at about this time so he'd assumed that she was dealing with Stuart and couldn't get to the phone. He'd tried again later but there was still no reply. Since she rarely went out in the evening, he'd gone back to the bar anxious and puzzled, and had soon begun to imagine various scenarios in which Mary was unable to reach the telephone. After another fruitless call he determined to walk to the flat.

When he'd arrived at the house the front door was locked as usual, but he could see a light in her sitting-room window, although the curtains were closed. He rang her bell several times but there was no reply, and he'd stood wondering what he should do. The landlord lived across the hall but Patrick was unwilling to rouse him. It was possible, after all, that Mary had pushed Stuart round to visit her parents, leaving her light on as a precaution in case they were late back.

Frustrated, he'd walked back to the pub and had another pint. There was no reason at all why Mary should stay in on a Saturday night . . . except that he nearly always managed to call her on a Saturday night. She always said how wonderful it was to hear him, and the thought of her sitting waiting for his call gave him a warm, possessive glow. His disappointment was out of all proportion, and he'd ordered a large Scotch in an attempt to cheer himself up. At last, after one final unrewarding telephone call, he'd set off home. The house had been in darkness, and he'd gone quietly upstairs to the spare room and had lain awake worrying. Eventually he'd persuaded himself that she'd gone to see her parents, that there had been an emergency that had kept her there, and, promising himself that he'd speak to her first thing in the morning, he'd fallen at last into a troubled doze.

He'd woken late, feeling ghastly, and Selina's news about Posy's departure had come as a shock. Now, as he made tea, some shadowy premonition, some shred of self-preservation kept him silent.

'The news of your affair with Mary upset her.' Selina sounded almost cosy, as if they were gossiping about friends. 'That's understandable. I felt the same when Daddy brought Maudie home. Do you remember, Patrick? You were so upset when I told you. You considered it quite shocking. You said some rather cutting things about Daddy, if I recall. A dirty old man was one of them, wasn't it? But then, you were very young, and Daddy seemed old to you. I suppose he was about your age. Fiftyish. Odd, isn't it, how the young consider that anyone over forty is past it. The thought of their parents having sex is bad enough, but to find out that your father is having a fling with another woman is terrible. I found it almost impossible to come to terms with. It's so utterly sordid. You feel sick and you don't want to be near him. All your respect vanishes. That's how Posy feels about you, of course.'

Patrick stood still, keeping his back to her, his hands trembling. He felt as if he were shrivelling inside as he imagined his daughter's clear-eyed, ruthless gaze. How cruel the young could be. Just so had he reacted when the young, tremulous Selina poured out her pain; how self-righteous he'd been. Safe in his own youth and virility he'd been the first to condemn Hector's need for another, younger wife.

'At least,' Selina was saying conversationally, 'Daddy was a widower. At least he wasn't an adulterous bastard.'

He took his hands away from the mug and pushed them deep into his pockets. 'Why did you tell her?' he asked, turning to face her. 'Why did you tell Posy before you even spoke to me about . . . your suspicions.'

She laughed contemptuously. 'Suspicions? You're not denying it, I see.' She waited, but when he did not answer she shrugged. 'Posy noticed that something was wrong with you. I told her what it was.'

His head rocked with pain. 'Since you'd suffered in similar circumstances, I suppose it didn't occur to you to protect her from it?'

She raised her eyebrows. 'My dear Patrick, don't accuse *me*! It's your job, as her father, to protect Posy. Don't expect to behave like a selfish, disgusting prat and then blame me if your daughter despises you. I notice that you're not concerned with how I feel about it.'

He was suddenly angry. 'Why should I be? You don't care about anything else that concerns me. You didn't give a damn until this happened. You still don't. You're a dog in the manger, Selina. You don't really want me, except to pay the bills, but you're damned if you'll let go. Why?' He laughed mirthlessly. 'Why keep up this pretence?'

'Because I choose to,' she said. 'You're mine, Patrick, and I intend that we shall stay together. And you can tell your little tart that if she doesn't lay off I shall write to the school governors. Don't forget that I'm friendly with Susan Partington. You tell Mary that. Then we'll discuss selling this house and buying Moorgate.' She stood up but, at the door, she paused, looking him over. 'You haven't forgotten that we're lunching with Jane and Derek, have you?' she asked sweetly—and went away upstairs.

Maudie placed a log on the fire, closed the door and settled again in her chair, adjusting her spectacles. She was about to pick up her knitting when the telephone rang. She reached for the receiver.

'Hello, Maudie. It's me.' Posy's voice was flat. 'How are you?'

'I'm fine, my darling. Are you OK? You sound tired.'

'I am a bit. I've just got back from London.'

'Oh dear. Were things a bit difficult? Is Moorgate a real problem?'

'Well, sort of. It was all a bit strained and stuff. Look, the good thing is that I can come for Christmas. They don't mind. Well, not really. Mum did her usual bit about my lack of loyalty but what's new?'

'Oh, darling, I'm so sorry.' Maudie cast about for words, feeling hopelessly inadequate. 'It would be wonderful if you could come. I should love it, but if it's going to make it unpleasant at home—'

'No. No, it won't.' She sounded defiant now. 'Anyway, who cares? It's all arranged. I'll go home first to leave them my presents and then come down to you the day before Christmas Eve. How's that?'

'It is simply perfect,' answered Maudie warmly. 'It's going to be such fun. I can't tell you when I last felt so excited. I shall tell Polonius.'

There was a small chuckle at the other end of the line and a more cheerful note in Posy's voice when she said goodbye. As she replaced the receiver and picked up her knitting, Maudie suddenly realised that Posy had not once called her 'babe'.

'Something's wrong,' she told Polonius, who thumped his tail sleepily but was disinclined to greater response. 'She's probably had a row with Selina over Moorgate. Damn and blast. If only I didn't have to sell . . .'

Posy went back into her room and closed the door. She'd been at Hyde Abbey Road for some hours, but she'd found it very difficult to speak even to Maudie. To her relief, Jude and Jo were out and she was able to be alone, attempting to sort out her emotions. Last evening, she'd heard her father come back quite late and go into the spare room.

To begin with, Posy had wanted to give him the benefit of the doubt, to let him deny or explain it. While her mother was watching television, she'd slipped out, hurrying round the corner to the pub.

'He's not here,' the barman had told her. 'He's been telephoning someone and he got a bit restless and suddenly dashed off. He'll probably be back in a minute. Give him a message, shall I?'

'No, don't do that. Thanks, anyway. It really doesn't matter.'

Later, as she lay in bed listening to her father creeping up the stairs, going into the spare bedroom, she had feared her mother's words were true, and knew that she simply couldn't face him in the morning.

Now, as she sat cross-legged on her bed, she felt comforted by her conversation with Maudie. Nothing had changed at The Hermitage.

Maudie was there with Polonius, waiting for her, and she could go for Christmas with a clear conscience. No matter how hard she tried to concentrate on this, however, other thoughts intruded. It hurt her to know that she had been replaced in her father's affections so easily, that it was more important to him to be with this woman than with his daughter.

Posy felt her lips trembling uncontrollably and dragged her hands fiercely through her hair. 'For heaven's sake! You're not a little kid,' she told herself. 'You're nearly twenty-two. Grow up and face facts.'

The bang on the door startled her so much that she cried out, and Jude opened the door and put his head inside the room.

'Are you OK?' he asked. 'I've just got back. How about some coffee?'

'Yeah. Great!' she answered casually, pretending to be rooting for something in her bag. 'I'll be right there.'

He disappeared and she stood up, drawing a deep breath, controlling herself. Nobody must know yet, not until she'd got used to the idea. She pulled her hair forward over her eyes and went out to find Jude.

CHAPTER FIVE

'I DO LOVE THIS OLD PLACE.' Ned Cruikshank cast his Filofax and mobile phone onto the work surface and smiled blindingly at Rob. 'If I had the money I'd buy it myself.'

'Would you, though?' Rob passed Ned a mug of coffee. 'Not a bit off the beaten track for you?' He glanced at Ned's shiny black loafers. 'You look as if the streets of London were more your natural habitat.'

'Oh, I'm a great countryman,' Ned assured him earnestly. 'Absolutely. I ride most weekends, if I can. Actually—'

The ringing of his mobile phone put an end to the conversation and Rob turned to look out of the window. It was a clear, bright day. Sheep grazed on the moor. The slate roofs of the village, huddled in the valley, gleamed in the wintry sunshine and, far away on the hill, a tractor was ploughing, seagulls screaming in its wake.

'Terrific view, isn't it?' Ned's voice at his shoulder made him jump. 'Gets 'em every time. Not that we've had too many people round yet. It's not a good time of the year for these isolated properties. I was really pleased we had sunshine this morning. Do you think they liked it?'

Rob looked noncommittal. 'Difficult to say. Some people think that they have to enthuse, don't they? I think the thought of having to ferry the kids everywhere didn't fill them with delight.'

Ned looked as put out as his round face and naturally cheerful expression would allow. 'You didn't have to lay it quite so firmly on the line,' he said. 'They were pretty keen, I thought, until then.'

'Sorry.' Rob shrugged. 'But they did ask about public transport. I don't think townspeople realise that out here you're not going to have a bus passing the gate every twenty minutes. They must have seen that it would be much too isolated for two teenage kids who've spent all their lives in a city. No point in stringing them along and then having the sale fall through at the last minute, is it? You might miss a genuine buyer.'

'You've got a point.' Ned brightened. 'I'm glad Lady Todhunter lets you keep the range alight. Makes all the difference, doesn't it? Don't you mind having to caretake, now that the work's finished?'

'Not particularly. I don't live far away. Pointless doing all that work and seeing it ruined through the winter. Have you got anyone else viewing before Christmas?'

Ned shook his head. 'Everything's dead as mutton at the moment and the office shuts tomorrow for a week. So.' He rinsed his mug at the sink and beamed at Rob. 'Good to see you again. Gave me a bit of a surprise to find you here, but it was just as well since I managed to get held up. At least they weren't hanging about in the cold.'

'Oh, I keep an eye on the place but I don't have a routine. Best to be unexpected. It's a lonely spot. Easy for someone to break in.'

'Mmm.' Ned glanced around nervously. 'Sounds creepy. Perhaps it is a bit off the beaten track.' He laughed, picking up his Filofax and mobile phone. 'But don't go saying that to the clients.'

'Of course not. But I shall tell the truth about transport and the weather, if they ask.'

'Fair enough. Well, I'll be off. Season's greetings and so on. See you in the new year.'

'Indeed. And the same to you.'

Rob strolled out, round the side of the house and into the yard, watching Ned climb into his car and shoot off down the lane. As the sound of the engine died away, he looked about him. The yard was tidy now: the stable repaired, the barn creosoted, rubbish cleared away. He passed through the gate that led to the front of the house, noting the first new green spears thrusting through the soil of the flower borders. Crossing in front of the windows, he stepped onto the lawn, which was divided from the moorland by the escallonia hedge. He remembered the rotting remains of a swing he'd found beneath its shelter, and for a moment he imagined Moorgate as it had been a hundred years before, with chickens in the yard, children playing on the swing and the men coming in tired and hungry from the fields. He turned, half expecting to see the farmer's wife watching him from the porch, but no one was there. Laughing aloud at his foolish fancies, he went back inside.

Mary, shivering on playground duty, saw Patrick come out of the door and look about him. She felt a newly familiar compassion for him, compassion and pity—and guilt because she no longer really loved him. As he approached she hardened her heart against his look of eagerness, checking that nobody else observed his transparent pleasure.

'I missed you on Saturday,' he said. 'Are you OK? I've been worried.'

Odd how the charm of his caring for her should have deteriorated into an irksome irritation.

'We're fine,' she said, smiling brightly at the children milling about them. 'I had to go and see Mum and Dad but we're all fine.'

'I've had a showdown with Selina. I simply must talk to you.'

Her heart was weighty with foreboding. Their little moment was finished, and she wanted him to let go, to relinquish his hold. She knew that he would not, that he would cling to her, possibly dragging them all down. Self-preservation stiffened her resolve, warning her against giving in to his need. Yet she wanted to be kind, to let him down lightly.

'Please, Mary.' His face was miserable.

'Isn't it bridge night?'

'Yes, it is.' He watched her hopefully. 'Can I come round?'

'Of course.' How weak she was to give way, but they needed to talk. 'Yes, come round as usual.' She gave him a swift smile. 'Better go now.'

'Yes. Yes, of course.' His relief was almost tangible. 'See you later.'

'I'll be there.'

She turned away from him, wishing that she could comfort him, reassure him, knowing that she couldn't.

'Are you going out tonight?' Selina was in the doorway, bright-eyed, inquisitive. 'Or have you work to do?'

'I'll probably go to the pub,' Patrick said casually. 'I'll see how I feel.'

'Only I'm wondering whether I'll go to bridge tonight.'

He did his best to hide his shock. 'Aren't you feeling well?'

'I'm a bit low, to tell you the truth. Well, who wouldn't be under the circumstances?'

He remained silent, praying for release. 'Perhaps,' he mumbled, after a moment, 'it would do you good to get out.'

She laughed, a loud, harsh laugh. 'Have you anything to tell me?'

'No,' he answered, confused. 'No . . . What do you mean?'

'Oh, I think you know what I mean.' She seemed amused at his discomfiture. 'Another thing. That weekend in Oxford. I'll come with you.'

This time it was impossible to hide his dismay. 'It's out of the question,' he said. 'It's . . . Everything is arranged.'

'Oh, surely not,' Selina said gently. 'I'm sure we can change your single room for a double. Or had you already booked a double? Anyway, it would do us good to get away for a weekend. I know you'll be busy but I'm sure we'll manage to have some time together. Oh, and Susan Partington's coming to lunch on Wednesday. She and I haven't had a good gossip for ages. I just thought you'd like to know that. Well.' She stretched, breathing deeply with satisfaction. 'That's that, then. Do you know, I'm feeling much better. I think I'll go to bridge, after all. It will give you the chance to get things sorted, won't it? See you later.'

Patrick put his head in his hands. It seemed that Selina held all the cards. His only hope was that Mary might love him enough to take a chance for him. As long as he could look after her and Stuart, surely they might scrape through?

He heard Selina call goodbye, heard the front door slam. He waited for a few moments, listening, before he stood up and went downstairs. Taking his coat, he stepped out into the wet evening, walking briskly, his head bent against the drizzle.

They made love almost immediately after he arrived. She saw the expression on his face and simply opened her arms to him. He seized her, kissing her hungrily, and she responded to his need. Afterwards she made them coffee and he poured out his plans, confident that she would be sympathetic. He explained that, although Selina would probably keep the house, he could support the three of them; they would find somewhere else to live, near Stuart's school, and even if they both lost their jobs they would soon find new ones . . .

She began to draw away from him, to free herself from his embrace. He talked on, urgently, but she became stiff and unresponsive.

'Let's try,' he pleaded. 'We can't just give in to her, Mary. You can trust me to look after you both. I love you. I can't bear the thought of us parting. Just think how wonderful it would be to be together properly without all this lying and subterfuge. Isn't it worth taking the risk?'

'No.' Mary shook her head. 'Absolutely not, Pat. I just can't.'

He stared at her, desperately, trembling with frustration, while she sipped distractedly at her coffee, miserable but unyielding.

'You don't really love me at all, do you?' he said at last. There was no self-pity in his voice, just a stating of bald fact.

'I do love you, Pat,' she said quietly, 'but I suppose I don't love you enough to take such risks. It's been hell, trying to cope with Stuart, nowhere to live, no money, and I just can't do it again. We work at a Church of England primary school and your wife is great friends with the governors. Sorry, Pat.' She shook her head. 'The odds are stacked against us. I only hope we haven't blown it already.'

'Selina hasn't said anything yet.' He stared down at his hands. 'She's giving me the chance to finish with you. We've got until Wednesday.'

'Wednesday?' She frowned at him, puzzled.

'She's invited Susan Partington to lunch on Wednesday.' He sounded tired, almost indifferent. 'She's one of the governors.'

Mary had to restrain herself from leaping to her feet, ordering him out of the flat. How could he be so calm when exposure and disgrace loomed so close? The thought of his selfishness nearly choked her, but she tried to control herself, tried to remember how he had helped her.

'Well, then.' She tried to steady her voice. 'It seems it's been decided for us, doesn't it? Even if we were prepared to take the chance, we can't put Stuart at risk. I'm sorry. I hate this, but we've got to finish it.'

'I suppose I knew it all along, really.' There were tears in his eyes. 'Selina always wins, one way or the other.'

'I had no idea that she was so . . . well, still in love with you. I'd imagined, from what you said, that she didn't care.'

'Oh, she doesn't.' He stood up. 'Selina doesn't love me. She owns me.'

She wanted to go to him, to hold him tightly and banish the empty look from his eyes, but she willed herself to remain seated. 'Thanks,' she said. 'I am truly grateful for . . . everything. It's been . . . good.'

'Yes.' He spoke on a deep breath, as if he were bringing a meeting to a conclusion, looking round him, checking that nothing was forgotten. 'Well, I'll be off then. See you in school.'

The door closed behind him. She sat, clutching her mug, tears trickling down her face. His dignity touched her as no pleading could have done, and she was suddenly aware of all that she'd lost.

'You're a selfish cow,' she whispered. 'But what else could I have done?'

She got to her feet and went into Stuart's room, staring down at him, biting her lips, holding his hand in hers.

Trendlebere Down was recovering from the fire that had burned across its slopes two years before, but charred trees still stood, bleak and twisted memorials to the flames, while new, pale, tufty grass grew among gorse and heather. Maudie parked the car on the road below Black Hill and let Polonius out. He dashed away, bounding among the rocks, nose to the ground, while she followed more slowly, looking away to the south towards Teignmouth, watching golden showers of sunshine slanting through the clouds, glinting on the grey waters of the estuary.

Polonius's excited barking recalled her attention and she saw a horse and rider picking their way down the hill. As they came closer she saw that it was Hugh Ankerton who, with Max Driver, ran the Adventure Training School. She raised her hand to him, holding Polonius firmly with the other, and he came up to her waving cheerfully, controlling the horse who was dancing a little at the sight of Polonius.

'Hugh,' she said. 'Good to see you. I'll be along in a minute for a chat.'

'That's nice.' He smiled down at Maudie. 'We haven't seen you for a bit. New friend?'

'He's Posy's.' Maudie stroked the dog's head. 'She rescued him last year. Her mother couldn't cope with him when Posy was at college . . .'

'And you were selected from a host of applicants,' he finished for her, grinning. 'He's enormous. What a pity Rowley's at school, he'd have loved him. What's his name?'

'Polonius. No, don't ask me. I have no idea.'

Hugh gathered up the reins. 'I'll tell Pippa to get lunch on the go.'

'I wouldn't dream of bothering Pippa with lunch.'

'It's not a problem.' Hugh was already cantering away, calling back over his shoulder, 'It'll only be soup or a sandwich. See you.'

As they started back towards the car, Maudie remembered how Hector had loved riding out over the moor. Max, Hugh and Pippa, the little group at Trendlebere, had made him very welcome. The adventure school had been Max's dream, and he'd taken on Hugh to run it with him. Pippa had joined later, as cook, matron and general factotum. She had a small son, Rowley, and by the time Maudie met them Pippa and Max were married. Over the years she'd come to know them well, taking Posy to Trendlebere to go riding with Hugh whenever she came to visit. As she and Polonius approached the car, Maudie found herself thinking about Posy again. Hugh was such a nice man, and a very good-looking one. She shook her head. He must be in his mid-thirties—much too old for Posy. Anyway, they'd been riding together for years . . .

'No matchmaking,' she told herself sternly, opening the door to allow Polonius to jump in. 'No interfering. On the other hand . . .'

Polonius turned himself round and licked her face enthusiastically, causing her to jump back, hitting her head on the still open door. Cursing eloquently she slammed the door, wiping her face with her handkerchief, romantic notions quite forgotten.

Posy finished wrapping the last present and sat staring at the festive-looking pile, confused and miserable. Ever since she'd been home she'd tried to avoid her father, and she longed to be away, off to Devon and Maudie. She hadn't imagined how difficult it would be to look at him. At times she loathed him, imagining him with the other woman, betraying his family and being undignified.

Posy dropped her head on her knees. Oddly, this was the worst thing—being undignified. Even when Mum was putting him down, being sarcastic, he'd stayed somehow outside it all. Oh, there had been times when she'd longed for him to stand up to Mum, to shout back, but she'd grown to admire his dignified refusal to descend to that level. She'd never cared about him being quiet and dull, as Mum called him, because he'd always been there, solid and unchanging. Now it was different. Now there was someone else he cared about. Someone he was being silly about. It was terrible, imagining him being silly. He was too old.

Posy sat up straight, listening, as she heard footsteps coming slowly up the stairs. They paused on the landing and she willed them past her door, into his study. The light tap brought her to her feet, and by the time he'd opened the door she was standing by the window.

'Hi.' He smiled at her but his eyes were wary. 'I was wondering if you needed a lift to Paddington?'

'Oh.' It was almost a gasp of fright before she controlled herself. 'Won't that be a bit of a drag? I mean—I can manage . . .'

He gave a ghost of a chuckle. 'I don't doubt that for a moment, but since I can't imagine you going away without enough luggage for a year or two I thought it might help a bit.'

'Well, thanks.' How could she refuse? It was Christmas and for the first time in her life they wouldn't be together. Tears gathered behind her eyes and she hastily seized her battered travelling bag, swinging it onto the bed. 'I haven't done too badly this time, actually, but I've got to put some presents in yet . . .'

'Posy.' His voice was quite gentle. 'I know that Mum's told you about Mary and I'm sorry. It must have been a terrible shock. I wish she'd left it to me. It's not quite how it might have sounded.'

She felt hot with distaste and pity. 'I don't want to talk about it.'

'Oh, Posy—'

'No.'

She was a small girl again, feet planted firmly, head lowered, eyes narrowed warningly. So Patrick had seen her on countless occasions in the past: defending herself against her brothers' teasing, against Selina's gibes about Maudie. He longed to hug her, to remove the pain, but, for the first time in their lives, it was he who was inflicting it.

'It doesn't change anything,' he said urgently. 'Try to understand that. You have new friends, now, new interests, new allegiances. We have to make ourselves big enough to contain them all. Nothing and nobody changes how I feel about you.'

'I don't want to talk about it.'

He sensed the panic behind the stubborn reiteration and took a deep breath. 'OK,' he said lightly. 'Fair enough. Don't worry. I won't start again in the car so you can have your lift quite safely. We ought to be away by half past eleven to be on the safe side.'

She waited until the door closed behind him and then she began to pack, jamming things into the bag. 'It does change things,' she muttered. 'He didn't care about me not being home for Christmas.'

She sat down, wrenching her hands through her hair. How childish it was to announce that you'd be away and then be upset when nobody minded! For a brief moment she allowed herself to imagine the bleakness of his Christmas. The boys would be told—if they hadn't been already—and she could already sense his isolation. Deliberately she hardened her heart. He shouldn't have started messing about. She zipped up the bag and flung her coat on top of it. Gathering up the pile of presents she went downstairs to put them under the Christmas tree. The house was decorated, ready for the boys' arrival, but she was glad to be going to Maudie—to Maudie and Polonius.

Driving back from the station through the busy streets, Patrick wondered why he hadn't told Posy, why he hadn't just said it.

'It's over.' He could have made it clear, even if she hadn't wanted to discuss it. 'It's finished.' The knowledge that the affair had come to an end might have comforted her. Yet he'd been unable to say the words and it was clear that Selina had not done so either. How shaming it had been, admitting to Selina that it was over, that Mary had been prepared to let him go rather than risk losing her job and her home.

Selina had been amused. 'So she's not going to put up a fight for you? What a shame. And you were prepared to risk your all for her. Poor old Patrick. So embarrassing to throw down the gauntlet and have people treading it into the mud, isn't it? At least I won't have to tell Susan. That's a relief, anyway. You're not much of a man, Patrick, but I still have some pride. So what about our weekend in Oxford?'

'I'm not going to Oxford. I never was, as you well know, and I don't intend to change my mind at this late date.'

She'd shrugged. 'Oh, well. I can't say I'm disappointed. Dreary place, if you ask me. Anyway, we must save our pennies for Moorgate. Don't look so surprised. Had you forgotten about Moorgate? Oh dear. Well, I haven't. It's been a comfort to me, while you've been off with your little tart, thinking about happier times. I'm not so sure, now, that we want to live there permanently, but it would be a comfort to know it was there.'

He'd gone away, then, leaving her to her triumph—and to her fantasies. The thought of Mary was a constant ache in his heart, and the realisation that Selina intended to pursue her romantic desire to possess Moorgate filled him with despair. He'd awaited Posy's arrival with trepidation and had seen immediately how it was to be. Selina was certainly right about Posy's reaction: she despised him. Yet he had not been able to say the words that might have healed the breach: *It's over. It's finished.*

It had been bad enough seeing Mary at school; it was a hundred times worse knowing that he would not see her for three long weeks. To protect Mary he'd told Selina that the affair was over, but at the bottom of his heart lay the hope that the miracle might happen, that Mary might relent. Each time the post arrived or the telephone rang, each time he saw her, he hoped that his misery would be relieved. He imagined scenes in which she told him that she'd changed her mind, that somehow they'd survive, that she loved him. As far as he was concerned it wasn't over. He needed her; he couldn't simply stop loving her at will.

As Patrick drove home he knew why he'd been unable to say the words to Posy: they simply wouldn't have been true.

Seated either side of the fire, Polonius stretched between them on the rug, Maudie and Posy seemed absorbed in their separate occupations: Maudie knitting, Posy reading. Although it was quiet, and she missed her friends, Posy knew that it had been right to spend Christmas here.

The thing that made Maudie such a good companion, Posy decided, was that she didn't fuss. There were no emotional confrontations, no hidden agendas. There was a detachment that gave you room to breathe. She didn't seek to possess you while offering her love. Several years ago, Posy had tried to explain this to her mother.

'It's easy for Maudie,' had been the answer. 'She's not related to you. She's not your real grandmother. You wait until you have children of your own and then you'll understand.'

This continual implication that Posy was ungrateful, disloyal, an unnatural daughter, was wearing—and hurtful. She'd never been able to see why she couldn't be allowed to love both her mother and her grandmother; couldn't understand why there had to be a choice.

'Of course you can't,' her mother had retorted. 'You've never made the least effort to understand my feelings. You choose to ally yourself with someone who's made my life miserable and expect me to be delighted about it. How Maudie must be laughing!'

'She doesn't laugh,' the young Posy had protested. 'We don't talk about you at all.'

This assurance, apparently, had not been as comforting as she'd hoped and the difficulty remained unresolved. Her father was much more reasonable, doing as much as he could to ease the situation.

Posy remembered the telephone conversation with her father on Christmas Day. He'd been cheerful, thanking her for his present, asking after Maudie. She'd managed to talk to him almost as if nothing had happened—it was easier at a distance—and then the boys had taken their turn. Her mother, it seemed, was too busy with the lunch to come to the telephone but sent her love, and Posy had felt irritated and hurt that she couldn't leave the turkey for five minutes to wish her a happy Christmas. The call had unsettled her, reminding her of past Christmases, making her feel guilty. Eventually, after several glasses of wine, she'd blurted it all out to Maudie and burst into pathetic weeping. Maudie's reaction had been so unexpected, however, that she'd been brought up short, sniffling into a tissue, wide-eyed with surprise.

'Good grief!' she'd said, bottle poised above her glass. 'You amaze me. Patrick, of all people. I'd never have believed he had the gumption.'

For a brief moment Posy had seen the situation through Maudie's eyes; seen her father as a man, independent of his family. The moment passed, but she'd been subtly changed by it. She'd realised that Maudie expected her to approach it as another adult might, and she'd felt flattered but at the same time affronted. Surely she couldn't approve?

Maudie had apologised. 'Sorry,' she'd said. 'You took me by surprise. It sounds so unlike Patrick. Are you absolutely certain?'

Posy had answered that she was quite certain but that she didn't really want to talk about it. This wasn't quite true, but she couldn't bear to discuss her feelings, even with Maudie, yet she'd felt rather deflated when Maudie had taken her at her word.

'I can understand that,' she'd said. 'It takes a bit of getting used to, I imagine. Just don't get things out of proportion.'

Easier said than done. It had seemed wrong, on Christmas Day, to spoil the festive atmosphere. Now, she wished she'd had the courage to talk it through, but it was difficult to raise the subject again. She couldn't just mention it casually, as though she were asking what they would be eating for supper. Perhaps an opportunity might arise naturally and she'd be able to take advantage of it. Posy settled back in her chair and tried to concentrate on her book.

Apparently absorbed in her knitting, Maudie was aware of Posy's pre-occupation with things other than her book. She'd been furious with herself for her reaction to Posy's disclosure, yet she'd resisted the urge to become affected by Posy's evident distaste. Maudie didn't approve of adultery but there were sometimes extenuating circumstances. She considered it either heroic or just plain stupid to remain married to Selina for thirty years and had a sneaking sympathy for Patrick's actions. She'd respected Posy's request, and they hadn't discussed it since, but she'd given it a great deal of thought.

Rooting about for another ball of wool, she was remembering Hector's reaction to Patrick's request for Selina's hand.

'Nice enough fellow,' he'd admitted privately to Maudie, 'but there doesn't seem much to him. Still, Selina seems very fond of him . . .'

Maudie had remained silent. The thought of a married Selina, living somewhere else, was too wonderful to contemplate. Guessing that enthusiasm on her part might make Hector suspicious, she'd held her tongue. To Daphne, however, she'd been more forthcoming.

'Oh, my dear,' Daphne had replied at once, 'I couldn't agree more. Much better all round if Hector gives his blessing cheerfully. Selina is determined to have her way. Of course, Hilda would have had a fit.'

'Would she?' Maudie had been intrigued. 'But Patrick's so . . . so spotless, so utterly nice. He's rather cool to me but that's because he's been brainwashed by Selina and regards me as the wicked stepmother. I should have thought that Hilda would have loved him.'

'She would have approved of his being a well-brought-up young man but she would have wanted a stronger character for Selina. I fear that once the first flush passes she'll walk all over him.'

Maudie had shrugged. 'You have a point. Still, there's nothing I can do about it. Selina wouldn't listen to me. Hector hates being cast in the role of unsympathetic father and she'll soon win him over. I have to say that Patrick shows up very well when Hector's doing the heavy father act. He stands up to him bravely and looks quite zealous on occasions.'

Daphne had chuckled. 'Young Lochinvar is come out of the west. Yes, Patrick's exactly the sort who needs a cause, isn't he?'

Now, as Maudie attached the new ball of wool to her knitting an idea occurred to her.

'I do begin to wonder,' she said thoughtfully, 'whether your father's so-called affair isn't little more than helping some damsel in distress. However, we won't talk about it if you'd rather not . . .' She hesitated, but Posy looked up from her book almost eagerly so she decided to continue. 'He's a chivalrous man, you know, and a very kind one. It's possible that things might have got out of hand but perhaps we shouldn't be too hard on him.'

She paused again but Posy seemed ready to talk. 'Mum did say that she wasn't a dolly bird, this . . . Mary.' It was still oddly difficult to use her name. 'She said she was a boring nonentity with a crippled child.'

Maudie swallowed down a sigh of relief. So her intuition was probably sound. 'Well then. It's just possible that they've got a bit tangled up emotionally. It can happen very easily, you know.'

'It's just,' Posy cast her book aside and drew up her knees, 'you know, it's not as if he's young or anything. It makes him look pathetic.'

'Lack of dignity in the old is so shocking to the young,' murmured Maudie. 'It's their prerogative to be shocking, outrageous or even simply sexy. We've all felt it. That's why your mother hates me, of course.'

Posy stared at her. 'Hates you?'

Maudie raised her eyebrows. 'Don't pretend it comes as a surprise.'

'No—well, perhaps "hates" is a bit extreme—but I just meant that I can't see the relevance.'

'Can't you? Well, think about it. Selina was nearly thirteen when her father married me. Her mother was not long dead and she felt a sense of betrayal, which is probably exactly how you are feeling now. It was a shock to learn that Hector was not satisfied with being a father, that he needed other company and stimulation. She also had to confront his sexuality. He was a little younger than Patrick, but as far as Selina was concerned he was old. To have to think about him like that in conjunction with me was appalling for her. She didn't want to blame him so I became the scapegoat. I didn't mind to begin with because I thought she'd grow out of it, but she never did.'

'I've never seen it like that,' said Posy slowly.

'It was like she had an obsession about you and I couldn't see why.'

'Well, now you can understand it. Supposing Patrick brought Mary home. How would you feel?'

'But Grandfather wasn't committing adultery,' protested Posy.

'That's what I kept saying,' sighed Maudie. 'But it made no difference to Selina. She felt I had supplanted her, as well as her mother. She was jealous. She didn't feel her father could love all of us and she was afraid.' She looked at Posy's downcast face. 'Sound familiar?'

'I do feel like that, I suppose,' she admitted at last. 'I feel hurt. As if he's risking his family for this woman, which means he must love her more than he does us.'

Maudie was silent for a moment, feeling herself on delicate ground.

'Patrick adores you,' she said gently, 'you know he does, but you're grown up and you've nearly left home. The boys have already flown the nest. I think you'd agree that your mother is not a comfortable person to live with. I suspect that your father has been feeling invisible for quite a while, and it's a heady experience to be noticed, admired even. This Mary probably makes him laugh, makes him feel good. He's probably been able to help her and feels valued, important. I'm not condoning adultery, Posy, but let's not be too harsh on him. As to his loving Mary more than he loves you, I think you'll find that Patrick is capable of a great deal of love. It isn't on ration, you know.'

'I know,' Posy mumbled, 'but it's like I don't know him any more.'

'That's because you want to think of him as some solid, dependable figure who is there when you need him but can be put on hold when you don't. That's very nice for you but where does it leave Patrick?'

'He's my father,' cried Posy. 'That's what being a parent is all about. I'd want to be there for my children.'

'Of course you would,' said Maudie. 'But we have all these complex sides and we respond to each one differently. This is what makes growing up so painful. We have to learn to adapt, to be generous. I'm afraid I haven't been generous with Selina. I tried for a while, but when she refused to meet me halfway I gave up on it. It's more difficult for you because you stand between Selina and Patrick. If you can walk a fine line between them it will be a very adult thing to do.'

'I don't want to take sides,' cried Posy, 'but it's not that simple. I can understand that Mum's asked for it, in a way, but I can't just say, "Oh, great, Dad. I think it's cool."'

'I'm not suggesting that. I'm simply asking that you don't condemn him out of hand. Try to detach yourself emotionally, to see that it needn't affect you. Remain affectionate and friendly to them both.'

Posy shook her head. 'It's impossible,' she said wretchedly. 'I can't just pretend nothing has happened, Maudie. I can't!'

'Of course not,' agreed Maudie. 'Sorry, Posy. I shouldn't have interfered. Talking about things isn't always helpful. Shall I make a pot of tea? And perhaps a piece of Christmas cake?'

In the kitchen she stood watching the kettle, cursing quietly to herself. It was too much, and probably quite wrong, to expect the child to be able to take such a detached view. Maudie smiled wryly. After all, disliking Selina as she did, it was hardly likely that her own point of view would be unbiased. The kettle boiled and she began to make tea.

When she went in with the tray Posy was putting logs on the fire. She smiled rather shyly at Maudie and hurried to clear a space on the table. As she put some books away, the envelope from The Scotch House was dislodged from between the pages and the woollen squares drifted to the floor. Posy bent to gather them up.

'Aha,' she said. 'Are you ordering a new skirt?'

'I'm thinking of it,' answered Maudie, grateful for a change of subject, remembering that it must be at least six weeks since the samples had arrived. 'Let's have a look at them and you can give me some advice.'

PART TWO
CHAPTER SIX

PASSING THROUGH THE HALL of the narrow terraced Georgian house in Oxford, Melissa bent to pick up the envelopes that lay scattered on the doormat. She wore an ankle-length bouclé wool cardigan over narrow jeans and a long tunic, and her feet were tucked into soft leather bootees. The effect was medieval, an image accentuated by the short, curly, fox-red hair, bound back from her thin, pointed face with a plaited silk scarf. She passed down the hall and into the kitchen, where her brother and his small son, Luke, were eating breakfast.

'Bank statement,' she said, flourishing the letters. 'House details. And someone telling you that you've won six hundred thousand pounds.'

Mike Clayton continued to spoon the soggy, milky mess into Luke's mouth. 'Chuck it,' he advised indifferently. 'I have a feeling that we're not the get-rich-quick kind.'

Melissa sat down at the end of the table and poured herself some orange juice. 'You're not doing too badly,' she said. 'The book's doing well and you've some good ideas for the new one. Think yourself lucky you managed the transition from playwright to novelist so painlessly.'

There was an uneasy silence. Melissa reached for the house details, aware of her tactlessness, while Mike watched Luke thoughtfully. He'd met Luke's mother during the staging of his second play and had rewritten her part with loving, brilliant fervour. She'd received such rave notices once it moved to the West End that hundreds of offers for work had rolled in and eventually even Hollywood had taken an interest in her. Had Mike been a little less besotted, his wife might still be here with him, looking after her child, instead of abandoning them both for a glittering career in America. He'd attempted a novel while looking after Luke, when Camilla had begun filming in the States. At the same time that he'd learned that Camilla would not be coming back, he'd been offered a two-book contract by a major publishing house, and the very respectable advance enabled him to concentrate on his second novel. He was glad to be done with the stage, and the permanent reminders of Camilla, but he had by no means recovered from his wife's defection.

Mike wiped milky bubbles from Luke's chin and glanced at his sister. She was absorbed with whatever it was she was reading and when she looked up at him her face wore a rapt expression.

'Oh, Mike,' she said. 'This house. It sounds simply perfect. We must buy it. You want to be in the country so you can write in peace and quiet, don't you? Well, this is it. Just look at the photographs.'

He studied the pictures of the old farmhouse and began to read the details. 'But it's on the edge of Bodmin Moor,' he said, surprised. 'Why on earth have they sent me something so far afield?'

'They've got a branch in Truro,' said Melissa. 'And what's wrong with Cornwall? The country is the country.'

'Well, not quite. It's a hell of a long way from London, for a start.'

'Oh, London.' Melissa made a face. 'Does that matter so much any more? Writing novels isn't quite the same as writing plays, is it? You can write novels anywhere. And think how wonderful it would be for Luke.'

He hated to pour cold water on her excitement. 'Perhaps we'll go down and look at it,' he said cautiously. 'A bit later on in the spring . . .'

Melissa had taken the details from him and was studying the photograph again. 'Isn't it odd?' she said. 'I feel as if I know this place. Oh, Mike, I want to see it. I've been thinking of going away for a little while, haven't I? Just a few days or, perhaps, a week. I think I'll go to Cornwall.'

'Look,' he said anxiously. 'It's a long way to drive, Lissy. Don't be silly about this. We'll all go if you really want to.'

'No, Mike,' she said quickly. 'It would be crazy to cart Luke down to Cornwall in February. I just feel I must do this. Please.'

He looked away from her, longing to agree, racked with worry.

'I'm OK at the moment,' she said gently. 'Robin said it could be six months, didn't he? Well then. A week or two out of six months. It would be such heaven, Mike.'

He swallowed hard, not wanting to be selfish. Well, it was her life, what was left of it, and they couldn't spend every minute of it together.

'If you're sensible,' he said. 'And don't overdo things.'

'I won't,' she said joyfully. 'How wonderful to have something to plan. A point for going on a jolly. We'll find somewhere for me to stay and I'll go and look at . . .' she peered down at the particulars '. . . at Moorgate. What a fantastic name. The gate to the moor.' She smiled at him. 'Don't worry, Mike. I'll be very good. I promise.'

Ever since Christmas, life had seemed rather dull. Walking in the woods with Polonius, Maudie wondered if the decision to sell Moorgate had triggered the unsettled sensations that possessed her: coming to terms with Hector's death, brooding over their life together, remembering the resentments caused by Selina's rejection. More recently there was the news of Patrick's infidelity and Posy's reaction to it. It was irrational to feel sympathy for Posy when she'd expected Selina to cope bravely with a similar situation.

'Perhaps I was too hard on her,' she murmured, pausing to watch a goldcrest flitting among the branches of a conifer, searching for insects.

Polonius appeared, crashing out of the undergrowth in pursuit of a squirrel, his barks splintering the silence. The squirrel raced for safety up the smooth grey bole of a towering beech, turning to chatter insults. Polonius hurled himself impotently skywards.

'Forget it,' advised Maudie. 'We all have our limitations and you might as well face facts. You'll never be able to fly. Come on.'

Polonius grumbled, but followed her away from the tree and soon picked up another scent. Maudie strolled after him, her thoughts with Daphne. They'd spoken at Christmas as usual, but, once Posy had gone, Maudie had telephoned Daphne again to tell her about Patrick.

'I cannot believe it,' Daphne had said firmly. 'Not Patrick. Selina will *marmalise* him.'

Maudie had laughed, for the first time for several days. 'I said more or less the same thing,' she'd said remorsefully, 'only out loud to Posy.'

Daphne had understood at once. 'That wasn't terribly tactful, was it?'

'I know, but I couldn't help myself. It's been a bit grim, Daffers. Posy is seriously upset. It came to me that she's feeling about this woman, Mary, exactly as Selina felt about me all those years ago. She feels betrayed, as if her father is putting the family at risk for this Mary. Now I'm wondering if I was very harsh with Selina.'

'But Hector was a widower.' Daphne had sounded surprised. 'Not quite the same, is it? And he always did his best to reassure Selina. Often at your expense, because he expected you to understand.'

'But I didn't.' Maudie had felt miserable again. 'Not always. I felt insecure, too. Poor Hector. If only I could get rid of these doubts and resentments. It's selling Moorgate that has brought all this on. I wish I could manage without selling it, but I can't. And I wish I knew what had happened to Hector's investments. It's like a worm, gnawing at my peace of mind.'

There was a moment of silence before Daphne spoke again.

'Oh, Maudie,' she'd said sadly, 'I hate you to be like this. It's so frustrating trying to communicate properly at this distance. Look, I'm hoping to come over later on this year and then we'll have a proper talk.'

'Are you really? How amazing.' Maudie had been swamped with delight. 'I was thinking of flying out to see you all, once Moorgate was sold. It was going to be my treat.'

'Well, now you can save your money,' Daphne had said, 'ready for us to have a good time together. I'll talk to Emily and make some plans. As for Patrick, let's hope the affair blows over. Selina will never let him go.'

'That's what I thought. But it's made me do a bit of rethinking.'

'Well, don't let it get out of proportion,' Daphne had warned. 'And Maudie, never forget how much Hector loved you.'

'I know he did. Of course I do. It was just that he was so different at the end. And then there's the thing about his investments . . .'

'Put it right out of your mind for the moment. Concentrate on all those wonderful times you had with him. I knew Hector for most of his adult life and I never saw him as happy as he was with you. Believe it, Maudie, hold onto it. Don't let it be ruined. Hector wasn't himself at the end, you know that. You know what Alzheimer's does to people. Think about the good times and make some plans for my visit . . .'

Turning for home, shouting for Polonius, Maudie realised that she was hungry—hungry and much more cheerful. Posy, back at college, had telephoned to ask if she could come down for the weekend and had muttered, in passing, that things were a bit better at home—much to Maudie's relief—and there was Daphne's visit to look forward to. All she needed now was a buyer for Moorgate.

Enjoying a well-earned rest from shopping, relaxing in Peter Jones's coffee shop, Selina, too, was thinking about Moorgate. The bank had refused to agree to lend the balance required for the deposit, and she was trying to bolster up the courage to speak to Maudie, to ask her for special terms. She'd spent several days trying to overcome her reluctance. It wasn't simply that she knew Maudie disapproved of her attempting to buy Moorgate; she also knew that Posy had told her grandmother about Patrick. She'd asked Posy outright and Posy had answered bluntly.

'Why shouldn't I tell her?' she'd demanded. 'I was very upset about it.'

'Oh, don't imagine that I expect loyalty from you,' Selina had snapped. 'Naturally you'd go round washing our dirty linen in public.'

'I haven't told anyone else,' Posy had said, stung by the accusation. 'You shouldn't have told me if you'd wanted it to be a secret. It isn't anyone's business but yours and Dad's. I wish you hadn't told me.'

'I expect you do.' Selina had shrugged. 'Anyway, it's all over. Your father has come to his senses.'

Posy's expression of overwhelming relief, the visible relaxing of her whole body, had almost shocked Selina. Assailed by an unfamiliar sense of guilt, she'd tried to make it up to Posy during the last week of her holiday and had been met, to her surprise, by a readiness to meet her halfway. Patrick, who seemed to be in a state of numbed indifference, was pleasantly polite to both of them, and a kind of truce had descended upon the household. Only Moorgate remained a subject of dissension.

Selina sipped her caffè latte thoughtfully. The old farmhouse should remain in the family, and she had to find a way to achieve her desire. At any moment, some other person might make an offer on it. There was no time to waste. She'd rather counted on exploiting Patrick's sense of guilt—a ploy that had worked in the past—but her suggestions that the purchase of Moorgate would be an excellent expiation for his sins fell on stony ground, and his cool, puzzled response made her nervous. At the same time, her determination to own Moorgate grew stronger. Perhaps an approach to Maudie, subtle and well prepared, was worth a try.

Melissa drove carefully, watching for the turning off the A38. Mike had written the instructions on an A4 pad which lay on the passenger seat, and the VW Polo contained every possible aid in case of emergency.

'It's only February,' he'd said, packing rugs and gumboots into the hatchback. A hamper was already on the back seat, containing flasks of tea and coffee, as well as biscuits and chocolate. 'You might get bad weather. You've got your mobile, haven't you? And the RAC card?'

She'd reassured him, feeling touched, hating to leave him and Luke, but driven by an inner need. They'd waved her off, standing on the pavement, and she'd suppressed the urge to stop the car and run back to them. They were all she had, and she loved them both so much— why waste precious time on a mad dash to the West Country?

'Because I must,' she'd told herself desperately, weaving her way out of Oxford. 'I need to feel normal, to pretend that I'm like anyone else, and I can't do that with Mike. However hard he tries, it's there at the back of his eyes. I want to be looked at by people who don't know.'

Gradually the panic and guilt receded. Slowly she thought herself into her other persona: the Melissa who had all her life before her, who was healthy and free and looking for adventure. She'd taught herself to do this as a means of escape from despair. Sometimes it was a slow, painful effort, but it was easier when there was something on which to concentrate. She glanced at the details of the farmhouse, also lying on the front seat, and excitement bubbled inside her. The day was bright and sunny, full of hope, and she sang to herself as the miles sped away. She'd promised not to attempt the journey in one day and had decided to break the trip just before she turned off the A38 onto Dartmoor.

'You could carry on into Cornwall on the A38,' Mike had told her. 'and shoot off at Liskeard. Much quicker.'

She'd wrinkled her nose. 'It's boring dragging through Plymouth when I could be driving over Dartmoor. You know I love moorland, Mike. I can go across to Tavistock and then Launceston. Much nicer.'

He'd agreed—but with the proviso that she had a night's sleep before crossing the moor. She'd laughed at him.

'Anyone would think it was the Kalahari,' she'd said teasingly. 'But OK. It'll be nice to take my time.'

He'd made certain that she'd booked a room in Bovey Tracey and another for two nights in Padstow, but she refused to do more than that.

'I want to be free to move about,' she'd insisted. 'It's an adventure, Mike, not a package tour.'

He'd agreed, understanding, and she'd promised to keep in touch daily, but slowly she was beginning to experience the sense of freedom that had become so elusive. By lunchtime, driving into Sherborne to find somewhere to eat, she could think about her brother and his child calmly, without guilt, and was managing to hold at bay the tiny demon of fear that lived in her mind and in her heart.

As she ate a large piece of apple cake and sipped her coffee, she looked again at the house particulars. The farmhouse, after all, was the reason for her journey. She was travelling to the West Country to look at houses for her brother who was a writer. If anyone asked she'd tell them that she was a lawyer working in one of the City law firms, living in a flat in Dulwich. Well, so she had been until a year ago. Apparently concentrating on the description of the kitchen, Melissa was aware of the attention she was receiving from a young man at a corner table. She felt a surge of gratitude for his admiration, which bestowed a kind of strength upon her. There was no compassion in his eyes, just a simple, natural interest shown by a man for an attractive woman.

Melissa put her hands to the scarf wound round her hair, which had grown back well once she'd refused any more chemo. She mourned the long, rippling bronze mane, but was grateful that, though still short, her hair curled into pretty tendrils. 'I've had enough,' she'd said to her GP. 'I know it's inoperable and I may not have much longer. I'm going to enjoy what's left to me,' and he'd agreed with her, defending her from the specialist and the other doctors, agreeing that she had the right to take her life back. It had been a relief when Mike had needed help just then, so that she could move to Oxford, free of that terrible, suffocating sympathy. Some of her friends had been unable to believe that she was 'giving up' and talked severely about denial; others attempted to persuade her to try homeopathic treatment. What she missed was the cheerful rough and tumble of daily life. The terrible privileges of the sick were paralysing, and she was determined to throw them off.

She finished her apple cake, drew her thick woollen ruana more closely about her, and slid the sheets of paper back into her bag. On her way out she smiled at the young man, rejoicing in the answering flash in his eyes, but was gone before he could react.

Back in the car she breathed deeply, feeling both stronger and more confident as she drove off. Yet later, as she left the A38, following the signs for Bovey Tracey, she acknowledged that she was weary. The day had been a busy one and she would be glad to rest. She would telephone Mike so that he would know she'd arrived safely, then a soak in a hot bath and a sleep before dinner would refresh her. Tomorrow, she promised herself as she parked the car, she would allow herself an hour or so to potter in the town before setting off on the second half of her journey.

The next day was Saturday and the town was busy. Melissa strolled along Station Road and crossed the bridge, pausing to watch the river flowing beneath it, past the now-defunct wheel on the Mill. The old stone building housed a craft shop, as well as an exhibition gallery and café, and she'd decided to have some coffee there before she set off to Tavistock. As she mingled with the locals she was aware of a delicious sense of anonymity. It was a holiday feeling, and a few early daffodils growing beside a cottage wall promised that spring was at hand, despite the icy breath of wind on her cheek.

Melissa browsed for a while in a bookshop, bought some chocolate and retraced her steps to the Mill. Despite the sunshine it was not warm enough to sit at one of the tables in the courtyard, and she headed for the café doors. Choosing from the array of cakes and asking for coffee took several minutes, and when she looked about her she saw that all the tables were occupied. She hesitated, dismayed, until she saw that only one person was sitting at the table by the window. She threaded her way between the morning shoppers and paused hopefully. The girl was young, twentyish, and rather striking. Her eyes, honey brown beneath the heavy fall of shiny dark hair, were bright and interested, and she gestured readily as Melissa asked if she might share with her.

'Of course,' she answered. 'It's rather busy this morning. Everyone's coming in to get warm.'

'The sun deceived me,' said Melissa cheerfully, putting her plate and her coffee on the table. 'I didn't realise how cold it was. Oh! How lovely the river is.'

Below the window the water raced by, silvery bright and glinting. On the bank opposite, trees leaned over the river and a grey wagtail bobbed among their roots. A bluetit clung to the nut container that hung from one of the branches, while a rival watched from a neighbouring twig.

'I've written down the bluetits and the wagtail,' said the girl. 'I always hope I shall see something really bizarre but I never have.'

Melissa looked puzzled and the girl pushed a diary towards her.

Under each day's heading, sightings were noted down by visitors, and she saw that binoculars and reference books stood on the windowsill.

'What a nice idea,' she said. 'I hope I see something. Only I'm not very good about birds.'

'There are other things too. Water voles and mice. Some people like to be funny. They've written "the Titanic, sinking" and "Free Willy" and things like that, but there's a really nice one here. "My darling wife, Anne, on our wedding anniversary, who, after thirty-five years and five kids, is still the best bird around for me." Isn't that lovely? Fancy having that written about you after all that time. Wouldn't it be brilliant?'

Looking into the younger girl's glowing face, Melissa felt a sudden, devastating sensation of loss. There could be no such epitaph for her. She broke the piece of sponge apart with her fork, trying to smile. The girl was leafing through the diary, and, watching her, Melissa was aware of an odd feeling of . . . of what? She frowned, trying to define it. The girl smiled across at her and Melissa felt absurdly touched, as if she had been offered something vital, included within a tight-knit circle of affection and kinship, and her sense of loss was diffused.

'You might see a dipper if you were really lucky. Or a kingfisher.'

'That would be wonderful.' Melissa sipped her coffee. 'Are you a local?'

'Sort of.' She sounded defensive. 'My grandmother lives here so I've been coming to Bovey all my life nearly. My parents live in London but I'm doing a theatre studies course at King Alfred's in Winchester.'

'What fun.' Melissa had regained her composure and now studied her companion afresh. 'Are you going to be an actress?'

The dark girl shrugged. 'I don't know really. I wish I did. It's awful not knowing what you want to do. People expect you to have a vocation from the age of ten, these days, and you feel a failure if you don't.'

Melissa chuckled mischievously. 'Perhaps you want five children and a husband that writes nice things about you when you're sixty.'

'That's the trouble. I probably would, but it wouldn't do my street cred any good to admit it to my mates.'

'Have you anyone particular in mind?'

'No, not really. There's someone I go riding with but he's much older. He's nice, though. I've had a thing about Hugh since I was a little girl, but it's not serious. I can talk to him, though. He listens properly.'

She sighed, propping her elbows on the table, chin in hands, and Melissa felt another wave of what she could only describe as an intense familiarity, a sense of comradeship. Before she could speak, however, the girl straightened, her eyes fixed on something beyond the window.

'Look,' she said. 'There's the nuthatch. Isn't he brilliant? I love the way he goes for the nuts, as if he has to kill each one before he can eat it.'

'And upside-down to boot,' agreed Melissa. 'He's very handsome, isn't he? Shall we put him in the diary?'

'You can have him,' the girl said generously, pushing the book across the table. 'Go on. Are you staying in Bovey?'

'Just overnight.' Melissa was busy writing. 'I'm on my way to Cornwall. House-hunting.'

'Oh, really?' She sounded interested, but before she could pursue it, someone called 'Posy' and she turned. 'It's my grandmother,' she said. 'I have to go. I hope you enjoy Cornwall. Bye.'

'It's been so nice to meet you . . . Posy.' Melissa watched as the girl collected her belongings and, with a farewell smile, made her way between the tables. She saw her greet the tall, elderly lady and, when they'd disappeared, Melissa turned back to the window feeling foolishly bereft.

'Posy,' she murmured. It was an unusual name and she decided that she liked it, that it had suited the dark girl who had been so friendly. Her spirit was brushed again with a sense of loss. Posy's vitality and youth had underlined her own frailty, and as she ate her cake, her eyes on the nuthatch, Keats's words drifted in her thoughts. The poem, his 'Ode to a Nightingale', had comforted her during those earlier, terrible months and now, today, pointed to a bittersweet contrast between herself and Posy. *''Tis not through envy of thy happy lot, But being too happy in thine happiness, That thou, light-wingèd Dryad of the trees . . . Singest of summer in full-throated ease . . . Now more than ever seems it rich to die, To cease upon the midnight with no pain, While thou art pouring forth thy soul abroad In such an ecstasy! . . . Thou wast not born for death, immortal Bird!'*

Odd that the girl's bright, young, eager face should make her own dark, cruel, secret terror easier to bear.

Melissa thrust aside such fanciful imaginings and turned her mind to the journey ahead. It was a wonderful day for a drive over the moor, and with luck she'd be in Padstow by tea time.

She picked up the diary again, her spirits rising, and wrote beneath her earlier entry: 'Met a great chick called Posy.' Perhaps she'd see it and it would make her smile, next time she came in for coffee. She hesitated for a moment, the pencil still in her hand, and quickly, lest she should change her mind, wrote a few more words. 'Thou wast not born for death, immortal Bird!' Gathering up her bag, shrugging herself into her ruana, she hurried out into the spring sunshine.

The cold blue air seemed to fizz like wine as they cantered over the slopes of Black Down on Sunday morning, the moor unfolding at their feet, stretching into an infinite distance. As they trotted beside the Becka Brook, Hugh reined in and brought his mount alongside Posy's.

'You're looking good,' he said, studying her. 'Better than last time.'

She smiled at him gratefully. 'I *am* better. Things are easier. Dad's . . . thing seems to have finished. Perhaps it wasn't as bad as I thought.'

'Things get out of proportion.' Hugh leaned forward to pat his horse's neck and the flesh twitched at his touch. 'Everyone gets a bit heated.'

Posy grimaced. 'I certainly did,' she admitted. 'Mum seems OK now. Dad's not his usual self, though. He's very quiet. Sort of abstracted.'

'He's probably had a bit of a fright,' said Hugh reassuringly. 'He might have got quite fond of this other woman and then realised that it was getting out of control. Could be anything. Don't start imagining things.'

She smiled, stretching a hand to him. 'I won't. Thanks, Hugh.'

He held her hand for a moment and then let it go. 'Mind you don't. Come on, let's make for Honeybag Tor, shall we?'

Single file they guided their horses down the bank, splashing through the brook, and set out together, beneath Greator Rocks, cantering over Houndtor Down in the bright sunshine.

In the end, Melissa came upon the house quite by chance. She'd lost her way in the winding Cornish lanes, driving slowly, peering at finger-posts that bore unlikely names, wanting to get a feel of the place before contacting the agents next morning. There were no precise instructions on the details, but Mike had drawn a circle on the map, noting the given distances from the A39, from the coast at Tintagel and from Launceston.

'Its name shows that it's at the edge of the moor,' he'd said, 'so it's got to be within this small area. It should be obvious.'

It might have looked obvious on the tourist map, but here in the twisty, unmarked lanes it could as easily have been a maze. She drove slowly through a small hamlet, granite cottages huddling about a grassy triangle with a stone cross set in it, and plunged once more into a deep, narrow lane that curved sharply left, uphill, and opened upon a grove of trees to the right. To the left, set back a little from the lane, was the old farmhouse: comfortable, solid, washed a deep, warm cream with dark red-painted window frames and gutters. The FOR SALE board leaned drunkenly against the low stone wall.

She edged the Polo in close to the wall, switched off the engine and stepped out into the sunshine. She became aware of the cawing of rooks and, further off, the plaintive bleating of lambs. The house wasn't particularly large or architecturally beautiful, just a stone and slate farmhouse, but she felt, quite simply, that it was hers. Crocus and daffodil were growing in the beds beneath the windows and jasmine climbed the porch. There was a small gate in the wall, which closed the garden off from the yard to the left, and the flagged path led across to the lawn, which spread away to the right of the house, encircled by tall shrubs.

Melissa closed the car door quietly and strolled to the wrought-iron gate. Moorgate—the legend was painted in black on a small wooden board attached to the gate. Moorgate. The gate to the moor.

She pushed it gently, passed into the garden and stood looking at the house. To prove that it was empty, she rang the bell. No one came hurrying to answer it. She turned the door handle, but the solid oak door remained firmly closed. Cupping her hands about her eyes she looked through the windows into the rooms on either side of the porch. They were similar: large, heavily beamed, with great granite fireplaces. Both were full of sunlight and empty of furniture.

She wandered back along the path, round the corner of the house, and stopped short with a cry of amazement. The moor, stretching as far as the eye could see, flowed like some great ocean up to the house. The path finished in a cleared turfed square, enclosed by a ring fence, and beyond it she could see the lambs with their mothers. Outcrops of granite burst haphazard from the peaty earth and she could hear the sound of water singing in some nearby hidden coomb. Here on the north side, out of the sun, the air was icy, and, pulling her ruana more closely round her, Melissa turned her back on the moor and gazed up at the house. A glassed porch enclosed the back door, and she went to peer in at the windows on either side. They let in to the same room: a huge kitchen with a range, and a sink unit directly below one window. Once again Melissa stepped back, staring up at the first-floor windows. What views the bedrooms on this side of the house must have! She crossed the turf behind the house and entered the yard. Logs were piled in the corner of an open-fronted barn next to a loose box, and a washing line was strung between two poles. Leaning for a moment on the five-bar gate, she watched the rooks, noisy but sociable, in the trees across the lane, twiggy nests conspicuous among the bare branches.

Melissa thought: How wonderful to live in a place where the only sounds you can hear from your front gate are made by rooks and lambs.

She let herself out, closing the gate carefully behind her, climbed into the car and drove slowly up the lane.

CHAPTER SEVEN

LATER THAT SAME DAY, arriving home from Newton Abbot, having seen Posy off on the train, Maudie was just in time to snatch up the telephone receiver.

'Yes?' she said. 'Hello?'

Maudie's peremptory telephone manner always irritated Selina, but this evening she could not allow herself the luxury of irritation. 'Oh, Maudie,' she said brightly. 'How are you? Is Posy with you?'

'Long gone, I'm afraid, Selina,' she said cheerfully. 'So sorry you've missed her. You'll catch her later on this evening, I expect.'

The finality in her voice hurried Selina into speech. 'Oh, right. I'll do that. But how are you, Maudie? Have you had a nice weekend together?'

'Very nice. It's such a treat to have Posy to stay.'

'It was good of you to take Polonius.' Selina couldn't resist a hint that she knew why Maudie had given a home to the wretched animal.

'It was a ruse on my part.' Maudie had no intention of letting the insinuation go unremarked. 'A bribe. You suspected that, didn't you?'

Selina gritted her teeth. 'Nonsense.' She laughed lightly. 'You've never needed bribes where Posy's concerned. She's always adored you.'

'Extraordinary, isn't it? And in the face of such determined opposition, too. Anyway, never mind all that. What can I do for you, Selina?'

Selina, who had hoped to work round to Moorgate by degrees, having invoked Hector's memory, abandoned subtlety and went straight to the point. 'I was thinking about Moorgate. I'm really serious about buying it, Maudie. I'm hoping you'll be prepared to talk terms with me.'

'Are you selling the London house?'

'No. I . . . We did think about it but decided against it. We want to keep Moorgate as a holiday home. As it was when we were children.'

'But it wasn't, Selina. When your mother was alive the tenants let you use it for a few weeks each summer and later on there was a gap between tenants. You know that if it's not lived in it will be damp and uninhabitable in a matter of months. Anyway, forgive me for being impertinent, but how could Patrick afford to buy it and run it on his salary?'

'It would be difficult,' said Selina stiffly, 'we realise that, but we think it's worth the sacrifice.'

'Whose sacrifice? What sacrifice will you be making, Selina?'

'I don't see that it's any of your business. I'm simply asking if you will take it off the market while we get our act together. I don't think that it's unreasonable given that really you have no right to it at all.'

'Oh, not that again, please,' said Maudie wearily. 'The answer is no. If you haven't been able to sort yourselves out since last November I can't see why you should now. If you want to sell up and live on the edge of Bodmin Moor that's one thing and I can't stop you. If you do, then you shall have every opportunity to buy Moorgate. Otherwise you'd be committing financial suicide and you know it.'

'So you won't help us?'

Maudie sighed. 'I thought that was exactly what I was doing. Very well. I'd like to speak to Patrick. I want to hear how he plans to finance this operation before I consider it. Is he there?'

'No,' she answered sulkily. 'Anyway, I speak for Patrick.'

'Oh, I know you do,' said Maudie. 'But just this once I want to hear him say it and I want to see how he plans to achieve it. Your father would have needed to be certain before he was a party to this, Selina, as well you know. So ask Patrick to call me when he gets in, will you?'

She winced as Selina slammed the receiver onto its rest.

'I behaved badly,' she told Polonius remorsefully as she hung up her jacket. 'I intended to be much nicer to Selina but she always rubs me up the wrong way. Oh, guilt! Guilt!' she cried angrily, opening the stove and thrusting logs into the glowing embers. 'How tiresome it is to feel responsible for people.' She shut the stove doors and Polonius lay down on the rug. 'The trouble is,' she muttered, 'Selina and I are incompatible. We all knew that on day one. How she disliked me!'

As she went into the kitchen to make tea she recalled a scene some twenty years before, when Hector had been told that he was to receive a knighthood. Selina had been beside herself with pride. To Maudie, however, she'd been unable to contain her resentment. 'You don't deserve it,' she'd said furiously. 'It's Mummy who should be Lady Todhunter, not you. It isn't fair.'

'I couldn't agree more,' Maudie had answered. 'I find it utterly embarrassing to be called Lady Todhunter. The whole thing is quite ludicrous.'

It had infuriated Selina even more that Maudie wasn't overwhelmed by such honour and her rage had become coruscating in its vehemence. Hector had been obliged to intervene and Daphne had taken Selina aside and pointed out that her sulks were spoiling her father's pleasure.

'Although I have to say,' she'd said later to Maudie, 'that you are being quite unnatural about this. We'd all give our eyeteeth to be Lady Whatever, and you're behaving as if it's simply rather tiresome.'

'It just seems so unreal,' was all Maudie had answered, though she'd tried to be thrilled for Hector's sake.

Maudie carried her tea into the living room and sat down at the table, still remembering. Her attempt had never really come off and she knew that Hector had been well aware of the sardonic gleam in her eye when people 'sirred' him. Poor old Hector, she thought. What a cow I am!

Yet she knew that she was right about Moorgate. It would be disastrous for Selina to buy it, and she could only hope that Patrick was not submitting to emotional blackmail. Maudie picked up the envelope from The Scotch House, tipped the pieces of tartan cloth onto the table and shuffled them absently. She needed a buyer; someone who would make an offer and put a stop to Selina's nonsense.

'Who was it?'

Selina whirled round on her chair, caught in the act, already mentally inventing a reason for slamming down the receiver.

'It was . . . I was just . . .'

'It was Maudie, wasn't it?'

'Yes, it was Maudie,' she said. 'I was talking to her about Moorgate.'

'Oh, Moorgate. You never give up, do you, Selina?'

His amused, casual reaction was unnerving. 'I still feel we could buy it if we made an effort. Especially now . . .' Her voice died under his puzzled scrutiny.

'Especially now? I think not. If you want to sell this house and move to Cornwall that's fine. As far as I'm concerned this house is yours and you can do what you like with it. You could sell it, buy Moorgate and have a bit over.' He shrugged. 'As for me. Well, I think I've had enough.'

'Enough of what?' Fear made her shrill. 'What do you mean?'

'Enough of you. Of married life. Of being dull old Patrick Stone. I'm going to pack it in. Go off somewhere. Live a bit before it's too late.'

'I hope you don't mind if I say that you sound like a corny character in some third-rate melodrama.'

He laughed. 'I don't mind what you say. I'm past caring. I just thought you should know where you stand regarding Moorgate. Count me out.'

'Don't be such a fool—'

'Oh, but I am a fool, Selina,' he cut in quickly. 'Nobody knows that better than you. I'm going to the pub. I'll get something to eat there.'

She heard the front door close but she seemed unable to rise from her chair. Of course, it was ridiculous and he didn't mean a word of it, she told herself. He was trying to make himself interesting, hoping to distract her from his unfaithfulness. Nevertheless, a tiny, panicky voice was asking how she'd cope if he'd really had enough? She had no answer.

In the pub, Patrick ordered a pint and stood waiting, staring reflectively at nothing in particular. Ever since Christmas an odd kind of lassitude had been growing in him. Even the pain of seeing Mary at school had lost its keen edge of misery and lately he'd felt merely sad. It was rather unpleasant, this lack of emotion. At least his desperation had carried with it the comfort of feeling alive; these days he simply felt detached.

He paid for his pint, remembering other evenings; marking time until he could go out to the telephone and speak to Mary. How vivid life had seemed then. She'd given a purpose to his existence. Now there was nothing. Nobody needed him and he was important to nobody.

Patrick swallowed some beer. Well, at least there was a freedom in that, an opportunity to begin something new.

'The world is my oyster,' he announced suddenly—and caught the surprised glance of the young barman. He took another draught, suppressing a rising desire to laugh, and almost choked. As he set his glass down on the bar, still trying to control the urge to giggle foolishly, he wondered whether he might be having a nervous breakdown.

The agent was already waiting for Melissa. His hatchback was in the yard and he was standing by the gate in the cold, bright sunshine. He raised a hand to her, swung wide the gate so that she could drive in, and then hurried round to open her door for her. She smiled at him as she climbed out, noting the fresh, newly scrubbed complexion and floppy fair hair. He wore a Barbour over his dark suit.

'Mr Cruikshank.' She shook his hand. 'What a fantastic morning.'

He beamed at her. 'It's simply perfect, Mrs . . . er, Miss Clayton?'

She made no attempt to clarify the matter, leading the way into the front garden while he fumbled with the keys. She waited impatiently as he opened the door and stood back for her to enter.

'I'm not too good at the official bit,' he told her. 'It always seems a case of stating the obvious, so I'll simply say that the place has been thoroughly renovated. No expense spared. New wiring and plumbing . . .'

She went before him into the sitting room, pulling the scarf from her hair, and stood rapt with delight, imagining a huge log fire burning in the massive granite fireplace.

'Impressive, isn't it?' he remarked.

She glanced at him absently and crossed the hall to the study. He followed her, watching as she wandered about.

'Is this the way to the kitchen?' Melissa asked, striding down the hall, flinging open a door. 'Ooooh . . .'

Mr Cruikshank stood at her shoulder. 'Breathtaking, isn't it?'

'It's utterly wonderful.'

'The stove is fantastic,' he said, happy that he'd had a positive reaction. 'It heats the water too, and supplies a heated towel rail in the bathroom and a radiator in the master bedroom. Lady Todhunter very sensibly keeps it alight to keep the house aired.'

'It feels very warm.' She glanced round the huge kitchen. 'It's north-facing, isn't it?'

'Wonderfully cool in summer,' he said quickly. 'This slate floor is a masterpiece. Now, at this end the old dairy has been converted into a larder and utility room. The other side is an office, a loo and a storeroom. Plenty of space. Do you have a family, um, Mrs Clayton?'

'Oh, yes. I have a family,' she answered airily. 'May I see upstairs?'

'Of course,' he said. 'Back into the hall. Lovely original oak staircase.'

She ran up lightly before him. The staircase turned to the right and opened into a passage with a room on each side. On she went: up two steps, round a corner, down three steps. She stopped, enchanted. There was a wide landing and a big window with a deep seat, where one could sit and stare out at the moor.

'. . . five bedrooms,' he was saying as he caught her up. 'One's very small but the biggest room has windows east and south. Here we are . . .'

'No en suite bathroom?' she asked idly, teasingly, as she followed him into the large, sunny room.

'Rob Abbot dug his heels in.' He sounded almost vexed. 'And Lady Todhunter agreed with him. She said it was a farmhouse not a hotel.'

'I couldn't agree more,' said Melissa, strolling over to the window and staring down into the lane. 'But there are two bathrooms?'

'Oh yes,' he replied quickly. 'One's tiny but it's there.'

The rooks were still busy in their tree, their cries ringing in the icy air. She leaned her forehead against the glass, aware of a deep happiness.

'I love it,' she said dreamily. 'I absolutely love it.'

A short silence.

'Well, then.' Mr Cruikshank sounded confused. 'Miss . . . er, Mrs—'

'I'd like another look,' she said, turning swiftly round. 'Alone.'

His startled expression made her want to laugh. 'Of course. I quite understand. I'll be downstairs. Take all the time you need.'

He went away, across the landing, along the passage, down the stairs. When she could no longer hear him she gasped, a huge, deep breath, and whirled lightly on her toes. Sunshine splashed on the warm cream wall and flowed down onto the bare varnished boards. Quickly she went from room to room, imagining them furnished and lived in, and when she could delay no longer she went downstairs. She saw the front door close tactfully behind the agent and paused in the hall before going into the sitting room, the study and the kitchen.

Finally she went to find him. He was on the lawn, examining the shrubs, but turned as she approached, watching her eagerly.

'It's . . . perfect,' she said.

He smiled at her. 'I agree. If I had the money I'd buy it myself.'

'Would you? You don't look like a countryman, Mr Cruikshank.'

'That's what Rob Abbot said.' He was too shy to insist that she should call him Ned. 'I *do* love the country but actually I'm transferring to the London branch. Should be fun . . .'

'Rob Abbot? You mentioned him before. Who is he?'

'He's the chap who did all the work on the place. Lady Todhunter had terrific faith in him, but he likes his own way, does Rob. He's a great guy, though. We've become good chums since the key business.'

'Key business?'

He told her about the mystery of the keys, the locked rooms, the fear of a squatter.

'How strange,' she murmured. 'How very strange.'

'All done with now, though,' he said quickly. 'It all came to nothing. It's a wonderful position, isn't it? So peaceful.'

'Mmm.' She turned away from him, biting her lip.

'Well. Seen enough inside? Want to have a look at the outbuildings?'

'What I'd really like,' she said, 'is to spend some time getting to know the place. I live a long way away, Mr Cruikshank, and I can't simply pop up and down. Do you think I could have the key for a couple of days?'

He looked dismayed. 'I couldn't do that. Company policy . . .'

'After all, the place is empty, isn't it? It's not as if I'm going to make off with the furniture.'

'We're simply not allowed, you see . . .'

'It's a lot of money . . .'

'I could come again, any time you like,' he said unhappily. 'I'm honestly not being difficult.'

'It's not quite that simple,' she said wistfully. 'You see, if I could have the key I shouldn't bother to go and see all the other houses I have lined up. I'm certain I should just settle for this one. On the other hand . . .'

He stared at her desperately. 'It's more than my job's worth.'

'But didn't you say that you were transferring to London?'

He looked alarmed. 'Same company . . .'

'But a long way off. When are you leaving?'

'Well, this weekend, actually.' He brightened. 'Listen. Rob Abbot has a set of keys. He sometimes shows clients round only I couldn't catch him this morning. Supposing I arrange with him—'

'What a good idea,' she interrupted swiftly. 'You can say that Mr Abbot has mislaid his keys and you've left him yours so that he can show people round. I'll take my time, measure a few things, then leave the keys with Mr Abbot. Brilliant! How clever you are, Mr Cruikshank.'

'Well.' He hesitated, his intention having been quite different, but somehow finding it impossible to say so. She was certainly very keen and, after all, it wasn't a bad story and he'd be gone by the weekend. 'I suppose so. But you mustn't drop me in it at the office.'

'As if I would.' Her smile was brilliant. 'Now, how can I contact Mr Abbot? I promise I shan't keep the keys a moment longer than I need.'

She accompanied him into the yard, promising to be in touch very soon, and went out into the lane to wave him off, shutting the gate behind her, the keys held tightly in her hand. When the noise of the engine had died away, and the only sounds she could hear were the rooks' strident conversation and the high, thin cries of the lambs, she turned very slowly and looked up at the house.

Rob Abbot locked the door of his mobile home, which was parked in the corner of the farmer's field, climbed the stile and set out over the moor. The house stood above him, washed warm by the evening sun, the grove of trees creating a dark backdrop. It was becoming more difficult, with spring drawing on, to make his entrances and exits unseen, but he'd dropped a few hints that he was caretaking the place and hoped that this was enough to satisfy inquisitive eyes. He knew that he was obsessed but he couldn't help himself; from the earliest days the house had charmed him. He remembered standing in the damp, empty rooms, seeing all the character and beauty beneath sagging wallpaper, peeling paint and dull varnish. The vision had remained before him as he'd worked. After a while it had been impossible to imagine anyone else living there. He'd needed to return, once he'd dropped the men off, to be alone in the house, to feel the peace settling on it again after the busyness of the day. He'd park the pick-up by his caravan and, packing up a few necessities, he'd slip away, over the stile and across the moor in the shadow of the thorn, letting himself in by the side door.

He laughed as he remembered the shock he'd had that morning when he'd come round the corner of the house and found Lady Todhunter standing in the yard, his fear that she might guess what was going on. He'd suggested she should move her car into the yard to give himself time to dash back into the house and hide all obvious signs of occupation, but at every step his heart had been in his mouth.

'It doesn't feel as cold as I'd expected,' she'd said, drinking her tea. 'And what's that smell? Bacon?'

His feeble suggestion of ghosts had distracted her—momentarily—and he was ready for her when they got to the sitting room and she'd asked if he'd been lighting fires. Nevertheless, it had been a nasty moment. Once she'd agreed that he should keep an eye on the place, light up the Esse, make certain that the house was warm, it had made life easier, giving him an excuse for being around at odd moments—but he'd lost his secret quarters. The office, with the loo and storeroom, had made a perfect base. He'd been able to keep his bits of furniture, a cache of food, some blankets, well out of the sight of prying eyes. How his heart had pumped when she'd suggested breaking the door down while she watched. The idea of squatters had bought him the time he needed but that was all. At least he'd been given the opportunity to carry on working in the house, but with Ned rolling up with potential buyers his peace of mind was shattered. Fortunately, nobody as yet had asked to see inside the locked cupboard under the stairs.

Striding over the sheep-nibbled turf, Rob smiled as he thought of how eagerly Ned had accepted him as a caretaker, responsible enough to show clients round. The fact that Lady Todhunter trusted him was enough for Ned, always glad to be saved the long drive from Truro, and how easy it had been to drop a word, here and there, to frighten those clients away. How much longer, he wondered, could he hold out before someone made an offer and pipped him at the post? He'd almost exhausted his cash-raising possibilities, and time was running out. It was easy to deter potential buyers when the rain was lashing down, or you couldn't see ten feet beyond the window because of rolling mist, but with the summer ahead it would be much more difficult.

Glancing up, as he neared the house, he frowned. He thought he saw someone standing at the kitchen window, staring out over the moor. He drew back into the shadow of the thorn. The dark window seemed to frame a pale, insubstantial form: a woman looking out. He mocked at himself—he was letting the house get to him—and when he looked again there was nothing there. He covered the last few yards swiftly, swung himself over the ring fence, checked that Ned Cruikshank's car was not in the yard and finally let himself in through the back door.

The kitchen felt warm and welcoming and he breathed more easily, relaxing as usual now that he was home. He took the frozen dinner from his backpack, peeled off the lid and put the foil dish into the oven of the Esse. Next he pushed the kettle onto the hotplate and took a tea caddy and a bag of sugar from the cupboard under the sink. A china mug stood upside-down on the draining board and he turned it the right way up. He laid the backpack on the floor, first removing his mobile phone and a carton of milk. Placing them beside the mug he went out into the hall, taking a key ring from his pocket as he went. At the foot of the stairs he hesitated, trying to identify the faint scent that lingered in the cooler air of the hall. Shaking his head, wondering if Ned had been round earlier with a client, Rob unlocked the small padlock and opened the cupboard door. He brought out a gate-leg table, a cane-seated chair and two large beanbags. He took the table and chair into the kitchen, set them up beside the Esse and then went back through the hall and into the sitting room. Here he picked up a cast-iron poker, pushed together the remains of burnt wood and hot ashes, and placed other logs on top. From the stack of wood at one side of the inglenook, he drew out a pair of bellows and began to blow new life into the ashes. When he was satisfied that the fire was well alight, he went out into the hall, returning with the beanbags, which he put together before the fire.

As he straightened up he paused, listening intently. Was that a footfall in the bedroom overhead? He glanced at his watch, shrugging off his jitters, and then out at the twilight, wondering whether to fasten the shutters. Unwilling to close out the gold-flushed evening, he went back to the kitchen and made himself a mug of tea. Stirring in the sugar, he stood looking out over the flowing, rippling moorland, enjoying the last of the sunset. He sipped the hot, sweet tea with pleasure, filled with a poignant sense of longing, aware of the house breathing around him. With a sigh, he set down the mug and went back to build up the fire.

The girl was standing by the inglenook, staring down at the beanbags. He checked just inside the door, with a barely concealed gasp, his heart hammering against his ribs, and she turned to look at him. She was beautiful, slender, with a sweet, bright face and an enchanting air of eager vulnerability.

'Hello,' she said. 'You must be Rob Abbot.'

Afterwards he could never remember exactly what happened next. He was plunged into madness, into magic, into love.

He stared at her, as if she were a ghost—'I thought you were,' he admitted later—and she began to chuckle, going towards him across the bare clean boards, her hand outstretched.

'I'm sorry,' she said. 'I tricked Mr Cruikshank into letting me keep the keys. I couldn't bear to leave Moorgate, you see. My name's Melissa.'

He cursed then, but laughing at himself, reaching for her hand, feeling an absurd desire to raise it to his lips.

'I knew that wretched boy would bring me down,' he said ruefully. Yet he smiled at her, not feeling in the least at risk. 'I realised earlier that my mobile has been switched off all day. You've caught me red-handed.'

She seemed to be in no hurry to reclaim her hand. 'I guessed,' she said, her eyes twinkling mischievously. 'He told me about the missing keys and I just knew what had happened. You see, I would have done exactly the same myself. Well, I have, haven't I? I've tricked him so that I could be here alone, pretending that Moorgate was mine.'

'After only one viewing?'

'Oh, yes. That's all it needed. What about you?'

'Not much longer. Once Lady Todhunter had gone, that very first time, and I was alone, the magic began to work. I felt I belonged here.'

'That's it,' she agreed eagerly. 'Oh, I was very taken with the photograph, but as soon as I saw the house I felt like that. As if I belonged.'

'Well.' He raised his eyebrows, teasingly. 'In that case, we have a problem, don't we?'

'Do we?' she asked provocatively—and he burst out laughing, in love, crazy, utterly happy.

'I've only enough supper for one,' he said. 'Never mind. We'll share.'

'I happen to have a delicious home-made steak and kidney pie in the hamper in my car,' she said demurely. 'As well as some fruit and chocolate and a rather good bottle of Chablis.'

He stared at her. 'You really meant to spend the evening here?'

She shrugged. 'I meant to stay as long as I could. So I came prepared. I saw that the stove was working, and when I touched that wood burner in the study it was hot, so I thought I'd manage quite well.'

He stared down at her, serious now. 'You didn't think you'd be frightened? Not all on your own out here on the moor?'

'I didn't expect to be alone,' she said candidly.

He took a deep breath. 'I could be a madman,' he told her, almost crossly. 'A psychopath.'

'But you're not, are you?' She smiled. 'You just love Moorgate. So do I.'

'Melissa.' It was as if he were tasting her name, experimenting with it—then he frowned. 'But where on earth is your car?'

She laughed. 'It's hidden up a little track a hundred yards down the lane. I was going to unload it when it was dark.'

'How very intrepid you are,' he said. 'Are you afraid of nothing?'

She turned away towards the fire. 'I'm afraid of being cold,' she said lightly. 'I do so feel the cold, which is why I was so pleased to see the Esse and the fires.' She touched the beanbag gently with the toe of her leather boot. 'You sleep on these?'

'Yes,' he said quickly, visited suddenly by an intimate image.

'I have some rugs,' she said. 'Nice warm rugs. Perhaps I could trade one of my rugs for one of your beanbags?'

'We'll manage somehow. We'll pile the fire high with logs and tell each other ghost stories until we fall asleep. How does that sound?'

'It sounds perfect.'

'Shall we get the car unpacked, then?' he asked. 'Then we can really settle in. Close the shutters and batten down the hatches.'

'I have a picnic chair and a table,' she offered, 'and knives and forks.'

'We'll go and forage,' he said cheerfully. 'The chair will be useful. I've only got one. Let's go before it gets too dark.'

She followed him out through the hall into the kitchen. Outside the back door they paused. The night was clear, stars twinkled frostily and a sickle moon was caught in a delicate net of black, bare branches. Their breath smoked in the icy air and he felt her shiver beside him.

'Come on,' he said. 'It's going to be cold tonight. Thank heavens we've got plenty of logs. Whatever happens, at least we won't freeze.'

Later, sitting at the kitchen table, which they'd placed as near to the Esse as they could, Rob and Melissa shared their supper and discussed how the kitchen should be furnished.

'It would make such a difference to have rugs on the floor,' Melissa said, watching as Rob dealt with the wine, 'and curtains, of course. Much more cosy. I'd have a really big kitchen table and a huge dresser.'

'Would it be possible to find a dresser large enough?' Rob poured the wine into the glasses from the hamper. 'I think that it might have to be a built-in one, along the whole of the back wall.'

'But then it would look new. Bright and shiny and rather horrid.'

'Not necessarily. It could be made from old, reclaimed wood. Then it would look old but be the right size. Same thing with the table.'

'Oh, I can just see it.' Her eyes shone as she looked at the wall. 'With lots of china on it. Not matching, or Grandmama's old Victorian tat, but treasured pieces that all seem to go together because they've been specially saved or bought. Because they're loved and because you simply couldn't live without having them. Do you know what I mean?'

'I'm beginning to think I do,' he said—and raised his glass to her.

She blushed fierily, and lifted her own glass to hide her confusion. 'It's the only way,' she said, ignoring the meaning behind his words, 'to make old and new live happily together. The trouble is, the shelves would be practically empty until the pieces built up over the years.'

'Sounds OK to me,' said Rob. 'It would be a lifetime's work.'

He looked at her, surprised at the sudden silence. She was frowning down at her plate, lips pressed together, almost as though she were trying not to cry. He decided that his comment must have been too near the mark. Of course, it was madness to feel so immediately happy with her, to feel that it was absolutely right that they should be contemplating a lifetime together. Even if she felt the same it was unfair to put her in a position where she was obliged to admit it.

'I'll show you the ford, tomorrow,' he said. 'There's a lovely old clapper bridge for wheeled traffic but we'll splash through the water properly. I hope you've brought some wellies with you.'

'Oh yes.' She seemed to have recovered herself. 'As you've seen I'm always well prepared. I would have been a first-rate girl guide if my mother would have let me join.'

'Why wouldn't she?'

'My mother was a recluse,' she said. 'She couldn't imagine anyone wishing to join anything. She made us feel inadequate if we asked to have friends to stay. It was odd, in her eyes, to need anyone.'

'"Us"?' he questioned gently.

'I have a brother,' she said. 'My mother died when I was fourteen. My father married again and had another family. He gave me and Mike twenty thousand pounds each and told us not to expect anything else from him. It was fair enough—very generous, in fact—but we've drifted a bit. His second wife isn't that keen on us. She feels she has to protect her own children, I expect.'

'You and your brother are close?'

'Oh yes.' Melissa smiled warmly. 'Very close. He's a dear. He has a small boy called Luke. And you?' She raised her eyebrows enquiringly. 'Tell me about you. Apart from loving Moorgate, I mean.'

'Oh, I come from quite a big family, all scattered about. We stay in touch at a distance. My mother went to live with her sister in Inverness when they were both widowed. We're all very fond of one another but not very close. Moorgate has been the only great passion of my life.'

They looked at each other a long, heart-stopping moment. The words 'until now' drifted unspoken in the air, and, quite involuntarily, Rob stretched out a hand to her across the table. After a moment, she laid her own hand in his and he held it tightly for a few brief seconds.

'You're cold,' he said, coming to his senses.

'"My tiny hand is frozen",' she sang. 'I told you, I'm always cold.'

'It's a bitter night,' he said worriedly. 'Let's make some coffee and take it in by the fire. I piled the logs halfway up the chimney. It should be roasting in there. If only we had comfortable chairs . . .'

'Big, squashy armchairs,' she said dreamily, watching him push the kettle onto the hot plate. 'And a sofa, don't you think?'

'Perhaps two, facing each other, either side of the fireplace?'

She wrinkled her nose, shaking her head. 'Too formal. What have you done with the chocolate?'

'Still in the hamper.' He peered inside. 'That's quite a selection.'

'I love chocolate,' she told him. 'The only great passion of my life, until,' she hesitated, smiling to herself, 'until Moorgate.'

'Take the chocolate,' he said, wrapping her ruana about her, 'and go and get warm. I'll bring the coffee.' He held the soft wool together under her chin and then kissed her lightly on the forehead. 'Shan't be long.'

She sat on the beanbag, her knees drawn up to her chin, staring into the flames, wondering if they were both quite mad.

She thought: What would Mike think if he knew what I was doing?

He would be desperate with anxiety, of course. 'Are you crazy?' he'd shout. 'He sounds an absolute nutter. Get out as quick as you can.'

Yet she was not afraid, perhaps because she had so little to lose, perhaps because her instinct told her there was no need of fear. When he'd raised his glass to her, she'd been filled with elation; when he talked as though he'd calmly accepted that they would share a lifetime together, she'd wanted to weep. How right it had sounded, but how differently he would behave if he knew that her lifetime was at best six months long.

It was such a relief, such a joy to act as if she were fit, ordinary, unhampered by such terrible knowledge. All the careless freedom of her young life had been done away with, nothing now could be taken for granted, but with Rob she could, for a short while, step out of time.

The door had opened behind her and Rob was smiling down at her. 'I forgot to ask how you have your coffee?'

'With milk and sugar,' she said. 'Shall I come and help carry?'

'Certainly not. Stay by the fire and keep warm.'

He went away again and she sat smiling to herself, liking his protectiveness, feeling ludicrously safe, terribly happy.

'Here we are.' He was back again, carrying the coffee.

She watched him covertly, liking the way his thick brown hair curled at the back of his neck, noting his deft hands, the long, strong back. He turned suddenly, meeting her eyes.

'This is so nice,' she said warmly. 'The fire and the coffee and—everything. It's as if I've stepped into a fairy tale. It's all so magical.'

'It's the same for me,' he mumbled. 'Crazy, isn't it?'

'Let's be crazy together,' she suggested. 'Tell me about the house. What it was like when you first saw it, Lady Todhunter and everything.'

'Everything is a tall order,' he said, settling down beside her, lounging easily. 'But I'll try. OK. Are you sitting comfortably? Then I'll begin.'

CHAPTER EIGHT

'THAT WAS YOUR AUNT MELISSA,' said Mike, putting down the telephone receiver and ruffling Luke's hair as he sat in his highchair. 'She's spent a comfortable night somewhere on the moor and is about to have her breakfast. Now we'll have ours, shall we?'

As he moved about, preparing Ready Brek for Luke, putting bread in the toaster, he was conscious of a relief from his anxiety. It was so difficult keeping his fears from Melissa, trying to live as if she were not under a sentence of death. To begin with she had been angry, railing against fate, but gradually her rage had subsided and a quieter resignation had taken its place, punctuated by periods of depression. Yet, once she had decided to let nature take its course, her natural resilience had reappeared along with a determination to enjoy what time was left. This opportunity to be normal was necessary for her emotionally and spiritually, whatever toll it might take physically. Mike put the marmalade on the table and rescued the milk in the saucepan from the electric ring.

Melissa had sounded enthusiastic about Moorgate, but the signal had kept breaking up and he hadn't been able to hear much, apart from the happy lilt to her voice. It was evident that she was enjoying herself, and that was all that mattered. He'd restrained himself from fussing, from reminding her not to get overtired. It didn't matter too much where she was—he could always contact her on her mobile—but it was necessary to know that she was safe and happy.

'It's good, Mike,' she'd said joyfully. 'Really good. But it's so cold.'

'You've picked the coldest week of the winter,' he'd told her. 'The weather's coming from Siberia. Be careful driving and keep warm.'

'I shall,' she'd said, 'don't worry. How are you? How's Luke?'

Amid the crackling, her voice fading and suddenly returning, he hadn't been able to do more than give her their love and ask her to stay in touch. She needed to feel free, normal, untrammelled by fear. If she could achieve it for a week or two then it would be a wonderful miracle.

'Go for it, Lissy,' he murmured, sitting down at the table beside Luke. 'Here we are, old son. Breakfast at last.'

'Hi, babe,' said Posy. 'I know it's an early one for me, but I thought I'd just check you're OK down there. I understand that the West Country is freezing hard and pipes are bursting and cars are crashing on black ice.'

Maudie was delighted at being addressed as 'babe' again. 'It's certainly cold,' she said, 'but everything's working properly. I saw the forecast yesterday, so Polonius and I went to Bovey to stock up. I shan't be taking the car out, so don't worry. How are you?'

'Great. This house is freezing, though. I went to bed in my clothes . . .'

She chattered on cheerfully while Maudie felt her spirits soar. When Posy finally rang off, Maudie returned to her breakfast, but before she could start on her toast the telephone rang again.

'Good morning, Lady Todhunter. It's Ned Cruikshank. Sorry to catch you so early but I wanted you to hear my news first hand. I'm being transferred to the London office at the end of the week.'

'Good heavens,' she said, startled. 'I'm sorry to hear this, Ned. I shall miss you. I hope your replacement is as enthusiastic about Moorgate as you've been.'

'That's what I wanted to tell you. I may have a buyer. A young woman, very keen. I hope to have good news for you by the end of the week.'

'But that's wonderful. I shall be very pleased to think that you brought it off and I hope you get a good commission.'

He laughed. 'So do I. Anyway, I'll ring you again before I leave, to bring you up to speed and to say goodbye.'

'That's very nice of you, Ned. Is it very cold down there?'

'Freezing.' He made shivery noises. 'They say it's going to snow but it's a glorious morning. Must dash. Goodbye.'

Maudie replaced the receiver feeling quite shocked.

'Well,' she said to Polonius. 'What a morning we're having. I do hope he's right. It would solve so many problems.'

For the third time she sat down to her breakfast, more light-hearted than she had been for many weeks. A genuine buyer would let her off Selina's hook and she might be able to stop feeling guilty.

'The G-word,' she murmured. 'How it rules our lives.'

Melissa woke to find Rob putting a mug of coffee beside her. She uncurled herself, shivering, glad to see the fire was newly made up.

'I didn't want to disturb you,' Rob said as he folded back the wooden shutters, 'but I didn't want you to be cold, either. It's quite warm in the bathroom if you feel you can brave it.'

He went away again, closing the door behind him, and she sat up, dazzled by the sunlight that poured into the room. She reached for the mug, cradling it in her hands, remembering. They'd sat together talking for hours, and when she'd come back downstairs from the bathroom he'd made up a bed for her: her sleeping-bag arranged on one of the beanbags with a rug tucked over it.

'In you get,' he'd said. 'I'm off for a quick sluice. Make yourself comfortable.' And she had been comfortable—and warm. She'd been aware of him during the night, moving quietly, making up the fire, before settling down again, and she'd lain awake for a while, watching the leaping shadows and listening to the hiss of the flames. For once these wakeful periods were brief, and she'd slept well and felt unusually rested.

Now she wriggled out of the sleeping-bag and went to the window, rug trailing. Frost sparkled in the sunshine and the rooks were arguing in the trees across the lane. She sighed with satisfaction, excitement fizzing. Today he would show her the ford, and they would walk on the hills, and she would imagine that they had a future together.

'Breakfast,' said Rob from the doorway, 'will be a little disappointing after the feast we conjured up last night. At least, I'm assuming that you haven't got a boot-load of porridge or bacon and eggs?'

Melissa shook her head, laughing. 'I'm afraid not. I'm not a big breakfast eater, but this morning I'd kill for a plate of bacon and eggs. Oh, and some big field mushrooms and a sausage.'

'I know a café in Tintagel,' he said thoughtfully, 'that could answer most of those requirements. How about we try it? I could go out and shop and cook it on the Esse, but it would be unfortunate if Ned Cruikshank turned up in the middle of it.'

She looked alarmed. 'Oh, heavens. Is that likely?'

'Since you've got his keys it's most unlikely, unless he telephones me first. I'll keep my mobile switched off.'

'Oh, no,' she said at once. 'Keep it switched on so that you can head him off. Or at least we'd be forewarned if he were determined.'

They laughed together, like conspirators.

Rob looked about the room. 'I'll clear the stuff away under the stairs. Hide the evidence. Hurry away, wench, and get ready. I'm starving.'

When she came back down to the kitchen, Rob was tidying things into the hamper. He wore a thick fisherman's jersey and jeans, and his hair was clean and shiny, curling a little from his shower.

'What a useful man you are,' she commented. And a very attractive one, she might have added. 'I can't tell you what fun I'm having.'

'We aim to please,' he said—and she went to him quite naturally and put her arms about him, hugging him. 'This is cheating,' he said, holding her tightly, his hands full of forks and plates, 'because you know I'm far too hungry to take advantage of you.'

She kissed him quickly and let him go. 'Let me do this,' she said. 'I know where everything lives. How far is Tintagel?'

'Not far,' he said, 'but we'll take your car, if you don't mind, and collect mine later.'

After a few minutes they went out, carrying the hamper and some rugs. Melissa waited while he locked the back door.

'Gosh!' she said, gasping, 'It's freezing.'

'The wind's from the north. Come on. It'll be warmer in the sun.'

The car was like a fridge and her teeth chattered as she drove away down the lane, following his instructions until at last they came to Tintagel. They fed lavishly on eggs and bacon, with toast and more coffee, in the company of the café proprietor, who watched them meditatively. Content at last they sat back and looked at one another.

'I hope,' said Rob, trying to sound casual, 'that you aren't going to abandon me now that you are replete with victuals.'

'Certainly not.' She sounded shocked. 'You promised me the ford. You said that I could splash through it if I'd brought my wellies.'

He sighed happily. 'We shall splash together. I just wondered if . . . you had any other engagements.'

She lightly touched his fist. 'None,' she said. 'I'm a free agent. I spoke to my brother earlier on my mobile so my duty is done for the day.'

He turned his hand, holding hers. 'Did you tell him where you were?'

She grinned. 'Not exactly. He knows that I'm staying on the moor and having a wonderful time. It's a pity, isn't it, that if you move about the signal breaks up and it goes all crackly and you have to shout? Things like, "Sorry. Can't quite hear but I'm fine. Don't worry. I'll call you later." I don't want him to worry, but he might not *quite* understand.'

Rob laughed. 'No, he probably wouldn't *quite* understand,' he agreed. 'In his place I'd have had a fit and ordered you back to a hotel.'

'Exactly,' said Melissa. 'You take my point.'

'You're in no danger from me. Always was a fool with women.'

'I expect Jack the Ripper used to say the same thing,' she said cheerfully, 'but it's too late. I'm in love.'

He looked at her sharply, eyebrows raised.

'With Moorgate,' she said sweetly, challengingly, and he chuckled. 'Those keys aren't going back just yet.'

'In that case we'd better stock up for the day . . .' He hesitated.

'Oh, at least,' she said at once. 'After all, tomorrow we could have a nice early breakfast, couldn't we? It's not that I don't like it here—the food's great—but I'd like to have breakfast at Moorgate.'

There was a short silence.

'In that case,' said Rob, 'we'd better do some shopping.'

It was just after break, in the staff room, that Patrick noticed the advertisement. The paper had been folded back to the classified ads page and the headline caught his attention: COULD YOU BE A L'ARCHE ASSISTANT? He'd heard of L'Arche: communities that looked after people with disabilities and learning difficulties. His eyes wandered over the column. 'There are no specific qualifications . . . except being at least 18 years old . . . Others decide upon L'Arche as a career change.' He remembered reading about Jean Vanier, a naval officer and then a philosopher, who gave up a promising career to help those who had been marginalised by society. He'd bought a little house and invited two such men into it— and so had started a worldwide movement.

Patrick stood holding the paper, an idea forming at the back of his mind. The door opened behind him and Mary came in.

'Oh,' she said, taken aback, clearly expecting the room to be empty. 'Hello. I left my paper. Oh, yes. That's it. Were you reading it?'

Patrick smiled at her quite easily, faintly saddened by her brittleness, still surprised by his own indifference. He felt in his jacket pocket for his pen and his diary. 'Mind if I jot down a number?' he asked. 'Won't take a moment. Just an advert that caught my eye.'

'Tear it out,' she said, almost impatiently.

'Thanks. I will. It's just this top corner. How's Stuart?'

'Fine . . . Well, you know.' She sounded flustered. 'Making progress.'

'That's good. Splendid.'

Patrick might have been talking about a distant acquaintance, more occupied with what he was doing than with Mary or Stuart.

'You don't sound all that interested.'

He looked up in surprise, folding the piece of paper into his diary. 'I had the impression that you preferred me to keep my interest to myself.'

He wasn't huffy, she noticed, merely amused.

'I didn't realise you'd be able to switch off so easily.'

'Switch off?'

She shrugged. 'Forget us. Stop caring. Whatever.'

He frowned thoughtfully. 'Is that what I've done? Yes, I suppose it is.'

His measured reply hurt her pride, and, as he handed her the paper, she drew closer, looking up at him.

'I miss you,' she said. 'I really do. I wish things could be different.'

He smiled rather absently. 'Never mind,' he said, as if comforting her. 'Perhaps it was for the best.'

He went out, tucking his diary into his pocket, and she stood looking after him, angry and miserable, and, worst of all, humiliated.

Shopping in Tintagel, choosing supper, waiting in the car while Rob disappeared on a mission of his own, Melissa was wrapped in the delightful holiday anonymity that she'd first experienced in Bovey Tracey. The local people, going about their business, barely spared her a second glance, so used were they to visitors in their midst.

Perhaps that's why Moorgate had appealed so much: its isolation attracted her, promising peace. Now that she'd met Rob, however, she didn't want to think about practicalities. How could she imagine Mike and Luke moving into Moorgate now that she knew how much Rob loved it? To own Moorgate was his dream. For these few days she wanted to forget her real reason for coming; she wanted to postpone decisions, put aside reality, and lose herself in this small, magical world.

Rob was coming towards her, a bulky parcel under his arm and a carrier bag in his other hand, his expression a mixture of satisfaction and embarrassment. She was puzzled but she did not question him.

'Right,' he said, settling himself beside her, the parcels stowed away. 'Would you like to continue to drive us or shall we get my pick-up?'

'I'm happy to drive. As long as you don't mind directing me.'

'Oh, I'm good at that,' he said. 'I've always enjoyed telling people what to do. OK, then. We'll head for the wide open spaces, shall we?'

'I'd like to get up onto the moor,' she agreed, pulling away from the kerb. 'I want to see Moorgate from somewhere else.'

'And so you shall. Do you have a hat as well as that scarf thing?'

She hesitated, foolishly sad that he would never see her with the long, bronze mass of hair that she'd had before the chemo. 'I have a hat,' she said, 'but you must promise not to laugh at it. Why do you ask?'

'It'll be seriously cold higher up,' he answered. 'The chill factor is supposed to be minus two. We'll cross the A39 in a minute. Not far now.'

The moor rose up ahead of them, but she looked in vain for Moorgate.

'Don't worry,' he said, guessing her thoughts. 'You'll see her in a minute. Straight over here and then right. That's it.'

Presently they came to the ford. The brown, peaty water flowed across the road and away under an old granite clapper bridge, but Melissa drove through the stream and came to a rest just beyond it.

'Come on,' said Rob. 'We'll have a stroll and I'll show you something.'

She dragged the sheepskin cap over her ears and climbed out. The wind was so sharp that she gasped, feeling the air freezing against her skin. Beyond the ford, ice had formed along the shallows beneath the bank, and the grass crunched like glass under their feet. Rob slipped an arm about Melissa's shoulder, turning her slightly.

'Look there,' he said, pointing.

They were looking at Moorgate from its north side. It should have appeared bleak, desolate, but Melissa thought that it seemed strong and welcoming and safe, safe as Rob's arm about her, holding her close. She looked up at him. He was staring at Moorgate, smiling, and she felt a sudden welling of desire, a tremendous need for him. He glanced down at her and his smile faded, his gaze intent.

His lips were burning cold but for once she was gloriously warm, the blood tingling to her fingertips. After a long moment she drew back a little and he clasped her close, his cheek against hers.

'You do pick your moments,' he murmured in her ear—and she burst out laughing, glad to take refuge in simple, uncomplicated happiness.

'I love you both,' she said, meaning it. 'Doesn't Moorgate look wonderful? Just as if she grew out of the ground. What's that tor over there?'

'That's Rough Tor,' he told her as they stepped out briskly, 'and beyond that is Brown Willy, but we can't see it from here. There's lots to show you before we go . . . home.'

'Home.' She looked up at him, unable to conceal a wave of longing. 'Oh, if only it were.'

'Perhaps it could be,' he said tentatively. 'Perhaps there's a way.'

She swallowed down her emotion, clutching his arm tightly. 'For today it is, anyway,' she said. 'And for tonight.'

Selina stood in the hall, listening. Supper was finished and Patrick had disappeared up to his study, but the situation was not resolved. All day she'd been building up the courage to confront him, to talk about this impasse. It was impossible to carry on in this miserable way, as if they were polite strangers who happened to share the same house. He was impervious to the tactics she'd used in the past and she felt helpless and frustrated. She'd planned to discuss it after supper, but Paul had telephoned at exactly the wrong moment. He'd been promoted and wanted to share the glad tidings with his parents, but by the time he'd finished telling her all the details, Patrick had cleared the table and vanished. He'd been particularly preoccupied, with a kind of suppressed excitement about him, and she was beginning to suspect that he'd revived his affair with Mary. Now, as she cautiously climbed the stairs, she could hear his voice: he was talking to someone on the telephone.

'That sounds fantastic,' he was saying. 'If you could, I'd be terribly grateful . . . No, no. I understand . . . Yes, Brecon sounds wonderful.'

She thought: Brecon? Whatever is he talking about?

She heard the receiver go down. Reaching the landing, she tapped at the door and opened it. He was sitting at the desk, deep in thought.

'Patrick,' she said, almost pleadingly, 'I need to talk to you.'

He raised his eyebrows in a friendly question, but didn't speak.

'We can't go on like this, can we? I mean, hardly communicating, and you going off to the spare room every night. It's silly.'

'It's difficult to know how to handle it, isn't it?' he agreed, almost cheerfully. 'But it won't be for much longer, I hope.'

She was staring at him, frowning. 'What do you mean?'

'Well, I've been trying to decide where I should go. What I might do.

But now I think I've found just what I've been looking for.'

'What the hell are you talking about?' Anxiety made her angry. 'If you think I'm impressed by this silly pretence you couldn't be more wrong.'

'I'm not pretending,' he answered. 'I thought we'd agreed that whatever we had together has outlived itself. It was bound to happen once the children were gone. Looking back, I can see that there wasn't much to begin with. You used me to get away from Maudie and Hector, and the children were the glue that held us together.'

'This is utter nonsense. Just because I stood up for myself over the Mary thing—'

'Precisely.' He gave a short laugh. 'You stood up for yourself. You didn't fight for me.'

She frowned again. 'What d'you mean? Of course it was for you.'

'No.' He shook his head. 'No, it wasn't. You didn't fight to get me back because you love me. You did it because I am one of your possessions.'

'You're wrong,' she said quickly. 'This has just got out of hand—'

'That's true,' he agreed. 'It has got out of your hands, Selina. For once my life is in my own hands. You've dominated and controlled us all— well, except for Posy—for nearly thirty years and I've had enough.'

'Oh, I see.' She folded her arms under her breasts, her lip curling. 'And so just because I refuse to condone your sordid affair with some little tart, you're reneging on your marriage vows, betraying your children and abandoning your wife.'

'Yes.' He looked almost proud. 'I suppose you could say that. I hadn't quite seen it in those terms—'

'May I ask how you had seen it?'

'I saw it as a relationship that was worn out. The boys have never been too bothered about me and I've nearly managed to alienate Posy, who will soon be too busy to care either way. As for you, I've annoyed and irritated you for more than a quarter of a century. You've decided where we live, who our friends are, where we have our holidays and how our money is spent, and you're still not happy. You've humiliated me, hurt me and ignored me.' He paused for a moment. 'I accept that to leave a wife to fend for herself is a disgraceful thing to do, but I intend to do it. This house is worth at least three hundred thousand pounds. You can downsize and have enough to invest for a reasonable living when you put it with the other pensions we have. You won't starve.'

'I'm beginning to wonder if you're ill. I think you've lost your senses.'

He shrugged. 'I'm fairly sane, I think. Just heady with freedom.'

'And you think I'll let you stroll off into the sunset? I don't want to sell this house. I like it here. I'm not moving into some grotty little flat.'

'Suit yourself. Thanks to your father we don't have a mortgage. Stay here and work. It's never too late to try something new.'

'You're having some kind of breakdown.'

'It's funny you should say that. I had the same thought myself.' He looked at her sympathetically. 'Poor Selina. It's come as a shock, hasn't it? The worm turning.'

'You're crazy,' she shouted. 'I'll speak to my lawyer in the morning.'

'Our lawyer,' he corrected her gently. 'Steve is my lawyer too.'

She glared at him. 'And have you told him that you're leaving me to go to Brecon? Got another little tart there, have you?'

She went out, slamming the door behind her, running down the stairs. Patrick stared reflectively at the door, then he picked up a piece of paper, studying it carefully.

Could you be a L'Arche assistant? Some people come from sixth form or college. Others decide upon L'Arche as a career change. Many find the vocation fulfilling enough to stay for many years. Assistants receive free board and lodging and a modest weekly income.

They returned as dusk was beginning to fall, after a day of exploration.

'It feels warmer,' Melissa said, as they unloaded the car. 'Or am I imagining it? I'll still be glad to get indoors, though.'

Rob paused, his arms full of parcels, looking away to the north. Pillowy clouds lay piled layer upon layer, advancing slowly, and he whistled thoughtfully under his breath as he followed her into the house. The kitchen was warm, and, leaving Melissa to put away their supplies, he went through to the sitting room to pile more logs on the fire. Back in the kitchen he washed and dried his hands.

'I've had a thought,' he said casually. 'I might bring a few things up from my place. Just to make us more comfortable.'

She glanced at him, surprised. 'I suppose you could take the car? You're probably insured to drive other vehicles.'

'Oh, I shan't bother. I'll walk down and bring back the pick-up. Not a problem. See you later.' He smiled at her, uncertain how to take his leave, and then went out quickly.

Standing at the window she watched him climb the rail fence and stride off across the moor, keeping in the shadow of the thorn.

After a while, she turned, leaning back against the sink, looking about her, alone again. It was at about this time yesterday that she'd watched him walking the same way, pausing to look up at the house.

She'd moved back, lest he should see her, and then she'd heard him enter. Standing in the shadow of the stairs, peering from the landing, she'd watched him moving about, heard him preparing the house. She smiled as she remembered his shocked gasp when he saw her standing by the fire; could it really be only twenty-four hours ago?

Melissa shivered, hugging her pashmina around her. She felt terribly tired. Passing through the hall into the sitting room, subsiding onto the beanbags, which Rob had brought out again, Melissa felt a twinge of guilt. She knew that Mike would have disapproved of such a long and active day, and that she should telephone him to reassure him that all was well. This weariness, however, the weighty limbs and a faint nagging pain, kept her pinned to her soft bed.

'I'll do it in a minute,' she murmured, watching the flames, conscious of the pain. 'I'm having such fun. Mike won't begrudge me it.'

As the light receded and the room grew dimmer, she felt the tears sliding down her cheeks. Never had she wanted so much to live, to be happy, uncaring and healthy. As she lay huddled in the firelight, she imagined she could hear the life of the house going on around her. She could hear voices and soft, intimate laughter, then the sound of a child calling. She tried to struggle up, but she was too tired, her limbs too heavy. They were calling to the child, a man was swinging him up into his arms, murmuring endearments. Melissa relaxed, drifting, dreaming, until she could see them. They were in the garden. The sun was hot and a girl was standing with her back to Melissa. She wore a cotton sunhat.

'Be careful,' she called to the small boy on the swing. 'Not too high.'

He was singing to himself as he swung, and the girl went to look into a pram that was standing in the shade of the escallonia hedge, rocking it with a proprietorial air. She turned suddenly, smiling at Melissa, who smiled back, recognising her, holding out her arms in welcome.

'It's you,' she murmured—and felt herself lifted, held tightly.

'You were dreaming,' Rob said. 'I was afraid of startling you.'

She clung to him, wrenched with a terrible sense of loss, quite unable to speak. He continued to kneel beside her on the floor, cradling her.

'Sorry,' she muttered. 'Really silly. Just a vivid dream. I'm OK now.'

He released her, going to close the shutters, piling more wood on the fire. 'Do you feel up to coming to see what I've brought back with me?'

'I certainly do.' The dream was fading now and some of her weariness was receding with it. 'It sounds very mysterious.'

In the kitchen was a wooden armchair with cushions and another dining chair. Two electric heaters stood beside them.

Melissa laughed. 'How clever of you. But why only one armchair?'

'I only have one armchair. Everything else is built in. It's for you.'

'It's a nice big one. Perhaps we could share it? Or am I being forward?'

He grinned. 'Wait until you see what's upstairs.'

She climbed after him, some of her weakness returning, but he was too tense to notice. On the floor of the main bedroom, plump and welcoming, lay a pumped-up king-sized air bed and several pillows.

'Now who's being forward?' he asked. 'I bought it earlier in Tintagel.'

'Oh, Rob,' she said, 'what a brilliant idea.'

He chuckled with relief. 'I thought you might slap my face and go off in a huff.'

'No you didn't. You knew it was exactly the right thing to do.'

He grimaced. 'I wasn't quite that confident, but never mind. I'll bring the heaters up to get the room really warm, although this radiator does pretty well, but I think it'll be another cold night.'

'Probably. Although I feel it's a bit warmer.'

'Mmm.' He followed her downstairs, grinning guiltily, secretly, to himself. 'I'm sure you're right. How's supper doing? I'm starving.'

Because Rob had taken the action needed to remove any further embarrassment, dinner was a relaxed affair and they were able to talk easily. Rob told her about his desperate bid to buy Moorgate, his race against time and how he was trying to raise the deposit.

'That's the real problem,' he said. 'I've got loads of work. I'm doing well, now. I can cope with the mortgage. But the deposit is something else. I'm terrified that some yuppie will come along and snap it up.'

'So how do you deter them?' she asked.

'Oh, it's easy. Most of them want to live in the country, but they have an image of a nice, clean, sanitised world. Moorgate still has the look of the farm about it. Then there's the weather. Driving rain and southwesterly winds are a turn-off. If they turn up on a glorious day it's not too difficult to convince them that that's the exception rather than the rule. If they have teenage children it's no problem at all. They can see that there are no discos, swimming baths and public transport, and they have no intention of allowing their parents to be so selfish.'

'It sounds as if you don't have much to worry about, after all.'

Rob shook his head. 'But then there are the people like us. People who want peace and quiet and don't mind a twenty-minute drive to buy a loaf of bread. People who want to walk out over the moor from the garden gate and like to see muddy, tired dogs lying by the kitchen stove.'

'You mean people like us—but with money.'

He nodded, leaning back in his chair. 'Did you really come from London because you fell in love with the photograph?'

She was silent for a moment, afraid of falling into a trap. She had to stick to the pretence that her life was as it had been before Oxford.

'I did,' she said. 'I'm getting tired of city life and I want to escape.'

'Forgive me for being personal, but could you afford a house like this?'

'Well, the London flat is worth quite a lot of money.'

'I see.' He was silent for a moment. 'So what now?'

Melissa couldn't quite meet his eyes. 'I love it,' she said. 'I really do. But I'd have quite a lot to do before I could make an offer.'

'Perhaps,' he said slowly, diffidently, 'perhaps between us we could manage something.'

She looked at him, hating to deceive him, unable to burst the golden bubble. 'It's possible,' she said. 'It's a bit . . . unexpected, that's all.'

'I know,' he said quickly. 'Of course it is. For me too. It's just . . . I seem to be falling in love with you, Melissa.'

'Oh, Rob.' She took his hand. 'It's the same with me. Are we crazy?'

'Probably,' he answered soberly. 'Does it matter?'

She laid her cheek against his hand, suppressing a terrible desire to tell him the truth. The fear of the love and admiration in his eyes being replaced by pity and anxiety held her back. His normal, natural, healthy love was all that was left to her now, and selfish though it might be, she couldn't bring herself to destroy it.

'No, it doesn't matter,' she said, releasing his hand, refilling their wineglasses. 'Here's to the routing of all yuppies and moneyed prospectors. You shall go the ball, Cinderella, and Moorgate shall be yours!'

'Ours,' he corrected her, raising his glass. 'Thank you, fairy godmother. What did we do with the apple pie?'

'In the larder.' She felt a flood of gratitude that he'd allowed the difficult moment to pass. 'With the cream. It seemed the coldest place, out there on the marble slab. I hope the milk doesn't go off.'

'We've got some powdered stuff, just in case.' He cut two generous portions of pie. 'We shall manage, never fear. So tell me about your life in London. No cutting corners, mind. I want to know everything.'

Later, much later, she leaned on an elbow, watching him sleep. He'd flung off the blanket—the room was much too warm for him—and his face, turned upon the pillow, was peaceful.

She thought: I should leave now. He'd grieve for a while but he'll

soon forget me. How could such a short time of love make a real difference to his life? Better to go now, before we get too deep.

Gently, carefully, she slid away from him, pushing herself to her feet,
feeling for her shawl. He'd left a paraffin lamp burning dimly, and in its
mellow light she trod on bare feet to the window. Rob had rigged up a
curtain; it hung unevenly, but lent an air of privacy and cosiness to the
room. Earlier, they had been too preoccupied with each other to take
much notice of anything but their deep, urgent need, but now, shivering, Melissa lifted the corner of the curtain and looked outside.

Snow whirled against the window, dancing in the wind, settling,
blowing, drifting. Her gasp of surprise became a soft chuckle. No
chance of going anywhere tonight; no hope of a quick flight down to the
car and away back to Oxford. The decision had been taken for her and
she felt almost weak with relief. She could stay with him a little longer.

'You'll freeze.' His voice made her jump. 'Is it still snowing?'

She turned quickly. 'Still snowing?'

She heard the rumble of his laughter. 'It had just started when I got
back with the pick-up. I thought it might when it turned warmer, but I
didn't want you deciding that you should rush off back to London while
there was still time. Come back to bed. I can hear your teeth chattering.'

She went back to him, laughing helplessly, and they rolled together,
holding tightly, forgetting everything but each other.

CHAPTER NINE

THE SNOW LASTED FOR TWO DAYS. It had drifted from the northwest, piling
up against the back of the house, but Rob was able to dig a path to the
woodshed and they had enough provisions to keep them from starving.

'Thank goodness we bought plenty of chocolate,' said Melissa,
munching happily, leaning against the Esse while Rob washed his hands
after ferrying logs into the sitting room. 'I must have had a premonition.'

He came across, smiling down at her. 'You should be as big as a
house. How do you stay so slender?'

She didn't answer, simply shaking her head, and he slipped his arms about her. She rested her cheek against his shoulder, staring out of the window at the snowy landscape.

'Let's go for a walk,' she said suddenly. 'Just a little one. It looks so perfect out there now the sun is setting. Shall we?'

'Why not? The snow is far too deep behind the house but it's not too bad in the lane. We'll see how far we can get.'

In the lane they turned up towards the moor, passing through the gate beside the cattle grid, wading slowly through the snow, pausing to stare about them.

'It's quite magical,' murmured Melissa. 'Everything is transformed.'

Her heart ached with the pain of it. She thought: How can I bear it? How can I face the end, now, knowing what I am losing? Yet as she stood gazing over the moor, she became aware of an unusual sensation of peace, as if her heart had ceased to grieve. The moor rolled away from beneath her feet, stretching to the earth's fiery rim, where the sun was dipping into the sea, and silence wrapped about them both.

She had no idea how long they'd stood together, before they heard a hoarse, eerie shriek and a barn owl passed above their heads and came to rest on a post some way below them.

'She nests in a barn below Moorgate,' said Rob. 'Beautiful, isn't she?'

'Beautiful,' agreed Melissa. 'And cruel,' she added, thinking of the sharp talons and strong, hooked beak.

'Well, that's life.' Rob tucked her hand under his arm. 'Owls have to eat, too. I admit, however, that I wouldn't want to be a part of the food chain. One long struggle for territory, food, or a mate. Living in permanent fear of death.' Misinterpreting the shudder she gave, he pressed her hand closely beneath his arm, dreading the moment that she would leave him. 'Don't go away,' he said foolishly. 'Stay with me at Moorgate.'

She hugged his arm, trying to laugh. 'I have to go. You know I do.'

'But you'll come back?'

'Of course. Part of me will never go at all. It will stay here always.'

'I shan't be satisfied with a bit of you,' he grumbled.

'I have to sort things out. But don't worry. Moorgate will be . . . ours.'

He sighed. 'Why can't I believe it?'

'Because you have no faith. I've told you that between us we can raise the deposit. Stop doubting. Once I'm back in London and have made the arrangements you can put in an offer. I'll sort out all the legal side. We've been through all this before, Rob. Stop fussing.'

'It's because you won't say when you'll be back. I hate not knowing.'

'I can't tell you. You know I have to go away on this big case I've got.

111

It's impossible to give you a date. But I'll stay in touch. I promise. You must get on with buying the house.'

'If Lady Todhunter knows I want to buy it she'll give me time to sort things out, I know she will.'

'Well, then. Let's not worry about the details.'

'I'm a fool, but I have this terrible feeling that once you leave I shall never see you again.'

Silence fell between them like a sword. The sun had set, a chill wind moved lightly over the land and the barn owl rose from his post with an unearthly cry. Melissa suddenly remembered that Chaucer had referred to this bird as a 'prophet of woe and mischaunce' and she shivered.

'I'm sorry.' Rob knew that he had distressed her. 'I had no idea that falling in love was so devastating. Take no notice of me.' He laughed. 'It's humiliating, feeling like an adolescent at my age. Ready to go back?'

'I think so.' She rose to his mood. 'Anyway, I'm getting hungry again.'

'I should have guessed.' He chuckled. 'I must remember not to travel any distance from home without supplies of food.' He stopped suddenly and she slithered to a halt, clutching him. Taking her face in his hands, he kissed her tenderly. 'I love you,' he said. 'Just never forget it.'

'I love you too, Rob,' she said. 'This has been the best thing that ever happened to me. And just you never forget that, either. Promise?'

They stared at each other, serious, intent.

'I won't,' he said gently. 'I promise. Bless you. Come on, my love. Let's go home.'

Maudie sat at the table, the tartan squares ranged before her. Months had passed since the package had arrived from The Scotch House, yet she seemed incapable of coming to a final decision. There was too much on her mind. Posy had telephoned earlier, sounding faintly anxious.

'Dad phoned,' she'd said. 'He's coming down to see me.'

'Well, that's very nice, isn't it?' Maudie had said encouragingly. 'You haven't seen much of him lately and you can show him round. I thought you wanted the chance to make up for Christmas.'

'I do. He just sounded a bit odd, that's all.'

'Odd? How?'

'He sounded . . . happy.'

She'd seemed so surprised that Maudie had burst out laughing. 'Poor Patrick,' she'd gasped.

'I don't mean it like that,' Posy had said defensively. 'He was more than just happy. There was something else . . . Perhaps he's agreed to buy Moorgate, but unless they sell up and move down I think it would be awful. They can't afford two houses.'

'Well, between you and me, I've heard that I may have a buyer. Someone's very interested, apparently, so keep your fingers crossed. It would certainly solve that particular problem.'

In the end, Posy had agreed that she must simply wait and see, and had gone off clubbing with Jude and Jo, leaving Maudie to brood. The description of Patrick's happiness puzzled her. But her conversation with Selina had made her feel quite confident that he had no intention of being party to buying Moorgate.

She pushed the pieces of cloth aside and went to sit by the fire, pulling her knitting out of its bag, spreading it across her knees. She was sure, too, that Hector wouldn't have approved of Selina buying Moorgate as a holiday home.

'I agree,' Daphne had said recently. 'It's crazy. Financial suicide.'

'I feel like an executioner,' Maudie had said. 'We've all had such happy times there, haven't we?'

'We can't hold onto everything,' Daphne had said firmly. 'Part of what we remember is our youth. For Selina, Moorgate represents her childhood before Hilda died, before her life changed, but it would be ridiculous to attempt to re-create it. She needs her feet on a pavement. Do stop ferreting, Maudie. Don't let Selina get you down . . .'

If only Ned Cruikshank's client made a genuine offer she could accept it thankfully and put the whole thing out of her mind. Tomorrow was Friday, so perhaps he might telephone with good news before he left for London. Maudie settled herself comfortably and began to knit.

Selina studied her image closely in the looking glass. She felt panicky and very angry. When had the wrinkles formed? Those grooves scored between nose and lips; the discontented lines about the drooping mouth? She was looking her age and was suddenly reminded of photographs of her mother—except that Hilda would have been smiling: bravely, determinedly, brightly, even grimly—but always smiling.

Selina thought: Well, she had plenty to smile about. Daddy would never have been unfaithful to her and then abandoned her.

For the first time ever, a tinge of resentment crept into her memories of her mother. She'd always been loved, respected, bathed in her husband's honours, lapped in comfort; why the hell shouldn't she smile? Selina leaned her elbows on the dressing table and sneered into the mirror. She'd perfected this look from an early age—she could date it

113

exactly—from the moment Maudie had arrived on the scene. It was meant to be a look of utter contempt. She'd always enjoyed being able to subdue her family with that practised curl of the lip, but soon there would be no one left to be impressed by it. The boys were already beyond her influence—their wives had seen to that—and Posy had never been truly cowed by it. Only Patrick had remained affected—until now. Now her power was going, she was losing control. Patrick was unmoved by rage, by contempt, even by a gentler approach. He remained remote and detached—and unbearably, infuriatingly happy.

'I've given in my notice,' he'd told her jubilantly, 'and it's been accepted. I have the feeling that perhaps I wasn't so discreet as I might have been over Mary and they're pleased to see me go without a fuss. If they can find a replacement I shall leave at Easter.'

'Easter?' She'd goggled at him, her fury at his casual mention of the little tart overborne by shock. 'You're leaving at Easter?'

'Why not? Why wait? Have you thought what you might do?'

'Is it any of your business?'

'Not really.' He'd shrugged cheerfully. 'I'm sure you'll cope. I'm going down to see Posy on Friday. I guessed from my conversation with her that you haven't told her that I'm leaving. Why not? You were quick enough to tell her that I was an adulterous bastard.'

'What should I tell her?' she'd said contemptuously. 'That you've found another little tart in Brecon?'

'You know exactly where I'm going, Selina, and why. You've looked through all my papers and I've made no secret of it.'

'You're such a hypocrite,' she'd shouted. 'Pretending to be holier-than-thou while betraying me and then abandoning me after nearly thirty years of marriage. How will you feel when I tell our friends that?'

'How will you feel?' he'd asked quietly. 'Happy, contented people don't walk out of loving relationships. How will you explain it, Selina?'

She'd had no answer for him. Already she'd shied away from telling even her closest girlfriends that Patrick was leaving her—especially for such a cause. How much easier to paint him as a weak philanderer! She almost wished she'd let him go to Mary. It would have been so much easier, as the injured wife, to gain sympathy. This was quite different: it was humiliating. Selina stared at herself, panic rising. Furiously, she seized a bottle and began to apply her make-up.

Later on in the morning, the west wind brought warmer weather and the thaw began. Snow fell from the trees in slabs, crashing to the ground, and dripped from the gutters. A tractor passed up the lane, turning the soft ice to slush, and, on the higher slopes, the drifts melted away into rivulets of sparkling water.

'I shall be able to go tomorrow, after all,' said Melissa, watching as the moor dazzled in the bright sunshine. 'No excuse now.'

For these few days she'd been able to believe that she might never leave, that the dream would become a reality. She smiled at Rob.

'I know,' he said. 'I know you have to go. I just don't want to think about this as our last day.'

'No, neither do I. Oh, Rob, we mustn't be miserable.'

He put his arm round her. 'We won't be miserable. We'll take the pick-up and go and forage. If the tractor's managed to come up from the village, we should be able to get down. How about it?'

'Oh, yes. That sounds fun. I'm nearly out of chocolate.'

'Well, we can't have that. We'll stock up for this evening and cook ourselves a slap-up meal.'

'Great.' She sighed contentedly and then looked at him more seriously. 'Rob, I think you should telephone Ned Cruikshank and make an offer. It's only fair. Today is his last day, after all. Tell him that we want to buy Moorgate and then he can phone Lady Todhunter.'

'You're absolutely certain?'

She nodded. 'I want to be sure that the house is . . . ours.'

He took a deep breath. 'That's fantastic.'

'Once the offer is accepted we'll have time to breathe,' she said, trying to sound casual. 'I'll sort things out when I get back. A girl I was at law school with works at a practice in Truro. I'll get her to do the legal stuff. OK? And as soon as I know where I am work-wise I'll let you know. We'll stay in touch by mobile, shall we? I may have to stay with friends while I wind up at the practice, but you'll always have my number.'

'I suppose so.' He didn't sound too happy. 'But I wish we could be a bit more definite.'

She tried to distract him. 'Ned will be surprised, won't he?'

'Not nearly so surprised as Lady Todhunter will be.'

'Do it,' she insisted. 'Telephone him now, Rob.'

'OK.' He kissed her quickly. 'I'll do it now, before we go out.'

'Fine.' She released him. 'I'll go and get my coat.'

Upstairs, she sat down on the window seat for a moment. She felt tired and weak, but quite determined to make certain that Moorgate should be Rob's. It was all she had left to give him. He had made her happier than she had ever been, enabled her to forget the horror that lay ahead, given her the opportunity to have some stake in the future. Soon he would be able to put these few days aside—to remember them always, yes, but begin to build a new life for himself here at Moorgate. She could give him that, at least: the chance to live in the house he loved more than anything in the world.

Downstairs in the kitchen, waiting for Ned to answer the telephone, Rob was thinking how odd it was that now that he was able to make an offer on Moorgate, the house mattered less than it had ever done before. Since Melissa had come into his life, everything else had taken second place. His passion for Moorgate had paled before his love for her. As long as they were together, he wouldn't really mind where they lived. She was so special, so beloved, that he couldn't imagine life without her now. Moorgate was a bonus, but she was all that mattered.

'Hello, there.' Ned's breathless voice broke into his thoughts. 'I've been trying to get in touch with you. What weather! Are you OK?'

'Very OK.' Rob was smiling. 'Hold onto your hat, Ned, I've got a bit of a surprise for you.'

Maudie kicked off her gumboots at the back door and hurried into the living room to pick up the telephone receiver.

'Yes? Hello?'

'Lady Todhunter?' Ned Cruikshank sounded quite jubilant. 'It's Ned. We've had an offer for Moorgate. A very good one.' He named a figure.

'That's wonderful, Ned. Is it the woman you were telling me about?'

He started to laugh. 'You'll never believe this. I didn't. It is the girl I told you about but it's Rob Abbot, too. They're buying it together.'

'You mean she's an old friend? What an odd arrangement. Of course, I know he loves the house . . .'

'Well, actually, it seems he's only just met her. It was love at first sight and they want to live at Moorgate.'

'Good grief! I do hope Rob knows what he's doing. He's so level-headed.' Suddenly she remembered her first meeting with Hector, the way they'd looked at one another, and she smiled to herself. 'It sounds wonderful. I hope they'll be very happy. I shall go down to meet her.'

'She's an absolute sweetie.' He sounded confiding, rather breathless as usual, and she felt an absurd surge of affection for him.

'I'm going to miss you, Ned. I hope you do splendidly in London.'

'So do I,' he said. 'I can't tell you how pleased I am to bring this one off, Lady Todhunter. It's the icing on the cake.'

'Bless you. And Ned? Make sure you get that commission.'

'I will.' He was laughing. 'The office will be getting in touch but I'll tell Rob you accept his offer, shall I?'

'You certainly may. Tell him I'm delighted. Thanks, Ned, and good luck.'

She replaced the receiver and stood for a moment, lost in a reverie. The relief was great but there was a measure of sadness, too. She remembered the summer she'd spent there with Daphne and Emily, and the baby Posy. How happy they'd been. Maudie sighed as she went to make her tea, hoping she'd made the right decision.

She thought: At least it solves the problem for Patrick. Perhaps now Selina can forget Moorgate and she and Patrick can make a new start.

It was terrible to leave him, to drive away, waving cheerfully, letting him believe that she'd be back soon. Only the thought of Mike, waiting in Oxford, and the arrangements to be made regarding Moorgate kept her steady. She felt tired—and the further she travelled so the weariness increased—but she knew that the greatest danger lay in the depression that hovered, waiting to convince her that there was no point in making any effort now. While she'd been with Rob she'd managed to believe that a miracle might happen. His love had strengthened her, his ignorance of her condition had allowed her to imagine that it did not exist. Now, without his vitality to warm her, his happiness to give her courage, the chill in her bones seemed to creep round her heart and weaken her. Even holding on to the steering wheel was an effort.

Nevertheless, she knew that she must not, this time, stop for the night. If she broke her journey to sleep she feared she might never find the energy to start off again. No, she must keep going, making do with short coffee breaks. Mike would be too relieved to see her to be cross for long. She considered turning off the A38 for a break at Bovey Tracey, half wondering if she might see Posy again, but decided against it. This time it would be different: the window table would be occupied by other people and her holiday feeling would be woefully absent. Better to remember things as they had been on that sunny morning. She could hardly believe that only a week had passed since she'd wandered in the town, browsed in the bookshop, and talked to Posy. Melissa wondered if Posy would ever see the message she'd written and remembered the odd feeling of friendship she'd felt for her. How she wished she could turn back the clock and be starting out again on her Moorgate adventure.

She swallowed down the tears and glanced at her watch. There was no reason why she shouldn't be at home for tea. It would be wonderful to see Mike and Luke. Concentrating on this, Melissa drove on.

Watching her go, Rob felt that his world was going with her. He could hardly remember how he'd managed before her arrival. He knew now that he'd only been half alive. The whole week had been extraordinary; even the weather had conspired. As he went back into the house, a thousand questions presented themselves. During this last week, buying Moorgate, being together, falling in love, these things had seemed perfectly reasonable. Now, walking from room to room, staring out at the drizzle, he wondered if he'd been seized by a form of madness. It would be quite easy to believe that he'd dreamed the whole thing. He longed to speak to her again, needing reassurance, looking about him for some sign of proof, but all evidence of her occupation had been cleared away; the hamper and her rugs packed into her car. She'd promised to telephone round about lunchtime, and he checked—not for the first time— that his mobile was switched on.

Rob locked the back door and walked round to the yard. Standing beside the pick-up he looked at the house. It was strange that Melissa, who loved it so much, had broken Moorgate's spell over him. The obsession had been a burden and it was a relief to be free from it. Nevertheless, it would be good to own Moorgate, to live in it with Melissa, to raise their children here on the edge of the moor. Moorgate had brought them together. He stood for a moment watching the rooks, thinking about the events of the last week. There were so many things he'd not asked her, so much still to learn about her. He glanced at his watch. In less than an hour he might be speaking to her. The thought raised his spirits, made his heart beat faster. Whistling to himself, he climbed into the pick-up and drove out of the yard and down the lane.

Posy, settled at a corner table in the bar of the Wykeham Arms, watched her father talking to the girl behind the bar, laughing with her, hands in his pockets. For the first time, Posy was able to see him as other people saw him: not as her father but as a man in his own right. Watching him coming towards her, carrying drinks, Posy remembered how often he had defended her to her mother. Immediately she was engulfed in guilt. He had always been so loving, yet she had been so critical when he'd had his own fall from grace. She had rejected him out of hand, not waiting to be certain that he was guilty, unable to be generous.

'The sandwiches will be along in a minute.' He put the glasses on the table and sat down. 'I was just telling the girl behind the bar that this place has hardly changed since I was here thirty years ago.'

'It must feel odd,' said Posy, 'coming back after all these years.

Meeting Mum here and all that.' She drank some lager to cover her confusion about how to proceed. She still didn't quite know why he'd come down alone to see her. 'Is Mum OK?'

He frowned. 'She's perfectly fit,' he said, 'but not particularly happy.'

Posy laughed. 'I'm not sure that Mum is ever particularly happy. It's not how she works, is it? What's the problem? Is she still going on about Moorgate? Honestly, Dad, it would be crazy to let her buy it.'

'No, it's not Moorgate. I'm afraid it's me.'

Posy stared at him. 'How d'you mean?'

He looked at her. 'I'm leaving your mother,' he said, gently but without hesitation. 'Not because of Mary—that's all done with—but because there's nothing left between us. Whatever we had is finished.'

'Finished?'

He sighed. 'This is going to sound callous. I'm hoping that you've had enough experience of both of us to understand. Your mother doesn't need me as a friend or a lover or a companion. I wonder if she ever did. I met her when she was anxious to get away from home and marriage was an escape. Of course it's wrong to imagine that we weren't happy. There have been some special moments, but there's nothing left. I don't want to waste any more time. Sorry. I'm not putting this very well.'

Posy was trying to stem a rising tide of anger. She swallowed, her hands twisting together between her knees, and tried to answer calmly. 'So, you're bored, fed up, but does that mean you can simply walk out on your marriage? Isn't that a bit extreme? Even irresponsible?'

He looked at her almost humorously. 'Probably. But I'm going to do it anyway. If Selina loved me—oh yes, I know it sounds pathetic—all the humiliations wouldn't matter. But she doesn't. She isn't unhappy that I'm going because she'll miss me; she is losing a possession, not a husband. Her main fear is how she will explain it to her friends.'

When Patrick had tried to talk to Posy about Mary there had been an element of guilt, a longing to be forgiven. Now, she realised, he felt she had a right to know, that it would be nice if she could see why he was leaving, but there was no pleading, no requirement for her approval.

Fear began to edge out the anger and Posy thrust her hands through her hair. 'But how can you just walk out on us all?'

'I hope that I shan't walk out on you. Just because I shan't be living with Selina in London doesn't mean that I shall stop caring about you.'

'But it's not the same.' She could hear her voice rising in panic and bit her lip. 'It won't be home without you. Anyway, where would you be?'

'I shall be in Brecon.' His voice was light with happiness.

She stared at him incredulously. 'In Brecon? What's in Brecon?'

'One of the L'Arche communities. They are committed to helping people with learning disabilities. I am going as an assistant. It's wonderful. I feel tremendously privileged and I can't wait to get started.'

Looking at his face, alight with anticipation, Posy wondered if she'd ever really seen him before.

'It sounds as if it's all been arranged. So when are you going?'

'Easter,' he said gently. 'There's no point in procrastinating. I thought Selina would have told you before this. I'm sorry it's such a shock.'

'So you won't be there when I come home for the holidays?'

'No.' He took a pull at his pint. 'Selina will keep everything. Hector's money paid off the mortgage so she doesn't have to move, although she might need to work. If she downsizes she could be quite comfortable.'

'Does she see it like that?' asked Posy drily.

'Probably not, but those are her decisions not mine.'

'You sound so . . . different.'

'Callous? Selfish? Yes, I know. So your mother has repeatedly told me. I don't care any more. I've done everything I had to do to support her and all of you and now it's at an end. Now I want to do something for other people. Teaching is changing and I don't enjoy it any more. I still have it within me to be useful and I don't want to waste the rest of my life pandering to the whims of a selfish woman or dealing with a new generation of children I no longer understand.'

'What about me?'

He smiled tenderly at her. 'You are Posy. I love you. Nothing changes that. I hope we'll still see each other, stay in touch, spend time together.'

'But how? How can we do that if you're not at home any more?'

'There will be ways. Come on, Posy. You're not at home too much these days, are you? As to the financial aspect, you'll find that the bank has had instructions to take care of you. Fees and allowances and so on have all been dealt with. You won't suffer because I choose to be callous and selfish.'

'It's not a question of money,' she mumbled. 'It just won't be the same.'

'I can't deny that. But I'm not abandoning you, Posy, just hoping we can do things differently and be flexible. I hope you'll come to Brecon to see me and I can come here . . .'

'One tuna and one beef?' The waitress stood beside them, holding two plates.

'Oh, yes.' Patrick smiled up at her. 'Thank you. Tuna for my daughter. Beef for me, please.'

Posy sat back in her chair, almost grateful for the interruption, her brain still reeling with the shock. She stared at the sandwich, her appetite ruined. Bravely she picked it up—and put it down again.

'So,' she said, almost conversationally, trying to be adult, 'tell me about this L'Arche place.'

On Sunday morning Mike bundled Luke into his clothes, whisked him out of his bedroom and hurried him downstairs. He was hoping that Melissa would be able to sleep as long as was necessary in order to recover from the journey back from Cornwall. She'd arrived just before six o'clock, climbing wearily out of the car and stumbling into the house, her face blurred with exhaustion. He'd been shocked by the way she'd looked, but had allowed the words of reproach to die on his lips.

'Oh, Mike,' she'd said. 'I've fallen in love with a farmhouse and with a man called Rob Abbot,' and he'd returned her hug, holding her tightly, a look of mingled compassion and bitterness on his face.

She'd sat beside the fire with Luke in her lap while he heated soup and put hot-water bottles into her bed, and then she'd talked and talked. By the time he'd persuaded her into bed she'd made it all clear to him: that she wanted to help Rob buy Moorgate.

'You don't mind?' she'd kept asking. 'Only it was so wonderful. I want to try to repay him. Oh, Mike, it was such heaven. I felt normal and fit and so happy'—and the tears had slid down her cheeks.

'Of course I don't mind,' he'd answered. 'If it's what you want . . .'

'If only you could see it,' she'd said. 'It's such a lovely house. You and Luke will have the insurance money after . . . afterwards. But I want to use the money from the flat for Moorgate.'

'Please, Melissa,' he'd said wretchedly. 'I don't care about the money.'

'I know that, Mike,' she'd said quickly, 'but I need you to understand.'

'I understand,' he'd said reassuringly. 'I'm glad for Rob to have Moorgate. He's given you a stake in the future. I understand that.'

'Yes.' She'd looked at him gratefully. 'It's foolish, but that's how I feel.'

She'd talked on and on, describing, laughing, crying, until she'd been too exhausted to do more than climb the stairs and fall into the warm bed. He'd returned to sit by the fire and think about all she'd told him.

Now, having fed Luke and settled him with some toys on his tray, Mike began to eat his own breakfast. He felt troubled. It seemed to him that Melissa wasn't thinking clearly. It was unlikely, to begin with, that Rob would remain tamely in Cornwall for as many weeks as it took to complete the sale. Melissa had looked so fragile that he'd been incapable of bringing her down to earth, but it was difficult to see how her dream might be achieved. As he wrestled with the problem, murmuring to Luke, his mind preoccupied, the door opened and Melissa came in. She wore a long green wrap, her feet in espadrilles, a pashmina round her shoulders. Her eyes were enormous, dark-circled in her thin face, but she was smiling cheerfully.

'Good morning,' she said, bending to kiss Luke's rosy cheek, taking the car that he held out to her. 'Isn't it a nice one?' She pushed it round his tray while he watched, chuckling. 'I wish I had a car like this.'

'How are you feeling?' Mike stood up to make more coffee. 'I was hoping you'd sleep in.'

'I slept very well,' she assured him. 'I really did. But I wanted to see you and Luke. I've missed you.'

'And we missed you, didn't we, Luke?'

Melissa gave Luke his car and sat down at the table. It was comforting to be back, in these familiar surroundings, without the need to pretend, but her heart ached when she thought of Rob.

'I've been thinking.' Mike turned to face her. 'I'm very happy to help organise this, I really am, but I don't think it's going to be quite as simple as you've imagined.'

'Why not?' She looked alarmed. 'Why shouldn't it be simple?'

'There are all sorts of reasons,' he said gently. 'To begin with, Rob is going to expect to hear from you regularly, isn't he?'

Her face cleared. 'Oh, I thought about that. He's got the number of my mobile but he thinks I'm at work. So we leave each other messages and I talk to him quite often. But he knows I've sold my flat and he thinks I'm staying with friends while I wind up my work. I've told him I've got a heavy case on so he doesn't expect me to be too available.'

'Right. OK. But it could take weeks to complete on Moorgate.'

'I know.' She watched him anxiously. 'I want you to have absolute power of attorney, Mike, so if anything happens you'll just carry on dealing with it. You don't mind, do you?'

'No, of course not,' he said, pouring the coffee. 'Look, I'm sure we can work through the legal bits. You're going to speak to Jenny in Truro and you can lodge the money with her for the deposit, and she has limited power of attorney to deal with the sale. Have I got that right?'

'Quite right. She can sign all the papers for me and I'll ask her to advise Rob to take out a simple repayment mortgage. It lets me out of having to have a medical. Jenny knows the truth. I can rely on her.'

'That's fine, but there's the other side to it.' He put the mugs on the table and sat down. 'Look, Lissy, don't you think all this is a bit tough on Rob? How is he going to feel when he finds out the truth? At what point will you stop taking his calls? Think of the shock it will be for him.'

She was staring at him, huddled in her wrap, eyes wide with anxiety. 'What else can I do? I don't want him to know, Mike. If I tell him he'll come and find me. I can't bear the thought of it. Everything will change. There will be all that pity and horror. I can't do that. I want to be free to . . . to just finish peacefully. Please, Mike, don't ask me to tell him.'

'I know how you feel.' He felt miserable, hating to upset her. 'I want to do it your way, but I don't want the shock of it to ruin everything for Rob. From what you've told me this has been really important for you both, something that would have gone on into a permanent relationship. I think Rob's going to feel terribly hurt that you couldn't confide in him. He might not understand, not unless it's explained to him. This poor guy is down there thinking you're going back, that you have a life together. Imagine how he'll feel when the letter arrives from the solicitor telling him that he's suddenly the sole owner. I'm sure he'll be delighted to have Moorgate, but I suspect that it's you he wants, not a farmhouse.'

'But what else can I do?' she cried. 'How could I possibly tell him now, even if I wanted to? I can hardly introduce it into light conversation on the telephone, can I? And I couldn't go back, Mike,' she added quietly. 'Even if I had the stamina, I simply couldn't do it. Oh, I can't bear it. It was all so perfect.'

'I know,' he said quickly. 'And we mustn't destroy the memory of all that, but if Rob suspects something's wrong I'd rather be prepared for it.'

'I wasn't really thinking. I've been so happy and, selfishly, I wanted to forget everything else except that happiness.'

She sounded dejected, all the joy gone, and he cursed himself for spoiling it for her. Why should he care how Rob felt, after all? He'd never met the guy, so why should he worry about his reaction?

'There's nothing wrong with that,' he said strongly. 'You were both happy and he's going to have Moorgate. He'll never forget that week, either. I just don't want anything spoilt for either of you.'

'But how could it be done?' she asked wretchedly.

'I have an idea,' Mike said slowly. 'Suppose I go down to see him and explain everything properly to him?'

She began to look hopeful. 'Would you? But would that work? Suppose he refuses to accept Moorgate once he knows the truth?'

'That is the danger.' They stared at one another.

'Let's see if we can get it through quickly,' Melissa said pleadingly.

'He's expecting me to be tied up for several weeks. Let's hope we can get to completion and then you could go down to see him.'

'OK.' He sighed with relief. 'We'll leave it like that, then. Tomorrow morning you can telephone Jenny and tell her to get her skates on. If she has limited power of attorney it will save weeks. There's no chain. It could be done in a fortnight if we really tried.'

'Bless you, Mike,' she said. 'And then you'll go down and tell him?'

'Whatever happens, I'll go and see Rob and tell him everything.'

Walking back from the station, having seen her father off on the train, Posy found that she was thinking of her mother. What a shock it must have been for her, how bitter and lonely it would be to face life alone after nearly thirty years of marriage.

As she turned into Hyde Abbey Road, Posy thought: She's got the boys. They'll be on her side.

Scrabbling in her bag for her key, Posy felt guilt creeping round her heart. She'd tried not to feel angry with her father. It was selfish to expect him to stay in an unhappy relationship and an unsatisfying job simply so that she could have him there on the few occasions when she wanted to go home. At the same time, she felt that it was wrong to walk out on a marriage because you'd had enough. She felt muddled and miserable and longed to talk it through calmly with someone.

She shut the door behind her. There was no sign of Jude, and Jo was out too. Posy stood for some moments beside the telephone before she dialled the number.

'Hello, Mum,' she said. 'It's me. Posy. Just wanted to see how you are.'

Her mother laughed mirthlessly. 'Your father has told you his news?'

Posy's heart sank. 'Well, yes. It's a bit of a shock, isn't it?'

'It's not a shock to me to know that your father is a coward. I can't expect you to understand how I feel, of course.'

'I just wondered if you wanted to talk about it.'

'Why? So that you can gloat?'

'No.' Posy tried to hold onto her temper. 'I don't particularly approve of his going, if you want to know the truth.'

'You amaze me. I thought he could do no wrong as far as you're concerned. I thought you'd encourage him to go off and help the disabled. Didn't you tell him how wonderful and noble he is?'

'Actually, no. No, I didn't. Well, never mind. I just thought you might like to know that I'm sorry . . .'

'I'm sure you are. You're going to miss him. It's not nice to be rejected, is it? Perhaps now you'll just begin to understand how I've felt about you and Maudie all these years.'

'Right. OK then.' Posy felt disappointment, along with the old familiar antagonism, burning inside her. 'I'm here if you need me. See you.'

She replaced the receiver, wanting to burst into tears. After a moment or two she dialled another number.

'Hi, babe,' she said. 'It's me. How are you? . . . Great. And Polonius? . . . Well, yes. I'm hoping to come down again next weekend if that's OK? Brilliant. Thanks, Maudie. Oh, and do you think you could arrange for me to go out with Hugh for an hour or two? . . . Thanks. I'll be really looking forward to it. So what's been going on down in Devon, then?'

CHAPTER TEN

'HOW ARE YOU?' asked Rob eagerly. 'How are things going? I've had a call from someone called Jenny at the solicitor's in Truro. She was really positive. Thinks it can all happen quite quickly.'

'There's no reason why not.' Melissa closed her eyes so as to imagine him more clearly. 'Where are you?'

'Up in our bedroom. I can get the best signal here.'

'Yes. Yes, I know.' It was there she'd telephoned Mike, sitting on the broad window seat. 'Can you see the rooks?'

'See them and hear them. It's a wonder you can't hear them too, the racket they're making.'

Hot tears slipped from beneath her closed lids. She could see the bulky, twiggy nests, propped in bare branches, silhouetted against a cloudy sky; she could hear the acrimonious argy-bargy, punctuated by the high, plaintive cries of the lambs on the moor below.

'Are you still there?' His voice was anxious.

'Yes.' It was barely more than a sigh. The pain in her heart was suffocating. 'Yes, I'm here. Wishing I was there with you.'

'Oh, Melissa.' His voice was strong with happiness. 'It won't be long now. I'm arranging for the building society to do a valuation. You're sure you're happy to leave it all to me?'

'Of course. You're on the spot. Only don't waste any time, will you?'

'I won't. But don't worry. We won't lose Moorgate now. Lady Todhunter was delighted. She telephoned and wished us every happiness. She wants to meet you.'

'That's . . . very friendly.' She felt exhausted. 'Rob. I have to dash. This was just a quick one. I wanted to say "hello".'

'It's wonderful to hear your voice. I love you, Melissa. It won't be long before we're here together.'

'No.' She made a tremendous effort. 'Of course it won't. I love you too, Rob.' She switched off her mobile, her mouth trembling with grief.

'Lissy,' said Mike from the doorway. 'Lissy. Should you be doing this?'

She stared at him, her eyes dark with pain. 'I have to speak to him,' she said. 'I have to, Mike. While there's still time.'

He went across to her, crouching beside her, holding her tightly. 'I'm just afraid that it's making it worse for you,' he murmured.

She leaned against him. 'He'll be all right, won't he, Mike?'

'Yes, he'll be all right.' He rocked her, feeling her bones beneath his hand. 'Of course he will. He'll need a bit of time, but he'll recover.'

'And you'll see him?'

'I shall see him. Perhaps, later, I'll go and stay with him. Luke and I might go together, for a weekend.' He spoke hesitantly, unwilling to describe a future in which she could have no share, but when she raised her head to look at him her face was full of wonder.

'Oh, that would be good, Mike. I'd like to think that you might go to Moorgate—you and Luke.'

'Rob might find it a comfort, too. I'm sure we'll be friends.' He wanted to weep, to scream, to vent his rage. Instead he loosened his hold, helping her up. 'You're cold. Come on. Hot coffee and chocolate time.'

She followed him into the kitchen, steadier now. As he filled the percolator he watched her covertly. She was thinner; the marks of suffering were drawn lightly but ineradicably on her face. The drive to Cornwall, the whole Moorgate experience had taken an even greater toll than he had feared. She sat at the table, wrapped in her long bouclé cardigan, breaking some chocolate into squares and eating it thoughtfully.

'Mike, how would it be if I were to write a letter to Rob?'

He frowned. 'What kind of letter?'

'Well.' She paused. 'I know that you'll go to see him, once the sale is finalised, but supposing I wrote it all out. Why I went to Moorgate in the first place and how I feel about him. And why I couldn't bring myself to tell him the truth. I could explain it, tell him what it's all meant. I want him to know what he did for me. It's been like a miracle. Something to hold onto when things are . . . difficult. In some ways it's made it worse, made it harder to let go. To know all that I shall be missing is simply agonising, but at the same time I can relive it all and lose myself in it. I had one glorious week when I had thought before that there was nothing left but waiting. I want him to know all that.'

'I think it's a brilliant idea.' He began to fiddle with the mugs lest she should see the heartbreak in his eyes. 'I can tell him, of course, but it will be better coming from you. Your own words will mean a lot to him and he'll be able to keep the letter. In his place I'd be really glad of it.'

'Well, then. I think I'll do it. Not anything morbid or self-indulgent, just saying how it was.' She smiled, comforted by this new sense of purpose. 'I'll get on with it.'

Maudie finished drying up the lunch things, put them away and went into the living room. She'd been putting off the moment when she should telephone Selina to tell her about the offer on Moorgate. Even now she was picking up Daphne's letter and glancing through it, anything to postpone the moment. With a sigh of irritation and a twinge of apprehension, she dialled the London number. Selina answered so listlessly that Maudie's anxiety increased.

'Hello, Selina,' she said, with an attempt at cheerfulness. 'It's Maudie.'

'Good heavens!' Selina laughed. 'The vultures are gathering. Who told you? Posy? Don't tell me Patrick had the courage to telephone?'

'What are you talking about?' Surprise lent an added crispness to Maudie's voice. 'I've phoned to give you some news. Not very good, I'm afraid, from your point of view.'

'That's par for the course, then.' Selina laughed again. 'So what now? Come along, Maudie, dear. Tell me this news. Is Polonius dead? Oh, no, of course not. You said the news wasn't very good, didn't you?'

'Whatever is wrong, Selina? Have you been drinking?'

'Ten out of ten, dear stepmama. And what business is it of yours?'

'None at all. It just seems rather early in the day for it.'

'Why shouldn't I?' Selena sounded sullen. 'I've enough worries to drive me to drink. Didn't Posy tell you?'

Maudie sighed. 'I have no idea what you're talking about, Selina. This is clearly a bad moment. Perhaps we should try again later.'

'Patrick's leaving me.'

Maudie was silent. She was surprised. Posy had been so certain that the affair with Mary was over.

'Are you still there?' Selina asked peevishly. 'Of course, I suppose it's too much to expect sympathy from you.'

'Why should he leave you?'

'You tell me! Probably because I intervened between him and his little tart last year and he's still sulking.'

'Do you mean he's going away with her?'

'Oh, no. No, it's nothing to do with *her*. He's giving everything up to go off and work with the poor. He's going to live in a commune in Wales. He's tired of being boring old Patrick Stone and he's decided that he wants to do something worthwhile.'

Maudie thought: So that's why Posy is coming down again so soon.

Aloud, she said, 'Isn't it rather drastic?'

'Rather drastic? It's bloody disgusting. After thirty years he's walking out just because he's bored. Bored!'

'I simply can't believe it.'

'Well try, dear. He's leaving at Easter. It's all arranged.'

Maudie was silent, too startled to speak. She heard a clink of glass and a gurgling of liquid.

'Are you still there? Did you hear what I said? He's like a child with a new toy. So. What was your news, stepmother?'

'It's not good, Selina. I have an offer on Moorgate.'

'Oh God!' There was a crash of glass, followed by sudden, noisy weeping. 'Oh, I can't stand this. Not now. This is just too much.'

'Selina,' said Maudie desperately, 'please listen to me. Moorgate would never have worked, with or without Patrick. You must know that.'

'I've got nothing,' sobbed Selina. 'Mummy and Daddy have gone. Patricia's so far away she might as well be dead. I hardly see the boys any more. And now Moorgate . . . Oh, God, I hate you, Maudie!'

The receiver was slammed down. Maudie replaced her own handset more slowly. She felt old and shaken, distressed by Selina's outburst, shocked by her news. How typical of Patrick to be prepared to give up everything for an ideal. It sounded as if he had simply come to the end of his tether. She looked in her address book for the number Patrick had once given her for emergencies. She dialled it, her hand trembling. His secretary answered and presently she heard Patrick's voice.

'Maudie?' He sounded concerned. 'What's the problem?'

'It's Selina.' She decided not to beat about the bush. 'I just phoned to tell her that I've accepted an offer on Moorgate. She took it badly. She sounded as if she'd been drinking, and she hung up in a terrible state.'

'I see.' He sounded noncommittal.

'I'm sure you can't speak openly at the moment, but I was hoping you could perhaps find an excuse for going home. You know I wouldn't be making a fuss about nothing, Patrick.'

'Yes, Maudie.' His voice was warm. 'I know you well enough for that. I'll attend to it.'

'Thank heaven! And Patrick? Don't tell her I called you.'

Maudie hung up and sat staring out into the garden. The warm weather, which had swept away the snow, had left a soft, grey dampness in its wake and the afternoon wore a muted, dun-coloured mantle.

She thought: Why can't I be nice to Selina, even for a few seconds? I didn't have to tell her about Moorgate when she was so upset. Surely I could have managed a word of sympathy or shown some compassion?

The trouble was that Maudie had never quite understood how Patrick had managed to live with Selina for nearly thirty years in the first place. It was only because he was so utterly self-effacing, so blessed with humility, that he'd been able to cope with her at all.

'It would be a mistake,' Daphne had once said, 'to believe that Selina is a strong character. Her aggressiveness and desire to control is rooted in fear. My anxiety is that Patrick will not help her to grow. He will simply acquiesce while protecting her from herself.'

Maudie groaned aloud. It seemed as if all that were about to change.

The café in the Mill was quiet on this cold, wet Saturday afternoon. Thick grey cloud obscured the higher slopes of the moor, and the rain drummed relentlessly in the valleys. Riding was out of the question, but Hugh had suggested tea, instead. Maudie had dropped her off.

For some reason, Posy had been unable to bring herself to relate to Maudie the latest instalment in her parents' drama, probably because she couldn't sort out her own feelings. Hugh had been so sweet last time, when she'd poured out her fears about her father. She'd had a massive crush on him when she was fourteen, which embarrassed her when she remembered it, although it was perfectly reasonable to believe that Hugh had noticed nothing. With her being at school in London, only able to visit Devon occasionally, the infatuation had soon dwindled, but she'd retained an affection for him, and lately she'd felt that she and Hugh were growing closer. Of course, it was silly to imagine anything romantic happening between them. After all, he was nearly fifteen years older than she was. To him, she must seem like a kid.

Hugh was watching her now.

'I met a really nice girl here a couple of weeks ago,' she said quickly, randomly. 'We sat by the window and talked about the birds . . .' She buttered her scone with great deliberation.

'So how are things at home?'

Posy heaved a silent sigh of relief. 'Terrible,' she said. 'Dad's decided that he's had enough. He's giving up his job and leaving Mum and he's going to work with an organisation called L'Arche.'

'Yes, I've heard about L'Arche. Wonderful places.'

She stared at him. 'But you don't think it's a bit bizarre? Giving up your job and abandoning your family at fifty? Not to say irresponsible?'

'You're angry with him?'

Posy closed her eyes—and then she laughed. 'Yes. Yes. I am angry with him. I admit it. But what I feel doesn't really matter, does it? As Dad says, I'm grown up now, I'm hardly ever at home. Why shouldn't he do what he wants for a change? He's done all the right things for thirty years and Mum's made his life hell. Now it's his turn.'

'Sounds reasonable. How does your mother feel about it?'

'She won't talk to me,' said Posy moodily. 'She thinks I'll be on his side and she's just sarcastic all the time.'

'It sounds as if he's just come to the end of everything, doesn't it? How will your mother manage without him?'

'She'll be OK. He's leaving everything for her—the house and their savings and stuff. He's suggested that she sells the house and downsizes, which won't have pleased her, but she won't starve.'

'Perhaps it might even be good for her.'

'Good for her?'

He shrugged. 'You can never tell. It might be a blessing in disguise.'

'And I thought you were going to be sympathetic.'

He smiled at her. 'Do you need sympathy?'

'Yes. I needed tea and sympathy and you've been . . . realistic.'

'Sorry.' He poured more tea. 'Shall we start again?'

'No. No, it's OK. I can hack it.'

'After all,' he said, 'you'll still be seeing him, won't you? He hasn't stopped caring about you.'

'No,' she agreed. 'I know that. It's just that there are special family moments . . .' Times like weddings, she wanted to say, and when babies are born. 'Moments when you want them there, being a proper family.'

'Well, in an ideal world that's what we'd all like. Unfortunately we don't live in an ideal world. Our expectations are not always attainable. People don't live up to our requirements. Sometimes they even die, usually at inconvenient moments.'

'Oh, shut up,' she said—but she was laughing now. 'I wanted to have a good whinge not a lecture.'

'Well, that proves my point,' he said comfortably, starting on his cake. 'Your expectation was unattainable. You don't even know whose side you're on. Or was that what you wanted to whinge about?'

'I don't know what I wanted,' she admitted. 'I still don't, really. But I feel better about it.'

'Good,' said Hugh. 'Now, this cake has lived up to my expectation of it and I intend to have some more. Do you want to try some?'

'Why not? Thanks.'

Feeling happier she began to eat. The couple at the window table began to gather up their belongings and Posy wondered whether to make a dash for her favourite seat. The rain was slanting down, the sky heavy and dark, and she decided that it wasn't worth the effort, but as she ate her scone she remembered the girl and how she'd told her about Hugh. There had been something special about her. How marvellous to look like that; to have those wonderful cheekbones and green eyes. She'd had such style, such confidence. Of course, she probably had some brilliant career and a host of admirers.

Posy thought: I wonder where she is now?

Rob drove into the yard, climbed out of the pick-up and felt in his pocket for the keys. It was odd that, now everything was in train, survey done, mortgage agreed but documents yet to be signed, he had no desire to continue his clandestine visits to Moorgate. Even thinking about it made him feel rather foolish, until he remembered Melissa saying, 'I would have done exactly the same myself.' She had understood, had been ready to behave in the same reckless way.

Letting himself into the kitchen, Rob longed to telephone her, to hear her voice. She was such an extraordinary girl that he was not yet quite able to believe his luck. He needed regular contact.

Upstairs in the big bedroom he sat down on the window seat. In his mind's eye he saw her standing at the window watching the snow. Unable to resist, he took his mobile telephone from his jacket pocket and pressed the buttons. Her voice was slow, dreamy, preoccupied.

'How are you?' He always asked this question.

'Busy.' He could hear that she was smiling. 'Where are you?' She always asked this question.

'In the bedroom.' He chuckled. 'It's true. It is the best place for a signal inside the house.'

'Oh, Rob.' She was laughing now. 'Our lovely air bed.'

'I was thinking about that, too. We'll keep it and use it on every anniversary.' A silence. 'It won't be long now,' he said urgently. 'We're getting on, aren't we? The mortgage's arranged and Jenny's being fantastic. I had no idea things could be moved along so quickly.'

'There are no chains. Nothing to hold it up.' She sounded tired.

'Are you OK?' he asked anxiously. 'Not overworking?'

'Probably, but never mind.'

'I wish I could see you. Are you sure I couldn't come up, for a day?'

'No, honestly, Rob. It would be such a muddle. Now the flat's sold I haven't anywhere to put you up. It's horrid having to stay with friends. I know it sounds crazy but I want to think of you there. At Moorgate. It won't be for much longer.'

'I know. I'm just being selfish, really. We had so little time together.'

'Oh, Rob, I know. I love you so much. Look, I really must go.'

'Sorry to distract you. I just needed to hear your voice. What's that noise? Sounds like a baby?'

'What? Oh, yes. A colleague's brought her new baby in to show us. Take care, Rob. I'll phone this evening. About eight? Love.'

He thrust the mobile back into his pocket and went downstairs. The brief contact had comforted him and there was the evening call to anticipate. Whistling to himself, Rob began to feed logs into the wood burner.

He'd spoken to his mother the previous evening, told her that he was buying a house. She'd sounded pleased. He'd been unable to tell her about Melissa. He knew it would be impossible to explain to his canny, pragmatic mother the effects of that magic week. She would be horrified to hear that he was buying a house with a girl he'd known for barely five days. She would have asked searching questions, demanded to know the date of the wedding. It was odd that he and Melissa never actually talked about commitment. It seemed implicit in all they were planning that their lives were bound together. He imagined that this was why he no longer needed to camp at Moorgate. Soon they would be here together, doing it for real; there was no need, now, for pretence.

The kitchen was deserted. Mike yawned, rubbing his hands over his unshaven jaw, noting that it was nearly nine o'clock. He'd worked well today, and he felt weary but at peace—and terribly hungry. A note was propped on top of the fridge: *Feel too tired to eat. Gone off to bed.*

Fear jolted him out of his other, imaginary, world back into the present. He went quietly upstairs. Luke slept peacefully, his thumb still half in his mouth. Mike had noticed that lately Melissa was having great difficulty in lifting the child, and he realised that he must be on his guard to protect her. Crossing the small landing, he gently opened her bedroom door. The light streamed across her bed and he saw that she was lying on her back, so flat and light that she seemed to make no impression on the bed, no shape beneath the quilt. Silently he raged against the pervasive, cruel, relentless disease, impotent with fury.

They'd heard earlier that completion should take place within the next few days, and Mike had realised, by the look on Melissa's face, that she was simply waiting. Ever since she'd returned from Moorgate it was as if she were being sustained by the need to see the sale through. Once it was accomplished she would feel able to let go. And then what? It was difficult to imagine life without Melissa, without her fun, her determination, her undemanding companionship. Without her love and support.

His attention was caught by a pale oblong shape on the table beside her bed. He stepped forward cautiously and picked it up, holding it angled towards the light. *For Rob* was written on the front of the bulky envelope. So she'd managed it. In the last few days she'd found the strength—and the courage—to write to him, to explain the reasons for the deception and to assure him of her love.

Mike thought: I said I'd go down to see him but how will I be able to leave her now? She's deteriorating so fast.

He replaced the letter gently and went out. As he made supper he wondered what he should do. Should he telephone Rob after completion and talk to him? Once he knew the truth it would be almost impossible to refuse to allow him to come to Oxford, yet Mike knew that his sister wanted Rob to remember her as she had been in Cornwall, and it would be cruel to weight her last days with the responsibility of comforting him, or the guilt of admitting that she'd misled him. The whole thing was impossibly foolish.

Yet it still might be achieved. His head aching with ideas and plans, Mike sat down to his supper.

Yet, when the end came, it was so quick that Mike found himself travelling down to Cornwall in the dawn light of a wild March day, speeding along wet, deserted roads, his whole mind concentrated upon the interview that lay ahead. Exactly six days after the keys of Moorgate had been officially handed to Rob, Mike found himself standing outside the gate, staring up at the house. The wind roared across the moor from the northwest, battering at the rooks' nests high in the trees, screaming round the house. The rain had cleared away and the sun was bright, casting sharp shadows, and daffodils gleamed in the borders beneath the windows. It was all exactly as Melissa had described it.

The front door opened and Rob stood, hands in pockets, watching him. Mike's heart thumped. He opened the gate and walked slowly along the path, pinned by Rob's unwavering stare.

'I'm Mike,' he said awkwardly, praying for guidance. 'Melissa's brother.'

'Yes,' said Rob, almost grimly. 'I thought you might be. I've been expecting . . . something.'

'Expecting?'

Rob shrugged and stood aside, indicating that Mike should enter. They stood in the hall, until Rob closed the door and turned to him.

'I knew something was wrong when I couldn't get an answer from her mobile and there were no more messages. She's changed her mind, hasn't she? Doesn't want to go through with it?'

His misery was palpable and Mike, in his overwhelming need to disabuse Rob of such suspicions, spoke baldly. 'She never changed her mind for a moment. It's not that, Rob. Melissa is dead.'

Dead? Rob's lips formed the word but did not utter it and he seemed to stagger slightly, as if from a physical blow. He put out an arm to steady himself, and Mike caught him, horrified by his thoughtlessness.

'Rob. I'm so sorry. Forgive me for being so brutal. She'd been ill for some time, but the end was quick. Look, can we go somewhere?'

Rob stumbled ahead of him into the kitchen. He went to the sink and stood staring out, gripping the edge.

'Why did nobody tell me she was ill?'

Mike looked compassionately at the straight back and clenched muscles, sharing the man's furious unhappiness. 'She left you a letter.' He took it from his pocket. 'Would you . . . ? Do you think you could read it, Rob? She'll have explained it all so much better than I could and then we can talk. I'll tell you anything you want to know.'

After some moments, Rob turned and took the envelope that Mike held out to him. He nodded, made to leave the kitchen, hesitated.

'There's coffee and sugar under the sink,' he mumbled. 'Milk's in the larder,' and went away, shutting the door behind him.

Shaken with grief, weary from the drive from Oxford after long days and nights of vigil, Mike stumbled about, pushing the kettle onto the hotplate, opening and shutting cupboards, dropping things in his clumsy distress. Then he stood at the window, holding the mug of coffee, staring out at the wild, majestic landscape. Hot tears ran down his cheeks. His own loss was so new, so raw, yet how to comfort Rob? He had no idea how long he stood, waiting, watching the changing colours of the moor, gold, indigo, lavender, as the clouds raced before the wind, but at length he heard the door open behind him. He turned eagerly—but glanced hastily away from the red eyes and ravaged face. At a loss for words he began to make more coffee, his hands trembling.

'When?' asked Rob.

'Yesterday morning. It was just getting light.' His voice wavered. He swallowed, gaining a measure of control. 'In the last few days she seemed to think that she was here. You were always in her mind. You and Moorgate. She was so happy.' He spooned coffee into the mugs, his face screwed up like a child's, and it was Rob who came to comfort him, dropping an arm along his shoulder. 'Don't blame her,' Mike muttered. 'She loved you, but she couldn't bear for it to be spoilt.'

'It's a very . . . wonderful letter,' said Rob gently.

'She wanted you to have it earlier.' Mike wiped away his tears. 'But the end came so fast, I couldn't leave her. I hoped you might come back with me to the funeral. I . . . . She . . . .' He bent his head and Rob tightened his grip on Mike's shoulder. 'We thought it would be right to scatter her ashes here at Moorgate. Where she longed to be.'

For a moment there was only the wild crying of the wind; then Rob spoke sadly, his eyes on the moor beyond the window.

'Yes, please, Mike. I'd like to come back with you. We'll have our own little ceremony here later.'

Mike nodded and Rob hugged him briefly and let his arm drop away. They stood together, each comforted by the other's presence, wrapped in their own thoughts, grateful for the shared silence.

'When you're ready,' Rob said at last, 'we'll get going. We'll talk on the journey, if you're up to it. There will be plenty of time for talking.'

Mike looked at him gratefully. 'I'd like to get back. There's Luke . . .'

'Oh, yes, your little boy. It was good of you to come, Mike.'

'I promised Melissa.' Mike stood his mug on the draining board and rubbed his eyes. 'I'm so tired. I feel I could sleep for a week.'

'Would you let me drive?' offered Rob. 'Just to give you a bit of a rest? I'm insured. I have to be in my kind of work.'

'Thanks. I'm not certain I should be driving, if I'm honest.'

'I'll throw a few things in a bag and be right down.'

Mike felt a brief lightening of spirits at the thought of companionship on the long drive back, relief that the worst was over. He opened the back door and stood, braced against the gale, letting it blow over him, cold and fresh and cleansing. A parliament of rooks argued in some trees somewhere out of sight, and, borne on the wind as it fled over the moor, he heard the high, plaintive crying of the lambs.

PART THREE
CHAPTER ELEVEN

IT WAS HOT. Spears of sunshine pierced the leafy canopies and thrust downwards into the water. In the cool, shadowy depths dark fish hung; a flick of a tail, a flash of gold, a sliding, glancing, silvery arrow. Tall yellow irises shone bright as flame, tiny wild strawberries trailed across the slate flags, and pansies edged the mossy paths.

In the deep shade of the verandah, Polonius lay, head on paws, utterly relaxed. He yawned massively, snapping at a passing fly, stretching himself upon the sun-warmed wooden planks.

Maudie, pottering happily, was in high spirits. In little more than a week, Daphne would be here. She was staying for a month.

'But not with you, love, don't panic,' she'd said. 'Not for all of it. I shall come and go. I shall be with you for just over a week to begin with, then go off for a few days to see Philip's brother. Oh, Maudie, we're going to have such fun!'

It was nearly two years since they'd been together last, at Hector's funeral. On that occasion Daphne had stayed for barely a week; this was to be a real holiday.

'And then I shall come out to see all of you,' Maudie had said. 'I long to see darling Emily and the children. Do bring some photographs.'

Maudie, kneeling beside the border beneath the hedge, prepared herself for the painful act of rising. The garden was looking delightful, the house was spring-cleaned, all was ready; but first, before Daphne was due to arrive, Posy was coming for the weekend. Perhaps they might make a visit to Moorgate, to see Rob and the girl whose name she'd forgotten. Maudie had sent a card once the house was finally, legally, his, but in the ensuing two months she'd had little time to spare. Somehow, the knowledge that Rob was there made her feel that Moorgate was still accessible, not lost to the family for ever.

As she kicked off her shoes, the telephone began to ring. Abandoning the search for her espadrilles, she fled barefoot through the French doors and snatched up the receiver.

'Lady Todhunter? Hello. It's Rob Abbot. How are you?'

Maudie sat down, took a deep breath and began to laugh. 'Rob, how good to hear from you. I was just thinking about you and wondering if I might come down and see you. Just a quick one, to say hello.' A short silence. 'Not if it's difficult, though,' she added. 'I don't want to be a nuisance. It would simply be nice to see you—both of you—settled in.'

'Yes. That would be good.' Rob sounded as if he'd made up his mind about something. 'Only, could you come this weekend?'

'This weekend? Well, I could. I'd have my granddaughter with me—'

'Bring her along. Would Saturday or Sunday be best?'

'I'd prefer Saturday. She travels back to Winchester on Sunday.'

'Saturday it is, then. About coffee time?'

'Excellent. I shall look forward to it. Goodbye, Rob.'

Polonius came padding in and sat down beside her chair. 'That should be fun,' she told him. 'If it's not too hot we might take you with us, but don't count on it.'

She patted Polonius consolingly, knowing how much he hated being left alone. She also knew that Posy would be loath to leave him. Posy had spent most of the Easter holidays with Maudie. Chris and his wife had invited Selina to go with them to Edinburgh. Selina had accepted with alacrity and Posy had felt free to travel to Devon without feeling guilty.

Maudie pushed Polonius's heavy head off her knee and stood up. It might be tactless to drag Posy down to Cornwall to see Rob and his partner happily settled into the house she'd always loved so much. On the other hand, they might all become friends. Either way it was too late to worry about it. Maudie went into the kitchen. Her knees and back ached from weeding and stooping, and she longed for a cup of tea.

'I'm an old, old woman,' she told Polonius, who had followed her and was now staring hopefully at the biscuit tin. 'And much you care. Oh, very well then. One biscuit and that's all, and now go away. I'm going to sit down with my cup of tea and read the paper.'

It was only much later that she'd realised that she hadn't asked Rob why he'd telephoned.

Rob stood at the kitchen window, gazing at nothing. He did a lot of this these days: staring out of windows. Fortunately he had a great deal of work at the moment, and for most of the time he was occupied, but during those other empty hours he was apathetic, unfocused and lonely. The odd thing was that, before Melissa, he had been quite content with his own company. It was as if she'd shown him how delightful life could be with the right companion and then departed, leaving him alone, dissatisfied and miserable. Only his friendship with Mike had kept him going. The shock of her death had momentarily unbalanced him, but Mike's need had steadied him, giving him something that enabled him to think his existence was worth preserving.

It seemed extraordinary that five short days could have changed his life, given it new, sweet meaning, while now the slowly passing hours were flat, empty, wearisome. It was ironic that Melissa should have supplanted Moorgate in his heart and then left both heart and house untenanted. Without her the house simply underlined all that he had lost. He saw her everywhere; expected to hear her voice. Missing her was a permanent, physical ache. Yet he was not bitter; he understood why she had allowed herself those five days of fun and love and he did not begrudge her a minute of them. So many things had become clear once he'd read her letter and talked to Mike, but he wished that she had not wanted him to have Moorgate. She hadn't foreseen that without her it kept his grief and loss at the forefront of his mind.

'I don't think I can go on here alone,' he'd said to Mike, one evening on the telephone. 'I keep expecting to find her, sitting by the fire or looking out at the moor. I think I can hear her voice. It should be comforting, to be here where we were so happy, but it isn't. It's agonising.'

'It's early days.' Mike had sounded almost as desperate as he was himself, and Rob had been struck by remorse.

'I know it is,' he'd answered. 'How are you managing? How's Luke?'

'He misses her. He looks for her and grizzles to himself. I don't quite know how to deal with it.'

'Why don't you come down?' Rob had suggested eagerly. 'You and Luke. Just for a weekend or something. It would distract him.' And me, he might have added. 'Or would it disrupt your work?'

Mike had laughed rather mirthlessly. 'I'm not getting much done. It sounds a great idea, Rob. Are you sure? Luke's a bit of a handful.'

'Just tell me what you need.' Rob had sounded almost buoyant. 'I can buy some secondhand bits and pieces. After all, I'm hoping you might consider this to be a second home.'

'Well.' Mike had hesitated. 'He still needs to sleep in a cot. And a playpen is an absolute necessity if we want a few moments of peace and quiet. Honestly, Rob, I can't put you to all that trouble.'

'It's no trouble. I might have been his uncle if . . . if . . .'

'You are his uncle,' Mike had said quickly. 'His only uncle. OK, I accept your offer with gratitude.'

So it was that Mike and Luke had made their first visit to Moorgate together. Once they'd settled in, joking at the makeshift arrangements, jollying each other along, Rob and Mike—with Luke slung papoose-like across his chest—had walked across the moor as far as Rough Tor. It had been a mild day and Mike had relaxed in the warm sunshine.

'I can see why Melissa loved it here,' he'd said. 'It's a different world. It meant so much to her, Rob. That glorious week of freedom coming out of nowhere, when there was nothing left to look forward to.'

Out there on the moor they'd talked naturally, easing their pain, sharing their grief. Even Luke had been soothed by the peace and had slept soundly in the old, white-painted cot. A few weeks later they'd made another visit. It was clear that Mike was puzzled by the continuing scarcity of furniture, although he said nothing.

'I can't bring myself to get on with it.' Rob had answered his quick glance around the kitchen, still furnished only with the gate-leg table and two chairs.

Mike had remained silent. Luke's playpen sat in the middle of the huge floor space and it was almost a relief when the usual detritus that gathers about small children began to spread around the house. When they'd gone, Rob left the playpen where it was.

Now, as he stared out of the kitchen window, he realised that he hadn't given Lady Todhunter a reason for telephoning. It was just as well that she'd jumped into the breach. He had no idea why he'd wanted to speak to her; a sudden need to hear her crisp old voice had possessed him. He'd remembered those cheerful conversations with her, her sharp humour and charming smile, and he'd simply picked up his mobile and dialled her number. He'd had no opportunity to explain about Melissa, and he could foresee difficulties there, but he'd had little choice. Mike and Luke were coming down again the following weekend, and he preferred to see Lady Todhunter without that added complication.

Rob frowned. He had the oddest sensation that Melissa was sitting at the table behind him, eating chocolate, smiling at him. He wouldn't turn round. He'd done it before and had always been disappointed. Yet, today, he'd felt her presence keenly. He clenched his teeth, tears starting in his eyes, his body aching for her.

You can't imagine what you gave to me, Rob, she'd written. *The most precious gift ever. Love and life when I'd thought it was all over. Forgive me, won't you? I shall always love you. Think of me when you see the rooks building and hear the new lambs each spring . . .*

He crossed his arms over his chest and allowed the tears to fall.

Mike sat at the kitchen table looking through his post, while Luke chuntered cheerfully in his highchair. He still occasionally received letters of condolence, as the sad news filtered out through close friends to acquaintances, but this morning he was studying the latest details sent from estate agents—photographs of cottages in idyllic Oxfordshire villages, rectories in Wiltshire and Gloucestershire. He had no plans to take out a large mortgage; his income was too uncertain for such a risk. And although the proceeds from the life-assurance policy that Melissa had taken out against the mortgage of her London flat were now his, it was a small sum compared with the prices of these houses. It seemed that he might have to move further afield than these expensive counties of middle England. The buzz of the doorbell disturbed his reflections and he piled the house details aside and went into the hall.

He opened the front door and hid his dismay behind a smile.

'Rebecca. How nice . . .'

'I shan't stay a minute. I'm sure you're much too busy. Just to say— what about supper on Saturday? We've got a little party going . . .'

'Come in,' he said, trying to keep the despair from his voice. 'Coffee?'

'Oh, well . . .' She clasped her hands together, a girlish gesture that sat uncomfortably with her years. 'Now, there's an offer I can't refuse.' She preceded him into the kitchen. 'Oh, good morning, Lukey.'

Mike grimaced at the percolator: *Lukey!* 'Black?' he asked.

'Fancy you remembering. No sugar. I'm desperately trying to lose weight. How do you manage to stay so lean?'

'It's Luke who keeps me in training,' he answered lightly.

'Well, I must say,' leaning towards him, voice pitched low with emotion, 'I think you are so brave. Not only about your sister. No'—a hand raised—'I know you don't want to talk about it, don't worry. No, I mean managing all on your own. Me and my chums are so impressed.'

'I can't imagine why.' Mike put the mugs on the table and sat down. 'I expect you looked after your children, didn't you?'

'Well, yes. I did. But it's different somehow, isn't it?'

He had a sudden vision of Melissa, appearing in the study doorway, grinning, finger to her lips. 'It's that frightful woman from round the corner. I told her that it was more than my life is worth to disturb you, but I'm going to have to give her coffee. I'll tell you when she's gone.'

The sudden wave of loss made it impossible to make another effort. He drank some coffee and remained silent.

'I hope you'll forgive me saying that you look tired.'

Mike looked at her. He thought that her impertinence was breathtaking but he managed to smile. 'So what was this about a party?'

Excitement kindled in her again. 'Just a little group of chums coming in for some supper on Saturday evening. They'd be so thrilled to meet you. We've all seen *Changing Places*, of course. Brilliant production! And we can't wait for the next book. Now, do say you'll come.'

'This Saturday?' He pretended disappointment. 'I can't, I'm afraid.'

Her face fell. 'But why not? We can easily put Lukey to bed upstairs.'

'No, no,' Mike said quickly. 'Nothing to do with Luke. The truth is'— his eye fell on the calendar pinned to the notice board behind her head, saw the thick green circle drawn around the date of the following weekend—'we're going down to Cornwall for the weekend.'

'Oh, that's too bad. We shall all be so disappointed. Never mind. Another time. I'll be certain to give you more notice.'

'You do that.' He remained on his feet. 'Look, sorry to break it up, but it's time for Luke's nap and then I have to get on.'

'I quite understand.' She leaned across the table, her expression a mixture of sympathy, admiration, coyness. 'Isn't there anything I can do to help? You must miss Melissa so much. Can't I be useful?'

'No.' Repugnance sharpened his voice and he bent over Luke, giving himself a moment to regain control. 'No, thanks.' He straightened up, smiling. 'I promise I'll ask if I have a real problem.' He herded her towards the door. 'Give me a buzz some time . . .'

He closed the door on her promises and leaned against it, wondering how he and Luke could hide for a whole weekend. Luke shouted and he hauled himself upright and went back to the kitchen. Murmuring to Luke, he reached for the telephone and dialled.

'Rob? It's Mike. How are you? . . . Good . . . Yes, I'm OK, but I've got a problem. Could Luke and I come down this weekend instead of next?'

Selina opened the cupboard door and stared at the line of clothes: suits, flannels hung neatly beneath jackets, shirts. She longed for the courage to drag them out and mutilate them; or at the very least bundle them up and take them to the local charity shop.

'I think it's Patrick's subconscious at work,' Chris's wife, Sarah, had stated. 'Deep down he knows he'll be back.'

Selina had retorted that she had no intention of taking Patrick back—

and made several pithy observations about his character—but Sarah's remark had taken root. As the days passed, and anger was replaced by a dull depression, she realised how much she missed him. Despite his gentleness, his dislike of confrontation, Patrick had a quiet strength and Selina was beginning to realise how much she'd leaned on it. She missed other things, too: the early cup of tea in bed; the washing-up unobtrusively completed while she watched a favourite television programme; the ready sympathy when one of her migraines took possession of her. He came of a generation of men who carried heavy objects and put up shelves, and she knew now how much she'd taken for granted.

Selina closed the cupboard door abruptly and went downstairs, feeling moody and irritable. The holiday in Edinburgh had not been a success. Chris was far too easy-going with Sarah and quite foolishly concerned about her now that she was pregnant. As for Sarah's mother, a bossy old woman who wanted them to move nearer to Edinburgh— well, Selina had made no bones about her opinion regarding that idea.

'But, Mum,' Chris had said pacifically, 'it's quite reasonable. She only has Sarah, after all, and now with the baby coming—'

'You're not intending to give up your job and move to Scotland?'

Chris had shuffled about, embarrassed. 'The company has a branch in Newcastle,' he'd mumbled. 'It's a kind of compromise. There's some beautiful countryside round there and the houses are cheaper than London. It would be a good move now that we're starting a family.'

Selina had made some sharp observations which embraced genetics, loyalty and weakness of character, but Chris had merely listened, shrugged and gone away. Paul, who worked in Bristol, was sympathetic—from a safe distance—while refusing to take sides, and as for Posy . . . well, Posy had always been a broken reed when it came to loyalty. The only good thing was that her own friends had never been selected from among Patrick's colleagues. As far as they were concerned, Patrick had decided to give up teaching and was away on a course, something to do with helping people with learning difficulties.

'How brave!' her friends cried, studying their hands at bridge. 'Darling old Patrick. So typical. Always doing something for somebody else.'

Occasionally, just occasionally, Selina looked at their complacent, well-maquillaged faces and felt a surge of antipathy. She longed to slam down her hand and storm out, but the thought of the empty house kept her in her seat. At these moments, she felt terribly alone.

Selina reached the bottom of the stairs and picked up the letters from the mat. A telephone bill, a circular offering yet another credit card, and a postcard. It was a scene of rolling Welsh moorland and she turned it over, her heart bumping unsteadily. *It's great here. Terrific challenge. Hope all is well with you.*

The sight of Patrick's looping signature engulfed her in a kaleido-scopic lifetime of memories. She swallowed painfully, then went into the kitchen and filled the kettle. While she waited for it to boil she continued to look at the card. Even now, with all the novelty and excitement of his new life, he had not quite forgotten her. She propped the card against the fruit bowl, made some tea and sat down, still staring at it.

'I'm feeling rather a fool,' admitted Maudie as they bowled along the A39, between the sea and the moor. 'I wish I'd asked Rob why he'd telephoned, instead of just butting in. After all, there's no real reason why I should go to see him now that he owns Moorgate. It's not the norm, is it? Going back to visit the new owners?'

Posy stared out at the grey granite mass of Rough Tor. 'But you and Rob have become friends, haven't you? So it's a bit different. So what? I think it's nice of him to invite us.'

'That's the problem. I have this feeling that I invited myself.'

'You're feeling guilty again,' accused Posy. 'We'll have to have a G-word box. What's his girlfriend's name?'

'I didn't even ask him,' wailed Maudie. 'I feel so . . . so idiotic.'

'I think it's going to be fun,' said Posy contentedly. 'I wasn't certain at first that I'd want to see Moorgate, now it's not ours any longer, but I have this feeling that it's going to be good. If we can be friends with them it won't seem as if we've really lost it. I love it here,' she added dreamily. 'It's so wild and rugged.'

Maudie struggled with another stab of guilt. 'Perhaps you should have trained for an outdoor kind of career,' she suggested. 'Something like Hugh does, for instance. You love horses and riding.'

Posy shifted in her seat. 'Mmm,' she murmured. 'Are we nearly there?'

'Not far now. What a day! It's quite hot. I'm sorry Polonius couldn't come, but if this girlfriend is anti-dog he might have had to stay in the car all morning.'

'I know. Don't worry. I gave him a good walk. He'll be fine. Don't we turn off soon?'

'Quite soon.' She peered at a fingerpost. 'Here we are.' She changed down into a lower gear and swung the car off the main road into the network of dim, narrow lanes. 'Not long now.'

They passed through the small hamlet, its cottages set about the grassy triangle with its stone cross. The lane curved sharply left, uphill, and there was the house. Set back from the lane, washed a warm cream with its window frames and gutters painted dark red, Moorgate looked comfortable, solid. As Posy gazed, the front door opened and Rob came swiftly out, down the path and into the lane. Maudie wound down her window, but before she could speak Rob was talking urgently.

'I'm sorry I have to break this news so abruptly, Lady Todhunter, but the situation is a bit tricky. I should have told you when I telephoned but . . . Look, I think you know that I was buying Moorgate with my partner. Well.' He glanced back at the house. 'She died quite suddenly two months ago.' He nodded in response to the shock on their faces. 'I wanted to tell you in a more . . . acceptable way but I have her brother staying with me unexpectedly. He was due next weekend but the situation changed and I don't really want to talk about this in front of him.'

'My dear fellow, of course not.' Maudie shook her head understandingly. 'Rob, I am so terribly sorry. Why don't we disappear and come back another time?'

'No, no. It's fine. Honestly.'

'But we shall be in the way. Why didn't you ring and put us off?'

Rob frowned. 'Mike only let me know on Wednesday. I did try to telephone but . . . look, it's OK. I just don't want to talk about it in front of him. They were very close. His wife left him with a small boy to look after, they're divorced, and now this. So it's all a bit dire. Never mind. I'll open the gate and you can put the car inside.'

'Hell and damnation,' muttered Maudie as she turned the car in through the gateway. 'This is going to be dreadful.'

'No, it won't.' Posy seemed quite composed. 'It's going to be OK. Not about the girl, of course—that's simply awful—but it'll be all right.'

Rob was opening her door, and she stepped out, smiling at him.

'I'm Posy,' she said. 'Hello. I'm just so sorry about all this.'

He nodded gratefully. 'It's been . . . rather fraught.' He raised his voice. 'It's good to see you again, Lady Todhunter.'

'You, too, Rob, even in these unhappy circumstances. I wanted Posy to see the miracles you'd performed on dear old Moorgate.'

'It's brilliant.' Posy looked about her. 'I love the colour you've painted the walls. It's so warm and mellow. Almost Mediterranean.'

'I know.' They stood together, studying the house. 'Perhaps it should have been left as bare granite, more in keeping, but this seemed right.'

'It is right,' she said confidently. 'It's a place of contrasts, isn't it? The open moor on one side and fuchsia and escallonia flowering on the other.'

He laughed. 'That's Cornwall for you. I'm glad you approve. Come and see what I've done inside.' He opened the front door and stood back to let them enter. 'Come and meet Mike,' he said.

Hearing their voices in the hall, Mike sat Luke in the playpen with his toys and put his hands in his pockets. Feeling unusually nervous he waited, leaning against the sink, ankles crossed, feigning indifference. Lady Todhunter came in first and he looked at her critically. She was a tall woman with a feathery cap of grey hair and large grey eyes. She paused for a moment in the doorway, still turned away from him, talking to Rob, and Mike was able to see the younger woman behind them. She was gazing eagerly about her, her face alive with curiosity. Shining dark hair was gathered loosely up into a knot from which long wisps had escaped, and warm, honey-brown eyes darted hither and thither until they finally rested on Luke. Her face lit with delight and she gave a small cry which moved the whole party forward into the kitchen.

'How do you do?' He straightened, holding out his hand. 'I'm Mike Clayton and this is Luke.'

'So what did you think of her?' asked Rob, casually, as they stood in the lane watching the car jolt away.

'I thought that they were both quite delightful,' answered Mike carefully, jogging Luke upon his hip.

Rob glanced at him sharply. 'Mmm. They are, aren't they? I hope you didn't mind showing Posy round. I thought it might be easier. Lady Todhunter and I are old friends.'

'So I gather. No, I didn't mind. Posy was very enthusiastic, and she loves the things you've done, but she can remember it from holidays when she was a child.' Mike sounded amused. 'I wondered if her memories were more to do with what she'd been told about it. Family stories and so on. But she was determined that it was her own memory.'

Rob smiled. 'I think Posy is a rather determined character. A chip off the old block, I'd say. Lady Todhunter certainly knows her own mind.'

'Actually, she's her step-grandmother.'

Rob raised his eyebrows. 'I didn't know that. Shall we have a beer?'

'Why not? Luke's ready for a sleep so I'll tuck him up. Shan't be long.'

Rob fetched two cans from the larder and looked for some glasses. It had been a good day, in the end. The clearly defined no-go zone had initially put a strain on conversation, but it had been fun. The two women had stopped in Camelford and bought some delicious pasties, which they'd produced when Rob insisted they stay for lunch. It was so warm that they'd been able to eat outside on the lawn. Luke had enjoyed himself immensely and, briefly, Rob had been able to put aside his own pain. Yet he'd been keenly aware of Melissa all day. He'd felt her friendly presence presiding, as it were, over the party. He shook his head, and smiled at Mike as he came into the kitchen.

'Is he OK?' He held out a glass of beer. 'Good. Was Posy surprised at the sparseness of the furnishing?'

'She didn't mention it. Did Lady Todhunter remark on it?'

'Much too polite.' Rob chuckled a little. 'She was the mistress of tact, for once.' He swallowed some beer, becoming serious again. 'But I want to talk to you about it. It's no good, Mike. I can't stay here.'

Mike stood his glass carefully on the table. 'Rob—'

'No.' Rob shook his head. 'We've been through it all before. I know it's early days. I know I'll come to terms with it. But I can't make a new start here at Moorgate. It should be wonderful to be here, where we were so happy together, but it isn't. It's as if I'm waiting for her all the time. It's not that I want to forget her—I don't—but I have to get on with my life. If we'd been here together for years it would be different, but we weren't. It'll be OK. I shall cope with it, but I can't do it here.'

'She thought it was what you wanted. More than anything.'

'Until I met Melissa that was true. But then I realised that I didn't give a damn where I lived as long as we were together. Ironic, isn't it?'

'Oh, Rob, I'm so sorry . . .'

'Don't be.' Rob was upset by Mike's distress, but he knew he must remain firm. 'But if I stay here I shall go under. I can see what she was trying to do, bless her, but it isn't going to work.'

'But what will you do?'

'I don't know. Sometimes I've thought of moving right away.' He looked directly at Mike. 'Of course, Melissa made a generous financial contribution to the house—'

'Forget all that,' said Mike abruptly. 'It's yours. She'd want that. And if it will help you get another place then that's great. Oh, Rob. This is . . . sad. But I want you to do what's right for you. I can understand how you feel, but after all you've done to the house and all you've been through here, won't you find it hard to leave it?'

'After losing Melissa this will be bad but not tragic. I know now about real loss. But the thing I wanted to say, Mike, was this. I wonder whether you might consider buying Moorgate.'

Mike stared at him. His shock was so great that Rob smiled a little.

'After all,' he said gently, 'that was the original intention, wasn't it? That's why Melissa came in the first place.'

'Well, yes.' Mike looked confused. 'Except that I always thought it was too far away from London. But . . . Good God, Rob! You're not serious, are you?'

'Absolutely serious. Why not? It's perfect for you and Luke. Peace and quiet. Glorious countryside. If you were to agree to it, I might buy a little cottage in Camelford or Boscastle and . . . well.' He shrugged. 'Will you think about it?'

Mike glanced round the kitchen, as if he were seeing it for the first time. 'I . . . simply don't know.'

'It needs thinking about,' Rob said reassuringly. 'Give yourself time to get used to the idea. Drink up and we'll have another. I think we need it.'

'So what do you think of him?' asked Maudie casually, turning out of the lanes onto the A39.

'I think they're really great,' answered Posy carefully, taking a suddenly intent interest in the passing countryside. 'All three of them.'

Maudie glanced at her sharply. 'They are, aren't they? Luke's a sweetie. And do you approve of what Rob has done to Moorgate?'

'It's perfect,' she said dreamily. 'Exactly right. Mike thinks so too.'

'I was rather impressed by Mike,' said Maudie. 'He coped very well with us, I thought. I must read his book. Rob says it's very good. It must be a great comfort for Rob to have him there.'

'It's so cruel. You can see by the way he's restored it that he must really love Moorgate, can't you?'

'Odd that he hasn't furnished it yet, though,' mused Maudie.

'Well, it must have come as a terrible shock for him.' Posy's face had a brooding look. 'It's thrown him into a kind of limbo. Poor, poor Rob. He reminds me of Hugh. He's attractive, isn't he? And he's so nice.'

'Yes,' said Maudie, after a moment. 'He's very nice indeed. And resilient, I should imagine. He'll soon recover, wouldn't you say?'

'Mmm,' said Posy absently. Suddenly she shook off her contemplative mood and looked about her. 'I hope Polonius is OK. I'll take him for a long walk through the woods when we get back.'

'Good idea,' said Maudie, with the strangest feeling that she'd been warned off. 'He'll enjoy that. I don't know why but suddenly I feel very tired. Shall we have a tape on?'

'Why not?' Posy sorted through the selection and presently the cheerful strains of Haydn's trumpet concerto filled the car.

There was no time for Maudie to think too much about the visit to Moorgate. Later that week, giving thanks that the fine weather was holding, she was driving to Exeter St David's to meet Daphne. The train was on time and Maudie, stationed near the exit, watched the doors as they swung open, suddenly nervous that she might not recognise her old friend. As soon as she saw her, however, she realised how foolish such a fear had been: the short fair hair, the small square jaw, those pansy-blue eyes had all been delightfully translated into old age. It was typical, too, that Daphne should be attended by a male. Even in her mid-seventies, she was still irresistible. Clearly the young man thought so: helping her with her case, laughing at her observations, refusing to be thanked. He stood by while the two old friends exchanged greetings.

'Maudie, this is Russell.' Daphne smiled upon him charmingly. 'Russell, this is my friend, Lady Todhunter. I've been telling him all about you. We've had such fun. Do get back on the train or it will go without you. Goodbye, Russell. Thank you for your company.'

'You're hopeless,' chuckled Maudie, taking the suitcase while Daphne slung herself about with small bags. 'No man is safe from you. Not even a schoolboy.'

'My dear.' Daphne's voice lowered confidentially, 'he's a married man with a child of two. Can you believe it? I was about to ask him if he was on his way home for half term. Such a shock!'

They laughed together, pausing to watch the train pull away, waving to Russell who had waited by the door, and then went out to the car. The luggage loaded in, they stood and looked at one another.

Maudie shook her head. 'I can't believe that you're really here. You look terrific.'

'Now that's very kind of you, Maudie. I happen to know that I look as if I've just been dug up and given a quick paint job. Is it appallingly old-fashioned to say that I would kill for a cup of tea?'

'Not a bit. Can you wait until we get home? It will be quicker than fighting our way into the city centre. Or we could have one here?'

Daphne closed her eyes. 'No,' she said quickly. 'No more rail-company liquid masquerading as tea or coffee, thank you. I can wait.'

'It'll only be twenty minutes,' promised Maudie. 'Let's get going.'

The journey was occupied with an exchange of news, but they were both relieved to pull into Maudie's drive, glad to be home.

'It's so peaceful,' remarked Daphne, looking up at the trees. 'I'd quite forgotten how beautiful it is here. Oh, Maudie! It's been much too long.'

Maudie smiled at her across the top of the car. 'Much too long,' she agreed. 'Aha! The kraken wakes. Here's Polonius to meet you.'

Polonius, who had been taking a nap in the woodshed, came yawning into the sunshine and was brought up short by the sight of a stranger on the other side of the fence. Daphne stared at him for a moment and then turned to Maudie.

'I feel overawed,' she admitted. 'He's rather impressive, isn't he?'

Maudie hauled out the suitcase. 'Don't be taken in by him. Come on in and we'll have that cup of tea.'

Daphne gathered up her belongings. 'There's so much to catch up on. I'm longing to hear about Selina and Patrick,' she said, following Maudie inside and pausing for a proper greeting with Polonius. 'Where am I? In here? Oh, it's so pretty, Maudie. I shall be very comfortable.'

'Well, I'll leave you to get yourself sorted out while I get the kettle on.'

The door closed behind her and Daphne sat down on the bed. Alone for the first time for several hours, her body relaxed and her expression grew thoughtful. This visit was not simply a holiday; there was another, more serious purpose behind it. She recoiled from the thought. Surely there was time for some fun, first; a few days to see how things stood with Maudie? Perhaps a right moment would come: a time for confidences and explanations that could be accepted and understood.

'Tea!'

Maudie's cry echoed along the passage. Daphne took a deep breath. She stood up and went out, closing the door behind her.

The table was set by the open French doors and Daphne exclaimed with pleasure. While Maudie poured the tea, Daphne wandered out onto the verandah. Afternoon sun slanted across the lawn so that the still, dark water glinted and secret, shadowy corners were briefly lit.

'This is perfect,' she sighed. 'So quiet. No wonder you left London for this, Maudie. I really can't blame you.'

'I was never a London person. Especially not without Hector.'

'No,' said Daphne, after a moment. 'No, I quite see that.'

'Hector was so good at all those things: exhibitions, concerts, first nights, the best restaurants. He had a kind of instinct which led him to the best seats, the best bars. You know what I mean.'

'Yes, love. Very well indeed. He had a knack of making people feel pleased to oblige him.' Daphne came back into the living room and sat down at the table. 'But it wasn't a heartless thing. He didn't use people, did he? Hector was naturally generous. He liked people to be happy.'

'Yes, that's true.' Maudie smiled. 'He had a huge capacity for fun.'

'Exactly,' said Daphne. 'Just that. Dear old boy!'

'Oh, it's good to have you here,' said Maudie impulsively. 'I've got things out of proportion lately and I've wondered if I'm going quite mad. You'll get me back on the rails again. I've been so bitter, Daphne.'

'Yes,' said Daphne quietly. 'Yes, I know you have, love. It hasn't been easy for you since Hector died.'

'I'm a jealous, cantankerous old woman,' said Maudie. 'We were so happy together, Hector and I. We enjoyed some blissful times and we were very good friends. Yet I could never quite get the wretched Hilda out of my system. I had long spells of peace but at the end all the bitterness came back. When Selina used to come to see him and he apologised to her for marrying me I thought I'd kill him. And her. Of course, it wasn't her fault. He thought she was Hilda, and he'd hold her hand and drone on and on. "I'm so sorry. I'm so sorry." Selina loved it, of course. And then there was the business of his stocks and shares. Oh, Daphne. I didn't mean to start on all this so soon. Let's forget it. Have some scones and some jam and clotted cream. A proper Devon tea.'

'It sounds delicious. Yes, please.'

'And now there's been the great drama with Patrick,' Maudie continued, ladling cream onto her scone. 'I cannot imagine what Selina is going to do without him.'

'It's quite extraordinary.' Daphne accepted the change of subject with a certain relief. 'I know you've kept me informed but it's not the same by telephone. Start from the beginning and tell me again properly.'

CHAPTER TWELVE

IN WINCHESTER, Posy lay on her bed, staring at the ceiling.

'I don't suppose you get back to London very often,' he'd said casually, and she'd answered that just now she went home quite often. She'd said that that there were a few problems and that her mother needed company. She'd been kneeling on the broad window seat on the landing, looking out over the moor, while he'd leaned beside her.

'I'm going up next weekend,' he'd said. 'I have to see my agent. Maybe we could meet up?'

She'd felt a tiny shock of surprise at the invitation—even anxiety—but had been rather flattered, too.

'That would be good,' she'd replied, very calm, very cool.

'Well, then.' He'd shifted his weight. 'Perhaps I'd better have your telephone number.'

'Oh yes.' She'd turned quite naturally, frowning a little. 'I think I can remember it. Or do you mean the London number?'

'I mean both.' He was smiling. 'Hold on a moment.'

He'd gone into the room he was using as a bedroom and returned with a pad and a pencil. She'd been able to give him both numbers and had watched while he tore out the page and tucked it into his wallet.

'Great,' he'd said. 'We'll talk, then. I don't like to leave Luke overnight, but perhaps we could have lunch?'—and she'd nodded, suddenly shy.

From the beginning she'd had a special feeling about the day, a certainty that something good might happen, but this was beyond her experience. After all, this was Mike Clayton, the playwright and novelist who had caused a sensation with *Changing Places*. She'd been given tickets for her eighteenth birthday. His wife, a beautiful, sophisticated woman, had been playing the leading role and Posy had been enraptured by the play. It seemed unbelievable that this was the same man, who'd laughed with Maudie and was so sweet with his baby son.

He'd telephoned on Tuesday afternoon. He'd been jokey, happy, amusing, and she'd fallen in with his mood, talking, listening, utterly happy until he'd had to go because Luke had woken from his nap.

'See you on Saturday, then,' he'd said.

She closed her eyes, imagining him, frowning slightly. He reminded her of someone, someone she'd met recently. Ever since last Saturday she'd been racking her brains, but it eluded her. She shook her head, suddenly seized by a mixture of anxiety and anticipation, and, rolling off her bed, turned her mind deliberately to her work.

Rob washed up his supper things, rinsing them, setting them on the draining board. He performed the task mechanically, the slow, almost rhythmical movements bringing a small measure of peace to his unquiet mind. The serene beauty of the evening beyond the window for once had no power to soothe his isolation. Before Melissa he'd sought out this seclusion, happy to be alone after a busy day. Solitude had begun to be an ideal to be sought, worked for, treasured—and then Melissa had arrived, demolishing the illusion with her vital presence. Strange that she, who was so near death, had been so full of life.

Rob removed the plug, letting the water rush away, and reached for the tea cloth. He knew that he must let Moorgate go. He knew he must resist the gentle path of melancholy, retrospection and self-pity.

As he put away the plates he considered the possibility of Mike buying Moorgate. He had no fears for Mike. Mike needed privacy and peace, but, once refreshed, he would seek out company with a friendly ease that would guarantee him companions. And there was Luke. Luke, as he grew, would keep Mike in touch with his own small world. Rob pushed the kettle onto the hot plate, wondering if he'd imagined the attraction that had flared between Mike and Posy last Saturday. His own heightened emotions had made him unusually aware, and he'd felt that the whole day was building towards some climax, yet to be fulfilled.

Now, as he made some coffee, he was visited by an odd sense of well-being, although his heart was heavy. He was waiting for something: some word or sign. Perhaps it would be Mike's agreement to buy Moorgate, perhaps something else that would release the weight of the pent-up pain in his breast into simple, ordinary grief.

'Hi.' Posy stood awkwardly in the sitting-room doorway looking across at Selina. 'I was just wondering . . .'

Selina did not remove her gaze from the flickering television screen. 'Wondering about what?' she asked indifferently.

'Supper,' Posy said brightly. 'I thought we might go round to the pub.'

At last Selina turned to look at her. 'To the pub?'

'Why not? It would save us having to cook. I'll pay. Come on, Mum,' she said, almost pleadingly. 'It'll be fun. It'll stop you moping.' Even as she said the words she knew she'd made a terrible mistake.

Selina stiffened. 'What makes you think that I should be moping?'

Posy sighed. 'OK, so you're not moping. It's just difficult to imagine anyone watching reruns of *Steptoe and Son* if they've got anything better to do. But perhaps you're enjoying it. So if you don't want to go to the pub, what are we going to eat? There isn't much in the fridge.'

'There's plenty to eat,' snapped Selina. 'I'm not running a hotel, you know. You think that just because you suddenly deign to grace the house with your presence I should be killing the fatted calf.'

'No,' said Posy wearily, 'I don't think that. I just thought we might try to have a fun evening together. Never mind. I'll make us an omelette.'

'Not for me, thanks,' said Selina. 'I'm not hungry.'

Posy stood holding the door handle, possessed by an urge to scream. 'Mum,' she said. 'Mum, why does it have to be like this? I thought we might spend some time together. I've got tomorrow off and we could go shopping or something, and have lunch.'

Selina sat quite still while her pride battled with a desire to break down and admit her loneliness. But how could she? This was nothing more than pity that Posy was offering; humiliating, degrading pity. She'd probably tell Maudie about it later. And here was another grievance. Maudie had Daphne staying with her. It was disgraceful that Daphne, Selina's mother's oldest and best friend, should have passed through London without coming to see her, without so much as a telephone call. Oh, she'd called earlier that evening from Maudie's, said that she'd be in London in a fortnight and would love to see her, but by then Maudie would have told her all about Patrick's defection. How they would enjoy it! All this passed through Selina's mind as Posy waited for an answer.

'Strange as it may seem,' she said, 'I have other plans for tomorrow. I do have a life, you know. I can't just drop everything because you suddenly decide to come home for a long weekend. Why should I?'

'Why indeed?' asked Posy. 'I can't think of a good reason. Great. I'll do my own thing, then. See you around.'

The door closed and Selina sat on, her hands clenched in her lap, staring at the flickering screen. As the laughter of the studio audience grew louder, Selina, locked in the prison of her insecurity and pride, was regretting her lost opportunity, the tears trickling down her cheeks.

All the way from Oxford, travelling on the Circle Line to Embankment, walking up The Strand and along William IV Street to the Chandos, Mike was thinking about Posy. Ever since last Saturday, she'd occupied his thoughts, distracting him from his work. Camilla had been beautiful, a boost to his ego, but Posy was the stuff of every day: interesting, funny, kind, inquisitive, enthusiastic. For one so young she'd handled the situation at Moorgate with great tact, without either descending into sentimentality or creating an atmosphere of false jollity. He was too experienced to be unaware of her interest, yet even the chemistry that had tingled between them had not rendered her tongue-tied or coy.

As he went up the steps and into the upstairs bar of the Chandos he was prey to a sudden attack of nerves. Perhaps today she might be different; perhaps his judgment had been clouded by the extraordinary circumstances. He was early, so he bought himself a pint and went to sit in one of the window seats, thinking of sensible explanations for the strange, magical influence that had informed that day. It had been a shock when Rob announced that he didn't want to stay at Moorgate. Yet, on reflection, it was easy to understand how he must be feeling. Melissa had not taken into consideration the essential fact that, without her, Moorgate would be a reminder of all that Rob had lost.

Yet to buy Moorgate himself was a big step. It was a large, isolated house, a long way from London and Oxford and his friends. On the other hand, it was exactly what he'd been considering: a place where Luke might grow up in a rural community. After all, he need not fear isolation. His friends would be delighted to spend weekends in Cornwall and he'd have Rob nearby.

Once he'd adjusted to Rob's announcement, one level of his consciousness was telling him that this was quite right, that all the pieces were falling into place. Surely Melissa would have been delighted to think that Mike and Luke were at Moorgate, with Rob near at hand. As for Posy . . . He was convinced that Melissa would have liked Posy . . .

He turned, sighing, and saw her standing in the doorway, looking anxious. As he stood up he saw her expression warm into eagerness and instinctively he held out his hand to her. She came quickly towards him and took it in her own, beaming at him, noticing his half-empty glass.

'You're early.'

'Oh, that was deliberate.' He grinned at her, releasing her hand, pulling out a chair. 'I needed to get a quick pint in to steady my nerves.'

'Excellent. I like to see myself as a scary character. How's Luke?'

'Fine. I have a very motherly lady next door who comes round for the day if I really need her. Now, what will you have to drink?'

She watched him go to the bar, his fair hair gleaming under the lights, his easy stance, the way he laughed at something the barman said. Once more a teasing memory flickered at the back of her mind; his resemblance to someone who had laughed just like that. He came across to her with her glass and the menu and went back for his own drink.

'This is fun,' he said. 'Now, what shall we have to eat?'

'So,' said Maudie, on the Tuesday evening after Daphne's arrival, 'what about these photographs? We've been meaning to look at them ever since you arrived.'

'The time has flown so fast,' said Daphne, 'and it's been such fun,' but she looked suddenly tired.

'It seemed a pity to waste the weather,' said Maudie cheerfully. 'I think we're in for a wet spell now, though, and it's chilly again. I think I was right to light the stove, only it seems such a luxury when it's nearly June.'

'Polonius is enjoying it.' Daphne looked affectionately at the recumbent figure. 'He must be exhausted after that long walk. I know I am.'

'Exactly,' agreed Maudie. 'A nice, quiet evening looking at photographs is just what we need.'

There was a silence. After a moment, when Daphne had made no move, Maudie glanced at her in surprise. Daphne's eyes were closed and her face wore a concentrated look. Maudie felt a spasm of fear. She leaned forward and touched her friend's knee.

'Are you all right?'

Daphne opened her eyes and smiled, but her face was strained. 'Yes,' she said, 'quite all right. I'll get them, then.'

'Shall I go?' Maudie was still concerned. 'I can fetch them if you tell me where they are. Or would you rather leave it?'

'No,' she answered, quite firmly. 'No, I think you're right. The time has come. It's been put off quite long enough.'

She got up and went out, leaving Maudie staring into the fire, puzzled by Daphne's choice of words. Maudie was still frowning when Daphne came back with several folders. She sat down again, holding them on her lap, looking preoccupied. Maudie watched her curiously.

Daphne shook her head and sighed. 'Very well,' she said, as though she had come to a decision. 'Where shall we start?'

'With young Tim,' said Maudie unhesitatingly. 'I've never seen a decent photograph of him. He's always blurred or has his back to the camera. I hope you've brought some good ones, Daffers.'

Daphne laughed. She laughed so much that Maudie began to feel uneasy. It reminded her of another occasion, years ago, when Daphne had laughed like that . . .

'Sorry,' Daphne was saying. 'It's simply so typical of you, Maudie. You always did go straight for the weak spot. Very well.' She shuffled through the photographs, found one, held it for a brief moment and then offered it to Maudie. 'That's young Tim.'

Reaching for it eagerly, Maudie did not see the anguished expression on Daphne's face. She scanned the photograph, looking intently at the young face that stared out at her.

'What a nice-looking boy. How dark he is! Not a bit like the other two, is he? He reminds me of someone. Not Emily, certainly . . . Oh, I've got it. How extraordinary.' She peered more closely, turning it to the light. 'It's Posy. He looks just like Posy when she was this age. She was so like Hector. In fact this reminds me of a photograph taken of him at just about this age. Isn't that amazing?'

She glanced briefly at Daphne, still absorbed by her discovery, not taking in the consequences, until her friend's utter lack of reaction caught her attention. Still holding the photograph, Maudie looked again at Daphne. Her words seemed to hang deafeningly in the silence. Daphne raised her head at last and their eyes met in a long look: Maudie's frightened, questioning; Daphne's compassionate, desperate.

'Hector?' whispered Maudie. The fears and doubts of the last year crystallised into terrible certainties. 'Hector and Emily?'

'No!' cried Daphne strongly. 'Good God, Maudie. No, of course not Emily. Forgive me, Maudie. It was me.'

'You had an affair with Hector,' said Maudie slowly, painfully. 'And Emily is his child.'

'It had finished long before he met you,' said Daphne quickly. 'I swear to you, Maudie. There was nothing between us then. It happened after Selina had scarlet fever. She took a long time getting over it and Hilda and both girls went home to Hilda's mother for a while. Hector was alone and . . . Well, it just seemed to happen.'

Maudie watched her bleakly. 'You were in love with him.'

'Yes,' said Daphne, after a moment. 'Yes, I was in love with him. Philip was a dear, but he was so terribly dull. And we couldn't have children, you see. Philip never wanted to discuss it. He was afraid it might be his fault, although it might just as easily have been mine. I simply didn't know, although by then I'd quite given up hope of a baby. We both had. He was so delighted when I became pregnant. Hector was furious when I told him. I pretended that it might be Philip's child, but I knew it wasn't and Hector knew it too. But I was so happy, and Philip thought it was some kind of miracle. A baby, after years of long- ing! But Hector regretted it always. He was never in love with me, Maudie. He never pretended to be. We'd known each other for years, and there was an easy, careless intimacy between us. But just that once it toppled over into something more. Hilda and Philip were good, upstanding people, but oh, the joy of being with someone who liked to laugh and have fun!'

'And that was why you were so passionate about Emily.' It was a state- ment. The pieces were fitting slowly into place.

'I was terrified it might be a boy and look like Hector. His dark colouring was so distinctive and Philip and I were both fair. I can't tell you the strain it was, with Hilda being so thrilled about it and giving me advice. And Hector and I pretending that everything was just the same between us. I was so relieved that she was a girl. Darling Emily never let me down. Not until Tim. Even so, I wasn't sure until he was three or four years old but then I could see quite clearly that he was beginning to look just like his grandfather.'

'Which is why I never had photographs of Tim, only of the girls.'

'I knew you'd spot the likeness, you see.' Daphne shook her head. 'I couldn't risk it. I picked the ones that weren't too clear but I suspected that one day I'd have to tell you.'

'Why now?' Maudie tried to control her hurt. Later, she would allow herself the luxury of feelings.

'Oh, love.' Daphne looked at her sadly. 'I couldn't stand it any longer. You see, he never loved me. I really faced that when I met you. For the first time in his life Hector was really in love and it simply shone out of him, so much so that I knew that the small piece of him that I'd had, our moment together, couldn't possibly hurt you. We became friends, you and I, and that was precious to me. Each time Emily became pregnant the old terror reappeared, but I might never have had to tell you if it hadn't been for the way you've suffered since he died.'

'I don't understand.'

'You can't come to terms with Hector's death because of two things. The first is the way that he apologised to Selina, thinking she was Hilda, for marrying you. But that wasn't what he was apologising for, Maudie. He was apologising for betraying her with me. Hector never forgave himself for that lapse. He might have been fun-loving, happy-go-lucky, but he wasn't by nature an adulterer. I got him at a low moment and he succumbed to it. He was horrified that I carried his child and that he couldn't acknowledge her. His guilt was tremendous, and he couldn't quite forgive me either. He lived in terror that I might spill the beans to you. He told me that he would never forgive me if I hurt you, Maudie. I didn't want to hurt you, which is why I've kept silent. But I can't see you tearing yourself apart with suspicion. The other thing is the money. Hector's stocks and shares. When Tim was killed in that car accident, Emily was left practically penniless. There were all sorts of complications. It was a terrible time. Hector came to me to see if he could help.'

'The money went to Emily and the children?' The last piece of the puzzle had slipped into place.

Daphne sighed heavily. 'He felt it was the least he could do. "She's my daughter," he said, "and they are my grandchildren. You must allow me to do this." He was convinced that you wouldn't suffer financially, and, you see, he'd always felt it so keenly that he could never acknowledge them. I always tried to show him the joy we'd had, Philip and I, because of Emily, but he was eaten up by guilt on both counts. Because of Hilda and because of Emily. I can't tell you, Maudie, how glad I was that he married you. You made him laugh. With you he grew young again.'

'I was often cruel to him.' There were tears in Maudie's eyes: tears of pain and tears of relief. 'I was often such a cow.'

'And Hector was often domineering and tiresome.' Daphne looked exhausted. 'But he loved you. There was never a moment's question of that. Try to remember how it was.'

'Does Emily know?'

Daphne rested her head against a cushion and closed her eyes. 'Yes, she knows. I didn't tell her until after Philip died, but I was afraid that she might guess. Tim is so like Posy, and Emily started to talk of coming over and seeing you all. She and Posy stay in touch and I began to be afraid that it was only a matter of time. I wanted her to hear it from me.'

'How did she take it?'

Daphne smiled. 'She was terribly sweet about it. She was always very fond of Hector, you know. She told me to tell you that she's always looked on you as her second mother and that now you can be step-grandmum to the children. She was so worried that you might be hurt.'

'Darling Emily,' said Maudie unsteadily. 'She belonged to all of us.'

'I'm so sorry about the money, Maudie.'

'It doesn't matter about the money,' cried Maudie impatiently. 'It was not knowing, thinking that Hector had kept things hidden from me.'

'I know,' said Daphne remorsefully. 'But you wouldn't have had to sell Moorgate if you'd had it. I've felt so guilty.'

'The G-word,' said Maudie. 'We all carry so much guilt. Poor Hector. I wish he'd told me at the beginning.'

'Do you?' Daphne raised her eyebrows. 'Are you sure?'

'No.' Maudie smiled reluctantly. 'No, I'm glad I didn't know. I might not have been able to feel so safe with you. Poor Daphne. How lonely you must have been. I can't believe that you didn't hate me.'

'I thought I was going to. Hector wrote to tell me, to warn me, and that was the final blow to any hope I had. After Hilda died, you see, I thought that I might have a little bit of him to myself. It was madness, of course, but there's always a tiny foolish dream we nurture, isn't there? Once I had his letter I knew my dream was just so much dust.'

'Oh, Daphne, I am sorry. And you were so generous, so kind. I've depended on you so much.'

Daphne stretched out a hand, her eyes filled with memories. 'It was so strange. I dreaded meeting you and yet, when I saw you, I felt a great liking for you. I knew that you were utterly right for him and that you would make him happy. It was very clever of Hector to find you. And, you know, gradually things began to work even better. We were all such friends, and, through you, I seemed to regain Hector's friendship and trust. That was very precious to me.'

'But what a weight you've carried.' Maudie held her hand tightly. 'And you came all this way knowing you were going to have to tell me.'

'You've been wonderful. I thought it would be so much worse.'

Maudie knitted her brows. 'I couldn't have borne it if it had happened after I'd met him but, as it is, somehow I feel that it doesn't matter. I can believe now that he didn't regret marrying me and that he didn't lie to me. That's what matters to me. You and Emily were to do with Hilda, not me. I can go on loving you just as I always have.'

Daphne took a deep breath. 'It was how I prayed you might feel, but I couldn't rely on it. Bless you, Maudie. Now, do you really want to look at photographs or shall we have a good stiff drink?'

'I can't see why we shouldn't do both.' Maudie got to her feet rather shakily. 'We've both sustained a shock and we need something to revive us. But you've kept this young man from me for quite long enough and I want to see more of him.'

Later, as they sat comfortably, a bottle on the table between them, Maudie asked suddenly, 'And what about Selina? Does she know?'

Daphne laid down the photograph she'd been studying. 'No, she doesn't. I've always thought that it would be cruel to tell her the truth. She found it difficult enough to cope with Hector remarrying. To know that he was unfaithful to her mother with me would be the last straw.'

'But I imagine she might meet Tim one day. Supposing she guesses?'

Daphne shrugged, shaking her head. 'Am I right, I wonder? It's so difficult to decide what is right for other people. I'd hate to alienate her. It sounds as if she has enough problems at the moment.'

'You're going to see her next week?'

Daphne nodded. 'I'm staying a couple of nights with her before I go to see Philip's brother. I'm rather dreading it now.'

Maudie stared reflectively into her glass. 'She's alienated her own family. The boys flee at the sight of her and Chris's wife can't stand her. Selina can't forgive Posy for loving me, or me for loving Hector, and it must be years since she saw Patricia. And now Patrick's left her. I wish I could help her, but we invariably rub each other up the wrong way. I'm ashamed of myself, to tell the truth. I've failed miserably with Selina.'

Daphne shifted uneasily. 'What are you saying?'

'I'm not too sure. It just occurred to me, while we were speaking, that

Emily might be able to help her. I can't imagine how, mind. Perhaps you should take the photograph with you, after all.'

'She'd turn me out of the house.'

'Join the club. We've all been turned out, why not you? Seriously, I'm probably talking nonsense. Too much whisky and the relief of knowing about Hector. I'm abrogating my responsibilities. I can't help Selina and I'd be grateful if someone else would. I'd feel less guilty. Anyway, let's not worry about it any more. Come on, Daffers. Fill up the glasses and pass some more photographs. I'm just beginning to enjoy myself.'

Rob stood the bags of shopping on the kitchen table, and opened the windows. Summer had arrived, overtaking the cool, green spring and rushing nature into a more generous and luxuriant growth. Below the house, red and white blossom lay thick along the thorn. He opened a can of beer and drank deeply, thinking about Mike.

He'd telephoned last evening, his voice charged with some kind of suppressed excitement mixed with another, different, emotion.

'I've thought it through,' he'd said, 'and I think you're right about me buying Moorgate. I'm going for it.'

Rob had felt weak with joy and relief. 'Oh, that's great, Mike.'

'Get it valued, Rob, will you? It's got to be done properly, although at least we can cut out agents. We'll talk about it when I come down.'

'And when will that be?'

A tiny pause. 'I'm hoping you can put me up this week.'

'This week? But that's great. When?'

'Midweek if you can cope. I'm busy next weekend. The thing is, Rob, I'd like us to inter Melissa's ashes. I think the time has come, don't you? She wanted them to be with you at Moorgate, and I think it's a wonderful idea but I know you were cautious about it—'

'Not because I didn't want them here,' Rob had interrupted quickly. 'It was only that I didn't know whether I'd stay and I didn't want her to be left with . . . strangers.'

'I know. I'm sorry, Rob.' Mike had known immediately that Rob was near to tears. 'It's just that I think the time has come, don't you? While you're still there but knowing we shall be there soon.'

'You're absolutely right.' His grief had seemed like a lump in his throat. 'So when will you come?'

'I thought Wednesday. Just me, by the way. Best to leave Luke here, this time. I'll set off early and be down midmorning. Is it a problem for you? You don't have to take time off.'

'Oh, an afternoon won't do any harm. I'll try to get back for lunch. Will you go back the same day?'

'No. I'll stay over and leave on Thursday morning. If you want me to, that is. Let's play it by ear.'

'Fair enough,' Rob had agreed. 'See you Wednesday, then.'

Rob finished his beer and began to unpack the shopping. His relief that Mike would buy Moorgate was very great. Any other solution would have felt as if he were betraying Melissa.

'I'm sorry, my love,' he murmured, as he went to and fro between the kitchen and the larder. 'I know what you tried to do. Forgive me that I can't cope here without you.'

He wondered if he would continue to feel so close to her in the small cottage he'd seen for sale in Tintagel. Perhaps it was only at Moorgate that he would be aware of her presence and hear the echoes of her voice, but at least he would still be able to come here, to visit Mike and Luke. It would be a comfort to have Mike at hand—the companionable comfort of shared loss. With Mike he could relax into his true self, and yet, even with Mike, he could not allow himself the luxury of real grief.

Rob threw the empty can into the rubbish bin. Keeping busy was the answer. It didn't do to have too much time to think. He would have a shower, put on some clean clothes, make up Mike's bed and mow the lawn. By then it would be suppertime. Concentrating on this necessary itinerary, Rob went out of the kitchen and ran quickly up the stairs.

CHAPTER THIRTEEN

MAUDIE SAT AT THE TABLE, the French windows open to the garden, some photographs spread before her. Yesterday afternoon, she'd driven Daphne up to Exeter to catch the train to London, and she was now enjoying the prospect of a few days alone to ponder. The strength of her reaction to Daphne's revelations—that glorious, swamping relief—had been the measure of her fear that Hector had never really loved her. Though startling, the truth had destroyed the enemy within and restored her, and to begin with nothing else had mattered. Yet it was a shock to know that Daphne and Hector had been lovers. A mental picture of them, intimately together, threatened to destroy her calm. Was it true that he had never loved Daphne? Had there never been other such moments after she herself had met him? If he'd betrayed Hilda, might he also have betrayed her, Maudie?

Perhaps the evidence of the past could help settle her mind. She rooted out photograph albums, and manila envelopes full of ancient snapshots, settled herself at the table and reached for her spectacles. She opened the first album and studied the black and white snapshots of the young Hilda with her two small children: sitting in a deckchair, a daughter on either side, laughing at the camera; posed beside Hector, her smile rather self-conscious as she held the girls' hands. Maudie stared curiously at this woman she had feared. She was so like Selina it was unsettling, but there was nothing else to give rise to jealousy. A rather ordinary young woman, whose life had been cut short, yet she had been the cause of so much pain.

Maudie held the album closer, examining Hector now. Dark, dashing, confident, he must have caused many a flutter in hearts other than Hilda's—or Daphne's. Maudie turned the pages slowly. Some of the photographs had been put in loosely between them, and one of these caught her eye. The camera had captured Daphne unaware. Her whole concentration was centred on Hector, who was laughing, head thrown back, hands on hips, unconscious of anything apart from whatever was causing him amusement. Hilda was there too, but it was Daphne's expression that riveted Maudie's attention. Her smile was wistful, tender, loving—such a wealth of feeling was expressed in that smile. Maudie felt tears pricking at the back of her eyes, and it was some while before, putting the photograph to one side, she continued to turn the pages.

At last she found what she had been subconsciously hoping for: a photograph of herself with Hector. She could remember when it had been taken. Staring at it, it seemed that she could hear the creak and flap of the sails, the gentle slap of water against the hull, the seagulls screaming overhead. She was leaning back against Hector's shoulder, her legs stretched along the thwart, dreamy and relaxed. They'd been swimming from the boat, and she wore his jersey, but her long brown legs were bare. His arm was round her and she held his hand in both of hers. He was looking down at her with a brooding, passionate intensity that even now, more than thirty years later, had the power to make her feel quite weak. How well she could remember that look— and yet, she had forgotten it; forgotten so many things about Hector that now came flooding back to remind her of his love.

Daphne was right: she'd had nothing to fear. Maudie held the two photographs together, comparing the way Daphne looked at Hector with Hector's expression as she, Maudie, lay in his arms on the boat. She had an idea. Fetching some scissors, she carefully cut Hilda out of the first photograph, trimming it so that it showed only Daphne and Hector. Keeping aside the other photograph, Maudie bundled the rest away into their carrier bags. It was after she'd found a leather folder and was carefully inserting the first photograph that the telephone rang.

'Hi, babe,' said Posy. 'How are things?'

'Things are splendid.' Maudie laid aside the folder. 'How are you?'

'Great. I thought I might come down at the weekend. Aunt Daphne's gone to see Mum, hasn't she?'

'She has indeed. She'll be with Selina for the weekend and back at the end of next week. I shall be delighted to see you. Usual train?'

'Yes.' A slight hesitation. 'I've got something to tell you, Maudie. You know Mike?'

Maudie frowned, searching her memory. 'Mike?'

'You know. We met him at Moorgate with Rob.'

'Oh, Mike. Of course I remember him. Sorry.'

'Well, the thing is . . .' a longer pause. 'It's just . . . I think it's getting a bit serious between us.'

Maudie was shocked into complete silence.

'I know it seems sudden,' Posy was saying, 'but I've actually been seeing him a lot. He's been up to London several times and I went to Oxford last weekend. It's just . . . well, I'm beginning to think I love him.'

Maudie's gaze fell distractedly on the photographs: Hector's look of love, Daphne's longing smile.

'Well,' she said weakly, 'well, my darling . . . of course, you haven't known him long but if you're sure . . .'

'Bless you, Maudie,' said Posy. 'I knew I could rely on you. Mum's making a dreadful fuss about Mike being divorced and having a child. As if it matters. And Maudie, you'll never guess what! Mike's going to buy Moorgate from Rob. Rob doesn't want to be there without Melissa, so Mike's buying it.'

'That sounds . . . wonderful.'

'Look, I'll explain everything at the weekend. And I want you to meet Mike again, properly. There's so much to talk about. If I don't phone again, I'll see you on Friday at the station. Love you lots. Byeee.'

Maudie put down the receiver and picked up the photographs,

hands trembling a little, her head rocking. Hector looked back at her with Posy's eyes. Posy: her baby, her child, her darling. Might Posy, too, become a second wife, a stepmother?

There was nothing to be done. She must wait patiently until the weekend and then find out as much as she could. It was quite possible, after all, that Posy and Mike were genuinely in love, just as she and Hector had been in love after one meeting at a snowed-in airport. Maudie picked up the second photograph and tucked it into the back of her wallet. Perhaps, one day, she might show it to Posy.

Mike was relieved to see that the pick-up was not in the yard when he arrived at Moorgate. He needed a little time alone to collect his thoughts. It was odd to approach the house, knowing that it was to be his. An exciting sense of ownership was infused with a Posy-induced joyfulness, yet he was aware of an overall sadness, the familiar weight of loss. He'd come to terms with these conflicting emotions. He was confident that Melissa would understand Rob's reason for leaving Moorgate, and would be delighted to know that her brother and Luke were to live there—he and Luke and Posy.

As he opened the gate and put the car away, Mike remembered the astonishing scene in Oxford last weekend. He'd fetched Posy from the station and taken her home, with Luke belted into his seat behind them. Her shyness had quickly dissolved into her natural friendliness, but they hadn't quite been at ease. An accidental touch, a glance that lingered, a casual phrase—these things found a nervous, quivering response which meant that the earlier intimacy had to be re-established.

He had an unexpected ally in his small son. Having already created a rapport with Posy in Cornwall, Luke had greeted her with an enthusiasm that was both gratifying and a welcome diversion from their own immediate problem. Carrying Luke in from the car, Posy perching with him at the table while Mike made tea, making themselves heard above Luke's delighted roars, had made it impossible for them to remain self-conscious. When at last Luke had been persuaded to be separated from Posy to be put into his highchair, and she'd settled herself more comfortably, her attention had been riveted by a photograph standing on the shelf. She'd frowned, about to speak, then paused, and he'd glanced in the same direction, immediately understanding her caution.

'That's Melissa,' he'd said at once, lifting the photograph and handing it to her. 'Taken a few years ago, just after she'd graduated.'

Posy had taken it, still frowning. 'This is so bizarre,' she'd said slowly, 'but I feel I know her. Or perhaps she reminds me of someone.'

'People say we're alike. Could it simply be a family resemblance?'

'I don't know.' She'd shaken her head. 'It might be. I've felt the same with you once or twice. It's like a kind of fleeting memory of something. I expect it will come back. She's so beautiful.'

'Yes,' he said. He took the photograph, looking at the bright, laughing face, the thick bronze-coloured hair. 'She was . . . lovely.'

'Oh, Mike.' Posy had stood up, putting an arm about him, and suddenly they'd been in each other's arms, everything else forgotten. It was Luke who had brought them back to the present, hammering on his tray, shouting for his tea, and they'd broken apart, laughing breathlessly.

It was the next day, when the weekend was nearly over, that Mike had talked to her about Rob, about being together, living at Moorgate.

'Oh, this is so amazing,' Posy had cried. 'I can't believe it can be happening!' And they'd talked for hours about their feelings, their hopes.

'I'm not easy to live with,' he'd told her. 'I get absorbed with what I'm writing and you'll probably feel neglected. Moorgate is rather isolated and I don't want you to be lonely.'

'I shan't be lonely,' she'd assured him. 'I like my own company and there will be Luke. Perhaps I'll get involved with the local playgroup when he starts going. I shan't sit about watching the grass grow.'

'No,' he'd said, 'no, I'm sure you won't. But it's all happened rather quickly. What will your parents say?'

She'd shrugged impatiently. 'Who cares? It's my life and I want to be with you. What's the point of waiting?'

'If you're certain . . .' He'd still sounded anxious.

She'd grinned. 'Trying to get rid of me before we've even started?'

'Of course not. I just don't want to be the cause of you missing out on anything. What will your grandmother say?'

'Maudie? Maudie will want me to be happy. Look.' Suddenly she'd become very serious. 'We don't want to waste time, do we? We know how precious it is and we know that you can't take it for granted.'

It was as if Melissa had materialised beside them, encouraging them, and his eyes had filled with tears.

'No,' he'd mumbled. 'You can't take it for granted.'

Posy had held his hand tightly, and, once he'd recovered, he'd begun to talk about his next visit to Moorgate.

'I was wondering,' he'd said, 'about giving Rob a keepsake. I think that when we've . . . dealt with the ashes, he might suddenly feel bereft. I've framed this photograph, a recent one of her. What do you think?'

He'd taken the leather case out of the drawer and shown it to her. Her response had been electrifying.

'Oh, my God!' She'd clutched the case with one hand, the other pressed to her mouth. 'I don't believe it! I know her. I met her.' She stared at him, her eyes almost wild with shock. 'Oh, Mike. I met her.'

'But where?' He'd felt almost angry with the surprise of it. 'Are you sure? Was it in London?'

'No.' Posy had stared down at the photograph and her eyes had filled with tears. 'It was in Bovey. We had coffee in the Mill. We talked about the birds. She was so lovely. I remember thinking how elegant and confident she was and wishing that I was like her. She said that she was on her way to look at a house in Cornwall and we talked . . .'

Posy had lapsed into silence, sitting quite still, then suddenly the tears had poured down her cheeks. Mike had tried to comfort her, still trying to come to terms with this revelation.

'We'll go there together,' Posy had said later, drying her tears. 'I'll show you. Oh, I simply can't believe this . . .'

Now, with the photograph and Melissa's ashes in his bag, Mike let himself into Moorgate, dreading the ordeal that lay ahead.

It was evening, however, before Mike and Rob had the courage to take the small box and go out into the garden.

After a walk across the moor and an early supper, conversation had begun to lag, and the atmosphere had grown heavy with suspense.

'Come on, Rob,' said Mike gently, at last. 'Shall we do this last thing?'

Rob nodded, pushing back his chair, his face grim, and Mike picked up the small casket from his bag and followed him outside. He was waiting on the lawn and Mike could see that the ground beneath the escallonia hedge had been freshly turned.

'Where do you think?' muttered Rob. 'I thought that it would be . . . safe there. But I don't really know . . .'

Mike held the casket tightly, staring down at the dark, peaty earth. 'No,' he said desperately, with a kind of revulsion. 'No. I can't put her there. Not in the cold and wet. Not Melissa.'

Rob stared at him. 'Let her go where she likes,' he said suddenly. 'Let her be free. That's how she was, wasn't she? Not tied down.'

On an impulse, Mike opened the lid, holding up the casket, letting the contents be taken by the wind which streamed over the moor from the west. They stood together until the casket was empty.

Rob was shuddering with reaction and Mike took a deep breath, steadying himself. The sun had disappeared beneath the horizon, the garden was washed in golden light and in the east a star was twinkling. Rob began to weep, almost doubling up, his body racked with sobs. Keeping control of his own reactions, Mike led him into the house and pushed him into a chair. Without thinking he dragged a rug from his bag, Melissa's rug, placing it round Rob's shoulders.

'There's nothing left now,' Rob said, raising his head to look pitifully at Mike. 'Nothing at all. How shall I manage?'

Mike took the photograph from his bag and placed it wordlessly before him, tucking the rug more closely over his shaking shoulders, before going to push the kettle onto the hot plate. Rob stared down at Melissa's face, his hand smoothing the soft wool. Growing aware of his unconscious action, he glanced at the rug. His face changed as a thousand memories possessed him and he began to cry in earnest, allowing, at last, the agonising weight of grief to dissolve in healing tears.

At the same hour, Posy was standing in the hall at Hyde Abbey Road talking to Selina. 'I know it's sudden,' she was saying. 'Of course it is. It's a sudden sort of thing, isn't it?'

'But you're talking about marrying this . . . Mike.' Selina's voice sounded strained. 'I can imagine you falling in love with someone suddenly, but marrying them after . . . how long? And what about your career?'

'I'll think about that later.' In her anxiety Posy managed to sound cockily defiant. 'After all, you were never terribly impressed by the thought of my having a career in the theatre, were you?'

'That's not the point.' Selina wanted to scream. She was tired, lonely and unhappy and she hadn't the strength for this. 'You're only twenty-two, Posy, and did you say this man is divorced? With a child?'

'I did say that.' Posy was on the defensive. 'So what? It's not his fault that his wife became famous and chose a career instead of motherhood.'

'Please, Posy.' Selina took a few deep, calming breaths. 'Please can we discuss this sensibly? Must we do it on the telephone?'

Various sarcastic answers presented themselves but, seized by an unexpected fit of maturity, Posy rejected them.

'I can't get home in the middle of the week,' she said, quite reasonably, 'and you've got Aunt Daphne staying the weekend, haven't you? Not much point me coming home while she's there. We wouldn't be able to talk properly. I just wanted you to know about me and Mike getting really serious. I'll come home the following weekend if you like.'

'Yes,' said Selina, with a gasp of relief. 'Yes, do that . . .'

'And I'll bring Mike to meet you.'

'Bring Mike?' cried Selina, alarmed. 'But isn't that rather premature? Can't we talk about this first, Posy?'

'We've already talked about it.' She paused, steeling herself. 'There's something else, Mum.'

'Oh God, you're pregnant, aren't you?' said Selina flatly. 'I might have guessed. That's what all this urgency is about, isn't it?'

'No,' shouted Posy crossly. 'No, it bloody isn't. I'm not pregnant. I just wanted to tell you that Mike's buying Moorgate. It's a long story and I'll explain when I see you. But . . .' She laughed almost hysterically. 'Isn't it amazing, Mum? I'll be living at Moorgate. You'll be able to come and stay with us. Aren't you pleased?'

'Buying Moorgate?' Selina was stunned. 'What are you talking about?'

'Mike's buying Moorgate,' explained Posy patiently. 'He knows the man who bought it from Maudie. He was engaged to Mike's sister but she died. Rob doesn't want to be there without her so Mike's buying it. Oh, Mum, I'm just so happy. Can't you be pleased for me?'

Selina's brain reeled. For once the usual cutting remarks deserted her. She felt bone-tired, exhausted, beyond all rational thought.

'Yes,' she said faintly. 'Yes, of course I'm pleased. We'll talk later, next weekend. Bring Mike. I shall be pleased to see him if he'd like to come.'

The line went dead and Posy stood for some time, eyebrows raised, staring at nothing in particular. After a moment she dialled another number and was eventually put through to Patrick.

'Hello, love,' he said cheerfully. 'I've had your letter. It's great news.'

'Oh, Dad,' she said, gratefully. 'Do you think so? You're not upset?'

'Upset?' He sounded surprised. 'Why should I be upset?'

'Well, it's a bit sudden, isn't it?'

'Falling in love is a sudden business. What else would you expect?'

'Nothing,' she said, pulling herself together. 'I mean, I'm being stupid. I've just been talking to Mum.'

'Ah.' His voice was guarded. 'Problems?'

Posy began to laugh. 'Not really. She took it quite well and invited Mike home to meet her the weekend after next. But she sounded a bit odd. Like she was too exhausted to care much. I wish you were going to be there that weekend. I want you to meet him.'

'So do I. Just tell me when he's got some time spare and I'll be there. He sounds a nice chap and a very interesting one. I've bought his book.'

'Thanks, Dad.' Posy was near to tears. 'Thanks for understanding.'

'Forget it,' he said. 'And let me know when we can all get together.'

'Of course I will. Thanks, Dad.'

She replaced the receiver, sighing with relief. Climbing the stairs to her room, she wondered how Rob and Mike were coping at Moorgate.

Selina wandered round the house, checking for the twentieth time that all was in order for Daphne's visit. So lonely was she that she was longing for the older woman's arrival, despite her own bitterness at Daphne's faithlessness. After ten days with Maudie it was only to be expected that Daphne knew all about Patrick and the situation that had led to his departure. It was humiliating, yet she needed company. It was so difficult being with her friends, keeping up appearances, pretending that Patrick was simply on a long course—she'd said that it was for a year, to give herself space—and acting as if nothing had changed.

She'd heard nothing more from him after the postcard, and she swung between hoping that he might suddenly telephone to say that he was coming home and deciding that she must get a job or sell the house. The problem was that those initiatives required energy, enthusiasm, and she was so tired. She slept the heavy, dreamless sleep of the depressed, waking unrefreshed, dreading the day ahead. She panicked at the least thing—the telephone ringing or the sight of the letters lying on the mat.

She knew that she must make an effort to pull herself together, but she did not know how, and now Posy's news was yet another anxiety: her only daughter marrying a divorced man with a small child! And what did Posy mean when she said that he'd bought Moorgate? Selina groaned aloud. She needed a drink. Since Patrick had gone, she tried not to start drinking before seven o'clock in the evening, but lately it had been hard to stick to her rule. She glanced hopefully at her watch, and, as she did so, the doorbell rang.

Hurrying out into the hall, she flung open the door and stood staring. In all the years she'd known her mother's old friend, Daphne seemed hardly to have changed: tall, fair, pretty, she smiled at Selina as she'd smiled at her when she was a little girl.

'Selina, darling,' said Daphne, holding out her arms. 'How are you?'

Forgetting her fears of betrayal, Selina flung herself upon the tall figure and burst into a noisy fit of weeping. Taken by surprise, her own terrors temporarily put to one side, Daphne led the howling Selina inside and closed the door firmly. Her instinct leading her unerringly to the kitchen, Daphne dropped her bag on the floor, her other arm still about Selina, and saw the bottle waiting invitingly on the dresser.

'A drink,' she said, relieved. 'Now sit down while I forage.'

Still sobbing, Selina allowed herself to be lowered onto a chair and Daphne hastened to find glasses and pour the wine—a nice Australian red, she noticed—which had been open and waiting for some time.

'Now that's what I call thoughtful,' said Daphne, pouring cheerfully. 'We'll feel better after one of these.'

Selina took her glass, her sobs diminishing, and smiled through her tears. 'Sorry,' she said. 'It was just seeing you there like that. Time swung backwards.' Her face creased up again. 'It was as if I was a child again.'

'Poor darling,' said Daphne, somewhat insincerely but ready to encourage Selina for her own ends, 'what a terrible time you've had.'

Selina groped for her handkerchief. 'It's been awful,' she agreed. 'I expect Maudie told you . . . ?' She began to cry again.

'Only a little,' lied Daphne diplomatically. 'She felt that it was better that you should tell me yourself.'

'Oh.' Surprise dried Selina's tears. She hadn't expected such consideration from her stepmother. 'I imagined she'd tell you all about it.'

'No, no. We had rather a lot of other things to talk about. Anyway, I want to hear it from you.'

'I'm absolutely desperate.' Tears were threatening again. 'And now, on top of everything else, Posy's dropped this bombshell.'

'Posy?' Daphne's surprise was genuine. 'What's Posy been up to?'

Selina took a swig of wine. She was beginning to feel slightly better. 'Doesn't Maudie know? She's fallen in love with a divorced man with a child. He's some kind of writer. She phoned just now to say that she's thinking of marrying him and says they'll be living at Moorgate.'

Daphne was silenced for a moment. She glanced round the kitchen, wondering how many empty bottles might be lying about, and took a firm grip on the situation.

'I can't believe it,' she said, with the air of one who was only too ready to be convinced. 'But I want to hear about everything. Now, I'm going to take off my coat, put my bag in my room—no, no, don't get up, I'm sure I'll find it—and then we'll have a good old session. I shan't be long.'

Selina finished her wine and poured another generous glassful. By the time Daphne returned a second bottle was waiting beside the first.

'Excellent,' said Daphne. 'Now where shall we start?'

'I don't know what I'm going to do,' Selina said, two hours later. The second bottle of wine was half empty, supper had been hastily assembled and disposed of, and Daphne was still trying to decide if Selina should know the truth. So far the conversation had related mainly to Patrick, his affair with Mary and his ultimate defection, with diversions into Posy's ingratitude and disloyalty and Maudie's insensitivity and selfishness. Nothing was Selina's fault, this much was clear. Daphne stirred restlessly. Advice, here, was pointless. Selina would stare at her blankly and immediately return to her first standpoint. The best she could do was to attempt to help Selina out of the maze of her apathy.

'Had you thought of anything that you might do?' she asked. They were still in the kitchen, sitting at the table, the bottle between them.

Selina looked helplessly at her. 'I'm feeling so tired. It's not like me to be doing nothing. I've always been the organiser in this family.'

'So you haven't had any ideas.'

It was a statement, and Selina frowned defensively.

'I wouldn't say that. It's just my options are a bit extreme.'

'Are they?' Daphne looked interested.

'Well, the obvious one is to sell the house.' Selina paused, waiting for Daphne to say how unfair it was that she should have to consider such a step, but Daphne merely refilled her glass and waited. 'I could move to a smaller place,' she said rather sulkily, 'and invest the money.'

'And would you move out of London?'

'I don't want to move anywhere,' snapped Selina.

Daphne pursed her lips. 'That sounds reasonable. So what are the other options? Can you afford to stay here?'

'Probably not. I'm living on savings at the moment, but when they've gone I'll have to do something drastic.'

'Like what?'

'Get a job, I suppose.'

Daphne straightened in her chair, her face alert. 'What could you do?' she asked brightly.

Selina stared at her, pride reasserting itself. 'I don't know. It's nearly thirty years since I was in the marketplace. I can't imagine that there would be many openings for a woman of my age.'

'Oh, nonsense,' said Daphne. 'Emily works, you know. She had to when Tim died. She had no choice. But she enjoys her work. The children are older, now, which makes it easier, but it was very difficult with the girls so young and Tim a baby.'

'But she cooks, doesn't she? She works from home.'

'She started like that,' said Daphne, 'but she's out much more these days, doing lunches and dinners and all sorts. She loves it, but then Emily always got on very well with people.'

'Of course it's almost easier if your husband dies than if he leaves you, isn't it?'

'I can't quite see why. Unless you're talking about pride. Naturally it's embarrassing to admit that your husband—or wife—has left you, isn't it? It suggests an inadequacy on your part. Is that what you mean?'

'Inadequacy?'

Daphne raised her eyebrows in surprise. 'Wouldn't you say so? Why else should he—or she—go? Nobody walks out of a happy, loving relationship voluntarily.'

'Are you suggesting that it's my fault that Patrick's gone?'

'Well, isn't it?'

'But I told you about Mary. That's when all this started.'

'Yes, you told me. But why was he attracted to her? What was missing in his relationship with you that he needed to look for elsewhere?'

'It was simply Patrick's pathetic need for gratitude. His ego has to be bolstered up by being told he's wonderful.'

'Sounds like the rest of us,' murmured Daphne. 'And I gather that you resented supplying that need?'

'Why should I?' demanded Selina. 'I've given him thirty years of support and he betrays me with a little tart and then leaves me. After everything I've done for him.'

'What have you done for him?'

Selina shook her head with an expression that asked if Daphne was in her right mind. 'I've supported him, brought up his children, run the home, taken all the responsibility. Patrick never had to think about anything but his job. Such as it was. And, even then, if it hadn't been for Daddy's generosity I'm not sure how we'd have survived.'

'Sounds very businesslike,' Daphne said judiciously. 'The perfect wife and mother. Rather like a job description, isn't it? But it tends to leave out the messy, human bits.'

'What's wrong with that? It worked for my parents.'

'Not altogether.' Daphne's calm voice belied her inward terror.

'What do you mean?'

'You are very like your mother, Selina. You keep to the letter of the law, but it leaves out all the warmth and frailty and fun. Hilda was the same, and although your father was devoted to her he needed fun. Hilda rarely condemned or criticised, but her forgiveness was cold. Hector was different. He was infuriating, overbearing, but he had a generosity and a kind of humility that made him great. Even he needed to breathe the ordinary air of lesser mortals.'

'If you mean Daddy was unfaithful to Mummy, I don't believe a word of it. He wasn't like that.'

'I don't know what "like that" implies. There are so many areas of grey in a relationship. Your father certainly wasn't promiscuous, he was like most of us are—human—and, like Patrick, he had a lapse.'

'How would you know?' asked Selina contemptuously.

'Because he had it with me,' said Daphne wearily.

They stared at each other. Daphne held her trembling hands clenched in her lap but she kept her eyes fixed bravely on Selina's.

'I don't believe you.' But she did. Her face showed it.

'He always regretted it. It was at a bad time and he needed simple affection, uncomplicated fun. He wanted to be seen as Hector, not just as a provider.' Daphne was pleading now, wondering how she could have destroyed Selina's trust so cruelly. 'Hilda never knew.'

'How could he do it to her?'

'It wasn't premeditated. It just flared up out of nothing—'

'And how could you do it? You were her best friend. Oh!' She covered her face with her hands. 'I can't believe this.'

'I loved him, you see.' Daphne spoke quietly, as if she were talking to herself. 'I loved him so much. Philip was rather like Hilda—punctilious, proper, kind, but there was no warmth, no hugs and silliness and fun. Hector and I were rather like brother and sister. No.' She shook her head. 'More like cousins. We could hug and joke and be silly but occasionally there was a flash of something else. I loved him, Selina.'

Selina raised her head. Her eyes were puzzled and Daphne was seized with guilt.

'But you loved Mummy, too. Didn't it bother you at all?'

'Oh, my dear child.' Daphne almost laughed. 'Have you never known that kind of passion? That mindlessness that sweeps everything before it? The kind of need that you'd sacrifice everything for gladly? No, clearly not. Well, it's a sort of madness that possesses you, and that's the only excuse I can offer you. For a few days your father and I were mad together. If it's any comfort, he never forgave himself. That's what he was apologising for at the end. It was nothing to do with Maudie. It was me he was apologising for.'

Selina sat in silence, staring back into the past, adjusting her ideas.

'And Mummy never knew?'

Daphne shook her head.

'How did you deal with it afterwards? Weren't you tempted again?'

'I was too busy having Emily,' she said almost bitterly, 'and Hector was too angry with me for it to happen again.'

Selina leaned forward. 'What do you mean?' she cried fearfully. 'Do you mean Emily is Daddy's child?'

Daphne looked at her compassionately. 'She's your half-sister. Your father was unable to acknowledge her. You can believe that, because you know it to be true, Selina. Nobody ever guessed.'

Selina looked so shocked that Daphne filled up her glass for her. She took it mechanically and drank, but she seemed dazed.

'I'm sorry,' said Daphne at last. 'I didn't know if I should tell you. It's just that Emily is hoping that you'll come out and stay with us. She was always very fond of you, Selina. But young Tim looks just like Posy did at that age, just like Hector, and it's only fair that you should know.'

'Emily knows, then?'

'I told her when Philip died. I wondered if she'd suspected. She took it so calmly. Philip never guessed, and she loved him very much, but she was always very fond of Hector and of you and Patricia.'

Selina's eyes filled with tears. 'Emily was like a little sister,' she said. 'I loved Emily . . .'

'I hope you'll go on doing so,' said Daphne gently. 'I can understand that you might not be able to forgive me, but none of it was Emily's fault.'

They sat in silence for a while. Selina felt as if she'd drifted from some safe mooring into a busy waterway and was trying to take her bearings, her head dizzy with wine and shock. Presently she looked at Daphne.

'I was thinking,' Daphne said carefully, 'if a visit to see us all might be good for you.'

Selina shook her head helplessly. How would she feel, visiting Emily, knowing her to be her half-sister, remembering what Daphne had said about her father—*their* father? Pride wearily raised its head. She thought: But I was first. Daddy loved *me*. Emily never had that. Somehow, though, she felt that, with Emily, it needn't be important.

'I keep wondering,' she said, dully, too tired to think clearly, 'whether Patrick might come home.'

'I think he might.' Daphne smiled encouragingly at her. 'I think Patrick needed to feel useful. The Mary thing isn't important—try to forget about it—but this was a challenge, a crusade. After a year or so he might like to come back. If you could cope with it. But wouldn't it be better if you weren't sitting and waiting? Don't you think you'd feel more positive if you'd been getting on with your own life?'

'What life?'

'For a start you could come out to Canada. You could meet your nieces and nephew and you could see how Emily runs her business. After that delicious supper I must say that I think you could do worse than start your own little outfit.'

Selina stared at her. 'Cooking, you mean?'

'Why not? There must be a tremendous demand for lunches and supper-parties in London. Emily meets all sorts of famous people. You could see for yourself. She'd love it.'

'I'd need to think about it.'

'Well, naturally. We'll talk about it again, over the weekend. That's if you want me to stay.'

Selina took a deep breath in and let it out very slowly. 'Yes, of course I do. I'm just rather . . . overwhelmed.'

'Of course you are. I'm sorry, Selina.'

'I think I'll go to bed. My head is beginning to pound. Do you think you can find your own way around?' She stood up, glancing about the kitchen as though puzzled that everything was still the same.

'Go to bed,' said Daphne gently. 'I'll clear up. Tomorrow is another day.'

'Thanks. Good night then.'

She went out and Daphne poured herself another glass of wine.

CHAPTER FOURTEEN

'THE THING IS,' said Posy, 'I love him.'

She stared at Maudie anxiously but with determination. Maudie knew that Posy had counted on her total sympathy and support. Yet her desire to be at one with this beloved child, her fear of risking her love, struggled with a requirement to show Posy the whole picture.

'I'm not suggesting that you shouldn't marry him,' she said gently. 'It's simply that you'll be sacrificing your own career to his.'

'That's what Mum said,' Posy sighed. 'The thing is that I want to be with Mike and Luke. I've never had any clear idea as to what I'd do once I've graduated. The theatre is a difficult world to break into. I know what you're all thinking. You want me to have some career of my own in case things go wrong later and Mike and I split up.'

'Something like that,' admitted Maudie. 'You mustn't be too hard on us for wanting to protect you.'

'I'm not.' Posy's face softened. 'I know you're only thinking about what's best for me. But I'll have my degree. And looking after Luke will be useful work experience. I could always get a job as a nanny.'

'Has Luke's mother completely abandoned him?'

Posy nodded. 'She's got this brilliant Hollywood career now, and she doesn't want to know. It's been sorted out legally, though. Mike didn't want her turning up five years on, deciding that she'd have Luke back. It's complicated, but Mike seems certain there won't be problems.'

Maudie sighed inwardly. How confident the young were.

'You don't mind being a stepmother?' She had to ask the question.

'I don't mind a bit.' Posy smiled at her comfortingly. 'It's not like it was for you, Maudie. Luke can't remember his mother. He's not even twelve months old. It's a bit different from two teenage girls.'

'I know it is.' Maudie smiled back at her, trying to relax. 'You must be patient. It's all rather sudden and I'm having to adjust my ideas.'

'But you liked Mike,' said Posy, 'didn't you? You said so.'

'I liked Mike very much,' agreed Maudie, 'but I didn't look at him in the light of being your husband. It makes a bit of a difference.'

'I want you to meet him properly,' said Posy. 'Could he come down? He could stay in Bovey. If you got to know him you'd be much happier.'

'That would be wonderful—if Mike agrees to it.'

'Oh, Mike's looking forward to it,' said Posy cheerfully. 'He's as worried as you are. He knows that a divorced man with a small child isn't everyone's idea of a good catch and he doesn't want me to miss out. The trouble is, I know that my heart wouldn't be in a career now. It would be down at Moorgate with Mike and Luke. If you love someone you want to be with them, don't you? Just because you're young doesn't necessarily mean that you have forty years ahead of you. Look at Melissa.'

'Yes, that's quite true,' said Maudie, remembering how she'd felt when she'd met Hector, and their absolute need to be together.

She thought: And we were middle-aged and supposedly sensible.

'Mike really misses her,' Posy was saying. 'Luke does, too. Isn't it bizarre that I met her? I can't get over it. I want to take Mike into the Mill when he comes down, to show him where we had coffee together. She was so pretty and such fun. I can't believe she was dying. Oh, Maudie.' She shivered. 'It makes you want to grab at life with both hands, doesn't it? Oh, I know that's what's worrying you, that I'm just going into this with my eyes shut, but it's not like that.'

'No,' said Maudie with an effort. 'I'm sure it isn't. We're all being too interfering. Bring Mike down, by all means. And Luke, too. It will be good to spend some time with him. Don't be too hard on us, Posy. It's too trite for words to say that we only want your happiness. It's hubristic, too. Who are we to suppose that we can ordain happiness for other people when we can't organise our own lives?'

'Dad said something like that,' said Posy. 'He wrote me a really nice letter after I'd telephoned him.'

'How's Selina taking it?'

Posy made a face. 'Dramatically. I'm hoping Aunt Daphne will take her mind off it this weekend. Do you think that's likely?'

Maudie, still in a state of shock at Daphne's revelations, wondered whether Selina also knew by now that Emily was her half-sister.

'Yes,' she said thoughtfully. 'I wouldn't be at all surprised.'

Selina watched Daphne climb into the taxi, waved again and closed the front door. She felt too tired even to think properly. It would have been better, once Daphne had told her this devastating truth, if she'd left at once. It had been difficult to sustain a polite exterior through the whole of Saturday, yet she'd got through it without sacrificing any of the rules of hospitality. Once or twice Daphne had attempted to broach the subject again, but Selina had maintained a calm attitude, which enabled them to discuss certain aspects, such as going out to Canada, as if it were nothing out of the ordinary. Looking back, she could congratulate herself that she'd acquitted herself without too much loss of pride.

Selina went into the kitchen and sat down at the table, staring at the remains of breakfast. Now she could give her thoughts free rein. Chin in hands, she frowned as she tried to create some kind of order out of the chaos. What was odd was that, terrible though Daphne's revelations had been, her observations about darling Mummy seemed even more shocking. Of course, Daphne was bound to try to shift the blame. She'd as good as confessed that she'd tempted Daddy when he was alone and feeling down, and she'd admitted that he'd always felt guilty about it, even when he was dying. Remembering, Selina felt a twinge of remorse. She'd been so sure that it was Maudie he was regretting and now it seemed that it was an affair with Daphne. How terrible to have carried such guilt all those years, but he'd only had himself to blame. It was ridiculous to hint that it was Mummy's fault. Mummy had been wonderful: always so good-tempered, so available, so . . . so motherly.

Selina shifted, folding her arms beneath her breasts. It was so typical of men to want you to have their babies but expect you to go on behaving like some kind of sex symbol. They should try looking after children all day long! Mummy had done wonderfully well; the house was always run beautifully, spotlessly clean, meals on time, everything orderly.

'Rather like a job description, isn't it?' Daphne had said. 'But it tends to leave out the messy, human bits.'

Was this why Patrick had turned to Mary—because she, Selina, had been unable to fulfil some essential need? Could it be true that, through some lack on her part, Patrick had looked elsewhere for comfort? Surely the lack was on Patrick's part. Yet Daphne's words stuck like a burr: 'Nobody walks out of a happy, loving relationship voluntarily.'

The words 'happy, loving' were not, she was forced to admit, ones that she'd apply to her marriage. She'd never been one for all that lovey-dovey business and it had been necessary to keep Patrick in line. Being cheerful and happy was all fine and good but pretty soon people took you for granted. A tiny memory struck into her mind. Despite Mummy's good temper there had, on reflection, been the tiniest air of long-suffering about her; little sighs escaping and a particular expression of . . . what? Of patience, of private suffering, nobly borne . . .

Selina got to her feet, rejecting such heretical thoughts, and started clearing the table, preparing to wash up. If Mummy had been long-suffering she'd probably had plenty to be patient about. It couldn't have been easy, moving from pillar to post, all that entertaining, two children to look after, while Daddy at the first opportunity was unfaithful with her best friend and remarried barely a year after she'd died.

Selina wondered what Emily had felt, suddenly discovering that Philip wasn't her father after all, that her real father had never acknowledged her. Selina was able to feel sorry for Emily, able to go on loving her. Yesterday, Daphne had shown her a photograph of Emily's little boy, Tim. It had been a shock to see him looking so like Posy; so like Daddy in the photos taken when he was small. It was odd how that photograph had moved her: it might have been of her own child.

'Come out and see us,' Daphne had said, then. 'Come and meet Tim. Emily would love to see you again. Won't you think about it?'

Still staring at the photograph, Selina had said that she would.

As she plunged her hands into the hot, soapy water the telephone rang. Cursing, she snatched a tea towel and went to answer it, still wearing her rubber gloves. It was Patrick.

'I wondered if you might want to talk about Posy,' he said, after a rather awkward greeting. 'It must have come as a bit of a shock.'

Hastily Selina gathered her rags of pride about her. 'Obviously,' she answered coolly. 'I'm really concerned that she seems intent on abandoning any ideas of a career. But then some members of this family don't have much staying power.'

'Well, it was just a thought.'

There was so much resignation and finality in his voice that she clutched the receiver tighter, regretting her sharp remark.

'Daphne's been staying with me.' She spoke at random; anything to keep him from hanging up. Suddenly she knew that she could not admit her father's indiscretions to Patrick; it would almost be as if she were condoning his own behaviour. 'She's invited me out to Canada.'

'Really?' His voice was warm with the acknowledgment of Daphne's generosity. 'And are you going?'

'Yes, I think so.' She managed a casual note. 'I don't see why not. I haven't seen Emily for years. Apparently she's running this very successful cooking business and I thought I might pick up a few tips.'

'She was such a sweetie.' He sounded so affectionately reminiscent that Selina was brought up short. Remembering Emily was clearly more important, more pleasurable, than asking why she should require any tips. If she thought that he might show an interest she was disappointed. 'Sounds like a great idea, Selina. Anyway, Posy is arranging for me to meet Mike. Have you met him yet?'

'No.' How she wished that she could have said 'yes', been the first. 'Not yet. I'd rather she wasn't marrying a divorced man with a child, but you know Posy. I'm sure my point of view will be ignored.'

'She sounds very much in love. That's how it was with us, remember? Luckily you were within a month or two of finishing your course at Miss Sprules's. I'm not sure we'd have wanted to be sensible and wait, are you?'

She swallowed. How underhand of him to speak of such a thing now; to make her remember . . .

'Daddy wouldn't have allowed us to marry if you'd been divorced with a child.' She spoke with difficulty.

He laughed softly. 'Oh, I don't think old Hector would have stopped us. He wasn't the sort who forgot what it was like to be young.'

She was breathless with surprise and indignation. 'He liked things to be done sensibly . . .' Even as she spoke, she faltered. Had her father behaved sensibly with Daphne, leaving his child to be raised by Philip?

'Perhaps. Anyway, Posy's twenty-two. I think we may have to give in gracefully. Aren't you pleased about Moorgate? You were so miserable about it going out of the family.' He chuckled. 'It all sounds quite extra-ordinary to me. However, I can see that I have forfeited all rights to comment so I just feel very lucky that Posy wants me to meet Mike. Poor Selina. You must be feeling a bit gobsmacked.'

She longed to reject his pity, yet she needed it. 'I'm managing.'

'I'm sure you are. Let me know if you need anything—'

'I was wondering,' she broke in quickly, 'if we might have a chat after we've both met Mike. After all, you are her father. I should be glad of your input.'

'Thank you,' he said, after a short pause. 'That's very . . . generous of you, Selina. I should appreciate it.'

'Well, then.' She felt almost ridiculously light-hearted, as if some great point had been gained. 'We'll stay in touch then, shall we? I don't quite know when she's bringing him to stay.'

'Me neither. If I haven't heard from you in a few days I'll give you a buzz. How does that sound?'

'It sounds fine. And thanks for phoning, Patrick. How . . . how are things with you?'

'It's tremendously hard work but terribly satisfying. It's being a real eye-opener. So what's this about professional cooking, then?'

She felt a strange desire to burst into tears. 'Oh, just an idea I had. I don't want to sit about being useless. We'll be in touch then. Bye.'

She replaced the receiver and went back to the kitchen, feeling strangely happy.

Several weeks later, Posy and Mike sat at the window table in the Mill. They were on their way to Cornwall, and Mike had spent the night at The Dolphin and renewed his acquaintance with Maudie.

'Maudie's a sweetie. I really like her,' he said, as he stirred his coffee. 'Your mother was much more intimidating.'

'It's weird, actually,' said Posy thoughtfully. 'I thought she'd be much worse. She was kind of muted. Having Aunt Daphne to stay must have loosened her up. I can't believe Mum's going out to stay with them. It was a real surprise. Poor old Mum. I feel a bit guilty now she's been good about it. And Dad's given us his blessing. No backing out now.'

Mike smiled at her. 'Your father was really nice. I rather admire what he's doing and I hope he'll come and visit us too. But not while I'm writing. They'll all have to wait until I'm between books.'

'We'll have big parties.' Posy sighed contentedly. 'Lots of quiet and then big celebrations. It's going to be so good.'

'I can hardly believe that you sat here with Melissa.' Mike looked out across the river, over the thatched roof of the pub, to the moor beyond. 'She didn't want to break her journey, but I insisted. We chose Bovey Tracey because it is the gateway to the moor. It's quite incredible.'

'It was a busy morning,' Posy said. 'This was the only table left. She watched the birds and I showed her the book. People write down what they've seen and some make funny remarks.' She paused, reaching for the diary. 'There's a nice entry a man wrote about his wife and I showed it to her. I wonder if I can find it.' She turned the pages and, after a moment or two, gave a cry of triumph. 'Here it is.'

She passed the book across the table and sat back, looking about her. She remembered how she'd had tea with Hugh here, weeks ago, and told him about her father. How kind he'd been then. She knew now that her feelings for Hugh had been a young girl's infatuation, a trying of the wings, a testing of the water, but she was still very fond of him.

She came out of her reverie with a start as Mike gave an exclamation. 'Good God!' he said. 'Look at this. Melissa wrote in the book, Posy. Did you know?'

'She put some birds in. A nuthatch, one was. I'd quite forgotten.'

'But she wrote something about you. It must have been after you'd gone. You said you went first, didn't you? Here it is. Look.'

'Maudie came for me.' Posy took the book and stared at the entry. 'Met a great chick called Posy.'

When she looked up she had tears in her eyes. 'I don't believe it.'

'You met each other and she wrote about you.' Mike shook his head, near to tears himself. 'It's like a little message to us, isn't it?'

Posy nodded, hardly trusting herself to speak. 'There's something else. A quotation, is it? "Thou wast not born for death, immortal Bird!"'

Mike was silent, shaken by a thousand memories. 'It's Keats,' he said at last. 'One of Melissa's favourites, especially . . . towards the end. I think your meeting was very important to her.'

He took the book and, after one long, last glance, put it back on the windowsill.

'Come on,' he said. 'Let's get going, shall we? I can't wait for us to be at Moorgate. Just the two of us for the first time. It's silly, I know, but it's like we've been given a special blessing.'

Rob shook the quilt into its clean cover and laid it on the air bed. He stood back and glanced about the room. Soon Moorgate would be furnished properly, lived in, alive, just as it should be. Its months of waiting were nearly over. Meanwhile he would be snug and comfortable in the small cottage in Tintagel. The purchase had gone through quickly and he was busy making it his own.

He went downstairs and into the kitchen. There were provisions in the larder and the Esse ensured that there would be hot water when they needed it. He placed a note with the word Welcome written on the outside against a bottle of champagne that stood on the kitchen table, and gave one last look round.

'So.' He picked up the photograph of Melissa and the rug that Mike had given him. 'Come on, my love,' he murmured. 'Let's go home.'

They arrived at about tea time. Posy jumped out to open the gate and Mike drove in, parking in the open-fronted barn. They stood together, looking about them, revelling in their sense of belonging.

'Rob said he'd leave milk,' said Posy. 'I'm dying for a cup of tea.'

They let themselves in through the front door, longing to explore the old house inch by inch now they could do so alone.

'Tea first, though,' said Posy. 'And then we can really savour it. Oh!'

'What is it?' He followed her into the kitchen. 'Champagne!' He began to laugh. 'What a terrific thing to do. I'll give him a buzz later.'

'We're going down to see him tomorrow,' Posy reminded him. 'To see how he's getting on at the cottage. He's trying not to be too thrilled about it but he's dead pleased, really.'

'It's such a relief,' said Mike, pushing the kettle onto the hot plate. 'I couldn't have felt really happy about Moorgate if Rob wasn't happy, too.'

Posy fetched the milk. 'He'll be able to come whenever he likes,' she said. 'It'll be his second home.'

They drank their tea, talking quietly together, making plans, then went to look round the house, arm in arm.

'Huge, comfortable sofas . . .' said Mike, in the sitting room.

'Oh, yes, but not too smart. No fussing if the dogs climb on them.'

'Or the children?' He was smiling at her.

'Of course not,' she said indignantly. 'It's their home, isn't it?'

They crossed the hall to the other room.

'So what about this as my study, then?'

'It would make a wonderful playroom.' Her voice was wistful.

'Perhaps you'd like me to work in the loose box?'

'The pony wouldn't like that.'

They laughed together, softly, intimately, as they climbed the stairs.

'It's such a lovely room.' They were standing together at the window of the big bedroom. 'We'll have the bed facing the window so that we can see the trees.'

'This is the nursery.' She was confident about it. 'Isn't it perfect?'

'I must put up a swing on the lawn, under the escallonia hedge.'

They paused on the landing to look out across the moor, and Mike slipped his arm about her.

'Don't you think old Rob made the bed look inviting?' he murmured.

She chuckled. 'I don't remember,' she answered teasingly.

'Then let's go and have another look,' he said.

Maudie poured herself some coffee, sliced the top neatly from her egg, and settled herself to look at her post: a letter from Daphne, a card from Posy and the autumn catalogue from The Scotch House. She slit open Daphne's letter and began to read it as she ate her egg.

'It's a success,' she'd written. 'Emily and Selina get on so well and Selina has really fallen for Tim. He adores her. It's such a relief.'

Maudie laid down the thin blue sheets for a moment. She'd been shocked to see how much Daphne had aged when she'd returned from London. They'd spoken on the telephone, and Maudie had realised that it had been a great ordeal for both of them, but she'd been quite frightened at the haggard appearance of her old friend.

'It's worth it,' Daphne had said, relaxing in an armchair, sipping tea. 'I cheated and said some brutal things, but we've worked our way through it and at least she's still speaking to me. If we can get her out to Canada we shall be home and dry. Emily will see to that. Emily and Tim.'

'It was very brave of you,' Maudie had said, 'and now you must relax for your last week. We'll have a wonderful time.'

'Have you forgiven me, Maudie?' she'd asked. 'For deceiving you and making you worry?'

'It's all over,' she'd answered. 'In fact, I wondered if you might like this.' She'd opened the drawer and offered her friend the leather folder.

Daphne had taken it wonderingly, opening it cautiously. As her gaze fell on the photograph of Hector and herself, her face turned pale. She'd sat immovably, studying it, and then she'd closed her eyes.

'Where on earth did you find it?' she'd asked faintly.

Maudie had kneeled beside her, putting an arm about her. 'I just found it,' she'd said, 'and I thought you might like to have it.'

Daphne had leaned forward and kissed her. 'Now I know that you've forgiven me,' she'd said. 'Oh, Maudie, how foolish we are.'

'It's certainly foolish to kneel down at my age.' Maudie had got up painfully. 'So tell me what you think about Posy's bombshell . . .'

With the mysteries solved and secrets shared and forgiven, the last week had been such a happy one.

'I shall come out to see you,' Maudie had promised, as they'd said goodbye at St David's. 'Perhaps for Christmas. Kiss Emily and the children for me . . .' It had been hard to watch her go.

'I miss her,' she said aloud—and Polonius stirred and wagged his tail, sitting up to look hopefully at the toast rack. Maudie frowned at him. 'I'm not surprised that Posy doesn't want you,' she muttered. 'We're stuck with each other, you and me.'

'It's not that we don't want him,' Posy had protested. 'It's because I'm not sure that he'll be able to adapt to Mike and a baby. He's just got used to you and it seems mean to ask him to start all over again. And he's so big and boisterous. Poor Luke will never learn to walk. He'll be knocked over every time he stands up. Do you really mind, Maudie? He can come to us if you ever want to go away.'

Maudie had grumbled, pretending that she'd known how it would be all along, but secretly she was relieved. She'd become surprisingly attached to Polonius and had been rather dreading being alone again. As for Polonius, he regarded Maudie as his own property and had settled so happily at The Hermitage that she wondered if he, too, was rather too old to cope with yet another change in his life.

She opened Posy's card, smiling at the familiar spiky writing: *Only another week, and I shall be finished here and can start organising the wedding. I can't believe it, Maudie. In three months' time I shall be married and living at Moorgate. Is it OK if I come down the weekend after next . . . ?*

Maudie stood the card against the marmalade with a little sigh. How strange that first Rob and Melissa, and then Mike and Posy, should meet and fall in love at Moorgate. It was extraordinary that the brief week in winter for Rob and Melissa had resolved itself into a happy future stretching ahead for Mike and Posy and little Luke. As for herself, after September there would be no more weekends . . .

'Don't start that,' she told herself sternly. 'I shall go and see them at Moorgate and there's my trip to Canada to plan. Perhaps I'll build an extension so that Posy and Mike and Luke can come and stay. And Emily and Tim . . .'

She spread some butter on her toast and opened the catalogue. The glossy pictures of rich tartans and supple tweed jogged at her memory. What had happened to the samples that Miss Grey had sent last autumn? Pushing back her chair, she went to look in the desk drawer.

There it was, the thick envelope, put away until she had the time to think about it. She sat down again, eating her toast, looking at the soft squares of tartan, recalling the day they'd arrived. That was the morning she'd had a card from Posy, asking her if she'd give Polonius a home, and the letter from Ned Cruikshank, telling her that Moorgate was nearly finished and wondering about the missing keys. How long ago it seemed; how much had happened since.

Maudie finished her coffee and picked up the samples. No reason, now, why she should not order something special: something for the trip to Canada at Christmas. She let the fine woollen squares slide over her fingers: Muted Blue Douglas, Ancient Campbell, Hunting Fraser, Dress MacKenzie. It was impossible to choose. Suddenly a memory slipped into her mind: Hector talking to someone at a party.

'My mother was a Douglas,' he was saying, 'descended from the Bruce, she used to say. It's a pretty tartan. Subtle and understated.' He'd smiled at her, sending her a tiny, private wink. 'Just the thing for you,' he'd said. 'We must buy some and have something made up for you . . .'

Maudie closed her eyes for a moment, the better to remember that intimate little wink, his heart-warming smile.

'Darling Hector,' she murmured. 'How I miss you.'

She removed her spectacles, selected the square marked 'Muted Blue Douglas' and, rising from the breakfast table, went to make a telephone call.

EPILOGUE

THE LONE WALKER ON THE HILL paused to remove his jersey. The late afternoon sun slanted from the west, touching the slopes with fire, warming the rough granite outcrops. He was looking forward to a cold drink, his own bottle of water long since finished. The early spring day had been unseasonably hot, the blue air still, the distant view hazy. As he tied the sleeves of his jersey about his waist, he watched the small figures in the garden below him. It was many years since he'd walked these hills, but the farmhouse was a familiar sight, a landmark. The cream-washed walls glowed warmly in the sunshine, and in the open-fronted barn, a man was piling logs into a barrow.

The last time he'd been here the house had been for sale, but now it was clearly occupied. Washing hung on a line stretched across the yard and he could hear children's voices as they clambered onto the swing beside the escallonia hedge. A young woman was pushing them gently as they clung together on the swing, shrieking with delight.

The schoolmaster smiled, touched by the simplicity of the scene, and then paused, staring intently. It seemed that another woman, tall and slender, was standing in the shadow of the escallonia, watching the happy group by the swing. Yet, as he watched, a rippling breeze shook the branches so that the sunlight danced and trembled, and he saw that, after all, the figure was simply a delicate fusion of light and shade.

As he set off, descending rapidly, his face to the west, the sun was dipping towards the sea and smoke drifted up from the chimneys of the cottages huddled in the valley. Long shadows, indigo and purple, crept upon the slopes and now, in the quiet spring evening, he could hear the rooks, quarrelling in the wood below, and the plaintive cries of the lambs.

MARCIA WILLETT

I met Marcia Willett a couple of months after *A Week in Winter* had been bought by an American publisher and she was still smiling from ear to ear at the thought of the deal. 'Breaking into the American market with this novel has completely changed my life,' she told me, pulling out details of a wonderful old Devon long house in the middle of Dartmoor that she and her husband, Rodney, had recently moved into as a result of the lucrative deal. 'We just fell in love with it and, of course, we've called it "The Hermitage" in honour of Maudie's home in *A Week in Winter*.'

Marcia's new home brings her and Rodney particular joy because they were, not long ago, on the brink of financial ruin. They met in Dartmouth, where Marcia was living with her son, Charles, and working as a market researcher in the wake of divorce from her first husband, a naval officer. 'Roddy and I share a love of words and books,' she says, with great fondness, 'and he was always encouraging me to write. Early in our marriage we had great fun living on Roddy's ketch in the Kingsbridge Estuary, before moving to Cornwall where he set up a computer programming company. Then the recession hit and we lost everything. I was forty-six and could not see our way out of the abyss. I just felt it was a matter of

holding on and eventually good would come out of this dark time. Then Roddy said, "Will you please just write that damned book."' And, to stop him nagging, Marcia did, calling on her memories of naval wives to write *Those Who Serve*. 'The day that book was accepted I felt all my dreams had come true,' she says with evident delight. 'I suddenly thought, *yes*, maybe I could be a writer, and I have never looked back.'

Marcia Willett would be the first to admit that she creates characters first, plot second. 'In the case of *A Week in Winter* it was definitely the characters that inspired me. I just let them lead, simply recording what they do and say in my head as faithfully as possible. Obviously I have some control but it is amazing how often they insist on doing something I know nothing about! So much so that, when I'm writing, I wake up most mornings to a voyage of discovery.'

With the American book deal enabling her to buy The Hermitage, everything has finally fallen into place for Marcia. 'Everything but the move,' she tells me, in a doom-laden voice. 'That was almost a total disaster. It was Trubshawe, you see.' Trubshawe is her huge, hairy, lazy but much beloved Newfoundland dog, who was not keen to move house. 'We had to sedate him and in order to move him we had to use the removal van's lift!'

With her sense of fun and general *joie de vivre*, long may Marcia Willett continue to enjoy her writing success on both sides of the Atlantic.

Jane Eastgate

LIBBY PURVES
a free woman

❧

Maggie Reave has been drifting
around the world, with just a
rucksack on her back, for years,
paying scant attention to her sister
Sarah's more conventional lifestyle
and her growing family back
in England.
But at last Maggie is coming home
and Sarah can't wait to see her
again. Her only concern is that she
and her sister will have little left in
common—a worry, she soon
discovers, that is very far from
the truth.

❧

Chapter One

THE STORM WAS PAST. For the first time in days the clouds scudding across the sky were white, high, harmless puffs; beneath them the sea was deep blue and barely ruffled by a steady westerly breeze.

Against the glare and dazzle of the noonday light, the doorway of the galley made a darker rectangle. From the hot shade of its interior a laden figure emerged, perspiring, dark tendrils of hair plastered to its head, a ragged vest slipping on tanned, glistening shoulders. It would have taken a moment or two for any outsider to recognise that the person advancing on the rail with a bucket of slops was female; but then, there were no outsiders on the *Evangelina*, and the men and boys of the little ship's company had long grown indifferent to the gender of the cook's mate. One flirtatious feint, one rebuff, were enough. A thousand miles out from Panama, a kind of grudging kinship bound them all together in a patient sexlessness. There would be time for soft delights later, in some harbour town, when all were clean and spruce in carefully hoarded shirts from the bottom of kitbags. For the moment, the expression of each man's desires was less pressing than the need to ensure he got a decent portion of potato soup or an unbruised apple from the keepers of the galley.

The woman vanished into the dim doorway again. Moments later she reappeared, and stooped to pick up another aluminium pail and lower it briskly on its long rope into the ship's wake. The new bucket jerked, filled, and was as rapidly hauled up. Without ceremony, the cook's mate upended the cold sea water over her head. She repeated the process, soaking her raggedly sawn-off jeans and cotton vest, shaking her shaggy

LIBBY PURVES

mane of hair; then she leaned on the wooden rail while the sun began gently to dry her clothes.

'Maggie!' called a rasping voice from the galley. *'Komm! Ich möchte . . .'* She whipped round. Dark eyebrows knitted together, and big green eyes narrowed like an angry cat's.

'Fuck off!' she said, into the gloom.

A deep, rather drunken-sounding laugh came from the darkness, and a slurred, *'Ich liebe dich!'*

The woman turned, and taking hold of the tarred wires and ropes that rose above her to the topmast, began to climb the rigging.

'Wiedersehen!' she called, from thirty feet above the deck. And added, in kitchen German, a routine obscenity. Two boys who were rubbing down the rusty side of the bridge looked up and laughed. Far aloft, the woman threw her knee over the yardarm and looked out ahead, eastwards across the illimitable wastes of the Atlantic.

A thousand miles away, a pair of very similar green eyes were wide and soft, dreaming beneath dark arching brows as Sarah Penn wiped down her kitchen worktops. The house was silent, for it was a schoolday; it smelt enticingly of fresh coffee, because it was the day when Sarah worked at home.

'*From* home,' she would correct friends. 'At home sounds as if you're doing housework.'

'But you do,' protested Nita, her neighbour and confidante. 'You use Fridays for cleaning and the weekend shop. I've seen you.'

'Sam Miller hasn't,' Sarah replied. 'And I can catch up on the practice invoices in odd moments at the weekend.'

Now she threw the cloth into the sink and crossed to the crowded notice board by the dresser. Among a chaos of timetables, notes, leaflets and bills there was a postcard pinned to the cork. Sarah took down the postcard and carried it over to the table. There, reaching for the coffeepot and absently pouring her third cup of the morning, she read the small, neat writing.

Acapulco Naval Base, it said. *July 13.* Sarah turned it over, but there was nothing in the photograph of sky, beach and sea to distinguish it from a thousand other postcards. She turned back, to the message.

Got a free lift, hooray! Ship is called Evangelina, *has been doing film location work and now has to get to Europe for winter in Canaries, lucrative charter to build characters of French kids. I am assistant cook but*

192

cook is German and mainly pissed. Small crew anyway, Chilean, Yanks and riffraff like self. Captain plays flute. Ten days max to Panama Canal, then eastward ho.

Have brought kids really disgusting presents from Mexico.
XXXX Mag

Sarah smiled. As she put it back, she glanced up at a small world map, torn by Jamie from an old diary months earlier when he decided to track his aunt's progress through South America. She found Acapulco, and traced the way to Panama. She looked at the blankness of the Atlantic and thought wonderingly for a moment of her sister, out on the ocean, and the long shared years of sisterhood.

The Reave sisters, Sarah and Margaret, were a piquant sight as children; elderly neighbours meeting the family on the Brackley estate would smile at how alike they were. When Sarah doggedly pushed new baby Margaret in her buggy, they would say, 'Aah! Look at that little face, and the hair, and those black eyebrows already! It's like having baby Sarah back again! She was a beauty, wasn't she!' And Sarah would try not to mind, even though she privately felt that she had not gone anywhere, and certainly did not need replacing with a newer, more beautiful model.

Later, while the elder sister with continued doggedness pushed her way through public exams, growing pale and flabby with constant studying, Margaret continued to be a physical reminder of her younger self: insouciantly nimble, as cheeky and skinny and wilfully disruptive as an elf. When Sarah glanced up from her A-level work to see Maggie practising handstands amid a pile of disregarded homework she would growl, 'Just you wait! Life isn't all fun when you get older!'

But Maggie would shake her shaggy head dismissively and run outside to hang upside-down over the top bar of the climbing frame.

The same neighbours would say, 'She's a wild one—but you can't put old heads on young shoulders. I'm sure she'll settle down like Sarah. Oh, that's a bright girl: all A grades they say she'll get—and going to London University to study chemistry.'

Sarah duly achieved her grades, her matchbox of a student room in the Imperial College hall of residence, and eventually her first-class chemistry degree and a promising traineeship at Intertech Industries UK, Paints and Wallcoverings Division. By contrast, when Maggie's turn came, the head of their sixth form, a sour man with little tolerance of female fantasy, observed tartly that he was not even ready to predict that the youngest Reave child would turn up to sit her exams, let alone pass them. Maggie had by then acquired an impressive record of truancy.

'Though you have to admit that she's always been original,' said her father, Ted, after the third or fourth major crisis. He was sitting at the kitchen table, tired from a six-hour trip to fetch his seventeen-year-old daughter home from the Isle of Wight, where she had been intercepted aboard an ocean-racing yacht whose horrified skipper had believed her to be a twenty-three-year-old veteran of the Fastnet Race.

'According to the head, most of the girls bunk off so they can hang around Etam and shoplift make-up from Woolies. At least Maggie's always had a reason.'

'I don't,' said her mother, Nancy, heavily, 'call going off with the circus much of a reason. Not for a twelve-year-old. Anything could have happened. Those men . . . two nights away . . .'

'It wasn't the men she went for,' said Ted stubbornly. Despite the stabs of terror she had so often inflicted on the whole family, he enjoyed his youngest daughter's wayward spirit. 'It was the elephant. She was learning about elephant-keeping.'

'The old man who did the elephants thought she was sixteen,' added Sarah, who was home from university for a weekend.

'Well, then!' said Nancy. 'You know what that means. To a man. And as soon as she *was* sixteen . . .' She closed her eyes in pained memory for a moment. 'It was a whole fortnight.'

'But she did phone home. We knew she was OK,' said Sarah gently.

'She was in *Turkey*!' exploded her mother. 'With no *money*!'

'She was looking for the site of Noah's flood,' said Ted. 'Remember— it was in the papers that year, about someone in Turkey thinking they'd found the Ark.'

'Anything could have happened,' said Nancy tightly. 'I blame you as much as her. You never reined her back.'

With practised diplomacy, her husband and elder daughter changed the subject. Although Nancy said 'anything' could have happened, they both knew that there was only one thing that the mother dreaded: that one of her pretty daughters would get pregnant.

Nancy scanned the newspapers daily for terrible tales of girls who got knocked up, dropped out of education, and subsequently led sordid lives in council flats. The fact that this fate had not overtaken any girl in living memory at Brackhampton High School hardly reassured Mrs Reave. Nor did Sarah's series of earnest, respectful boyfriends or Maggie's tomboy scorn. The fact was that neither of them ever showed the slightest tendency to get into that particular kind of trouble.

But still the mother fretted. 'Women,' she would say, 'live under a curse. A mother of girls can never really rest until they're safe.' By safe she meant married.

'Married alive. Ugh,' said Maggie, and grinned at her father, who would try not to grin back while his wife was watching.

Somehow the head of the sixth form coaxed Maggie into the exam room, to emerge with a set of grades that guaranteed her a place at a lesser university to read geography. It was a canny move on his part to point out to her the advantages of the subject for an adventurous spirit.

'There's a sandwich year,' he said. 'Field-work camps. There's a forestry project in South America, and a survey they've got on in Iceland. You get your fares paid.'

So as Sarah moved decorously up through the ranks at Intertech, and conducted a slow, shy, happy courtship with an assistant bookshop manager called Leonard Penn, Maggie Reave gazed out of the windows of Midlands lecture halls. Her reward, in the year that Sarah and Leo became engaged, was to walk among steaming geysers and camp at night beneath the northern lights.

Her father, who was privately amazed that his younger daughter had got through two years of ordinary student life without breaking free, read her ecstatic postcards and said confidentially to one of his friends at the bank that he found it hard to believe that his Margaret would ever go back to a desk. 'She's my wild bird,' he said sentimentally. 'If you try to hold her, she'll fly off. I'm afraid my wife's never understood that.'

He managed, however, to feign decent surprise and disapprobation for his wife's benefit when, at the end of her eight months in Iceland, Maggie fired off a postcard to explain that she was giving up the university course and travelling on.

Before this news was digested there was another bulletin: a crackling telephone call to Sarah. Maggie was edging along the Greenland coast as cook on an oil-company tugboat.

'She'll come home pregnant!' lamented her mother. 'She'll ruin her life!' And, inconsequentially, 'She's a terrible cook, anyway!'

By the time Sarah had extricated herself from work and come home to discuss the crisis Maggie was in Newfoundland, and represented at the family table by a grimy postcard.

Sarah had brought her newly affianced Leo home with her. He had become a familiar of the tidy little house on the Brackley estate, and was tranquilly approved of by the elder Reaves. He was ten years older than

Sarah, an alumnus of both Cambridge and Harvard. Ted and Nancy found themselves instinctively turning for help to his apparent sophistication. Even the less impressionable Sarah said, 'You know that part of the world, Leo. What do you think we ought to do? Do you reckon she'll be OK?'

In love, flattered, Leo said, 'I could go out there if you like. Speak to her. Persuade her to finish her education.'

The Reaves collectively leapt on the idea.

Later that night, sitting on the sofa with his arm round Sarah, Leo said, 'Oh God. I'm going to have to do it, aren't I?'

'Your fault for offering,' said his beloved, unkindly. 'It's a fool's errand. Nobody's ever persuaded Maggie to do anything she didn't fancy.' She paused. 'But yes,' she added, illogically. 'You've got to go. I don't think Dad is terribly well just now. They're not saying anything but . . .'

Ted, indeed, was looking thin and grey. It was, as it turned out, his last summer.

So Leo flew to Boston on the cheapest fare available and took a train northwards into Canada. By this time Sarah had had a brief call from Maggie, saying that she had found a job cooking for some entomologists camped northwest of Halifax. She named the leader of the expedition, which was her big mistake. Once Sarah had telegraphed him the name, it took Leo a mere three days to track down his sister-in-law-to-be.

He found her sitting outside a log cabin in a forest clearing with a red scarf wound round her head. She was mixing a panful of powdered mashed potato.

She looked up, and her big eyes widened. '*What*,' she asked incredulously, 'are *you* doing here?'

Leo slept for two nights in the entomologists' hut, and for two days relentlessly unrolled before Maggie the arguments for finishing her degree. By the end of the first day she knew she was beaten. That night she wept, but kept up a show of resistance for a further twenty-four hours. When it was all over, Leo made a mistake. He produced her train and air tickets home.

'They're *dated*,' said the girl angrily. 'You were *sure* you'd get me home. You patronising bastard!'

He was shattered by the emotional force of the anger he had unleashed. On the plane back to Heathrow, Maggie did not speak one civil word to Leo Penn. Looking at her huddled in her seat, her big eyes hard and hostile, Leo thought that she was a scrawny feral version of his soft-hearted, gentle Sarah. Indeed there was an almost comical similarity in the two women's eyes, their straight dark brows, the way their hair fell, the timbre of their voices. But this ungrateful angry creature was compounded of fire and air, mountain and storm. His Sarah, he thought poetically, was rather earth and water: a gentle breeze through a cornfield, a stream through cool green woods . . .

Later, as they stood beside the baggage carousel at Heathrow, Maggie turned to him and spoke in a tight, small voice.

'I suppose you have to escort me all the way home?'

'No,' said Leo tranquilly. 'You won't bolt. It was your decision to come home. I'm going back to my flat, and I presume you're going home to Brackhampton.'

Maggie snorted, and ran her hand angrily through her shaggy dark hair. She was, he thought, still very young. He looked down at her, a tall, awkward figure in his black-rimmed glasses and crumpled jacket, and added, 'You've got all your life to go travelling. Once you've finished university.' Deftly, he hooked their bags off the carousel.

She shrugged and walked away from him with her kitbag swinging.

She never sulked for long. Back home, Maggie saw her father's new pallor and threw her arms around him; she even took care to turn a reassuringly flat-bellied profile to her mother at every opportunity.

That was in 1983, the year before Ted died. Maggie became quieter during that year. To Sarah's surprise she spent her university vacations at home, sitting with her father as he grew weaker and tolerating her mother's tearful, capricious moods with a new gentleness. Her sister never doubted how much this forbearance cost her. When Sarah came down at weekends, Maggie would vanish until Sunday night with the ragged old tent from their childhood. It took her the best part of a day to walk along the verge of the roaring trunk road to the coast, where she pitched her tent on the beach with utter unconcern for bylaws and sat by a driftwood fire. The next morning she would swim in the sea, whatever the season, and walk home.

'Why don't you get the bus?' Sarah asked once. 'It seems such a waste of your free time walking ten miles along that miserable road with all the container lorries when you could get there in half an hour.'

'Ugh!' said Maggie. 'That's like picking all the raisins out of a bun. You see, you have to measure out a journey,' she said. 'You measure it best in steps. And the shorter the journey is, the more important it is to use your own legs as a measure.'

'You mean,' said Sarah, intrigued, 'that you can turn any trip into an adventure provided you make it difficult enough for yourself?'

'No,' said Maggie. 'Not an adventure. But you can pace up and down the cage a bit, can't you?'

'I worry,' said Nancy to Sarah during one of these absences, 'about her being out in that tent alone. Anything could happen.'

Sarah had suffered her mother's troubling obsession for too long to fall into the trap of responding. Instead, kindly, she said, 'Oh, Mum, while you're here, I did want to talk through a few things about the wedding . . .' So Nancy's easier daughter led her up to the bright, safe, happy realm of weddingland, where nothing mattered but embossing, bouquets, and fork lunches.

Ted Reave lived just long enough to give away his elder daughter in Brackhampton church, amid great sprays of lilies and yellow roses. Sarah and Leo had their fortnight's honeymoon in France, but arrived home barely in time to say goodbye at a hospice bedside and arrange his funeral. It was the same church, and again Nancy ordered lilies.

'They made him sneeze,' said Maggie, *sotto voce*, to her sister when she saw the coffin lying tranquilly in the aisle between the white waxy blooms. The two of them had gone early into the church to make sure that all was well. 'Remember, at the wedding?'

'Well . . . Mum likes lilies,' said Sarah. 'Surely that's the point.'

Maggie began suddenly to cry, with raw childish sobs. Sarah stood quietly apart, resisting the urge to hug her: Maggie hated to be pawed when she was upset. The surge of grief passed, and Sarah handed over a wad of tissues.

'Poor Dad,' said Maggie. 'I wish he'd had more of a life.'

'He was happy with it,' said Sarah. 'He had a family, he liked the bank, and they liked him. He had Mum, and the garden, and us. It was a good life.'

'He never went anywhere,' spat Maggie with sudden vehemence. 'He never went anywhere hotter than Margate or colder than the Lake District. He never saw anything that lives wild in a jungle. He lived fifty-eight years and never saw coral, or coconuts on the tree. It's desperate.'

She began to cry again. Sarah knew perfectly well that it was not only their father she was weeping for.

'You've been home too long, pacing the cage, Magpuss,' she said. 'All you have to do now is finish college, then you're free. Go and be a jackeroo or a pirate or a coconut farmer—whatever you fancy. I promise that I'll never, ever send Leo to bring you back again.'

Maggie almost smiled at that; for the intervening months had soft-ened the Canadian forest outrage to a well-worn joke.

They walked out into the thin Easter sunshine, and shortly the organ began to play.

The year of Sarah's wedding and Ted's death saw Nancy just as worried about pregnancy as before, but now anxiety consumed her that her elder daughter should conceive as fast as possible. The newspaper cut-tings that littered her kitchen table were about IVF and ageing ova.

'You don't want to leave it too late,' the mother was crackling down Sarah's telephone line a mere month after the wedding. 'Women's, you know, *equipment* doesn't last for ever. And the older you are, the more tiring a baby can be. I was twenty-two when I had you, and twenty-seven when Margaret came, and there was a difference. I was drained . . .'

Sarah would sit patiently in her bright new London flat, grimacing humorously at her husband to indicate that the subject had come up again. She and Leo were intensely happy in those first days; it seemed to her indeed that she had never been so much at home with another human being before. Each day they woke and smiled, embraced with easy passion, amicably split the morning papers and berated Mrs Thatcher together in total harmony. After breakfast Sarah would shower, carrying on the conversation while Leo shaved. Then they would embrace one last time and set off for their work.

Leo was increasingly disillusioned about the big chain bookstore where he had worked for close on a decade.

'Philistines,' he said. 'The books don't matter, the customers don't matter, only their money. I might as well be selling burgers. At least there's less hype and tinsel in the burger trade. Do you know who they want me to have in for a so-called book event next month? *Fifi de Mornay!* The one who slept with two Cabinet ministers in the same week. No, I tell a lie, the bald one wasn't even in the Cabinet.'

After a while his complaints ceased to sound like jokes and, when evening came, he had sometimes poured and finished his first drink before he could bear to discuss his day.

Sarah, happily in love and naturally of a more philosophical nature, was less inclined to complain of her lot. She had begun to wonder whether departmental team leadership in the world of specialist paint marketing was really a goal worth being groomed for. But then, she told herself, it was different for a woman. The idea of her being trapped for ever in Intertech was an absurdity, even in 1984.

Sarah Penn knew perfectly well that some time—perhaps when she was thirty—there would be a baby. Just as the fun of work began to pall, she would find herself with a new and exciting function. She would be a Mother. And although Sarah entirely applauded the idea of equal working rights for women, she had no intention of going into her fourth decade of life exhausted by working with a carry-cot under the desk. Nor would she hand over any baby of hers to some hireling or nursery for ten hours a day. She foresaw without repining that when she returned from the inevitable break, it would be to a different kind of work, a lesser commitment.

Sarah looked forward to this future of compromise, and rarely glanced beyond the child-rearing years to any future work. The child who had pushed her sister's pram knew beyond any doubt that motherhood would suit her. Therefore it did not matter if Intertech was less than fulfilling. It was only a prelude, after all, to the real tune of her life.

For Leo it was different. A man's work went on and on until he retired. It was therefore more important for him to be satisfied. And so Sarah worried ever more about Leo's frustrations at work, but bore her own with a shrug, because there was a time-release key on her shackles that a man could never have.

Towards the end of 1984, Sarah said to her increasingly morose husband, 'Look, you don't have to stay with the company. You could set up as an independent. You've got the flair, you've got the contacts. I can support both of us for three years or so on what I earn. We can use my New Year bonus to help with the first stock. Why don't we just go for it?'

'I can't live off my wife!' said Leo, with old-fashioned horror. 'And suppose you had a baby?'

'I shall have a baby when I'm good and ready for it,' said Sarah. 'I'm only twenty-four. I've got six years before I need bother. And by then you'll be doing terrifically well, and I can go back part-time. And it'll be ever so much cheaper living out of London anyway.'

'Living out of London?' said Leo wonderingly. 'You've got it all worked out, haven't you?'

'Well, you aren't going to start off by paying London rents, are you?' said Sarah scornfully. 'We could go to—I don't know, Ramsgate? Or Brackhampton? There's nothing but a couple of tacky newsagents there, doing best sellers and puzzle books. I could commute. Intertech's only three minutes from Waterloo.'

Leo thought for a moment or two then said slowly, '*Brackhampton*. Near your mother.'

'Well, we wouldn't live out on the Brackley estate, obviously. But would you mind? Being near Mum, I mean?'

'No,' he said. 'Not really. I suppose she can't actually make you pregnant just by sending out rays of magic 'fluence, can she?'

But somehow, she did. Leo and Sarah sold the London flat and bought a bankrupt butcher's shop on the corner of Friar's Alley and the High Street, with a cellar for a stockroom and a one-bedroom flat over half of it.

'Which we can open up for a children's department—or a coffee shop—when we can afford to move out to a house,' said Sarah.

The premises smelt unpleasantly of meat, but there was nothing wrong with them that a bit of paint would not cure.

Within a week of the move, though, the smell of paint itself was too much for Sarah.

'Tummy bug,' she said, groaning as she knelt to stir the leaf-green paint. 'I've been feeling queasy all morning.'

'You felt queasy all yesterday morning too,' said Leo. 'You don't think—'

She looked up. On the top of the stepladder, scraper in hand, her husband stood frozen in horror, looking down. Sarah stood up slowly, and gazed at him. After a moment contemplating his pale, wretched wife, Leo said emphatically, 'No. No, you can't be!'

But she was. The two of them fled along the High Street to Boots, bought a pregnancy-testing kit and ran back to the shop. Sarah vanished into the bleak lavatory, then together they stared at the test tube and watched the brown ring of sediment form, clear and unmistakable.

The shock of that moment never left them. It was, Sarah told Maggie, like being hit with a hammer. 'Or hijacked at gunpoint.'

'Should bloody think so,' said her sister. In contrast to Sarah's pale, eight-month bulk she was thin and brown, fresh back from a spell of travel in the USA. 'What are you thinking of? I turn my back for a few weeks—'

'Months!' said Sarah miserably.

'Well, a few months then, and first of all you decide to support Leo's business with your salary, then you get up the spout. It's madness!'

'It's my baby!' said Sarah angrily. The child was moving now; she had become reconciled to it. 'It's my baby, even if I didn't want it just yet.'

'OK,' said Maggie equably. 'But a shop and a baby—a ball and chain. Talk about being tied down. I'm glad you're happy, but bloody glad it isn't me.'

Nancy, of course, was delighted. 'You've got your anchor now. You can put down roots. *You* won't go drifting through life like your sister. Did you hear this harebrained scheme of hers about Australia?'

Nancy had stopped worrying about Maggie becoming pregnant; her younger daughter seemed, these days, to be hardly a daughter at all. She was more like a son: high-spirited, evasive, always off on some mystifying expedition. There had been no boyfriends either; at least, none brought home for approval.

Leo was reconciled to the baby too. Sarah remained resolute about returning early to work, so he thought they could cope financially; the shop had had a surprisingly good launch and he faced its first Christmas with optimism. He quickly grasped—by way of a few mistakes—what books the denizens of Brackhampton would actually buy. There was no point despising the rock music biographies, celebrity froth and sumptuously gimmicky cookbooks; yet his gentle, scholarly manner and wide enthusiasm for his wares won him friends among those who thought of themselves as Brackhampton's intelligentsia. He had plans to start a specialist service finding rare books on military and naval history and sending them out by post. There was profit in that, if you were organised. Leo was always organised.

The young couple decided to rent a little house behind the High Street rather than try to live in the flat with the baby. When Sarah got back to work they would be able to afford a local girl to help out. Babies, he had heard, grew up very fast these days. In no time it would be at school, and the difficult bit would be over. Despite his many talents, Leo was still in many ways an innocent.

Samantha Margaret Penn was born in February 1985, two weeks late, after a long and difficult labour. Her aunt got the news over a crackling radiotelephone link in Western Australia, where she was imparting the basics of world geography to a dozen inattentive children.

'I long to see it!' yelled Maggie over waves of static. 'Give it my love!'

'Not *it*!' shouted Sarah. 'Her!'

'Sorree!!' said the distant voice from down under. 'Look, I have to go. They wander off outside if I turn my back. Write! Tell me about her. Photos. All that. I'm here for at least two more months, then I'll see if I can work a passage on a ship pointing north.'

'Mags, why can't you FLY home like everyone else?'

'There speaks a yuppie. Intertech executives fly. Me, I know my place. I earn peanuts here, Sarah, less than peanuts.'

A FREE WOMAN

'I want to see you!' Sarah twisted the telephone cable and tears pricked her eyes. Maggie's strong, happy, careless voice tormented her like the singing of a bird outside a prison cell.

'I want to see you too. But I have to finish term. Look, I can't talk now, I really do have to go and shout at them. Bye. Take care.'

Leo, who was walking up and down with his baby in his arms, saw his wife's face twitch as she put the phone down. Gently he laid Samantha down in the cot. He went to Sarah and put his arm round her.

'Tired? Did she keep you up a lot last night? You're doing so, so well. I'm proud of you. Both.'

Sarah did not relax into his arm at once. She glanced at the cot.

'It's for ever now, isn't it?' she said. 'That's the thing that never sinks in till it happens. I'll never be a free woman again.' And she wept, with great tearing sobs.

'Fourth day blues,' said the consultant next morning, after he had checked Sarah and signed her off as fit to go home. Leo had intercepted him on the way into the ward. 'Sometimes we call it fifth day blues, depending when it turns up. But fourth or fifth, it nearly always does happen. You've got help at home, I suppose?'

They had Nancy. She came to sleep in the spare bedroom, not even complaining at having to share it with boxes of unsold books. Adept and delighted, she doted on baby Samantha, cuddled and cooed and very soon took over the job of feeding her. Sarah had tried, but her breasts ached and bled.

'Not every woman can manage it,' said Nancy with happy confidence, holding the baby to her. 'Better a bottle than a hungry baby, izzen't dat so, precious popkin?'

Sarah retreated into a sullen dreamworld, and did not much care. The suckling hurt, anyway; and sitting anchored to the sofa with the child latched to her bosom made her feel powerless, bloated and irritable. She took to walking aimlessly round the town centre during the periods when her mother would be feeding and caring for the baby.

Leo saw his wife pass the bookshop almost every day, and guessed that she was escaping. In the evening he would nurse the baby and try to create an affectionate circle of the three of them; but his mother-in-law would chatter excitedly about vests and colic, and Sarah would go early to bed, silent and morose. Then Nancy would take the baby from him and cluck off upstairs, leaving him alone.

At first Leo filled the void by pulling out his account books and working late into the night. He did not yet feel confident enough to hire a proper assistant; he was overstretched in those early days, and not a little frightened of what he had taken on.

But after a fortnight he could no longer bear the dark, cold feeling in the pit of his stomach. Halfway through a working day, when Nancy had just wheeled the baby past the shop window in her buggy, he went up the alley to the little house. Cautiously, he climbed to the bedroom and found Sarah lying on her back on the bed, staring at the ceiling. For once he did not speak gently to her.

'This,' he said, 'has got to stop. Either you are ill and you've got to get treatment. Or else you're angry with me, or the baby, or something. I don't know what it is, I don't know about women and babies. But it's not going to go on. It's got to stop.'

Sarah sat up and stared at him, her face unreadable.

'The baby's all right,' she said defensively. 'Mum's got her.'

'Shall we offer to let your mother adopt her, then?' said Leo with studied callousness. 'Or perhaps hand her over to someone younger. There's a shortage of babies for adoption, they say. If her own mother doesn't want her, obviously that's the answer.'

He had hardly ever spoken to anybody so cruelly. All he knew was that he must get a reaction from his wife.

The shock worked. Sarah's face crumpled, and she began to cry. 'My baby—how dare you—you don't care . . .'

Leo crossed the room, took her in his arms and let her cry. After a while he said, 'Your mother had better move out. We've got to do this properly. Samantha is ours. Not hers.'

'But the shop—you can't help—I can't cope alone—I don't know how to do any of it—oh, Christ, Leo!'

'We'll cope,' said her husband kindly, stroking her hair. 'People cope. People always have.'

Everything had gone better after Leo's remonstrance. Nancy had been persuaded back into her proper grandmotherly place, Sarah had learned her way round the problematical baby ways of Samantha, and suddenly one afternoon, between a windy smile and a small flailing fist patting her cheek, Sarah felt an almost physical sense of relaxation; her hard-edged dreams of liberty and control melted into a warm nurturing broth. 'I'm your mummy,' she whispered to the wriggling creature in her arms. 'For always.'

Going back to work was a torment, even though Nancy jealously and vigilantly monitored successive au pairs; but after two short hectic years commuting up to Intertech, the birth of Jamie put an end to Sarah's progress up the executive ladder. The shop was doing fine, and so was the rare-book catalogue, administered by two part-timers, General Madson and Rear-Admiral Havelock. This time, Sarah accepted severance pay and a boisterous farewell party in the tapas bar behind Waterloo Station.

When Sarah did at last return to earning, it was as a part-time clerical assistant to Samuel Miller, senior partner at the local veterinary practice.

Seven months later Maggie, who had by now based herself rather loosely in Spain, came home to see Teddy, the newest baby.

'At least working for a vet you must get some laughs. I couldn't have worked in that paint place for six months,' she said, 'let alone three years.' She had Jamie on her knee, playing with her ropes of carved amber beads. 'I'll tell you a thing about life, boy—the crap jobs are far more fun than the good ones.'

'*You* couldn't work *anywhere* for more than a few months,' said Leo. 'How many jobs did it take you to get round Australia?'

'Six,' said Maggie. 'Schoolteaching, cooking, washing cars, packing fleeces, grape-picking, and mending smelly wet suits in the dive centre at Cairns. That was the worst. And all so that I could get the fare back every two years to see what you'd sprogged. I've had to stick to Spain lately, just so I can afford to commute to your ever-fertile bedside.'

'I would have thought the fleeces were the worst of your jobs,' said Sarah, who was nursing the newborn Teddy, light-headed with the hormones of lactation and the pleasure of having her sister home. 'All full of fleas and sheep shit, I should think.'

'Nah,' said Maggie. 'Lovely, they were. Lots of lanolin, my hands have never been so soft.'

'When are you going to settle down and get a real job?' asked Leo, from the sink. Maggie's visits always made him a little stiffer and more pompous than usual, which in turn made the two women playfully gang up against him. 'I've heard of gap years, but you seem to be taking a gap decade.'

Maggie looked at him, her dark brows arching satirically. 'Were you offering me a job, brother-in-law? Do you want me to step into Miss Mountjoy's cardigan when she resigns again?'

Leo had at long last hired a full-time assistant: an angular, Anglican churchwarden who had twice handed in her notice on grounds of principle, the principle usually involving books about what she referred to as 'unnatural practices'.

'I wouldn't hire you with a ten-foot pole,' said Leo. 'But you'll have to decide what you're going to do some time, won't you?'

'No,' said Maggie. 'No, I don't think so. In my increasingly global experience of life, people are always deciding things with great solemnity, and then events come along and change their direction. I thought I'd just let fate have its way.'

'Drift, you mean?'

'No, no, no. There's an art to it.' As the child scrambled down from her lap, Maggie looked across at Leo. 'The more places I put myself, the more interesting and different will be the things that happen. That's why I'm learning Spanish. There are three hundred and fifty million Spanish speakers in the world, so that's three hundred and fifty million new conversations I can have. Good, eh?'

'If you don't mind the prospect of still being a chambermaid when you're knocking thirty,' said Leo repressively.

'Temporary chambermaid,' said Maggie cheerfully.

'I looked in my old diary the other day,' said Sarah, propping the baby upright and rubbing his back. 'And it seemed really weird that there used to be a time when I had absolutely bugger-all to do apart from earn a living and keep myself amused. I don't know how I filled the time. But I suppose you're still in that phase, Mags. Stay alive, stay roughly solvent, stay amused, and that's your day's work done.'

'Correct,' said Maggie. 'Except I'm better than solvent. If nobody will lend you any money, you don't have any debts. In Australia once I ran out of everything—technically, I suppose I was destitute. So I went to the petrol station, and that's when I started the car-washing. It was a breeze. One day and I had a big steak dinner and a night in the hostel. Two more days and I had enough to buy a bus ticket to the coast.'

'And what did you do on the coast?' asked Leo.

'Err . . . stuck new crotches in skanky wet suits for fat tourists,' said his sister-in law, who was good-natured enough not to grudge him his victories. 'OK, I give in. I'm a bum.'

Years later, Sarah, the mother of three, baked a cake in a sunny kitchen, remembered these things and shook her head in wonder. That baby, Teddy, was eleven now. Even Sarah, who knew Maggie best, had not really believed back in 1989 that her sister would still be rootless in the new century; but she was. Slotting the cake into the oven, she washed her hands and then looked at the postcard again. It was a bigger house now, further up the High Street with a more comfortable kitchen. Samantha was a moody, clever, fifteen-year-old; Jamie's voice was just beginning to break. Sarah herself was softer and rounder in the face and body; the pretty, sharp young marketing executive had vanished, swallowed up in the plump blandness of a nice efficient motherly lady who did accounts for a small-town vet.

Leo was a little heavier too, almost jowly, and even more anxious for his evening drink. He was still running the shop with only Miss Mountjoy and an ever-changing cast of part-time sixth-formers. Attempts to bring the General and the Rear-Admiral in to man the shop for the odd hour had foundered; after gamely trying it, both stated firmly that they preferred to work at home, sending out book lists and parcelling up orders. As for Nancy, she had grown quite suddenly into an old woman, with parchment skin and sunken cheeks.

Maggie, on the other hand, came home once or twice a year and seemed at first glance unchanged: merry, unattached, always full of adventures. Sarah read the card: ten days to the canal, it said. Ten days, then the Atlantic—four weeks? Five?

It would be nice for the children. They always looked forward to Auntie Maggie.

Chapter Two

CAPTAIN LOPEZ SHADED HIS EYES and looked aloft. He ran his eye over his web of rigging, and saw that it was good. On the upper fore-topsail yard two figures worked, his boatswain and one of the Chilean boys left over from the film job. There were ten or eleven of them on board, and he was glad enough to have them. They paid for their food and skivvied at any job going. But he would be glad to have a proper payload again: a paid crew and paying passengers.

His eye rested on the figure which sat lightly astride the lower yard, looking out at the eastern horizon. Captain Lopez smiled; his assistant cook, too, was good. Of all the riffraff crew, she was the treasure. Gunther was drunk and dirty in his habits. When they docked in Spain Gunther would have to go, and he knew it.

They had sailed together two years earlier from Kiel, and Gunther had been a good enough cook then. What harm had come to him in the hot Americas and made him the useless liability he now was, Captain Lopez did not know. A woman, probably. Women were terrible trouble.

But this one, perched neatly in his rigging, was no trouble, and he approved very much of her. So much that now he cried, 'Hola, Maggie!' and returned her wave with an almost boyish glee. Not so bad-looking, but thin. Thin, however, was good in the circumstances, with so many men together on the sea. This woman was friendly, kind even, but neither scoldingly maternal nor flirtatious. Perfect!

The first he had seen of this treasure was a pair of long, ragged denim legs, dangling over the side of the quay in Acapulco.

'You need a cook?' she said. 'No pay, just the passage to Europa. You are going to Europa, sí?'

'Sí,' he said. 'And I have a cook.'

'I do not think he is a good cook. I have been drinking with some of your crew, and I think this cook is a man who needs help if he is to make good food for sailors.'

'Is that what they say?' The captain bristled, his professional pride wounded by the notion that every bartender in Acapulco knew by now how badly managed was the galley of the *Evangelina*. 'Ignorant men will always talk when they are drinking.'

'OK,' said the girl on the quay. 'But I have a UK passport, I can land in Spain with no trouble, and I don't want any pay. I have also worked on deck before. It is a pity that you do not want me. I am sorry to waste your time. To show my sorrow I will do a penance. Now.'

She swung down from the quay and before he could stop her had invaded the galley and begun to ferret energetically for mops and cloths. He made as if to stop her but could not bear to; Gunther's horrible domain remained a source of shame on his otherwise excellent ship. An hour later she reappeared and said, 'OK. And now *adios*, Captain.'

So of course it had not been *adios*, and he had taken her on for the passage to Santander. And there she was, a very great deal of help.

'Maggie!' he said softly as he padded back to his quarters. He shook his head sadly. The night before, he had formally asked her to sail on as paid cook for the winter. 'Come,' he said. 'My owners will pay you well.'

She had turned him down, smiling all the while. 'No. With regret, Captain, I must go home to see my family.'

'You have a husband?' he said, fixing her with eyes of brown doglike devotion.

'*Nunca!* Never!' she said. 'No, no, no. You know what bad things marriage does to a cook. Look at Gunther.'

Joaquim Lopez had never particularly thought about Maggie Reave's sexuality before, but at that moment, looking at her bright, spare, tanned face he said with a conviction so strong that it made him vehement, 'It is not a joke! You should marry!'

She had laughed at him. She generally did.

'Yes, but when is Auntie Maggie coming?' asked Teddy for the third time that meal.

'I don't know,' said Sarah patiently. 'Teddy, you know what it's like. She's coming on a ship. A sailing ship to Spain, which should be nearly there by now—then she's got to get back to England. It could be weeks.'

'It only takes 'n hour and a bit from Spain,' insisted the small boy.

'She hates aeroplanes,' said Samantha firmly, 'unless they're really, really small, with propellers, like in the jungle.' Her recent veneer of fifteen-year-old cynicism was breached by the prospect of Maggie's arrival. Her eyes were sparkling nearly as much as the boys'.

'She goes on planes that are really, really old and dangerous, like in Russia,' added Jamie. 'She told me that on some of them you could decompress the cabin by taking off the top of the lavvy cistern.'

'So you see,' said Leo, reaching for the wine box, 'your aunt cannot possibly be expected to travel like a normal twenty-first-century human being on a fast and comfortable aeroplane. If there's a truly frightful way to get here, that's the one she'll choose.'

'It's not *fair*,' said Teddy. 'I want to see Auntie Maggie.'

Samantha shrieked suddenly, her sophistication finally deserting her. 'Mum!' she said. 'At the *window*! I *saw* her!'

The whole family turned together to follow Samantha's pointing finger. Sure enough, in the autumn evening gloom a familiar face was grimacing through the panes above the sink. A fist tapped, then uncurled to give a flippant little wave towards Samantha. Then Maggie stuck her tongue out at the entranced, staring Teddy. His own shot out in reply. Sarah went to the window. Leo, more practical, went out of the kitchen door and addressed his sister-in-law's back as she perched on top of the wheelie bin.

'Don't you *ever* just ring the bell?' he asked.

She turned and looked at him in the dusk, surprised at the genuine irritation in his voice.

'Well, of course I do,' she said. 'I just couldn't resist, that's all.'

By now the other four Penns were outside.

'Hello, friends!' said Maggie. 'Oh, this is nice. Teddy, you have grown a foot. Jamie, you're virtually adult. Samantha—you look amazing. I mean, shit, I'd forgotten about how big you all were. I've brought you the most unsuitably kiddie presents.'

An extra plate was found, and family supper continued in agreeable uproar as Maggie produced from her vast backpack a series of sugar skulls and coffins from Mexico.

'For Christ's sake don't eat them! They could have any kind of germs on them.'

There were glass beads and bracelets too, carefully wrapped in layers of newspaper so garishly redolent of another continent that Samantha and Jamie were almost equally fascinated by them. They spread out these exotic treasures between the plates, crowding the table and making Sarah worry even more about germs (Oh God, I am turning into my mother, she thought in horror). They fired questions at their aunt.

'Was *Evangelina* ever so slow?'

'Well, not very fast. Especially with the wind against us.'

'Did you climb the mast? Did it lean over? Is it scary?'

'Lots of times. No, not scary at all. Very nice up there. Like being a monkey up in the jungle canopy. There's always a rope or a wire to hold on to.'

With the bluntness available only to the very young, Teddy asked, 'Did you have a boyfriend on the ship?'

Leo and Sarah both pricked up their ears.

'Nope. If you'd seen the crew, you'd know why.'

'You shouldn't *ask* those things,' said Samantha crossly to her brother. 'It's not polite.'

'Samantha's got a boyfriend,' said Jamie smugly. 'He's called Duane and he's from the council estate and he's a really, really rough biker yob.' He ducked as his sister aimed a swipe at his head, almost falling off his chair.

As Jamie clutched at his little brother, Teddy dissolved in fits of laughter, adding, 'He's a biker, but he hasn't actually got a *motorbike!*'

Sarah intervened swiftly. 'Behave yourselves. Jamie, you can shut up about Sam's private life. Or go to bed now. I mean that.'

Samantha's face burned red, and she stood up, her droopy wide jeans flapping over her toes, swayed tall and awkward across the room and ran water noisily into the sink, bringing back a glass of water which she then ignored. Sarah smiled at her and was met with a ferocious scowl.

Leo looked uncomfortable. Although he might not have used precisely the same words, he too was of the view that Duane was indeed a really, really rough biker yob. He felt that Sarah's strategy was all wrong ('Make him welcome, let her make her own judgments as to how this new friend fits into the world she knows'). He suspected it of coming straight from one of the family self-help books in the shop. He frowned at Jamie; it was easier than looking at his daughter. He did not like to think of her being anywhere near Duane, let alone—He reined in his thoughts, sharply.

Maggie had assumed an air of serene unconcern at this family ruction, and was winding spaghetti round her fork. Teddy continued the questioning.

'Daddy says you never take planes like a modern lady. He says you always do things in the difficultest way, just to be contrary. How did you get here from the harbour that the ship went to?'

'British Airways standby from Bilbao,' said Maggie demurely, throwing a sidelong glance at Leo, who pressed his lips together in real annoyance. She smiled, relenting. 'But I did hitch a lift from Santander to Bilbao on a cheese lorry. Mountain goat cheese, Cabrales. Cor, it did smell. Like a wagonload of dirty old feet.'

The children giggled, delighted.

'And I can prove it!'

Maggie lugged her rucksack over, and unzipped a front pocket. From it she drew a plastic packet. 'Go on then,' she said. She handed Jamie the packet and watched him tear the plastic away. As soon as he had done so a ripe, overpowering odour filled the kitchen.

'See? Imagine a great big lorry full of cheeses. Taste it.'

With a gleeful pantomime of disgust, the children gathered round, daring one another to taste the strong cheese.

Later, in bed, Leo laid down his book and said to Sarah, studiedly casual, 'How long is Maggie staying, this time?'

'Here, you mean?' She knew perfectly well what he meant. There was only one guest room. Leo had set up his laptop computer and files there, so that he could come home to a glass of wine and the comforting sounds of home rather than work on in the shop after closing time. With Maggie and her rucksack ensconced there now, his books and files were back downstairs in the living room. It was not satisfactory.

After a pause Sarah continued, 'She's learning Chinese, apparently. So it might be a few months.'

'That wouldn't be local, would it?' said Leo in a tone of careful neutrality, pretending to look at his book. 'She'd have to go to London, to the School of Oriental and African Studies, or wherever.'

'She might go to Mum for a bit,' said Sarah feebly. She was a bad liar. While Leo had been out of the room after supper, Maggie had mentioned that it might be worth her trying some of the colleges in East Kent. Sarah had said, 'Then you could stay here—oh, Mags, do!'

Leo now turned sharply to look at his wife. 'Come off it. She's never stayed with Nancy. They'd drive each other insane.'

Sarah acknowledged the fact with a dip of her head, and then said with a new firmness, 'Sweetheart, I haven't seen her for years. The way she lives, the odds are that I might not see her for years more. You know what she's like. She'll vanish off with some camel train and then get hooked up with some project or other. She's my sister. I think it would be really lovely to have her here for a couple of months.'

'How?' said Leo, dangerously bleak.

'Well—why don't we move your desk into the alcove in here?' She pointed at the space beside the chimney breast. 'It's got lots of light, we could have a neat little filing cabinet. Nobody's ever up here till bedtime. We could run a phone point up if you wanted to get online.'

Leo understood that she had thought all this through. He hunched his shoulders and said, 'Right. I see.' He looked down at his book, and after a moment or two, without apology or concealment, let out a loud and vinous burp. Burping men were one of Sarah's small phobias; she flinched, threw aside her book, and lay down with her back to him.

'It's the half-and-half places that are so interesting,' Maggie was saying to Samantha and Jamie at breakfast, for all the world as if they were adults. 'If you follow the great Silk Road, you find countries which were part of the USSR, but actually if you look at the people and listen to them you see that they're basically Chinese. It looks like fabulous country. Mountains. I'm hoping to get into the Taklimakan Desert, too.'

'Jamie,' said his mother, 'Have you got your gym kit together?'

The child grimaced. 'Uh.'

'Do you ever get scared, travelling round on your own?' Samantha asked her aunt, intently.

'Not really,' said Maggie. 'You stay alert, and if it's really dodgy you generally hook up with someone else for a week or so. But honestly, if you dress unobtrusively you're safer than you'd think. Most men in most countries have some kind of code of respecting women.'

'More than they do at my school,' said Samantha feelingly.

'Jamie, *gym kit!*' said Sarah. 'Come on, I'll help you.'

When they had left the room, Maggie grinned at her niece and said, 'I never had a brother. Let alone two.'

'Brothers suck,' said Sam bitterly.

The aunt remained silent, head cocked, dark brows arched in sympathy. She liked this thin, dark, spiky, uncertain girl. It was difficult to connect her, as yet, with the chattering rosy-cheeked Girl Guide she remembered from last time home, but this was part of the fascination of watching her sister's family.

Samantha added, 'Jamie's a spy and a peeping Tom and an arsehole. He spies on me and Duane.'

'Arsehole behaviour,' agreed Maggie.

There was a silence, during which Samantha pressed her lips together and stared down at the table, as if angry at having offered a cue and not had it taken up. After a moment her aunt, who preferred more directness in her dealings, gave her what she wanted.

'So, Duane,' she said. 'Is it going well?'

There was another silence. Samantha, Maggie thought, looked more preoccupied and depressed than a girl in love ought to do. Clearly there was something she wanted to say. Samantha finally answered with a little rush, 'Boys don't think about anything 'cept doing it. Do they?'

Before Maggie could answer the question, the door opened and Sarah came in, flushed, followed by Jamie and his sports bag, and Teddy wearing a furry spider backpack.

'School!' she said. 'Sam, you coming? Dad says he'll drive you.'

Samantha stood up and shucked on her school blazer over untucked blouse and abbreviated grey skirt.

'See you, anyway,' she said casually.

'Yeah, right,' said Maggie. 'Don't let the bastards grind you down.' She raised a fist in a rather dated Black Power salute.

When the children had gone, Sarah spooned coffee into the machine and said, 'What was that all about? Who's grinding Sam down? I can't get a word out of her about anything these days.'

The answer was a question. 'What's the boyfriend like?'

'Nightmare,' said Sarah briefly, pouring in cold water and clapping the machine shut. 'Thick, sneering, stupid, sexist. Dodgy family. With an earring. And another ring in his nose, like a pig. Real yob. Leo goes purple at the sight of him.'

'Have you spoken to her about it?'

'She'd only dig in her heels if I did. So I try to welcome him to family meals so that she can compare him with normal people. He's come twice now, and both times it has been ap-pall-ing. Leo starts coming on like he's the Duke of Edinburgh, and the little boys just stare. But you're supposed to bring the dodgy boyfriend into the family circle.' Sarah rattled on, as if she was trying to convince herself. 'Everyone agrees that you have to hang loose, these days. Remember how Mum used to go on and on about us getting in "trouble"? I couldn't bring myself to lay that stuff on Sam. Anyway, they're totally sussed by the time they're twelve these days. Sex education seems to start at about seven years old at Brackhampton. The boys know more about condoms than I do.'

'Not working, though, is it?' said Maggie. 'I mean. Sam's still stepping out with the sexist pig with the ring in its nose.'

'Well, I suppose the flaw in the theory is that the only men she can actually compare him with are a harrumphing father and two annoying little brothers,' Sarah conceded. 'I can see that Duane might look mildly attractive as a sort of contrast, when Leo's glowering into his drink and the boys are having a belching competition.'

The coffee machine was working now, hissing and bubbling with promise. She clattered mugs, and drew a firm line under the subject with, 'But it's all part of growing up. My theory is you have to stay cool. Not interfere.'

Maggie thought of the troubled look on Samantha's face a few minutes earlier, and wondered.

Sarah left for the vet's after breakfast. When the house was quiet, Maggie washed, dried and stowed the remaining breakfast things. Then she poured the dregs of the coffee into her mug and took it upstairs. The house felt strange around her: solid, unchanging, British. It was a kind of carapace, she thought; a bricky garment smelling faintly of shoes and damp and soap powder and warm towels, a whitewashed costume which her sister and brother-in-law wore like a crinoline, with their children tucked under its skirts. To be alone inside it felt unnervingly intimate. She stood for a moment or two at her bedroom window, absently picking flakes of old paint off the sill and watching the flat plastic greyness of the English sky.

Then she turned to the bed and began to unpack her rucksack, sorting the clothes—T-shirts, jeans and shorts, fleece and sweater, two cotton skirts, socks, one bra, and a rabble of tangled knickers. In the attic at Nancy's house there would still be a trunk containing the rest of her meagre wardrobe, and a wicker hamper into which she was prone to throw any souvenirs which had retained her fancy for long enough to prevent her giving them away. The hamper also contained a dozen fat, closely written notebooks of various sizes, detailing her travels.

'You should write a book,' Sarah had urged her. 'Loads of people who do much feebler journeys write travel books.'

'I might,' said Maggie. 'Only the book wouldn't ever be as good as the life, would it? I'm not a poet.'

'You don't have to be a poet,' began Sarah.

'Yes, you do. If you really wanted to do it right, a poem or a song would be best. I know the kind of travel book you mean. Lists of places, and grumbles about boots, and undigested chunks of history to show they did research, and badly remembered conversations with locals. Oh, and all that shit about their *feelings*. Nope. Can't be bothered.'

Now Maggie turned over the notebook she had kept aboard the *Evangelina*. She supposed that it would end up in the hamper with the rest, never to be read. The thought filled her with a reluctance she had never felt before. The ship had stirred something new in her. Although she had often cooked aboard charter yachts, something about the old brig and the long, slow Atlantic crossing tugged at her heart in a new and troubling way. It had been harder to leave *Evangelina* than any job, any country, any journey she could remember.

'You do not have to go, Maggie,' Captain Lopez had said, his brown eyes sorrowful. They were together in a harbour-front bar in the confused days before their farewell. 'You can sail on with us. Chief cook, real pay. We go to Cádiz and the Canarias.'

But of course she had said no. She had gone, because going was what she did best. The day after that last drink she was off aboard the cheese lorry in the dawn. *Adiós*.

When she had organised her few possessions to her satisfaction, Maggie locked up her sister's house and set off, towards her mother's. It was never her favourite part of a homecoming, but it had to be done. She left the notebook, though, tucked carefully into the front pocket of her pack. It was not yet time to relegate it to the hamper of history.

'My aunt,' said Teddy impressively to his cronies at break, 'has come home from the Americas.'

'Whatchoo mean, Americas?' said Colin Byfleet derisively. ''S' only one America, right?'

'Wouldn't be room for two,' said Adrian, who regarded himself as something of a wag. 'It'd fill up half the ocean.'

'That's stupid,' said Joanne from behind Adrian's ear. She was a stout, confident and clever child who had known Colin and Teddy since play-group and had not yet learned that in secondary school a girl did well to retreat to the company of her own gender; at least for a couple of years, while everyone sorted out the troubling mystery of their identity. She did not see why they should be so sniffy with her now. She elaborated on her point.

'There's North America and there's South America. And Central America, like Mexico. So Ted's right, OK? You *can* say the Americas.'

Teddy, with breathtaking ingratitude, switched sides to line up with the boys. 'Yeah,' he said. 'But nobody ever does, really. Just people like my aunt. She doesn't live in England much. She brought us sugar skulls from Mexico.'

'Eugh! Gross! Did she bring you anything else?'

'No,' said Teddy. 'She's only got a rucksack. She goes all round the world with just that, in canoes, and on a bike, and hitching, and dangerous Russian planes and stuff.'

Little Joanne hovered, agonised. She was torn between a wish to walk away from these scornful boys to prove she didn't care, and a need to know more about this captivating new model of adult female life. Already at eleven she felt a pressing need to explore more options in life.

She blurted out, 'Does she have a job? Is she, like, a journalist?'

'Doesn't have one,' said Teddy uncertainly. 'But she does all sorts of jobs for a bit, then stops and goes somewhere else. She was a cook on a sailing ship.'

As he said it, the enormity of his aunt's way of life abruptly struck him in turn, and he fell silent. His aunt, his mother's sister, had no house or job. Just a rucksack. Yet she seemed perfectly content and cheerful; indeed, rather more so than most of the grown-ups around him who led proper grown-up lives.

Colin Byfleet broke into his thoughts. 'On a *ship*! Like, with sails?'

'Yep,' said the proud nephew. 'She went up the mast a lot.'

'I'm going on the Tall Ships Race when I'm fifteen, like my cousin did,' announced Colin. 'We saw them at Southampton.'

'I'm prob'ly going when I'm *fourteen*,' said Teddy.

'Can't. S'not allowed.'

'Might be for me. My aunt could fix it.'

'Dickhead.'

The boys began to scuffle. Eventually a football, strayed from a game across the playground, bounced between them and set them running and kicking until the bell went.

A FREE WOMAN

Samantha was, thought her geography teacher, unusually quiet. It was a big class, and not all of the pupils even in her GCSE set were truly individuals to Mrs Ellerman; but she had taught Samantha Penn for two years at primary school, and this earlier acquaintance gave her a fair sense of the girl's hinterland.

Until this term the child had been consistent, careful, and apparently interested. The staffroom saw her as one of the brighter hopes for the exam season. She was no trouble, gave no cheek, and had a real flair for some of her subjects, notably history. Yet two weeks ago Mrs Ellerman had found herself remarking tentatively to the head of Year 11, 'Sam Penn's very quiet. I think there might be something going on there.'

Nobody else had picked it up, but now the teacher's unease sharpened into real concern. From the dark head, a single tear could be seen to fall on the photocopied map which she had just told the class to study. She frowned, uncertain what to do. While she stood thinking about it, her eye travelled automatically to the back of the classroom where the bad boys sat. There they were, the awful triumvirate of Andy, Duane and Paulie, hulking in a sullen row. As she watched, Andy nudged Duane in the ribs, jerking his head forward. Duane's thick mouth formed into an unappealing sneer, and with the elbow and arm which rested on his desk he achieved an almost imperceptible but unmistakably obscene gesture. The other boys sniggered.

When Mrs Ellerman followed the gesture's direction, she found without much surprise that it was aimed at Samantha Penn's back.

'I went to the Internet café,' said Maggie at suppertime. 'On the way back from Mum's.'

'How was Mum?' asked Sarah, clattering plates. 'I haven't seen her for weeks, I'm ashamed to say.'

'Fine. The same. Older. Fussy. Officially glad to greet roving child, but telly nonetheless kept permanently on,' said Maggie. 'Anyway, I went to that Internet café that's opened, and did a surf. Guess where they're doing external courses in Mandarin?'

'Pass.' Sarah began ladling the cauliflower cheese onto the six plates.

'Southwick Community College! They got a grant for it, from the Ethnic Diversity Board or something.'

Sarah said nothing. The boys listened, interested. Samantha was still up in her room, despite having been called three times.

'You'll have missed part of the first term,' said Leo, accepting his supper. 'You'd have trouble catching up.'

'Only missed two weeks,' said Maggie. 'There are still places. It's a one-year course but the summer term is mostly placements in China, which I don't need. So I booked in. It's amazingly cheap.'

'Where are you going to live?' said Leo.

Sarah cut in smoothly. 'You'll stay with us for the winter, then? That'll be lovely!'

She had finished filling the plates now and, avoiding her husband's eye, made a great show of looking around for her daughter. She began a maternal shout towards the stairwell, '*Saaam!*' but stopped when she heard the front door slamming. Quick on her feet, she was out of the house in time to catch Samantha on the path.

'And where do you think you're going?'

'Out,' said the girl economically.

'It's suppertime!' her mother remonstrated.

'Not hungry. Feel sick.'

'Where are you going?' demanded Sarah.

'Nadine's. We're working on a project, all right?'

Sarah returned to the house, her step heavy. Leo said in a low, angry voice, 'I wish you wouldn't let her just roam around on her own. She's only fifteen.'

'She's got to have her freedom. I remember what it was like at that age, and how we hated Mum fussing. We have to keep lines of communication open, and you don't do that by confrontation.'

Recognising again the voice of the self-help family book, Leo gave an angry, hissing sigh. 'And I bet she's gone to meet that boy—'

'She's gone to Nadine's.'

'Huh!'

In the diversion of the argument, the issue of Maggie's staying all winter was forgotten; or rather, went by default. By the end of supper it seemed generally accepted that the guest room was, for the duration of her studies, 'Auntie Maggie's room'. It was only when Sarah had gone upstairs to help Jamie with his maths that Maggie said to her brother-in-law, 'Leo, I won't stay if I'm in the way. It's a bit steep to expect you to put up with a lodger.'

'You hardly count as a lodger,' said Leo politely, but without warmth.

'Yes, I do. What's the proverb? Guests and fish stink on the third day. If I do stay, I am going to pay board and lodging. I'll be getting a part-time job, obviously.'

'As you wish,' said Leo. 'But Sarah's delighted. We all are.'

His welcome rang hollowly on the air.

Samantha dug her hands deep in the pockets of her jacket and hunched her thin shoulders against the cutting autumn wind. It was a wild night, and growing dark. In the High Street, a knot of boys lounged outside the Wimpy Bar, among them a silhouette she knew very well. She walked towards them, tentative but defiant.

Andy Moss greeted her first. 'Duane—it's your ho'!'

The others joined in.

'Gi's a blow job, darlin'!'

'Hot bitch!'

She ignored them. 'Duane, I want to talk to you about something.' Her voice had tightened with tension, and slid treacherously up the social scale from the normal slouchy, classless patois of the school day. The three boys mimicked her with glee, while Duane stayed silent.

'*Ay wawnt to talk to yew abeyout some-theeng,*' they jeered. 'Oh, oh, oh. Orf to Benenden in the maw-ning, are we?'

'Duane,' said Samantha, squeaky and breathy now. '*Pleeeease.*'

The boys erupted in obscene babble.

'She wants you, man!'

'Man, do we get a share? She've got plenty for everyone!'

Samantha instinctively backed away from them. 'Come on!' she said again, with diminishing hope. Duane looked uneasy. Then one of his companions played into Samantha's hands by taunting the boy.

'You shagged out already, man? No stamina.'

'Fuck off!' said Duane, but moved towards Samantha and roughly took her hand, half dragging her away from his friends. When they were out of sight, however, he dropped her hand and said ungraciously, 'You wannna make me look stupid, or what?'

'I wanted to talk to you,' said Samantha. Her voice was shaking now. 'It's two weeks now you've been avoiding me. Why've you gone horrible? What've I done wrong, anyway?'

He looked her up and down, and lust stirred mindless within him. He took her arm, not gently.

'Le's go to the railway hut, then.'

'No, it's cold,' said Samantha. She pulled her arm away; it felt bruised. 'I didn't mean that. Let's get a coffee.'

'Oh, fuckit!' said the boy angrily. 'Teaser! You winding me up? Serve you right if I call the boys over. Give them all a go.'

'That's a horrible thing to say,' said Samantha, fighting back tears. 'Just because I, just because we—'

'Slag!' said Duane. 'Posh slag!' With a lightning twist and stab he slammed an open hand between her legs, as if to force his fingers inside her. She wrenched his arm aside and with a sob she turned and fled.

'And where have you been, young lady?' asked her mother angrily when the child arrived, trembling, inside her own front door. 'I rang Nadine, and you certainly weren't there.'

'Decided to go for a walk,' said Samantha with all the surly confidence she could muster. 'Do the project tomorrow. It's only half past nine.' Sarah's face made her momentarily hesitate, but the sound of Leo's laughter from the sitting room hardened the girl again. She wasn't fooled by all that tolerant stuff. They both thought she'd been stupid to go near Duane. And now he and his friends mocked her as well. Samantha summoned all her hauteur. 'I got homework. G'night.'

When Maggie went upstairs to fetch something from her rucksack, she heard sobbing from the room next door to hers. Without a moment's hesitation she walked in on her niece without knocking.

'Hello,' she said.

Samantha was face down on the narrow bed. Her aunt sat down by her feet, and regarded them gravely.

'Throw me out if you like,' she said conversationally, 'but are you sure that this Duane bloke is worth all the trouble?'

There was a snort, then a just audible, 'No. He's an arsehole. I thought he was really nice, different, but nice. But he's just as horrible as all his mates.'

'So dump him.'

Samantha twisted over and sat up. She sniffed. 'Yeah, but I already . . .'

'You already had sex,' said Maggie, unruffled. 'I guessed.'

'Do you think Mum . . .' The girl was horrified now.

'Nope. Hasn't a clue. It takes a bad girl like me to spot something like that. Promise.'

Samantha looked carefully at her aunt, and decided after a moment to trust her. She rolled onto one elbow, dragged a tissue from the box on her bedside table, and blew her nose.

'So what's the main problem?' Maggie prompted.

Samantha stared at her in amazement. 'Well, how can I dump him?'

'Oh, come on!' said Maggie. 'It wasn't that good, surely?'

'It was *horrible*.' There was savage relief in her tone as she admitted it even to herself. 'He said it would get better, but *six times*, and it didn't at all. Then he tells all his mates, and they tell the girls, and half the school starts giggling about me, and my friends give me funny looks, like they're thinking "gross". And then tonight he says . . .'

She stopped, close to tears, and Maggie saw how thin and drawn her face had become. She laid a hand on the girl's ankle and said, 'There's nothing special about being a virgin, you know. One minute you are, one minute you aren't, so what? You're still you. It's just an incident. Good if it's a good incident, but if it isn't, you move on. Think of it as a seriously bad kebab.'

Samantha sniffed, childish again. Then morosely she said, 'I wish I didn't have to go back to school.'

'Well, you do,' said Maggie. 'But you can always leave and go to Southwick College for A levels, can't you? It's a big world, Sammy. It's all out there waiting for you. Stuff Duane.'

'He'll tell people I'm no good at it,' said the child mournfully.

'So? Tell them he's even worse. Blokes are more scared of that than girls, trust me.'

'His mates call me a whore and a slag and stuff.'

'So call them dickheads! Sticks and stones may break my bones, but names will never hurt me.'

'Oh, Maggie!' said Samantha, who had decided she was too old to give her the title of Auntie. 'I'm glad you're here. I couldn't talk to Mum about it. I'd die.'

'You should,' murmured Maggie dutifully. 'She'd be broad-minded, you know.'

'But I can't,' said Samantha firmly. 'Apart from everything else, she'd tell Dad. Then I *would* die. Oh shit, that's her coming.'

By the time Sarah poked her head round the door for a conciliatory word with her daughter, Maggie was nowhere in sight. She had swung her long legs out of the window and eased herself down the drainpipe onto the wheelie bin. She hesitated by the back door, then decided to take a walk round the town.

As she passed the Wimpy Bar she looked speculatively at a knot of scruffy, big-booted louts, who hunched around emitting occasional shouts of 'Oy oy!' and 'Wooor!' She shook her head and smiled, but then the smile faded.

The small, sniffing voice came back to her. '*He said it would get better, but six times....*' Maggie found herself hoping, very much, that the ring-nosed sexist pig had taken every precaution in the book. She was fairly certain that her niece would not have. Looked too skinny to be on the pill, for one thing.

'Hell,' she said aloud into the dimmed window of Woolworth's. 'I really am turning into my mother now, aren't I?'

Chapter Three

AUTUMN WORE ON, under damp leaden skies. Maggie lived with the Penns but in a parallel world. Her energies flowed from a different source to theirs. Sometimes Sarah thought that it was like having an older teenager in the house and had to remind herself that there were barely five years between them.

She seemed to feel none of the plodding weariness that was the defining quality of Sarah and Leo's lives. They sank into their routines as into a feather bed, watched the news together, desultorily discussed their day, read a chapter of their books at bedtime and turned the light out early. Maggie, on the other hand, could barely watch television for five minutes without growing bored. When she started a book she became engrossed, and read for most of the night; or else threw it aside and plunged into a game of table football or Snap with the boys.

She rose at dark, incredible hours of the morning to go loping through the town and round the park. Back home for breakfast she teased the children, and then changed rapidly to catch the bus to Southwick. By midafternoon she was back in town for a three-hour shift chopping vegetables and laying tables at the Blue Lady Restaurant, then she brought her books home and sprawled on her bed, making notes and practising her Chinese intonations with strange chiming cries which, inevitably, drew Teddy to sit on the end of her bed copying her.

In the evenings she either worked relief bar shifts at the Black Lion or went out in search of music. Almost any music would do; she made friends with a teenage rock band who practised in the Black Lion at weekends, and even persuaded Leo—once—to join her and Sarah at a folk pub in Southwick. Maggie herself led a set on tin whistle and mouth organ, neither of which her sister had known she could play.

On Saturdays she went back to the Blue Lady to serve lunches. It seemed incredible to Sarah and Leo that the pay she got for twenty hours at the café and a few at the pub somehow stretched to cover her bus fares, lunches, occasional cinemas and the fifty pounds a week which she insisted on paying for her keep. But then, they had to admit that Maggie's only luxury was melons—'Can't live without them. God knows what I'll do in the Taklimakan Desert.' Her clothes never cost more than fifty pence at the charity shop, and in any case Sarah had given her two pairs of jeans and some white shirts which no longer fitted her plumper frame.

'I'm really fine,' said Maggie one Saturday night when Sarah as usual disputed the need for the fifty pounds. 'It's years since I earned so much hard currency. I'm actually saving.'

'But you ought to have real savings,' protested Sarah. 'At least let me invest your rent money for you.'

'If you do, I shall go and live with Mum,' said Maggie threateningly. 'And if I do that there will be bloodshed, sooner rather than later. Look, Sare, Leo doesn't much like me being here. The least I can do is pay for my food.'

'He *loves* you being here. We all do,' said Sarah stoutly.

'Leo—well, never mind,' said Maggie. 'Anyway, you keep the damn money.'

'All right,' said Sarah, folding it into her purse. 'I'll put it in the account with the child benefit. It's their university fund. OK?'

'Fine.'

Samantha, after the first burst of confidence, withdrew slightly from Maggie, who in turn decided not to intrude by asking for bulletins on the Duane situation. The boys just artlessly revelled in their aunt. She read their bedside books voraciously, discussing Harry Potter plots with as much impassioned argument as they did. She listened to their music, she taught Jamie to play the harmonica. She passed on what she learned day by day at Southwick College.

The boys were enthralled. At school, Teddy developed quite a following for his tales of the eccentric house guest. 'My aunt says,' he informed a knot of respectful Year 7 listeners in the playground, 'that if you want to speak Chinese right, you have to watch Chinese people, when they say words. You have to stand like a Chinese, and put your neck like a Chinese, because it's like singing. You have to get the note right. *Aha-ching-wa!*'

'You look more like sunnink in *Star Trek*,' said Adrian witheringly. 'So who's she going to talk Chinese to, then?'

'She's going there in the summer. To the *borders*,' said Teddy with an insouciant air. 'I will probably go with her.'

'You won't,' said Joanne, who was still hanging around the boys, despite their lack of interest. With all her heart she wished to know the Penns' marvellous Aunt Maggie. 'She won't take a stoopid little boy along. She's a free spirit. I heard your mum say that to Miss March.'

Teddy rose to the barb, as she had intended, and turned to glare at the square, dark, stubborn child.

'She *is* taking me, so. That's why I have to learn Chinese too. *Ahha! Ching chaa cheng!*'

'That is *so* not real Chinese,' said Joanne. 'Will you tell us again the story about the snake in the wall?'

Teddy could not resist this, and nor could the others.

Nor, indeed, could Jamie, who at that very moment was telling it at the other end of the playground to his gruffer-voiced peers. Of the three children, the only one who did not talk much about the exotic aunt was Samantha. But then, she did not talk to anybody very much in that autumn term.

Down at the bookshop, meanwhile, Leo was being confronted by Miss Mountjoy. She was sixty-nine now, and he supposed that he should have been expecting her retirement. All the same, it came as a shock.

During the first few turbulent months in his employ she had spiritedly handed in her notice several times over the content of modern novels on the shelves. After a while, however, she had reached a personal accommodation with the spirit of the age. Instead of refusing any contact with the more distressing works, she resolved to intercede with heaven for their authors.

'I am *praying* for Will Self,' she would say serenely. 'I made a special intention for him this morning at Communion. I have also prayed for Mr Jeffrey Archer since his tribulation.' She made a whole novena once, before the statue of the Virgin in her favoured High Anglican church, for immodest young female novelists.

Leo soon found that provided he listened with apparent respect to her bulletins on the relationship between prayer and modern literature, she would work on, contentedly and efficiently, for the very modest salary the bookshop was able to pay her. She had been doing accounts all her life, and made an impressive transition from handwriting to the computer ('I have prayed about these unmapped memory exemptions, and I think I have found Guidance'). She was capable of surprising firmness, even asperity, with the credit controllers of publishing houses when they rang up trying to chase their money days before it was due. 'I don't think Mr Penn has ever defaulted, and nor would he. We are rather busy here. Good morning.' Her brisk, unbending, kindly presence had steadied him through bad Christmases, panic shortages of hot titles and disastrous misjudgments which left his shelves full of dross.

And now here she was, resigning. He stared at her angular, honest old face in dismay.

'I have not decided this lightly, Mr Penn,' she said. 'It is time that I retired. My friend Louise is not well, and needs more daily help than the council will give her. My duty is plain.'

'Oh dear,' said Leo. 'I hardly know how I shall cope.'

'Would you like me to pray about a successor?' asked Miss Mountjoy.

'That would be kind,' said Leo. 'But when must you go?'

'On the 8th of December, which is a Saturday. This gives you more than a month, although I am, as you know, weekly paid. I hope that is satisfactory?'

So with less than a month to Christmas, Leo's permanent staff of one would leave him. Hot books would be flowing in, reorders would become critical for the season's important titles, customers would be rushed and impatient. He swallowed. But it was, he knew quite well, useless to argue with her.

'Well, thank you for the generous period of notice. I know it hasn't been as highly paid a post as your talents deserve, but—'

'Heavens, Mr Penn,' said Miss Mountjoy. 'It has been a privilege to plough this furrow with you.' She smiled graciously, and returned to check a delivery of pictorial biographies of the Queen Mother. Leo watched her with real affection, glad that on this momentous day she had a box to open which could give her only pleasure.

That night, he told Sarah. 'I don't know what to do really. I can't believe I'll get anybody for what I've paid her. Not anybody I can leave in sole charge. And the shop won't stand much of a hike in the payroll.' He poured the dregs of a bottle of wine into his glass. 'God, what a nightmare.' He looked across the glass at Sarah, suddenly foxy.

'I don't suppose you . . .?'

'No,' said his wife firmly. The question had occasionally arisen of her giving up the job with the vet Sam Miller and working in the bookshop, making it a true family business. Sarah always refused. She had a deep, warning sense that if she agreed she would compromise her freedom more gravely than either of them understood. In the shop Leo would always be the boss. They would spend all day together, every day. The business would inevitably come home and be discussed between them over the family table. There would be no place of refuge. She tried to explain these things to him, but her refusal remained a bleak grey area between them.

'Leo, it would be awful.' she said now. 'I would be bad at it, and get things wrong, and you would get annoyed with me, and then how do you sack your own wife?'

Samantha had recently said much the same when he asked her to be a Saturday morning assistant.

Leo sighed. He felt a great deal of bitterness over this. The bookshop paid the family's way, for God's sake, yet none of them seemed to care about it. All he said, though, was, 'All right. I'll look around.'

'God,' said Sarah, looking out of the window into the night. 'It's raining again. That's four days now it's hardly stopped.'

Maggie's morning runs took her up to the top of the town, along a bare track round the park, then down alongside the slow-moving River Brack and over the bridge to rejoin the High Street.

She had always loved rivers, although this one, in its concrete gutter, was unattractive. In the first days of a rainy October she noted with pleased interest that it was taking on a livelier aspect than usual: rising higher, moving faster; the high winds even whipped up some tiny wavelets. Maggie's life had made her into an observant stranger in all lands. Besides, she had once been a geographer. After a few mornings of running beside the newly extrovert river, she began to take a different route to survey its relationship with the town, hopping on parapets and squinting along sight lines before heading home for breakfast. One morning, she said to her sister and brother-in-law, 'Do you have an Ordnance Survey map with the town on it? With contour lines?'

'Somewhere,' said Sarah vaguely. 'Sammy, weren't you doing a project last year?'

Samantha looked up from the plate on which she was crumbling toast. 'Dunno,' she said.

'Of course you know, young lady. Answer your mother's quite reasonable question,' said Leo, who was riffling through the coat pegs in the kitchen lobby in search of something more waterproof than his usual tweed. 'Coat, coat, coat . . . oh, I am sick of this rain.'

'That's why I want the map, really,' said Maggie. 'I want to look at the flood profile.'

'Miss Mountjoy says there hasn't been a flood in Brackhampton since the war,' said Leo. 'They built up the town embankment pretty well, according to the locals.'

'Mmm,' said his sister-in-law, taking her plate to the sink. 'But suppose it broke through further upstream than the town. In the park,
where there's just that sort of concrete V-section, and then grass. I
reckon Abelard Street is a kind of gully. A natural conduit.'

Leo frowned. 'What do you mean, if it broke through in the park?
Near the oaks?'

'Yup.'

'It'd soak into the grass, surely.'

'Only the first inch or so. It's clay soil, I tested it.'

Sarah, quietly wiping the worktop, ignored the subject matter but
registered pleasure in the fact that Leo and Maggie were having a co-
operative conversation, neither spiky nor unnaturally polite. This was a
novelty. Although the slight chill of their relationship was casually camouflaged by the noisy flow of family life, there had been some uneasy
moments in the past month. Once or twice she had thought the pair
seemed almost overtly hostile. She was not sure that Leo had forgiven
Maggie for causing the loss of his spare-room office.

At a further goad from her father about the map, Samantha heaved
herself up from the table and said ungraciously, 'Prob'ly in the geo file
from last year. Hangon. Gettit.' She vanished.

Maggie was moving things round on the kitchen table now, building
a street out of butter dish and milk bottle and flowing the river down it
with her finger.

'So if it broke through *here*, see, there's nothing to stop it creating a
quite deep stream along that sort of trench that the path runs in, right to
the bottom of Abelard Street. And there are slopes either side, and terraced houses. So everyone's looking at the main river and thinking it's
fine because the embankment is nice and high, when sloosh! Up comes
the floodwater from behind.'

'You seem very expert at all this,' said Leo.

'Seen it happen. Floods don't always come from where everyone
thinks. The lie of the land gets camouflaged by familiar buildings.'

'Where'd you see it?'

'Guatemala.'

Leo snorted. 'Yes, but it didn't happen here in 1953, or that other
time in the '70s. If the river broke out there—' he tapped the milk
bottle—'it would just soak away in the meadows. Even if it lay, it would
just lie in the park. It's happened once or twice; I remember people skat-
ing on it in the really cold winters in the '80s.'

'Yes, but look—' She broke off. Samantha had brought the map in and slapped it down on the table. Maggie pushed aside her makeshift objects and spread the map flat.

'Look. It can't soak away there now because there's the new estate with the embankment and the wall to protect it. It can't go *that* way, because there's the bypass embankment. Neither of those lumps of concrete was there in 1953. Or even when I left, in the '80s. I reckon the new development has created a lovely alternative riverbed, just waiting to be used by any spare water.'

'Only with incredible rainfall all the way upriver,' said Leo. 'And the council have allowed for that. This isn't Mozambique.'

'Hmm,' said Maggie. 'That's probably what they said in Guatemala.'

That afternoon, when she had finished at the Blue Lady, she walked down in the rain to the bookshop and stood outside it, looking carefully up the street in each direction. She squatted down to peer through a wall-grating by her feet and frowned, then with swift strides walked to the bridge and the brown river.

She stared for a while at the bridge at the point where water met air. When she had first come home, that line had been as she remembered it, green with river ooze. Today the water lapped against clean, mellow red brick: brick more used to sunlight than to slime and darkness. The dark arches were shallower too, thin slivers of space rather than the mysterious glinting tunnels she remembered.

It was eight o'clock when she reached the house; the rain still fell in great sheets, turning her black hair to rat-tails. The seams of her thin plastic jacket had leaked, leaving stripes of soaked darkness over her shoulders.

'Look at you!' said Sarah. 'Get changed, supper's nearly ready.'

'Where's Leo?' asked Maggie. 'Only it's urgent. The shop.'

'Oh, *not* a break-in!' said Sarah agitatedly. There had been a spate of minor but irritating High Street vandalism.

'No, not a break-in,' reassured Maggie. 'But it could be worse. Leo—' he had appeared in the doorway—'I'm really sorry, but the flooding, I think it could be tonight. I seriously do. Your shop is at one of the lowest points of the High Street. And if water did come down Abelard Street it would get into your basement. At least.'

'There haven't been any warnings for Brackhampton,' said Leo, for it had been a season of flood warnings. 'The Brack isn't a big river, like the Medway or the Ouse. We aren't even on the list.'

'Fuck the list!' said Maggie roughly. 'Lists just make everyone else feel smug. Leo. Listen. Please. What is in your shop basement? What?'

'Books,' said Leo. 'It's a bookshop. Stock.'

'Insured to full value? Including labour for clearing out the pulp, loss of profits, all that stuff?'

'Ummm . . . there's an excess,' said Leo, wavering. He thought for a moment. 'And I did agree to a cap on the profit compensation so it doesn't include fluctuations like Christmas.'

Maggie said sharply, 'Kiss your excess goodbye, then. Either that, or let's all get down there and shift stuff up higher. Truly. I mean it.'

Leo hesitated, then glanced at his wife.

Sarah said, 'Might as well check anyway. See if there's any sign of trouble. Supper can wait ten minutes.'

'There won't *be* any sign,' said Maggie. 'It'll be really quick when it happens. And we'll need everybody. And for more than ten minutes.'

Samantha was summoned from her bedroom and the boys from the television, and in the pelting rain the family skittered to Brackhampton Books. Leo unlocked the shop.

'Come on then.'

There was a steep flight of wooden steps to the stockroom. With Sarah at the bottom, pulling boxes from shelves, they made a human chain: Sarah passed her load to Samantha on the first step, Samantha gave it to Maggie, who twisted and reached with strong, agile movements on the precarious middle step, passing boxes up to Jamie on the top one, hence to Teddy struggling manfully to and fro across the main floor, finally to Leo. After a moment's hesitation, he had constructed a plinth of upended plastic milk crates in the middle of the shop, and on this he began building a tower of cardboard boxes. When it was too high for further progress, he began carrying boxes up the few steps to the children's department, and stacking them there.

'God knows what Miss Mountjoy will say,' he said. But there was an edge of enjoyment in his voice. The children caught it, and began singing catches from *Noye's Fludde*, which the school choir had done last year, and then 'One More River'. Sarah, down in the basement, heard the note of buzzing cheerfulness above her and smiled. It was an absurd manoeuvre, probably unnecessary, but it had created a Blitz spirit among the family and for that she was grateful. Even Samantha's clear soprano, unheard (she now realised) for many months, rose joyfully above the rest as she sang, 'Oh, River! Keep 'way from ma door!'

'Can we have supper now?' said Teddy, tiring. 'I've got homework.'

'I'll walk you back and get it hotted up,' said Sarah comfortingly, emerging from the trap door. 'Come on, Jamie, Samantha. Job done, I think.'

'Shall Leo and I follow on?' asked her sister. 'We might as well finish the job.'

'If Brackhampton is not visited by flood tonight,' said the bookseller, 'I am going to look bloody silly in the morning.'

'We can make the shop look OK,' said Maggie. 'You don't use the tops of the bookcases, we can move all this low stuff up there.'

'Right . . . oh God, sheep as a lamb and all that. Ten minutes, Sarah, and we'll be up.'

They worked in silence. After a while Maggie grew uncomfortable with the silence and said, 'Leo, if it doesn't happen, it doesn't. You can blame me for all this. I'll round up some volunteers from college to put it all back if you like.'

'No,' he said. 'I am truly grateful. For you thinking of the shop. You took trouble.' He smiled. It lit his face, and eased her mind.

'It's just that I've seen floods,' she said more conversationally. 'They're horrible even in simple countries, and here . . . well, you do always get the sewage thing. The drains overflow.'

'You're right. It'd be horrible, especially with all this paper. The damp. Makes you wish you sold something a bit more robust.'

'Like, um, ironmongery?'

'That'd go rusty,' said Leo.

'Well, rubber goods. Beach toys. Inflatable women . . .'

They began to laugh, easy now and comradely. Leo went round the shop checking windows, then turned off the spotlights and made his way to the door in the dim security lighting. As he reached it Maggie, who had pushed it open, abruptly froze.

'Sh!' she said. 'Listen.'

It was the smell that Leo caught first: a dank, graveyard, drainpipe breath. It was a moment or two before his ear caught the stealthy lapping. 'Flaming Norah!' he said fervently. 'You were *right* . . .'

It was only a shallow current, not high enough to mount the pavement. But as their eyes grew accustomed to the dimness they saw that it was flowing, down from Abelard Street and towards the row of shops where they stood. As they watched, a fat gout of water broke over the pavement's edge and joined the slick of rainwater already weeping over the flagstones. Another came from further along and joined it. Leo watched with fascinated horror as the main water level rose unhurriedly over the pavement. Then his eyes widened at the unmistakable sound as water poured down the ventilator into the basement beneath them.

'Christ, half an hour back . . .' he said with horror.

'I didn't really think it would be tonight,' said Maggie in a faint voice. 'To be honest, I thought it would take two days to talk you into it, so I just thought I'd make a start with the propaganda campaign. Jee-sus!'

They peered down the trap door, shining the shop torch onto the water. 'Almost knee-deep down there already,' said Leo. 'What's the physics of this? Does it come up under us and through the floor?'

'It finds its own level,' said Maggie. 'I reckon it won't quite reach the basement ceiling, unless it comes up much higher outside.'

'Is it going to come over the doorstep?'

'Yes. Probably. Got any sandbags?'

'Of course I haven't got any sandbags!' said Leo. 'Until this morning not one living soul had, to my knowledge, predicted that the River Brack would bloody creep up from behind and flood Brackhampton.' He turned to her. 'What are you, psychic or something?'

'The stranger's eye,' said Maggie. 'It's a well-documented phenomenon. People don't expect disrupting things to happen among familiar buildings. We all close down our primitive fear mechanisms most of the time. You have to. Otherwise you'd never drive, or go in a plane.'

There was a silence while they watched the first trickle of water pushing its way through the cracks round the doorframe. Then, 'Oh God, my floor!' said Leo helplessly. 'It'll be wrecked.'

'Veneer strips, laid on concrete?' said Maggie.

'Yes, blast you. I like to think it looks real.'

'Well, concrete dries faster. Better than if it was planks. This stuff'll curl up and die, and you can just lay it again in a fortnight. Look.' Maggie laid a hand on Leo's shoulder. He had begun to shiver, shocked. 'You go home, tell Sarah what's happening, bring us a Thermos of soup. I've had an idea that might help with this sill.'

'Will you be safe?'

'Never happier!' said Maggie, with a grin.

And indeed, she was suddenly happy. Although she did not show it, the weeks in Brackhampton had been oppressing her. Arriving from the *Evangelina*, she had reasoned with herself that it could be no worse staying in England for a few months than staying anywhere else. Although more than anything she loved to be on the road from day to day, her travels had often kept her in one country for a year or more. But she had not reckoned with the steady deadness of Brackhampton or the autumn darkness of British skies. Although she dearly loved Sarah and enjoyed her nephews and niece, the town itself possessed a quite unexpected ability to get her down. She had fought the feeling; the purpose of the morning runs was as much to preserve her optimism as to keep up her traveller's fitness. Yet it was harder with each passing day; on recent mornings Maggie had been waking up as reluctant as any of them to get out of her warm bed.

But this crisis brought the surge of joy in action which had marked most of her adult life. She stood looking down at the seeping water, then ran over to the open trap door. She climbed down into the basement, ignoring the cold water welling round her knees, and waded to the corner under the grating. She bent, plunging arms and shoulders into the flood, grasped something, then straightened up. In her hands was what she had been looking for: a solid laminated board, the base of a discarded set of shelves. She let it float alongside her while she groped again and wrenched out two more planks. The shelving was only slotted together; now that she had removed the first piece, the remains came away easily.

Dripping, she took the three best boards up the ladder with her, closed the trap, went to the sales desk and pulled out the lowest filing drawer. To her delight there was a hammer and some tacks. The tacks were too short for her purpose but the hammer had a claw, with which she swiftly drew nails out from the skirting board in the children's section. Before more than a few pints of water had found its way into the ground floor of the shop, she had nailed the boards securely across the bottom of the doorway and reduced the flow to a trickle.

Straightening up, she looked around. 'Sandbags,' she said. 'What do sandbags actually do? They absorb water. They shape themselves to where they are. Hmmm . . .' Forgotten in the haste were the copies of the pictorial tome on the Queen Mother, which Miss Mountjoy had been unpacking. The first of the water had ruined them.

'OK, Queen Mum! Time to save the nation!' Grinning, Maggie began to stack them behind her barricade of boards, sometimes pulling out handfuls of pages to stuff tightly into cracks. Outside, in the darkness, the water rose. It pushed against her planks and their backing of glossy monarchism, gave up, and turned to swirl on down the street towards the Blue Lady and the Wimpy Bar. Maggie found the cleaning cupboard, pulled out some cloths and a mop.

By the time Leo got back with the soup, almost tripping over the barricade in his confusion, his ground floor was dry and his sister-in-law posing in comedic triumph, leaning on her mop.

It was a famous autumn for floods, a season of deluge all across England. Night after night the rescue helicopters and the news photographers hovered over towns and villages that had turned to vast brown lakes with islets of red brick and slate, and the television news showed streets that were canals. From Yorkshire to Kent, haggard householders waded helpless through a stinking sea of wrecked possessions.

The Brackhampton flood, everybody agreed, was slight in comparison. The Brack never burst its embankment in the town centre, despite two anxious nights when citizens stayed up to watch it. The floodwater, in the event, only made one major incursion into the town and that was just deep enough to affect a dozen houses, and the lowest shops of the High Street. The next belt of rain dealt lightly with them, and the waters subsided rapidly.

Maggie's shop-door barricade held good through the worst two days, reinforced with extra nails and the five old pillowcases which Sarah filled with builder's sand. The flood defence was, the children agreed, a 'wicked' feat of instant civil engineering on the part of their aunt.

It also cost Maggie her jobs at the Blue Lady and the Black Lion.

When Maggie arrived at her usual shift time, the Blue Lady, four doors along from the bookshop, was still an inch deep in foul water. The kitchen would be unusable for months, the flooring and much plaster in the restaurant would have to be replaced.

Mrs Pritt said sourly, 'I gather you warned your brother-in-law about this flood. Family first, I suppose.'

'It wasn't that,' said Maggie. 'I wasn't sure. I just thought that his basement might flood, and it was full of books.'

'Well,' Marion Pritt said. 'I'm sure he'll be anxious to employ you, if only as a soothsayer. There's no work here, as you can see.'

'Can I at least help sort out the mess?' offered Maggie. 'Just as a volunteer, you understand.'

'No, thank you,' said Mrs Pritt. 'That won't be necessary.'

Two days later up at the Black Lion, which had merely had its garden flooded, the landlord, mildly embarrassed, told her that following the flooding in the town they were 'downscaling' the bar staff. Shortly, however, it was to be observed that an eighteen-year-old boy was working Maggie's shifts.

'Your sister's name,' said Leo to his wife in bed, 'appears to be mud in the town. People think it wasn't cricket for her only to warn me.'

'What could she have done?' demanded Sarah heatedly. 'Run through Brackhampton with a bell, shouting "Doom, doooom, prepare to meet your God"? Who'd have paid any attention? Really, it's terrible. Leo, I wondered . . .'

Leo turned off his light and rolled over, his back to Sarah. 'Yeah, so did I. You mean, p'raps I should see if she wants to work in the book-shop?' He made no attempt to look at his wife and gauge her reaction.

'Well, it's logical,' said Sarah slowly. She was still sitting up, causing a chilly draught to get beneath the duvet. 'She could only do afternoons, obviously. Till term ends. But it might help with the run-up to Christmas. Then you could get someone permanent later, when you've time to interview.'

'Mmm,' said Leo. 'Lie down, you're making me cold. Love you. G'night.'

You don't have to employ me,' said Maggie, astonished, when Leo made the suggestion at breakfast time. 'I can get pub or café work in Southwick easily. There's never a shortage of jobs.'

'There's people on the dole,' said Jamie, who had taken to frowning his way through the newspapers. 'You know, unemployment. We did it in Citizenship with Mr Glover. Mum, where's my games kit?'

'You're right about the unemployment thing, I suppose,' said his aunt. 'But what that probably means is there aren't enough proper decent jobs for people who've got families and houses to keep up. There are always jobs for casuals, and students, and underpaid bums like me.'

'You could do a proper job,' said Teddy. 'You could be a meeter-meety-meeteryologist. You could tell people about floods.'

'P'raps,' said Maggie. 'But I don't want to stay put and have a career. Never did. Take each day as it comes, I say.'

'It wouldn't suit everybody,' said Sarah, handing Jamie his sports bag. 'Come on, you'll be late. And don't you start thinking that the way your Auntie Maggie lives is easy, either. She works jolly hard, for not much money and no security whatsoever. That's the price of freedom.'

'God, you sound like Mum,' said her sister with kindly scorn. 'Sam, since the sun is at last shining, I'm going to get the bus from the top of town today. D'you want to walk up with me? Get some fresh air, ultra-violet light, all that good stuff?'

Leo was growing impatient. Somehow, between his question and any coherent answer from Maggie, the whole topic had been driven away by his family.

'So what do you think?' He tried to regain control: 'It'd be doing me a favour, not you. It was Sarah's idea. I can only pay pretty casual wages, but you wouldn't have to peel carrots.'

Maggie glanced at Sarah.

'Go on,' said Sarah encouragingly. 'Solve Leo's problem, solve your problem, and you can both rethink at New Year.'

'I'll walk with you,' said Samantha abruptly. 'Lemme just get my bag.'

'Oh, all right,' said Maggie to Leo. 'But I've never worked in a book-shop. Don't know anything about it.'

'Can read, can't you? How about today? Half past two?' said Leo. 'Miss Mountjoy can show you round.'

'Two, if you like. C'mon, Sam.' Samantha abandoned her uneaten toast and, schoolbag hanging from one hunched shoulder, began searching through the kitchen bowl of rubber bands and paperclips for something to tie back her barely brushed hair. Maggie, seeing her dilemma, yanked a green cloth scrunchie from her own hair and prof-fered it, silently.

'Bye, darling. Have a good day,' said Sarah to her daughter, brightly.

'Bye,' said Samantha, not brightly at all.

'Well, there you are then,' said Leo when they had gone. 'Christmas reasonably solved, anyway. She can work with Miss Mountjoy for a couple of weeks. Learn the ropes.'

'She'll be invaluable,' said Sarah. 'Perhaps . . .'

Leo threw her a sharp glance. He knew what she was thinking. Perhaps she'll settle down, get a little flat, stay in Brackhampton.

'Don't count your chickens,' he said with unaccustomed gentleness.

Chapter Four

MAGGIE AND SAMANTHA walked up the road together. Neither spoke until they had left the old town and were on the suburban street that led up to Brackhampton High School.

Then Maggie said casually, 'How's the work going?'

'Pants,' said Samantha briefly. Her aunt glanced sideways at her. Too thin, she thought, not wiry and actively thin but scrawny and pale.

'Yup, I remember the feeling,' she said. 'It gets better. After filthy GCSEs.' Then, her voice neutral, 'That's not the problem, though, is it?'

'You being nosy?' Samantha challenged. 'Like Mum?'

Maggie paused as if considering the charge. 'I was just—you know, concerned, because I like you. And I seem to remember that we did have a conversation once about your Duane . . .'

'He is NOT my Duane!' burst out Samantha. 'He is a stupid yob, he's just a little boy, he's disgusting—it's been weeks since we even spoke to each other.' There were tears in her eyes.

'Ha! So you did dump him, as I advised,' said Maggie. 'Well done. And are people being vile to you at school?'

'N-no,' said the girl, kicking a stone neatly off the pavement. 'Not nearly 'smuch as I expected. To be honest. Not many people like him any more 'cos he and his mates beat someone up quite badly by the Wimpy Bar and two of them got excluded, and Duane nearly did.'

Maggie noticed, in passing, that whereas her brothers always sounded much the same, Samantha's argot and accent were subject to quite violent changes. Once away from the gentility of home and the town centre, her manner dropped by several social classes. Aloud she merely said with studied lightness, 'Well, that's fine. They do like you, and they don't like him, so they'll be all right to you. So all's well. But you say it's not?'

Samantha stopped as if to turn to her aunt, but then changed her mind, speeded up, and fired the killer question at the beech hedge instead.

'I wanna know something. Do people, I mean women, always know, like, straight away, if they're, you know . . .'

Maggie's heart skipped and a horrible dread came on her. Since the night in Samantha's room she had tried not to allow herself to entertain this particular fear. With an effort, she said levelly, 'You mean, do women always know if they're pregnant?'

Hell! The girl was nodding, speechless, her dark hair falling from its elastic to hide her face.

'Well,' said Maggie. 'Things happen. Your periods stop.'

Samantha walked on, silent and alert. Every line of her thin body said, scornfully, *I know that.*

Into the emptiness the older woman continued, 'But lots of other things can stop your periods. Stress. Being too thin. Working too hard. That sort of thing. So it's not a sure sign.'

The girl grimaced. 'What other signs d'you get? I mean, like, without doing a test?'

The child should be asking her mother these things, thought Maggie in a panic. Sarah should cope with this. But she took a grip on herself.

'Oh, I don't know, feeling sick and not wanting coffee and things. Your mum always said, anyway. Look, it's best to do a test. There are kits. You buy them at the chemist.'

Samantha strode on, her thin back eloquent.

After a few paces Maggie asked tentatively, 'Do you want me to buy you a kit? From the chemist in Southwick, where nobody knows us?'

The dark head nodded. Of course, thought Maggie. How on earth could a schoolgirl buy a kit in Boots in Brackhampton High Street? A schoolgirl, moreover, who was the daughter of a leading citizen and shopkeeper? A wave of protective pity swept over her, and echoes of confused feelings from her own secretive adolescence. Poor bloody kid!

She said, as comfortingly as she knew how, 'Tonight, then. I'll go past the chemist near college.'

'Mum,' began the girl pleadingly, 'you won't tell Mum . . .'

'I won't tell her. But, Sam, look, if it turns out that you—'

'I'm not. I just want to be sure,' said Samantha.

'Yes,' said Maggie. 'I can see that you would.'

When she had left Samantha at the school gate, she walked on to the bus stop in a daze. Looking down, she saw that her hands were trembling. When had they ever trembled? When had she ever felt the ground so treacherous beneath her feet? Not in the desert, not in the jungle, not on the ocean. Only once, in a time she rarely thought about these days.

'Christ,' she muttered aloud. 'Oh Christ Almighty.'

Panic tightened in her breast. The octopus of family life was throwing tentacles round her, one after the other. She should have been more wary. She should have made her usual brief convivial visit before going off to lodge somewhere alone and anonymous. She should never have allowed herself to be furred by the soft insidious moss of family. She should have kept on rolling.

She shuddered, staring out of the bus window at the fleeting country-side. Maggie's inner equilibrium had depended for fourteen years on the fact that she was tied to nobody and to no place. It was an article of faith to her that wherever she was, whatever she was doing, whatever friend-ships she had made, she could leave any time at half an hour's notice with-out reproach. Twice in those years she had come close to commitment, even to domesticity; twice she had, with implacable rigour, disconnected herself from the encroaching tendrils. Once, she had wept as she left. Yet always, deep within her, lay the certainty that she was right.

So how had she let this happen? How had she not seen how sticky were the fingers of the Penn family?

Swinging off the bus at the stop before the college, suddenly Maggie understood why. It was because things had been so different last time she had been in England, four years ago. Samantha was eleven, proud of her Patrol Leader uniform and big-school status. Jamie was nine, Teddy a romping small child who still climbed on his mother's knee. The little ones still had bedtime stories, often from Leo. Leo and Sarah themselves were always rushed, but given to hugging one another exhaustedly in the kitchen, moaning humorously about their busy-ness. In 1996 the house was relatively new to them and still a source of pride and constant discussion about shower fitments and carpet bargains. Maggie had stayed for three weeks but never once felt at the slightest risk of being entrapped by her relatives' needs. They had no needs, frankly; they were a snug, complete, almost hermetically sealed little city-state all on their own.

Now they were not. Leo was harassed, and drank too much in the evenings. Sarah seemed impatient with her husband, and openly bored by his complaints about the book trade. The children were as much fun as ever—more fun, thought Maggie, who had little taste for mewling infancy. But the family was—yes, definitely cracking open, she thought. The obvious symptom was that, with the exception of Leo, they had been just a little bit too keen to see her. They needed to be distracted from themselves. Sarah wanted a companion, the boys wanted fun, Samantha wanted a confidante in her awful dilemma. And now even Leo had decided that there was, after all, a place for her. In his shop.

And here she was, standing outside a chemist's shop preparing to buy, in secret, a pregnancy test for Leo and Sarah's only daughter, a child who had every reason to suspect that she was up the spout at fifteen. I did not want this kind of life at all, thought Maggie. I ran halfway round the world to escape it.

Squaring her shoulders, she marched into the shop, spotted what she needed more by luck than judgment, and stood for a moment irresolute. There were four different kinds where she remembered only one. They were unbelievably expensive: over ten pounds each. How did schoolgirls manage? Only one was cheaper and that, she noticed, was also marked '2 TEST PACK'. Her eyes filled unaccountably with tears and, with a half-blind, embarrassed grab, she laid her hand on a discreet little blue and white box and handed over £7.95.

Poor Sam, she thought, poor bloody Sam.

'These all need signing,' said Sarah, putting down a sheaf of letters on the vet's desk. She was in the office behind the surgery, in the familiar smell of antiseptic. 'I could get them to the post tonight if you like.'

Privately, she thought that Mr Miller's habit of personally signing all the practice invoices was daft, but he had been doing it for all of the twelve years she had worked for him, and there seemed little chance of his changing now.

'Did you ring Mrs Pritt about her dog?' he asked, flipping over a set of notes. 'I really have to take those stitches out. You'd think people would remember.'

'The flood probably drove it out of her mind,' said Sarah. 'It's going to be months before the Blue Lady's dried out properly.'

'The flood,' said Samuel Miller irritably, 'makes the dog all the more susceptible to infections. If people won't take proper responsibility for their animals—'

'Anyway, I did ring her,' said Sarah. She grimaced, remembering that the conversation had mainly consisted of herself listening resignedly, with the phone held an inch from her ear, to a tirade on the subject of Maggie's lack of loyalty in the matter of flood warnings. 'I put her straight through to the desk, when she'd finished going on about my sister, and Louise has made her an appointment.'

'Yes, how *is* that sister of yours? Saw her running by the river,' said Miller, beginning to sign the letters. 'She's an active creature. Wish half the dogs I see were as fit to run through the park.'

Sarah perched on the end of his desk. She enjoyed talking to the old vet. His acerbic, cynical view of the world provided a bracing counterpoint to her own soft-hearted optimism.

'Maggie's fine,' she said, idly admiring the silver wings of hair which swept up with senatorial elegance behind the old man's ears. 'She's even going to help Leo in the shop over Christmas.'

Samuel Miller looked up sharply. 'She's going into the *bookshop*?' he said incredulously. 'What'll all the old tabbies make of that? Bit of a change from Mountjoy. Like replacing a chicken with a kestrel. Some people are not made for shop life. She'll drive poor old Leo insane.' He bent to his task again.

'They've always got on really well,' protested Sarah. '*Now* they do, anyway. Leo was very grateful to her for all the work she did the night of the flood. She's keen to do it.'

The vet snorted. 'Not a restful girl. She never was. My wife taught her, you know, at the High School. Never there, always off with the circus or whatever. Not like you. You got all the steadiness in the family genes, she got all the Vikings and pirates and troublemakers.'

'Well, I know,' said Sarah, laughing and climbing off the desk to smooth down her sensible dark wool skirt. 'But people calm down as they get older.'

'Hah!' said the vet. 'That's what they say about dogs, but in my view it's once a biter, always a biter.'

'I think it's a great idea,' said Sarah stoutly. 'Who knows, she might even stay in Brackhampton and settle down. Be lovely for all of us.'

The vet glanced up, his blue eyes fixing her from their nest of wrinkles.

'Can't believe you're saying that,' he said. 'Butter her paws, like a kitten, to stop it running away? Think you can do that? I doubt it.'

'She's my sister,' said Sarah defensively. 'I was only thinking—'

'I suppose that somewhere in the world,' said the vet, 'there's some idiot following a Bengal tiger around with a tub of butter and a spatula, thinking he'll eventually succeed in making it lie down and purr by the fire.' He laughed, but there was kindness in it. 'Sarah, dear, don't count your chickens.'

'Leo said that,' replied Sarah, glumly.

While this conversation was going on at the veterinary surgery, Maggie was meekly undergoing her first session of training with Miss Mountjoy. She received praise for her facility with the computer, and nodded keenly through a lecture on the proper handling of books and the need to prevent customers from using their covers to rest on when they wrote out cheques.

'And another thing,' said the old lady. 'There are certain people you have to watch: they'll clip over a page or dent a spine in order to ask for a discount. If you've any suspicion at all, you must always insist they have a perfect copy from the stockroom, at the full price. That discourages them from being so dishonest again.'

'Why's it so important that books are spotless?' asked Maggie. 'It's the words that matter.'

'That's true, dear,' said Miss Mountjoy surprisingly. She smiled, and Maggie saw that she could once have been a handsome woman. 'But we sell a lot of books to people who never actually read the words. They either give them away as presents, or just look at the illustrations.' A delicate little shrug of disdain. 'And on these customers relies the prosperity of the shop. Books,' she concluded, 'partake not only of the divine spark of the understanding, but of the crudity of materialism. That is why they are so very fascinating to work with.'

'She's *wonderful*,' said Maggie to Leo later. 'You *can't* let her go. She's a national treasure. I know Americans who would cross half the world to do business with her.'

'I have no kind of control over her,' said Leo. 'You'll have to do, for the moment, until fate throws me another real assistant.'

'Not fate,' said Maggie. 'God, surely. Isn't Miss Mountjoy praying for someone?'

Leo grinned. 'She told me she already had prayed. And the answer has come already. You're it.'

'I totally am *not*! I'm going to China in May!'

'I'm only telling you what she said. You've been sent.'

Maggie stared at him, amused and horrified. 'A dog is not only for Christmas, but I bloody well am. Leo. You know that? Leo? Hello?'

'Well, she could be wrong,' said Leo, turning back to the cardboard dump bin he was filling with paperback editions of a saucy political diary. 'But she's never been wrong yet.'

During the hours in the bookshop, Maggie briefly forgot about the pregnancy-testing kit in her bag. When she did remember it, dismay rose in her, chill and murky as the floodwater, at the thought of giving this cold clinical test to the child and standing by while she did it. As confidante she must be there, to share the guilty relief or the cold shock of disaster.

She still hoped to persuade Sam to confide in her mother. Walking home, the reluctant aunt rehearsed her speech. 'She'll understand . . . I'm sure she won't tell your father unless it's absolutely necessary . . .'

Samantha was already home. The boys were not, and Sarah had left a message to say that she was dropping in on her friend Nita Syal, who was recovering from a hysterectomy. Leo had closed the shop door and said he needed an hour to look through catalogues. When Maggie turned her key in the lock, Samantha heard the sound and was in the hall to meet her.

'Well? Did you get it?'

'Yes,' said her aunt, heavily. 'But look, I think we should talk before you do it.'

'Why? Mum'll be home soon, and the boys, and Dad, and—look, give it here. I'll pay you later.'

'I don't want paying,' said Maggie patiently. 'But the point is, honey-bunch, if this test is positive it's going to mean a lot of thinking. And it might be sensible to do some of the thinking first. Like, about who you'd tell.'

'I am not preg—I just need to be sure, OK?'

Still Maggie kept her hand on her canvas bag, holding it shut. She opened her mouth to speak again, but Samantha—pale and angry now—looked at the bag and jerked forward as if planning a snatch.

'Give it me! Please!'

So Maggie did, and silently followed Samantha upstairs. She stood outside the bathroom. After a few minutes her niece burst out again and said, 'I can't read the fucking thing! My eyes just go—fuzzy. It does my head in. What do I do? You read it!'

Maggie began reading the leaflet, while Samantha leaned in the bathroom doorway fiddling distractedly with a little clear plastic tub she had taken from the box.

'There's two stick things in sort of paper packaging,' she began, but her aunt hushed her.

'Do shut up. I'm trying to get the idea, it's different from when I—'

'Have you done one before, then?'

'I said shut up!'

Maggie read. *Excessive fluid intake before testing may dilute the hormone and invalidate the testing process . . .*

'You're reading the wrong side,' said Samantha in an exasperated tone. 'The stuff about dipsticks and swim rings is all on the other side.' She snatched for the paper. 'Look!' She dropped the little plastic trough, which bounced and skittered down the stairs.

'You have to understand what it is before you do it,' said Maggie, snatching back the leaflet. 'And I bet you've been drinking.'

'Have not, so! I don't drink since, since . . .'

'Not alcohol, dummy. It's your PE day, you drink your sports bottle, then you come in and drink all the fridge water. You always do.'

'So? What's water got to do with it?'

'Everything. Look, it's best to do it first thing in the morning. It says here. It's more accurate.'

Samantha wailed, a baby herself. 'I want to do it now!'

'No,' Maggie said. 'You can't do it now, you're all diluted. So it's quite likely to give you a negative result. And you'll have a sneaky suspicion it's a false negative, and you'll still be worried. What's the point of that? Do it in the morning!'

Suddenly Samantha crumpled, her defiance melting. 'If I do, will you walk to school with me again?'

'Yes, of course.' Maggie looked at the pale face and red eyes beneath the tangle of dark hair so like her own, and felt a treacherous tug at her heart. 'Of course I will. We'll leave early. Say we want to look at something in a shop window. I'll fix it.'

The front door opened, crashing back in a manner which signalled the arrival of the two boys. Quick as a flash, Maggie stuffed the leaflet back and slipped the box into the sleeve of her sweater. Samantha gave her a grateful glance and went into her room. As Teddy thundered upstairs he trod heavily on the little clear plastic trough.

'Whassat?' he said, picking up the crumpled plastic and flicking it disdainfully. 'Looks like a Barbie's rain hat.'

Maggie took it. 'Mine,' she said. 'God, though, it does, doesn't it?' She grinned at the child, then when he had clumped onward to his bedroom, studied it with care. It would go back into shape, she thought. A bit of Sellotape round the edge to stop it leaking. 'Oh God, Oh God,' she muttered under her breath. 'I fought so hard not to live like this . . .'

'Auntie Mag!' shouted Jamie from downstairs. 'D'you wanna see the new Eminem single video? It's coming up after the break.'

Maggie woke abruptly before dawn. She rolled out of bed, reaching for the sweatshirt and jeans in which she took her morning run. Before she could do more than pull on the ragged top, however, a low scratching sound at the door made her pause. Stealthily, she moved over to open it.

Samantha stood there, wearing a nightshirt with a fluffy cat appliquéd on the front. She looked about ten years old.

'I heard you,' she said. 'I can't go back to sleep. Anyway I need a wee.'

Maggie put her finger on her lips. Crossing to the chest of drawers, she pulled open the top one.

'Here it is,' she whispered. 'I read the proper instructions in bed. You've got to collect some wee in this trough thing. Then you push the cardboard stick through the floating ring thing, and float it, and leave it for ten minutes until you see whether there's a faint blue line under the other blue line.'

'And if there is, you're . . .?'

'Yup.'

Samantha took the box and shook out its contents on the bed, grimacing at the crumpled and mended plastic trough. She peered into the bottom. 'There's another,' she said. 'Look. There's two tests.' She sat on the bed and shivered. 'Oh God, I know I'm not going to believe the result anyway. How do I know whether it's the right kind of blue stripe? You can't ever quite tell, my friend once said. You need to see an unpregnant one as well.' She looked sidelong at Maggie and said, 'Suppose you do the other one? Then we'd know. We could compare them.'

'You ought to save the other one, in case you want to do it again to be sure.'

'But I *would* be sure, if I had a control. Like in chemistry at school. I could look at your unpregnant one and see if mine was different.'

'Oh, all right.' Maggie picked up the crumpled plastic container. 'Let's get on with it. Or we'll both go mad.'

A few minutes later the girl and the woman were both back, each holding her specimen. Silently, each assembled her testing kit.

'Don't muddle them up, for God's sake,' said Maggie. She placed hers carefully on the bedside table. 'Put yours on the windowsill.'

'We can't muddle them up because you've got the crumply tub.'

Maggie said, 'Right. Ten minutes. No looking. Get your shoes and jeans on, we're going for a run round the block.'

'I can't!'

'Bloody can. Come on.'

Together they crept downstairs, put the door on the latch and went out into the dank morning. Jogging slowly, Maggie led the way down the alley and turned left. Shafts of fog lay across the silent High Street; only the newsagent was outside her shop, hauling in heavy bundles of papers. In silence they ran past the Blue Lady, Woolworth's, the shining brass plaques of vet and dentist, the whole crooked jigsaw of Tudor and Victorian, Georgian and 1930s brickwork.

'We should go *back*,' puffed Samantha at her elbow. 'If it's more than ten minutes it might go *funny*.'

'Be fine,' said Maggie briefly. 'Stop worrying.' But she turned and led the way back up the High Street.

They slipped back into the house and crept upstairs. On the landing, Maggie turned to Samantha and said, seriously, 'Whatever the result says, no hysterics. Either way. No noise. We'll look, and think, then you and I will get properly dressed. *Without talking about it*, right? Then we'll leave a note and nip out to the Costarica for coffee and a bun. We can talk there.'

'Come *on*,' said Samantha impatiently. Maggie reached out and pulled her hand from the doorknob.

'Agreed? Stay cool, whatever? Until we're safe out of the house?'

'Yesss!'

They walked into the room. Samantha went straight to the windowsill. She picked out the little cardboard stick, shook it, and stared. Then she turned and said, 'Give me yours. I need to see if they're the same.'

Maggie sat on the bed, watching her warily. 'So?'

'It's positive,' said Samantha, in a low choked voice. She had taken Maggie's stick out of the tub, looked at it, and after a moment's hesitation, put it back in the tub. She turned. Maggie saw that she was white, shaking violently. 'They're different. Two blue lines there, one thick blue line there.' She held her stick out to her aunt. 'What am I going to do?' Tears started in her eyes.

Maggie pulled her down to sit beside her on the bed, and threw an arm over her shoulders.

'Steady. Steady. It's all right. Whatever happens, it's all right.'

Samantha choked out something which her aunt did not quite catch. After a moment she said it again. 'Don't wanna kill a baby. S'wrong.'

'It isn't exactly like—' began Maggie.

'Oh, don't worry. I'll have to do it, I'll have to have an ab—a termination. S'just I don't want to. But I'll have to, won't I?'

'You don't have to do anything. You make your own choices,' said Maggie. 'But look, your parents will be up soon. Go and get dressed for school, and we'll get out of here.'

Tears coursing down her face, Samantha obeyed, absently laying the stick back on the windowsill as she went. Maggie stood up, shuddered, and pulled on her college clothes. Then she looked with intense dislike at the paraphernalia and prepared to clear it up. She reached out a hand for the control test, then froze.

Moments later, with the instruction leaflet in her hand, she knocked cautiously on Samantha's bedroom door.

'Did you switch the sticks?'

'What do you mean?'

'Did you put your stick in my wee?'

'No. Obviously. I put yours back, once I saw they were different. I've got one thick blue pregnant stripe, you've got two thin ones.'

'You're not pregnant.'

'What?'

'One blue stripe means you're not pregnant. Two stripes means you are. *Look!*' She held up her own testing stick, and with her other hand brandished the leaflet, stabbing at the diagram with the strip of cardboard.

'What?' Samantha stared at her, not understanding.

'You—are—not—pregnant.' Maggie spat the words.

'But then that means . . .' The girl stared.

'Right. Yes. It means that I am.'

Deafening, apocalyptic in the silence between them, Sarah's tin-plate alarm clock sounded high and strident as a fire alarm. Aunt and niece, of one accord, fled downstairs in silence. Maggie had the presence of mind to scribble a note and stick it to the kitchen table.

Gone to watch the sun rise, walking to school, Mag & Sam.

Chapter Five

SILENT IN STUNNED ACKNOWLEDGMENT of their new bond, aunt and niece walked rapidly down the alleyway to the Costarica coffee house.

As they sat down Samantha began a question, but Maggie frowned a warning until the waitress had moved away. At last, with an impatient wriggle, Samantha began.

'So you're saying it's the two blue stripes that mean yes?'

'Yes, yes, yes. It's in the leaflet. You read it, didn't you?'

'Yes. No. Sort of. My brain must have sort of switched things. I just never thought—'

'You just thought it couldn't be that way round.' Maggie tried to smile, with little success.

'You aren't—I mean, I didn't know—'

'You mean, I'm not married.' Her hand, Maggie saw to her annoyance, was shaking so much that black coffee spilt hot over her fingers. She put it down, sharply.

Samantha was hurriedly correcting herself: 'No, I mean I just didn't know . . . I didn't think you had a boyfriend at the moment.'

'I don't.'

'But how . . .?'

'Not a virgin birth,' said Maggie. 'Not a miracle. Miss Mountjoy need not roll out the red carpet for the Second Coming.'

Samantha wriggled unhappily in her chair. After a moment's silence the girl spoke again, awkwardly.

'Auntie Maggie.' After the morning's events, the renewal of this childish appellation hung oddly between them. 'I'm really, really sorry, but the thing is I have to be sure.' She took a deep breath. 'And if it's sort of, you know, impossible that it's you that's pregnant, and one of us in that room *was* pregnant . . .Then it's me, isn't it?'

Maggie found her hand becoming steadier, and took a draught of black coffee, shuddering a little at its sour, metallic taste.

'No,' she said. 'It isn't you. For one thing, you didn't switch the sticks round. I'd have seen you. And anyway . . .'

She did not know how to put it, but in the past few minutes, a dozen memories, perceptions and doubts had come to her. Her breasts ached as they had never ached; her coffee was each morning less welcome, and at odd times of day in college she had felt passing nausea. Her monthly cycle, never regular, had last manifested itself in mid-Atlantic aboard the *Evangelina*. Every arrow pointed the same way, towards the accusing blue stripes.

'Oh, I'm pregnant,' she said. 'And I'm a complete fool not to have suspected it earlier. Therefore you are not pregnant. Rejoice! I would, if it was me.'

The child struggled not to smile, but her face split at last into a grin. 'Sorry. It's just—oh God, it's like being let off death row.' She finished her cup of coffee and looked round. 'I'm starving. Do you mind if I ask for a croissant?'

'Go and get one.' Maggie shivered. 'I need a minute.'

When Samantha returned, Maggie was sitting with her head in her hands, almost as if she were crying.

'Are you . . .?'

'No. It's just a shock. I was counting how long.'

'How long?'

'Has to be three months.' She looked up, and saw the anxious pale face opposite. The girl's tact and worry touched her, and resolutely she said, 'I'll tell you about it. If you want.'

'You don't have to. You've been ace to me, honestly. I don't know what I'd have done. But it's your business.'

'No, we're in it together. And I suppose I'm better off than you would have been. He may have been a one-night stand, but I enjoyed it more than you did. And he was a lot nicer than your Duane.' She gave a watery smile. 'A dear, good man.'

'Are you in touch? Now?'

'No. He's married with children, thousands of miles away. Like I say, it was a bit of an impulse thing. I don't do it often, hardly ever in fact.' She drummed her fingers on the table. 'But this was a sort of celebration. Home is the sailor, home from the sea. That sort of thing.'

'What was his name?'

'I mainly called him Captain.' Maggie tried to smile. 'But Joaquim—Joaquim Lopez.'

'What are you going to do?'

'I don't know. You'd better get to school. Don't worry about me. I'll have to think it over. I might not go to college.'

When Samantha had gone, lighter of step than she had been for weeks, Maggie emerged into the High Street, where once again it was beginning to rain. The impulse to run to Sarah was intense. But first she had to think. She would walk, that was it; she would walk to the sea.

She would not, she realised as she strode rapidly towards the edge of town, be back in time to go to the bookshop for another afternoon's training. Leo would wonder where she was. At the thought of Leo a hot, unexpected surge of fury overtook her, and with it came a wave of nausea stronger than any before. The tinny taste of black coffee rose in her throat, making her gag. Leaning on a garden wall, coughing her discomfort, she suddenly felt a weakness in her legs and fought to stop their trembling.

'Panic attack,' she said aloud. 'Breathe.'

She breathed deeply, leaning on the wall, head back against the safe brick, her knees locked straight in case they should betray her. Movement, energy, a journey . . . if she could walk to the sea, stride the beach, clear her head . . .

She would ring the shop when she got to the coast, tell Leo she was held up. Against the driving rain, in her thin, light waterproof and on shaking legs, Maggie Reave walked out of the grey town and took the bleak road to the sea.

'Heaven knows what my sister and my daughter were up to this morning,' said Sarah to Nita Syal. 'They were stumping around the house at crack of dawn, then left a note about watching the sun rise. And look at it.' She gestured towards the window, and the weeping rain. 'Sunrise, my foot.'

She was sitting on a high hospital bed. In the last two years its occupant, the soft-spoken Nita, had become her closest female confidante; she was the mother of a twin girl and boy in Teddy's class and a gentle, dark-eyed daughter of fifteen who had stayed in the Guide troop amassing badges, when Samantha left. Now Nita lay in a side ward at the nursing home, recovering from a hysterectomy.

'Recovering from daily life, too,' she had said lightly when Sarah tiptoed in. 'Truly, it is wonderful to lie in clean sheets, and quietness, with flowers, and no need to cook.' She seemed genuinely happy and comfortable, so the women rapidly exhausted the subject of her operation and moved on to family matters.

'It must be an excitement for Samantha, to have a bachelor auntie,' Nita said wistfully. 'All that my girls ever see within the family is the life of a good Asian wife—me, my mother, their aunties—all of us running so nicely on the rails and doing our duty.'

'Well, yes. I'm not sure Maggie's exactly a role model,' said Sarah thoughtfully. 'I mean, it isn't as if Mags was a whizzy professional or anything sort of—solid. She does rather doss around the world.'

'But she is free!' said Nita. 'She is not defined by serving a man and a family. She works, her work earns money, and she can spend or keep it according to her own judgment.'

'But I'm not sure I'd want any of my children to live the way she does.'

Nita looked at her, her big dark eyes alight with amused intelligence.

'The important thing is to show them many different ways,' she said. 'So they can choose, and not follow rails. I am hopeful for Uma, who is clever and asks the world many questions. But I wish we could arrange for Maggie to meet my Leela and shake her up a bit. My youngest daughter is too fond of taking instructions. I sometimes think she is practising to be a bride bossed around by a good Indian mother-in-law, as I was. I tell you one thing clearly, whatever Ravi says, no daughter of mine will have a husband found for her by family. Or be made to have one at all.'

'You're a bit of a rebel, in your way, aren't you, Nita?' said Sarah admiringly. 'Do you know, I think I'm more suitable to be an Asian wife than you are.'

'So your parents arranged your marriage, hey?'

'N-no,' said Sarah. 'But they approved very much. And as soon as he was set to join the family, they seized on him as an instrument of discipline to bring Maggie back under control.'

'No! Tell me,' said Nita, agog and amused.

'Well, Maggie was on a field trip, in Iceland. And she was meant to come back to university, but she decided to travel on instead, so she got a job on a tugboat and landed in Newfoundland, and sort of vanished into Canada as cook for a camp of scientists.'

'So your parents made Leo this—what did you say? Instrument of family discipline? Oh, very Asian!'

'Well, he offered to go out and persuade her to come back and finish the course. So Leo went, and found her in the forest. I've often wondered what he said to her to make her come back. I think it might have been about Dad being ill. He died, the next year.'

'So was that good, or bad, to tell her?'

'I don't *know*,' said Sarah. 'I just know that when they got back, and for years afterwards, and even now, if I'm honest, there's been something not quite right between them. I'm amazed Leo's having her in the shop, actually. He's desperate for an assistant for Christmas, and he's grateful about the flood thing, but all the same—I dunno.'

'You think, as a good chemist, that they are a dangerous mixture?'

'Yes,' said Sarah. 'Yes, I do.'

The rain did not stop all morning, as Maggie walked. The wind eased a little, though, and she grew hot; by the time she saw the seafront, she had taken off her plastic jacket and was letting the rain cool her. Her head was clearer now. The old route reminded her of her youthful nights in the tent, trying to forget the overheated little house that held her anxious mother and dying father. She had walked away once, she thought, and could walk away again from the cloying, sticky domestic traps that nature and culture laid for women.

Eschewing the track, she clambered over the rain-pocked dunes and stood between two faded beach huts to stare at the ocean. The wind was at her back, and her face was whipped and stung by tendrils of black hair. The rain was passing now, scudding away eastwards across the grey North Sea. She thought of other seas and oceans: Atlantic and Pacific, Tasman and Caribbean. From babyhood, it seemed to her, she had known that there was a world out there to be discovered. From child-hood she had understood that if she was to see its strangeness and its riches, then she must labour to make herself strong and free and resolute. She had struggled to be at all costs quite unlike her parents.

Or her sister. Dear Sarah: kind and thoughtful, devoting her whole life to the children, and to Leo.

What kind of diabolical ill luck did it take, for Christ's sake, for a woman long accustomed to infertility to be undone by one carefree night with Joe Lopez in an upper room at the Bar Europa? It was true, she reflected bitterly, that she had not often put to the test the verdict of that snake-faced college doctor in Coventry all those years ago. On being told by the unsympathetic cow that infertility was the price she paid for having managed a private crisis badly, the young Maggie had responded with characteristic bravado, 'Good. Excellent. Maternity is not my scene.'

Only one man had ever made her waver, and that was Adam. He had said when they parted, 'But it doesn't have to end there, does it?' She had told him that it did, not least because she could never bear him children for his family dynasty. Judging by their meeting two years later at Cape Cod, he was far better off with his preppy little blonde. She had loved Adam the student in his bare chest and frayed shorts on the beach, but she would have been a poor partner for Adam the rising realtor in a Ralph Lauren blazer and monogrammed shirt.

There had been a long blank time after Adam, but all the same, she thought now, she had taken enough risks over the years to be pretty certain that Dr Snake-face was right. On the night with Joaquim, drinking sour Spanish cider and revelling in the knowledge of an ocean well crossed, it had never occurred to her to take the slightest precaution. Nor to him, apparently. Ah well, he was a Hispanic and a Catholic, and probably assumed that all foreign Protestant women were on the pill.

She smiled, remembering. *Is that an order, Captain? Are you sure?* How flippant, how happy, it had been. A night could only be taken in that spirit if you knew for certain it was the only one there would ever be. Like—

No, not like that. The smile faded on her lips. She turned back, facing the wind; glanced at her watch: two o'clock. She had better go back. Winter darkness would fall at four. She should hitch a ride, perhaps. At the thought, the memory of Samantha swam back into her mind, for one of the few things her sister expressly forbade her to do was to mention hitchhiking to any of her children as a norm. Maggie had acquiesced, referring in all her traveller's tales to 'a lift from a friend' or 'the local transport'. Samantha, she thought, would be wary of all men and boys for a while now anyway. Just as she herself had been, back in the '80s after the abortion. Thank God the kid didn't have to make that hardest of choices.

But she did. Again! Her anxiety returned in an overwhelming, choking torrent. She had been managing in the last few minutes to think about the pregnancy as a stroke of ill luck like having your money stolen. Now it came home to her with sickening force that the moment of discovery was the smallest part of it. Pregnancy was a continuum, a roller coaster. Even during the morning, this thing had been growing within her. On the way back to Brackhampton she would become more pregnant still, and lose another half-day on the way to her decision.

But as the word abortion came to her, so did memories: of invasion, instruments, masked faces, pain, ignominy, the horror of a certain covered bowl. She had made a death happen. Long ago, to be sure, and for the very, very best and kindest of reasons. Christ, yes. Better reasons than anybody would ever know.

All the same, there were tears on Maggie's face as she turned her back on the sea and began slowly to walk towards the long road home.

'Where *is* she?' asked Leo, not for the first time.

Miss Mountjoy looked up from the shelf she was arranging. 'Don't keep *on*, Mr Penn. She's probably delayed.'

'Well, it can't go on,' said Leo with a petulant slap of his folder on the table. 'You're leaving us next week, and she did accept the job. It's too bad! Unprofessional!'

The afternoon wore on, and still Maggie did not appear. Nor was Leo's temper improved when his daughter came in after school, accompanied by Uma Syal, and he saw that both of them had studs in their noses. Uma had always had one, accepted by school as a legitimate part of her commitment to her ethnic roots. Pink and white Anglo-Saxon Samantha, on the other hand, had been specifically banned from any form of body piercing. Leo exploded in fatherly rage, which turned to fleeting horror and then to irritation as Sam casually pulled the gilt stud from the outside of her nose and a magnet from the inside, saying,

'Chill, Dad. It's the temp'ry kind.'

'Well, if you've nothing better to spend your money on—'

'One pound eighty-five for two. Get a *life*, Dad. Can we have some Christmas catalogues to cut up, for the art club collage?'

He gestured towards Miss Mountjoy, who rose stiffly and led the way to the catalogue drawers. Even through his irritation, Leo dimly noticed that his daughter was more cheerful than he had seen her for months.

Maggie was cold in her damp clothes, and her legs ached. When she reached the main road to Brackhampton the tight flow of traffic made her realise that she would do better to hitch a lift on the grass by the slip road, catching the eyes of drivers before they got up to cruising speed.

A sudden sense of vulnerability made her hesitate.

The cars that pelted down the bypass wailed on the wet road like demons; the light, feeble all day, was perceptibly dying. She stood for a moment irresolute, arms by her sides, and was startled when a black car, unbidden, pulled into the lay-by beside her. Its electric window hummed open and an elbow emerged, in a white shirtsleeve, followed by part of a man's head.

'Hoy! You OK? Wanting a lift?'

Maggie hesitated, miserably aware as she did so that hesitating was not one of her normal habits. Where had she gone, that clear, determined, happy woman of yesterday? But as she approached the open window she suddenly felt an emanation of warm air from the car's heated interior and she made up her mind. She said, 'Thanks. I wouldn't mind. But my clothes are wet. Even if I take off my jacket, I'm worried about your upholstery.'

'Dog blanket,' said the man economically, twisting and hauling something from the back seat. 'Sit on that.'

'Well, if you're sure,' said Maggie.

She went round to the passenger side, sat down and kicked her wet jacket into the passenger footwell. She saw that the man's suit jacket swung on a hanger inside the back door of the car, in the immemorial fashion of the travelling sales rep. A briefcase lay on the back seat.

'Brackhampton? Or beyond?' he asked, sidling the car out of the lay-by into the traffic. 'I'm going right on to Maidstone, if it's any help.'

'Only Brackhampton, thanks. Bypass will do,' said Maggie. The man was silent for a moment, but she sensed in the silence that he, like many drivers in her hitchhiking experience, had picked her up at least partly in the hope of conversation. She would have preferred to be alone and quiet with her dilemma, but the questioning silence defeated her.

'You got a dog, then?' she said with all the brightness she could muster.

'Nope,' said the man. 'Wife got the dog. I got the blanket. Christ knows why. Story of my life.'

Hell, thought Maggie, an embittered divorcé. Still, it was only nine miles. She had once spent eight hours bumping across the Western Desert with a lorry driver whose wife had run off with a male nurse in the hospital where she had her baby.

But this man showed no sign of wanting to pursue the subject, asking instead, 'Where you travelling from, then?'

'Mexico,' said Maggie, thankfully identifying an escape route. She could go onto autopilot with a traveller's tale or two, and that would easily fill the quarter-hour to the Brackhampton bypass.

She began to explain about her journey up through South America, but after a moment he broke in with, 'In Mexico. Go to Cancún?'

'Nope. Tourists, very expensive. Very crowded, too, they say.'

'Good,' said the man, grinning. 'The more money flows in there, the better. I was there in February last year. Sold a whole lot of computer peripherals to the biggest American hotel complex. Great business.'

Maggie was momentarily nonplussed, then the man said teasingly, 'See? I stand revealed as the filthy enemy. I'm the capitalist West. I fly in, sell hard, piss off.'

'Why do you think you're *my* enemy, in particular?' said Maggie. 'How do you know what I think?'

''Cos I've got your number. You're a nice, caring, respectful, cultural traveller, right? Leave only footprints, take only memories, like it says on the Greenpeace T-shirts. Aren't you?'

'Well, I try.' There was, Maggie thought unexpectedly, something oddly enjoyable about having to defend herself. His aggression, in any case, was delivered so lightly that there was no sting in it. 'Yes, I try. I don't think Westerners should impact—'

'Ah, but I do. Memories are no good to people like me. I take contracts, and leave thousands and thousands of inkjet cartridges and office consumables. You are a tourist, and tourism is decadent. I am part of world history. I am a merchant traveller, in the tradition of Marco Polo.'

Maggie smiled, for the first time since early morning. 'Maidstone next stop, was it?' she asked sweetly, and the man turned his head towards her momentarily and laughed aloud.

'Nice one,' he said. 'Yup, you got me bang to rights. I'm grounded now. Gave up most of the travelling job last Christmas. Flying a desk in head office for a spell.'

'Where else did you travel?' Generous now, she wanted to give him back the upper hand.

'St Petersburg, Moscow, Belgrade before the war, Tokyo, Seattle, Santiago, Brisbane . . .' and she rose excitedly to match him, comparing notes. 'Hellhole, isn't it? . . . Fabulous mountains . . . were you there in summer or winter . . .?'

As they approached the Brackhampton turnoff, there was a tiny pause in their flow of reminiscence. Impulsively, liking this glib, cheerful man in spite of herself, Maggie offered him a small tribute.

'You know, actually, there is an argument for saying that guys like you are the real travellers now. You have to get right down into the commercial nitty-gritty of a place.'

'And you have to meet the people,' he said, with a shudder. 'You dippy-hippy backpackers can hang out with shepherds and share weird brews with nomads. Me, I have to go to hideous karaoke nights in Kodo with bonsai chief executives. I have to make small talk on balconies with trophy wives while sinister Panamanians in white suits decide whether to give you a quarter-mill contract or shoot you in the kneecap.'

Maggie laughed. 'So you'd rather hang out with the nomads?'

'Probably not,' he conceded. 'If I wanted to get covered in animal turds I'd get a job in the elephant house at London Zoo.'

'I was an elephant keeper once,' said Maggie, before she could stop herself. 'When I was twelve, I ran away to be one.'

'Excellent,' he said. The car was slowing, close to the Brackhampton sign.

'Here would do,' said Maggie. 'I can walk into town.'

'Ah, bollocks,' said the man, turning left. 'It's still bloody raining. I'll drop you further down.' He turned his face to her, and she saw that he was younger than she had thought. Younger than her, certainly. 'Don't panic. I'm not going to insist on taking you home and then spend the next six months hanging round outside the house.'

'I didn't think—'

'Yes, you did. All women do. Very wise, too.'

When he dropped her at the top of the High Street, Maggie got out of the car and leaned into the open door to thank him, suddenly formal. 'Really, really kind of you. Much obliged.'

'I'm called Steve,' he said. 'And I know *your* name.'

She was nonplussed, and began to stammer in confusion.

He grinned. 'The old gag. Gets 'em every time,' he said. 'Vera. Mavis. Rumpelstiltskin. Lorna Doone. Mopsa. Any or all of the above. Bye-bye, Rumpelstiltskin. Hope you get dry soon.'

She watched his red lights vanish. Heard his tyres squish down the road. She was halfway up the alley to the Penn house when she remembered that her waterproof jacket was still on the car floor.

Chapter Six

SARAH WAS ALL SOLICITUDE when Maggie came in, her hair and clothes bearing every mark of having been soaked through. She gesticulated with a kitchen knife across a pile of onions.

'God! You haven't got as wet as that just coming up from the shop, have you? This weather!'

'Well, no,' said Maggie. 'I'm afraid I bunked off college and the shop today. Went for a walk to the sea.'

Sarah glanced sharply at her. 'Pacing the cage again,' she said in a sad voice. 'Oh, Mags, I've been having stupid delusions that you might put off China and settle down with us for a bit. I do miss you, you know. When you go away. It takes me weeks to cheer up, every time.'

Maggie looked at her feet, unwontedly abashed. Their affection was rarely made so explicit by either of them. Then she said, 'I wasn't pacing the cage, actually. I just had something to think through.' It would be an unutterable relief to tell her sister. *Sarah, I'm pregnant, I'm three months gone, what in hell's name can I do* . . . But even as she opened her mouth, an unshared fragment of their history came between them, and she only said, 'So I took a thinking walk. S'good. S'fine.'

'Well, go and have a bath,' said Sarah, turning back to the chopping board. 'You can have a good long soak. The boys are at Scouts, and Sam's doing some art project. She's brought Uma Syal home to help. Now *there's* a nice girl.'

Upstairs, in the bath, Maggie looked down at her body and immediately the hollow, sick panic returned. How could she not have suspected earlier? Three months! Samantha, hardly more than a child, had been more sophisticated.

Even when she fondly remembered the *Evangelina*, her thoughts had always gone to the weeks of slow, beautiful progress across the ocean rather than to that one aberrant night of overenthusiastic friendship in the Bar Europa. Now, gazing down at the slight swelling of her belly, Maggie remembered the morning after, when she had woken at Captain Lopez's side and seen him, innocently asleep.

He had stirred and thrown out an arm. She stroked it briefly, then with infinite stealth slid from the bed and pulled on her clothes. It was early, and the street outside was empty; with her pack on her back she walked to the main road and almost immediately found the cheese lorry pulled in at the roadside.

She doubted that Joaquim Lopez would be surprised by her absence. It was only after she had made it utterly clear that she was leaving the ship that they had grown so rapidly, instinctively, lustfully close. Lopez would not, she felt sure, have deluded himself that one intimate encounter would change her mind about leaving. He would have taken it for what it was: a traditional harbour celebration. She grinned, in spite of herself. She could not regret it. He was a dear man, and they had gone through gales together.

She had assumed that the college doctor was right. It had been made perfectly clear to her in 1985 that any girl so stubborn and secretive that she fixed herself an ill-managed, dubiously legal abortion in an unregistered clinic had only herself to blame for infection and permanent infertility. After that it had been five years before Maggie slept with another man. She had done it without precautions, still obscurely angry enough to dare the consequences and there had been none. Nor ever again, not even in the six months with Adam. Thenceforth, she took her infertility for granted.

She breathed in, a deep shuddering breath, and her newly rounded belly broke the surface of the bathwater. She leaned forward and turned on the hot tap to cover it. 'Gin and hot baths,' she said aloud, under her breath, as the water rose. 'And hunting used to do it for the Mitford generation, didn't it?' Her eyes filled with tears.

At supper, when Maggie had made her peace with Leo, Samantha threw her a troubled, enquiring look under cover of a spirited argument between the boys and their parents.

'OK?' she mouthed. Maggie gave her a slight nod. Aloud, Samantha said, 'I liked walking up the town early with you, Mags. Can we do it tomorrow?'

'Yep,' said Maggie, smiling. 'We might have better luck with the sunrise.'

'Great,' said Samantha. But her troubled eyes continued to rest on her aunt until the family meal was over.

Maggie slept badly that night. After an hour of turning over her situation in her mind, she went to the window. Looking out at the little town, she saw that the rain had stopped and the clouds lay broken into pale fragments around a misty moon, still moving in some high-altitude wind. She thought about the *Evangelina*.

'That's what I love,' she said aloud. 'The open road, the open sea, the ship, the journey. I wouldn't love a baby, I couldn't. I would hate it for tying me down.'

A silent voice inside her said, 'It already has. So what'cha going to do about it? Kill it? Again?'

She opened her mouth to say 'It's not the same' but could not. The light intensified as the moon trailed through between the clouds. But I love what I love, she thought, silently this time. I have to be free. Sarah wanted all this stuff. I don't. I never will.

She went slowly back to bed and rolled herself in the duvet. She closed her eyes defiantly, but the moon, the sky, the memory of the ship pressed in on her, making it impossible to take a solution involving death. There was a third option, she thought. She could let the creature live, but give it away instantly. She could go away, have it somewhere quietly, hand it over and carry on.

Go *away*? The thought jolted her back into wakefulness. Why? Was she ashamed? What hideous hangover from her mother's terrors was this? Every kind of woman had babies outside wedlock these days. Why did she think she had to go away?

Not because of the baby. Where Sarah was concerned, the shame would lie not in the pregnancy, but in the adoption. Your first child at nearly thirty-six, and you give it away! You might as well get a T-shirt with SELFISH UNNATURAL BITCH printed across the breast. Whereas if you had an abortion, some would dislike you for it but most would understand and few would know.

But the baby would still be dead.

Maggie curled up into a ball of concentrated fear and self-disgust. After a time of suffering, she slept.

Leo slept badly too. He kept waking, squirming with irritation, aggrieved and full of formless dread. More and more often in the past months he had felt a sense of impending doom, of something just out of sight flapping dark wings. Middle-aged depression, he thought. Existential angst. Nothing worth paying attention to. The shop was fine, Sarah as serene and comfortable as ever, the children healthy and, apparently, happy. He was not, he knew, getting enough exercise; the presence in his household of Maggie's rangy, restless energy had borne that truth in upon him. He should walk at weekends, maybe frequent the soupy chlorinated warmth of Southwick Pools.

Next to him Sarah lay, beautiful and calm, fast asleep. He edged towards her, hoping that her serenity would seep into him. But the black wings flapped at the edge of his mind. There was something nearby, something bad and dangerous. Leo shuddered and a single, unmanly tear rolled down his cheek.

Maggie was woken from a heavy dawn sleep by a soft scratching at the door. Samantha, fully dressed, put her head into the room.

'Sorry,' she said. 'Only, if we're to get out before breakfast . . .'

'Right,' said her aunt. Yesterday's jeans were still wet through, and the other pair were in the wash. She pulled out some white trousers from her pack, unworn since Mexico; they were too summery, but she put them on anyway.

They were too tight. Dismay overcame her, and she sat down on the bed with a bump. The truth of her situation almost overwhelmed her and tears pricked behind her eyes. Eventually she put on a pair of track-suit bottoms and a sweater, and grabbed her folder.

'You going to college, then?' asked Sam in a low voice as they crept out of the front door.

'Well, obviously,' said Maggie. 'I've got to get notes on yesterday. It's a very intensive course.'

Samantha digested this information. Still going to China, then, she thought. They walked down the road to the Costarica coffee shop.

When Sam's coffee and Maggie's tea had come, the niece said, 'I don't want to be nosy, but I was wondering all day whether you were all right. 'Cos I know I wouldn't have been, if it had been me.' She shuddered. When Maggie remained silent, touched almost to tears, Samantha added, 'But I'm sorry if it's a cheek. You're probably, like, totally sussed about it. It's only 'cos I'm a kid really that I'd panic like that.'

Maggie recovered herself, and gave her a fond, watery smile. 'No, it's sweet of you. To be honest, I'm not sussed. You see, I thought I couldn't have children.' She looked down at her hands, playing with a spoon. 'I was *told*, once, that I couldn't.'

Samantha's eyes widened. A whole romantic understanding came to her: this, of course, was the reason why her aunt stayed on the road! It was like a really sad song, or a novel.

She said, a little breathless, 'Well, gosh, then—are you, like, I mean—thrilled?'

Maggie threw the spoon down with a little clatter which made heads turn at nearby tables. 'No!' she said vehemently. Then in a lower voice, 'And I shouldn't be troubling you with any of it. I wish you didn't know. I don't want the—the thing at all. It's a disaster.'

Samantha looked down at the table, and deliberately poured some sugar off her spoon and began to make patterns in it. She did not want to hear what her aunt would say next. Although in theory Samantha knew all about the law on abortion, the sources of termination advice and the moral rationale of a Woman's Right to Choose, a darker thread of intelligence also reached her. Girls told stories about friends of friends. Pro-life pamphlets circulated, full of horrid pictures. A girl at Southwick had cut her wrists, unsuccessfully, six months after a termi-nation, and Sarah had shaken her head over the local paper and said,

'It's never as easy as they think, poor lambs. We're not made for it.'

Samantha, freed herself from having to contemplate the horrid need, felt unwilling to contemplate the fact that her aunt was clearly about to do it. Yet Maggie had been good to her, so it was her duty to help.

She summoned up all her chivalry and said, 'D'you need any phone numbers? You wouldn't have to go to our doctor. There're some in the library at school.'

'For terminations, you mean?' Maggie looked at her directly. 'I don't know that I want to do that.'

A great wave of relief swept over Samantha, but she still did not understand.

'You mean you *do* want to have it?'

'I mean, I can't terminate it.' She sighed. It was a relief to talk about it to Samantha, but at the same time she felt achingly guilty that it was not Sarah, her faithful, adult, experienced sister, to whom she was turning. 'There's other ways. A lot of people want babies to adopt.'

Samantha stared at her in dismay. More scraping at the sugar pattern on the table, then, 'So you reckon to have it adopted?'

'Maybe. I've got no money, remember. I don't live anywhere. It wouldn't have a father. Kindest thing, don't you think? Someone would give the kid a really good life.'

'Mum might—' began Samantha, but her aunt cut her off with a frown. Maggie had thought about this herself, in the night. After all, the child would only be eleven years younger than Teddy. She could send home money regularly for its keep. It would keep it in the family. But it could not be asked of Sarah. She had given fifteen years of her life to motherhood, and had another decade in front of her if you counted universities. A new baby would double her sentence. Impossible.

Samantha, however, was not giving up.

'She might really, really love it,' she said stubbornly. 'She was joking with Mrs Syal the other day about how broody she gets round Uma's big brother Sanjay's new baby, and they were giggling about how appalled Dad looks when she says it—' She stopped, crestfallen. 'Oh, yeah. I see. You think Dad wouldn't want us to keep it, even if Mum did.'

'I think,' said Maggie sadly, 'that it's my responsibility, not theirs.'

'So when are you going to tell them?'

'Before the bump does, I suppose.'

'Well, whatever Dad says,' concluded Samantha, 'once it's born, I reckon you'll have a struggle to stop Mum wanting to keep it. Unless you keep it yourself.' She stood up, took the empty cups to the counter and then came back with a cloth to clear up the sugar.

Maggie watched her. *A struggle to stop Mum wanting to keep it, if you don't . . .* It might be a struggle to stop Sarah from making Leo angry and resentful, from endangering her marriage and her family. *Once it's born . . .* Well, it didn't have to be born, did it? But she did not want to choose between killing an unborn child and torpedoing her sister's happiness. Not again. *Unless you keep it yourself.* And be a single mother, broke and grounded. With an effort, she wrenched her mind away from all three horrible possibilities.

'You'd better go. What have you got on first today?' she asked Samantha with an air of idle interest.

'History. Drama project work, on exploration. Me and Uma have got to do a duologue about Marco Polo.'

Maggie smiled. 'Oh, I know about him,' she said. 'He sells a lot of inkjet cartridges to the Mexicans.'

'She's crazy, my aunt,' said Samantha to Uma later. 'But she's cool.'

Meek and punctual, Maggie turned up at the bookshop that afternoon and unpacked Christmas stock and reorganised the shelves. Leo was busy with the insurance loss-adjuster, displaying soggy boxes and crinkled Queen Mother books in the children's library. Miss Mountjoy, seeing that Maggie was competent enough on her own, slipped off early to help her sick friend Louise choose an electric wheelchair. Maggie worked on steadily. At last Leo saw off the insurance man with great cordiality. Turning to Maggie, who had moved over to the desk and begun ticking off stock, he said, 'He was amazed by how little we lost. We've got great Brownie points there. It's all down to you, you know. You saved our bacon that night.'

'The insurance would have paid,' said Maggie, dismissing the compliment.

'They'd have paid wholesale value. Any loss-of-profit payment would just be based on an ordinary month. I know a lot of shops that got flooded are finding that they can't replace lost stock before Christmas, so they're going to lose the peak trade of the year. Honestly, Maggie, if I'd lost my Christmas profit we might have been in a lot of trouble.'

The door pinged, and two women bustled in. Leo looked at them, then at Maggie. 'You OK to serve on your own?'

'Yes, of course.'

He went back up the steps and watched unobtrusively from behind a pile of Harry Potter books.

Maggie smiled at the women. 'Can I help you?'

The larger, more commanding of the women pulled from her hand-bag a Sunday newspaper review page. Maggie took it and together they went over to the Biography shelf.

You would think, thought Leo contentedly, that she had been a book-shop assistant all her life.

It was, in the event, hardly more than a week before the rest of the Penns heard about Maggie's condition. Samantha hated keeping secrets but drew on all her reserves of heroic discretion, only sometimes darting anguished glances at her aunt, when related subjects came up during family supper.

'Adrian's sister's up the duff,' announced Teddy one night, through a mouthful of spaghetti. 'She's at Southwick College but she's going to keep the baby, only her boyfriend doesn't want to pay for it, Adrian says.'

Jamie squirmed on his chair. With his newly gruff voice and growing awkwardness around girls, he found such subjects unfit for mealtimes. Leo would normally have been inclined to agree but was too engrossed in his catalogue of spring books to bother.

Sarah, on the other hand, had read a great many articles about the importance of taking natural opportunities to discuss sex and procre-ation in an open manner with your growing children. She plunged in now with enthusiasm.

'Well, what do you all think?' she said. 'It's a terribly difficult decision for a girl to make.'

Teddy said, 'I think she ought give the baby to one of those test-tube ladies that have to have babies grown in a bottle. 'Cos that's really expensive, innit? And Suzy's baby's, like, free.'

'It's very *hard* to give away your own child,' said Sarah. 'I wouldn't have wanted to give any of you away.' She smiled fondly. Reinforce their own sense of being secure and wanted, the books said. Teddy betrayed his loss of interest with a yawn, and Jamie concentrated fiercely on his food. Sarah turned to Samantha. Brightly she asked, 'What do you think, Sam? Do you suppose it's best to struggle with a baby on your own when you're not ready for it, or have it adopted, or—well, the other thing.'

Samantha could bear it no longer. 'Don't say "the other thing" as if it was a piece of poo!' she snarled. 'Termination. Live with it, Mum. Move on.'

Sarah stared in astonishment. As the emotional temperature in the room rose, she noticed through the corner of her eye Leo starting to pay attention. Why was Samantha so savage all of a sudden? Surely . . .

A horrid suspicion came over her. Duane was not a nice boy at all. Samantha had been morose of late. No, surely not. Sarah's stomach sank with unfamiliar terror. She then looked closely at her daughter. But Sam, unaccountably, was looking at Maggie. Maggie's lips were pressed together, as if she were contemplating a difficult decision.

'Mum,' said Jamie, 'can I go out? I said I'd go down to the Scout Room.'

'You're not *in* the Scouts,' said Sarah, surprised.

'No, but there's a meeting. About helping the Sally Army, Christmas stuff, collecting toys and cleaning them up an' that.'

'Oh, I remember! I thought you weren't going to do it.'

'He is now,' said Teddy, 'because Toyah Robinson's going to do it.' He sniggered. 'Fancies her.'

'Piss off, moron,' said his brother angrily.

'Teddy, you've got homework,' said Sarah swiftly. 'Go upstairs *now*, and get on with it.'

Teddy dragged his feet out of the room, sniffing as irritatingly as he knew how. Jamie slipped out through the kitchen door.

Leo put down his catalogue. 'I dunno,' he said to nobody in particular. 'Do you reckon Jeffrey Archer's finished now? I suppose the market—'

Maggie cut across him. 'Leo. Sarah. Sam. While we grown-ups are together, there's something I have to tell you all.'

Samantha sat stock-still, nervous. Inclusion in the circle of 'we grown-ups' was not, at this moment, a welcome promotion.

'And what I have to say may come as a bit of a shock. Certainly did to me.' Maggie had their full attention, and did not draw out her narrative. 'I'm pregnant. Just over three months. And no, nobody in England, nobody I want to contact. This is a solo expedition, I'm afraid.'

Sarah's mouth hung open, foolishly. 'Darling, are you all right?' It was the wrong question, but rightly intended.

Maggie put a hand on her arm, fondly. 'Yes,' she said. 'I am now. It was a shock at first.'

Leo was silent, stunned. Maggie and pregnancy did not go together. It was Sarah who had babies. Maggie had rucksacks instead. He needed a drink. The wine box was nearly empty, but he reached for it and began to concentrate very hard on getting out the last drop. Samantha, too, was silent.

'What are you going to do?' asked Sarah. 'Have you decided?'

'I'm not going to have an abortion,' said Maggie.

There was a discernible relaxation of muscles round the table. Maggie thought with brief bitterness that they had suspected that she was going to burden her family with vicarious guilt and now they were pleased at being let off.

'Do you have plans?' asked Leo and Sarah together.

Maggie avoided Leo's eye and answered her sister. 'I've been thinking about how to play it, obviously. And, obviously, I can't bring it up.'

'Why not?' It was torn from Sarah. 'You could, you're perfectly—I mean, I never expected Sam so early, but it was bliss, truly. Anyone can—'

'Not me,' said Maggie sadly. 'I really can't do it. I don't want to, I don't know how to, I never meant to. One might as well be honest. I'm no more fit to be a mother than all those fallen fourteen-year-olds Mum used to go on and on about.'

Samantha began to jab the tabletop viciously with her fork.

'So you're thinking of—ummm—adoption, then?'

'Probably.'

'But it's so difficult—I mean, for a new mother. Let's talk about it . . .' Sarah was floundering. What she meant was, 'Let's talk about it without Leo in the room.'

Leo, however, had every air of being thoroughly engaged and involved in the conversation. Sarah's last words had irritated him. He felt unreasonably needled and sidelined by Sarah's assumption that only women had feelings for new babies.

'It's not just difficult for a new mother,' he said. 'I think a father has some right to know if his child is to be given away to strangers.' As he said it, he heard the words fall on the warm kitchen air and knew that they were unforgivable.

Maggie looked directly at him for the first time since she had delivered her news.

She never knew why at this precise moment she chose to destroy at a blow a safe and ancient structure of decorative falsehood. Malice, pique, hormones? It was not planned. When she had first spoken, earlier, she was convinced that she was back in control, after long days and nights of working out what would produce the best result. She had concluded that the child must be adopted: she would give birth, sign every necessary paper renouncing the baby, and leave for China to forget it. Meanwhile she needed shelter for a while with Leo and Sarah, but was planning financially how she could spend the last two months elsewhere, to avoid distressing her sister with the sight of a fruitless pregnancy. Her plan was not ideal; she dimly saw that there would be more than one kind of pain involved. But she had made it with care and was dully, staunchly proud of having made it.

And now Leo had the nerve to lecture her on fathers' rights—her, whose body was suffering, who wept at nights alone, a bound, trussed captive of biology.

Ignorant bastard! As if poor Lopez would even want to know, him with his good Catholic wife back home in Chile! The unforgivable words hung on the air, and Maggie said in a hard, shaking voice, 'Yes. I'm sure a man worries about these things. Dreadful people, strangers. I knew you wouldn't like that sort of thing, Leo. That's why I got rid of your baby instead.'

Chapter Seven

THREE PAIRS OF EYES stared at Maggie. Leo spoke first.

'What do you mean?'

'I got rid of it. Your baby. After Boston.'

Samantha knew the story. From early childhood she had been told, as part of family lore, how poor Daddy was sent out to persuade Auntie Maggie to come back to college and not to live in the woods, and how he had to walk through a forest which might have bears in. He had had the wrong kind of shoes, and got bitten by mosquitoes, and found her at a log cabin. It was part of the Maggie legend.

She understood immediately. White, shocked, the girl stumbled to her feet. She was starting at her father, and in his face she read the truth.

'You bastard! You bloody—you didn't—' Tears overcame her. 'You were engaged to *Mum!*'

Sarah put out a restraining hand towards her daughter, an instinctive gesture of protection that made Samantha's tears run even faster. She flinched away from her mother, unable to bear contact with anybody so grievously betrayed. Small relief came from turning on her aunt.

'And how *could* you? You slept with Dad and then you killed his baby. You killed my big brother!' Confusion overcame her. It could have been a sister, she knew that, but she had often dreamed when she was small of having a big brother. Perhaps the dream had come because somewhere, inside her, she *knew* . . .

She heard whimpering, fast breathing, a cry in the room, and did not know it was her own.

'Sammy,' said Sarah in an odd voice. 'Sammy, I think the three of us need to talk about this quietly, by ourselves. Sweetheart, don't cry. Shall I take you up to bed?' She talked as if the tall young woman was a baby.

''S'please,' said Samantha, running a sleeve across her nose.

Sarah turned to her husband and her sister. 'Don't move,' she said. 'Don't move, either of you. Maggie, don't go out. I'm asking you. Five minutes.'

Upstairs, she helped Samantha out of her clothes as if she were five, not fifteen, handed her a nightshirt and in silence pulled back the bedclothes. Samantha slid in, still shaking. Sarah bent and kissed her forehead. 'I'll be back later,' she said. 'Good girl. Sweetheart. Breathe deep. Read your book. Forget it for a while.'

Samantha clung to her for a few moments, then fell back on the pillow. Sarah kissed her again. On her way downstairs she looked in on Teddy and said quite brightly, 'How's it going?'

'Nearly finished. Mum, can I watch *The Vicar of Dibley*?'

'Yes. Use Jamie's television, lie on his bed, he'll be out for another hour at least.'

Teddy grinned. Telly-on-a-bed was a luxury not granted to under-thirteens in the Penn household. He gave his mother a hug. All in all, it was nearly ten minutes before she rejoined the adults in the kitchen.

Leo glared across at his sister-in-law, who sat pale and still, elbows on the table, her face framed between thin hands.

'What the hell did you mean by that?' he asked. 'What baby?'

'I was pregnant, after Boston.'

'And you say it was mine?' he asked, his voice brittle with anger. 'I mean, it's not as if we—'

Maggie slapped her palms down on the table and sat upright. 'Of course it was bloody well yours! And yes, it does only take one time to do it. Think of Tess of the d'Urbervilles, Mr Bookseller! How dare you ask whether it was yours! What do you think I am?'

'Well, why didn't you tell me?'

'At the wedding, perhaps? And you'd have said what, exactly? "Oh yes, go on, have the baby, Sarah'll be thrilled"? Grow up, Leo. You'd have wanted me to do exactly what I did do. And I did you and Sarah a favour by not telling you.'

Leo was silent. Next to the horror of the present moment, he weighed the alternative, hypothetical horror of having Sarah told this thing before their wedding. It probably had been best for her to neutralise their terrible, culpable mistake in the swiftest possible way, however brutal. And yes, Maggie was right. Yes, she was probably right not to tell him. In that moment he acknowledged his own weakness. He would not have coped as well as she had with the knowledge of what they had done.

They heard Sarah's footsteps upstairs and the soft closing of Samantha's door. It reminded both of them of the present moment. They stared at one another, appalled.

'Why now?' said Leo, his voice cracking. 'I can see that you were right. Yes, you were. But why'd you do this to Sarah?'

Maggie dropped her eyes. 'I don't know,' she said miserably. 'Bloody hormones. And you being so pompous and snotty about fathers' rights.'

'But I didn't *know*!' Leo almost howled it. 'I had no idea, no idea. You don't think of a stupid one-night stand as being—'

'As being full of eternal consequences? No,' said Maggie sadly, 'I suppose men don't think that. And I suppose I always thought more like a man than a woman myself. Which is probably why I'm pregnant now.'

'Oh Christ. That,' said Leo, who had forgotten how this all began. 'Yes. Well. That's another thing.'

'The main thing,' said Maggie, hearing the footsteps moving towards the stairs, 'is what to say to Sarah.'

Leo hunched in his chair. 'Well . . . the truth,' he said.

The door opened and Sarah came in, quiet and composed. She had stopped in the hallway and practised the old deep-breathing tricks remembered from childbirth. *In . . . one, two, three . . . out, one, two, three, four . . . in . . . and out . . .*

At the sight of the guilty pair, looking terrified at the sight of her, she had a fleeting instinct to reassure them. It passed.

She sat down, and looked first at Leo.

'OK. Now you tell me. How long did it go on for?'

'Once. Just a stupid, stupid . . .' Leo could not go on. 'I've only ever loved you, since we first met. I don't know what happened.'

His sheepish, pleading face was new to her. Unaccustomed to this sort of power, Sarah found to her horror that she quite liked it. The pain, she suspected, would kick in later. Harshly she said, 'Well, I suppose I can work out what happened. Since it resulted in my sister—' Maggie flinched. Could Sarah not say her name, even? '—getting pregnant and needing the services of an abortionist.'

'I mean I don't know why I was so stupid,' said Leo. 'I was shaken up, we both were, it was a long way from home, nothing felt real.'

'That's true,' said Maggie. 'And I was upset. He'd told me about Dad, how ill he was. And the plane got delayed and we had to stay over at an airport hotel. It was all just a muddle.'

'So he put a brotherly arm round you, and you carried on from there, huh?' said Sarah. 'Were you at it for very long? Just so I know, you understand.'

'No!' They almost shouted it, together. From Leo, 'Once, I swear it. And we felt terrible, terrible . . .'

'Terrible,' said Maggie. 'So we said to each other that we'd scrub it out, never remember it, never talk about it. We said that it just didn't happen.'

'But then you found you were pregnant? And you just did it, just like that? Aborted it?'

'It was hard to get the two doctors. I took some short cuts. It had to be done quickly, because I was coming home every week to see Dad.'

Sarah was silent. Waves of outrage kept rising in her, and then subsiding to reveal to her that she still loved her little sister. Leo was another matter, one she did not yet dare think about. Unwillingly she muttered, 'Were you all right?'

'I got an infection. They reckoned I was infertile.'

'And now you're pregnant again. Bit of a coincidence.' The rage was rising once more, and she wanted to lash out and do harm. 'I don't suppose by any chance it's the same father. One-take Charlie, Mr Miracle Sperm here?'

'Jeezus Christ Almighty,' said Maggie. 'I hope you're joking!'

Leo was looking at her with wide, spaniel eyes, too shocked to speak. Sarah felt suddenly weary.

'Yes,' she said, 'I was joking. God knows why. Leo, I'm going to bed. Make sure Jamie's back from the Scout Room by ten. Maggie . . .'

Her practicality deserted her. There was nothing she could say to Maggie now. She shrugged, and left the room.

When Sarah left the kitchen Maggie got up from the table, went into the lobby and pulled on an old waxed jacket, belonging to nobody in particular, which she had adopted since losing her own. It had a rip in the sleeve which let in water. Leo still sat, motionless, at the table.

'I'm going for a walk,' she said in a flat, expressionless voice.

'Fine,' he said.

Rapid walking and the night air began to revive her, cutting through the stupefaction of the scene in the warm kitchen. After carrying her burden alone for years until she hardly noticed it any more, she had cast it at the feet of this kind, steady, dutiful, secretless family. With only one sentence, a sentence she need never have uttered, she had brought their whole security crashing down in ruins. She could not bear to think about Samantha. She could not let herself envisage the grief and confusion of the two boys if their parents were sundered because of this moment of mad wickedness.

She should never have stayed more than a fortnight. She should have moved on. It was what she had to do now; as soon as she was confident that Sarah truly believed in the unimportance of those short hours with Leo. She had sworn at him, she remembered, straight after it was over.

'*Sod* you, you stupid bugger! What have we done? You ought to have known better, you're older than me.' He was: thirty-five to her twenty. And he was in a kind of authority over her during those days: the envoy sent by a trusting sister to persuade her home. He knew perfectly well that he was in the wrong. When she shouted at him he had been meek, appalled by his own behaviour.

She walked swiftly down the High Street, intending to seek comfort from the river. After a few steps, though, she saw the warm lights of the Costarica café.

Her legs ached unwontedly, and a phantom pain darted around her lower back. More than that, she found herself longing for casual, uninvolved human contact: for the silently potent comfort of strangers. She pushed the heavy glass door and went in.

'Rumpelstiltskin! Mavis! Minerva-Louise!'

The man from the car was sitting at a table alone, the wreckage of a chicken Kiev spread before him. 'Boudicca! Esmeralda! Remember me, Marco Polo from Maidstone? I've got your coat here. Look!' He pulled her rain jacket from the bench beside him.

Maggie took it, wonderingly. 'Oh, that is kind. How did you . . .?'

'I have to get my supper somewhere, on my way from here to there. So whenever it makes sense, I come here, with the coat. Persistence pays off in the end. All the world flows through the Brackhampton Costarica.'

'That's extraordinarily kind. This one leaks,' said Maggie.

'Do you suppose it'll ever stop raining?' asked the man. He kicked the chair opposite him so that it scraped back, inviting her to sit down. 'Go on, join me. Humour me. I can amuse myself guessing your name for the next half-hour.'

'Maggie,' she said firmly. 'Margaret Minerva Louise Reave.'

A grin spread across his face. 'Well, coffee?'

'I can't. I'm—' She nearly said 'pregnant'. 'I'm off it at the moment.'

His eyes appraised her with a new sharpness. 'Yes,' he said. 'My ex-wife went right off it, I remember. It was the first sign.'

Maggie sighed, and said resignedly, 'That obvious, is it?'

'You could say I'm sensitised to it,' he said. 'Anyway, my name is Stephen Arundel.'

He ordered herbal tea for her, and they talked, calmingly, of Ireland and the Hebrides, Brittany and Asturias. The travel talk was balm to her.

After a while he asked, 'Where are you off to next?'

She was grateful for his assumption that she was, despite the pregnancy, off on her travels again.

'China,' she said. 'I want to get into Hunan Province.'

'Language?' he asked. 'Speak much?'

'I'm doing a course at Southwick. It's not bad.' She saw that they were alone in the café now, and the waitress was clearing the tables in a huffy manner. 'We'd better get out.'

'Bugger,' said Steve. 'Don't you just hate Middle England, the way everything bloody shuts just as you're settling down?'

'People go home,' said Maggie. The edge of bitterness in her tone was not lost on him, she saw, and she regretted letting it show. For all his jokey glibness, this man had efficient antennae. But he said nothing, merely paying at the counter and turning back towards her with an easy grin.

'Would you,' he asked, 'tell me something?'

'Probably,' said Maggie. 'Come on outside though. I've done that job,' Maggie said in a low voice as they pushed the door open. 'I know how much you detest the customers who hang around.'

The damp air struck them as they left the fuggy, warm-lit room. Coloured Christmas bulbs along the street only gave it an air of dank desperation. Three boys lounged outside the Wimpy, but otherwise the street was empty. Steve Arundel turned to face her and for the first time she saw his height: six foot four or five, he cast a long, gangling shadow under the streetlight.

'You wanted to ask me something,' said Maggie.

'Yes.' He hesitated, an almost crafty look coming over his thin and constantly amused face. 'You won't hit me, though, will you?'

'No,' said Maggie resignedly. Oh God, a proposition. All she needed.

'All it is,' said Steve, 'is to ask you whether this, er, expectant state of which you speak—or rather of which you don't speak—'

'My pregnancy,' said Maggie flatly.

'Well,' he said, 'whoever it is that the condition, er, emanates from . . .' He squirmed, polishing a shoe on the back of his trouser leg like a schoolboy; it was deliberately arch and theatrical. Maggie watched him, silent, amused despite herself.

'This guy,' he said. 'Is he by any chance a) local, b) bigger than me, and c) of an aggressive and territorial temperament?'

Maggie smiled, and ticked off points on her fingers. 'No, no, and no. Well, he may be territorial, but his territory is in Chile.'

'So he could be back any minute? Chile doesn't seem very far away to me.'

'No,' said Maggie. 'He is out of the frame, and far in the past.' Suddenly an image of *Evangelina* came to her, the ship bending to the wind and shuddering with its power, and tears sprang to her eyes. She tightened her lips and said as lightly as she could, 'I am a fallen woman, since you ask so nicely.'

'So he's definitely far enough away for me to ask you out to dinner?'

'I don't know,' she said. 'I'm tired, and life has just taken an unfortunate turn. I can't take on anything new.'

'I'm not new,' he said. 'I am very definitely secondhand.'

She said nothing.

'Someone has to make the decisions,' he said with a sigh. 'First law of business. So, Friday, then. I'll meet you outside the Costarica at seven. We'll go to a pub. If you don't come, I'll just go into the Costa, order another of their undercooked Chicken Kievs and die of salmonella. And it'll be your fault.'

She was on the verge of refusing, but something about him stopped her. Beneath the jokes lay something she recognised: a yawning uncertainty, not quite loneliness but not far from it.

'Just be friends?' she said suddenly. 'Just friends?'

'Possibly not even that,' said the tall man, smooth again now. 'You have to remember that I am an insensitive capitalist bastard.'

'Not friend material at all,' agreed Maggie gravely. He raised a hand in salute and strode off towards the car park. She stood watching him, then with a heavy heart walked back towards her sister's house.

Everything was quiet. Jamie, she thought, must have got back in time. Leo would be upstairs with Sarah. She hung up the torn jacket, tiptoed to her room and closed the door very quietly.

When Leo had seen Jamie upstairs he climbed the stairs, his stomach icy, to face his wife. He undressed in the bathroom and crept into their room without switching on a light; for a wild moment of hope he thought she was already asleep. But as he sat carefully on his side of the bed, the hunched shape opposite reared up, and he saw a glimmer of white face turned towards him.

'Did you love her?' came the hoarse, exhausted whisper. She must have been crying for over an hour.

'Christ, no!' said Leo, his voice shaky. 'I was in love with you. Always. I still am.'

'No, you're not,' said Sarah into the darkness. 'In-love doesn't last. Not for anybody. You graduate from that, into properly loving each other, which is better.'

'And I love you.'

'But the long-term love has to grow out of the in-love thing. And now I don't know if that was ever real. If the root was a fake, the whole thing could be a fake.'

'Of course it was real. I only ever loved you.'

'You slept with her. You went to Canada for only a week, only a week away from me, and you had to sleep with her. Men in love don't do that.'

Leo could have said, 'Yes, they do' but he dared not. He could not explain, if only because he had so completely lost touch with the younger man he used to be. Why had he done it? His memory was hazy. He remembered he was lonely and shaken up after the excursion into the wild alien forest world. He remembered how like Sarah Maggie had looked, and how instinctive was his move to comfort her about Ted's illness. That was all. Nothing to it, really. It seemed absurd to him, looking at the lean, assured, mocking, weather-beaten Maggie of today, that he had ever had the slightest inclination to take her in his arms. Even when they had stood together in that incredible moment watching the flood-water rise in the moonlight, his hand on her shoulder, there had been no tremor of sexuality between them.

He said, 'There isn't an excuse. But it was you I wanted, always. It was one mistake, just one. Before we made our vows. It's always been you.'

Sarah sat up properly, shaking her head as if to free herself from nightmare. 'Were you drunk?'

Leo grasped at the lifeline. 'Yes.' He lied, and knew that she knew he was lying. But it was enough for the present. She lay back, exhausted, on the pillow. Her back was to him; Leo rolled over until he was facing it, but not touching. They had begun. They had put into place the first brick of the new edifice that would shelter the family. He would persevere in telling her that he made a drunken mistake that night. For the moment, that would have to do.

Two doors away, Samantha lay sleepless, hot-eyed, staring at the ceiling. There was a yawning hole in the roof of her life, a jagged gap ripped through the overarching branches of her parents' lives. Beyond it stretched illimitable blackness. But if it had to be faced, she would face it. Plenty of other kids had divorce happen to them. It was part of modern life. It was only when she heard the footfall of Maggie in the passage, and the soft closing of her door, that she began to cry again.

When Maggie woke, she saw to her horror that it was gone eight o'clock; the family was on the move downstairs. She lay beneath the duvet, afraid to get up and face them. But Teddy came to her rescue, bursting in to say, 'Dad says anybody who wants a lift uptown has to be ready in five minutes flat.'

'Oh, uh, I must have overslept.'

'You'll miss your bus then if you don't come with us. And Mum won't drive you because she's having a headache day at home.'

Maggie had been considering skipping college again, but the fear of being alone in the house with Sarah galvanised her.

The drive was silent, or as silent as any drive could be with Teddy among the passengers. Jamie sat in the front and turned on Radio 1, and turned it up, little by little. Leo did not react, driving on in a dream. Both boys kept glancing at their father with fascination. Usually it took only ninety seconds from the switching on of Radio 1 to his eruption. His silence almost worried them. In the end it was Maggie who startled them by snapping abruptly, 'Look, turn it down, we'll go insane.'

When the boys jumped out, Maggie made as if to follow them, but Leo said, 'Stay put, I'll take you to the bus stop.'

'I can walk. I've got ten minutes before the bus.'

'Stay put!'

She closed the door obediently.

As he pulled away, Leo said, 'I haven't spoken to Sarah yet about the bookshop. About you carrying on working there.'

'Oh,' said Maggie. 'I did wonder. I was going away quite soon anyway; I can't face being pregnant in the same town as Mum.'

'You won't go before Christmas?'

'I'm not sure you'll all want me in the house at Christmas.'

'I meant, in the shop. Look, I couldn't say it to her, but I really do have to have an assistant. And I'm not going to find another.'

'Well,' said Maggie, 'it's between you two. But I don't imagine she'll really suspect us of falling on each other lustfully in the shop, will she?'

'Don't joke about it. We're fighting for our lives here.' He stepped on the brake, jolting the car to a halt by the bus stop.

'What shall I do then? Today?'

'Just come into the shop. I'll nip up at lunchtime and have a word with her.'

Maggie got out of the car, pulling her coat round her. Enjoying the familiar setting of the old waterproof on her shoulders, she thought of the tall, dry, oddly kind Steve and how he had kept vigil in the café for her. She turned back towards Leo as he prepared to drive away.

'Is today Friday?'

'No. Tomorrow. Don't forget, late-night opening till eight.'

'Oh, bugg—Well, OK.' She could, she supposed, nip out to the Costarica at seven and tell Steve she would be late. She hoped he'd wait.

'Bye, then. I'll be in the shop. But not at supper. I'll go out somewhere tonight, and I'm out tomorrow too.'

'Good.'

As Leo drove back into town he saw Samantha walking the last few hundred yards to school. She would be late. He slowed down, but she looked straight through him and clipped on along the pavement. Leo, who had not wept for years, found himself sniffing, awash with self-pity. The boys, he thought, the boys must never know.

When the house was empty, Sarah got up straight away. She did not have a headache. Of all the family, she had spoken only to Samantha, when she woke in the dawn to hear her in the bathroom. She had put her head round the door to find her daughter sitting on the edge of the bath, stirring the fluffy bathmat around with one bare foot.

'All right, sweetheart?'

'Are *you* all right, Mum?' The blue eyes looked up at her, swimming.

'Yes. Don't worry. It was all a long time ago.'

'Mum, shall I stay at home today? With you?'

'Absolutely not. Go to school. Be normal.' And, seeing the tears welling in Samantha's eyes again, she added. 'Brave girl. No fussing. I'll sort it all out.'

'Will you leave Dad?' said Samantha, standing up.

'Darling, I am not up for questions like that. Not now,' said Sarah. 'Don't ask. But we both love you, all of you, and we'll do what's best for everyone.'

Now she moved around automatically, straightening curtains and cushions and rinsing the breakfast mugs and plates. When her coffee had brewed, she sat down and pulled the morning paper towards her. She could not concentrate, though, and after a while stood up and set off for the vet's. His grumpy presence was what she needed. She would not tell him anything about the crisis. Of course not.

Sam Miller was scrubbing his hands at the basin in the consulting room when she arrived, and raised his eyebrows.

'You don't come in till two on Thursday, woman,' he said. 'Are you going to tell me you can't do this afternoon? Because I've got a long, long letter to the Royal College—'

'I'll be here all day,' said Sarah. 'I don't want to be at home.' And she burst into tears and told him everything in the short time between his kicking the door shut and the young veterinary nurse pushing it open again to bring in a drooping shih-tzu. Sarah pretended to check the notices on the wall while the girl flopped the dog on the table and said, 'He's due to go home today, post-op, but I don't think he looks right, Mr Miller, do you?'

'Hmmph. Look, Mrs Penn can hold him if need be. You'd better go and check the other night kennels.'

'Righty-ho,' said the girl amiably, and vanished.

Sarah said, 'I'm sorry to burst out at you like that.'

'No, you're not. You feel much better for it. People always do, when they've told you about their lives. That's why I decided not to be a doctor. Animals don't relate long atrocious sagas about their love lives.' He rolled the dog's eye open and grimaced. 'Bloody thing. I knew he'd do this to me.'

Sarah wondered, not for the first time, how the old vet got away with it, and why she was so stubbornly fond of him.

'I said I'm sorry,' she insisted. 'But I've had an awful shock. It just came over me.'

The vet reached for a syringe, holding the dog down with his free hand. 'Just hang on to him for me a sec,' he said, and filled the syringe to plunge its needle deftly into the dog's hindquarters. 'There you are, boy. No, I do see it was a shock. You've never quite grasped that your sister is designed by nature to give people shocks, it still surprises you every time. You know whose he is, don't you?' said Miller. Sarah was momentarily distracted from her own troubles by a professional misgiving.

'Oh no, not Mrs Harrison!' she said.

'Oh yes, Mrs Harrison,' said the vet. 'So I'll cut you a deal, if you like.'

'What?'

'You ring the old bat and tell her that Muffy-Poo or whatever its name is has had a slight allergic reaction and has to stay here for another night. Then you listen to her squawking for half an hour, and tell her I'm tied up with a dying pussycat and on no account put her through. And in return I will give you wise counsel as to what a woman should do when she discovers that her husband slept with her sister sixteen years ago before the wedding.'

'OK,' said Sarah. 'Shoot.'

'The wise woman's best course of action is . . .' He paused impressively. 'Forget it.'

'Why?'

'Because it doesn't matter. Because it's in the past and can never happen again. Your sister is a wandering albatross. She'll be off again soon, baby or no baby.'

'But I just feel so—'

'Hysterical and irrational,' completed the vet. He reached over to the buzzer, and before Sarah could gather her wits to reply to this insult, the nurse came in.

'Come on, darling!' she cooed to the dog. 'Back to the ward, then?'

'Yes. Mrs Penn will ring Mrs Harrison,' said the vet. When the nurse had gone, he washed his hands and said over his shoulder, 'You know I'm right. Just forget it. Women have no idea how little sex can mean to young men.'

'But what about my sister?'

'I told you. She's a pirate. A Viking. Different rules. Get treated rougher, treat other people rougher. Is she still working in the bookshop?'

Sarah stared at him in wide-eyed dismay. 'I'd forgotten that,' she said.

'See? Forgetting's quite easy, when you get the hang of it.'

Leo went through the morning like a sleepwalker. At lunchtime he went up to the house to speak to Sarah, but found it locked and empty. Unreasonably disconsolate, he made himself a sandwich and mooched around the kitchen, trying not to imagine how it would be if Sarah were never there at all.

Except, of course, that it would be him who had to move out, if anyone did. That was how it worked when there were children in the case, and he supposed that was the right thing. He, Leo Penn, could be imminently thrown out just for something he did more than fifteen years earlier, for no motive that he could remember.

Where had she gone? To a solicitor?

At two he dragged himself back down to the shop, and unlocked it. Maggie arrived, and without a word went up to the children's department to unpack a delivery.

Leo called up to her, 'Since you're here, can you man the barricades while I go out for twenty minutes?'

'Course,' she said, glaring at him over a pile of Grinch books.

He wandered along to the vet's surgery. The nurse glanced up at him as he came in.

'Mr Penn. You looking for your wife? She's taking some letters from Mr Miller before afternoon surgery.'

'Can I see her?'

'All righty! You sit down-io and I'll grab her.'

Sarah appeared a moment later, looking annoyed.

'What d'you want? I'm working.'

'Had to ask you something.' The nurse was pretending to tidy up prescription forms but eyeing them with interest. He lowered his voice. 'Maggie. Her working in the shop. Is it OK with you? For the moment?'

'Course.' She turned away, leaving him faintly shocked and not knowing why. Then he realised.

It was what Maggie had said, and in the same contemptuous voice, and with the same glare.

Maggie walked up towards the house. She longed to lie down. Her legs ached, her head was swimming, and she yearned for sleep. Teddy and some freckled friend waylaid her at the door, with demands for instruction in street magic.

'Will you show us how you do the one where you sort of burn the name on your arm?'

'We could do it for the school revue. Hardly any Year Sevens ever get to be in it.'

Maggie shivered. It was not just that she was tired. After what she had done it seemed unfitting for her to frolic as she used to with her sister's child. Had she stripped herself even of aunthood? Behind the boys, she could see Sarah's back view in the kitchen, deliberately not turning to greet her.

'Look,' she said, 'I can't do the arm trick now because I need special wax. But if you like, you can get the magic coin trick out. It's in the bedside-table drawer in my room. OK?'

'Wicked!' said Teddy, and to his friend, 'I'm going to be a street magician when I'm fourteen. I'm not doing GCSEs.'

Sarah still did not turn.

When the boys had gone, Maggie went up to her and said, 'Talk to me. Sare, talk to me. I'm leaving town pretty soon, but Leo wants me to work over Christmas in the shop. Is that all right, if I stay in the house till then?'

Sarah turned, her eyes hard. 'I don't see that it makes the slightest difference,' she said coldly. 'Not to me, anyway. To Samantha, perhaps. She's very upset. It's a difficult age for a girl. Not the time you want to drop this kind of bombshell on her.'

'I wish I could tell you how sorry . . .' began Maggie miserably. But Sarah snapped.

'You keep out of her way. I'll explain to her that you're needed for the shop.' She slapped a wedge of pizza dough down hard, and ground her knuckles into it.

'Well, I'll keep out of everyone's way,' said Maggie with sad finality.

On Friday morning Maggie hauled herself out of bed before first light. In the bathroom mirror she saw that she looked suddenly older, the lines on her temples more pronounced, her skin yellow as its old tan faded in the Kentish rain; her wide reflected eyes looked out at her from a thin face.

She pulled on Sarah's old jeans and white shirt with the ache of guilt which had, over the past thirty-six hours, become as familiar a pain as the ache of her back and the constant faint nausea. It was colder today under the clear skies, and with dismay she realised that she owned virtually no clothes suitable for winter. Her one fleece and store of tattered sweaters might not take her far into the cold season. She must go to the charity shop, but most of the stuff there would hang like sacks on her . . .

Not for much longer. The thought froze her in the act of combing her long hair. Jesus Christ, but she was pregnant! She would *need* huge clothes soon. Tears pricked her eyes. Imagine buying maternity clothes, wearing them, all for a baby she would never even see. It was pathetic. Not because she wanted the baby, but because of the lumbering figure she would cut, all the more ludicrous for not intending to be a mother. But there was no alternative. She must endure what was coming.

She felt sick, and knew she would have to eat. She could not take any more of the Penns' food, not just now, even as a paying lodger. Maggie hurried down the stairs, grabbed her jacket and bag and stepped out into the frosty air. She must watch every penny now. From the corner shop she bought a waxed carton of fruit juice and a Danish pastry, and ate this dreary breakfast as she walked up to the bus stop.

'If I tell you something awful,' said Samantha to Uma Syal, 'will you promise to keep it, like, totally secret?'

Of all the girls in the school, this quiet, dark-eyed, self-possessed creature was the most likely to keep such a promise. They had been inseparable friends during the first years at the High School, only losing one another during Samantha's defection to Duane. When the dust of recent alarms had settled, it was with relief that she saw the dark, kind eyes still willing to look in her direction, and they had renewed the friendship.

'I can keep secrets,' said Uma calmly, 'if it is not dangerous or wicked to keep them. If you tell me you have murdered Mrs Harvey then I will tell the police.' She grinned. 'Go on then. Tell. What is it? You've looked so pissed off these two days!'

Samantha sighed, and stretched her long legs. They were sitting together on a bench in the gym, waiting for Mrs Randall, the PE teacher, to come back from answering the phone.

'Well,' she said. 'Basically—you know my aunt?'

'The famous Aunt Maggie? My mother talks about her.'

'Yes. Well, she's pregnant.'

'Aie, aie! Difficult. No husband. Will she have the baby at your house?'

'It's not that. She says she's moving out of town anyway, and it'll be adopted. But it's not that.'

Uma looked at her friend, surprised by her dismissal of Maggie's momentous and—to her—appalling decision. 'There's something even more secret than that?'

'Yes. The other night Dad was being a bit pompous about her having it adopted, saying fathers had rights, all that. Which I do believe, actually, I suppose.' Confusion overcame her; she had not thought about Duane when she thought she was pregnant, had she? 'But anyway . . .'

'What?' Uma was impatient now.

'It was awful. Maggie burst out and said that, huh, when she was pregnant by Dad she got rid of it. It turns out that just before Mum and Dad got married, he slept with her.'

'Aie, aie, aie!' said Uma again. 'Oh, that's terrible!'

'Yes. It made me go all weird, and I keep crying when I don't mean to.' Samantha's eyes filled with tears. 'Mum says it's all right, they'll sort it all out. But! I mean, it's awful, why did he do it?'

'What about your Aunt Maggie? What does she say?'

'I'm never going to *speak* to her again. Bitch!'

'And your father?'

Samantha stared at her in horror. 'Oh, come on. If it was *your* father, would you ask him? I mean!'

Uma shook her head in shared dismay at the dreadful prospect of knowing anything about a father's sex life. Then, frowning, she asked, 'Do the boys know?'

'No. Unless Mum's told them, and she wouldn't.'

'That's good.'

'Yes. That's something.'

They brooded together, then the gym door swung open violently and Mrs Randall reappeared.

'Right, girls! Sorry! Now, warming up—round the walls, jog!'

As they jolted obediently off, Uma turned to whisper to her friend. 'Will your aunt go away now?'

'I hope so,' said Samantha, but there were tears in her eyes again.

Chapter Eight

WHEN MAGGIE STEPPED into the bookshop she hardly recognised it. Leo was wrestling with a trestle table, assisted by two elderly men in tweed jackets, battered trousers and highly polished shoes. Another table already dominated the centre of the room. Cardboard boxes of books were stacked against the wall on the left. A large cardboard effigy of Raymond Briggs's cartoon Father Christmas was propped on the right, obscuring the travel shelf. As she watched, a gust blew through the door and the creature began to topple sideways towards the desk.

With a lightning reaction, Maggie dived forward and caught the collapsing Santa, ending up slightly breathless with one arm round the cardboard figure's waist and the other clutching the desk.

'Oh, well saved!' said one of the two men. 'That's the sort of customer you need, Leo.'

Leo flickered a smile and said, 'This is my sister-in-law, Maggie Reave, who is helping out over the Christmas rush. Maggie, you haven't met General Madson and Rear-Admiral Havelock. They run the rare-book catalogue. This is the only time of year I manage to get them in the shop for an hour or two.' He beamed nervously at the old men.

'Bobby Madson,' said one, extending a polite hand.

'Tim Havelock,' said the other. 'Don't, for Christ's sake, call me Admiral. These days they're just a kind of butterfly as far as I'm concerned. Leo here likes to use the ranks. Gives him credibility among collectors of militaria.'

'Also makes him feel less guilty about forcing poor old men with dodgy hips to help him move heavy tables. He feels as if he's got troops, not dupes.' They laughed, a bluff, wrinkled Tweedledum and Dee.

Maggie, unspeakably relieved to see that there would be company in the shop for a while, gave the old men a smile.

'Let me help with the tables,' she said. 'How do they go?'

Leo explained that during the Christmas rush, he always abandoned the spacious, peaceful layout of the bookshop in favour of narrower aisles and higher heaps. It was not to his taste, but experience revealed that it was not only a practical measure to keep fast-moving star books on display. It actually attracted a different class of customer. The shop became more welcoming to those who liked bustle and garishness.

Soon Maggie was at work, ripping open boxes, while the two old men tacked up the Santa in the children's library and wound tinsel along the spotlight tracks. Maggie sold a good number of books, and Leo took orders which, trying not to cross his fingers, he assured the buyers would arrive by Christmas Eve.

At five o'clock the old servicemen made their exit and soon the shop was filled with late-night shoppers. Maggie was kept busy, for these were the hurriers rather than the browsers, anxious people who would pounce on a book as a quick, easily wrapped way of ticking off another family duty.

At five past seven Maggie finished a transaction and turned to Leo. 'Do you mind if I nip out for five minutes?' she said. 'I need to speak to someone. I'll be right back.'

'OK. Be quick.'

She half ran down the road to the Costarica. Peering through the clouded windows she saw a dozen resting shoppers in there. None was the tall, familiar shape. She was surprised at the treacherous power of her disappointment. But turning resignedly away, she found herself staring up at Steve Arundel, and gasped.

'Oh! I thought—'

'Sorry. Couldn't park. Forgot about Christmas shopping.'

'The thing is, I'm working in a shop down the road. The bookshop. And I forgot too—it's open till eight tonight. I'm terribly sorry. Perhaps another evening . . .'

'Why?' he said. 'Do you need a couple of hours to go home and run up a dress out of the green velvet curtains before you can face a gentleman? Why, Scarlett!'

'No! I can come straight from the shop at eight, if you don't mind the jeans—but you don't want to wait around in this lot.'

In fact she longed for him to wait, yearned for an evening's easy company. But she would not say so. She could not do the slightest thing which might be construed as Leading A Man On.

Steve looked at her, consideringly. 'I'm not bloody well going into the Costarica,' he said, finally. 'Can't face it.' He watched her.

Maggie began, with all the brightness she could muster, 'Well, another day perhaps . . .' She was suddenly conscious of her lank hair and tired countenance. But smoothly the watcher cut in.

'No, I was going to ask, would you consider driving off somewhere else? My dad always said it was inconsiderate to ask a strange woman to go in a car with you on the first date, in case she thought you were a kidnapper. But seeing how we met . . .'

Maggie looked up at him again and smiled. 'Which car park?'

'Top. Near the cinema. Black Saab.'

He pulled out his wallet and handed her a card. It bore his company's name embossed with a logo, his own name and a grainy photograph of Steve himself. 'Just give that card to someone you work with. Then if you're found dismembered in a trunk tomorrow, they can pull me in, and I can explain, with shifty rolling eyes, that it was a very determined and tidy-minded suicide.'

She hesitated, not quite knowing whether to laugh. He pressed the card on her, suddenly very serious.

'No, take it. It's a wicked world. Women have to be suspicious. Men have to be cool about being suspects. Go on, feel safe.'

She took the card. There was no point explaining the impossibility of her giving it to Leo just now. But she saw that he was trying to reassure her and she was touched. She smiled up at him, and nodded.

On the way back to the shop she met Miss Mountjoy, flushed from the cold, hurrying along with a carrier bag. They had not met for a week, and again Maggie was touched, this time by the enthusiasm with which the old woman greeted her. 'Maggie dear!' On an impulse she handed her the card.

'That's a man I'm going out with tonight,' she said. 'I don't know him very well, and he thought it would be a good idea if I made sure someone knew who he was. So that I felt safe.' She blushed.

Miss Mountjoy beamed. 'How very considerate. He must be a gentleman. I'll pop into the shop tomorrow to make sure you're safe. Have a lovely evening.'

When Maggie joined him in the car park, Steve said, 'Hop in. Mystery tour begins. Anywhere but Christmasland.'

'Mmm. It has been a bit overpowering,' she said.

Steve made his way to the bypass and put his foot down. 'Where are we going?' she asked.

'Sea,' he said briefly. And indeed, for a few minutes they followed the same road they had first travelled. It was the shortest way to the coast, but moments later he took the left fork, off to the north.

'Where *are* we going? Which sea?'

'North Sea. Well, Thames Estuary.'

He drove on. Maggie found that she could relax in his silence. It was a novelty to be taken somewhere she had not chosen. She closed her eyes; it had been a long day, and her traitorous body was more sluggish than it once had been. The car was warm, its pace on the clear road smooth.

With a jolt she woke. They had come to a halt, and through the windscreen she could see a bright moon shining a hole in dark, ragged cloud. Again the memory of nights on *Evangelina* came to her, so powerfully that she gasped. She turned and saw Steve Arundel sitting beside her, reading a book.

'God, I'm sorry. What—?'

'You fell asleep. Seemed a pity to wake you.'

'How long?'

'Half an hour. We got here twenty minutes ago. I haven't white-slaved you, honestly. Frankly, there's not much of a white slave trade in Whitstable. In spite of all the oysters.'

'Whitstable! Do you know, I've never been here.'

'You have now. Fish restaurant. Very good. Booking's in fifteen minutes. Time for a walk, if you like.'

Maggie tumbled from the car, stretching stiff limbs. There was salt air all around them and she could hear a faint susurration of waves. They were barely ten feet from a sea wall and a shingle beach. She clambered onto the concrete wall and looked out across the estuary.

'Oh, thank you!' she cried, transported. It was as if she had woken from the whole bad dream to find herself on the edge of freedom. She forgot all the troubles and exulted on the seashore. 'Thank you!'

'You haven't had your dinner yet,' protested Steve mildly, amused. In his experience, girls who fell asleep in your car spent their first minutes of consciousness looking at the mirror, not the scenery.

Maggie turned, her thin face alight. 'No, it's something else. I'll tell you about it. Come on. There's a harbour!'

'Oooh, a harbour!' he mocked, and held out a hand to get her down from the wall. When she had alighted, he kept it.

'C'mon,' he said. 'Harbour's this way.' They wandered along to the little dock where dark water lapped at the stones and the still darker shapes of fishing boats tugged gently at their lines. In the outer approach lay a small sailing ship, its mast rearing high above the level of the harbour wall.

'Brixham trawler,' said Steve. 'Don't often see them in here.' There were lights in the boat's cabin, and the faint sound of an accordion playing. They peered down, hand in hand, enjoying the bittersweet sense of being outsiders. After a while, not yet ready for their supper, they walked the other way. It was a silent little town that night, with closed-up holiday cottages and only a few lights along Sea Road. Maggie admired the wooden walls of the old buildings, with their white overlapping planks. She ran her hand over them, lovingly.

'Shiplap, is it called?' said Steve. 'Americans call it clapboard. Or is that different?'

'Built by people who normally built boats, I suppose. I love it,' said Maggie. 'You feel so different in brick.' She kicked the low wall of a Victorian cottage. 'Brick just slowly crumbles. With wood, if a bit rots, you can put a new bit in and get on with your life. And you know that somewhere there's a live forest growing more for the next generation. Wood is optimistic. Brick is fatalistic. It assumes the worst.'

She thought of the house she must go back to, the brick garment that Sarah's family wore. She halted, suddenly choked with emotion, and found to her dismay that she was crying. A loud sniff in the darkness alerted Steve.

'Dear oh dear,' he said. 'Blood sugar dropping. Time to eat, I think.' He led her back to the restaurant.

'It's all right,' he said kindly as they approached. 'Look, it's all made of wood. An old oyster shed. Hardly a brick in sight.'

'Sorry,' said Maggie. She sniffed, and grinned.

'*De rien*,' said Arundel, smooth again.

'So,' said Steve, when they had ordered. 'You said you'd tell me why you were so pleased to see Whitstable.'

'It was just that when I opened my eyes, and smelt the harbour, and heard the waves, it reminded me of *Evangelina*,' said Maggie.

'Who's Evangelina?' Crikey, thought Steve to himself. A lesbian. I should have guessed. But a pregnant one? Well, that would explain why she's not looking too happy. He looked at Maggie with almost brotherly fondness. Poor kid. 'Where did you meet her?' he said evenly.

Maggie stared at him. 'She's a *ship*,' she said. 'Did you think . . . oh my God!' Her mouth fell open. 'You thought it was a girlfriend?'

'Well, how was I to know . . .' He blushed fiery red.

Maggie began to laugh properly for the first time since he had picked her up, on the sea road.

'*Where did I meet her*, indeed?' Maggie added remorselessly. 'All set to listen understandingly to tales of dyke clubs in Acapulco, huh? What happened to your judgmental right-wing capitalist bastard instincts?'

'Oh, bugger!' said Steve. 'I am so embarrassed. Ooh, look, the relief column—gimme!' He took his plate of mussels from the surprised waitress's hands, and snipped one out expertly with the double shell of another. 'Mm, delicious! Let's talk about mussels. Did you know they change sex all the time? It was probably them that I was thinking of.'

Maggie began to eat her scallops. After a moment she said, 'Can I tell you about *Evangelina*, though?'

'Shoot.'

She told him the story of how she came upon the ship, the passage and her growing sense of wonder on the ocean. 'I'd sailed on quite a few boats, some of them really big yachts, but always faffing about in the Caribbean, with spoilt tourists. And I'd never been aloft before, working on yardarms.'

'You'd not get me up there,' said Steve. 'So the view was good?'

'Oh yes. The moon, the sunrise, a pod of whales, eternity all around. I never wanted to arrive, but when we got near Spain, and I saw the Picos de Europa rising out of the sea . . . and all the crew just going wild . . .' She sipped her wine, smiling. 'Oh God, Steve, it was amazing. Spain's always a sort of mother country to South Americans. I got caught up in it like they did . . .' She paused. 'Well, it was sad to arrive and leave the ship, but sort of wonderful too.'

'The voyage wouldn't have been a voyage without the landfall?' he said quietly.

'That's right. Things have to end.'

They were silent. The waitress cleared away the plates and brought them cod and skate wings. Then Steve said, 'And from what you said outside the Costarica, I assume the proposed infant is a sort of farewell present from the voyage. Half Chilean?'

Maggie found that she no longer minded talking to Steve about her situation. 'Yes. A reprehensible one-night stand. In my defence I would stress that he *was* the captain. I obviously took my duties too far.'

He did not react to the joke, only asking quietly, 'But you want it?'

She looked him in the eye. 'No.' She paused, and he held her with a questioning look so that she continued, less willingly, 'It's completely impractical. I have no money, I have no fixed home. My life doesn't suit a baby. Anyway, babies ought to have fathers.'

'Amen,' said Steve, with an edge of bitterness.

She remembered his fleeting mention of his wife, she who hated coffee in her pregnancy, and asked, 'Do you have kids?'

'No. Jill—my wife—was pregnant. It was brilliant. I thought life couldn't get better. But she lost the baby. Seven months. Stillbirth.'

'Oh God . . .' Maggie felt treacherous tears rising again. 'That's terrible. Oh, how awful. I mean, I don't want this baby, it's going to be adopted, but I'd be horrified if it died.'

'We did want ours,' said Steve flatly. 'But when Jill lost it, I handled everything wrong.'

'How?' she said.

'I said the wrong things. Blokey things, I suppose. I was trying to be helpful. Stuff about going forward, trying for the next time, all that.'

'Well, fair enough. You'd *have* to look forward.'

'Not so soon. I see that, now. Jill—well, it had lived inside her, hadn't it? Moved. Blokes don't get that. Emotional illiterates, they call us. I should have kept out of it.'

'But someone had to talk to her,' objected Maggie.

'Her mother did that. No Men Past This Point.'

Maggie rubbed a piece of bread in the sauce from her cod, and ate it. After a moment she said, 'Was that why you separated?'

'Probably. It was six months later. She left a note, and that was it. Off with her fitness coach.'

'Is she all right now?' Somehow, Maggie felt she had to go on asking. The sisterhood of pregnant women, she thought, must be grasping her to its soft bosom already.

'Yes,' said Steve. 'I would say so. I heard she's pregnant again. There's no medical reason it shouldn't work out OK. Last time was some sort of one-off poisoning. I don't know, cream cheese or something.'

To her dismay there were tears in his eyes. She put her hand on his, patting it like a mother.

'I'm sorry. Shouldn't have pried.'

He recovered. 'Anyway, I hadn't finished grilling you. You're expecting a semi-Chilean baby but you don't want it, you're off to Hunan, and meanwhile you're doing what?'

'Oh, God, you don't want to know. My life at the moment is like an edition of the Jerry Springer Show,' said Maggie bitterly.

'I *love* Jerry Springer,' said Steve. 'Come on, let's have pudding and tell me all the unspeakable details. It'll cheer me up.'

'Well,' said Maggie slowly. 'It begins in the year my dad died. Sixteen years ago.'

Sarah prowled restlessly round the sitting room, unable to sew or watch television, unwilling to read. Leo sat with a book; the children had retired to their rooms.

'I ought to talk to Samantha,' she said.

Leo looked up. 'Sarah. Sweetheart.'

She looked at him coldly. 'Yes?'

'We have to sort it out between ourselves first. It's you and me.'

'You and *her*, more like.'

Leo flinched. 'There is no me and her. There never was. There was one night, one confused night.'

'All night?' Sarah could not help herself.

'No,' said Leo, understanding her perfectly. 'Not even all night. We knew what a disaster it was straight away. She was angry, she went off to her room.'

'People don't get pregnant that easily.'

'Maggie did. I swear to you. And I swear, Sarah, that until Wednesday, I had no idea at all. God, do you think I would have let her do that? She didn't even do it properly, legally. She did herself harm, apparently.'

'So now she's spreading the harm, messing us up.'

Leo sensed he was being unwise, yet could not prevent himself. 'To be fair, love, Maggie wasn't that much older than Sam is now.'

Sarah turned away from him and left the room. Leo looked down at his book as if he had never seen such an object before. Then he threw it from him with some force, and stared into emptiness.

'So you see,' concluded Maggie, 'Jerry Springer would love to have me on. I Secretly Aborted My Brother-In-Law's Child.'

'Not to mention I Did Secret Pregnancy Test With My Teenage Niece,' said Steve. 'And I Don't Want To Bring Up Married Sea Captain's Bastard Child Alone. You could do a whole edition of Jerry Springer all on your own, no trouble.'

Maggie smiled at him, and he saw that she might sometimes be a beauty. 'Look, I *am* grateful. I didn't think there'd be anyone I could tell the whole awful story to. And confession is good for the soul. Such a *string* of crimes against decent society. I haven't even begun to think about Mrs Lopez.'

'Oh, for God's sake,' said Steve bracingly. 'Leave her out of it. What she doesn't know won't kill her.'

'I tried to tell myself that about Sarah, sixteen years ago,' said Maggie bitterly. 'But she knows now, doesn't she?'

'Well, you're not likely to end up at the Lopez kitchen table in sixteen years' time, are you?' he said. 'Talking of terrible house guests, how long are you staying there?'

'I promised to work in the shop until Christmas Eve,' said Maggie. 'I'll find some way of not being in the house by Christmas Day.' The restaurant was emptying. She glanced around. 'We'd better go.'

Outside, the moon was brighter now, the tattered clouds in retreat. Silently, by common consent, they walked away from the car park and along by the sea, buffeted by the wind, admiring the glimmering track of the moon. Then they went back to the black Saab and climbed in, glad to be out of the rising gale. Maggie felt a brief, absurd wish that the journey home was longer. She could sit in this warm car with this dry, comradely man for hours in contentment. She felt a dread of Brackhampton.

'Off to get bricked up again,' she said aloud.

He turned to look at her. 'You're tired,' he said. 'You need some sleep.'

But she didn't go to sleep on the way back to Brackhampton. She stayed awake, watching the lights of the little town grow clearer.

Teddy had stayed overnight with his freckled friend, and on Saturday morning he came in to the bookshop. He crashed against the Christmas table with a cheerful 'Oops!' and announced to Leo and

Maggie and the shop in general, 'Hey, hot news. Duane's in *prison*.'

'Who?' said Leo. 'Don't barge around like that.'

'Sam's old boyfriend, remember?' said Teddy. 'He came to supper and then afterwards you said he was a yob.'

'Yes, yes,' interrupted his father hastily. There were half a dozen people up in the children's department. 'But what do you mean, prison?'

'Young offender place at Normanfield. For agg-agger-avated burgling. Remanded in custody. He hit this bloke on the way out, when he was doing the place over.'

Leo winced at his young son's fluency on the subject. 'Well,' he said vaguely. It was for Maggie to ask whether Samantha knew.

'Noooh,' said Teddy. 'S'why I came down here, to tell her, thought she'd be here 'cos she said she had Christmas shopping to do, and Dad gives us discounts here. If she comes in for mine, I want the Blackadder book.' He left to rejoin his friends in the record shop.

Samantha did come in, minutes later. She had appeared slightly less frosty at breakfast time, so when Samantha was ensconced in a quiet bay Maggie came up behind her and said hesitantly, 'Sam. Teddy was in. He had a bit of news about Duane. He's in custody at Normanfield. Burglary with violence.'

Samantha started, turning to her wide-eyed. 'Oh shit! Stupid idiot! I always knew—' She stopped.

'You knew that he went burgling?' Maggie kept her voice low, and Samantha followed suit.

'I knew his brother did. Jake. He's horrible. Was Dooze with his brother?' It was the first time Maggie had heard Sam use the nickname; she was strangely affected by the unwilling proof of old affection.

'I don't know. Teddy didn't seem to know much.'

'The thing is,' said Samantha, 'he was actually quite scared of his brother. I reckon he used to threaten him, to make him come out on jobs, 'cos Duane is really good at climbing, and really thin for windows, and Jake and his mates are all quite fat.'

'Right,' said Maggie. Once again, she was being confided in; the warmth it lit within her was astonishing.

'Yeah, 'cos once he was meant to go and help them break into a house, and I made him stay with me at a party instead. But next morning he had this big bruise down the side of his face.'

'His brother?'

'He said he had a fall and hit the cooker at home.'

Leo noticed them talking, kept his distance, and he, too, was relieved at the apparent truce. His daughter was still cool and uncommunicative with him, but if she was thawing towards her aunt, perhaps he would be next.

He was right. Samantha had been thinking hard for two days, and discussing the matter with the level-headed Uma at school.

'I don't think you should be too angry with your aunt,' Uma had said that very afternoon. 'If you stay furious with her, you have to be just as angry with your dad. And that wouldn't help, right? Hating him is, like, no point. You've only got one dad. And it's not like fathers who run off.'

Uma's reasoning suited Samantha's instincts better than the almost mawkish sympathy which her mother kept offering, in whispering visits to her bedside, or in oversweet gestures of unspoken female empathy at mealtimes. *We are victims, you and I*, said Sarah's manner. *Men stray, women weep*.

Samantha found a small, hard core of resistance growing within her. Her mother could think what she wanted. The fear of her parents' separation still struck cold panic into her stomach, but with an effort she quelled it. As for the crime itself, with Uma's assistance, her own view had come to encompass several aspects which had not at first been apparent to her. It happened before she was born, years ago, before they were married. It was, her father had said, a mistake. He clearly loved his wife and children. He was very meek and sorry and putting up with no end of ratty treatment from Mum.

As for Maggie, she too was acting so meek and sorry that she didn't even eat meals with them any more. And she had had a horrible time, thought Samantha, all alone and deciding about the abortion. All in all, when Maggie spoke to her in the bookshop, Samantha leapt at the chance to be reasonably civil.

Leaning on her father's bookshelves, she said, frowning slightly, 'I s'pose I'd better go and see him.'

Maggie was taken aback. 'I didn't mean that,' she began. 'I only told you because I thought you had a right to know early. But you're not Duane's girlfriend now.'

Sam stared at her. 'That's got nothing to do with it,' she said simply. 'I *was* his girlfriend, at least I *tried* to be. We were sort of friends, before— all the sex stuff. I sort of liked him. He was funny in class. I even felt sorry for him about his crappy family.'

Maggie raised an eyebrow, almost in her old teasing way.

Sam snapped, 'No, I don't still fancy him. No way. But I *liked* him. I might be able to help.'

'How?' Maggie was impressed, but unwilling to encourage this line of thought; she dimly saw more trouble ahead.

'Character reference. If I could tell the police, like, that he got beaten up for not going on the robbery the other time, it could be intimidation, or mitigation, or something.'

'That's brave, but don't do anything sudden,' Maggie said slowly. 'Please. Getting mixed up with him has already cost you.'

'I'll ring his mother,' said Sam flatly. 'I'm not a baby.'

Samantha walked home, and in through the kitchen where Sarah sat listlessly turning the pages of the newspaper.

"Lo, Mum,' she said, and made for the stairs.

'Oh darling, just a minute—while we've got a chance on our own . . .' began Sarah.

Samantha stopped walking, but shifted restlessly. 'Ya?' 'On our own' could only mean more sticky emotional talk.

Sarah perceived her daughter's reluctance, but did not want to give up her chance. She was particularly low that morning, despondent and afraid. The burden of righteous victimhood lay heavy on Sarah's solitude. But whenever she felt an instinct to forgive and carry on, a small raging voice inside her would begin again.

He never loved me, it was a sham, I was just the available one and he wanted to settle down, wanted a wife who earned enough for him to set up the shop. I was never exciting, never what he wanted—he preferred Maggie, they always go for the youngest they can, even now he's only thinking about how hard it was on her, poor little Maggie, everybody's baby, Dad's pet. What about how I feel? I'm the one who has to look after everybody. Who bothers to look after me, what about me?

In more rational moments Sarah knew that the voice was twisting truth, but she could not help it. It was as if a whole stretched life of cheerful hard-working endurance and thought for others had sprung back on itself, with every slight and resentment and small exploitation giving energy to the murderous coiling rage within her.

Sarah persuaded herself that she watched and comforted her daughter because it was needed. In fact, as Sam herself had spotted, it was Sarah who needed these sessions.

'Sweetheart, the thing is, Christmas. It's going to be difficult for you, I know. We ought to talk about how to manage it.'

'Well, the usual,' said Samantha, surprised. 'I s'pose Gran's coming round, and the family, and the normal stuff.'

Sarah's voice dropped into a low, hurt register. 'It can't be normal, though, can it?'

Samantha said, 'Whatever you think. Only the boys would be surprised if it wasn't the usual stuff.'

Sarah knew perfectly well that this would be the deciding factor, and that somehow they would conduct Christmas along normal lines. Leo's role in the feast, anyway, was to arrive home exhausted from the shop on Christmas Eve, sleep in till eleven on Christmas Day, and then try unsuccessfully to persuade everybody to go on a nice walk before lunch; after which, he once again slept. Nancy would talk nonstop until she, too, fell asleep over Christmas tea, and everybody left awake would watch the big film. There was no particular reason to put a bomb under Christmas, except that she, Sarah, wanted to detonate something—anything—to ease her own anguish.

Sulkily she said, 'Well, what about Maggie?'

Samantha searched for something to say, something safe. She happened to come up with the least safe thing of all.

'Well, I don't mind,' she said, 'And she is pregnant, so p'raps we ought to be looking after her at Christmas.'

Her mother had often told them to think of the vulnerable at Christmas. Sam, in her innocence, thought that it would help to portray her aunt not as desirable company but as a charity case. She did not expect the reaction she got.

'Right!' screamed Sarah. 'Out of my sight! You, of all people! Go and run the poor-dear-Maggie club with your bloody father! Just FUCK OFF!'

Sarah never swore. Never. Tears misting her eyes, Samantha stumbled from the room and ran upstairs. Bloody Mum. Bloody parents, fucking everything up. Bloody Aunt Maggie, shooting her mouth off.

It did not take long, though, before she dried her eyes, composed herself, and took out her mobile phone to ring Duane's mother.

'Mrs Atherton?' she said. 'It's Sam here. Remember, I went out with Dooze . . . it's just that I'm ever so sorry . . .'

Downstairs, Sarah sobbed on the newspaper.

Without spare money, for she was still anxiously hoarding all she could, Maggie was exercised over the best way to spend the two Sundays before Christmas. Leo would not open the shop on a Sunday even for a few hours.

In the first week, the day dawned sunny, and it was easy enough to say that she needed a hike and head out of town towards the sea. Another week passed, with Leo reserved and depressed and Sarah maintaining a frosty silence. Maggie persuaded Leo to stay open late each night, and manned the shop alone until eight, eating a cheese sandwich and avoiding the family meal.

On the second Sunday it rained. Maggie thought of going to Nancy's house, to combine a duty visit with sorting out some of her possessions in the attic. But when she phoned, her mother informed her that no, it wasn't convenient, as she would be out all day on a Townswomen's Guild outing to a Christmas fair and turkey dinner.

Finally she resolved to stay in her room working on her Chinese until noon, then go out for a long walk in the rain.

At noon she set out from the house, trying not to smell Sarah's Sunday roast. Glancing back, she saw Leo relaxed in the sitting room, with Teddy sitting sedately at his feet, reading aloud from a book. Leo ruffled his small son's hair, laughing at him. In the doorway she could see Jamie, and for once his moody face, too, was alight with the joke.

Cast out of Eden, thought Maggie to herself in the rain, and smiled at the absurdity of the thought. It wasn't Eden, not with Sarah nursing her cold wounded fury and Leo scared sick that she would leave him. But it would heal itself. Probably all the faster once she had gone. She had announced to Sarah, or rather to Sarah's back view in the kitchen, that she would definitely go on the 23rd. Leo was not planning to open on the Christmas Eve Sunday, so she would have discharged her duty to the bookshop. Sarah had said, 'Suit yourself,' in a flat, nasty voice.

Now, walking down the alley to the High Street, Maggie wondered whether to use the afternoon to look for somewhere to stay. But her soul revolted at the thought of lodging in Brackhampton when her job and family ties were gone. If you were going to be an outcast, you might as well cast yourself somewhere you wanted to be.

She was so preoccupied, her head so bowed against the driving rain, that Steve Arundel had to call her name twice when he stopped his car at the bottom of the alley.

'Oh—hi,' said Maggie, surprised. She had heard nothing from him since they parted nine days ago, but then she had not given him a telephone number. She had vaguely thought that he might look in at the bookshop, and she had glanced in the Costarica each morning, but never saw the tall familiar form. So she had deliberately let this new friend slip from her thoughts. She had, after all, done it often enough before. You met someone, you exchanged stories, you had a laugh, you moved on.

But here he was again, leaning out of his sleek black company Saab, grinning. She was immoderately pleased to see him.

'First time lucky!' he said. 'No, truly. I would hate you to think I had been cruising around all week looking for you.'

'Oh yeah?' said Maggie happily.

'Nope, I've been in St Petersburg,' he said. 'Saturday morning, boss rang, said his wife's been ill. Boss said in his tactful way, "You can always rely on the gay divorcés to step in." I just got back from Heathrow this morning.'

She was in the passenger seat beside him now, motioned there by expansive welcoming gestures, glad to be out of the rain. 'You think I haven't been anywhere at all, just couldn't be bothered to stay in touch,' he said teasingly. 'Oooh, men! They're awful!'

With a flourish he pulled out the remains of an airline ticket.

'*Now*,' said Maggie, 'I really do think you're a suspicious character. No honest man ever hangs on to his alibi like that.'

'You don't know many reps, do you, hippie-chick?' said Steve scornfully. 'Expenses claims! Never discard anything!'

Maggie laughed. 'Where are you heading?' she asked.

'Fancy lunch?'

'That's kind, but . . .' She was troubled now. 'Look,' she said. 'I really can't spend money. I've got to move out in a week's time and find another job. So I can't go Dutch. And in the circumstances I ought to. Couldn't we just—I don't know—drive?'

Steve glanced at her. 'I want my *dinner*,' he said plaintively. 'Oh, go on, let me have lunch. You can eat the bits off the plate I don't want or you could sit under the table, if you like, and beg.'

'I don't want to stop you—' began Maggie primly.

'Shut up. *One*, I'm still on subsistence expenses, travelling home. *Two*, I've spent the last week's meals negotiating with spivvy Slavs. I just want to eat food and have somebody talk to me about something other than ultraspeed data back-up protocols. Is that too much to ask, woman?'

'No,' said Maggie, settling back. 'As long as I can think of it as necessary social work for the victims of capitalism.'

He drove through the rain, up to the sea road and then off to the left again, and after a while she said, 'Whitstable?'

'Where else?'

'Lovely.' And once again they settled into the companionable silence which was becoming as natural to them as their joshing conversations. Maggie glanced at his profile, wondering about Steve Arundel. He liked to amuse; he took life as lightly as he could, yet had not been unwilling to admit his pain about the lost baby. He was a traveller, but not as she had been; drifting and seeing was not enough for him. He liked a goal, a project. He must be good at what he does, thought Maggie, to be sent to do a deal in a new country without preparation. A troubleshooter, then; a safe pair of hands.

Steve's thoughts were on her, too. She was not at all the kind of girl he generally took out, nothing like his pretty doll of a wife or his silver-blonde secretary Ingrid. It baffled him slightly that each time he had left her he had felt a pang of worry that he might not find her again. She was not pretty, or not all the time; right now she looked both thinner and more pregnant than a week ago. Her face had subtly aged, too, the lines of tension and anxiety more marked even than on the day he picked her up on the sea road.

Suddenly, with a force that surprised and shook him, Steve felt the impulse to solve her problems. Or at least, some of them. He frowned, looking at the road ahead with fierce concentration. The germ of an idea came to him almost at once, and he smiled into the rain.

Samantha chose that Sunday lunch to drop another bombshell into her family circle. Sarah laid great store by family meals, and it had been a successful enough policy to make her daughter instinctively feel that the gap between roast pork and apple pudding was the safest forum in which to introduce a dangerous subject. There were witnesses, and a variety of different points of view. So she took a deep breath and said, 'I saw Duane. I got a visiting order and went to Normanfield.'

'Isn't he out?' asked Jamie, amazed.

'No. His mum hasn't got the money for bail, and she's pissed off with him anyway. He's still remanded in custody. It'll come off his sentence if he gets convicted, but I don't think he ought to be, anyway.'

'Why didn't you ask before you went?' said Sarah, her voice as cool as she could make it. 'I don't know what I feel about you going to that place on your own.'

'I went with his cousin,' said Sam stoutly. 'And I went because I want to help, and I knew you'd want to stop me.'

'What sort of help?' asked Leo suspiciously.

'Character witness. I know for sure that his brothers beat him up if he didn't help them do burglaries.'

'God Almighty!' exploded Sarah. 'What sort of school is this? Some sort of thieves' kitchen?'

Leo looked nervous. From time to time, the question of private education had come up when Jamie was slow to read, when Teddy came home
swearing. Sarah had several times become concerned enough to wonder
whether she ought to try going back into a full-time city career to pay for
a private day school. Leo, however, had been of the view that
Brackhampton was a perfectly good school and that it did middle-class
children no harm at all to mix with all sorts. Besides, women in their for-
ties were expected to have longer CVs than Sarah had, and he shrewdly
guessed that the working world might reject her. Better for her, he
thought, to keep the illusion that she could step back instantly into that
high-paid world, but chose family and community instead.

Now, however, the venom of her irritation was aimed directly at him.
'I suppose now you'll say how wonderful it is that Sam's mixing with a
wide social spectrum. Normanfield!'

Samantha was rattled by her mother's reaction, but pressed on. 'He's
not that bad, Mum. He shouldn't have to go to prison. He's just got a
crap family, right? And his barrister thinks it'd be really helpful if he had
my evidence about the brothers threatening him . . . And apparently I
have to have parental permission.'

'Well, I don't think you should be involved,' said Sarah flatly. 'You're
too young.'

'Same age as Duane,' muttered her daughter.

'An' *he* might be going to *prison*,' said Teddy.

'Don't *you* think she's too young, Leo?' said Sarah combatively.

Leo looked at his daughter. She looked right back, catching his eye,
and he understood with a sinking heart what he must do.

'These young offender institutions are really rough,' he said slowly.
'They turn more kids onto crime than off it. If he does get acquitted
now, it could make the difference to a whole life. Perhaps it's what she
ought to do.'

'And you'd be the moral expert around here?'

Leo dropped his eyes, defeated.

Now it was Samantha who shook with rage. 'Mum, that is *so* below
the belt!'

Sarah looked warningly towards the boys, but Samantha blundered
on. 'Just because Dad goes wrong once, sixteen years ago, you're making
him into a—a criminal! And you're virtually throwing Auntie Maggie
out of the house when she's *pregnant*, and it's not fair!'

'Is she pregnant?' asked Jamie, and 'What did Dad do wrong?' asked
his brother.

'Now look what you've done!' This from Sarah. 'Now look here, madam—'

'No, you look here!' Samantha grew dangerously voluble when roused. 'You're being so unfair! Maggie has to go out wandering around in the rain because of you—she's all miserable and sorry, and it's not fair, when she's pregnant and stuff. Because she respected me for wanting to help Duane, and she was brilliant to me when I thought *I* was preg—'

She stopped, too late.

Chapter Nine

BOTH PARENTS STARED in horror at Samantha's flushed cheeks.

'When you *what*?' Leo said, in a voice unlike his own.

Samantha took a deep breath. 'I had a scare, right? It's not that big a deal, lots of girls do. But I was really frightened and I didn't want to worry you, and Maggie helped me do the test. And I wasn't. It was fine. And that's how she found out *she* was, actually. And I think she's really cool and brave, letting it get adopted. I would've probably got rid of mine because I'm not brave like she is.'

Part of Sarah wanted to hug her daughter, but there was too much anger and unfocused terror in her. Coldly she said, 'And would you, I wonder, have mentioned this abortion to us at all? Or would Maggie have arranged everything for you without thinking to consult us?'

'She said I ought to tell you anyway.'

'She should have told me herself.'

'I didn't want her to, and it was my business.'

'You are only *fifteen*!'

Leo broke in. 'I think we ought to talk about this calmly,' he said. He did not like the way that Jamie and Teddy had withdrawn from their usual flow of commentary and begun to concentrate fiercely on their almost empty plates—particularly Jamie, whose blush was visible beyond his curtain of hair.

Samantha had recovered herself. She stood up and said, 'I'm going round to Uma's, right?'

'You are going nowhere!' said her mother. 'And who was responsible for this—what you call this scare of yours, anyway?'

'Duane,' said Samantha flatly. 'He *was* my boyfriend, right? Because whatever you think, I am not a *complete* tart.'

'And now you want to stand up in court for this little yob?'

Leo remembered, wonderingly, how often Sarah had rebuked him for referring to Duane as a yob. He was alarmed by this new Sarah, and sorrowful at the part he had played in her creation. But his children were around him and he must take some kind of lead.

'Let her go,' he said firmly. 'We'll all talk later.' And to Sarah, 'Why don't you go and take some time for yourself, sweetheart. The boys and I will wash up.'

Sarah, startled by the firmness of his tone, hesitated but eventually went upstairs. Samantha grabbed a coat and went out into the rain. Leo and the boys washed up, and haltingly, kindly, the father tried to put the upheaval into perspective for his sons.

When the car drew up in Whitstable, Maggie and Steve were deep in conversation about the Inca trail. She was joshing him for having abandoned his Marco Polo salesmanship in Lima to walk like a useless tourist for four days.

'So I'm not allowed a soul now?'

'You virtually told me you didn't have one. Didn't believe in them. Called me a tree-hugger.'

'Well, I was pressurised into it by a keen guide I met.'

'So what did you make of it?'

'Too many tourists. Bloody packed. Litter all along the way. Touts. Made me angry. It made me feel as if there was nowhere to escape to, no parallel world after all.'

Maggie looked at him. They had both got out of the car, and stood facing one another across its sleek black roof. The rain had died away here at the coast, and the sky was lightening.

'God, I know what you mean. I've always had a vague idea that if I stopped travelling, there was another universe I could step into. Happy families and dull solid little houses and washing the car at weekends and everyone quite contented and not wanting to get out.'

'And there wasn't?' He led the way to the restaurant.

'Well, I thought it existed. I suppose I've always used my sister's home as a sort of theme park. I visit, I ride the roundabouts of aunthood, fold up one of the kids' paintings as a souvenir, and go back to my own life.'

They reached the restaurant, but its doors were unpromisingly closed.

'Bugger!' said Steve. 'Look!'

There was a sign, announcing a seasonal closure until January 3. He glanced at his watch and said, 'Have to be the pub. Quick.' He led her running along the seafront towards a faded sign that swung in the wind, depicting seven unlikely-looking fruits attached to a curling vine. They pushed open the door and found a half-empty saloon, its shabbiness only slightly alleviated by some swags of tinsel.

'Lovely,' he said. 'Used to come here with my uncle when he was alive. Watch out, it's the sort of place where your feet stick to the floor.'

A cadaverous, sullen man stood behind the bar, sniffing. There was, however, a menu on the wall and within fifteen minutes they each had a plateful of hake and chips to go with their beer.

'Good fish,' said Maggie.

'Always is here. Local.' He glanced around. 'God, I haven't been in here since Uncle Anton died.'

'You never said you had family connections here.'

'Used to have. Anton was a sort of uncle once removed. Half Russian. Don't ask, my family's complicated. He lived here because he used to be in the navy, in submarines, and he had to be by the sea.'

'Yes, I can see that. Remember how I cheered up when we first came here?'

'You're a bit fixated about that trip, aren't you?'

'It's just . . .' She found that she could not go on.

'Captain Whatsit? You miss him?'

Her green eyes met his with a stare of astonishment.

'Noooh! That was a mistake. No. It's because I wonder whether I will ever go on a journey like that again, a journey that blows your mind, gives you, I dunno, a direct line to, to . . .' She did not know what the direct line might lead to. She shrugged, and ate another chip. 'So I panic, and when I have bad dreams it always seems to be about the *Evangelina*, sailing away without me.'

'You said you could have stayed on.'

'Yes, but . . . it's not what I do.'

'If you had stayed on,' said Steve, pushing his plate away from him, '*Evangelina* would have become ordinary, and you'd have felt as if you'd married it and settled down in a little brick house to wash its underpants and go to Tesco's with it every Saturday. Am I, or am I not, one of the leading analytical psychologists of the age?'

For an answer she smiled at him, a heart-stopping smile, and his cautious heart turned over.

They finished their meal, paid, and stood up. As they left, Maggie noticed a curling sign tacked to the upright wooden beam over the bar.

'Due to defection of ungrateful slut,' it said, 'bar staff wanted from Dec 26 until student labour reappears in June. Full- or part-time, poor pay, depressed landlord, all the damaged crisps you can eat. Experience preferred, no complete morons, please.'

Maggie laughed. 'My kind of job,' she said, pointing. 'If only it was Whitstable I was looking for a job in.'

He stopped in his tracks, stock-still, understanding that by some providence the last piece of his vague, quixotic plan had fallen into place. 'Why isn't it?'

'Nowhere to live. It's not the kind of place for cheap lodgings, is it? From Easter it'll be all ritzy holiday lets.'

'Come with me.' He took her out through the drizzle, down the narrow gut between the old oyster sheds, until he was by a peeling door, next to a dilapidated chandlery. He found the key and unlocked it. He gave a sharp kick to the bottom of the door and it came open and revealed a dim yawning space and a stairway.

'Don't tell me you live here!' said Maggie, amused.

'No. Uncle Anton did. Come and see.' He went up the stairs first. At the top he took out another key and opened another door. Maggie hurried after him. Steve was standing triumphantly in the centre of an attic with a great skylight and a high window looking out towards the sea.

Glancing round, Maggie saw a wide mattress on a makeshift wooden platform, a plastic garden table and two chairs, and a long set of shelves. There was a wooden chest, too, and a pile of broken utensils cast into the corner which, judging by the ancient and rusting cooker, had served as a kitchenette. There was a yellowing, chipped electric radiator standing unplugged beside it. One corner of the big square space was partitioned off, with a sliding door half falling off its tracks.

'All mod cons,' said Steve as her eye fell on this unpleasing corner. 'Shower and bog.'

'Uncle Anton's flat?' asked Maggie.

He nodded. 'Good, isn't it? He left me a twenty-three-year lease, much to the disgust of the chandler underneath, who wants to use it as a store. But I haven't been able to bring myself to sell it on to him. It used to have all Anton's model ships, and bits of purloined RN crockery. I've been moving them gradually, but the flat remains a millstone.'

'You could use it for holiday lets.'

'With that bathroom? And kitchenette? In the twenty-first century?'

'You could convert it.' She had guessed his offer before he made it, but a mixture of fear and excitement made her stall.

'Hardly worth it for the length of the lease. My best bet is to let it to someone who isn't fussy,' he said. 'You, for instance. Go for the bar job, hole up in Whitstable, look out at the sea every morning. Get it all over with, and make your plans.'

Maggie gazed around her. There was the faint, comforting aroma of wood and tar. In the silence, a sudden gust of wind blew, pattering more rain on the roof; the building creaked comfortably, like a sailing ship.

'Oh God, that is so, so kind,' she began. 'Oh, Steve, but I can't afford anything as wonderful . . .'

He looked from her transported face to the crooked sliding door of the lavatory, and back again, with such a theatrical expression on his face that she began to laugh.

'I admit,' he began, in oleaginous imitation of a Knightsbridge estate agent, 'that its many period details and sympathetic architectural originalities command a substantial rental income. Say, fifteen quid a week?'

'That's ridiculous!'

'Ten, then. Seriously, I haven't known what to do with it. I don't want to leave it empty. Go on. Six months or so. A couple of days with a screwdriver and a mop, and you could be in here for Christmas.'

It was irresistible. She did not resist. Steve even sat in on her brief interview with the dour landlord of the Seven Grapes, and refused to let her work more than a thirty-hour week.

'No maternity pay rubbish,' said Ardriss, the landlord, a calculatedly morose, cadaverous figure with an unhealthy high colour in his cheeks. 'Don't care what the law says. Temps ain't got no rights.'

'Fine,' said Maggie. 'I don't want rights. I don't even live here, really.'

'Australian?' asked Mr Ardriss. 'I like Aussies. They don't mind washing floors. No class-consciousness. Bloody English students think it's beneath them.'

'Nothing's beneath Miss Reave,' said Steve loftily. 'Speaking as her pastor and psychiatric social worker, I am happy to say that she has few delusions about her status.'

'You're not a social worker,' said the landlord witheringly. 'You're Anton Arundel's nephew. He used to bring you in here and cheat you at poker.'

'Kept him in whisky, didn't it?'

When Steve dropped her back in Brackhampton that evening, impulsively, Maggie kissed him on the cheek. He laughed, and gave her a thumbs up; they had already arranged to meet on Saturday evening.

As he pulled away, a spry figure, which had paused to watch them, detached itself from the shadows and walked off along the street. Miss Mountjoy was pleased to see that Maggie and her new boyfriend were still getting along. She mentioned as much to nice Mrs Penn outside the vet's office in the morning, thus accidentally hardening Sarah's heart still further against her wayward, ungrateful, infuriatingly buoyant little sister.

'There is such an atmosphere at home,' said Samantha despairingly to Uma, 'that I don't want to live there any more. Can't I come and stay with you?'

'Oh yes, with my mother such best friends with your mother, I can just *see* how well that would work,' said Uma with bracing sarcasm. 'Especially at Christmas, oh yes.' The two girls were leaning against the brick wall of the science block, sharing a Mars bar out of sight of censorious dieting friends.

'I wonder how much Mum's told her,' mused Samantha. 'She'd probably think Nita would be shocked by it all.'

'Well, *you* thought that I would be shocked about you doing that preggy test,' said Uma accusingly. For the afternoon before, a tearful Sam had finally unrolled the whole of her story to her friend. 'Like I didn't *guess* anyway! The way you were round Duane at school, the way that you broke up then got more miserable and not less. It was obvious what you were scared about. Then one morning you're dead cheerful. Doesn't take Inspector Morse to work it out.'

'Well, Mum didn't guess.'

'She knows now, though. So you have to get back and face her. Just tell her it was a mistake, and you handled it, end of story.'

'All very well for you, you've never had anything like that,' said Samantha, but her friend's words gave her hope. Painful though life was at the moment, it seemed to her as if she was being renewed: shedding a skin, leaving behind the useless shreds and rags of childishness that she had, for too long, been trying to patch together for protection. It was colder out in this adult world, but the air was clearer too. 'I s'pose you're right. I'm not a kid.'

'Right!' said Uma. 'And if you wanna give evidence for Duane, you do that too. They can't stop you.' Uma frowned, and went on, 'But what about your auntie? I think that's sad, about her and your ma.'

'So do I,' said Samantha, her brow clouding over again. 'Maggie's moving out for Christmas. I don't know whether she's even got anywhere to go.'

After Miss Mountjoy had innocently revealed to her the existence of Maggie's supposed boyfriend, Sarah could hardly complete her morning's work for rage. Eventually, exasperated beyond endurance at the frosty atmosphere of his surgery, Sam Miller said, 'For God's sake, Sarah, draw a line under it, for everyone's sake. Forgive the poor bastard and all get on with your lives.'

'It's not *Leo*,' said Sarah scathingly. 'It's *Maggie*, and all she's done, and the nerve of her keeping it secret about little Sam—who does she think she is, swanning in to our family and taking over—'

Miller's dry, quizzical look arrested her in mid-sentence.

'Good,' he said quietly.

'What's good?'

'Good that you've turned it outside the family. If you and Leo gang up on your sister, it gives you common cause. Already you're much less cross with him, aren't you?'

Sarah examined her own feelings and discovered, to her slight astonishment, that this was indeed the case.

Later that day, in Nita's tidy kitchen, she admitted as much to her friend. Privately, Mrs Syal thought that Sarah was being unduly hard on her sister. But she was a practical woman, and considered it wiser to rip up a sibling relationship than to endanger a marriage with children. With delicate caution, therefore, she let Sarah rant on.

So gradually, as the two women talked, Leo ceased to be a monster of infidelity and became a fellow victim and an admirably caring father. It helped further that the man himself—tipped off by old Sam Miller when he dropped in to the shop—took the trouble to leave early, buy a side of sliced smoked salmon, and drive round to Nita's house to offer his wife a lift home.

'I could do us scrambled eggs and smoked salmon,' he said. It had been a staple supper in their early, child-free days.

'That would be nice,' said Sarah, and smiled at him.

Steve Arundel was smiling too, grinning at the screen as he rapidly deleted unwanted ranks of emails.

'You look perky,' said his colleague, Malcolm. 'St Petersburg obviously agreed with you. Get lucky?'

'No I did not!' said Steve, flicking aside an unopened attachment which would, he knew, be the musical Christmas wishes of some cartoon reindeer, capable of taking two full minutes to download. If time-wasting electronic mail oppressed him, so did the way that all his colleagues expected every divorced and unattached man to lead a life of dissipation and tell them all the details. 'You family men are all the same,' he grunted. 'Desperate for vicarious sex.'

'Doesn't have to be sex,' said Malcolm, turning back to peek at his own keyboard. 'A hot glamorous date would do. Anyway, who's the girl?'

'What girl?'

'The one you're grinning to yourself about.'

'There is no girl,' said Steve firmly. 'I'm just pleased that I've got a winter tenant for Uncle Anton's flat.'

'Is this dream tenant by any chance a female girl?' began his colleague, but was distracted by the appearance on his screen of a reindeer singing 'Jingle Bell Rock'. 'Did you just forward me this crap? It won't stop opening.'

'Serve you right.'

But Steve was light-hearted, as he had not been since the ending of his marriage. The rest of the team noticed it and were happy for him. Ingrid, his pale and elegantly groomed secretary, was less happy than most, for Steve was a generous escort. Shrugging, she hid her mild dismay with typical competence. The old Steve would, she thought, be back before long, needing her.

And in the shop Maggie smiled too; more restrainedly, with lines of sorrow and apprehension beginning to shape her mouth into a new set. It would be better, she thought, when she had left the Penns' house and the bookshop, and at least she had somewhere to go and a job. She would be able to save for the time when her body would make her helpless. The thought made her shudder, but she squared her shoulders, set her lips, and resolved to bear it.

She packed her rucksack in advance, and on the last day of trading she brought it in to work. Steve had telephoned the bookshop to tell her that he would drive her to Whitstable, and fix the lavatory door while he was at it. She said her light-hearted farewells to the boys the night before, spoke briefly and clandestinely to Samantha, and told Nancy vaguely that she was 'off away again' on Christmas Eve. Her mother seemed so little interested that there were no questions.

She had worked it all out to avoid any need for a formal farewell. On that Saturday, however, she suddenly thought, I can't leave it like this! 'I go away,' she said aloud, to nobody in particular. 'But I don't *run* away!' There was a lull in trade and she asked Leo, 'Can I take half an hour? Lunch break?'

'OK,' he said. 'Might get busy again around two, though.'

She pulled on her jacket and half ran up the street. As she expected, Sarah was in the Penns' kitchen kneading pastry for mince pies. As her sister's shadow fell across the doorway, she looked round.

'Oh, it's you,' she said coldly, and went back to her pastry. 'You forgotten something, then?'

'No. Sarah,' began her sister desperately, 'we can't just leave it like this. You've hardly spoken a word to me since—since all that. I'm going away. But can't we just mend a bit of the fence? You're my sister.'

'That didn't seem to bother you when you slept with Leo.'

'Sixteen years ago! It was the stupidest mistake—'

'Nor when you conspired to drag my underage daughter into your scummy, immoral, promiscuous subculture of . . . of . . .' Sarah heard herself, and did not like it, and stammered enough to let Maggie break in.

'That isn't fair. I tried to make her tell you. All I did was help her do the test because she was so, so scared, and I remember how awful—'

'Oh, very experienced in these things, you are! Though it isn't exactly the kind of experience I want my daughter to plug into. You've been a baleful influence on all of them these past months. Samantha nearly pregnant, Teddy in trouble at school for doing magic tricks, and Jamie upset over me and his father. The sooner you get out of town the better.'

'I came to say goodbye,' said Maggie sadly. 'And to say thanks for putting me up all these months. I might not see any of you again before I go abroad. Please, Sare, please couldn't we just shake hands? Call it a day? Then I'll go.'

Sarah turned her back and began to roll the lump of pastry flat, with short, vicious strokes. Nothing that Maggie said could make her speak again, and after a few minutes the younger sister took her heavy heart back down to the bookshop.

That evening, in the car, she said to Steve Arundel, 'She won't forgive me. It's frightening, it's not like Sarah at all.'

'Never mind,' said Steve comfortingly. 'I've got a screwdriver, and some tracking for the bog door, and a gas bottle for the cooker, and two bottles of wine.'

'I've got no food,' said Maggie suddenly, surprised that this was the first time she had thought of it.

'I've got some watery ham and half a dozen eggs in the back. I even got some nasty cardboard mince pies from the supermarket. Uncle Anton would have liked to think of a social rejects' Christmas party going on in his flat. We could invite Evan Ardriss from the pub and make it *really* miserable.'

'You're a mate,' said Maggie. 'God knows why. Perhaps you're an angel, like in all those Christmas films.'

He glanced at her. She was staring ahead, her eyes misty, her thoughts not really with him at all. With a small pang he realised how unlike she was to the other women he knew. She had no notion of flirtation or conquest; to her he was a crewmate, a chance comrade doing her a favour. She had not the slightest notion of anything more than matehood between the two of them.

Not, of course, that he did either.

The sickness began on Christmas Eve. At first she thought it was the effect of Steve's ham and eggs and wine. It wore off by noon, to be replaced by a deep lassitude; she slept on the lumpy old mattress all afternoon. On Christmas morning it came again, worse than before. Retching in the bleak lavatory she wondered if this could be morning sickness.

But wasn't that supposed to happen sooner? Why should it suddenly start at three months? Was it reaction, after the last tense weeks at the Penns'? Shuddering back to her sleeping-bag and the two old blankets Steve had donated from the back of his car, Maggie reflected that it really was time she saw a doctor. So, on her way to the pub the day after Boxing Day, she signed on with the local clinic. The nausea wore off each day before her lunchtime shift started, and she thanked her stars that the job was one that started late.

The doctor was sympathetic but brisk. 'No, it's not abnormal. Sickness takes different mothers at different stages.'

But I'm not a mother! Maggie wanted to say. I'm just temporarily carrying it.

The doctor spoke of taking it easy, of eating a proper balanced diet and going to a hospital clinic to arrange for the birth, which they agreed would probably be in mid-May. She went to the maternity clinic a few days later, on her day off from the pub, and afterwards, rebelling against the overheated room and the pall of vague anxiety which hung over her fellow patients, she tried to go for a run along the seafront. After a few hundred yards she was exhausted, puffing and wincing with heartburn.

She sat on the sea wall, staring out bleakly at the water, and realised that she could not after all carry on as if nothing was happening. Particularly, she accepted the end of her studies at Southwick. She had worked out the system of buses and fast walking which would get her there for eight thirty and back to the pub by half past one, and had persuaded Evan Ardriss to let her start her shift late once term began. But there was not a chance, she thought now, of her being able to complete such a challenge. The very idea of a bus, of diesel fumes and swaying, brought back her morning nausea.

Sadly she walked towards the harbour, dismayed at the beginnings of a waddle in her gait and at the unseemly stretching of the stitches of her sweater in front. The tide was out; beneath her lay not the bobbing, shifting gaiety of the community of boats but an expanse of dully gleaming mud. The boats hung at crazy, ugly angles in the slime, as helpless as she was herself. Tears sprang to her eyes.

'Beached,' she said aloud. 'Beached!'

She wondered whether Steve would appear, as she had wondered on her last day off; but the evening brought no sign of him. She laid aside his rent each week, in cash in a jam jar, and hoped to give it to him personally. She supposed, a little ruefully, that he went to his family for Christmas like everybody else. Perhaps he was skiing. She knew little enough about the man, for God's sake. He was just a mate.

She climbed into bed early, reflecting that one of the few perks of pregnancy was the sleepiness. If she could just lie like Rip Van Winkle for the next five months, she thought, and wake up to find it all over, that would be good . . .

Thirty miles away Steve Arundel paced around his bare, anonymous flat in Maidstone. He had come here when the value of the marital home was split between him and Jill; he had no interest in furniture, so the white modern box had been furnished entirely by one trip to IKEA. Every piece of furniture reminded him of how much he had disliked the task of putting it together, all alone. Except for the bed, which reminded him only of two evenings spent with the cool, willing and unnervingly expert Ingrid.

Since his travelling had become curtailed, he had vaguely wondered whether it might be nice to get a more homelike place to live. But he had no heart for it.

On Christmas Day he visited his father in an old people's home near Hastings and went home, alone. It was his own fault. Malcolm had tried to get him to Christmas dinner with his flourishing family, and Ingrid had kept leaving newspaper travel features open at pages about hotel breaks in Paris, but he had resisted kindness and rapacity alike. 'You're becoming a monk, then, are you?' Ingrid had teased, with an edge of anxiety in her wide kitten eyes. But he had only smiled, and offered a comradely pat on the shoulder which was met with an angry shrug.

He wanted very much to call on Maggie. It hurt him to think of her alone, shut out by her furious relatives. But at Christmas and New Year, he thought, he could not trust himself. There was too much emotion in the air, and he would only betray himself, step further forward than he truly wanted, and alienate and embarrass her.

The thought of Maggie's baby also filled him with confused unhappiness. She said she would give it up, hand it over and not look back. But how could she? Wasn't that the hardest thing in the world for women?

Then his own pain came back, and he paced faster, until the confines of the flat were too much for him and he went outside to walk the deserted suburban streets in the rain, wearing himself out before the last half-bottle of whisky, and oblivion.

When term began, Samantha and Uma hatched a plan. They would wait for a morning of free study periods, get a pass to go to the public library, and go to Southwick instead on the midmorning bus. They would find Maggie and see how she was and ask where she was living.

'She's really keen on college,' said Sam. 'All we have to do is find the right lecture room for her course, and hang about outside till they have a break.'

But when they got to the college, a bespectacled young American told them that Ms Reave had withdrawn from the course 'on health grounds'. He would say no more; but a student, overhearing, chattered on more freely about how surprised they had all been because she had serious plans to go to China in the summer.

'Well, bog!' said Samantha dispiritedly, as they took the bus back to school. 'Now what? Honestly, it's awful what Mum and Dad are doing. Imagine being *pregnant*, and all on your own.'

'I thought she had a boyfriend.'

'Mum says she has. But she never said anything to me. I think she's in some skanky *hostel*!'

Uma shuddered. 'Yeah, that is grim.' They contemplated it together, as the bus roared round the Brackhampton bypass. 'C'mon, we'd better ring for our stop.'

'You look better,' said Samuel Miller to his secretary, who was holding down a groggy terrier. 'Sorted it all out at home, have you?'

'Yes, I think so. Leo and I are *really talking*,' said Sarah. 'Samantha's being difficult, but the boys are back on an even keel.'

'Hmm,' said Miller, reaching for the hind leg of the dog and plunging a hypodermic needle into it. 'And the wildcat sister?'

'Good riddance,' said Sarah viciously. The dog gave a faint protesting kick.

'Careful,' Miller said. 'These things can kick right back at you.'

Sarah had an uneasy feeling that he was not talking about the dog.

Chapter Ten

JANUARY PASSED, AND FEBRUARY; Maggie's morning sickness grew better. Or perhaps, she thought, she was merely growing used to it. Slip out of bed and hold on to the edge of the platform, head down against the faintness; make your way to the bathroom, vomit, drink a long glass of water; sit in the folding chair for a while, then make your way carefully to the kitchenette and eat a slice of dry bread. Sit down, and wait. When the time comes, put on clothes and go to work. Fresh air might make it better.

The clothes were, for a while, a serious problem. The town's charity shop had no maternity wear and their only large dresses were so sprigged, so garish, that she recoiled from them. In the end she found two men's blue guernseys and some dark blue tracksuit trousers. This uniform just about passed muster down at the pub, though Evan Ardriss would occasionally grumble about her lack of glamour.

'What's a barmaid for, if not to show a bit of tit?' he demanded.

'For serving and stacking the shelves, you sexist arsehole,' replied Maggie tranquilly.

Their working relationship was satisfactory; he was just nasty enough for her to feel she owed him nothing, and just funny enough in his misanthropy to give her the occasional therapeutic laugh. She longed to tell someone about him, to imitate his curmudgeonly ways. She did not, though; the only person she could imagine telling was Steve. Who was nowhere to be seen.

There was company, though, of a kind. Her weariness in the evenings had abated a little by mid-March. Sometimes after closing time, she would play dominoes or cards for an hour with a couple of the regulars, usually fishermen. They were for the most part as bored and as skint as she was, waiting for the extra work brought by the spring and summer. A new face at the bar was more than welcome to them. Sometimes Maggie played her whistle or mouth organ, but not often. Music troubled her too much, stirring up feelings best unexamined.

'It's all right as long as you bloody lock up,' Ardriss would snarl as he retreated to bed. These, after all, were his best winter customers. 'But you're not burning my bulbs out.' Sometimes Maggie's natural high spirits returned momentarily, and a peal of laughter would unite the odd little company that sat round two candles in bottles, with the roar of the winter sea outside. Sometimes it was so like the old times on the road that she even wondered whether the travelling had genuinely been what she needed all those years. Maybe, after the painfully respectable caution of her upbringing, it was that sense of hand-to-mouth lowliness and casual unattachedness that she had needed, rather than the exotic places themselves. Sure, she loved them; yet in a curious way she was coming to love this wintry Kentish backwater as much as anywhere she had been. It was not a bad life, when she could forget about the pregnancy.

But the baby leapt and kicked within her. Every time it moved her heart beat faster, unpleasantly, so that whatever she was doing she had to stop, suddenly paralysed with shock. The heart of the shock was her own feeling for the curled thing within her. She had been warned of this by the social worker to whom she had announced her intention of giving the baby up.

'You'll have strong biological feelings of bonding to overcome,' the woman said assuredly. 'It won't be easy, you know.'

Maggie knew with equal assuredness that she could slap down a biological urge as easily as she could a drunken fumbler. Yet now that the baby was stretching and turning within her with such vitality, it was as if her hard, cool, competent core was liquefying. Her fight took the form of another visit to social services.

'I want a definite arrangement,' she said. 'I think you should have a family standing by, ready for the baby.'

She had lain awake for many hours thinking about this: her first instinct, simply to hand the baby to authority, had been weakened by an unwilling attention paid to news headlines and to documentaries that ran on the pub TV. Britain, her impression was, did not show very much competence in the matter of children in care. If this half-Lopez within her was to be handed over, then she wanted it to go straight to a family. Not into some scabby children's home full of damaged angry teenagers and run by people like the tired, lank-haired, humourless woman across the desk.

'It isn't that simple,' said the woman. 'Suppose you change your mind? A lot of women do, although usually,' she glanced at Maggie with mild distaste, 'where there is this intention of giving the baby away, we are dealing with far younger girls. Or suppose baby is born with a disability, or something else—unforeseen.'

'Like what?'

'We have policies on interracial adoption,' said the woman smoothly. 'There is talk of a new government guideline, but—'

'It's not black, you know,' said Maggie irritably. 'And anyway, so what if it was?'

'As I say, there are guidelines and procedures and cooling-off periods.' The woman was almost snapping now. 'It would be very unusual indeed for an adoptive family to take the child on immediately from birth these days. Foster families—'

'No,' said Maggie. 'Not fostering. Not pillar-to-post. It ought to know its mother and father straight away.'

'I can't do what you ask,' the woman said dismissively. 'If you opt to put the child voluntarily into the council's care, you will have to leave such judgments about his or her welfare to us, the professionals.'

Maggie stood up, balancing her new bulk in front of her. The baby kicked hard, twice. That moment of shock kicked in again; her chin dropped to her chest and she breathed carefully. Then her head came up, resolutely. 'Thank you for your time,' she said. 'I'll give it more thought.'

It was April when Steve came to see her. She was wiping down the bar counter at three o'clock, and for a second or two he barely recognised her. The thin mischievous face had filled out, not puffily but enough to make her look more like her sister Sarah than her old self. Maggie's wild hair was tied back for work, and the bony grace of her shoulders was blurred and padded by an unwonted layer of female softness. But her eyes were the eyes he remembered, and so was the sudden leaping joy of her smile.

'Hey, stranger!' she said. 'I've got great wads of rent for you! Didn't know where to send it!'

'I feel bad about that. Should've told you. Suppose something had gone wrong in the flat?' he said with an awkwardness that she, in turn, found strange in him. 'What a crap landlord I am.'

'Well, it did go wrong. Bit of rot in the floorboards, so I ripped it out and got Dinksie to nail some old lump of boat there instead. And the wiring went funny after the snow got in from the broken gutter, and Evan's brother's sorted that.'

'You're well dug in, then,' he said admiringly. 'Be getting the freedom of the city any minute, I should think.' He was in his business suit, fresh from a meeting; he made an odd sight in this grimy pub, awkwardly dapper next to Maggie's draggled guernsey. 'I came to ask if you might come out to supper. It's your night off, isn't it?'

Maggie looked suddenly embarrassed. 'Well, depends where,' she said cautiously. 'Clothes, you see . . .' She laid a hand on her bump, gingerly, then blushed.

'Caftan? Poncho? Shower curtain?' he suggested 'Go on, come.'

'Yes, of course I will. But not one of your smart county watering holes with BMWs outside.'

'All right. Meet you at six o'clock at Anton's.'

They were back on course, thought Maggie happily. Joking, taking nothing seriously, a pair of mates. In recent weeks she had been troubled in her dreams by a different notion of Steve Arundel. This was, she fully recognised, nothing but a matter of hormones. All pregnant vulnerable female animals latch on to the strongest alpha male in sight. Sarah used to fall in love with her obstetrician for the duration of delivery. ('Honest, Mags, you do. It's because he seemed more competent than Leo.')

At six o'clock, her hair loose, she was waiting for him in her cleanest blue tracksuit trousers and a bright pink baggy fleece jumper. It was the day's great find in the Oxfam shop, a casually smart style and a colour that made her hair, brushed into a great dark wing, look all the glossier. She had tidied the flat meticulously and thrown a jumble-sale rug over the scruffy chair. There was a candle in a bottle on the table, and with only the standard lamp lit, it did not look too bad at all.

Steve looked round with proper admiration. 'Homelike,' he said. 'I have to admit, when I first showed it to you I was a bit embarrassed.'

'It's wonderful,' said Maggie with feeling. 'It's private, it's easy to warm up, it's cheap, it's even a bit shippy, and I am incredibly grateful.' She smiled at him, and the disturbing thought flitted through her mind that a few months ago she would have kissed him gratefully on the cheek.

Now she could not. Her looming belly came between them, and her meaningless dreams.

Steve said, 'I'm glad. And I'm sorry I just abandoned you here without checking things were OK. I've been working quite hard.' He glanced down. He had also been reviving his old fling with Ingrid, in the hope of extinguishing some confused and dangerous feelings. He had confided these to Malcolm in the pub. 'I can't risk it,' he said. 'I should not be getting involved with an unmaternal, pregnant maverick who's leaving for China any minute. For all I know I only fancy her because she's pregnant, like poor Jill was. But it's wrong for me. If I ever trust a woman again, it's got to be someone who wants what I want.'

'Like?' said Malcolm, into his beer. 'Like what do you want?'

'A home. A wife and family. Somewhere I can think about when I'm away, and look forward to. You have to make sensible decisions about things like that. Like you did.'

'I was in *love* with Moira,' said Malcolm with dignity. 'If you aren't in love, it's hopeless.'

'Well, you must make sure you fall in love with someone who wants to be married and have a home. There's got to be some sense applied to it. I wish I was Asian or Jewish, then I could have an arranged marriage.'

'Ingrid?' said Malcolm. 'Perhaps Human Resources could arrange it.'

Steve laughed, without much mirth. 'No, the thing with Ingrid is that she just likes sex and expensive outings, and she doesn't really like me all that much otherwise.'

But he may have been wrong. It was only days later that Ingrid informed him that it was over for good this time.

'I don't care who she bloody is that you think of all the time,' she said crisply, tossing her neat pale hair. 'But I'm not playing substitute for a minute longer.'

'You're not a substitute! I'm not in love with anybody else!' protested Steve, avoiding her eye. 'I'm not ready. Jill and everything.'

'Ha bloody ha,' said Ingrid. 'You haven't given Jill a thought for months.'

He had been planning to sleep with her again that night, as they did once every week or so; but all the same it was a relief when the door slammed, and he knew it was for the last time.

Now, he looked at the heavily pregnant, flushed Maggie and found himself smiling like an idiot, lurching forward onto dangerous and uncertain ground. Enjoy tonight, he said to himself. Just have fun, go for broke.

'Come on then,' he said. 'Canterbury, I think. Bright lights. We might even do the late movie. I think they're showing *Bride of Frankenstein.*'

'Bit near the bone,' said Maggie. 'Bit tactless.'

'You look beautiful,' said Steve, lurching another step joyfully into the unknown. 'Totally lovely. A big pink party balloon.'

'Some women,' said Maggie happily, 'would be seriously offended at that remark.' And she too smiled, and put her hand in his as they made for the dark stairway.

The winter had passed slowly, healingly, in the Penn family. Leo drank less and was careful of Sarah's feelings, almost wooing her. Unaccustomed to such solicitude, she paid him more attention, even at times putting his comfort ahead of the children's. Samantha defiantly went to the defence solicitor and offered to be a witness for Duane, but in the event was not called. At the last minute one of his more respectable sisters unexpectedly stepped forward, to give such a spirited account of his persecution by elder brothers that the court let him off with a caution.

Jamie developed a passion for natural history under the tutelage of an enthusiastic new biology teacher, and began making an exhaustive record of the signs of spring in a notebook. Teddy carried on with his magic tricks at school, but took care never to discuss such aunt-engendered skills at the family table. Sometimes at school he was asked about her.

'Where's your auntie gone? She in China already?' asked little Joanne when she could bear the dearth of news no longer.

'Dunno. She moved on,' said Teddy.

'She's pregnant, right?' said Adrian. 'Only my mum said—'

'Are you getting a microscooter on your birthday?' asked Teddy, with guile beyond his years. The dangerous moment passed. He missed his aunt, but she had come and gone before.

One night at the end of April, with fear in his heart, Leo said to his wife, 'Your sister's baby must be due quite soon.'

They were in bed, reading their books companionably, with their shoulders touching. They had made love that morning and the warmth of it still lay over them. Maggie's name had been mentioned rarely since Christmas but the thought of her troubled him.

Perhaps, he often told himself, there was no reason to worry. Perhaps she had terminated the pregnancy and taken off for China weeks ago. He tried to visualise her, carefree in a coolie hat on the edge of some great rice-field or pointed mountain range. But another vision obtruded: of a pale starveling creature in a sordid hostel, alone and friendless and about to give birth without sympathy or support. Sarah had always said childbirth would have been hell without him, and that she didn't know how single mothers coped. 'I like having someone around who has nothing much to do except be thrilled,' she once said. 'It sort of reminds you that babies really are something to be thrilled about. Not just pain.'

Who would be thrilled for Maggie? Who would mop her sweating brow? Raising the subject, he half hoped that Sarah would respond with: 'Oh yes, we ought to get in touch and see if she needs anything.'

Instead, she said carefully, 'Leo, I think it'll be easier for all of us if we just forget about Maggie. The boys are settled now, Sam's fine. You and I are fine. Maggie is just a load of trouble.'

Now it was Leo who was silent. There were many things he wanted to say, but he had learned the perils of frankness.

Eventually he said, 'Well, if you're sure it doesn't worry you, sweetheart. It was you I was thinking of. I didn't want you worrying and not saying anything because of me.'

Sarah cuddled closer. 'I talked to Mum about it. Maggie, I mean. She thinks the same. Don't trouble trouble.'

Leo found it hard to get to sleep.

After their evening in Canterbury, Steve resolved to call on Maggie twice a week, once on her evening off and once at closing time on Sundays. On the first Sunday he found her setting up a game of pontoon with the fishermen Dinksie and Martin; he feigned delight and sat down to join them for the evening. He had been half planning to say some new things to Maggie Reave, alone on a moonlit waterfront; but a fine judgment told him that it would be safer to go along with her normal routine.

The following Sunday, after another cheerful midweek dinner in Canterbury, he arrived to find no card players, and Maggie putting her jacket on ready to go home. She greeted him with a convincing start of surprise.

'Hey—hello. Would you like some rent at all?'

'Lead me to it. This is all so new, having women give me money just for existing. I could get used to it.'

He took her hand, drawing it into his elbow as they walked along the seafront. It was a warm dusk still, with the lengthening days of spring.

'Walk by the harbour?' he said carelessly. 'See what's in?'

'OK,' said Maggie. She seemed listless and, he thought, breathless. Was it too late for her to be at work? Jill, he remembered with a pang, had planned to give up at seven months and rest.

When they reached the harbour they saw tall masts and yardarms, and he felt her arm stiffen against his. Glancing round, he saw her looking aloft, with concentrated care.

'Did you think it might be *Evangelina*?' he asked softly.

'My lesbian lover, you mean?' She tried to make a joke of it, but tears were in her eyes. 'It's just that—oh Christ, Steve, it's just that I dream all the time, *all* the time, about being back out on the ocean.' She stopped. 'And if you don't mind, let's go back. I don't want to look at a ship, not ever again. It hurts too much.'

All he could think of to say, as they came to the door beside the chandlery, was, 'You'll go travelling again, you know. It probably feels impossible now, but it's just that your tide's down. It'll come up again. When it's all over.'

'Yeah,' said Maggie, and he had never heard her so bitter. 'When it's all over.' She turned, lumbering heavily along the sea wall, and his heart went out to her graceless vulnerability.

'Careful,' he said. 'Let me give you an arm.'

She turned to him, the tears still in her eyes. 'Why do you do this? Why? Even my sister doesn't want to know me now—did you know I wrote to her? She didn't answer. Why should you bother with me? I'm a waste of space.'

'You're not, you're doing brilliantly under the circs,' protested Steve. 'You've arranged everything, saved up, fixed about the adoption—'

'That's just it,' said Maggie flatly. 'I haven't. I've pulled right out. I don't trust social services. They're clearly going to shove it into some foster home, then another, then another, and take years to let anybody have it properly as their own, by which time it'll be miserable and confused and fucked-up. When I come out of the hospital it'll be with a sodding, bloody baby in my arms that I don't know what to do with.'

Steve's heart leapt, and hammered so hard that he could hardly answer. Her words opened a new vista.

'So you'll bring it up? Yourself?' he asked eventually. He thought of Maggie, running with a toddler and swimming with a child, and a wave of tenderness shook him.

'Christ, I don't know.' She shook herself. 'Sorry, sorry, sorry. Look, forget it. Come and get your rent and have a cup of hot chocolate for the road. I've got no coffee, but lots of milk.'

He followed her up the dark stairs with a song in his heart.

In the flat, she lit the candle and the standard lamp, motioned him to one of the white plastic chairs, and clattered her saucepan on the aged stove. Her dark hair was tied back lankly in a rubber band and the tracksuit trousers stretched uncomfortably across her stomach. He remembered Ingrid's pale slender grace, and marvelled at himself for wanting only Maggie. *I must not*, he told himself sternly, *I must not, not, not fall for a woman just because she is having a baby.* Besides, she needed a friend right now, not some importunate suitor.

She turned to him in the lamplight, a mug in each hand, and every resolution crumbled.

He stood up, took both mugs, set them down on the table and said, 'I love you.'

Maggie glanced round for the other plastic chair and sat down, heavy and afraid. 'No,' she said. 'No, we aren't like that. Are we?'

'I am,' said Steve. His head was swimming with risk and exhilaration. 'I am. I've been in love with you since I met you.'

Maggie recovered herself a little. 'You have not! You thought I was a dippy tree-hugger. You took the piss out of me.'

'You are, and I did. But, Maggie, I love you. Please. I'm serious.'

'I'm having someone else's baby!'

'So?'

'I've got to keep it! It isn't just the social bloody services woman, it's that I can't let it go to some stranger. I can't!' She mistook his expression for disbelief and repeated, 'Look, Steve, I can't! I've tried and tried, but I can't do it!'

'Good.' He smiled at her, so tenderly that she had to look away, in order to hold herself to her resolve.

'It is *not* good! It's the end of everything that I've done, and been, and all the freedom that kept me alive. I've just got to accept that I had my fun and my freedom, and it's over!'

'I could look after you,' Steve said steadily. 'Both of you. I want to. Please, Maggie. I love you. You don't have to love me back as much as I love you, nobody possibly could. But stay with me, let me look after you.'

Maggie got up, came towards him and gingerly, so that her swollen belly would not touch him, put her arm round him from the side and kissed his cheek.

'You're a dear soft man. But it's impossible. You lost your baby, you lost your wife, you're just convincing yourself you want an instant replacement. But it's not your baby, and you'd resent it. And anyway, I'm not your cup of tea really. You want someone cosy, a proper wife like Sarah. I'm just a piece of chaos.' She stepped away and sat down again.

'Not with a baby. You won't be chaos with a baby. And I bloody *would* love it. I like babies!' He told himself that he had not expected instant success, but all the same a cold dismay was gripping him. He remembered what he had told Malcolm about the need to marry calmly and sensibly. 'I don't care,' he cried, too loud. 'I don't care if you go on being chaos—and you won't be.'

Maggie was looking at him, sadly. 'Of course I won't be bad to the baby,' she said gently. 'It'll be safe with me. But I don't think I can live in England for long, it's a killjoy sort of place for single mothers. I'll probably go abroad. Find a housekeeping job with a room, somewhere warm.'

'I'll come too!' said Steve desperately, reaching for her hands.

Maggie looked at him with great, sad eyes. 'I do, sort of, love you,' she said. 'How couldn't I, after all you've done? And you make me laugh more than anyone. But it's no good, Steve. I don't love you that way. Don't kid yourself.' She winced, and touched her side. 'Please just be friends. If you can bear it.'

'Well, I can't,' he said, his voice harsh. 'I wish I was bloody dead!'

He dropped her hands, picked up the rent she had left on the table, and without another word let himself out of the studio.

When he had left, Maggie began to cry.

Chapter Eleven

HE DID NOT GO HOME. Instead of taking the road to Maidstone and the sterile flat, he drove along the Brackhampton bypass and down into the dark town where she had lived. Parking behind the town hall, he sat and wept through the night until he fell into an uncomfortable sleep.

When he woke it was full daylight, and curious passers-by were pausing to peer at him through the misted windows. He did not care. He got out of the car, glanced around him, and walked stiffly to the High Street, where he stood for a moment looking in through the plate glass of the bookshop. It was already a quarter past nine; he could see a grey, stooping, scholarly man in conversation with an early customer.

Leo Penn! The creep! This dull-looking man was the cause of Maggie's misfortune sixteen years ago. He was the chief author of all the sorrow she had dragged round the world with bright, brittle gaiety through her travelling years. No wonder she had never trusted a man! No wonder she could not trust him now!

Tears of rage choked him. He had his hand on the door, ready to storm in and tell Brackhampton's favourite bookseller his fortune with a fist.

'Hello! I do believe I know you!' He turned, to see a spry elderly woman in a purple coat and woolly scarf behind him.

'Maggie Reave gave me your business card when you were taking her out the first time in your car. *Such* a nice gesture, I thought. Are you still in touch? We miss her.'

Something in the old woman's sharp eye made Steve aware that she was not merely waffling in the manner of her kind. She had a purpose.

He said, 'I have her address, if you like.' It seemed to him that if he could no longer be a friend to Maggie, it would be good if someone who wished her well knew where to find her.

'Thank you. It's her mother, you see. She's dead. Two days ago. It was a heart attack. Nobody was expecting it. Simply taken, just like that.'

Steve rubbed his chin perplexedly. Maggie had rarely spoken of old Nancy except with mild exasperation, but all the same a mother was a mother. Doubtfully he said, 'Her relatives should be the ones to tell her.'

Miss Mountjoy looked at him with scornful sharpness. 'Oh, come on, Mr Arundel,' she said. 'You must know how things stand. Family rifts are reprehensible, and I have not only prayed about it but *spoken* seriously to Mr Penn. He is not being entirely straight with himself, in my view. But I do not think that in her present state Mrs Penn is going to see her duty very clearly. She is extremely upset.'

'Well, *you* could tell Maggie about her mother,' said Steve. He pulled out a pen and another business card, rested it against the wall and began writing the address in Whitstable.

The old woman peered at it over his shoulder. 'I do not drive a car, and there is no telephone number. You go and tell her. A man friend is very comforting to a woman at times like this. The funeral is on Thursday. St Chad's, two o'clock. You should bring her. It must be divine mercy that we met like this.'

Steve nodded, still speechless.

'Oh, she'll come,' said Miss Mountjoy, answering an unspoken question. 'She'll come with you, in your nice black car.'

Sarah had wept, on and off, for two days. Her competence deserted her; Leo had to deal with the chapel of rest, and Samantha rose magnificently to the occasion, cooking for the boys over the confusing, troubled weekend. On Monday Sarah woke in a calmer state and said to Leo, 'I want to sort out her things.'

'We don't need to do anything till after the funeral,' said Leo.

'I want to,' said Sarah. As the shock abated, she was beginning to see that a powerful ingredient in her sorrow was a sense of unfinished business, unasked questions.

'Almost everyone feels that when a parent dies,' said Leo when she told him this. 'It was with both of mine.'

'Then you see why I have to go and be in her house,' said Sarah flatly.

'OK,' said her husband. 'I'll drive you over.' He wondered whether to mention Maggie, but dared not.

Sarah was dry-eyed on the journey to the Brackley estate, and maintained her composure as she entered the living room. Nancy had died here, alone in her chair, to be found later by a neighbour coming to tea. Sarah stared at the empty chair.

Leo said inadequately, 'I doubt she suffered. The doctor said—'

'I know what he said. Look, go for a walk round the block. I want to be on my own for half an hour.'

Obediently, he left her. Sarah sniffed, then went to the roll-top desk to collect the family documents and take them safely home. She found a key on Nancy's ring, and unlocked the desk.

It was a moment before she could pull out the first folder, marked 'Accounts to 1967'. God, did these old people never throw *anything* away? She peered at it: 'Mortgage £24.7s 6d'. She smiled in spite of herself.

She began to fill the folding plastic crate she had brought with her. After a few minutes she reached a cardboard pouch marked 'Certificates'. She pulled out first Ted's birth certificate, then Nancy's. Clipped behind them was Maggie's—dated April 11, 1965—and her own, August 3, 1960. She had last seen it when she applied for her first passport, to go on honeymoon.

She turned over the papers, and came on her parents' marriage certificate. How many years had it been? How many years? Would she and Leo make it that far? Sentimentally she gazed down at the paper, and then went rigid.

June 4, 1960 was the date. No, it must be a mistake. Must be 1959. Yes, of course—she remembered their twentieth anniversary party in

September 1979. She had come home from her first term in college for it. She remembered how insistent Nancy had been to mark the date, and how full of reminiscence about how Ted had courted her, and how pleased they were to find Sarah on the way soon afterwards, and what a tragedy it was that their wedding pictures had been destroyed in a fire at the photographer's.

She also remembered that Ted dwelt on how delighted they had been to have a baby. 'Both of us,' she could hear him saying, oddly. 'Both of us were pretty excited!' Now it was only too clear why the poor man felt he had to say this so emphatically. Nancy, lifelong deplorer of unmarried mothers, had walked up the aisle seven months gone.

There were tears in her eyes as she closed the folder. No wonder Nancy had always fretted about her daughters. How had such a disaster happened to her mother? Had quiet, considerate Ted been an importunate wooer, back in—Sarah frowned—November 1959? Had he left her for half a year before making an honest woman of her? It was hard to imagine.

Very hard. Something else stirred in her mind, and some time later, when Leo returned, he found the front room empty and bangings reverberating from the attic. He climbed the ladder and stood, puzzled, on a top rung. Flushed, Sarah looked across at him from where she knelt behind a barrage of cardboard boxes.

'Darling, you don't have to go through every last thing now,' he said. 'Only the main documents, surely?'

'I was conceived in 1959,' said his wife gnomically. 'In November. And do you know what?'

He was afraid for her; there had been more anger and tears in recent months than he could ever remember, and he mistrusted the weird intensity of her look. He could not tell if she was horrified or exalted.

'What's the matter?' he asked gently.

'*They weren't married then.* It was another seven months.'

'Well,' said Leo. 'By 1959 . . . well, the world was changing, surely? There must have been lots of brides with big bouquets.'

'Yes, but he wasn't the father,' said Sarah flatly. 'Look.' She shoved a paper at him. It was from one of Ted's old boxes, the ones he had brought with him to the marriage and put straight in the attic.

Obediently, Leo read the paper. Under a printed bank heading, it was a letter about a temporary promotion to the Skipton branch from June 1959 to February 1960 'to replace our Assistant Manager Mr Inglebrough during his journey to the Far East'.

'He was there all right,' said Sarah. 'Here's his notebook.' Again the small, neat writing; again the dates.

'So,' said Leo, 'he came down from Skipton to see his girlfriend, and they were glad to be together again, and all that . . .'

'No,' said Sarah. 'Because Dad used to tell us about his bachelor days. He had a girlfriend in Yorkshire whose father ran a farm. He talked about it lots. Maisie taught him how to milk. Then he'd laugh and say that when he left the Skipton job and got properly promoted and posted to Maidstone, this Maisie girl told him she'd never come south or live in a town. So he got off the train feeling a bit low, and then he'd always say, "And then I met your mother in the station buffet, just like in *Brief Encounter*, and saw her shining black hair, and that was that!"'

'See? Sarah concluded. 'By the time Mum met Dad, she was three months gone. And he still married her.'

Leo shifted uneasily on his rung of the ladder. After a moment, he said, 'But you're so like Maggie to look at. And you're both so like Samantha.'

Sarah riffled among the photographs, and thrust one at him. 'We're both the spitting image of Mum,' she said. 'But there are things that are different between Maggie and Sam. Sam's got a square jaw, with that dimple. She didn't get it from me, and Dad didn't have it, nor Mum. But look who did. It's just skipped a generation. Look.' She delved in her cardigan pocket, and opened a pale, flat, shagreen card case. 'It was right at the back of her bedside-table drawer.'

It was a tiny, black-and-white contact print, cut from one of those sheets that studio portraitists used to give to clients. The subject was a handsome man in his mid-thirties, with dark crinkled hair brushed back, a slightly hooked nose and a dimpled jaw which Leo recognised instantly as belonging to Samantha and also to Teddy.

'Bloody hell!' he said softly.

'At least we know that Dad was willing,' said Sarah softly. 'And he bothered to keep telling me how thrilled he was when I was born. He was my dad. He'll always be my dad. But poor old Mum, with her romantic secret.'

'Who is this? I don't suppose we'll ever know,' said Leo, gazing at the photograph.

'Oh, I know,' said Sarah. 'I've seen the twin of it. I know perfectly well who it is. Take away his beard and you'd see that dimple down the High Street any day. The nice thing is that he'll be at the funeral, ex officio anyway.'

'Who?' Leo asked. 'What are you talking about?'

'Samuel Miller,' said Sarah. 'Remember? Sam Miller is filling in on the organ for services at the moment. And this very photograph is also in old Mrs Miller's Victorian silver locket. She showed it to me once. It was taken when they got engaged.'

'The bastard!' said Leo. 'Somehow you don't think about your parents' generation carrying on like that.'

'No,' said Sarah. 'But, do you know, it makes me fonder of Mum and Dad than I've ever been. He loved her, you know. And he loved both of us, though I always had a hunch Maggie was more special to him, and I was more special to Mum. But it's like that in families sometimes. And it wasn't a bad family really.'

That night Sarah did not cry, but slept close and warm with an arm round her husband all night. In the morning she was composed, and spent a long quiet time with Samantha and the boys choosing hymns and making sausage rolls and quiches for the funeral tea. It was a strangely happy afternoon. Sam and the boys were touchingly careful of their mother, hugging her often and washing up her dishes.

'Don't you have to go to work this week, Mum?' asked Teddy solicitously. 'Will Mr Miller be cross?'

'No,' said Sarah, and smiled at the little boy with the dark, crinkling hair and the dimple in his chin. 'Not him!'

Steve ran up the rickety stairs two at a time, because of the sound beyond the door. He had gone to the Seven Grapes first, only to find a surly Evan Ardriss behind the counter on his own.

'Bloody unreliable bitches, barmaids, every bleeding one of them,' said the landlord, only to receive a blast of invective before his guest clattered from the room.

Panting and terrified, Steve pushed open the unlocked door of his late uncle's flat. Maggie lay on the platform bed, white as chalk.

'I can't—breathe properly,' she gasped, without preamble. 'I don't— get this. I thought it was different. Sarah said . . .' Her voice tailed off into a long, dragging moan.

'You're in labour, fool,' said Steve, whose arm was round her shoulder.

'Not for a couple of weeks yet,' she said faintly. 'Not due.'

'It's not a *bus*,' he said. 'We'd better get you to hospital quick. May I?' His hand was on her stomach, and she nodded, and let it lie there until the next pain gripped her. It came very soon indeed.

'Oh, bloody hell,' said Steve, snatching his hand away as he felt the terrible tightening. 'How long have they been so close together?'

'Half an hour?' said Maggie vaguely. 'It hurt last night, but I thought it was indigestion. I thought labour contractions were something different. Sort of lower down.'

Steve ripped his mobile phone from an inside pocket, and dialled 999. Maggie moaned again twice while he had a tense geographical altercation with a distant Vodafone operator.

When he snapped the phone shut she said, 'Look, the thing is, Steve, it's sort of—aah—coming out!'

'Are you meant to push it out? What position? Do you sit up or lie down? What did they say in the antenatal classes?'

'I only went to one. They were such awful women.'

'You are hopeless!' He felt panic and joy all at once: panic that she might come to harm and guilty joy at being her helper.

'It is really, seriously coming out. Oh God, the mess—oh God, your flat—this mattress will have to go . . .'

They were both prone to say, in after days, that the next few minutes passed in a blur. They both lied: every detail of it was fixed in their minds. Steve had the presence of mind to run for a clean sheet and towel, stumblingly. Maggie, as her gasps declined and the red, waxy, kicking new thing lay between them, reminded him about 'cutting the rope' and tying a shoelace round it.

When the ambulance crew came they found Maggie cross-legged on the high bed platform with Steve next to her, both of them gazing down at an alert, beady-eyed infant wrapped in a threadbare towel.

'Looks like you hardly need help,' said the woman paramedic, grinning. 'Is it a boy or a girl?'

The couple exchanged a horrified glance.

'Oh, bloody hell,' said Steve. 'We haven't actually looked.'

'If it's a girl I'm not sure I want to know,' said Maggie, faintly. 'It's altogether too bloody tough to contemplate, this being female.'

The woman gently unwrapped the towel and said, 'It's a boy.'

'That's pretty tough too,' said Steve. He put his arm round Maggie again. 'Never mind. As they say in *Three Men in a Boat*, humankind is born to trouble, as the sparks fly upward. Either way, we're all stuffed.'

The paramedic raised an eyebrow at her colleague, and together they carried Maggie to the waiting ambulance.

Inside, Maggie said shyly, 'I didn't think you'd come any more. I thought I blew it,' and Steve remembered with a plummeting heart what it was that he had come to tell her. After some evasion she got the truth from him.

'Miss Mountjoy, from the bookshop, told me. I'm really sorry. It's your mother. She died suddenly.'

Maggie was quiet for a moment Then she said, 'Is Sarah OK?'

'Don't know. I only know that Miss Mountjoy thought you should be told about the funeral. Nice old trout, I like her.'

'Yes,' said Maggie. 'Well, I'll go, obviously. I'll keep out of Sarah and Leo's way, but I have to go.'

'Well, I'll drive you. Both of you. We can get a baby seat thing.' He looked down at the sleeping boy with shining eyes. 'Hello again, sprog. Welcome!'

Maggie watched him, and her heart rose and swelled with irrational, treacherous joy.

He read her face, and said, 'It was all bollocks, that stuff you said yesterday. About being wrong for me. Wasn't it?'

'Complete bollocks,' said Maggie happily. She reached up and stroked his stubbled chin.

'So can I come with you next time you run away?'

'If you don't, I shan't go.'

'You must always go, if you need to,' he said seriously. 'And somehow or other we'll come along too.'

'Always,' said Maggie.

Tentatively, he touched the baby's tiny cheek. 'You're my witness, Lopez junior,' he said. 'Always.'

The organ played a soft regretful voluntary as the mourners filed in to their benches beside the coffin. Miss Mountjoy saw the Townswomen's Guild deputation into their allotted benches behind the family, then discreetly met Leo and Sarah and the three dark-suited children by the door and led them forward. Sarah glanced up at the organ loft and the back view of the old vet, with his wings of silver hair. Leo's eye followed hers and he put a steadying hand on her waist, but Sarah was composed, even faintly smiling. The time would come, she thought, when she would inform her acerbic employer of what she knew. Dear Samuel, with his spiky cynical pragmatism and exaggerated respect for the marital art of forgiving and forgetting.

As she stepped into the pew, she laid a hand briefly on her mother's coffin. *Goodbye, Mum. We know everything, and we're happy about it. You did all right, considering.* Joyful, lilting, from above them fell Brother James's Air: 'The Lord's my shepherd, I'll not want . . .'

Maggie and Steve were very quiet; not one head in the small congregation turned as they slipped into the back of the church with their sleeping new child in a carrier between them. Only later did the two sisters' eyes meet. Across the grave, under the pale green of the spring leaves, Sarah mouthed one word.

'Sorry.'

Gravely, Maggie nodded. Then she stepped forward, and stooped to throw her handful of earth, dust to dust, on the coffin. Looking up at Sarah, she in turn mouthed one word.

'Later?'

Sarah inclined her head.

Then, unremarked by any but the interested eye of Miss Mountjoy, Maggie turned back to where Steve Arundel stood with her baby just waking in his arms. The three of them withdrew from the company as silently as they had come.

LIBBY PURVES

Libby Purves has presented Radio Four's *Midweek* programme since 1984 and is an award-winning columnist for *The Times*. Married to fellow writer and broadcaster, Paul Heiney, she has two children and has written twenty-four books, including three amusing guides to surviving and enjoying family life. How does she manage to fit everything in? 'I never, ever do any housework if I can avoid it,' she says. 'I've had someone in to do it two or three times a week for the past fifteen years. I don't waste time faffing about with fashion and special shoes. And my children are big teenagers now; they need to talk and be listened to, but they don't need watching all the time! I was much less productive when they were small.'

Like Maggie in *A Free Woman*, Libby Purves is a keen sailor and takes to the water regularly with her family. In fact, it was their shared passion for sailing that brought Libby and her husband together. They met while working on Radio Four's *Today* programme, but it was through their regular sailing trips together that their relationship developed and they married in 1980. Over the years Libby has written several books about sailing, including *One Summer's Grace*, an evocative account of a sailing trip she and her husband took with their young family around the British Isles.

A Free Woman, Libby Purves's seventh novel, was inspired by some of

the free-spirited people she has met over the years through sailing. 'I was interested in exploring why people who turn their backs on conventional ways of living unsettle us and make us feel dissatisfied with our own lives, and how we sometimes drive them away as a result.' In creating Maggie, however, Libby Purves was careful not to base her on any one person in particular. 'It doesn't work if you base your characters on real people,' she says. 'You're too limited by the person you copy and, besides, it isn't really fair on them. So the characters in my books are composites and imaginary, but they become real to me as I write and think about them.' As a journalist she loves the freedom of writing fiction. 'I like being able to make up stories and thereby place a satisfying shape on lives and relationships. It's like sculpting; sometimes you even surprise yourself.'

Part of the novel is set in Whitstable, which she fell in love with one windy winter's night while having supper there with friends. 'I suddenly realised this would be where Maggie would run to when things went wrong. I ran out of the restaurant and toured the town. Our friends thought I was mad and my dinner went cold, but I had found the perfect setting. Now I long for a film to be made so that Whitstable can be the star!'

Sally Cummings

The Villa

NORA ROBERTS

❦

For many years the Giambelli winery has
been under the firm control of Tereza
Giambelli, who now faces some hard
decisions if the company is to survive. What
she proposes is a merger with the MacMillan
vineyard—a union that will depend on the
cooperation of her spirited granddaughter,
and MacMillan's headstrong heir.
But as Sophia and Tyler reluctantly work
together, the winery comes under threat from
someone determined to sabotage its
reputation. And that's not the only danger,
for Tyler and Sophia's business relationship
soon explodes into a passion as intoxicating
and irresistible as their finest wines.

❦

PROLOGUE

ON THE NIGHT he was murdered, Bernardo Baptista dined simply on bread and cheese and a bottle of Chianti. The wine was a bit young, and Bernardo was not. Neither would continue to age.

Like his bread and cheese, Bernardo was a simple man. He had lived in the same little house in the gentle hills north of Venice since his marriage fifty-one years before. His five children had been raised there. His wife had died there.

Now at seventy-three, Bernardo lived alone, with most of his family a stone's throw away, at the edges of the grand Giambelli vineyard, where he had worked since his youth.

He had known La Signora since her girlhood and had been taught to remove his cap whenever she passed by. Even now if Tereza Giambelli travelled from California back to the *castello* and vineyard, she would stop if she saw him, and they would talk of the old days when her grandfather and his had worked the vines. Signore Baptista, she called him. Respectfully. He had great appreciation for La Signora and had been loyal to her and hers the whole of his life.

For more than sixty years he had taken part in the making of Giambelli wine. There had been many changes—some good, in Bernardo's opinion, some not so good. He had seen much.

Some thought, too much.

The vines, lulled into dormancy by winter, would soon be pruned. Arthritis prevented Bernardo from doing much of the handwork, as he once had, but still, he would go out every morning to watch his sons and grandsons carry on the tradition.

On this last night of his seventy-three years he looked out over the vines, seeing what needed to be done, and listened as the December wind whistled through the bones of the grape.

From the window where that wind tried to sneak, he could see the skeletons as they made their steady climb up the rises. They would take on flesh and life with time and not wither as a man did. Such was the miracle of the grape.

Bernardo sipped the good, full-bodied wine by his little fire. He was proud of his life's work, some of which was in the glass that caught the firelight and gleamed deep, deep red. The wine had been a gift, one of many given to him on his retirement, though everyone knew the retirement was only a technicality. Even with his aching bones and a heart that had grown weak, Bernardo would walk the vineyard, test the grapes, watch the sky and smell the air.

He lived for the wine.

He died for it.

He drank, nodding by the fire. Through his mind ran images of sun-washed fields, of his wife laughing, of himself showing his son how to support a young vine, to prune a mature one. Of La Signora standing beside him between the rows their grandfathers had tended.

Signore Baptista, she had said to him when their faces were still young, we have been given a world. We must protect it. And they had.

The wind whistled at the windows. The fire died to embers.

And when the pain reached out like a fist, squeezing his heart to death, his killer was 6,000 miles away, surrounded by friends and associates, enjoying a perfectly poached salmon and a fine pinot blanc.

PART ONE
THE PRUNING

~

THE BOTTLE OF CASTELLO di Giambelli Cabernet Sauvignon, '02, auctioned for $125,500. A great deal of money, Sophia thought, for wine mixed with sentiment. The wine in that fine old bottle had been produced from grapes harvested in the year her great-great-grandfather, Cezare Giambelli, had established the Castello di Giambelli winery on a hilly patch of land north of Venice.

THE VILLA

At that time the *castello* had been either a con or supreme optimism, depending on your point of view. Cezare's modest house and little stone winery had been far from castlelike. But his vines had been regal, and he had built an empire from them.

Sophia made a note of the final bid and the buyer's name, though she was unlikely to forget either, for the memo she would send to her grandmother when the auction was over.

She was attending the event not only as the public relations executive who had designed the promotion and catalogue for the auction but as the Giambelli family representative at this exclusive precentennial event. As such, she sat quietly in the rear of the room to observe the bidding, her legs crossed in a long, elegant line, her back convent-school straight. She wore a black pinstripe suit, tailored and Italian, that managed to look both businesslike and utterly feminine.

It was exactly the way Sophia thought of herself.

Her face was sharp, a triangle of pale gold dominated by large deep-set brown eyes and a wide, mobile mouth. Her cheekbones were ice-pick keen, her chin a diamond point, sculpting a look that was part pixie, part warrior. She had, deliberately, ruthlessly, used her face as a weapon when it seemed most expedient.

Tools, she believed, were meant to be used, and used well.

A year before, she'd had her waist-length hair cut into a short black cap with a spiky fringe over her forehead.

It suited her. Sophia knew exactly what suited her.

She wore the single strand of antique pearls her grandmother had given her for her twenty-first birthday, and an expression of polite interest. The corners of her wide mouth curved slightly as the next item was showcased.

It was a bottle of Barolo '34, from the cask Cezare had named Di Tereza in honour of her grandmother's birth. The label carried a picture of Tereza Giambelli at the age of ten, the year the wine had been deemed sufficiently aged in oak, and bottled.

Now, at sixty-seven, Tereza Giambelli was a legend, whose renown as a vintner had overshadowed even her grandfather's.

This was the first bottle of this label ever passed outside the family. As Sophia expected, bidding was brisk and spirited.

The man beside her tapped his catalogue where the photograph of the bottle was displayed. 'You have the look of her.'

Sophia smiled first at him—a distinguished man hovering comfortably somewhere near sixty—then at the picture of the young girl staring

333

seriously out from a bottle of red wine in his catalogue. 'Thank you.' Marshall Evans, she recalled. Real estate, second generation of one of the top US companies listed in *Fortune* 500. She made it her business to know the names and vital statistics of wine buffs and collectors.

'I'd hoped La Signora would attend today's auction. She's well?'

'Very. But otherwise occupied.'

The beeper in her jacket pocket vibrated. Annoyed at the interruption, Sophia ignored it to watch the bidding. Her eyes scanned the room, noting the signals. The casual lift of a finger from the third row brought the price up five hundred. A subtle nod from the fifth topped it.

In the end, the Barolo outdistanced the cabernet sauvignon by fifteen thousand, and she extended her hand to the man beside her.

'Congratulations, Mr Evans. Your contribution to the International Red Cross will be put to good use. On behalf of Giambelli, family and company, I hope you enjoy your prize.'

'There's no doubt of it.' He took her hand, lifted it to his lips. 'I had the pleasure of meeting La Signora many years ago. She's an extraordinary woman.'

'Yes, she is.'

'Perhaps her granddaughter would join me for dinner this evening?'

He was old enough to be her father, but Sophia was too European to find that a deterrent. Another time, she'd have agreed, and no doubt enjoyed his company. 'I'm sorry, but I have an appointment. Perhaps on my next trip east, if you're free.'

'I'll make sure I am.'

Putting some warmth into her smile, she rose. 'If you'll excuse me . . .'

She slipped out of the room, plucking the beeper from her pocket to check the number. She detoured to the ladies' room, pulling the phone from her bag. With the number punched in, she settled on one of the sofas and glanced at her watch.

It had been a long and demanding week in New York, and she needed time to change before her dinner date. Jeremy DeMorney, she mused, meant an elegant, sophisticated evening. French restaurant, discussion of travel and theatre. And, of course, of wine. As Jeremy was descended from the Le Coeur winery, DeMorneys, and was one of their top account execs, and she sprang from Giambelli stock, there would be some playful attempts to prise corporate secrets from each other.

And there would be champagne. Good, she was in the mood for it.

All followed by an outrageously romantic attempt to lure her into bed. She wondered if she'd be in the mood for that as well.

He was attractive, she considered, and could be amusing. Perhaps if they hadn't both been aware that her father had once slept with his wife, the idea of a little romance between them wouldn't seem so awkward.

Still, several years had passed . . .

'Maria.' Sophia tucked the evening to come away when the Giambelli housekeeper answered. 'I've had a call from my mother. Is she available?'

'Oh, yes, Miss Sophia. She hoped you would call. One moment.'

Sophia imagined the woman hurrying through the wing, scanning the rooms for something to tidy when Pilar Giambelli Avano would have already tidied everything herself.

Mama, Sophia thought, would have been content in a little rose-covered cottage, where she could bake bread, do her needlework and tend her garden. She should have had half a dozen children, Sophia thought with a sigh. And had to settle for me.

'Sophie, I was just heading out to the greenhouse. I didn't expect you to get back to me so quickly. I thought you'd be in the middle of the auction.'

'End of it. And I think we can say it's been an unqualified success. Is everything all right?'

'More or less. Your grandmother's ordered a summit meeting.'

'Oh, Mama, she's not dying again? We went through that six months ago.'

'I'm sorry, baby, but she insists. I don't think she plans to die this time, but she's planning something. She's sending for everyone. You need to come back.'

'All right, all right.' Sophia blew a mental kiss goodbye to Jerry DeMorney. 'I'll finish up here and be on my way.'

Two hours later she was flying west and speculating whether in another forty years she would have the power to crook her finger and have everyone scrambling. Just the idea of it made her smile as she settled back with a glass of champagne.

Not everyone scrambled. Tyler MacMillan was only minutes away from Villa Giambelli, but he considered the vines a great deal more urgent than a summons from La Signora. And he said so.

'I'm sorry, Granddad. You know how vital the winter pruning is, and so does Tereza.' He shifted the portable phone to his other ear. He hated portables. He was always losing them. 'MacMillan's vines need every bit as much care as Giambelli's.'

'Ty,' Eli explained calmly, 'Tereza and I are as dedicated to MacMillan wines as we are to those under the Giambelli label, and have been for

twenty years. You were put in charge because you're an exceptional vintner. Tereza has plans. Those plans involve you.'

'Next week.'

'Tomorrow.' Eli didn't put his foot down often, only when necessary.
'One o'clock. Lunch. Dress appropriately.'

Tyler scowled down at his ancient boots and the frayed hems of his
trousers. 'That's the middle of the damn day.'

'Are you the only one at MacMillan capable of pruning vines, Tyler?
One o'clock. Try to be on time.'

'Yeah, yeah,' Tyler muttered, but only after he clicked the phone off.

He adored his grandfather. He even adored Tereza. When his grandfather had married the Giambelli heiress, Tyler had been eleven years
old. He'd fallen in love with the vineyards, the rise of the hills, the great
caverns of the cellars. And in a very real sense he'd fallen in love with
Tereza Louisa Elana Giambelli, that whip-thin, ramrod-straight, somewhat terrifying figure he'd first seen dressed in boots and trousers, striding through the grapes.

She'd taken one look at him, lifted a razor-sharp black eyebrow and
deemed him soft and citified. If he was to be her grandson, she'd told
him, he would have to be toughened up.

She'd made him. Pruned him back at the age of eleven and trained
him to grow into what he was.

But she didn't own him.

Tyler started out of the office and detoured through the charming ramble of the house that had been his grandfather's into the kitchen to refill
his Thermos with coffee. Absently he set the portable phone on the
counter and began rearranging his schedule in his head.

He was just over six foot tall with a body sculpted by fieldwork. His
hands were wide, and tough with calluses, with long fingers that knew
how to dip delicately under leaves to the grape. His hair tended to curl
if he forgot to have it trimmed, which he often did, and was a deep
brown that showed red, like an aged burgundy in the sunlight. His raw-
boned face was more rugged than handsome, with lines beginning to fan
out from eyes of calm blue that could harden to steel.

Those who worked for him considered him a fair man, if a single-
minded one. They also considered him an artist, and that would have
baffled him.

To Tyler MacMillan, the artist was the grape.

He stepped outside into the brisk winter air. He had two hours before
sunset, and vines to tend.

Donato Giambelli had a headache of outrageous proportions. Her name was Gina, and she was his wife. When the summons from La Signora had come, he had been happily engaged in eye-crossing sex with his current mistress. Unlike his wife, she did not require conversation.

There were times he thought Gina required nothing else.

She babbled at him. Babbled at each of their three children. Babbled until the air in the company jet vibrated with the endless stream of words.

Between her, the baby's screaming, little Cezare's banging, and Tereza Maria's bouncing, Don gave serious thought to opening the hatch and shoving his entire family off the plane and into oblivion. Instead he could only sit, his temples throbbing, and damn his aunt Tereza to hell and beyond for insisting his entire family make the trip.

He was executive vice-president of Giambelli Venice and a nephew of La Signora, was he not? Any business to be conducted required him, not his family. Why had God plagued him with such a family? Was it any wonder he sought his comfort elsewhere?

'Donny, I think Zia Tereza will give you a *big* promotion, and we'll all move into the *castello*.' Gina lusted for the great house of Giambelli—all those lovely rooms, all the servants, her children raised in luxury, and one day the Giambelli fortune at their feet. She was the only one giving La Signora babies, wasn't she? That would count for quite a bit.

'Cezare,' she said to her son as he tore the head off his sister's doll, 'stop that! Now you made your sister cry. Here now, here, give me the doll. Mama will fix.'

Little Cezare, eyes glinting, tossed the head gleefully over his shoulder and began to taunt his sister.

'English, Cezare!' She shook a finger at him. 'We're going to America. You'll speak English to your zia Tereza and show her what a smart boy you are.'

Tereza Maria, screaming over the death of her doll, retrieved the severed head and raced up and down the cabin in a flurry of grief and rage.

Don lurched up, stumbled away, and locked himself in the sanctuary of his in-flight office.

Anthony Avano enjoyed the finer things. He'd chosen his two-storey penthouse in San Francisco's Back Bay with care, then hired the top decorator in the city to furnish it for him. Silk moiré walls, oriental carpets, gleaming oak furniture, modern art. Tony Avano relied heavily on decorators, tailors, brokers, jewellers and dealers to surround him with the best. Money, as Tony saw it, bought all the taste a man required.

He knew one thing. And that was wine.

His cellars were arguably among the best in California. Every bottle had been personally selected. While he couldn't distinguish a sangiovese from a sémillon on the vine, he had a superior nose. And that nose had steadily climbed the corporate ladder at Giambelli California. Thirty years before, he had married Pilar Giambelli. And it had taken that nose less than two years to begin sniffing at other women.

Tony was the first to admit that women were his weakness. There were so many of them, after all. He had loved Pilar as deeply as he was capable of loving another human being, and he had certainly loved his position in the Giambelli organisation as the husband of La Signora's daughter and as the father of her granddaughter. He had attempted to be discreet. He had even tried, a number of times, to reform.

But then there would be another woman, soft and fragrant or sultry and seductive. What was a man to do?

The weakness had eventually cost him his marriage, in a technical if not a legal sense. He and Pilar had been separated for seven years. Neither of them had made the move towards divorce. They maintained a polite, even friendly relationship. And he kept his position as president of sales, Giambelli California.

Seven years they had walked that civilised line. Now he was very afraid he was about to fall off the edge of it.

Rene was insisting on marriage. Like a silk-lined steamroller, Rene had a way of flattening all barriers in her path. She was violently jealous, overbearing, demanding, and prone to icy sulks.

He was crazy about her.

At thirty-two she was twenty-seven years his junior. Knowing she was every bit as interested in his money as the rest of him didn't trouble him. He respected her for it. But he worried that if he gave her what she wanted, he would lose what she wanted him for. It was a hell of a fix.

Studying his view of the bay, sipping a small vermouth, Tony waited for Rene to finish dressing for their evening out. And worried that his time was up.

The doorbell had him glancing over, frowning slightly. They weren't expecting anyone. As it was his major-domo's evening off, he went to see who was there. The frown cleared as he opened the door to his daughter.

'Sophie, what a lovely surprise.'

'Dad.' She rose slightly on her toes to kiss his cheek.

Ridiculously handsome, as ever, she thought. Good genes and an excellent plastic surgeon served him well. She did her best to ignore the quick and instinctive tug of resentment and tried to focus on the equally quick and instinctive tug of love.

'I'm just in from New York and wanted to see you before I headed up to the villa.' She scanned his face—almost unlined and certainly untroubled. The dark hair wisped with grey at the temples, the deep blue eyes were clear. 'I see you're going out,' she said, noting his tuxedo.

'Shortly.' He took her hand to draw her inside. 'But there's plenty of time. Sit down, princess, and tell me how you are. What can I get you?'

She tipped his glass towards her. Sniffed, approved. 'What you're having's fine. Are you going up tomorrow?'

He walked over to the liquor cabinet. 'Going where?'

She tilted her head. 'To the villa.'

'No, why?' He crossed back to her.

She took the glass, considering as she sipped. 'You didn't get a call?' Loyalties tangled inside her. He'd cheated on her mother for as long as Sophia could remember and, in the end, had left them both with barely a backward glance. But he was still family, and the family were being called to the villa. 'La Signora. One of her summits with lawyers, I'm told. You might want to be there.'

'Ah, well, really, I was—'

He broke off as Rene walked in.

If there was a poster girl for the trophy mistress, Sophia thought as her temper sizzled, Rene Foxx was it. Tall, curvy, and blonde on blonde. The Valentino gown showcased a body ruthlessly toned. Diamonds shimmered against polished skin.

'Hello.' Sophia sipped vermouth. 'Rene, isn't it?'

'It has been for nearly two years. It's still Sophia?'

'Yes, for twenty-six.'

Tony cleared his throat. 'Rene, Sophia's in from New York.'

'Really? That explains why you're looking a bit travel-frayed. We're about to leave for a party. You're welcome to join us. I must have something in my closet that would work on you.'

'That's so considerate, but I'm on my way north. Family business.' Sophia set her glass down. 'Enjoy your evening.'

She walked to the door, where Tony caught up with her. 'Why don't you come along, Sophie? You're fine as you are.'

'No, thank you.' She turned, and their eyes met. His were full of sheepish apology. It was an expression she was too accustomed to seeing for it to be effective. 'I'm not feeling particularly festive.'

He winced as she shut the door in his face.

'What did she want?' Rene demanded.

'She just dropped by, as I said.'

'Your daughter never does anything without a reason.'

He shrugged. 'She may have thought we could drive up north to-gether in the morning. Tereza's sent out a summons.'

Rene's eyes narrowed. 'You didn't tell me about that.'

'I didn't get one.'

'What do you mean you didn't get one? Your position at Giambelli is certainly more important than your daughter's. If the old woman's call-ing the family, you go. We'll drive up tomorrow.'

'We? But—'

'It's the perfect opportunity, Tony, to tell Pilar you want a divorce.' She crossed to him, slid her fingers down his cheek. 'And when we get back tonight, I'll show you just what you can expect when we're married.' She leaned in, bit teasingly at his bottom lip.

'Let's just skip the party.'

She laughed, slipped away from his hands. 'It's important. Get my sable for me, won't you, darling?'

She felt like sable tonight, Rene thought. She felt rich.

The Napa Valley, and the hills that rose from it, wore a thin coat of snow. Vines climbed the slopes, their naked branches spearing through the quiet mist that turned the circling mountains to shadows. Under the pearly dawn the vineyard shivered and slept.

This peaceful scene had spawned a fortune, a fortune that would be gambled again and again, season after season. Wine-making was a busi-ness, a science. But it was also the biggest game in town.

From a window of her grandmother's villa, Sophia studied the playing field. It was pruning season, and she imagined that while she'd been travelling, vines had already been accessed, considered, and those first stages towards next year's harvest begun. She was glad she'd been called back so that she could see that part of it. Still, she couldn't stay long. She had duties in San Francisco. A new advertising campaign to be polished. The Giambelli centennial was just getting off the ground. And putting her mind to it would keep it off her father and the scheming Rene.

None of her business, Sophia reminded herself. None of her business at all if her father wanted to hook himself up with a former underwear model with a heart the size and texture of a raisin. He'd made a fool of himself before, and no doubt would again.

She wished she could hate him for his pathetic weakness of character, and his benign neglect of his daughter. But the steady, abiding love just wouldn't shift aside. Which made her, she supposed, as foolish as her mother.

He didn't care for either of them as much as he did the cut of his suit. And didn't give them a thought two minutes after they were out of his sight. He was utterly selfish, sporadically affectionate, and always careless. And that, she supposed, was part of his charm.

She wished she hadn't stopped by the night before, wished she wasn't compelled to keep that connection between them. Better, she thought, to keep on the move. Travelling, working, filling her life with professional and social obligations.

Two days, she decided. She would give her grandmother two days. Then it was back to work with a vengeance.

As she scanned the hills, she saw two figures walking through the mist. The tall, gangly man with an old brown cap on his head. The ramrod-straight woman in mannish boots and trousers with hair as white as the snow they trod. A Border collie plodded along between them. Her grandparents, taking their morning walk with the ageing and endlessly faithful Sally. The sight of them lifted Sophia's mood.

At sixty-seven Tereza Giambelli was sculpted, razor-sharp, body and mind. She had learned the art of the vine at her grandfather's knee. Had travelled with her father to California when she'd been only three, to turn the land of the ripe valley to wine. She'd become bilingual and had travelled back and forth between California and Italy the way other young girls had travelled to the playground. Eventually, she had married a man who had met with her family's approval. With him she'd had a daughter, Sophia's mother, and to her lasting grief, two stillborn sons.

Tereza had buried her husband when she was only thirty and never taken his name. She was Giambelli. Her second marriage, to Eli MacMillan, had been a carefully considered business merger, as his vineyards were prime and nestled below hers in the valley, but she was surprised to find comfort, pleasure and simple satisfaction in a marriage now approaching its twentieth year. He was a good man and a fine-looking man still. Though he was ten years Tereza's senior, Sophia saw no sign of him bowing to age.

She scanned the land again. The mist was raw and the air damp. The winter sun would not burn through it that day, she was certain. Then tossing aside her thoughts, Sophia dashed from the window to grab her coat and join her grandparents.

Villa Giambelli sat on a knoll above the centre of the valley, beside a forest that had been left to grow wild. Its stones showed gold and red and umber when the light struck them, and its windows were many. The winery had been built to replicate the one in Italy, which had been expanded and recently modernised.

The villa boasted twelve bedrooms and fifteen bathrooms, a solarium, a ballroom and a formal dining room. There were rooms dedicated to music and rooms celebrating books; rooms for work and for contemplation; Italian and American art and antiques that were second to none. There were indoor and outdoor pools. A central courtyard was tiled in Chianti red and boasted a fountain where a grinning Bacchus forever hoisted his goblet. When the winter cold had passed, dozens of pots would be set out so that the space was alive with flower and scent. The gardens were a fantasy.

Balconies and terraces laced the stone, and a series of steps afforded both family and guests private entrances and exits. But despite its size, its scope, and its priceless treasures, it was very much a home.

The first time Tyler MacMillan had seen Villa Giambelli, he'd thought of it as a castle, full of enormous rooms and complicated passages. At the moment he thought of it as a prison, where he was sentenced to spend entirely too much time with entirely too many people.

He wanted to be outside in the raw air tending his vines and drinking strong coffee out of a Thermos. Instead he was trapped in the family parlour sipping an excellent chardonnay. A fire was snapping gaily in the hearth, and elegant little hors d'oeuvres sat on platters of colourful Italian pottery.

Tyler couldn't understand why food had to be such a damn event. He imagined that if he uttered such heresy in a household of Italians, he'd be lynched on the spot.

He'd been forced to change out of his work clothes into slacks and a sweater, but at least he hadn't strapped himself into a suit like . . . what was the guy's name? Don. Don from Venice with the wife who always seemed to have a shrieking baby attached to some part of her body.

The little boy, if you could call a demon from hell a boy, was sprawled on the rug smashing two trucks together. Eli's Border collie, Sally, was hiding under Sophia's legs.

Great legs, Ty noted absently. She was looking as sleek and polished as ever, like something lifted off a movie screen and dropped down in three dimensions. She appeared to be fascinated by whatever Don was saying to her, and kept those big, dark chocolate eyes of hers on his face.

But Ty watched as she discreetly slipped Sally hors d'oeuvres. The move was too slick for her to have had her full attention on the conversation.

'Here. The stuffed olives are excellent.' Pilar stepped up beside him with a small plate.

'Thanks.' Tyler shifted. Of all the Giambellis, Tyler was most comfortable with Pilar. 'Any idea when we're going to get rolling?'

'When Mama's ready and not before. I can't pin down what this is all about, but Eli seems content. That's a good sign.'

Ty started to grunt, remembered his manners. 'Let's hope so.'

'We haven't seen you around here in weeks, Ty. What are you up to, other than business?'

'What else is there?'

With a shake of her head she pressed the olives on him again. 'Weren't you seeing someone last summer? A pretty blonde? Patty?'

'Patsy. Not really seeing. Just sort of . . . you know.'

'Honey, you need to get out more.'

He had to smile. 'I could say the same about you.'

'Oh, I'm just an old stick-in-the-mud.'

'Best-looking stick in the room,' he countered, and made her laugh.

'Mama, you're hoarding the olives.' Sophia dashed up, plucked one off the plate. Beside her lovely, composed mother, she was a fireball, crackling with electricity. The kind that was always giving you hot, unexpected jolts if you got too close.

Or so it always seemed to Ty.

For that single reason, he'd always tried to keep a safe distance.

'Quick, talk to me. Were you just going to leave me trapped with Don the Dull for ever?' Sophia muttered.

'Poor Sophie. Think of it this way. It's probably the first time in weeks he's been able to say five words without Gina interrupting him.'

'Believe me, he made up for it.' She rolled her dark exotic eyes. 'So, Ty, how are you?'

'Fine.'

'Hard at work for MacMillan?'

'Sure.'

'Know any words with more than one syllable?'

'Some. Thought you were in New York?

'Was,' she said, mimicking his tone as her lips twitched. 'Now I'm here.' She glanced over her shoulder as her two young cousins began to shriek. 'Mama, if I was ever that obnoxious, how did you stop yourself from drowning me in the fountain?'

'You weren't obnoxious, sweetie. Demanding, arrogant, temperamental, but never obnoxious. Excuse me.' Pilar handed the plate to Sophia and went to do what she'd always done best. Make peace.

'I suppose I should have done that,' Sophia said with a sigh as she watched her mother scoop up the miserable Tereza Maria and carry her to a window. 'But I've never seen a pair of kids less appealing in my life.'

'Comes from being spoilt and neglected.'

'At the same time?' She considered, studying Don ignoring his screaming son and Gina making foolish cooing noises to him. 'Good call,' she decided. Then she turned back to Tyler.

He was such a . . . man, she decided. He looked like something carved out of the mountains that guarded the valley. Now if she could just prise a reasonable conversation out of him.

'Any clues about our little gathering today?' she asked.

'No.'

'Would you tell me if you knew?'

He shrugged a shoulder and watched Pilar murmur to little Tereza. Sophia started to speak, then broke off as her father and Rene walked into the room.

At the window, Pilar tensed, and all the simple pleasure she'd had from distracting the unhappy girl drained away. She felt instantly frumpy, unattractive, old, fat, sour. Here was the man who had discarded her. And here was the latest in the long line of replacements. Younger, lovelier, smarter, sexier.

But because she knew her mother would not, Pilar set the child on the floor and walked over to greet them. Her smile was warm and graced a face much more compelling than she thought. Her simple slacks and sweater were more elegant than Rene's power suit. And her manner carried an innate class that held more true sparkle than diamonds.

'Tony, how good you could make it. Hello, Rene.'

'Pilar.' Rene smiled and trailed a hand down Tony's arm. The diamond on her finger caught the light. She waited a beat, to be certain Pilar saw it. 'You look . . . rested.'

'Thank you.' The backs of Pilar's knees dissolved. She could feel the support going out from under her. 'Please, come in, sit. What can I get you to drink?'

'Don't fuss, Pilar.' Tony leaned down to give her an absent peck on the cheek. 'We'll just go say hello to Tereza.'

'Go to your mom,' Ty said to Sophia under his breath.

'What?'

'Go, make an excuse, and get your mom out of here.'

She saw it then, the diamond glint on Rene's finger, her mother's blank shock. She shoved the plate at Ty and strode across the room. 'Mama, can you help me with something? It'll only take a second.' Pulling Pilar from the room, Sophia just kept moving until they were well down the hall and into the library. There, she pulled the sliding doors closed. 'Mama, I'm so sorry.'

'Oh.' Trying to laugh, Pilar ran an unsteady hand over her face. 'So much for thinking I pulled that off.'

'You did beautifully.' Sophia hurried over as Pilar lowered to the arm of a chair. 'But I know that face.' She cupped her mother's in her hands. 'Apparently so does Tyler. The ring's ostentatious, just like she is.'

'Oh, baby.' Her laugh was strained, but she tried. 'It's stunning, it's gorgeous—just like she is. It's all right.' But already she was turning the gold band she continued to wear round and round her finger. 'Really, it's all right.'

'The hell it is. I hate her. I hate both of them, and I'm going back in there and telling them right now.'

'You're not. Sophie, there's no point.'

Be angry! Be furious and bitter. Be anything, Sophia thought. *Anything but defeated.* 'To just walk in and shove it in our faces. He had no right to do that to you, Mama, or to me.'

'He has a right to do what he wants. Don't let it hurt you. He's still your father, whatever happens.'

'He was never a father to me.'

Pilar paled. 'Oh, Sophia.'

'No. No.' Furious with herself, Sophia held up a hand. 'This isn't about me. It's not even about him. He's oblivious, but she's not. She knew what she was doing. How I hate her lording that over you.'

'You're ignoring one factor, baby. Rene may love him.'

'Oh, please.'

'So cynical. I loved him. Why shouldn't she? He's the kind of man who makes women love him—effortlessly.'

Sophia caught the wistfulness in her mother's voice. She'd never loved a man, but she recognised the sound of a woman who had. Who did. She kissed both her mother's cheeks, then hugged her. 'Will you be all right, Mama?'

'Yes. Nothing really changes, does it? Let's go back.'

'I'll tell you what we're going to do,' Sophia began when they were in the hall again. 'I'm going to juggle my schedule, and you and I are going to the spa. We're going to sink up to our necks in mud, have facials, spend wads of money on overpriced beauty products, and lounge around in bathrobes all day.'

The door of the powder room opened as they walked past it, and a middle-aged brunette stepped out. 'Now that sounds wonderfully appealing. When do we leave?'

'Helen.' Pilar leaned in to kiss her friend's cheek.

'Had to make a dash for the loo.' Helen tugged at the skirt of her stone-grey suit over hips she was constantly trying to whittle, to make certain it was back in place. 'All that coffee I drank on the way up. Sophia, aren't you gorgeous? So . . .' She shifted her briefcase, squared her shoulders. 'The usual suspects in the parlour?'

'More or less. I didn't realise you would be coming.' And, Sophia thought, if her grandmother had called in Judge Helen Moore, it meant serious business.

'Your grandmother insisted I handle this business personally.' Helen's shrewd grey eyes shifted towards the parlour. 'She keeping all of you in the dark?'

'Apparently,' Pilar murmured.

Helen adjusted her black-rimmed glasses. 'It's her show. Why don't we see if she's ready for the curtain?'

La Signora never rushed her cue. She had planned the menu personally, wanting to set the tone for the lavish, and the casual. The wines served were from the California vineyards, both Giambelli and MacMillan. That, too, was meticulously planned.

She would not discuss business at the meal. Along with family and Helen, she had invited her most trusted wine-maker, Paulo Borelli, who had been with Giambelli for thirty-eight years. Despite his age, he was still called Paulie. The final addition was Margaret Bowers, head of sales for MacMillan, a sharp-featured, divorced woman of thirty-six who was currently being bored senseless by Gina's chatter and wishing desperately for a cigarette.

Tyler caught her eye and gave her a sympathetic smile.

Margaret sometimes wished desperately for him too.

When the food was cleared and the port passed, Tereza sat back. 'Villa Giambelli has been making wine in the Napa Valley for sixty-four years, MacMillan for ninety-two. That is one hundred and fifty-six years combined.' She scanned the table. 'Five generations have been vintners and wine merchants.'

'Six, Zia Tereza.' Gina fluttered. 'My children give you six.'

'From what I've seen, your children are more likely to be serial killers than vintners. Please, don't interrupt.'

She lifted her port, nosing the wine, sipping slowly. 'In those five generations we have earned a reputation on two continents for producing wine of quality. The name Giambelli *is* wine. We have established traditions and have blended them with new technology, without sacrificing that name or what it means. Twenty years ago we established a partnership with MacMillan of Napa Valley. The partnership has aged well. It's time for it to be decanted.'

She felt rather than saw Tyler tense. She gave him high marks for holding his tongue, and met his eyes now. 'Changes are necessary for the good of both. Donato.'

He snapped to attention. '*Sì*. Yes,' he corrected, remembering she preferred English at her California table. 'Yes, Aunt Tereza.'

'Giambelli Italy and California have been run exclusive of each other. Separate. This will no longer be the case. You will report to the chief operating officer of the newly formed Giambelli-MacMillan company, which will have bases in both California and Venice.'

'What does this mean? What does this mean?' Gina exploded in Italian, shoving awkwardly from the table. 'Donato is in charge. He is next in line. He is your sister's son. He carries the name. He is your heir.'

'My heir is who I say is my heir.'

'We give you children.' Gina slapped a hand on her belly. 'No one gives the family children but me and Donato. Who will carry on the name when you're gone?'

'Do you bargain with your womb?' Tereza said evenly.

'It's fertile,' she snapped. 'More than yours, more than your daughter's. One baby each, that's all. I can have a dozen.'

'Then God help us all. You'll keep your fine house, Gina, and your pocket money. But you will not find yourself mistress of the *castello*. My *castello*,' she added coolly. 'Take what you're given or lose a great deal more.'

'Gina, *basta!* Enough,' Don ordered and had his hand slapped for his trouble.

'You're an old woman,' Gina said between her teeth. 'One day you'll be dead and I will not. So we will see.' She swept out of the room.

'*Zia Tereza, scusi*,' Donato began and was cut off by a sharp gesture.

'Your wife does you no credit, Donato, and your work falls short of my expectations. You have this year to correct matters. Then we will reassess. If I am pleased, you will be promoted, with a salary and the benefits that apply. If I am not, you will remain with the company on paper only. I will not see one of my blood removed, but you will not find your life so easy as you have. Is this understood?'

His tie was suddenly too tight, and the meal he'd just eaten threatened to revolt in his belly. 'I've worked for Giambelli for eighteen years.'

'You worked for twelve. You have put in appearances for the last six. Do you think I am not aware of what your *business* is when you take trips to Paris, to Rome, to New York at Giambelli expense?'

She waited for this blow to land, saw the faint sheen of sweat skin his face, and was disappointed in him yet again. 'Your wife is foolish, Donato, but I am not. Have a care. Now, Margaret. You'll pardon the family histrionics. We're temperamental.'

Margaret Bowers spoke quietly. 'Of course, La Signora.'

'You will, if you choose to accept, oversee the heads of sales of Giambelli-MacMillan, California and Venice. This will require considerable travel and responsibility, with the appropriate salary increase. You'll be needed in Venice in five days to familiarise yourself with the operation there. You have until tomorrow to consider this.'

'I don't need time to decide, thank you,' Margaret kept her voice brisk and even, and her heart pounded like wild surf. 'I'm grateful for the opportunity.' She shifted to Eli, nodded. 'Grateful to both of you.'

'Well said. Tomorrow, then, we'll discuss the details. Paulie, you'll coordinate the operation in the fields. You know the best men here and at MacMillan. You'll serve as foreman.'

'I have nothing but respect for Paulie.' Ty's voice was calm, even if temper and frustration had twin grips on his throat. 'But we have topflight people at MacMillan. I won't see our operation overshadowed by yours, La Signora. You're proud of what your people have accomplished, of the legacy you've inherited and intend to pass on. So am I of mine.'

'Good. So listen. And think.' She gestured to Eli.

'Ty, Tereza and I didn't come to this decision overnight,' Eli said. 'We've worked out, with Helen, how to implement this merger to the benefit of all involved.' He leaned forward. 'Do you think I want any less for MacMillan than you?'

'I don't know what you want. I thought I did.'

'Then I'll make it clear, here and now. By doing this, we'll become not only one of the biggest wine-makers in the world but the best in the world. You'll continue to oversee MacMillan.'

'Oversee?'

'With Paulie as foreman and you as vintner. With some addenda.'

'You know the fields, Ty,' Tereza said. She understood his resentment. It pleased her. That hot, choking anger meant it mattered to him. 'You know the vines and the casks. But what you do stops at the bottle. It's time to go on from there. There's more to wine than the grape. Eli and I intend to see our grandchildren blended.'

'Grandchildren?' Sophia interrupted.

'When is the last time you worked in the fields?' Tereza demanded of her. 'When is the last time you tasted wine that wasn't uncorked from a pretty bottle taken from a cabinet? You've neglected your roots, Sophia.'

'I've neglected nothing,' Sophia shot back. 'I'm not a wine-maker. I'm a publicist.'

'You'll be a wine-maker. And, Ty,' she said, pointing at him, 'you'll learn what it is to sell, to market, to ship. You'll teach each other.'

'Oh, really, Nonna—'

'Quiet. You have the year. Pilar, Sophia won't have as much time to devote to her usual duties. You'll fill that gap.'

'Mama'—Pilar had to laugh—'I don't know anything about marketing or promotion.'

'You have a good brain. It's time you used it again. To succeed, we'll need all the family.' Tereza shifted her gaze to Tony Avano. 'And others. You will remain in sales, and will, for now, keep your title and privileges. But you will report to the chief operating officer, as will all department heads. From this time on, we have a business relationship only. Do not come to my house again uninvited.'

It was a downslide. His title was one matter. His salary, and long-term benefits, another. She had the power to strip him clean. He used the single shield he had.

'I'm Sophia's father.'

'I know what you are.' Tereza scanned the faces round the table. 'You'll excuse us. Helen, Eli and I must speak to Sophia and Tyler. Coffee will be served in the parlour. Please enjoy.'

'You say it,' Sophia began, trembling with anger as the rest filed out of the room, 'and it's done. Have you become so used to that, Nonna, that you believe you can change lives with a few words?'

'Everyone has a choice.'

'Where is the choice? Donato? He's never worked outside the company. Tyler? He's given all his time and energy to MacMillan since he was a boy.'

'I can speak for myself,' Tyler said.

'Oh, shut up.' Sophia rounded on him. 'Five words in succession tie your tongue in knots. And I'm supposed to teach you how to market wine.'

He got to his feet and, to her shock, grabbed her hands and turned them palms up. 'Like rose petals. Pampered and soft. And I'm supposed to teach you how to work?'

'I work as hard as you do. Just because I don't sweat and stomp around in muddy boots doesn't mean I don't give my best.'

'You're off to a hell of a start, both of you.' Eli sighed and poured more port. 'You want to fight, fight. It'll be good for you. The problem is that neither of you has ever had to do anything that didn't suit you. Maybe you'll fail trying to do something else. Something more.'

Sophia tossed up her chin. 'I don't fail.'

'You have a season to prove it. Would you care to know what you'll have at the end of it? Helen?'

Helen lifted her briefcase onto the table. She took out files, laid them down. 'I'll keep this simple and in layman's terms. Eli and Tereza are merging their respective companies, which will cut some costs and incur others. Each of you will carry the title of vice-president, operations. If at the end of one year your performances are unacceptable, you will be shifted back to a lesser position.' As she spoke, she slid two thick contracts from the files. 'Ty, you will remain in residence at MacMillan. Sophia, you will be required to move here. Your apartment in San Francisco will be maintained by Giambelli for your use when you're required to do business in the city. Ty, when you're required there, accommodations will be provided. The *castello* in Italy is available to either of you.'

She glanced up, smiled. 'So far, not so bad, right? Now the carrot. If at the end of this contract year, Sophia, your performance is acceptable, you will receive twenty per cent of the company, one-half interest in the *castello*, and the title of co-president. Reciprocally, Tyler, you will receive a like twenty per cent, full interest in the house where you now reside, and the title of co-president. You will both be offered ten acres of vineyards to develop your own label, or the market value thereof should you prefer.'

She paused and added the final weight. 'Pilar receives twenty per cent as well. In the event of Eli's or Tereza's death, their respective share passes spouse to spouse. On that unhappy day when neither of them is with us, their forty per cent share will be disbursed as follows: fifteen per cent to each of you and ten per cent to Pilar. This will give each of you, in time, thirty-five per cent of one of the biggest wine companies in the world.'

Sophia waited until she was certain she could speak. She was being offered more than she'd ever imagined and being slapped down like a child as well. 'Who decides on the acceptability of our performances?'

'In the interest of fairness,' Tereza said, 'Eli and I will give you evaluations, as will the COO.'

'Who the hell is COO?' Tyler demanded.

'His name is David Cutter. Recently of Le Coeur and based in New York. He'll be here tomorrow.' Tereza got to her feet. 'We'll leave you to read your contracts, to discuss, to consider.' She smiled warmly. 'Helen? Coffee?'

Tony Avano's smile was charming as always. 'Pilar, could I have a word with you? A private word.'

A dozen excuses ran through her head. She was, in her mother's absence, hostess. The room was full of guests. She should order more coffee.

But they were only that, excuses. 'Of course,' she murmured. 'Shall we use the library?' At least, Pilar thought, he wasn't bringing Rene with him. Even as they passed, Rene shot her one look, hard and bright as the stone on her finger.

A victor's look, Pilar thought. How ridiculous. There'd be no contest to win and nothing to lose.

Tony stepped into the room and sat in one of the deep leather chairs. Once he'd thought that he would live in this house, or at least maintain a base there.

'Well, Pilar.' His smile was easy. 'What do you intend to do about La Signora's suggestion you take a more active part in the company?'

'It wasn't a suggestion, and I don't know what I intend to do about it.' The idea of it was still buzzing through her head like a swarm of hornets. 'I haven't had time to think it through.'

'It'll be good for you to get out more, to be occupied. You may even find you have a talent for it. A career might be just what you need.'

She had wanted a family. Husband, children. Never a career. 'Are we here to talk about my needs, Tony, or yours?'

'They're not exclusive of each other. Not really, Pilar. I think we should look at this new direction Tereza has plotted out as an opportunity for both of us to start afresh.'

He took her hand, cupping it protectively and provocatively in his. 'Pilar, I realise that the idea of divorce has been difficult for you.'

'Do you?'

'Of course.' She was going to make it sticky, he thought. 'Pilar, our marriage failed, and by not ending things legally, I've been unfair to you. Clearly, you've been unable to start a new life.'

'Which hasn't been a problem for you, has it?' She pulled her hand from his and walked over to stare into the fire. Why was she fighting this? Why did it matter? 'Let's at least be honest here. You came here today to ask me for a divorce, and it had nothing to do with my mother's decisions. I won't stop you. I doubt I could in any case. Rene won't be as easily handled as I was,' she added, turning back. 'Maybe that's good for you. Maybe she's right for you. I certainly wasn't.'

All he heard was that he would get what he wanted without trouble. 'I'll handle the details. Quietly, of course, and—'

'You got what you came for, Tony. I'd suggest you take Rene and leave before Mama finishes her port. I think there's been enough unpleasantness in this house for one day.'

'Agreed.' He started for the door, hesitated. 'I do wish you the best, Pilar.'

'Yes, I believe you. I wish you the same. Goodbye, Tony.'

When he closed the doors behind him, she walked carefully to a chair, sat slowly as if her bones might shatter. She remembered what it was like to be eighteen and wildly in love, full of plans and dreams. She remembered what it was like to be twenty-three and sliced through the heart by betrayal. And thirty, fighting to raise a child and hold a husband too careless to pretend to love.

Now, she thought, she knew what it was to be forty-eight, alone, with no illusions left. She lifted her hand, slid her wedding ring up to the first knuckle. Tears burned at her eyes as she slipped it from her finger. What was it, after all, she thought, but an empty circle. The perfect symbol for her marriage.

She had never been loved. Pilar let her head fall back. How sad to sit here now and accept what she had refused to admit for so long. No man, not even her husband, had ever loved her.

When the doors opened, she closed her fingers around the ring.

'Pilar.' Helen's lips tightened. She crossed to a painted cabinet, opened it, and selected a decanter of brandy. She poured two snifters, then sat on the footstool in front of Pilar's chair. 'Drink up, honey. You look pale.'

Pilar opened her hand. The ring glinted in the firelight.

'Yeah, I figured that, when the rock of ages kept flashing. They deserve each other. He never deserved you.'

'Stupid, stupid to be shaken like this. But thirty years, Helen.' She held up the ring. 'Thirty damn years. She was in diapers when I met Tony.'

'That's the big ouch.' Helen shrugged. 'But think of this. By the time she's our age, she'll be feeding him baby food and changing *his* diapers.'

Pilar let out a moaning laugh. 'I hate where I am, and I don't know how to get someplace else. I didn't even fight back.'

'So you're not a warrior.' Helen rose to sit on the arm of the chair, wrapped an arm round Pilar's shoulder. 'You're a beautiful, intelligent, kind woman who got a raw deal.'

Pilar smiled a little. 'Helen, what the hell am I going to do with the new life that's been dumped in my lap?'

'We'll think of something.'

Sophia was doing a lot of thinking herself. She was already getting a headache from reading the pages of the contract. The gist of it was that La Signora maintained control as she always had. Over the next year Sophia would be expected to prove herself, which she'd thought she already had. If she did, to her grandmother's satisfaction, some of that much-desired control would be passed to her hands.

Well, she wanted it. But she didn't care much for the way she'd have to go about getting it.

She glanced over at Tyler, who was scowling at his own contract.

'You don't like it,' she said.

'What's there to like about it? It was a goddamn ambush.'

'Agreed. That's Nonna's style. But how do we get what we want out of it?' She pushed to her feet, paced. 'And who the hell is David Cutter?'

'A suit,' Ty said in disgust.

'More than that,' Sophia murmured. 'We'll just have to find out how much more.' That was something she could take care of very shortly, and very thoroughly. 'And we're going to have to find a way to work with him and each other. The last part shouldn't be that hard. We've known each other for years.'

She was moving fast where he preferred to pace himself. But he was damned if he wasn't going to keep up. 'No, we haven't. I don't know you, or what you do or why you do it.'

She put her palms on the table, leaned forward. Her magnificent face moved close to his. 'Sophia Tereza Maria Giambelli. I market wine. And I do it because I'm good at it. And in one year, I'm going to own twenty per cent of one of the biggest, most successful and important wine companies in the world.'

He rose slowly, mimicked her pose. 'You're going to have to be good at it, and a lot more for that. You're going to have to get your hands dirty, and get mud on your designer boots and ruin your pretty manicure.'

'Do you think I don't know how to work, MacMillan?'

'I think you do what you do because you're good at it. I do what I do because I love it. I've got nothing against you, Sophia, but if it looks like you're going to cost me my vines, I'll cut you out.'

Intrigued and challenged, Sophia studied him from a new angle. Who'd have thought the boy next door could be ruthless? 'All right, so warned. And same goes, Ty. Whatever I have to do, I protect what's mine.'

Blowing out a breath, she looked down at the contracts, then lifted her gaze back to his. 'I guess we can witness each other's.' She drew a deep breath, held it. 'On three?'

'One, two. Three.'

In silence, they signed, slid contracts across the table, witnessed.

Sophia topped up their glasses, waited for Tyler to lift his. 'To the new generation,' she said.

'To a good season.'

'We won't have one without the other.' With her eyes on his, she clinked glasses. '*Salute.*'

The rain was razor-thin and mean with cold, a miserable drizzle. It turned the light blanket of snow into a mire of mud and the dawn light into a gloomy smear on the sky.

It was the sort of morning when a reasonable person snuggled in bed. Or at the very least lingered over a second cup of coffee.

Tyler MacMillan, Sophia discovered, was not a reasonable person.

The phone woke her, had her sliding a hand reluctantly out of the covers, groping for the receiver. 'What?'

'You're late.'

'Huh? I am not. It's still dark.'

'It's not dark, it's raining. Get up, get dressed, get out and get over here. You're on my time now.'

'But . . .' The drone of the dial tone made her scowl. 'Bastard,' she muttered. Yawning, she tossed back the covers and got out of bed. She might have been on his time now, she thought, but before long he'd be on hers.

The rain dripped off Ty's cap and seeped under his collar. Still, it wasn't heavy enough to stop the work. And a rainy winter was a blessing. A cool, wet winter was the first crucial step towards a rare vintage.

He watched Sophia trudge through the mud in her $500 boots. 'I told you to wear rough clothes.'

She puffed out a breath, watched the rain dissolve it. 'These are my rough clothes.'

He studied her sleek leather jacket, the tailored trousers, the Italian boots. 'They will be before it's over.'

'I was under the impression rain delayed pruning.'

'It's not raining. It's drizzling. Where's your hat?' Annoyed, he pulled his own cap off, tugged it over her head. Even its wet, battered ugliness couldn't detract from her style.

'There are two primary reasons for pruning,' he began.

'Ty, I'm aware there are reasons for pruning.'

'Fine. Explain them to me.'

'To train the vine,' she said. 'And if we're going to have a lesson, why can't we do it inside, where it's warm and dry?'

'Because the vines are outside. We prune to train the vines for easier cultivation and harvesting, and to control disease.'

'Ty—'

'Quiet. A lot of vineyards use trellising techniques instead of hand pruning. Here we use both. Vertical trellising, the Geneva T-support and other types. But we still use the traditional hand-pruning method. The second purpose is to distribute the bearing wood over the vine to increase its production, while keeping its ability to produce top-quality fruit.'

He slapped the pruners in her hands and pushed a cane aside, exposing another. Then he guided her hands and made a cut with her. 'We want the centre—the top—left open. It needs room to get enough sun.'

'What about mechanical pruning?'

'We do that, too. You don't.' He shifted her to the next cane. 'You work by hand, plant by plant. Row by row.'

She scanned the endless stream of vines waiting to be tended. The pruning, she knew, would run into February. She imagined herself bored senseless with the process before Christmas.

'We break at noon,' she reminded him.

'One. You were late.'

'Not that late.' She turned her head, and her body angled into his. He was leaning over her, his arms round her so that his hands could cover hers on cane and tool. The slight shift was uncalculated. And potent.

Their eyes met, irritation in his, consideration in hers. She felt his body tense, and the tingle of response inside her own. A slightly quickened pulse, a kind of instinctive scenting of the air.

'Well, well.' She all but purred it. 'Who'd have thought it?'

'Cut it out.' He straightened up, took a step back as a man would on finding himself unexpectedly at the edge of a very long drop. But she simply continued her turn so that their bodies brushed again.

'Don't worry, MacMillan, you're not my type. Usually.'

'You're not mine. Ever.'

If he'd known her better, he'd have realised such a statement wasn't an insult, but a challenge. 'Really? What is?'

'I don't like cocky, aggressive women with fancy edges.'

She grinned. 'You will.' She turned back to the canes. 'We'll break at twelve thirty.' Once again she looked over her shoulder at him. 'Compromise. We're going to have to do a lot of it to get through the season.'

'Twelve thirty.' He pulled off his gloves, held them out. 'Wear these. You'll get blisters on those city-girl hands. Tomorrow bring your own, and wear a hat. No, not there,' he said as she started to clip another cane.

He moved in behind her again, put his hands over hers, and angled the tool correctly.

And didn't see her slow, satisfied smile.

It was a long way from coast to coast. It was, in some ways, another world, a world where everyone was a stranger. He'd ripped out the roots he'd managed to sink into New York concrete with the hope he could plant them here, in the northern California hills.

If it had been only that, David Cutter wouldn't have been worried. He'd have found it an adventure, the kind of freewheeling gamble he'd jumped at in his youth. But when a man was forty-three and had two teenagers depending on him, there was a great deal at stake.

If he'd been certain remaining with Le Coeur in New York was what was best for his kids, he'd have stayed there. He'd have stifled there, trapped in the glass and steel of his office. But he'd stopped being sure when his sixteen-year-old son had been picked up for shoplifting and his fourteen-year-old daughter had started painting her toenails black.

He'd been losing touch with his kids, and in losing touch, losing control. When the offer from Giambelli-MacMillan had fallen in his lap, it had seemed like a sign.

Take a chance. Start afresh.

'This place is in the middle of nowhere.'

David glanced in the rearview mirror at his son. Maddy had won the toss in San Francisco and sat, desperately trying to look bored, in the front seat. 'How,' David asked, 'can nowhere have a middle? I've always wondered that.' He had the pleasure of seeing Theo smirk, the closest his son came these days to a smile.

'Why does it have to be raining?' Maddy slumped in her seat and tried not to let her eyes gleam with excitement as she studied the huge stone mansion in front of the car.

'Well, it has something to do with moisture gathering in the atmosphere, then—'

'Dad.' She giggled, and to David it was music.

He was going to get his children back here, whatever it took. 'Let's go and meet La Signora.'

'Do we have to call her that?' Maddy rolled her eyes. 'It's so medieval.'

'Let's start out with Ms Giambelli and work from there. And let's try to look normal.'

'Mad can't. Geeks never look normal.'

'Neither do freaks.' Maddy clumped out of the car on her ugly black boots with their two-inch platforms. She stood in the rain, looking to her father like some sort of eccentric princess with her long pale hair and pouty lips. Her little body was swathed in layers of black. Three silver chains dangled from her right ear.

Theo was a dark contrast. Tall, gangly, with his deep brown hair a curling, unkempt mass straggling towards his bony shoulders. His eyes were a soft blue, and too often clouded and unhappy. He slouched now in jeans that were too baggy and a jacket that sagged past his hips.

Just clothes, David reminded himself. Clothes and hair, nothing permanent. But he wished they'd at least wear things that fitted.

He walked up the wide fan of steps, then stood in front of the deeply carved front door of the villa and dragged a hand through his own thick, dark blond hair.

'What's the matter, Dad? Nervous?'

There was a smirk in his son's voice, just enough of one to strain David's composure. 'Give me a break, OK?'

Theo opened his mouth, but he caught the warning look his sister gave him. 'Hey, you can handle her.'

'Sure.' Maddy shrugged. 'She's just an old woman, right?'

With a half-laugh David punched the buzzer. 'Right.'

'Wait, I gotta get my normal face on.' Theo put his hands on his face, shoving, pulling at the skin, drawing his eyes down, twisting his mouth. 'I can't find it.'

David hooked an arm round his neck and the other round Maddy's. They were going to be all right, he thought, and held on. They were going to be fine.

'I'll get it, Maria!' Pilar dashed down the hall, a spray of white roses in her arms. When she opened the door, she saw a tall man holding two children in headlocks, all three of them grinning. 'Can I help you?'

Not an old woman, David thought as he released his children. Just a beautiful woman, with surprise in her eyes and roses lying in the crook of her arm. 'I'm here to see Ms Giambelli.'

Pilar smiled. 'There are so many of us.'

'Tereza Giambelli. I'm David Cutter.'

'Oh. Mr Cutter, I'm sorry.' She held out a hand for his. 'I didn't realise you were expected today.' Or that you had a family, she thought. Her mother hadn't been forthcoming with details. 'Please come in. I'm Pilar. La Signora's daughter.'

'Do you call her that?' Maddy asked.

'Sometimes. When you meet her, you'll see why.'

'Madeline, my daughter. My son, Theodore.'

'Theo,' Theo mumbled.

'Maddy, OK?'

'I'm delighted to meet you. Come into the parlour. There's a nice fire. I hope it wasn't a terrible trip.'

'Not so bad.'

'Endless,' Maddy corrected. 'Awful.' But she stared at the room when they entered. It was like a palace, she thought. Everything was in rich colours and looked old and precious.

'I bet it was. Let me have your coats.'

'They're wet,' David began, but she simply plucked them out of his hand and draped them over her free arm.

'Please, sit down, make yourselves at home. I'll let my mother know you're here and see about something hot to drink. Would you like some coffee, Mr Cutter?'

'I absolutely would, Ms Giambelli.'

'So would I.'

'No, you wouldn't,' he said to Maddy, and had her sulking again.

'A latte, perhaps?'

'That's cool. I mean,' she corrected when her father's elbow reminded her of her manners, 'yes, thank you.'

'And Theo?'

'Yes, ma'am, thank you.'

'It'll just take a minute.'

'Man.' Theo waited until Pilar was safely out of the room, then plopped into a chair. 'They must be mega-rich. This place looks like a museum or something.'

THE VILLA

'Don't put your boots up on that,' David ordered.

'It's a footstool,' Theo pointed out.

'Once you put feet into those boots, they cease to be feet.'

'Chill, Dad.' Maddy gave him a distressingly adult pat on the back. 'You're like COO and everything.'

'Right.' From executive vice-president, operations, to chief operating officer in one 3,000-mile leap. 'Bullets bounce off me,' he murmured, then heard footsteps.

He started to tell his kids to stand up, but he didn't have to bother. When Tereza Giambelli walked into a room, people got to their feet.

He'd forgotten she was so petite. They'd had two meetings in New York face to face. And still he'd walked away from them with the image of a statuesque Amazon rather than the fine-boned, slim woman who walked towards him now. The hand she offered him was small and strong. 'Mr Cutter, welcome to Villa Giambelli.'

'Thank you, La Signora. You have a beautiful home in a magnificent setting. My family and I are grateful for your hospitality. I'd like to introduce my son, Theodore, and my daughter, Madeline.'

'Welcome to California.' She offered her hand with a hint of a smile. 'Please, sit. Be comfortable. Pilar, you'll join us.'

'Of course.' Pilar had stepped into the room.

'You must be proud of your father,' Tereza began as she took a seat, 'and all he's accomplished.'

'Ah . . . sure.' Theo didn't know much about his father's work. In his world his dad went to the office, then came home. He nagged about schoolwork, burned dinner, sent for takeout.

'Theo's more interested in music than wine,' David commented.

'Ah. And you play?'

'Guitar. And piano.'

'You must play for me some time. I enjoy music. What sort do you prefer?'

'There's just rock. I go for techno and alternative.'

'And you,' Tereza said to Maddy, 'do you play?'

'I had piano lessons.' She shrugged a shoulder. 'I'm not really into it. I want to be a scientist.'

'Arts and science.' Tereza leaned back. 'You take after your father, then, as wine is both. I assume you'll want a few days to settle in,' she continued as a trolley was wheeled in. 'A new location, a new school and routine for your family.'

'I'm at your disposal, La Signora,' David said, and watched Pilar as she rose to serve coffee and cakes. 'I appreciate, again, the use of your guest-house. I'm sure settling in will be a pleasure.'

When the coffee was served, they fell into light conversation. David followed Tereza's lead and left business out of it. Time enough, he concluded, to get to the meat.

In precisely twenty minutes, Tereza got to her feet. 'Pilar, will you show the Cutters the guesthouse and see they have all they need?'

'Certainly. I'll just get our coats.'

What was this? Pilar wondered as she retrieved jackets. Normally she had her finger on the pulse of the household, yet her mother had managed to slip an entire family in.

So many changes, and practically overnight. It was time she paid more attention, she decided.

Still, when she returned, she geared herself up to play hostess. 'It's a short drive. An easy walk, in good weather.'

'Winter rain's good for the grapes.' David helped her into her jacket.

'Yes. So I'm reminded whenever I complain about the wet.' She stepped outside. 'There's a direct line from house to house, so you've only to call if you need anything. Our housekeeper's Maria, and there's nothing she can't do. Thank you,' she added when David opened the door of the car for her.

'There's a pool,' she said, shifting round to speak to the children when they climbed in the back. 'Of course, you won't be able to enjoy that just now, but you're welcome to use the indoor pool here whenever you like.'

'An indoor pool?' Theo's mood brightened. 'Cool.'

'That doesn't mean you drop in wearing your bathing trunks whenever you feel like it,' his father warned. 'You don't want to give them the run of the house, Ms Giambelli. You'll be in therapy in a week.'

'We'll enjoy having young people around. And it's Pilar, please.'

'David.'

Behind their backs Maddy turned to her brother and fluttered her lashes wildly.

'David, just take the left fork. There, you can see the house.'

'Is that it?' Theo leaned up. 'It's pretty big.'

'Four bedrooms. Five bathrooms. A lovely living room, but the kitchen/dining room is friendlier, I think. Anybody cook?'

'Dad pretends to,' Maddy said. 'And we pretend to eat it.'

'Smart-ass. Do you?' David asked Pilar. 'Cook?'

'Yes, and very well, but rarely. Well, perhaps your wife will enjoy the kitchen when she joins you.'

The instant and absolute silence had Pilar cringing inside.

'I'm divorced.' David pulled up in front of the house. 'It's just the three of us. Let's check it out. We'll get the stuff later.'

'I'm very sorry,' Pilar murmured when the kids bolted from the car. 'I shouldn't have assumed—'

'Natural assumption. Don't worry about it.' He reached across to open her door. 'You know, they're going to fight over bedrooms. I hope you don't mind screaming scenes.'

'I'm Italian,' was all she said, and stepped out into the rain.

Italian, David thought later. And gorgeous. Aloof and gracious at the same time. Not an easy trick. In that area she was her mother's daughter.

He knew of Pilar Giambelli. He knew she was married, and to whom, but since she hadn't been wearing a ring, he assumed the marriage to the infamous Tony Avano was over or in serious trouble. He'd have to find out which.

There was a daughter. Anyone in the business had heard of Sophia Giambelli. A firecracker who had style and ambition in spades. Wondering how she'd taken to his induction as COO, he reached for the cigarettes in his pocket. Only to remember they weren't there because he'd quit three weeks and five days earlier.

And it was killing him.

Think about something else, he ordered himself, and tuned in to the music played at a brutal volume in his son's new room.

The expected combat over bedrooms had been without real heat, as every room in the house was appealing. Damn near perfect, he thought, with its gleaming wood and tiles, silky walls and lush furnishings. The absolute order gave him the willies, but he expected the kids would soon put that to rights.

Down the corridor, Maddy wandered out of her room. She'd tried to act casual about it. The fact was she was thrilled. For the first time in her life she didn't have to share a bathroom with her idiot brother. And hers was done in blues and deep reds. Big splashy flowers, so she imagined taking a bath there would be like swimming in some weird garden. Plus she had a huge four-poster bed.

Then she'd remembered that she wouldn't be able to call her friends or walk to the movies. She wouldn't be able to do anything she was used to doing in New York. Homesickness settled so hot and heavy it ached. The only person she could talk to was Theo. It was the poorest of choices, but the only one left.

She pushed open his door to a blast of the Chemical Brothers. He was lying on his bed, his guitar across his chest as he tried to match the riff. The room was in chaos, as she imagined it would stay until he moved out to go to college.

He was such a pig.

She flopped down on his bed. 'There's nothing to do here.'

'You just figuring that out?'

'Maybe Dad'll hate it, and we'll go home.'

'No chance. Did you see how he slicked up for the old lady?'

'He sounded like something out of a movie.' She rolled over on her back. 'He was looking at that woman.'

'Huh?'

'The Pilar woman.'

'Get out.'

'Guys don't notice anything. He was checking her out.'

'So what?' Theo gave a little jerk of the body, a horizontal shrug. 'He's checked out women before.'

'Gee, you think?' While the sarcasm dripped, she pushed off the bed to pace to the window. Rain and vines, vines and rain. 'Maybe if he has sex with his boss's daughter, he'll get caught, he'll get fired, and we'll go back home.'

'Home where? He loses his job, we've got no place to go. Grow up, Maddy.'

She hunched her shoulders. 'This sucks.'

'Tell me about it.'

Down in San Francisco, Ty MacMillan was thinking the same thing about life in general. Sophia had whipped him into a meeting—a brainstorming session, she called it. She'd rattled off names at him as she'd zipped through the advertising section, gesturing, calling out orders and snatching up messages as she went.

There were three other people in the room now, all with trendy clothes and trendy hair and little wire-rimmed glasses and electronic organisers. Two female, one male—all young and handsome. He couldn't for the life of him remember who was who.

He had some kind of fancy coffee he hadn't wanted in his hand, and everyone was talking at once and munching on *biscotti*.

'No, Kris. What I'm looking for is a strong image with an emotional message. Trace, quick sketch: couple—young, late twenties. Relaxing on a porch. Sexual, but keep it casual.'

Since the man with the blond, choppy hair picked up the pencil and sketch pad, Ty assumed he was Trace.

'It's sunset,' Sophia continued. 'End of day. This is a working couple, no kids, upwardly mobile but settled.'

'Porch swing,' the perky black woman in a red T-shirt suggested.

'Too settled, P.J. Too country. Wicker love seat, maybe,' Sophia said. 'Strong colour in the cushions. Candles on the table. Fat ones, not tapers.' She leaned over Trace's shoulder, made humming noises. 'Good, good, but have them looking at each other, maybe have her leg swung over his knees. Friendly intimacy. Roll up his sleeves, put her in khakis.'

'You should have water.' The second woman, a redhead who looked annoyed, stifled a yawn. 'Suburban scenes bore me. At least water adds a subliminal sexuality.'

'Kris wants water.' Sophia nodded. 'Water's good. A pond, a lake. Reflections. Take a look, Ty. What do you think?'

'I don't know. It's a nice sketch.'

'You look at ads,' Sophia reminded him, 'whether you consciously take in the message or not. What does this say?'

'It says they're sitting on the porch drinking wine. Porch usually means house. So how about some kids?'

'We don't want kids in an ad for an alcoholic beverage,' Kris Drake said quickly.

'Evidence of kids, then. You know, some toys on the porch. Then it says these people have a family, have been together for a while, and are still happy to sit on the porch together and have a glass of wine at the end of the day. That's sexy.'

Kris started to open her mouth, then closed it again.

'That's good,' Sophia said. 'Toss toys on the porch, Trace. Here's our cosy yet hip suburban couple. Celebrate the sunset,' she murmured. 'It's your moment. Relax with Giambelli. It's your wine.'

'More cosy than hip,' Kris muttered.

'We use an urban setting for hip. Friends getting together for an evening. Apartment scene, city lights out of the window.'

'Coffee table,' P.J. put in, already sketching. 'A couple sitting on the floor, others lounging on the couch.'

'Good, perfect. Celebrate Tuesday. Same tags.'

'Why Tuesday?' Ty wanted to know in spite of himself.

'Because you never make big plans for Tuesday.' Sophia crossed her legs. 'You make plans for the weekend. Tuesday night with friends is spontaneous. We want people to pick up a bottle of our wine on the spur.'

'The wine's Giambelli-MacMillan.'

She nodded. 'Correct. We need to identify that as well within the campaign. A wedding. Celebrate our marriage. Champagne, flowers, a gorgeous couple.'

'Honeymoon's sexier.' Trace refined his other sketch. 'Same elements but in a snazzy hotel room. Wedding dress hanging on the door and our couple in a lip lock with champagne on ice.'

'If they're in a lip lock, they're not going to be thinking about drinking,' Ty said.

'Good point. Hold the kiss, but the rest is great. Show me . . .' Her hands began to move. 'Anticipation. Eye lock instead of lip lock. Go, see what you can get me in the next couple of hours.'

Her team headed out. 'Not bad, MacMillan. Not bad at all.'

'Good. Can we go home?'

'No. I've got stuff to deal with.' She frowned into space. 'I need a half-hour. Why don't you head over to Armani, and I'll meet you there.'

'Armani?'

'You need clothes.'

He wanted to argue, but didn't want to waste time. The sooner they were driving north, the happier he'd be. 'Where's Armani?'

She stared at him. The man had lived an hour out of San Francisco for years. How could he not know? 'See my assistant. She'll point you in the right direction.'

'One suit,' Ty warned as he walked to the door. 'That's it.'

'Mmm.' They would see about that, she thought. But before the fun started, she had work. She picked up the phone. 'Kris, can I see you a minute? Yeah, now. My time's pretty tight.'

She'd worked with Kris for over four years, and was very aware there had been considerable resentment when the fresh-out-of-college Sophia had taken over as head of promotion. They'd come to terms, delicately, but she had no doubt that Kris's nose was now seriously out of joint.

Couldn't be helped, Sophia thought. Had to be dealt with.

There was a brisk knock, and Kris stepped in. 'Sophia, I've got a pile of work.'

'I know. Five minutes. It's going to be rough shuffling things around between here and Napa for the next few months. I'm in a pinch, Kris.'

'Really? You don't look pinched.'

'You didn't see me pruning vines at dawn.' Sophia met Kris's eyes dead on. 'Look, if you think I'm going to enjoy juggling my time between the work I love and mucking around the vineyards, you're crazy. And if you think Tyler is gunning for a position here in these offices, think again.'

'Excuse me, but he now *has* a position in these offices.'

'And one you believe should be yours. I'm not going to disagree, but I'm telling you it's temporary. Ty's position here is titular. He doesn't know anything about promotion and isn't particularly interested in it either.'

'Interested enough to make comments this morning.'

'Just a minute.' She could be patient, Sophia thought, but she would not be pushed. 'Do you expect him to sit here like a moron? He's been tossed off the cliff without a parachute and he's coping. Take a lesson.'

Kris set her teeth. She'd been with Giambelli nearly ten years and was sick to death of being passed over for their precious bloodline. 'He has a parachute and so do you. You were born with it. Either one of you screws up, you bounce. That doesn't go for the rest of us. But I'll do my job.' Kris turned to the door, yanked it open. 'And yours.'

'Well,' Sophia murmured as the door slammed, 'that was fun.'

'**N**o, we want classic. This very subtle chalk stripe to start.'

'Fine, great. I'll take it. Let's go.'

'Tyler.' Sophia pursed her lips and patted his cheek. 'Go and try it on, like a good boy.'

He snagged her wrist. 'Mom?'

'Yes, dear?'

'Cut it out.'

'If you'd done more than brood for the last thirty minutes on your own, we'd be practically out of the door. This one,' she said, handing him the rich brown with narrow stripes, 'and this.' She selected a classic black three-piece.

She moved from suits to shirts and ties and had a small mountain of choices when Ty came out of the changing room.

He looked annoyed, faintly mortified and absolutely gorgeous. Take the farmer away from the land, she mused, and just look what you got. Big, broad shoulders, narrow hips and long legs in a classic Italian suit.

'My, my.' She angled her head, approving. 'You do clean up well, MacMillan. All sturdy and sexy.'

'They're just clothes.'

She pressed a hand to her heart, staggered back a step. 'MacMillan, if you can think that, we have a long way to go with you.' She plucked up a tie, draped it over a shirt. 'Yes, definitely. How do the trousers fit?' she began, and reached down to check the waistband.

'Do you mind?' Flustered, he batted her hand away.

'If I was going to grope, I'd start lower. Why don't you put on the black suit? Then the tailor can fuss with you.'

Tyler was relieved to escape to the privacy of the changing room, and stripped off the chalk-striped and put on the black.

He glanced at himself in the mirror, shook his head. Who the hell were either of them going to fool by dressing him up in some snappy three-piece suit? He was a damn farmer, and happy to be one.

Then he made the mistake of looking at the price tag. He'd never realised a series of numbers could actually stop the heart.

He was still in shock when the tailor came into the changing room.

Pilar was nearly asleep, finally, when the phone rang at 2.00am. She shot up in bed, snatching at the phone as her heart slammed into her throat. An accident? Death? Tragedy?

'Hello. Yes?'

'You ignorant bitch. Do you think you can scare me off?'

'What? Who is this?' She groped for the light, then blinked in the sudden flash.

'You know damn well who it is. You got a nerve calling me, spouting off. Shut up, Tony. I'll say what I have to say.'

'Rene?' Recognising her husband's placating voice in the background, Pilar struggled to clear her head. 'What is this? What's the matter?'

'Just cut the innocent act. It might work with Tony, but it doesn't with me. I know what you are. You're the whore, sweetheart, not me. You're the liar. If you ever call here again—'

'I didn't call. I don't know what you're talking about.'

'Either you or your bitch of a daughter, and it's all the same to me. Get this straight. You're out of the picture. You're a frigid, dried-up excuse for a woman. Fifty-year-old virgin. There isn't a man out there who wants you.'

'Rene, Rene. Stop. Stop now.' Pilar heard Tony's voice through the rush of blood in her head. 'Pilar, I'm sorry. Someone called here, said perfectly vile things to Rene. She's upset.' He had to shout over the shrieks. 'Of course, I told her you'd never do such a thing, but she . . . she's upset,' he repeated. 'I have to go.'

The dial tone buzzed in Pilar's ear.

She tossed back the covers. She was trembling as she yanked on a robe, as she dug deep into a drawer for her secret emergency pack of cigarettes. Stuffing them into a pocket, she pushed through the French doors out into the night.

She needed air. She needed a cigarette. She needed peace.

She strode away through the gardens, keeping to the shadows so that if anyone in the house was awake, they wouldn't see her through the windows. Pretences, she thought, furious to find her cheeks were wet. We must maintain pretences at all costs. Wouldn't do to have one of the servants see Ms Giambelli smoking in the shrubbery in the middle of the night. Wouldn't do for anyone to see Ms Giambelli doing her best to stave off a nervous breakdown with tobacco.

A dozen people might have called Rene, she thought bitterly. From the tone of Tony's voice, Pilar knew he had a pretty good idea who'd made the call. Easier, she supposed, to let Rene believe it was the discarded wife than a current lover.

Easier to let Pilar take the slaps and the insults.

'I'm not fifty,' she muttered, fighting with her lighter. 'Or a virgin.'

'Me, neither.'

She whirled, dropping the lighter with a little crash of metal on stone. Temper warred with humiliation as David Cutter stepped from shadow to moonlight.

'I'm sorry I startled you.' He bent down for her lighter. 'But I thought I should let you know I was here.'

He flicked the lighter on, studying her tearstained cheeks. 'I couldn't sleep,' he continued. 'New place, new bed. Took a little walk. Want me to keep on walking?'

It was breeding, she supposed, that prevented her from making a fast, undignified retreat. 'I don't smoke. Officially.'

'Neither do I.' Still he took a deep, appreciative sniff of the smoke-stung air. 'Quit. It's killing me. Want to walk?'

She wanted to run back inside, bury herself under the covers, but she walked with him.

'Are you and your family settling in?' she asked as they fell into step together.

'We're fine. Period of adjustment. My son got into some trouble in New York. Kid stuff, but there was a pattern to it.' He dug a handkerchief out of his jeans, silently passed it to her. 'I'm looking forward to getting a good look at the vineyards tomorrow. They're spectacular now, with a bit of moon and a hint of frost.'

'You're good at this,' she murmured. 'At pretending you didn't come across a hysterical woman in the middle of the night.'

'You didn't look hysterical. You looked sad and angry.' And beautiful, he thought. White robe, black night.

'I had an upsetting phone call.'

'Is someone hurt?'

'No one but me, and that's my own fault.' She stopped, stooped to crush the cigarette and bury it under the mulch on the side of the path. Then she turned, took a long look at him.

It was a good face, she decided. A strong chin, clear eyes. Blue eyes, she remembered. And she remembered the way he'd been grinning when he'd had his arms round his children. A man who loved his children inspired Pilar's trust.

In any case, it was difficult to maintain pretences when you were standing in your robe in the middle of the night.

'You're all but living with the family,' she told him, 'so you'll hear things. My husband and I have been separated for years. He informed me very recently that we are getting divorced. His bride-to-be is very young. Beautiful, sharp-edged. And . . . very young,' she said again with a half-laugh. 'It's an awkward and difficult situation.'

'It'll be more awkward and difficult for him if he ever takes a good look at what he let go.'

It took her a moment to adjust to the compliment. 'That's very kind of you.'

'No, it's not. You're beautiful, elegant, and interesting.'

And not used to hearing it, he realised as she simply stared at him. That, too, was interesting. 'That's a lot for a man to let go. Divorce is tough,' he added. 'Especially if you took your marriage seriously.'

'Yes.' She felt comforted. 'Yes, it is.'

He touched her shoulder, leaving his fingers there, lightly, when he felt her tense and shift slightly away. 'Some of the daylight rules don't apply at three in the morning, so I'm going to tell you straight out. I'm very attracted to you.'

She felt a little clutch in her belly. 'That's flattering.'

'It's not flattery.' His eyes, dark in the shadows, were quiet, serious. 'The minute you opened the door today, it was like I was hit by a thunderbolt. I haven't felt that in a long time.'

'David'—she took a step back—'we barely know each other. And I'm . . .' *A fifty-year-old virgin.* No, she thought, she damn well wasn't. But close. Close enough.

'True enough. I didn't intend to bring this up quite so soon. But a beautiful woman, moonlight in a garden. You can't ask a man to resist everything. Besides, it gives you something to think about.'

'Yes, it certainly does. I should go.'

'Will you have dinner with me?' He reached for her hand and brought it to his lips—it seemed like the moment for that, too. 'Soon?'

'I don't know.' She tugged her hand from his and felt like a foolish and fumbling young girl. 'I . . . Good night.'

She rushed back down the path and was breathless by the time she reached the steps. Her stomach was fluttering, her heart skipping in her chest. They were sensations she hadn't experienced in so long, it was almost embarrassing.

But she no longer felt angry. And no longer felt sad.

It was just midnight in New York when he took the call. He considered the person on the other end of the phone no more than a tool, one to be wielded as necessary.

'I'm ready. Ready to move to the next stage.'

'Well.' Smiling, he poured himself a snifter of brandy. 'It's taken you a considerable amount of time to make up your mind.'

'I have a lot to lose. The reorganisation hasn't changed that.'

'For the moment. But now there's David Cutter. He'll be taking a serious look at all areas of Giambelli. A serious look that could very well turn up certain . . . discrepancies.'

'I've been careful.'

'Poisoning an old man, for instance?'

'That was an accident. You said it would only make him ill. How was I to know he had a weak heart?'

The panic, the hint of whine in the tone made him smile. It was all so perfect. 'Is that what you call it, an accident?'

'I'm not a murderer.'

'I beg to differ. You've killed. If you want my help, and my financial backing to continue, you'll start by getting me copies of everything. The legal papers, the contracts, the plans for the centennial ad campaign. Every step of it. The vintner's logs, Venice and Napa.'

'I need money. I can't get what you ask without—'

'Give me something I can use. Then I'll give you payment.'

'They're grapevines. Big deal.'

'Grapevines,' David informed his sulking son, 'are what's going to buy your burgers and fries for the foreseeable future.'

'Are they going to buy my car?'

David glanced in the rearview mirror. 'Don't push your luck, pal.'

'Dad, you can't live out in Nowheresville without wheels.'

David turned into MacMillan Vineyards. 'The minute you stop breathing, I'll check out the nearest used-car lot.'

Three months before—hell, David thought—three weeks before, that comment would have resulted in his son's frozen silence or a snide remark. The fact that Theo's response was to clutch his throat, bug out his eyes, and collapse gasping on the back seat warmed his father's heart.

'I knew we should've taken those CPR classes,' David said absently.

'It's OK. He goes, it's more fries for us,' Maddy said.

'Pretty place.' David stopped the car, got out to look over the fields and the workers steadily pruning vines in the frosty morning. 'And this, all this, my children,' he continued, sliding an arm round each of them when they joined him, 'will never be yours.'

'Maybe one of them has a babe for a daughter. We'll get married; then you'll work for me.'

David shuddered. 'You're scaring me, Theo.'

Ty spotted the trio heading down through the rows and swore under his breath. Tourists, he thought. He didn't have time to be friendly.

He crossed to Sophia, noted grudgingly she was doing the job, and doing it well. 'We got some tourists,' he told her. 'Why don't you take a break here and steer them to the winery?'

Sophia straightened, turned to scope out the newcomers. The father and son were pretty much out of L.L. Bean, she concluded, while the daughter had taken a left turn into Goth land.

'Sure, I'll take them. But a quick look at the fields and an explanation of pruning would lead nicely into the winery and make Dad more inclined to pop for a couple of bottles.'

'I don't want civilians tromping through my fields.'

'Don't be so cranky.' She put on a bright smile and deliberately grabbed Ty's hand and dragged him towards the family.

'Good morning! Welcome to MacMillan Vineyards. I'm Sophia, and Tyler and I would be happy to answer any questions you might have. Are you touring the valley?'

'In a manner of speaking.' She had La Signora's eyes, David thought. The shape and the depth of them. Pilar's were softer, lighter, hinted of gold. 'Actually, I was hoping to meet both of you. I'm David Cutter. These are my children, Theo and Maddy.'

'Oh.' Sophia recovered quickly, taking David's offered hand.

'Well, welcome again. All of you. Would you like to come into the winery—or the house?'

'I'd like to take a look at the fields. Been a while since I've seen a pruning in process.' David turned to Tyler. 'You've got a beautiful vineyard, Mr MacMillan. And a superior product from them.'

'You got that right. And I've got work to do.'

'You'll have to excuse Tyler.' Setting her teeth, Sophia wrapped her arm through his like a rope to hold him in place. 'He has no discernible social skills. Do you, MacMillan?'

'Vines don't need chitchat.'

'All growing things do better with audio stimulation.' Maddy didn't flinch at Ty's annoyed expression. 'Why do you prune in winter,' she demanded, 'instead of early spring?'

'Maddy,' David began.

'It's OK.' Ty took a closer look at her. She might dress like an apprentice vampire, but she had an intelligent face. 'Pruning over the winter decreases the yield. Overbearing vines produce too many inferior grapes, and what we're after is quality, not quantity.'

'Can you show me how to do it?' Maddy asked Tyler.

'Well, I . . .'

'I'll start you off.' Taking pity on Tyler, Sophia radiated cheer. 'Why don't you and Theo come with me?' She herded the kids out of earshot.

Ty let out a sigh. 'OK, Cutter, let's clear the air. I don't like someone looking over my shoulder, giving me grades like I was in high school, and I don't care how they did things at Le Coeur. I run this vineyard.'

'MacMillan, I'm not here to get in your way. You're the vintner. But I do intend to keep abreast of every phase of the vineyards.'

'You've got the offices. I've got the fields.'

'Not entirely. I was hired because I know the vines. I'm not just a suit, and frankly, I was tired of trying to be one. Mind?' He plucked the pruners out of Tyler's belt sheath. Gloveless, he lifted canes, studied, and made his cut.

It was quick, efficient and correct.

'I know the vines,' David repeated, holding the tool out to Tyler, 'but that doesn't make them mine.'

Irritated, Tyler took back the tool, shoved it into its sheath like a sword into a scabbard, and strode away.

Hardheaded, inflexible, territorial, David mused. It was going to be an interesting little battle. He strolled over to where Sophia entertained his children. Theo's throbbing hormones were all but sending out bolts of sex-crazed red light. And that, David thought wearily, was going to be complicated.

Judge Helen Moore rushed into her chambers.

'Sorry, dear, we ran a little over.'

'It's all right,' Pilar told her. 'I really appreciate your making time for me today. I know how busy you are.'

Helen stripped off her robe and hung it up. 'If I ever lose this extra fifteen pounds, I'm going to start wearing a bikini under that.' Instead she wore a quiet brown suit.

Too matronly, Pilar thought. Too boxy. And very Helen.

'We've got two hours.' Helen flopped into the chair behind her desk and pulled off her shoes. 'Want to go out for lunch?'

'Not really. Helen . . . I know you're not a divorce lawyer, but—Tony's moving to finalise things. I don't know what to do.'

'I can handle it for you, Pilar. Or I can recommend someone.'

'I'd feel a lot more comfortable if you handled it, and if it was kept as simple as possible. And as clean.'

'Well, that's disappointing.' Helen frowned. 'I'd love to leave that man bleeding from the ears. I'll need your financial papers,' she began, pulling over a yellow legal pad for notes. 'Fortunately, I browbeat you into separating your finances years ago, but he may make demands. You are *not* going to agree to anything.'

'It's not a matter of money.'

'Not for you. But he's going to want to continue living high. How much have you funnelled to him over the last decade?'

Pilar shifted uncomfortably. 'Helen . . .'

'Exactly. Loans that are never repaid. The house in San Francisco, the house in Italy. The furnishings in both. And I know damn well he slid plenty of your jewellery into his pocket.'

'I loved him, and part of me thought that if he needed me enough, he'd love me back. Something happened last night, and it's changed things. Changed me, I suppose.'

'Tell me.'

Rising from her chair, Pilar told Helen of the phone call. 'When I listened to him making those careless apologies, cutting me off to placate Rene after she'd attacked me, I was disgusted. And later, after I'd calmed down, I realised something. I don't love him any more, Helen. Maybe I haven't for years. That makes me pitiful.'

'Not any more, it doesn't.' Helen picked up the phone. 'Carl? Order me two chicken clubs, with side salads, two cappuccinos and a big bottle of fizzy water. Thanks.' She hung up. 'Now, sweetie, I'll explain what needs to be done.'

Sunday slid into the week like a balm on a mild, nagging itch. Sophia wouldn't be spending her morning hours covered in wool and flannel and pruning vines. She could drive into the city, do some power shopping, see people. But first she was going to nag her mother into taking that girls' day.

Sophia knocked briskly on her mother's bedroom door, then pushed it open. The bed was already made, the curtains open to the wavering sunlight. Maria walked in from the adjoining bathroom.

'Mama?'

'Oh, long up and about. I think she's in the greenhouse.'

'Maria, I've barely seen her all week. Is she all right?'

Maria's lips tightened. 'She doesn't sleep well. Eats like a bird, and then only if you insist. She says it's holiday stress. What stress?' Maria threw up her hands. 'Your mama, she loves Christmas.'

'Maria, I'll hunt her down now.'

Christmas, Sophia thought as she jogged downstairs. The perfect excuse. She'd ask her mother to give her a hand with some last-minute Christmas shopping. She scanned the house as she hurried through. Her mother's poinsettias, red and white stars in dozens of silver pots, were mixed with miniature hollies throughout the hall. Fresh greenery twined with tiny white lights swagged doorways.

The three Giambelli angels were displayed on the long refectory table in the parlour. Tereza, Pilar and Sophia—their carved faces reflecting each of them at the age of twelve. It was always a little jolt, a little tug of amused pleasure to see them. Sophia had been thrilled when she was given her angel all those years ago. And she still was.

She turned to study the room. Candles in spears of silver and gold, more greenery artfully arranged. The grand tree, laden with precious ornaments from Italy, stood regally by the windows, presents already tucked under it.

The annual Christmas party was nearly on them, she thought guiltily. And she'd done nothing to help.

She went out of the side door, ran down the winding stone path, cut left, and sprinted to the greenhouse.

The warm, moist heat felt so inviting. 'Mama?'

'Down here. Sophie, wait until you see my paper-whites. They're spectacular. Very festive.' Pilar stopped, looked up.

Sophia leaned over and kissed her mother's cheek. 'Mama, I'm so behind on my shopping. Come to the city with me. I'll buy lunch.'

'Sophia'—with a shake of her head, Pilar shifted her long trough of narcissi—'you finished your holiday shopping in October. Just as you always do to make the rest of us hate you.'

'OK, caught me.' Sophia boosted herself up on the work counter. 'Still, I'm dying to go into the city and play. It's been a brutal week. Let's run away for the day.'

Pilar frowned. 'Sophie, is this new order of things your grandmother's set up too much for you? You're up at dawn every day, and then you spend hours in your office here.'

'I thrive on pressure. Still, I could use an assistant, and since I'm not about to admit to Nonna, or to MacMillan, that I'm feeling the least bit squeezed, you could help me out. With filing and typing.'

Pilar blew out a breath, tugged off her gloves. 'You're doing this to keep me busy, just as Maria hounds me to eat.'

'Partially,' Sophia admitted. 'But if I could pass work over, I might actually begin to date again in this decade.'

'All right, but don't blame me if you can't find anything.' Pilar laughed. 'I haven't done basic office work since I was sixteen, and then Mama fired me.'

'Fine. But for now, let's escape to the city.'

For over fifty years Giambelli California had held lavish Christmas parties on the Saturday before Christmas. The house was open to family and friends, and the vineyard winery to employees. Associates, depending on their position, were placed in the proper location.

Invitations to the main house were prized like gold and often used as a symbol of status or success. Still, the Giambellis didn't stint on the festivities in the winery. Food was elegant, wine flowed freely, the decorations and the entertainment were topnotch. And there were fewer irritating relations.

Sophia could hear her cousin Gina's progeny shrieking at the other end of the hall. Her hopes that Don and his herd would remain in Italy had been dashed when they'd arrived the evening before.

Still, even their presence wouldn't be as annoying as that of her father and Rene. Her mother had stuck firm on their being invited. The consolation was their invitation had been to the winery.

That, she thought as she fastened on her diamond teardrop earrings, would stick sharply in Rene's craw.

She stepped back, studied the results in her cheval glass. The shimmering silver gown with its short, fitted jacket worked well. The scooped neck was a nice frame for the diamond necklace. Both it and the earrings had belonged to her great-great-grandmother.

She turned, checked the line of her skirt, then called out an invitation at the knock on her door.

'Look at you!' Helen came in, pretty and plump in frosty pink. 'You sparkle all over.'

'Not too much with the diamonds?'

'Diamonds are never too much. Honey, I only wish Linc were here to see you. He takes the bar next month, you know.'

'He'll pass, of course. He's your son, so he can't help being brilliant.' Sophia winked.

Lincoln Moore was the closest thing Sophia had to a brother. Their mothers' friendship had ensured that neither of them had ever felt like an only child.

'Of course,' Helen said, 'but now I want a minute with you.' She shut the door. 'I hate to bring this up, but Pilar told me Tony and Rene will be here.'

'What is it?'

'The divorce is final. Yesterday.'

'I see.' Sophia picked up her evening bag, opened and closed the catch. 'Have you told Mama?'

'Yes. Just now. She's fine. Or she's holding up. I know it's important to her you do the same.' She squeezed Sophia's hand. 'Don't let Rene have the satisfaction of seeing this hurts you, on any level.'

'I won't.'

'Good. Now I've got to go down and run herd on my husband.'

Alone, Sophia let out a long breath. Then she marched back to her mirror. Opening her bag she took out her lipstick and painted her lips bloody-murder red.

David sipped a full-bodied merlot, mingled with the crowd packed into the towering stone walls of the winery, tried to tune out the hot licks from the band that was currently thrilling his son, and scanned the area for Pilar.

He knew the Giambellis would put in an appearance. He'd been well schooled on the holiday protocol. He'd be expected to split his time between the winery party and the party in the house, which—though it hadn't been put precisely that way—was both a privilege and a duty.

He was learning fast that nearly every assignment in this organisation came under the heading of both.

He could not complain. Everything he'd seen in the past weeks had confirmed that Giambelli-MacMillan was a tight, family-orientated ship. Money was respected, but it was not the goal. Wine was.

'David, good to see you.'

He turned, surprise registering briefly as he looked into Jeremy DeMorney's smiling face.

'Jerry, I didn't know anyone from Le Coeur would be here.'

'I try never to miss an annual Giambelli bash. Very democratic of La Signora to invite reps from the competition.'

'She's quite a lady.'

'One of a kind. How are you taking to working for her?'

'It's early days yet, but the move's gone well. I'm glad to get the kids out of the city. How are things back at Le Coeur?'

'We're managing to grope along. Hated losing you, David.'

'Nothing lasts for ever. Anyone else here?'

'Duberry flew in from France. He's known the old lady for a hundred years. Pearson's representing the local group. A few top levels from other labels. Gives us all a chance to drink her wine and spy on each other. Got any gossip for me?'

'Like I said, it's early days yet. Great party, though. Excuse me, there's somebody I've been waiting for.'

Maybe all my life, David thought as he left Jerry without a backward glance and worked through the crowd to Pilar.

She wore blue. Deep blue velvet with a long rope of pearls. She looked warm and regal, and he would have said utterly confident if he hadn't noticed the quick flicker of panic in her eyes.

Then she shifted her head a little and focused on him. And God help him, she blushed. Or at least more colour came into her face. The idea that he'd put it there drove him crazy.

'I've been watching for you.' He took her hand before she could do anything about it. 'Like a kid at a school dance. I know that you have to mingle, but I want a minute first.'

It was like being swept away by a warm wave. 'David—'

'We'll talk about business, about the weather. I'll only tell you you look beautiful five or six dozen times. Here.' He plucked a flute of champagne from a tray.

'I can't keep up with you.'

'I can't keep up with myself. I'm making you nervous. I'd say I was sorry for that, but I'd be lying. It's best to start out a relationship with honesty, don't you think?'

'No. Yes. Stop.' She tried to laugh. He looked like some sort of sophisticated knight in his formal black with his rich blond hair glinting in the light. 'Are your children here?'

'Yeah. They whined about being dragged here, and now they're having the time of their lives. You're beautiful. I did mention I was going to tell you that, didn't I?'

'Yes, I believe you did.'

'I don't suppose we could find a dark corner and neck.'

'No. That's a definite.'

'Then you'll just have to dance with me, and give me a chance to change your mind.'

It staggered her that she thought he could change it. That she wanted him to. Inappropriate, she told herself firmly. Ridiculous. She was years older than he.

God, what was she supposed to do? Say? Feel?

She drew in a breath. 'David, you're very attractive—'

'You think so?' He touched her hair, couldn't help it. He loved the way it curved against her cheek. 'Could you be more specific?'

'And charming,' she added, struggling to keep her voice firm. 'But I don't know you. And besides . . .' She trailed off. 'Hello, Tony. Rene.'

'Pilar, you look lovely.' Tony leaned over to kiss her cheek.

'Thank you. David Cutter, Tony Avano and Rene Foxx.'

'Rene Foxx Avano,' Rene corrected. She lifted her hand to send the diamond circlet wedding ring flashing. 'As of today.'

It wasn't a stab in the heart, Pilar realised. More of a burn, a quick shock. 'Congratulations. I'm sure you'll be very happy together.'

'Oh, we already are.' Rene slid her arm through Tony's. 'We're flying out to Bimini right after Christmas. You really should take time for a little vacation yourself, Pilar. You're looking pale.'

'Strange. I was thinking how vital she looks tonight.' Gauging the ground, David lifted Pilar's hand, kissed her fingers. 'Delicious, in fact. I'm glad I had a chance to meet you, Tony, before you left the country.'

Smoothly, David slid an arm round Pilar's waist. 'I've had trouble reaching you the last few days.' He gave Rene a glance, just a few degrees short of polite. 'Now I see why. Let my office know your travel plans. We've business to discuss.'

'My people know my plans.'

'Apparently mine don't. You'll excuse us, won't you? We need to make the rounds before heading up to the villa.'

'That was unkind,' Pilar whispered, as they moved away.

'So what?' Gone was the flirtatious charm. In its place was power of the cold and ruthless sort. It wasn't, she thought, any the less appealing on him.

'Over and above the fact that I didn't like him on principle, I'm COO and he's been avoiding my calls.'

'He's just not used to having to report to anyone.'

'He'll have to adjust.' Over her head, David spotted Tyler. 'So will others. Why don't you help clear the way a little and introduce me to some of the people who are wondering what the hell I'm doing here?'

Ty was trying to be invisible. As far as he was concerned, the music was too loud, the winery too crowded, and the food too rich. He'd already calculated his plan. One hour here, one hour in the main house. Then he could slide away, go home, and go to bed.

'Why are you standing over here all by yourself?'

Tyler looked down, frowned at Maddy. 'Because I don't want to be here.'

'Why are you? You're an adult. You can do what you want.'

'You keep thinking that, you're doomed to disappointment.'

'You just like being irritable.'

'No. I just *am* irritable.'

She pursed her lips. 'OK. Can I have a sip of your wine?'

'No.'

'In Europe, children are taught to appreciate wine.'

She said it so grandly, standing there in her layers of black and dead-ugly shoes, Ty wanted to laugh. 'So go to Europe. Around here it's called contributing to delinquency.'

'I've been to Europe, but I don't remember it very well. I'm going to go back. Maybe I'll live in Paris for a while. I was talking to Mr Delvecchio, the wine-maker. He said wine was a miracle, but it's really just a chemical reaction, isn't it?'

'It's both. It's neither.'

'It has to be. I was going to do an experiment and I thought you could help me.'

Tyler blinked at her, a pretty, badly dressed girl with an enquiring mind. 'What? Why don't you talk to your father?'

'Because you're the vintner. I thought I would get some grapes, put them in two bowls, and see what happens. One bowl would be left alone—Mr Delvecchio's miracle. The other I'd process, using additives and techniques. Pushing the chemical reaction. Then I could see which worked best.'

'Even if you use the same type of grapes, you'll have variations between your tests.'

'Why?'

'You're talking store-bought this time of year. They may not have come from the same vineyard. Even if they do, you get variations. Soil type, fertility, water penetration. When they were picked. How they were picked. You can't test the grapes on the vine, because they're already off the vine. The must in each bowl could be considerably different even if you left them both alone.'

'What's must?'

'Juice.' Bowl wine, he thought. Interesting. 'But if you wanted to try it, you should use wooden bowls. The wood'll give the must some character. Not much, but some.'

'A chemical reaction,' Maddy said with a grin. 'See? It's science, not religion.'

'Baby. Wine's that and a whole lot more.' Without thinking, he offered her his glass.

She sipped, delicately, her gaze shifting just in case her father was nearby. Experimentally she let the wine roll around on her tongue before she swallowed. 'It's pretty good.'

'Pretty good?' He took the glass back. 'That's vintage pinot noir. Only a barbarian would call it "pretty good".'

She smiled, charmingly now because she knew she had him. 'Will you show me the barrels and the machines some time?'

'Yeah. Sure.'

'Sophia. Stunning as always.'

'Jerry. Happy holidays.' She leaned in, kissed both of his cheeks. 'How's business?'

'Le Coeur's had a banner year. And we expect another. A little bird tells me you're planning a brilliant promotion campaign.'

'Those little birds chatter entirely too much, don't they? Another from the flock was singing about you launching a new label. Mid-market, with an American target.'

'Someone's going to have to shoot those birds. I saw the write-up in *Vino* on your cabernet '84. And the auction went well. Shame on you, Sophia, for standing me up in New York. I'd looked forward to seeing you.'

'Couldn't be helped. Next trip.'

'I'm counting on it.'

He was an attractive man, smooth, almost silkily attractive. The faintest sprinkling of silver at the temples to add distinction, the slight dip in the chin to add charm.

Neither of them would mention her father or the poorly kept secret of Jerry's wife's infidelity. Instead, they would keep it light, flirtatious, friendly.

They understood each other, Sophia thought, very well. The competition between Giambelli and Le Coeur was high, and often exhilarating. And Jeremy DeMorney was not above using whatever means came to hand to push his edge. She admired that.

'I'll even spring for dinner,' she told him. 'And the wine. Giambelli-MacMillan. We'd want the best, after all.'

'You're a cruel woman, Sophia.'

'You're a dangerous man, Jerry. How're your kids?'

'The children are fine. Their mother has them in St Moritz for the holidays.'

'You must miss them.'

'Of course.'

She caught a movement out of the corner of her eye, watched her mother slip off towards the ladies' room. With Rene a few feet behind.

'Jerry,' she said, 'lovely to see you. I have something I have to deal with right now.'

Rene pushed through the door of the ladies' lounge one step behind Pilar. 'Managed to land on your feet, didn't you?'

'You got what you wanted, Rene.' Though her hands wanted to tremble, Pilar opened her evening bag and pulled out her lipstick. 'I shouldn't be an issue for you any more.'

'Ex-wives are always an issue. I tell you, I won't tolerate you calling and spewing out your neurotic abuse.'

'I didn't call.'

'You're a liar. And a coward. I go after what I want in the open. If you think I'm going to let Tony slink away because you've gone whining to your family, you're wrong. You're not going to shove him out, and if you try . . . just think of all the interesting information he could pass along to your competitors.'

'Threatening the family or the business isn't going to help secure Tony's position. Or yours.'

'We'll see about that. I'm Mrs Avano now. And Mr and Mrs Avano will be joining the family at the villa tonight.'

'You'll only embarrass yourself.'

'I don't embarrass easily.'

Deliberately, Pilar turned to the mirror and slowly, carefully painted her lips. 'How long do you think it will take for Tony to cheat on you?'

'He wouldn't dare.' Secure in her own power, Rene smiled. 'He knows if he does, I'll kill him. I'm not the passive, patient wife. Tony told me what a lousy lay you were. We laugh about it. My advice? If you want to keep Cutter on the string, pass him down to your daughter. She strikes me as someone who knows how to entertain a man in bed.'

Even as Pilar whirled, Sophia opened the door. 'Oh, what fun. Girl talk? Rene, how brave of you to wear that shade of green with your colouring.'

'Fuck you, Sophia.'

'Erudite as always. Mama, you're needed at the villa. I'm sure Rene will excuse us.'

'On the contrary, I'll leave the two of you alone so you can hold your mother's hand while she dissolves into helpless tears. I'm not finished, Pilar,' Rene added as she opened the door. 'But you are.'

'That was entertaining.' Sophia studied her mother's face. 'You don't look like you're about to dissolve into tears, helpless or otherwise.'

'No. I'm done with them.' Pilar dropped her lipstick back into her bag. 'Sophie, your father married her today.'

'Well, hell.' On a long sigh, Sophia stepped over, put her arms round her mother, laid her head on Pilar's shoulder. 'Merry Christmas.'

Sophia bided her time. She needed to catch her father alone, not when Rene was draped all over him like poison ivy on a tree trunk. She worked the crowd, danced once with Theo. When she spotted Rene on the dance floor with Jerry, she made her move.

It didn't surprise her to see her father tucked into a corner table, flirting with Kris Drake. It revolted her slightly, but didn't surprise her that he'd turn on the charm for another woman on his wedding day. But as she approached, she caught the subtle signals—a light touch, a promising glance—that told her it was more than flirtation.

'Kris, I'm sorry to break up this tender moment, but I need to speak with my father.'

'Nice to see you, too. It's been so long since you've bothered to come by the office, I nearly forgot what you look like.'

'I don't believe I report to you, but I'll send in a photo.'

'Now, princess,' Tony began.

'Don't push it.' Sophia kept her tone level. 'We'll have a meeting, Kris, when my schedule permits. For tonight you can consider yourself lucky I saw you before Rene did. Now I need to speak to my father on family business.'

'With you at the wheel, your family's not going to have much of a business.' Kris got to her feet, skimmed a fingertip over the back of Tony's hand, and strolled away.

'Sophie, you have the entirely wrong impression. Kris and I were just having a sociable drink.'

Her gaze cut like a blade. 'Save it for Rene. I've known you longer. Please don't interrupt,' she said before he could protest. 'This won't take long. I hear congratulations are in order.'

'Now, Sophie.' He stood, reached for her hand, but she snatched it out of reach. 'I know you're not fond of Rene—'

'I don't give a damn about Rene, and at the moment I don't give much of one about you.'

He looked sincerely surprised, sincerely hurt. She wondered if he practised the expression in his shaving mirror. 'You don't mean that. I'm sorry you're upset.'

'No, you're not. You're sorry I cornered you.'

'Princess—'

'Quiet. You came to a family function, and under the business cloak this is a family function, flaunting a new wife and a side piece for good measure. That's insensitive enough, but you didn't have the decency to tell Mama about the marriage first.'

Her voice had risen, just enough to turn some heads. Uneasy, Tony took her arm. 'Why don't we go outside and I'll explain. There's no need to cause a scene in here.'

'Oh, there is. Every need. Because here's the kicker. You pushed that woman in my mother's face.' Sophia jabbed a finger into his chest. 'You let Rene corner her, let her spew all over her, while you sit and slobber over yet another woman. You stay away from her and see that your *wife* does the same. Or I promise you, I'll make you bleed.'

She stepped away before he recovered. Then her arm was gripped and she was being swept away into the crowd.

'Bad idea,' Ty said quietly. 'Really bad idea to murder staff members at the Christmas bash. Let's go outside.'

'I don't want to go outside.'

'You need to. It's cold. You need to cool off. So far you only entertained a handful of people who were near enough to hear you rip into Avano. Nicely done, by the way. But with the steam puffing out of your ears, you're going to end up putting on a show for the whole party.'

He all but pushed her out of the door.

'Stop shoving. I don't like being manhandled.' She jerked free, rounded and nearly, very nearly struck him.

'Go ahead. First shot's free. After that, I hit back.'

She sucked in a breath, blew it out, sucked in another while she continued to glare at him. With every breath her glittery gown threw out sparks in the moonlight.

She was, Ty thought, outrageous and magnificent. And dangerous as a handful of dynamite with the fuse already hissing.

'There you go,' he said with a nod. 'A few more and you might be able to see past the blood in your eyes.'

'The bastard.'

'Let's walk up to the villa. Give you time to calm down.'

The gardens of the Villa Giambelli sparkled with thousands of fairy lights. Table groupings invited guests to spill out onto the heated terraces to enjoy the starlight and the music that slipped through the doors and windows of the ballroom.

Sophia drew Ty up the steps to a terrace decked with flowers and ornamental trees. 'Smile, MacMillan,' she told him.

'Why?'

'Because you're going to dance with me.'

'Why?' He bit back a sigh as she took his hand. 'Sorry. Been hanging around with Maddy Cutter too long. The kid just never stops asking questions.'

'The two of you seem to be hitting it off. We'd dance better if you actually touched me.'

'Right.' He laid a hand at her waist. 'She's an interesting kid and bright. Have you seen my grandfather?'

'Not for a bit. Why?'

'I want to see him and La Signora. Then I figure I'm done with this and can go home.'

'You're such a party animal.' She slid her hand over his shoulder and tugged playfully at his hair. There was so much of it, she thought. All thick and unruly. 'Live a little, Ty. It's Christmas.'

'Not yet. There's still a lot of work to be done before Christmas.'

'Hey.' She tugged his hair again so that he stopped scanning the crowd for his grandfather and looked at her. 'There's no work to be done tonight, and I still owe you for coming to my rescue.'

'You weren't in trouble. Everyone else was.' It wasn't gratitude he was looking for, but distance. A safe distance. She was always dangerous, but pressed up against a man, she was lethal. 'And I have some charts and some graphs I want to go over. Why is that funny?' he demanded when she chuckled.

'I was just wondering what you'd be like if you ever loosened up. I bet you're a wild man, MacMillan.'

'I get loose,' he muttered.

'Tell me something.' She skimmed her fingers down his neck. 'Something that has nothing to do with wine or work.'

'What else is there?'

'Art, literature, an amusing experience, a fantasy.'

'My current fantasy is to get out of here.'

'Do better. Come on. The first thing that pops into your head.'

'Peeling that dress off you, and seeing if you taste like you smell.' He waited a beat. 'Good, that shut you up.'

'Only momentarily, and only because I'm assessing my reaction. I find myself a great deal more intrigued by the image than expected.' She tipped her head back to study his face. Oh yes, she liked his eyes when there were sparks of heat in them. 'Why don't we go to your place?'

'Is it that easy for you?'

'It can be.'

'Not for me, but thanks.' His tone turned careless and cold as he looked away from her and around the room. 'But I'd say you've got plenty of alternatives here if you're up for a quick one-night stand. I'm going home.'

He stepped back, walked away.

It took her nearly ten seconds before she had her wind back, and another three before the fury spurted up and scored her throat. The delay allowed him to get out of the room and down the stairs before she came after him. 'No, you don't.' She hissed it under her breath, then stalked past him. 'In here.' She strode into the family parlour, banged the sliding doors closed.

'*Cazzo! Culo!*' Even now her voice was quiet, controlled. He couldn't know how much that cost her.

'You're right.' He cut her off before she could spew all the venom. 'That was out of line and I'm sorry.'

The apology, quietly given, turned temper to tears, but she held them back by sheer raw will. 'I'm a slut, in your opinion, because I think of sex the way a man does. Because I'm honest, I'm cheap.'

'No. You got me worked up. You always have. I shouldn't have said what I did. Look, you're beautiful, outrageous, and over my head. I've managed to keep my hands off you and I'm going to keep them off.'

'I get you worked up, do I? And your answer to that is to take a slap at me.'

'I said I was sorry.'

'Not good enough. Try this.'

She was on him before he could act. All that was left was reaction.

Her mouth was hot and soft and very skilled, her body lush and smooth and very female. It pressed intimately against his.

His mind blanked. He pressed her close before he could stop himself. She tasted like she smelt; he learned that much.

One minute she was wrapped round him, and the next he was cut loose. 'Deal with it,' she said, then turned to shove the doors open again.

'Just a damn minute.' He had her arm, spun her round. Then he saw the utter shock on her face. Before he could react, she was racing across to the refectory table.

'*Dio! Madonna,* who would do such a thing?'

He saw it then, the three Giambelli angels. Red ran down the carved faces like blood from slash wounds. Written across the chest of each were vicious messages:

BITCH #1

BITCH #2

BITCH #3

It was very late when Tony let himself into the apartment. He wondered if anyone knew he had the key after all this time.

He'd brought his own bottle of wine from his personal cellar. The Barolo would keep things civilised. Business discussions—and the word 'blackmail' never entered his mind—should always be conducted in a civilised manner.

He uncorked the bottle in the kitchen, left the wine on the counter to breathe, and selected two glasses. Though he was disappointed not to find fresh fruit in the refrigerator, he made do with the wheel of Brie.

Even at three in the morning, presentation mattered.

Money was the main matter, of course. The Giambellis intended to cut him loose. He was certain of that now. But he had other options. Any number of options. The first of which should be coming along any minute.

The knock on the door made him smile.

PART TWO
THE GROWING

'I DON'T KNOW why we had to come back here.'

'Because I needed a few more things.' She could have put it off, Sophia admitted, but no reason to waste a trip into San Francisco without stopping by her apartment.

'Look, Ty,' she continued. 'I explained that at the beginning I'm going to have to spot-check the offices. Kris is going to continue to resist the new feeding chain. She needs to see you and me together, a team.'

'Some team.'

'I'm managing.' She pulled into her parking slot, set the brake. 'I think we should call a holiday truce. At the moment, Ty, I just don't have the time to fight with you.'

She climbed out of the car, slammed her door, jammed her keys in her briefcase.

'What's the problem? Are you still upset about the angels?'

'No. I cleaned them, didn't I? Red nail polish. Good as new. You want to know the problem? I hate getting up at the crack of dawn every day, tromping around the fields in the cold, then going back to do the work I'm trained to do. And I have a second-in-command who's not only slept with my father but is ready to mutiny.'

'Fire her.'

'Oh, that's an idea.' Her voice dripped disdain. 'Why hasn't that occurred to me? Could it be because we're in the middle of a huge promotion and I have no one qualified to take over her work? Yes, you know, I think that might be the reason. And now I can't get through to my father, who hasn't been to *his* office for two days. It's imperative I speak with him about one of our top accounts.'

They stepped onto the escalator. 'Work round him.'

'If I work round him, it makes him look like a . . . Damn it. He *is* a fool. I'm so angry with him for putting me into this spot.' She let out a breath, stepped off the escalator and put her key in the lock.

She pushed open the door, took one step inside, froze.

'Dad?'

She had a brief impression, no more than a blur, before Ty was shoving her out of the door again. But that blurred image stayed in her mind, was all she could see.

Her father, slumped in her chair, the side of his face, the glinting silver at his temples, the front of his shirt all crusted and dark. And his eyes—his handsome, clever eyes—filmed over and staring.

'Dad. He's . . . I have to . . . My father—' She was pale as a sheet and beginning to shudder.

'Listen to me, Sophia. Use your cellphone. Call nine-one-one. Do it now.'

'I have to go to him.'

'No. You can't help him.' He pulled Sophia to the floor, opened her briefcase and dug out her cellphone.

Sophia lowered her head to her knees as Tyler gave the police the necessary information. 'I'm all right.' Her voice was quiet. 'I know he's dead. I have to go to him.'

'No.' He settled beside her and draped an arm over her shoulders. 'I'm sorry, Sophia. There's nothing you can do.' He tightened his grip until she laid her head on his shoulder.

'Someone killed my father.' Her voice broke, and the tears that were scalding her throat poured up and out.

'I don't know what he was doing in my apartment,' Sophia said again. She tried to study the face of the man who questioned her. Like his name—Detective Lamont? Claremont?—his features kept slipping out of focus.

'Did your father often use your place?' The name was Claremont. Alexander Claremont.

'No, I . . . I gave him a key not long after I moved in. He was having some decorating work done on his place, and I was going to be out of the country. I offered him my place. I don't think I ever got the key back. I never thought of it again.'

Hadn't there been times she'd come back from a trip and felt someone had been there? Little things out of place.

'Ms Giambelli?'

'I'm sorry. What did you say?'

'When was the last time you had contact with your father?'

'Two days ago. Saturday night. There was a party at our vineyard. It's an annual event.'

'What time did he leave?'

'I couldn't say. He didn't say goodbye to me.'

'Did your father have any enemies that were known to you?'

'No. I don't know of anyone who would have killed him.'

'When were your parents divorced, Ms Giambelli?'

'I believe the decree was final the day before my father married Rene.' Though her knees shook, she got to her feet. 'I'm sorry, I have to go to my family. I don't want them to hear about this on the news. Can you tell me what arrangements need to be made?'

'My partner is working with the crime-scene unit. We'll discuss arrangements with next of kin.'

'I'm my father's only child.'

'His wife is his legal next of kin, Ms Giambelli.'

Her mouth opened, closed. 'I see. Of course. I have to go home.'

Alexander Claremont liked French wine, Italian shoes and American blues. The middle son of solidly middle-class parents, he had planned to be a lawyer, but he'd been born to be a cop.

For a lawyer the law was there to be manipulated. To a cop it was the line. Claremont worshipped the line.

Now, barely two hours after walking onto the crime scene, he was thinking about the line.

His partner drove. 'What do you think of the daughter?'

'Rich,' he said at length. 'Classy. Tough shell.'

'Big, important family. Big, juicy scandal.' Maureen Maguire braked at a light. Tapped her fingers on the wheel.

At thirty-six, she was four years Claremont's senior, comfortably married where he was radically single, cosily suburban where he was uptown urban.

'From the looks of the body, he'd been dead at least thirty-six hours. Three hundred in his pocket. A gold Rolex, gold cuff links. The apartment had plenty of easily transported items. Two glasses of wine, only one with prints—his prints. No signs of struggle. From the angle of the shots, the killer was sitting on the sofa. Nice little wine-and-cheese party and *bam, bam, bam.* You're dead.'

'Guy was divorced and remarried within a day. Romantic interlude gone bad?'

'Maybe.' Maguire parked, glanced up at the snazzy building. 'Funny, huh, how a new husband doesn't come home and the new bride doesn't report him missing.'

'Let's find out why.'

Sophia looked round the grand entrance hall like a stranger. Nothing had changed. How could it be that nothing had changed?

She watched Maria come down the hall. 'Maria, where is my mother?'

'Upstairs. She's working in your office, Miss Sophia.'

'And La Signora?'

'She is in the fields, with Mr Mac.'

'Would you send someone for them, please?'

Maria went quickly while Sophia turned towards the stairs. She could hear music coming from her office. When she stepped into the doorway, she saw her mother, bent over the keyboard of the computer.

'Mama?'

'Oh, thank goodness! Sophia, I've done something. I don't know what. An illegal function! I've been practising for an hour and still I'm useless on this thing.'

Pilar pushed back from the desk, glanced up—and froze.

'What is it? What's wrong? What's happened?'

Everything changes now, Sophia thought. Once it was said, nothing was ever going to be the same again. 'Mama, it's Dad.'

Word spread. In whispers over cocktails, in gleeful articles in the press. Across the country and across the Atlantic. Tony Avano was dead.

The current Mrs Anthony Avano lost some of the colour in her face when Detective Maguire informed her of her husband's death. 'Was there an accident?'

'No, ma'am. Could you tell us when you last saw your husband?'

Rene stared hard at the detective. 'Saturday night, early Sunday.'

'You weren't concerned when you didn't hear from him?'

'We'd had an argument. Tony often goes on little sulks afterwards. What happened to him? I have a right to know what happened.'

'Anthony Avano was shot and killed.'

Her head jerked back, but almost immediately the colour rushed back into her face. 'I warned him she'd do something crazy.'

'Who is that, Mrs Avano?'

'His wife.' She sucked in a breath, turned and stalked over to pick up her drink. 'His *ex*-wife, Pilar Giambelli. The bitch killed him. Or her little tramp of a daughter did.'

Donato Giambelli sat in the office on the ground floor of his home, drank brandy, and considered the new circumstances.

The meeting scheduled with Margaret Bowers, head of sales, the next morning would be postponed. That would buy him time. He'd preferred business dealings with Tony. He'd known just where he stood.

Now Tony was dead, and there would be talk, gossip, delays. He could use that to his advantage.

He must go back to California, of course. To offer his support and assure La Signora that he would do whatever she required him to do in order to maintain Giambelli's production.

Yes, this would give him time to figure out what had to be done and how to do it.

Poor Tony, he thought, and lifted his brandy. Rest in peace.

Over the long winter, the vines slept. The fields stretched, acre upon acre, drinking the rains, hardening under frosts, softening again with the quick and teasing warm snaps.

Sophia spent the month of January handling her father's murder like a business assignment. She made calls, made arrangements, asked questions, answered them, and watched her mother like a hawk.

The police gave her nothing but the same repetitive line: the investigation was ongoing. All leads were being actively pursued.

They treated her, she thought, no differently than they would a suspect.

On the second floor of Villa Giambelli, Tereza kept her office. The desk had been her father's. It was old, the oak dark and the drawers deep. That was tradition. On it sat a two-line phone and a high-powered computer. That was progress. Beneath it, old Sally snored quietly. That was home.

She believed, absolutely, in all three.

Because she did, her office was now occupied by her husband and his grandson, her daughter and granddaughter, and David Cutter and Paulo Borelli. Rain beat like soft fists on the roof.

Tereza folded her hands. 'I'm sorry,' she began, 'we've been unable to meet before this. The loss of Sophia's father postponed certain areas of business. And Eli has been ill.'

She glanced towards him now. He still looked a bit frail to her. The cold had turned so quickly into fever and chills.

'I'm fine,' Eli said, more to reassure her than the rest. 'A little shaky on my pins yet, but coming round.'

She smiled, because he wanted her to, but she heard the faint wheeze in his chest. 'Sophia, I have your projections regarding the centennial campaign. I'd like you to bring everyone up to date.'

'Of course.' Sophia got to her feet, opened a portfolio that contained mock-ups, along with full target reports on message, consumer statistics, and venues.

'Phase one will begin in June,' she began as she passed advertising packets around. 'We've created a three-pronged campaign.'

While she spoke, Tyler tuned her out. He'd heard the pitch before. Had been in on the various stages of its development. The exposure had taught him the value of what she did, but he couldn't drum up real interest in it.

In February heavy rains had delayed the pruning cycle. Long-range weather reports forecasted a warming trend, but too much too soon would tease some varieties out of dormancy. He needed to keep a keen eye out for signs of slight movement in the buds, for the soft bleeding at the pruning cuts.

'I see we're keeping Tyler awake,' Sophia said sweetly.

'No, you're not. But since you interrupted my nap, the second phase deals with public participation. Wine-tastings, vineyard tours, auctions, galas—both here and in Italy—which generate publicity. Sophia knows what she's doing.'

'And in the fields?' Tereza asked. 'Does Sophia know what she's doing?'

'She's all right, for an apprentice field hand.'

'Please, Ty, you'll embarrass me with compliments.'

'Very well,' Tereza said. 'David? Comments on the campaign?'

'Clever, classy, thorough. My only concern, as a father of teenagers, is that the ads targeting the twenty-one-to-thirty market make wine look like a hell of a good time. If we could do some sort of disclaimer . . .'

'Disclaimers are boring and dilute the message,' Sophia began, but she pursed her lips and sat again. 'Unless we make it fun, witty, responsible, and something that blends with the message. Let me think about it.'

'Good. Now, Paulie.'

Now it was Sophia who tuned out while the foreman spoke of the vines, of vintages being tested in the casks and tanks.

Paulie was excused and David called up. Instead of the marketing projections, the cost analyses, the forecasts Sophia had expected, her grandmother set his written report aside.

'At the moment I'd like your evaluation of our key people.'

'You have my reports on that, La Signora.'

'I do,' she agreed, and simply lifted her eyebrows.

'All right. Tyler. He doesn't need me in the vineyards, and he knows it. The fact that it's my job to oversee them hasn't taken the edge off his resistance and that does get in the way of efficiency. Other than that, the MacMillan vineyards are as well run as any I've ever been associated with. As are Giambelli's. Tyler's work on merging the operations, coordinating crews is excellent.

'Sophia does well enough in the vineyard, though it's not her strength. However, there are some difficulties in the offices in San Francisco.'

'I'm aware of the difficulties,' Sophia said.

'Sophia, you have an angry, uncooperative employee who's been trying for weeks to undermine your authority. Are you interested in how I know just how angry and uncooperative Kristin Drake's been? Her résumé's landed on half a dozen desks in the last two weeks. One of my sources at Le Coeur tells me she's making claims and accusations, with you her favourite target.'

Sophia absorbed the betrayal, nodded. 'I'll deal with her.'

'See that you do,' Tereza advised. 'And Pilar?'

'I think you misuse her, Signora.'

'I beg your pardon?'

'In my opinion, your daughter would be more useful as a spokesperson for the company, where her charm and elegance wouldn't be wasted. I wonder you don't ask Pilar to help with the tours and the tastings. She's an excellent hostess, La Signora. She is not an excellent clerk.'

'You're saying I've made a mistake expecting my daughter to learn the business of the company?'

'Yes,' David said easily, making Eli fall into a fit of coughing.

'Sorry, sorry.' Eli waved a hand as Sophia leapt up to pour him a glass of water. 'Tried to suck down that laugh. Shouldn't. Tereza, he's right and you know it.' He took the glass, sipped carefully. 'Hates to be wrong and hardly ever is. Sophia, how's your mama working out as your assistant?'

'She's hardly had time to . . . She's terrible,' Sophia admitted, and burst out laughing. 'Oh, Mama, I'm so sorry, but you know you hate every minute you're stuck in my office.'

'I'm trying. And obviously failing,' Pilar said as she got to her feet.

'Mama—'

'No, that's all right. I'd rather you be honest. Let me make this easier on everyone involved. I quit. Now, if you'll excuse me, I'll go and sit somewhere looking elegant and charming.'

'I'll go and talk to her,' Sophia began.

'You won't.' Tereza lifted a hand. 'We finish the meeting.'

It was, she thought, encouraging to see her daughter show a snap of temper and a hint of spine. Finally.

With Maria's help, David tracked Pilar down in the greenhouse. He found her there wearing gardening gloves and an apron, repotting seedlings.

'Got a minute?'

'I have all the time in the world,' she said without sparing him an ounce of warmth. 'I don't do anything.'

'You don't do anything in an office that satisfies you or accomplishes a goal. I'm sorry my evaluation hurt your feelings, but—'

'But it's business.' She looked him in the eye.

'Yeah, it's business. Do you really want to type and file, Pilar?'

'I want to feel useful.' She yanked off her gloves, then tossed them down. 'I'm tired of being made to feel as if I have nothing to offer. No skills, no talents, no brains.'

'Then you weren't listening.'

'Oh, I heard you. I'm to be charming and elegant.'

She started to push by him, yanked her arm when he closed his hand over it, then stared in shock as he simply took her other arm and held her in place.

'Take your hands off me.'

'In a minute. First, listen. Charm is a talent. Elegance is a skill. If you think handling tourists and accounts at tastings is fluff work, you'll find out different. If you work up the guts to try it.'

'I don't need you to tell me—'

'Apparently you do.'

She remembered how he'd dealt with Tony the night of the party. He was using that same cold, clean slice with her now.

'I'll remind you, I don't work for you.'

'I'll remind you,' he countered, 'essentially you do. Unless you're going to stalk off like a spoilt child, you'll continue to work for me.'

'Va' al diavolo.'

'I don't have time for a trip to hell,' he said equably. 'I'm suggesting you put your talents in the proper arena. You've let yourself be wasted, and it's starting to piss me off.'

'You have no right to say these things. Your position with Giambelli doesn't give you a licence to be cruel.'

'My position with the company doesn't give me the right for this, either,' he said, and jerked her against him. 'But this time it's personal.'

She was too shocked to stop him, to manage even the slightest protest. When his mouth was on hers, she could do nothing but feel.

The blood rushed into her head, one long tidal wave of power. And her body, her heart, starved, leapt into the flood of pleasure. Everything seemed to waken at once as her knees went weak.

'What?' She was breathless. 'What are we doing?'

'We'll think about it later.'

He had to touch her. Already he was tugging at her sweater. Rain slapped against the glass walls, and the air was warm and moist, fragrant with flowers. She was quaking against him—quick, hard trembles. Delicious little sounds were humming in her throat. He couldn't remember when he'd last felt this ferocious rush.

'Pilar, let me . . .' He fought with the button of her slacks. 'Pilar, I want you.'

She pushed against him. 'David, I'm not ready for this.' Pleasure sprinted into her, chased by panic. 'I'm—'

'Don't.' He spoke curtly. 'Don't say you're flattered.'

'Of course I am, and—' And she couldn't *think* straight when he was touching her. 'Please. Would you step back? I think we took each other by surprise,' she began.

'Pilar, we're not children.'

'No, we're not. I'm forty-eight years old, David, and you're . . . Well, you're not.'

He hadn't thought anything in the situation would make him laugh, but that did. 'You're not going to use a handful of years as an excuse?'

'It's not an excuse. It's a fact. Another is that we've only known each other for a short time.'

'Eight weeks.' He trailed his fingers over her hair while she stared at him. 'I didn't plan on tearing off your clothes in the middle of your peat pots. You want something more conventional? I'll pick you up at seven for dinner.'

'David, my husband's been dead only a few weeks.'

He took her by the shoulders. 'Tony Avano has stopped being your safety zone, Pilar. Deal with it.' He kissed her again, hard and long. 'Seven o'clock,' he said.

Maddy eyed her father shrewdly as he knotted his tie. It was his first-date tie, the grey with the navy-blue stripes. He'd said he and Ms Giambelli were just going out to dinner, that it was a business kind of thing, but the tie was a dead giveaway.

She had to think about how she felt about it.

But at the moment she was pushing his parent buttons.

'It's a symbol of self-expression.'

'It's unsanitary.'

'It's an ancient tradition.'

'It's not a Cutter family ancient tradition. You're not getting your nose pierced, Madeline. That's it.'

She sighed and put on a good sulk. Actually, she had no desire to get her nose pierced, but she did want another third piercing in her left ear lobe. Working down to it was good strategy. 'It's my body.'

'Not until you're eighteen, it's not.'

She rolled onto her back on her father's bed, lifted her legs to the ceiling. They were clad in her usual black, but she was starting to get sort of tired of it. 'Can I get a tattoo instead?'

'Oh, sure. We'll all go and get one this weekend.' He turned and scooped her up, carting her from the room with her feet dangling off the floor.

The habit, as old as she could remember, never failed to bring a bubble of happiness to her chest. 'If I can't do the nose, could I just do another in my left ear? For a little stud?'

'If you're bound and determined to put more holes in yourself, I'll think about it.' He paused by Theo's door, knocked.

'Get lost, creep.'

David looked at Maddy. 'I assume he means you.' He pushed open the door to see his son stretched out on the bed, the phone at his ear. David felt twin pulls. Annoyance that homework was certainly not done and pleased relief that Theo had already made new friends at school.

'Call you back,' Theo muttered, and hung up. 'I was just taking a break.'

'There's plenty of stuff you can nuke for dinner. No fighting, no naked strangers in the house, no touching the alcoholic beverages. Finish your homework, no phone or TV until it's done. Did I leave anything out?' He kissed the top of Maddy's head, then dropped her to her feet. 'I should be home by midnight.'

'Dad, I need a car.'

'Uh-huh. And I need a villa in the South of France. Go figure. Lights out at eleven,' he added as he turned away.

'I've *got* to have wheels,' Theo called after him, and swore under his breath as he heard his father walk down the stairs. He flopped back on the bed to brood up at the ceiling.

Maddy just shook her head. 'You're such a moron, Theo.'

'You're so ugly, Maddy.'

'You're never going to get a car if you nag him. If I help you get a car, you have to drive me to the mall twelve times without being mean about it.'

'How are you going to help me get a car, you little geek?'

She sauntered into the room. 'First the deal. Then we discuss.'

The caves always made Sophia think of a smuggler's paradise. All those big, echoing spaces filled with huge casks of ageing wine. Even as a child, one of the wine-makers would let her sit at a little table and sample a small glass from one of the casks.

She'd learned, very young, to tell the difference between a premium vintage and an ordinary one. To understand the subtleties that lifted one wine over another. But it wasn't wine she was thinking of now, though wine had been drawn and glasses set out for sampling. It was men.

'It's their third date in two weeks.'

'Mmm.' Ty held a glass of claret to the open fire. He rated it a two for both colour and clarity, noted the marks on his chart.

'My mother and David.' Sophia punched him lightly on the arm.

'What about them?'

'They're going out again tonight. Third time in two weeks.'

'And that's my business because?'

She heaved out a breath. 'She's vulnerable. I can't say I don't like him, because I do. And I didn't want to.'

'Sophia, it may surprise you, but I'm working, and I really don't want to talk about your mother's personal business.'

He swirled the wine gently, inhaled and focused.

'They haven't had sex.'

He winced. And lost the wine's bouquet. 'Damn it, Sophie.'

'If they'd had sex by now, that would mean it was just a nice little physical attraction. I think it's becoming a thing. And how much do we really know about David? He might be a womaniser or an opportunist. When you think about it, he started after my mother right after my father . . .'

Tyler nosed the wine again, noted down his numbers. 'You're saying your mother wouldn't appeal to him on her own?'

'I certainly am not.' Insulted, Sophia snatched up a glass of merlot, scowled through it into the light. 'She's beautiful, intelligent, charming, and everything a man could want in a woman.'

But not what her father had wanted. She marked the sample down for cloudiness, then sipping, let the wine rest, touching it with her tongue to register the sweetness before moving it to the sides to judge its acidity and tannic content.

She swished it around, allowing the elements to blend, then spat it out. 'It's immature yet.'

Tyler tested it. 'We'll let it age a bit. A lot of things become what they're meant to if you leave them for a while.'

'Is that philosophy I hear?'

'You want an opinion or just somebody to agree with you?'

He picked up the next glass, but he was looking at Sophia. It was hard not to. Here they were in a cool, damp cave, a fire snapping, the smells of smoke and wood surrounding them, shadows dancing.

Some people would have said it was romantic. He was doing his best not to be one of them. Just as he'd been doing his best for some time not to think of her as a person, much less as a woman. She was, he reminded himself, a partner at best. And right now she was worried. Maybe she was borrowing trouble, but if he knew one thing about Sophia, it was that she loved her mother unreservedly.

'His ex-wife dumped him and the kids.'

Sophia's gaze lifted from the wine she held, met his. 'Dumped?'

'Yeah, decided there was a big old world out there and she was enti- tled to it. She doesn't contact them often.'

'How do you know this?'

'Maddy talks to me. Theo got in a little trouble, and Cutter took the position out here to get him out of the city.'

'So he's a good father. That doesn't mean he's good for my mother.'

'That's for her to decide, isn't it? You look for flaws in every man you see, and you're going to find them.'

'That's not what I do.'

'It's exactly what you do.'

'You barely look at all. Easier to keep wrapped up in the vines than risk getting wrapped up in a human being.'

'Are we talking about my sex life? I must've missed a step.'

'You don't have one.'

'Not compared to yours.' He set down the glass to make his notes. 'Then again, who does? You go through men like a knife through cheese. You can't set those standards for Pilar.'

'I see.' Hurt rippled through her. He'd made her sound cheap again. Like her father. Needing to punish him for it, she moved closer. 'I haven't gone through you yet, have I, Ty? Haven't even managed the first cut. Why don't you expand your horizons?' She tipped her face up, inviting him. 'Dare you,' she teased.

'I'm not interested.'

Still testing, she wound her arms round his neck, tightening them when he lifted his arms to pull them away. 'Which one of us is bluffing?'

Her eyes were dark, fiery. The scent of her slid round him, into him. She brushed her lips over his, one seductive stroke.

'Why don't you sample me?' she asked softly.

It was a mistake, but it wouldn't be his first. He gripped her hips and ran his hands up her sides. The scent of her was both ripe and elusive. A deliberate and effective torment for a man.

'Look at me,' he ordered, and took the mouth she offered.

Took what and how he wanted. Long, slow, deep. And he let the taste of her slide over his tongue, as he would with a fine wine, then slip almost lazily, certainly pleasurably, into his system.

His lips rubbed over hers, turning her inside out. Somehow he'd flipped it all around on her, and the tempted had become the tempter. Knowing it, she couldn't resist.

There was so much more here than she'd imagined. More than she'd ever been offered or had accepted.

He watched her, intensely. Even as he toyed with her mouth, sent her head spinning and her body churning, he watched her with all the patience of a cat. That alone was a fresh and shocking thrill.

He ran his hands down her sides again, those wide hands just brushing her breasts. And drew her away.

'You push my buttons, Sophia. I don't like it.'

He turned away to take a pull from the bottle of water used to cleanse the palate.

'A vintner's also a scientist.' The air felt thick as she drew in a breath. 'You've heard of chemical reactions.'

He turned, held the bottle out to her. 'Yeah. And a good vintner always takes his time, because some chemical reactions leave nothing but a mess.'

The stab disappointed as much as it stung. 'Can't you just say you want me?'

'Yeah, I can say it. I want you, enough that it sometimes hurts to breathe when you're too close. But when I get you into bed, you're going to look at me the way you looked at me just now. It's not going to be just another time, just another man. It's going to be me and you're going to know it.'

'Why do you make that sound like a threat?'

'Because it is.' Moving away from her, he picked up the next glass of wine and went back to work.

David Cutter had a meeting with department heads in twenty minutes and needed to review his notes. Because time was short, he wasn't pleased to be interrupted by the police.

'Detectives, what can I do for you?'

'A few minutes of your time,' Claremont told him.

'A few minutes is exactly what I can spare. Have a seat.'

Big, cushy leather seats, Maguire noted. In a big, cushy corner office with a spectacular view of San Francisco. Biscuit-and-burgundy colour scheme, glossy mahogany desk.

'I assume this has to do with Anthony Avano.'

'The case is still open, Mr Cutter. How would you describe your relationship with Mr Avano?'

'We didn't have one,' David replied matter-of-factly.

'You both worked primarily out of this building.'

'Very briefly. I'd been with Giambelli less than two weeks before Avano was killed. We had only one discussion, which took place at the party the evening before his murder. It was the only time I met him face to face.'

'Why hadn't you met him?'

'Scheduling conflicts.' The tone was bland.

'Yours or his?'

David didn't care for the direction of the questioning or the implication. 'His, apparently. In the time between my arrival and his death, Avano didn't come to the office, nor did he return my calls.'

'Must've annoyed you,' Maguire said.

'It did. During our brief conversation at the winery I made it clear that I expected him to make time to meet up with me. Obviously, that never happened.'

Claremont got to his feet. 'Do you own a handgun?'

'No, I don't. There are no guns in my house.' David kept his voice even. 'While I understand you have to explore every avenue, I think you're scraping bottom if you're looking at me as a murder suspect.'

'You're dating his ex-wife.'

'I don't believe that crosses any legal or moral line.'

'Were you aware Mr Avano was having financial difficulties?'

'Avano's finances weren't my concern. And that's all we're going to discuss until I consult my attorney.'

'That's your right.' Maguire rose and played what she banked was her trump card. 'Thanks for your time, Mr Cutter. We'll question Pilar Giambelli about her ex-husband's finances.'

David slipped his hands into his pockets. 'She knows less about the business than either of you.' And thinking of her, David made his choice. 'Avano had been, for the last three years, systematically embezzling money from Giambelli. Padded expense accounts, inflated sales figures, travel vouchers for trips not taken. To a total of just over six hundred thousand. Never a great deal at a time, and he picked various pockets so that it went unnoticed. No one questioned his figures.'

Claremont nodded. 'But you did.'

'I caught some of it the day of the party and, in double-checking it, began to see the pattern. It was clear to me he'd been dipping for some time. I reported this to Tereza Giambelli and Eli MacMillan.'

'Why was this information withheld?'

'It was the wish of the senior Ms Giambelli that her granddaughter should not be humiliated by her father's behaviour becoming public. The man was dead, and it seemed unnecessary to add to the scandal by painting him as a thief as well as a philanderer.'

'Mr Cutter,' Claremont said, 'when it's murder, nothing's unnecessary.'

David had barely closed the door and taken a breath to steady himself, when it opened again. Sophia didn't knock, didn't think to.

'What did they want?'

He scooped up his notes. 'They had questions, Sophia. Follow-ups, I suppose you'd call them.'

'Why you and not me or several other people in this building? You barely knew my father. What could you tell the police that they haven't already been told?'

'Little to nothing. I'm sorry, Sophia, but we'll need to table this, at least for now. People are waiting.'

'David, give me some credit. They came to your office.'

He said nothing for a moment, but studied her face. Then he picked up his phone. 'Ms Giambelli and I will be a few minutes late for the meeting,' he told his assistant. He nodded to a chair as he hung up. 'Sit down.'

'I'll stand. You may have noticed, I'm not delicate.'

'Fair enough,' he said. 'Your father had been embezzling from the company. The amounts were spread out and relatively moderate, which is one reason they went undetected as long as they did.'

The colour drained out of her face. 'There's no mistake?'

'I confirmed it the day of the party. I intended to meet him to ask for his resignation. As per your grandparents' instruction, he would have been given the opportunity to pay back the funds and resign. They did that mostly for you. I'm sorry.'

She nodded, turning away as she rubbed her hands over her arms. 'I appreciate your being honest with me now.'

'Sophia—'

'Please, don't apologise. I'm not going to fall apart. Isn't it odd? Now he's stolen money, so much less important than stealing a person's self-respect, as he did with my mother. But it takes this for me to face that he was worthless as a human being. I wonder why that is? Well, I'll see you at the meeting.'

'Take a few minutes.'

'No. He's already had more of my time than he was entitled to.'

She was, he thought as she walked out of his office, very much like her grandmother.

Margaret Bowers tracked Tyler MacMillan down in the winery. She'd had several satisfying and successful meetings since her return from Venice. Her career was advancing well; she was developing the polish she'd always believed international travel sheened on a woman.

There was one last goal she intended to achieve while she was state-side: bagging Tyler MacMillan.

'Ty, when are you coming over to take a look at the operation in Italy? I think you'd be impressed and pleased.'

'There're noises about it. I don't have time now. Sorry. I've been swamped.' February was a slow month in wine-making, but that didn't mean there wasn't work. Sophia had scheduled a wine-tasting party that evening on his turf. While he wasn't pleased, he understood the importance of making certain everything was in place.

'I can imagine. I looked over the plans for the centennial campaign. You've done a terrific job.'

'Sophia has.'

Margaret wandered with him as he moved into the tasting room. 'You don't give yourself enough credit.'

'I hear you've been busy, too.'

'I love it. There's still a little resistance with some of the accounts that were used to Tony Avano and his style of business. They're not as open to sitting around drinking grappa and smoking cigars with me.'

He stopped, smiled at her. 'That's a picture.'

'I have to head back at the end of the week. I was hoping we could get together. I'll fix you dinner.'

'That's—' He broke off as he saw Maddy come in. The kid always lifted his spirits. 'Hey, it's the mad scientist.'

Secretly delighted, Maddy sneered at him. 'I've got my secret formula.' She held up two jars filled with dark liquid.

'Looks pretty scary.' Ty tipped one and watched it swish.

'Maybe you could try it tonight. See what people say.'

'Hmm.' He could only imagine the comments of the wine snobs after a sip of Maddy's kitchen wine, and because he could, he began to grin. 'It's a thought.'

'Tyler, aren't you going to introduce me to your friend?'

'Oh, sorry. Margaret Bowers, Maddy Cutter.'

'Oh, you must be David's little girl. Your father and I had some meetings today.'

'No kidding. Can I stay for the tasting? I'm going to do this report on the wine, so I want to, like, observe and stuff.'

'Sure.' He opened the jar, nosed it.

'Ty, how about tomorrow night?'

'Tomorrow?'

'Dinner.' Margaret kept her voice casual. 'There's a lot regarding the Italian operation I'd like to discuss. I'm hoping you can pump up my weak areas. Talking to an expert vintner who has English as his primary language would really help.'

'Sure.' He moved behind the bar to get a glass.

'Seven? I've got a lovely merlot I brought back with me.'

'Great.' The liquid Ty poured into the glass would never be a lovely anything.

'See you then. Nice to have met you, Maddy.'

'OK.' She gave a quick snort when Margaret went out. 'You're such a dork.'

'Excuse me?'

'She was hitting on you, and you're, like, oblivious.'

'She wasn't, and you're not supposed to talk that way.'

'Was, too.' She slid onto a stool. 'Women know these things.'

'Fine. Great.' It wasn't a debate he wanted to enter into. He let the wine, such as it was, lie on his tongue. It was unsophisticated to say the least, highly acidic and oversweet. Still, she'd succeeded in making wine in a kitchen bowl. Bad wine, but that wasn't the point. 'Did you drink any of this?'

'Maybe.' She set the second jar on the counter. 'Here's the miracle wine. No additives.'

A brave man, he poured a swallow, nosed, sipped. 'Interesting. Cloudy, immature, and biting, but it's wine.'

'Will you read my report when I'm done?'

'Sure.'

'Good.' She fluttered her lashes. 'I'll fix you dinner.'

Pilar chose a simple cocktail suit, the sage green with satin lapels. Perfect, she hoped, for hosting the wine-tasting.

She'd taken on the role to prove herself—to her family, to David, and even to herself. She'd spent a week assisting with tours, being trained—delicately, she thought now. Staff members treated family members with kid gloves. It had jarred her to realise just how little she knew about the winery, about the vineyards, about the process, and about the public areas and retail venue. It would take more than a week and some subtle education to learn how to handle tours, but surely she could handle a group at a wine-tasting.

She was going to learn how to handle a great many things, including her own life.

She had forgotten, for example, what it was like to sit across a candlelit table from a man and talk, just talk. Experiencing it again, with David, was like being offered a cool sip of water. Still, the idea of an intimate relationship terrified her. And that irritated her.

Terrified and irritated, she had made herself a nervous wreck.

The knock on her door had her fixing what she hoped was a confident expression on her face. 'Yes? Come in.'

She sighed hugely when she saw Helen. 'Thank goodness it's you. I'm so tired of pretending to be a twenty-first-century woman.'

'You look like one. Fabulous outfit.'

'I'm glad you and James are here for the tasting.'

Helen sat on the curvy velvet chaise, made herself at home. She patted the spot next to her. 'Now sit down. Catch your breath and tell me all about your romance with David Cutter. With nearly thirty years of marriage under my belt I have to live vicariously.'

'It's not really . . . We're enjoying each other's company.'

'No sex yet, huh?'

'Helen.' Giving up, Pilar dropped onto the chaise. 'How can I have sex with him?'

'If you've forgotten how it works, there are good books on the subject.' Behind her lenses, her eyes danced.

'Stop it.' But she laughed. 'David's been very patient, but he's not going to keep settling for necking on the porch—'

'Necking? Come on, Pilar. Details, all the details.'

403

'Let's just say he has a very creative mouth, and when he uses it, I remember what it's like to be twenty.'

'Oh.' Helen fanned a hand in front of her face. 'Yes.'

'But I'm *not* twenty. And my body sure as hell isn't twenty. How can I possibly let him see me naked, Helen?'

'Honey, James doesn't seem to mind.'

'But that's the point. You've gone through the changes together. Worse, David's younger than I am.'

'Worse? I can think of a lot worse than that.'

'Try to be on my side here. He's a forty-three-year-old man. I'm a forty-eight-year-old woman. There's a huge difference there. A man his age most usually dates younger women.'

'Pilar, the fact is, he's dating you. If you're self-conscious about your body, make sure it's dark the first time.'

'You're a big help.'

'Yes, I am. Do you want to sleep with him? Just yes or no.'

'Yes.'

'Then buy yourself some incredible underwear and go for it.'

Pilar bit her lip. 'I already bought the underwear.'

Nearly twenty-four hours after the tasting, and Tyler could still form a picture in his mind that made him laugh. Two dozen snooty, slick-faced wine-club members had got the shock of their narrow lives with a sample of what he was calling Vin de Madeline.

'"Unsophisticated",' he said, cracking himself up again, '"but nubile". Nubile! Where do they get that stuff?'

'Try to contain your hilarity.' Sophia sat behind the desk in her office in the villa and continued to study pictures of the models that Kris had chosen for the ads. 'And I'd appreciate it if you'd warn me the next time you decide to add a mystery vintage to the selection.'

'Last-minute candidate. And it was in the name of science.'

She glanced up briefly, gave up when he just grinned at her. 'OK, it was funny, and we'll maybe even get a little anecdotal press out of it.'

'Does your blood run on publicity?'

'You betcha. Which is fortunate, as some people would've been very offended if I hadn't been there to spin it.'

'Some people are pompous, tight-assed idiots.'

'Yes, and those pompous, tight-assed idiots buy a great deal of our wine and talk it up at social events. Next time you want to experiment, give me some warning.'

He stretched out his legs. 'Loosen up, Giambelli.'

'That, from the king of the party animals.' She picked up an eight-by-ten glossy, held it out. 'What do you think of her?'

He took the picture, studied the sloe-eyed blonde. 'Does this come with her phone number?'

'That's what I thought. She's too sexy. I told Kris I wanted wholesome.' Sophia scowled into middle distance. 'She's ignoring direct orders, giving the rest of the team grief.' She sighed. 'But cutting her loose is going to mean more work for the rest of us.'

'That sure cheers me up.'

'I was thinking about asking Theo if he wanted a part-time job. We could use a gofer a couple of afternoons a week.'

'Great. Then he can moon over you on a regular basis.'

'Daily contact'll take the edge off his hormones.'

'You think?'

'Why, Tyler, is that a twisted sort of compliment or just your cranky way of saying I make you edgy?'

'Neither.' He studied the glossy again. 'I go for sleepy-eyed blondes with full, pouty lips.'

'Peroxide and collagen.'

'So?'

'God, I love men.' She got up from the desk, walked to him, cupped his face in her hands, and gave him a smacking kiss on the mouth. 'You're just so cute.'

One hard tug on her hand had her tumbling into his lap. An instant later her laugh was cut off and her heart was pounding.

He kissed her with impatience and heat and hunger all mixed together. He kissed her as if he couldn't get enough. Her body quivered once—in surprise, in defence, in response. Then her fingers raked through his hair.

More, she thought. She wanted more of this. When he would have drawn away, she went with him, sliding up against the hard lines of him even as he broke the kiss.

'What was that for?'

'I felt like it.'

'Good enough. Do it again.' She pulled him to the floor.

Fast. He could imagine it fast, and hard and furious. A mindless coupling, all heat and no light. It was what she wanted. What they both wanted. He clamped his mouth over hers again.

The office door swung open. 'Ty, I need to—' Eli stopped in mid-stride

NORA ROBERTS

as he started at his grandson, at the girl he thought of as his grand-daughter, tangled together on the floor. 'Excuse me.' Colour flooded his cheeks as he stumbled back.

When the door slammed, Tyler was already rocking on his heels. Mind swimming, body churning, he rubbed his hands over his face. 'Oh, perfect. Just perfect.'

'How do we handle this?'

'I don't know. I guess I have to talk to him.'

'Ty, I'm really sorry. I'd never do anything to upset Eli or to cause trouble between the two of you.'

'I know.' He pushed to his feet and helped her up.

'I want to make love with you.'

His already jangled system suffered. 'I think what we both want's pretty clear. I just don't know what we're going to do about it. I have to go after him.'

Tyler found his grandfather walking towards the vineyards. He didn't speak, hadn't worked out what he would say once he did. He merely fell into step beside Eli.

'Going to have to keep a frost watch,' Eli commented. 'Warm snap's teased the vines.'

'Yeah, I'm on it. Ah . . . it's nearly discing time.'

'Hope the rain doesn't slow that down.' Eli studied the canes and racked his brain for the right words. 'I . . . should've knocked.'

'No. I shouldn't have . . . It just happened.'

'Well'—Eli cleared his throat—'hell, Ty. You and Sophie?'

'It just happened,' he repeated. 'I guess it shouldn't have, and I guess I should tell you it won't happen again.'

'Not my business. It's just—Ty, you were almost raised together. I know you've got no blood tie, and there's nothing stopping either of you from such a thing. Just a shock, is all.'

'All round,' Tyler agreed.

Eli walked a little further. 'Do you love her?'

Inside his gut Tyler felt the slippery knots of guilt tighten. 'Grandpa, it's not always about love.'

Now Eli stopped, turned, and faced Tyler. 'I know it's not always about love, boy. I was just asking.'

'We've got this heat going on, that's all. If it's all the same to you, I'd rather not go into that end of things.'

'You're both adults. Next time, though, lock the damn door.'

It was nearly six when Tyler got home. He was worn out, worked up, and irritated with himself. Reaching for a cold beer, he saw the note he'd stuck on the refrigerator handle: 'Dinner at M's—7'.

'Hell.' He lowered his forehead to the appliance. He just didn't have it in him. He wasn't in any mood to discuss business, even if it included a decent meal and good company.

He reached for the phone, only to find he'd misplaced it. Swearing, he yanked open the fridge, and there was the phone, tucked between a bottle of Corona and a carton of milk.

He'd make it up to Margaret.

She didn't hear the phone ring. Her head was under the shower, and she was singing. She'd looked forward to the evening all day, shuffling meetings, writing reports, and, finally, stopping on the way home for a man-sized steak and two huge potatoes. She'd bought an apple pie at the bakery and fully intended to pass it off as her own.

A man didn't have to know everything.

She stepped out of the shower, slid into silk. She took out the wine she'd earmarked for the evening and noticed the message light blinking on her kitchen machine.

'Margaret. It's Ty. Listen, I'm going to have to take a rain check on dinner. I should have called sooner, but something came up. I'm really sorry. I'll call you tomorrow.'

She stared at the machine, struggling against tears of disappointment. The hell with him. There were plenty more where he came from. Plenty, she reminded herself as she yanked her grill open to cook the steak. She'd had a number of interesting offers in Italy. When she got back, she might just take one.

But for now, she was opening the damn wine and getting drunk.

Pilar approached the guesthouse by the back door. It was a friendly habit. She felt she had become friends with Theo. He seemed to enjoy her company when he came by the villa to use the pool or play the piano. Maddy was a different matter. The girl was polite but always cool. She watched, Pilar thought, everything and everyone.

She hitched her shoulder bag as she started up the back path. The contents weren't bribes, she assured herself. Just tokens. And she wouldn't stay any longer than was comfortable for all of them, though part of her hoped they'd want her to stay for a while and fix them lunch.

She knocked briskly on the kitchen door and had her smile ready.

It wobbled a bit when David answered. He wore a work shirt and jeans and held a cup of coffee. 'Now this is handy.' He took her hand to draw her inside. 'I was just thinking about you.'

'I didn't expect you to be home.'

'Working out of here today.' He leaned down to kiss her.

'Oh, well. When I didn't see the car—'

'Theo and Maddy ganged up on me. Professional day, no school. Every parent's nightmare. We solved it by letting them nag me into giving Theo the keys and driving off to the mall and the movies for the day. Which is why your visit's perfectly timed.'

'Really?' She tugged her hand free, fiddled with the strap of her bag. 'It is?'

'Keeps me from sitting here imagining all the trouble they could get into. Want some coffee?'

'No. I really should . . . I just stopped by to drop off a couple of things for the kids. Maddy's so interested in the wine-making process, I thought she'd like to read this history of Giambelli California.' Pilar tugged a book out of her bag. 'I brought Theo sheet music, thought he might get a kick out of trying some of the classics.'

'*Sergeant Pepper.*' He grinned. 'Where'd you dig this up?'

'I used to play it and drive my mother crazy.'

'Did you wear love beads and bell-bottoms?' he teased.

'Naturally. I made a terrific pair out of paisley.'

'So many hidden talents. You didn't bring me a present.'

'I didn't know you'd be here.' She tried to laugh, to keep it light. 'I really should get back. I'm helping with a tour at four thirty.'

'Mmm.' He glanced at the kitchen clock. 'An hour and a half. I wonder what we could do with ninety minutes?' Hands at her waist, he drew her slowly towards the inside door. 'Nobody home but you and me,' he said. 'You know it's a complex business. My girlfriend lives with her mother. And I live with my kids.'

'David, it's the middle of the day.'

'The middle of the day.' He paused at the steps. 'And an opportunity. I hate wasted opportunities, don't you?'

She was walking up the steps with him, which seemed a miraculous feat to her, since her heart was labouring as if she'd already scaled a mountain. 'I wasn't expecting . . . I'm not prepared.'

'Sweetheart, I'll take care of that.'

Take care of it? How could he arrange for her to be wearing sexy underwear or turn the merciless daylight into the soft shadows of night?

How could he . . . Then it struck her that he meant protection. 'No, I didn't mean . . . David, I'm not young.'

'Neither am I.' He eased back slightly at his bedroom door. 'Pilar, I have a lot of complicated feelings for you. One that isn't complicated, for me, is that it's you I want. All there is of you.'

Nerves were swimming now, in a stream of heat. 'David, you need to know. Tony was my first. And last. It's been a long time.'

'That flatters me, Pilar.' He brushed his lips over hers. 'It humbles me. It excites me.' His mouth came back in a kiss that trembled on the edge between seduction and demand. 'Come to my bed.'

He slipped off her jacket. He kept his eyes on hers as he unbuttoned her blouse, while his fingers whispered along exposed flesh. 'Put your hands on my shoulders. Step out of your shoes.'

She was trembling, and so was he.

The late winter sun was a whitewash of light through the windows. In the silence of the house he could hear every catch of her breath. His fingers skimmed lightly over her.

'Smooth. Warm. Beautiful.'

He was making her believe his words. And if her fingers shook as she unbuttoned his shirt, he didn't seem to mind.

It made her want to weep to be touched again. It seemed natural to lie back on the bed, to have his body press down on hers.

It seemed natural and glorious. She forgot about the sunlight and all the flaws it would reveal. He didn't want to rush, but her hesitation had become eagerness. He forgot about patience and all the doubts he wanted to assuage.

The soft, damp skin that smelt of spring, the subtle curves. He wanted to take all, to give all he had. She moved with him, reached for him as if her arms had always held him close. She watched him as he ranged himself over her. They moved together in the light, a pace that quickened, a need that pulsed.

She cried out, muffling the sound against the side of his throat as her heart took the final leap.

The sun was shining in San Francisco, too, but it only added dimension to Sophia's headache. She faced Kris across her desk and took a steadying breath.

'You don't want to be here, Kris. You've made that clear with your deliberate rejection of company policy and your attitude towards authority.'

'You mean my attitude towards you.'

'Here's a bulletin for you. I am authority.'

'Because your name's Giambelli. If Tony was still alive, I'd be sitting behind that desk.'

Sophia swallowed the bitterness that rose in her throat. 'Is that how he got you into bed? Promising you my job? That was clever of him, foolish of you. My father had no weight here.'

'You saw to that. All three Giambelli women.'

'No. He saw to it. But that's beside the point. The fact is, I'm head of this department, and you no longer work for me. You'll be given the standard termination package. I want your office cleared of your personal property by the end of business today.'

'That's fine. I have other offers.'

'I hope you get just what you deserve at Le Coeur,' Sophia replied, and watched Kris's jaw drop in surprise. 'There are no secrets. But I'll warn you to remember the confidentiality clause you signed when you joined this firm.'

'I don't need to pass anything on. Your campaign's ill-conceived and trite. It's an embarrassment.'

'Isn't it lucky, then, that you won't have to be associated with it?' They both got to their feet. Sophia reached the door, opened it. 'I think we've said all we have to say to each other.'

'When I go, others will go with me. Let's see how far you and the farmer go on your own.' Kris paused for one smirk. 'Tony and I had a good laugh over the two of you.'

'I'm shocked you took the time for conversation.'

'He respected me,' Kris shot back. 'Bitch number three.'

Sophia's hand clamped down on Kris's arm. 'So it was you.'

'Call a cop . . . then try to prove it. That'll give me one last laugh.' She yanked her arm free, strolled away.

Sophia went straight back to her desk and called security. She wanted Kris escorted from the building. She wasn't surprised that it had been Kris who'd defaced the angels. She couldn't do anything about computer files Kris might have already copied and taken out, but she could make certain there wasn't a last-minute foray.

Far from satisfied, she sent for both P.J. and Trace.

While she waited, she paced. And Tyler walked in.

'I saw Kris steam down the corridor,' he commented, and dropped comfortably into a chair. 'I figured it didn't go well when I noticed the tongues of fire shooting out of her ears.'

'She called me bitch number three.'

'What?' He caught her hand.

'She did it. She's the one who smeared nail polish on the Giambelli angels. And she said my father was going to help her to land my job. I imagine he promised her that.'

He watched her face. 'I'm sorry.'

'You're thinking they deserved each other. So am I. Gotta calm down, gotta calm down,' she repeated like a mantra. 'It's over and done, and we have to go forward. I have to talk to P.J. and Trace to start, and then we have a meeting with Margaret.'

The little tug of guilt had him shifting in his chair. 'I was supposed to meet her myself last night. I haven't been able to get in touch with her today. She missed two morning meetings.'

'That's not like Margaret. Try her at home.'

'You up for a lunchtime meeting thing if she wants to?'

'Sure, but that's not going to make her happy. She has the hots for you,' Sophia said.

Women, Tyler thought as he hunted up the number in Sophia's Rolodex. Just because he and Margaret got along—

He shifted his thoughts when a man answered on the third ring. 'I'm trying to reach Margaret Bowers.'

'Who's calling?'

'Tyler MacMillan.'

'Mr MacMillan.' There was a brief pause. 'This is Detective Claremont.'

'Claremont? Sorry, I must've dialled the wrong number.'

'No, you didn't. I'm in Ms Bowers's apartment. She's dead.'

PART THREE
THE BLOOMING

⌒‿⌒

MARCH ROARED ACROSS the valley on a raw, galloping wind. It hardened the ground and rattled the naked fingers of the vines. The dawn mists had a bite that chewed through the bones. There would be worries about damage and loss until the true warmth of spring arrived.

There would be worries about many things.

Sophia stopped at the vineyards first, and was disappointed that Tyler wasn't stalking down the rows examining the canes for early growth. She knew the discing phase was about to begin—weather permitting. Men with disc harrows would pulverise and aerate the soil, breaking up the crusted earth, turning the mustard plants and their nitrogen into the ground.

He'd be brooding in his office, she imagined as she changed directions for the house. Going over his charts and records, but brooding all the same. Time to put a stop to it.

She started to knock on the door. No, she decided, when you knocked, it was too easy to be told to go away. Instead she opened the door and stepped inside. 'Ty?' She tossed her jacket over the newel post and following instinct, headed upstairs for his office.

'I've got work to do.' He didn't bother to look up.

'You look like hell.'

'Thanks.'

'No word from the police yet?'

'You're just as likely to hear as I am.'

It had been nearly a week since Margaret's body had been found. On the floor by a table set for two, with an untouched steak on the platter and an empty bottle of merlot.

'I spoke with her parents today. They're going to take her back to Columbus for the funeral.'

'If I hadn't cancelled—'

'You don't know if it would have made any difference.' She went to stand behind him, began to rub his shoulders. 'If she had a heart condition no one knew about, she could have become ill at any time.'

'She was too young for a goddamn heart attack. And don't give me the line of statistics. The cops are looking into it and not passing on information. That means something.'

'Ty, until we know differently, it's just routine.' Without thinking, she hooked her arms round his shoulders, rested her cheek on his head. 'Come downstairs. I'll fix soup. It'll give us both something to do besides think. And wait.'

She pulled at his hand, pleased when he let her tug him to his feet.

Downstairs, at the base of the steps, he turned to her. With a casual tap of his finger he tipped up her chin. 'You're not a half-bad person, as people go.'

'Oh, I can be bad.' Her eyes changed as he looked into them. And her blood began to move. 'Ty.' She lifted a hand to his face as he leaned towards her.

And the knock on the door had her cursing. 'For God's sake! What is wrong with our timing? I want you to remember where we were. I really want you to remember it.'

'I think I've got it bookmarked.' No less irritated by the interruption than she, he stalked to the door, yanked it open, and felt a clench in his gut.

'Mr MacMillan'—Claremont stood beside Maguire in the chilly air—'can we come in?'

They moved into the living room where the atmosphere was masculine and messy. Tyler dropped into a chair, Sophia edged onto the arm of it beside him. And made them a unit.

Claremont took out his notepad and set the rhythm. 'You said you and Margaret Bowers dated.'

'No, I didn't. I said we went out a couple of times.'

'You were supposed to have dinner with her on the night she died.'

'Yeah. As I told you before, I got hung up here, called her somewhere around six. I got her machine and left a message that I couldn't make it.'

'Have you ever had dinner in Ms Bower's apartment before?'

'No. Look, I'm sorry about what happened to Margaret. She was a nice woman. I liked her. And maybe if I hadn't cancelled I could've called nine-one-one when she had the heart attack. But I don't see what these questions have to do with anything.'

'Did you ever give Ms Bowers a bottle of wine? Wine carrying the Giambelli label, the Italian label?'

'No, I use my own. Why?'

'Ms Bowers consumed nearly an entire bottle of Castello di Giambelli Merlot on the evening you were to dine with her. The bottle contained digitalis.'

'I don't get it.' Even as Tyler reared up in his seat, Sophia was clamping a hand on his shoulder.

'She was murdered?' Sophia demanded. 'Poisoned? Margaret was . . . If you'd been there. If you'd had the wine . . . I have to call my grandmother.' She sprang to her feet. 'If there's been product tampering, we have to deal with it quickly. I need all the information on that bottle. The vintage. I have to have a copy of the label to run it down.'

He watched the evening newscast: 'Giambelli-MacMillan, the giant of the wine industry, has suffered another crisis. It has been confirmed that a tainted bottle of wine was responsible for the death of Margaret Bowers, an executive with the company. Police are investigating, and the possibility of product tampering is being considered. Since the merger of Giambelli and MacMillan wineries last December . . .'

Perfect, he thought. Absolutely perfect. They'd scramble, of course. Already were scrambling. But what would the public hear?

Giambelli. Death. Wine.

Bottles would be poured down the sink. More would sit unsold on the shelf. It would sting. It would cut into profits.

People had died, and when the police caught the one at fault, the damage to Giambelli would only be compounded.

He'd wait a while. Bide his time. Watch the show. Then, if it seemed advantageous, there could be another anonymous call.

Not to the media this time. But to the police.

The family was in the front parlour, with David standing by the window talking on the phone. Eli paced back and forth in front of the fire. The strain seemed to have weight and caused his face to sag. Tereza sat, soldier-straight, sipping coffee. She nodded when Ty and Sophia came in, and merely gestured to chairs.

'Mr Cutter is talking to Italy now, getting damage control started.' She glanced towards David, who lowered the phone. 'So?'

'We're tracking it. We'll recall all Castello di Giambelli Merlot, 1992. We should, very shortly, be able to determine which cask the bottle was drawn from. I'll leave in the morning.'

'No. Eli and I will leave in the morning.' Tereza lifted a hand. 'This is for us. I leave the California operation to you and Tyler.'

'Paulie and I can start with the wineries,' Tyler suggested. 'David can look at the bottling.'

David nodded. 'We'll go over the personnel files one by one.'

Sophia already had her memo pad in her lap. 'I'll have press releases, both English and Italian, ready in an hour. I'll need all the details on the recall. We'll want a story on how exacting the wine-making process is for Giambelli-MacMillan. How safe, how secure. We'll need to allow camera crews in the vineyards and wineries. Nonna, with you and Eli going over to Italy, we'll be able to show that Giambelli is family-run and that La Signora continues to take a personal interest.'

'It is family-run and I take a very personal interest,' Tereza said flatly. 'But we do nothing else until we meet with James Moore.' Helen Moore's husband was a top criminal defence attorney in California. 'Sophia, draft your release. Then we'll let James look at it. And everything else.'

It was the blow to her pride that was the hardest to accept, Tereza thought. What was hers had been violated, threatened. The work of a lifetime besmirched by one tainted bottle of wine.

Now, in so many ways, she had to trust others to save her legacy.

'Digitalis comes from foxglove.' Maddy knew. She'd looked it up.

'What?' Distracted, David looked over briefly. He had a mountain of paperwork on his desk. In Italian. He was much better at speaking it than reading it.

'Would they have grown foxglove near the vines? Like they grow mustard plants? I think they'd know foxglove had digitalis. But could it infect the grapes if the plants were turned into the soil?'

'I don't know. Maddy, this isn't for you to worry about.'

'Why? You're worried.'

'It's my job to worry.'

'I could help.'

'Honey, if you want to help, you could give me a little space here. Do your homework.'

Her lips began to pout. 'I've done my homework.'

'Well, help Theo with his. Or something.'

'But if the digitalis—'

'Maddy.' At his wits' end, he snapped at her. 'This isn't a project. It's a very real problem. Go find something to do.'

'Fine.' She shut the door of his office and let the resentment burn as she stomped away.

She bet he wouldn't have told Pilar Giambelli to find something to do.

She stalked to Theo's room. He was sprawled on the bed, his music blaring and the phone at his ear. From the dopey look on his face it was a girl on the other end.

Men were so lame.

'Dad wants you to do your homework.'

'Beat it.' He crossed his ankles. 'Nah. It's nothing. Just my idiot sister.'

The phone knocked hard against his jaw when Maddy launched herself at him. In seconds Theo was dealing with the shock of pain, the squeals in his ear and the pummels and kicks of a furious Maddy.

'Ow! Wait! Damn it, Maddy. Call you back.' He managed to drop the phone. 'What the hell?'

After a long, sweaty minute, he managed to flip her and pin her down. 'What's your problem?'

'I'm not *nothing*.' She spat it at him.

'No, you're just nuts.' He licked the corner of his mouth, cursed at the unmistakable taste. 'I'm bleeding. When I tell Dad—'

'You can't tell him anything. He doesn't listen to anybody except her.'

'Her, who?'

'You know who. Get off me, you big fat jerk. You're just as bad as he is, making gooey noises to some girl, and not listening to anybody.'

'I was having a conversation,' he said with great dignity to counter the gooey snipe. 'And if you hit me again, I'm hitting you back. Even if Dad grounds me for it. Now, what's your problem?'

'I don't have a problem. It's the men in this house making asses of themselves over women that's the problem.'

Theo shook back his mop of curly hair. Yawned. 'You're just jealous.'

'I am not.'

'Sure you are. I don't know why you're having a fit because Dad's hanging out with Pilar. He's hung out with women before.'

'You're so stupid.' Every dreg of disgust gathered in her voice. 'He's not hanging out with her, putz-face. He's in love with her.'

'Get out. What do you know?' But his stomach did a funny little jump.

'It's going to change everything. That's the way it works.' There was a terrible pressure in her chest, but she got to her feet. 'Nothing's ever going to be the same again, and that sucks out loud.'

'Nothing's been the same. Not since Mom took off.'

'It got *better*.' The tears wanted to escape, but rather than let them fall in front of him, she stormed out of the room.

Sophia hoped cold air would blow some of the clouds from her mind. She had to think, and think precisely.

She stood at the edge of the vineyard. It was guarded, she thought, against pests, disease, the vagaries of weather. Whatever threatened to invade or damage it was fought against. This was no different.

She caught a shadow of movement. 'Who's there?' Her mind leapt towards trespasser, saboteur. Murderer. Without hesitation she charged, and found her arms full of struggling young girl.

'Let go! I can be here. I'm allowed.'

'Sorry. I'm sorry.' Sophia stepped back. 'You scared me.'

She hadn't looked scared, Maddy thought. But she had looked scary. 'I'm not doing anything wrong.'

'I didn't say you were. I said you scared me. I guess we're all a little jumpy right now. Look . . .'

She caught the glimmer of tears on the girl's cheek.

'I just came out to clear my head. Too much going on in there right now.' Sophia glanced back at the house.

'My father's working.'

There was just enough defence in that statement to have Sophia speculating. 'There's a lot of pressure on him. On everybody. My grandparents are leaving for Italy first thing in the morning. I worry about them. They're not young any more.'

After her father's rebuff, Sophia's casual confidence soothed. Still cautious, Maddy fell into step beside her. 'They don't act old.'

'No, they don't, do they? But still. I wish I could go instead, but they need me here right now.'

Maddy's lips trembled as she looked towards the lights of the guesthouse. Nobody, it seemed, needed her. Anywhere. 'At least you've got something to do.'

Sophia slanted Maddy a look. The kid was wound up and sulking about something. Sophia remembered very well what it was like to be fourteen, wound up and sulking.

'I guess, on some level, we're in the same boat. My mother. Your father. It's a little weird.'

Maddy shrugged, then hunched her shoulders. 'I gotta go.'

'All right, but I'd like to tell you something. Woman to woman, daughter to daughter, whatever. My mother's gone a long time without someone, without a good man, to care about her. I don't know what it's been like for you, or your brother or your father. But for me, after the general strangeness of it, it's nice to see her have a good man who makes her happy. I hope you'll give her a chance.'

'It doesn't matter what I do. Or think. Or say.'

Defiant misery, Sophia mused. Yes, she remembered that, too. 'Yes, it matters. When someone loves us, what we think and what we do matters.' She looked over at the sound of running feet. 'From the looks of it, somebody loves you.'

'Maddy!' Breathless, David plucked his daughter off her feet. He managed to embrace and shake her at the same time. 'What are you doing? You can't go wandering off like that after dark.'

'I just took a walk.'

'And cost me a year of my life. You want to fight with your brother, be my guest, but you're not to leave the house again without permission. Clear?'

'Yes, sir.' Though secretly pleased, she grimaced. 'I didn't think you would notice.'

'Think again.' He hooked his arm round her neck, a casual habit of affection Sophia had noticed. And envied. Her father had never touched her like that.

'Partly my fault,' Sophia told him. 'I kept her longer than I should have. She's a terrific sounding board. My mind was going off in too many directions.'

'You should give it a rest. You're going to need all circuits up and working by eight o'clock tomorrow. Now, I'll drag this baggage home.'

'I'll be ready. 'Night, Maddy.' She watched them walk through the fields towards the guesthouse, their shadows close together.

Hard for the kid to make room for changes. For adults too, when your life seemed just fine as it was. But changes happened. It was smarter to be a part of them. Better yet, she decided, to initiate them.

Tyler kept the radio and the TV off. One thing he could control was his own reaction to the press, and the best way to control it was to ignore the press altogether. At least for a few hours.

He was working his way through every record he had available. He could, and would, ascertain that MacMillan was secure.

The current crisis was going to pull his time and energy away from the vineyards when he could least afford it. Long-range forecasts warned of frost. Casks of wine were on the point of being ready for bottling. Discing had already started.

He didn't have time to worry about police investigations, potential lawsuits. Or a woman. And of all of them, he was finding the woman the hardest to shove out of his mind.

Because she'd invaded his system, he thought. And she'd be stuck there, irritating him, until he got her out again. Thinking about Sophia muddled up the mind, strained the body, and complicated an already complex business association.

So why didn't he just march over to the villa, storm up her terrace steps, and deal with it? Finish it?

He knew exactly how pathetic and self-serving that was as rationalisation. And decided he didn't give a damn.

He grabbed a jacket, strode to the front door and yanked it open. And there she was, stalking up his steps.

'I don't like irritable, macho men,' she told him as she slammed the door at her back.

'I don't like bossy, aggressive women.'

They dived at each other.

He rapped her back against the wall and began dragging her sweater over her head. He tossed it aside, took his mouth over the soft swell of breast that rose above her bra.

It was hard to know where she was, who she was. Hands were pulling at clothes; mouths ran hot over flesh. Everything blurred. Over the wild beat of blood she could hear her own whimpers, pleas, demands, a kind of mad chant that merged with his. She heard his breath heave and tear, thrilled that she could weaken him.

'Now.' She anchored her hands in his hair and shuddered. 'Now, now.' Pleasure careened through her, left her shattered, stupefied.

Tyler managed to hold on to her as both of them slid to the floor.

Some time around midnight, she found herself in Tyler's bed. The sheets were tangled and hot, and her bones were limp as water.

'Water,' she croaked. 'I need water. I'll give you anything—wild, sexual favours—if you'll just give me a bottle of water.'

'You've already paid out the wild, sexual favours.'

'Oh, right.' She groped over, patted his shoulder blindly. 'Be a pal, MacMillan.'

'OK, be right back.' He staggered up, and since he'd been crossways on the bed, misjudged direction and rapped smartly into a chair.

Listening to his muttered curses, Sophia smiled. God, he was cute. Funny. Smarter than she'd given him credit for. And incredible in bed. On the floor. Against the wall. She couldn't remember any man appealing to her on so many levels. Especially when you considered he was the type who had to be held at gunpoint to put on a suit and tie.

Which was, she supposed, why he always looked so sexy in them. The caveman temporarily civilised.

Lost for the moment in that thought, she yelped when Ty held the iced water to her bare shoulder. 'Ha ha,' she muttered, but was grateful enough to roll over, sit up and gulp down half the glass.

'Hey, I figured you'd share.'

'I didn't say anything about sharing.'

'Then I want more sexual favours.'

'You couldn't possibly.'

'You know how much I like proving you wrong.'

It had been, Sophia mused, a long time since she'd sneaked into the house at two in the morning. Still, it was one of those skills, like riding a bike or, well, sex, that came back to you. She dimmed her headlights before they flashed against the windows of the villa and eased the car gently, slowly round the bend and into the garage.

She crept out into the chilly night and stood under the brilliant wheel of stars. She felt outrageously tired and wonderfully alive.

Tyler MacMillan, she decided, was a man full of surprises.

Odd, she thought as she walked quietly round the back of the house, she'd wanted to stay with him. Sleep with him. All curled up against that long, warm body. Safe, cosy, secure.

She'd trained herself over the years to click off emotionally after sex. A man's way, she liked to think. Sleeping, and waking, in the same bed after the fun and games were over could be awkward. It could be intimate. Avoiding that, making certain she didn't need that, kept things from getting messy.

But she'd had to order herself to leave Tyler's bed.

Perhaps she was more attracted to him than she'd expected to be. But that didn't make him different to anyone else. Just . . . new. After a while the polish would wear off the shiny excitement, and that would be that.

That, she considered as she navigated through the shrubbery, was always that.

If you looked for love and lifetimes, you were doomed to disappoint, or be disappointed. Better, much better, to seize the moment, wring it dry, then move on.

Rounding the last bend in the gardens, she came face to face with her mother. They stared at each other, the surprised breath each puffed out frosting into little clouds.

'Um. Nice night,' Sophia commented.

'Yes. Very. I was just, ah . . . David . . .' Stumped, Pilar gestured vaguely towards the guesthouse. 'He needed help with some translating.'

'I see.' A wild giggle tried to claw its way out of Sophia's throat. 'Is that what your generation calls it?' A small, choking sound escaped. 'If we're going to sneak the rest of the way in, let's do it. We could freeze out here trying to come up with reasonable excuses.'

'I *was* translating.' Pilar hurried to the kitchen door, fumbled with the knob. 'There was a lot of—'

'Oh, Mama.' The laughter won as Sophia clutched her belly and stumbled inside. 'Stop bragging.'

'I was merely . . .' Floundering, Pilar pushed at her hair. She had a very good idea how she looked—tumbled and flushed. Like a woman who'd just slid out of bed. Or in this case, off the living-room sofa. Taking the offensive seemed to be the safest course. 'You're out late.'

'Yeah. I was translating. With Ty.' Sophia opened the refrigerator. 'I'm starving, how about you? I never got round to dinner.' She spoke casually, with her head in the fridge. 'Do you have a problem with me and Ty?'

'No—yes. No,' Pilar stuttered. 'I don't know. I absolutely don't know how I'm supposed to handle this.'

'Let's have pie.' Sophia pulled out what was left of a deep-dish apple pie. 'You look wonderful, Mama.'

Pilar brushed at her hair again. 'I couldn't possibly.'

'Wonderful.' Sophia set the dish on the counter and reached up for plates. 'I had a few emotional bumps about you and David. But when I run into you sneaking into the house in the middle of the night, looking wonderful . . .' Sophia cut two huge hunks. 'It was a long, lousy day. It's nice to end it well.'

'Yes. Though you gave me a hell of a shock outside.'

'Me? Imagine my surprise, reliving my teenage years, then running into my mother.' Sophia carried the plates to the kitchen table while Pilar got forks.

'Reliving? Really?'

'Oh well, why dwell on the past?' Grinning wickedly, Sophia licked pie from her thumb. 'David's very hot.'

'Sophie.'

'Very. Great shoulders, that charmingly boyish face, that intelligent brain. Quite a package you've bagged there, Mama.'

'He's not a trophy. And I certainly hope you don't think of Ty as one.'

'He's got a terrific butt.'

'I know.'

'I meant Ty.'

'I know,' Pilar repeated. 'What, am I blind?' With an unladylike snort, she plopped into a chair. 'This is ridiculous, it's rude and it's—'

'Fun,' Sophia finished. 'We share an interest in fashion, and more recently in the business. Why shouldn't we share an interest in . . . *Nonna.*'

Pilar dropped her fork. 'Mama, what are you doing up?'

'You think I don't know when people come and go in my house?' Somehow elegant in a thick chenille robe and slippers, Tereza swept into the room. 'What, no wine?'

'We were just . . . hungry,' Sophia managed.

'Ha. No wonder. Sex is a laborious business if done properly. I'm hungry myself.'

Sophia slapped a hand to her mouth, but it was too late. The burst of laughter erupted. 'Go, Eli.'

421

Tereza merely took the last piece of pie, as her daughter stared down at her plate, shoulders shaking. 'I believe the occasion calls for wine. You needn't look so stunned, Pilar. Sex is a natural function, and since you've chosen a worthy partner this time, we'll have wine.'

She chose a bottle of sauvignon blanc from the kitchen rack and uncorked it. 'These are trying times.' She poured three glasses. 'I approve of David Cutter, if my approval matters.'

'Thank you. It does, of course.'

Tereza turned towards Sophia. 'If you hurt Tyler, I'll be both angry and disappointed in you. I love him very much.'

Deflated, Sophia set her fork down. 'Why would I?'

'Remember what I said. Tomorrow we'll fight for what we are, what we have. Tonight'—she lifted her glass—'tonight we celebrate it. *Salute.*'

It was a war waged on several fronts. Sophia fought her battles on the airwaves, in print, and on the telephone. She spent hours updating press releases, reassuring accounts. And every day she started again, beating back rumour and speculation.

She worried about her grandparents forging their front on the Italian line. Every day the reports came in. A recall was being implemented, bottle by bottle; the wine would be tested. She couldn't think about the cost, short- or long-term. That, she left in David's hands.

When she needed to step back from the hype and spin, she stood at her office window and watched men with harrows work the earth. It would be a year of rare vintage, she promised herself. They only had to survive it.

She jumped at the next ring of her phone, and buried the very real need to ignore it.

'Sophia Giambelli.'

Ten minutes later she hung up, then released pent-up rage with a vicious stream of Italian curses.

'Does that help?' Pilar asked from the doorway.

'Not enough.' Sophia pressed her fingers to her temples. 'I'm glad you're here. Can you come in, sit down a minute?'

'I've just finished up a tour.' Pilar settled into a chair. 'They're coming in droves. Curiosity seekers, for the most part. Some reporters, though that's down to a trickle since your press conference.'

'I just got off the phone with a producer of *The Larry Mann Show.*'

'Larry Mann.' Pilar wrinkled her nose. 'Trash television. You aren't going to give them anything?'

'They've already got something. They've got Rene. She's going to tape a show tomorrow revealing family secrets, supposedly, telling the true story of Dad's death. She's been giving interviews right and left. I'm going to talk to Aunt Helen and Uncle James about legal action.'

'Don't. Taking legal action only gives her credence.'

'I've thought of that. But when it comes down to it, you fight fire with fire.'

'Not always, honey. Sometimes you just drown it. We'll just drown her out, with good Giambelli wine.'

Sophia inhaled, exhaled slowly as she sat back. Behind her, the fax beeped and whined, but she ignored it.

'That's good. That's very good. Drown the flames with one good flood. We're going to have a party. Spring ball, black tie. Rene opts for trash; we'll opt for elegance. How much time do you need to put it together?'

To her credit, Pilar only blinked. 'Three weeks.'

'**A** party?' Tyler raised his voice over the rumble of discing. 'Ever hear of Nero and his fiddle?'

'Rome's not burning. That's my point.' Impatient, Sophia dragged him further from the work. 'Damn!' She swore as her cellphone rang. 'Wait.'

She pulled the phone from her pocket. 'Sophia Giambelli . . . *Sì. Va bene.*' With an absent signal to Ty she paced a few feet away.

He stood watching the discing progress. The noisy, systematic turning of earth and cover crop. Warmth teased the vines to bud, even as the breeze that shivered down from the mountains promised a night of chills. In the middle of it all, in the centre of the ageless cycle, was Sophia, her voice a kind of fascinating foreign music.

He didn't bother to curse, didn't even bother to question when he felt that last lock click open inside him.

He was crazy about her. Gone. Over the line. And sooner or later he'd have to figure out what to do about it.

She jammed the phone back in her pocket. 'Italian publicity branch,' she said. 'Sorry for the interruption. Now, the party—'

She stared up at him. 'What are you grinning at?'

'You're not so hard to look at, even in fast-forward.'

'Then why haven't you come sneaking through my terrace doors in the night?'

His lips twisted. 'Thought about it.'

'Think harder.'

'OK. Leave your terrace doors unlocked.'

'They have been.'

And the phone in her pocket began to ring again.

She dragged it out. 'Sophia Giambelli . . . Nonna, I'm glad you caught me. I tried to reach you earlier, but . . .'

She stopped walking, stood at the edge of the vineyard. Despite the wash of sunlight, her skin chilled.

She was already whirling back as she broke the connection. 'Ty! Nonna—She and Eli—' She had to stop, organise her thoughts. 'There was an old man, he worked for Nonna's grandfather. Started in the vineyard when he was just a boy. Late last year he died. He had a bad heart. His granddaughter, the one who found him, says he'd been drinking our merlot. They're having his body exhumed.'

It felt odd sneaking into a house where he'd always been welcome. Odd and exciting, knowing she'd be waiting for him. He could see the candlelight beating against the glass. The turn of the knob in his hand barely made a click and rang like a trumpet in his head.

He braced for her, closing the door at his back. Then he saw her, curled in a ball of fatigue in the chair.

'Ah, hell, Sophie. Look at you.'

He crossed the room quietly and studied her. Soft skin that hinted of rose and gold. Thick, inky lashes and a full, lush mouth.

'You're one gorgeous piece of work,' he murmured. 'And you wore yourself out, didn't you? Come on, baby'—he slid his arms under her—'let's put you to bed.'

She stirred, shifted, snuggled. 'Hmm. Ty.'

'Good guess. Here you go,' he said, laying her down.

Her eyes fluttered open. 'Where are you going?'

'Baby, you're beat. I'll take a rain check.'

'Don't go. Please, I don't want you to go.'

'I'll be back.' He leaned down again to kiss her good night, but her lips were soft and tasted of lazy invitation.

'Don't go,' she said again, reaching for him. 'Make love with me. It'll be like a dream.'

It was dreamlike. Slow and tender where neither had expected it. He slid into bed with her, floated with her on the easy stroke of her hands. And the sweetness of it drifted through him like starlight.

His hands were rough from work and smoothed over her like velvet. His body was hard and covered hers like silk. His mouth was firm and took from her with devastating patience.

No wildness here. No brilliant flashes of urgency. Tonight was to savour and soothe. To offer and welcome.

She skimmed her fingers in his hair, saw the shades of it shift in the light. Her fingers curled, drawing him down.

In the dark he could see the glint of the candlelight in her eyes, gold dust splashed over rich pools.

'This is different,' he told her, and touched his mouth to hers as she shook her head. 'This is different. Yesterday I wanted you. Tonight I need you.'

Her lips trembled with words she didn't know how to say.

What did a seventy-three-year-old wine-maker from Italy have in common with a thirty-six-year-old sales executive from California? Giambelli, David thought. It was the only link he could find between them. Except the manner of their deaths.

Tests on the exhumed body of Bernardo Baptista had confirmed he'd ingested a dangerous dosage of digitalis with his Chianti. It couldn't be construed as a coincidence. Police on both sides of the Atlantic were calling it homicide and the Giambelli wine the murder weapon.

But why? What motive linked Margaret Bowers and Baptista?

David left his children in their beds and drove towards MacMillan. As the temperature had dropped, he and Paulie had turned on the sprinklers, had walked the rows as water coated the vines and the thin skin of ice formed a shield against the threatening hard frost. He knew Paulie would stand watch through the night. Predawn temperatures were forecast to hover near the critical twenty-nine-degree mark.

He could see the fine mist of water swirling over the MacMillan vines, the tiny drops going to glimmer in the cold moonlight. He pulled on his gloves, grabbed his Thermos of coffee, and left the car to walk in the freezing damp.

He found Tyler sitting on an overturned crate, sipping from his own Thermos. 'Thought you might be by.' In invitation, Ty banged the toe of his boot on another crate. 'Pull up a chair.'

David settled down, uncapped his Thermos. 'Where's your foreman?'

'Sent him home. No point in both of us losing sleep.' Ty shrugged, scanning the rows that turned to a fairyland of sparkle under the lights. 'Frost alarms went off just after midnight, but the system's running smoothly.'

'Did you know Baptista?'

'Not really. My grandfather did. La Signora's taking it hard. And I guess Sophia thought of him as a kind of mascot. Said he used to sneak her candy. Poor old bastard.'

David hunched forward, the Thermos cup of coffee between his knees. 'I've been thinking, trying to find the real connection. Probably a waste of time, since I'm a corporate suit, not a detective.'

Tyler studied him. 'From what I've seen so far, you're not much of a time-waster. And you're not so bad, for a suit.'

'Coming from you, that's a hell of a kudo.'

'Damn right.'

'Well, from what I can tell, Margaret never met Baptista. He was dead before she took over Avano's accounts and started the travel to Italy.'

'Doesn't matter if they were random victims.'

David shook his head. 'It matters if they're not.'

'Yeah, I've been thinking that, too.' Tyler got up to stretch his legs, and they began to walk the rows together. 'They both worked for Giambelli, both knew the family.' Tyler paused. 'Both knew Avano.'

'He was dead before Margaret uncorked the bottle. Still, we don't know how long she had it. He'd have had plenty of reason to want her out of the way.'

'Avano was an asshole,' Tyler said flatly. 'But I can't see him as a killer. Too much effort and not enough guts.' He stopped walking for a moment, his breath streaming out as he scanned the rows. It was colder now, edging down towards thirty. 'I'm not a suit, but I've got to figure all this trouble is costing the company plenty. If somebody wanted to cause trouble, they found a nasty way to do it.'

'Between the recall, immediate public panic and long-term consumer distrust in the label, it's going to cost millions.'

'I figure Sophia's smart enough to take the edge off long-term distrust.'

'She's going to have to be more than smart. She'll have to be brilliant.'

'She is. That's what makes her a pain in the ass.'

'Stuck on her, are you?' David waved the comment away. 'Sorry. Too personal.'

'I was wondering if you were asking as a corporate suit, an associate or as the guy who's dating her mother.'

'I was aiming towards friend.'

Tyler thought about it a moment, then nodded. 'OK, that works for me. I guess you could say I've been stuck on her on and off since I was twenty. Sophie at sixteen,' he remembered. 'Christ. She was like a lightning bolt. And she knew it. Irritated the hell out of me. I've always thought if you had to be stuck on a woman, which is an annoyance

426

itself, you might as well get stuck on one who's easy to be around and doesn't make you jumpy half the time. I put considerable effort into that theory the last ten years. Didn't do me a damn bit of good.'

'I can beat that,' David said after a moment. 'Yeah, I can beat it. I had a wife, and we had a couple of kids—good kids—and I figured we were chasing the American dream. Well, that went into the toilet. But I had the kids. Maybe I screwed up there a few times, but that's part of the job. And my focus was on the goal. Give them a decent life, be a good father. Women, well, being a good father doesn't mean being a monk. But no serious relationships, not again. No, sir, who needs it. Then Pilar opens the door, and she's holding flowers. There are all kinds of lightning bolts.'

'Women, they fry your brain.'

Together in companionable silence, they walked the rows in the coldest hour before dawn, while the sprinklers hissed and the vines glittered.

Two hundred and fifty guests, a seven-course dinner, each with appropriate wines, followed by a concert in the ballroom and ending with dancing. It had been a feat to pull off, and Sophia gave her mother full marks. She added a pat on the back for herself for carefully salting the guests with recognisable names and faces from all over the globe. The United Nations, she thought as she sat with every appearance of serenity through the aria by the Italian soprano, had nothing on the Giambellis.

And the quarter of a million dollars raised for charity would not only do good work, it was damn good PR. Particularly since all four generations of the family were there. Unity, responsibility, tradition, all bound together by blood, wine, and the vision of one man, Cezare Giambelli, the simple farmer who'd built an empire on sweat and dreams.

'You're not paying attention.' Tyler gave her a quick elbow jab. 'If I have to, you have to.'

She leaned towards him slightly. 'I hear every note. And I can write mental copy at the same time. Two different parts of the brain.'

'Your brain has too many parts. How long does this last?'

The pure, rich notes throbbed on the air. 'She's magnificent. And nearly finished. She's singing of tragedy, of heartbreak.'

'I thought it was supposed to be about love.'

'Same thing. You're such a peasant.' She linked her fingers with his, allowed herself to think of nothing but the music.

When the last note shimmered into silence, she rose, along with the others, into thunderous applause.

'Can we get out of here now?' Ty whispered in her ear.

'You go,' she said under her breath. 'I need to play hostess.'

She watched him escape, then moved forward, hands extended. *'Signora, bellissima!'*

It looked like socialising, but it was work. Putting on the confident front, answering questions from interested guests and the invited press, expressing sorrow and outrage.

'Sophia! Lovely, lovely event.'

'Thank you, Mrs Elliot. I'm so glad you could attend.'

'Wouldn't have missed it. You know our restaurant contributes generously to homeless shelters.'

And your restaurant, Sophia thought as she made appropriate noises, cancelled its standing order on all Giambelli and MacMillan labels at the first sign of trouble. 'Perhaps we could work together on a fund-raiser. Food and wine, after all, the perfect marriage.'

'Blake and I couldn't be more sorry about your recent troubles, Sophia, but business is business. We have to protect our clientele.'

'As do we. Giambelli stands by its product. Any of us at any time can be the victim of tampering and sabotage.'

'Be that as it may, Sophia, until we're assured the Giambelli label is clean, we can't and won't serve it. I'm sorry, dear, but that's the reality. Excuse me.'

Sophia marched directly to a waiter, took a glass of red, and, turning a slow circle in case anyone was watching, drank deeply.

'You look a little stressed.' Helen hugged an arm round Sophia's shoulders, squeezing hard. 'Sophie, you're trembling.'

'I'm just angry. And scared,' she admitted. 'Aunt Helen, I poured money into this event. Money, given the situation, I should have been more careful with. The Elliots aren't going to budge.'

'My dear, I know things are shaky now, but I've talked with a number of people tonight who're solidly behind you, who are appalled by what happened.'

'Yes, and some of them may even be swayed to put their money where their sentiments are. But there are more, too many more, who won't. I had reports from the waiting staff that a number of guests are avoiding the wine or watching others drink it, and live, first. It's horrible. And such a strain on Nonna. I'm starting to see it, and that worries me.'

'Sophie, when a company's been in business a hundred years, it has crises. This is just one of them.'

'We've never had anything like this. We're losing accounts, Aunt Helen.

We're the victims here. Why can't people see that? We're *still* being attacked—financially, emotionally, legally. The police . . . For God's sake, there are rumours drifting around that Margaret and my father were in some sort of conspiracy together, and Mama knew.'

'Just Rene's blathering.'

'Yes, but if the police start taking it seriously . . .'

'Now, you listen. The police may look, but only to eliminate.' She patted Sophia's back, grateful that attorney-client privilege with Tereza prevented her from adding to the girl's fears.

Just that morning, all company financial records had been subpoenaed.

Tiny flowering buds, bursting open as the lengthening days bathed them in sunlight, covered the vines. The earth was turned, opened to hold the promise of new plantings. Trees held their spring leaves in tight fists of stingy green, but here and there sprouts, brave and young, speared out of the ground.

April, Tereza thought, meant rebirth. And work. And hope that winter was over at last.

'The Canada geese are about to hatch,' Eli told her as they took their morning walk.

She nodded. From her father she had learned to watch the sky, the birds, the ground, as much as she watched the vines. 'It'll be a good year. We had plenty of winter rain.'

'I think we've timed the new plantings well.'

She looked over the rise of land to where the ground was well ploughed. She'd given fifty acres for the new plantings, vines of European origin grafted to native rootstock. They'd chosen prime varieties—cabernet sauvignon, merlot, chenin blanc—and, consulting with Tyler, had done much the same on MacMillan ground. 'We'll have been together a quarter of a century, Eli, when we see them bear fruit.'

'Tereza'—he took her shoulders, turned her to face him, and she felt a shiver of alarm—'this is my last harvest.'

'Eli—'

'I'm not going to die.' To reassure her, he ran his hands down her arms. 'But I want to retire. I've been thinking of it since you and I travelled to Italy. We've let ourselves become too rooted here. Let's do this last planting, you and I, and let our children harvest. It's time.'

'We talked of this. Five years or so, we said, before we stepped aside. A gradual process.'

'I know. But these last months have reminded me how quickly a life, even a way of life, can end. There are places I want to see. With you, Tereza. I'm tired of living to each season's demands.'

'My life, the whole of it, has been Giambelli. Eli, how can we pass something to our children that's blighted?'

'Because we trust them. Because they've earned the chance.'

'I don't know what to say.'

'Think about it. I want to give Ty what he's earned while I'm alive. There's been enough death this year.' He looked over the buds to the new plantings. 'It's time to let things grow.'

Maddy read the note stuck on the refrigerator and grimaced:

> *We're getting a home-cooked meal tonight. Pilar's cooking. I don't know what's on the menu, but you will like it. I'll be home by six. Until then, try to pretend you're human children and not the mutants I won in a poker game. Love, Dad*

Why did they have to have company? Did he really think she and Theo were so brain-damaged they'd believe a woman came over and fiddled around in a guy's kitchen just to cook?

Please.

Taking the note, she jogged upstairs. Theo was already in his room, ruining his eardrums with the music up to scream.

'Ms Giambelli's fixing dinner.'

'What?'

'The woman Dad's sleeping with is coming to fix dinner.'

'Yeah?' Theo's voice brightened. 'Like, on the stove?'

'Don't you get it?' Disgusted, Maddy waved the note. 'It's a tactic. She's trying to squeeze in.'

'Hey, anybody wants to squeeze into the kitchen who can actually cook is fine with me. What's she making?'

'It doesn't *matter* what she's making. How can you be so slow? She's showing him what a big, happy family we can be.'

'Get off it, Maddy. I mean—Dad's entitled to have a girlfriend.'

'Moron. I don't care if he's got ten girlfriends. What are we going to do if he decides he wants a wife?'

Theo considered it. 'I dunno. Ms Giambelli's cool.'

'"I dunno,"' she mocked. 'She'll start changing the rules, start taking over. She's not going to care about us. It'll all have to be her way.'

Maddy stomped to her room, slammed the door. She intended to stay there until her father got home.

She made it an hour.

Maddy could hear the music, the laughter. Something smelt really good, and that was just another strike against Pilar. She was just showing off, that was all. Making some big, fancy dinner.

When she walked into the kitchen, she had to grit her teeth. Theo was at the kitchen table, banging on his electric keyboard while Pilar stood at the stove.

'Hi, Maddy.' Pilar turned, set down her spoon.

She didn't answer. She opened the refrigerator, took her time selecting a soft drink. 'What's this gunk in here?'

'Depends. There's cheese gunk for the manicotti. The other's a marinade for the antipasto. Your father tells me you like Italian food.'

'I'm not eating carbs today. Anyway, I made plans to go to a friend's house for dinner.'

'Oh, that's too bad.' Casually Pilar got out a bowl to mix the filling for tiramisu. 'Your father didn't mention it.'

'He doesn't have to tell you everything.'

It was the first directly rude comment the girl had made to her. Pilar calculated the barriers were down. 'He certainly doesn't, and you're old enough to eat where you like. Theo, would you excuse us?'

'Sure.' He grabbed his keyboard, sent Maddy a disgusted look.

'Why don't we sit down?'

Maddy's insides felt sticky. She sat with a look of boredom. Pilar poured herself a demitasse of the espresso she'd brewed for the tiramisu, sat across from Maddy at the table, and sipped.

'I don't expect you to throw out the welcome mat for me, Maddy, but I'm hoping you won't lock the door in my face.'

Maddy frowned. 'Why do you care what I do?'

'Couple of reasons. I like you. I imagine if I wasn't involved with your father, we'd get along very well. But I'm taking his time and attention away from you. I'd say I was sorry about that, but we'd both know it wasn't true. Because I'm in love with him.'

'My mother loved him, too. Enough to marry him.'

'I'm sure she did. She—'

'No! You're going to make all the excuses, all the reasons why. And they're all bull. When it wasn't just exactly the way she wanted, she left us. We didn't matter.'

Her first instinct, always, was to comfort. Console. There were a dozen things she could say to soothe, but this little girl with wet, defiant eyes wouldn't hear them.

Why should she? Pilar decided.

'No, you're right. You didn't matter enough.' Pilar wanted to reach out, to draw this young girl close. But it wasn't the way, or the time. 'I know what it's like not to matter enough. I do, Maddy,' she said firmly, laying her hand over the girl's before she could jerk away. 'How sad and angry it makes you feel, how the questions and doubts and wishes run through your head in the middle of the night.'

'Adults can come and go whenever they want. Kids can't.'

'That's right. But your father didn't leave. You mattered to him. You and Theo matter most to him. You know that nothing I could say or do or be will change that.'

'Other things could change. And when one thing does, others do. It's cause and effect.'

'Well, I can't promise you that things won't change. Things do. People do. But right now your father makes me happy. And I make him happy.'

'He was my father first,' Maddy said in a fierce whisper.

'And he'll be your father last. Always. If I wanted to change that, if I wanted for some reason to ruin that, I couldn't. Don't you know how much he loves you? You could make him choose. Look at me, Maddy. Look at me,' she said quietly and waited for the girl's gaze to lift. 'If it's what you want so much, you could make him choose between you and me. I wouldn't have a chance. I'm asking you to give me one. If you can't, just can't, I'll make an excuse and be out of here before he gets home.'

Maddy wiped a tear off her cheek as she stared across the table. 'Why?'

'Because I don't want to hurt him, either.'

Maddy sniffled, frowned. 'Can I taste that?'

Pilar silently slid her espresso towards the girl. She wrinkled her nose, but lifted the cup and tasted.

'It's horrible. How can anybody drink that?'

'An acquired taste, I guess. You'd like it better in the tiramisu.'

'Maybe.' Maddy pushed the cup back across the table. 'I guess I'll give it a chance.'

'Oh no.' David laid a hand over Pilar's before she could stack the dishes. 'House rule: He who cooks, cleans not.'

'I see. Well, that's a rule I can get behind.'

'Another house rule. Dad gets to delegate. Theo and Maddy will be delighted to do the dishes.'

'Figures.' Maddy heaved a sigh. 'What do you get to do?'

432

'I get to work off some of this excellent meal by taking the chef for a walk.' Testing the waters with his kids, he leaned in and kissed Pilar warmly. 'That work for you?'

'Hard to complain.'

She went with him, pleased to be out in the spring night. 'That's a lot of mess to leave two teenagers to handle.'

'Builds character.'

He turned her into his arms, drawing her closer when she lifted her mouth to his. A long, slow thrill rippled through him. 'Haven't had much time to be together lately. I look out of my window some nights, across the fields, and see your light. I want to tell you not to worry, but until this is settled, you will. We all will.'

She rested her head on his shoulder. 'If it helps, I feel better knowing you're so close.'

'Pilar, there're some problems in the Italian offices. Some discrepancies in the figures that turned up during the audit. I might have to go over for a few days.'

'The kids can stay at the villa while you're gone, David. You don't have to worry about that.'

'No.' Tereza had already decreed that his children would be guests of the villa during his travel. 'But I don't like leaving you. Come with me.'

'Oh, David.' There was a rush of excitement at the thought. 'I'd love that. But you'd do what you have to do faster and easier if I was here with your children.'

'Do you have to be practical?'

'I don't want to be,' she said softly. 'I'd love to say yes, to feel young, foolish, ridiculously happy.' She turned in a circle. 'To make love with you in one of those huge old beds in the *castello*. When all this is over, ask me again.'

Something was different about her, more free.

'Why don't I ask you now? Go with me to Venice when this is over.'

'Yes.' She gripped his hands. 'I love you, David.'

He went very still. 'What did you say?'

'I'm in love with you. I'm sorry, it's too much, too fast, but—'

'This is handy. Very handy.' He lifted her into his arms and spun her round. 'I had figured it was going to take at least another two months before I could make you fall in love with me, which was tough, because I was already in love with you.'

She pressed her cheek to his. Her heart glowed with the joy of it. 'What did you say?'

433

'Let me paraphrase. I love you, Pilar. One look at you, and I started to believe in second chances.' He brought her close and kissed her. 'You're mine.'

Venice wasn't a city to be wasted on meetings with lawyers and accountants. Venice was a woman, *la bella donna*, elegant in her age, sensual in her watery curves, mysterious in her shadows. The sight of her, rising over the Grand Canal with her colours tattered and faded like old ball gowns, called to his blood.

He wished he could stroll the ancient streets and bridges with Pilar and buy her some ridiculous trinket. Watch Theo inhale a *gelato* like water, listen to Maddy interrogate some hapless gondolier over the history and architecture of the canals.

Still, the accountant was droning on. In Italian.

'*Scusi.*' David held up a hand, flipped a page of a report an inch thick. 'I wonder if we might go over this area again.'

'The numbers,' the Italian said, switching out of compassion to English, 'do not match.'

'Yes, I see. They don't match in a number of departmental expenditures. Across the board. This perplexes me, signore, but I'm more perplexed by the activities attributed to the Cardianili account. Orders, shipments, breakage, salaries, expenses—all very clearly recorded.'

'*Sì.* In that area the figures are correct.'

'Apparently. However, there is no Giambelli client by that name, no Cardianili.'

The accountant blinked. 'There is a mistake?'

'Of course there's a mistake.' David swivelled in his chair. 'Signore, have you studied the documents I gave you?'

'I have,' the accountant said.

'And the name of the executive in charge of this account?'

'Listed as Anthony Avano.'

'And the invoices, the expense chits were signed by Anthony Avano?'

'They were. Until December of last year. After that time it is Margaret Bowers's signature that appears in the file.'

'We'll need to have those signatures verified as genuine. And the signature approving the shipments, expenditures and payments on the account. Donato Giambelli.'

'Signore Cutter, I will have the signatures verified and advise you of your recourse when you have contacted La Signora herself. This is a delicate matter.'

'**D**on, thanks for coming in. Sorry to keep you waiting.'

'You made it sound important, so I made time.' Donato Giambelli stepped into David's office. 'If I'd been informed before you made your travel arrangements, I would have cleared my calendar so that I could have shown you Venice.'

'The arrangements were made quickly. I look forward to seeing the *castello*, though. Have a seat.'

'If you let me know when you plan to go, I'll escort you. I go there myself, regularly, to make certain all is as it should be.' He sat, folded his hands. 'Now, what can I do for you?'

'You could explain the Cardianili account.'

Don's face went blank. 'I don't understand.'

'Neither do I,' David said pleasantly. 'That's why I'm asking you to explain it.'

'Ah, well, David, you give my memory too much credit. I can't remember every account. Give me time to pull files—'

'Oh, I already have them.' David tapped a finger on a file on his desk. 'Your signature appears on a number of expense chits.'

'My signature appears on many such account papers.' Don was beginning to sweat visibly. 'I can hardly remember all of them.'

'This one should stick out. As it doesn't exist. There is no Cardianili account, Donato. There's considerable paperwork generated for it, a great deal of money involved. Invoices and expenses, but no account. No man by the name of'—he drew out a sheet of Giambelli letterhead— 'Giorgio Cardianili, with whom you appear to have corresponded several times. He doesn't exist, nor does the Rome warehouse to which wine was shipped. This warehouse, where you, on company expense, travelled to on business twice in the last eight months, isn't there. How would you explain that?'

'I don't understand.' Donato sprang to his feet, but he didn't look outraged. He looked terrified. 'What are you accusing me of?'

'At the moment, nothing. I'm asking you to explain this file.'

'I have no explanation. I don't know of this file, this account.'

'Then how is it your signature appears in it? How is it your expense account was charged more than ten million lire in connection with this account?'

'A forgery.' Donato snatched the letterhead. 'Someone uses me to steal money from La Signora, from *la famiglia*.' His hand shook as he thumped it against his heart. 'I'll look into this immediately.'

'You have forty-eight hours.'

'You would dare? You would dare give me such an ultimatum when someone steals from my family?'

'The ultimatum comes from La Signora. In the meantime, all activity on this account is frozen. Two days from now, all paperwork is to be turned over to the police.'

'The police?' Don went white. 'This is ridiculous. It's obviously an internal problem of some kind. We don't want an outside investigation, the publicity—'

'La Signora wants results. Whatever the cost.'

'With Tony as account executive, it's easy to see the problem.'

'Indeed, but I didn't identify Avano as the account exec.'

'Naturally I assumed . . . A major account.'

'I didn't qualify Cardianili as major. Take your two days,' David said quietly. 'And think of your wife and children. La Signora will be more likely to show compassion if you stand up for what's been done, and stand up for your family.'

'Don't tell me what to do about my family. About my position. I've been with Giambelli all my life. I *am* Giambelli. I want that file.'

'You're welcome to it.' David ignored the outstretched hand. 'In forty-eight hours.'

Donato was not innocent, David thought as he crossed St Mark's Square. He had his arm in the muck up to his elbow, but he hadn't put the scam together. Avano, possibly. Quite possibly, though the amount skimmed under his name was petty cash next to what Donato had raked in.

And Avano had been dead four months.

He moved towards one of the tables out on the pavement. He sat, and for a time simply watched the flood of tourists pour across the stones, in and out of the cathedral.

Avano had been milking the company, he thought. That was a given. But what David now carried in his briefcase took things to another level. Donato stepped it all up to fraud.

And Margaret? There was nothing to indicate participation in any skimming prior to her promotion. Had she turned so quickly? Or had she learned of the false account and that knowledge had led to her death?

Whatever the explanation, Donato Giambelli would have to be replaced. The investigation would have to continue until all leaks were plugged. David's own time in Italy would likely be extended, and at a point in his life where he wanted and needed to be home.

He ordered a glass of wine, checked the time, then took out his cell-phone. 'Maria? This is David Cutter. Is Pilar available?'

'One moment, Mr Cutter.'

He tried to imagine where she was in the house, what she was doing. It was easier, he found, to imagine her sitting across from him while the light dimming towards dusk struck the dome of the cathedral like an arrow, and the air filled with the flurry of pigeons on the wing.

'David?'

The fact that she was a little breathless made him smile. She'd hurried. 'I was just sitting here, in St Mark's Square.' He picked up the glass of wine the waiter brought him, sipped. 'Drinking an interesting little Chianti and thinking of you.'

'Is there music?'

'A small orchestra across the plaza, playing American show tunes. Sort of spoils the moment.'

'Not at all. Not for me.'

'How are the kids?'

'Maddy came out to the greenhouse yesterday and gave me a lesson on photosynthesis. Theo broke up with his girlfriend.'

'Julie?'

'Julie was last winter, David. Keep up. Carrie. He moped for about ten minutes. He's sworn off girls and intends to dedicate his life to his music. How's everything there?'

'Better now, for talking to you. Will you tell the kids I'll call them tonight? I'll make it about six your time.'

'All right. You don't know when you might be coming home?'

'Not yet. There are some complications. I miss you, Pilar.'

'I miss you, too. Drink your wine, listen to the music. I'll think of you there.'

'I'll think of you here, too. Bye.'

When he hung up, he lingered over the wine. Talking to Pilar about his children that way connected them, made them almost like family. And that, he realised, was what he wanted. He wanted a family again.

On an unsteady breath, he set down his wine. He wanted Pilar to be his wife. Too fast? he wondered. Too much?

No. No, it wasn't.

He got to his feet, tossed some lire on the table.

Why should he waste another minute? What better place to buy a ring for the woman he loved than in Venice.

He climbed the stairs on the packed Rialto bridge, where the stores were cheek by jowl above the water. He bumped his way past stalls offering leather goods and T-shirts. Shop windows ran like rivers with gold and gems. A dazzle that confused the eye.

Then he turned, looked into one more window. And saw it.

The ring was set with five stones, all in delicate heart shapes that made a quiet stream of colour. Five stones, one for each of them and their children. He imagined the blue was sapphire, the red ruby, the green emerald. The purple and the gold he wasn't sure of. What did it matter? It was perfect.

Thirty minutes later he walked out, the ring tucked in his pocket, engraved with the date he'd bought it. He wanted her to know, always, that he'd found it on the evening he'd sat in Campo San Marco while the light went soft, talking to her.

He ducked under the awning of a pavement trattoria, ordered the turbot, a half-carafe of the house white, and idled his way through the meal. He smiled sentimentally at a couple obviously honeymooning, enjoyed the little boy who escaped from his parents to charm the waiters. It was, he supposed, a typical reaction of a man in love that he'd find everyone and everything a simple delight.

Most of the squares were empty as he headed back across the city. Now and then he saw the little beam of light from a gondola carrying tourists down a side canal. He crossed another bridge, walked through the shadows of another twisting street. He glanced up when light poured out of a window above him, and smiled as a young woman began to draw in the washing that fluttered faintly in the breeze. She was singing, and the cheerful bell of her voice rang into the empty street. She caught his eye, laughed, a sound full of fun and flirtation.

David stopped, turned, intending to call a greeting up to her. And in doing so, likely saved his own life.

He felt the pain, a sudden, horrendous fire in the shoulder. Heard, dimly, a kind of muffled explosion.

Then he was falling, falling forever until he lay bleeding and unconscious on the cool cobbles of the Venetian street.

'You're a very lucky man, Mr Cutter.'

David tried to focus. Whatever drugs the doctors had pumped into him were strong. He wasn't feeling any pain, but he was hard-pressed to feel anything. 'It's difficult to agree with you at the moment. I'm sorry, I've forgotten your name.'

'DeMarco. I'm Lieutenant DeMarco. Your doctor says you need rest, of course. But I have just a few questions. Perhaps if you tell me what you remember?'

He remembered a pretty woman drawing in the washing, and the way the lights glimmered on the water, on the stones. 'I was walking,' he began, then struggled to sit up. 'Pilar's ring. I bought a ring.'

'Calm yourself. I have the ring, your wallet, your watch.'

DeMarco was a little dumpy, a little bald, with a luxurious black moustache and precise English.

'Did you see who shot you?'

'No.' David grimaced. 'I must've passed out.'

'What is your business in Venice?'

'I'm chief operating officer for Giambelli-MacMillan.'

'Ah. You work for La Signora.'

'I do.'

'Do you know anyone in Venice who might wish you harm?'

'No.' As soon as he denied it, he thought of Donato. 'No,' he repeated. 'I don't know anyone who'd shoot me down on the street. You said you had my valuables, Lieutenant. The ring I bought, my wallet, my watch. My briefcase.'

'No briefcase was found.' DeMarco sat back. 'What were the contents of this briefcase?'

'Papers from the office,' David said, and shut his eyes.

It was difficult, Tereza thought, to stand up under so many blows. Under such constant assault, the spirit began to wilt. She kept her spine straight as she walked with Eli into the family parlour. She knew the children were there, waiting for the call from their father.

Innocence, she mused as she looked in to see Maddy sprawled on the sofa with her nose in a book, and Theo banging away on the piano. Why did innocence have to be stolen this way?

She gave Eli's arm a squeeze, then stepped inside.

Pilar glanced up from her needlework. One look at her mother and her heart froze. The embroidery hoop slid out of her hands as she got slowly to her feet. 'Mama?'

'Please sit. Theo.' She gestured to quieten him. 'Maddy. First I must tell you, your father is all right.'

'What happened?' Maddy rolled off the couch. 'Something happened to him. That's why he hasn't called. He's never late calling.'

'He was hurt, but he's all right. He's in the hospital.'

'An accident?' Pilar stepped up, laid a hand on Maddy's shoulder.

When previously the girl would have shrugged her off, she merely clung tighter.

'No, not an accident. He was shot.'

'Shot?' Theo shoved himself away from the piano. 'That's wrong. That's a mistake. Dad doesn't go around getting himself shot.'

'Listen to me.' Eli moved forward, took Maddy's hand, then Theo's. 'We wouldn't tell you he was all right if he wasn't. I know you're scared, and you're worried, and so are we. But the doctor was very clear. Your father's healthy and strong. He's going to make a full recovery.'

'I want him to come home.' Maddy's lip trembled. 'Just make him come home, OK?' She walked into Pilar's arms and felt better for crying there.

Over Eli's and Pilar's objections, Tereza Giambelli had allowed David's children to attend the emergency meeting. They had a right to know why their father had been hurt.

She smiled at them as she took her place behind her desk. 'With his doctor's approval your father will fly home in just a few days. Meanwhile, I've talked to the man in charge of the police investigation. There were witnesses. They have a description of the assailant. I don't know that they'll find him or that he particularly matters.'

'How can you say that?' Maddy jerked up in her chair. Her eyes were dry now. Raw and dry. 'He shot my father.'

Approving the reaction, Tereza spoke to her as she would to an equal. 'Because I believe he was hired to do so, as one buys and uses any tool. To take away papers in your father's possession. It became clear earlier today, through David's work, that my nephew, Donato, has been funnelling money from the company into a dummy account.'

'Donato.' Sophia felt a sharp pinch in the heart. 'Stealing from you?'

'From us. He had a meeting with David, on my orders, this afternoon in Venice and would have realised his actions would soon be uncovered. This was his response. My family's caused your pain,' she said to Theo and Maddy. 'I'm head of the family and responsible for that pain.'

Theo clenched his teeth. 'It's Donato's fault, not yours. Is he in jail?'

'No. They've yet to find him. It appears he's run.' Disdain edged her voice. 'Left his wife and his children. But I promise you he will be found; he will be punished.'

'You'll need someone in Venice to clear this up.' Sophia rose. 'I'll leave tonight.'

'I won't put another of mine in danger.'

'Nonna, if Donato was using an account to skim funds, he had help.

440

My father. It's my blood,' she continued in Italian, 'as much as yours. You can't deny my right to make amends.' She took a breath, switched to English. 'I'll leave tonight.'

'Hell'—Tyler scowled—'we'll leave tonight.'

'I don't need a baby sitter.'

'Yeah, right.' He lifted his gaze now, met hers with chilled steel. 'We've got an equal stake in this, Giambelli. You go, I go.'

'Agreed.' Tereza ignored Sophia's hissing breath. 'Your mother will worry less if you are not alone.'

'Mama,' Pilar said, 'Gina and her children?'

'They'll be provided for. I don't believe in the sins of the father.' Tereza shifted her gaze to Sophia's, held it. 'I believe in the child.'

David was released from the hospital—or more accurately, he released himself. He was fed up with doctors, and even in Italy they couldn't seem to make hospital food palatable.

It wasn't easy manoeuvring through the crowded streets of Venice with one arm in a sling, and by the time he made it back to his rooms, his shoulder was screaming and his legs were unsteady. He found himself gasping for air and leaning limply on the wall outside his door as he fought left-handed to work his key into the lock. The door jerked open. 'There you are!' Sophia jammed her hands on her hips. 'Are you out of your mind? Checking yourself out of the hospital, wandering around Venice by yourself. Look at you, pale as a sheet. Men are such morons.'

'Thanks. Mind if I come in? I think this is still my place.'

'Ty's out hunting for you right now.' She took his good arm and helped him inside. 'We've been worried to death since we went to the hospital and found out you'd left, against doctor's orders.'

He sank into a chair. 'What did you do, beam yourselves here?'

'We left last night. I've been travelling on very little sleep, so don't mess with me.' She uncapped a bottle.

'What is that?'

'Pain medication. You left the hospital without your prescription.' She stalked to the mini-fridge for a bottle of water. 'David, I'm so sorry about this.'

'Yeah. Me, too. The kids are OK, right?'

She handed over the bottle. 'They're fine. Worried about you, but re-assured enough that Theo's starting to think it's pretty cool that you got shot. And Maddy said something about keeping the bullet. According to my mother, she wants to study it.'

'That's my girl. Sophie, is Pilar all twisted up about this?'

'Of course she is. Come on, let's get you into bed.'

He leaned heavily on Sophia as she led him to the bedroom.

When Tyler got back, she was making minestrone. It knocked him back a step to see her working in the kitchen.

'He's here,' she said without looking round. 'Sleeping.'

'I told you he could take care of himself.'

'Yes. He did a wonderful job of that by getting shot, didn't he? Stay away from that soup,' she added as he leaned over the pot. 'It's for David.'

'There's enough for everybody.'

'It's not done yet. You should drive up to the vineyard. You can stay at the *castello* tonight. I'm having files messengered over. I can work on the computer here.'

'Well, you worked all that out, didn't you?'

'We're not here to sightsee.' She walked out of the kitchen.

He took a moment to make sure his temper was on a leash, then followed her into the small office. 'Why don't we just have this out? I know why you didn't want me to come.'

'Really?' She booted up the computer. 'Could it be that I have a great deal of work to do in a short amount of time?'

'It could be that you're feeling pissed off, betrayed, hurt. Those things slice at you. And when you're hurt, you're vulnerable. You're afraid I'll get too close.' He took her chin so that she had no choice but to look at him. 'You don't want me too close, do you, Sophia?'

'I'd say we've been as close as it gets. And it was my idea.'

'Sex is easy. Don't try to boil everything down to that.'

Moving too fast, she thought. Too many things with too much speed. If she wasn't at the wheel, how could she maintain the right direction? 'Anything else is too much trouble.'

'Maybe that's part of the problem.' He strode to the door. 'I'll be back.'

She frowned after him. 'Don't rush on my account.'

Why didn't the man ever do what she expected him to do?

They'd acted on some pure, healthy animal lust. Had some stupendous sex. She'd expected him to cool off in that area, but no.

And what if it was true that she was a little worried because she didn't show any signs of cooling off, either? She'd never had any intention of developing serious feelings for Tyler MacMillan.

It was infuriating to know she had.

Worse, he'd been exactly right in his run-down of her. She was pissed off, she did feel betrayed, she was feeling vulnerable, and she wished Tyler was 6,000 miles away in California. Because she wanted so desperately for him to be right here. Within easy leaning distance.

She wasn't going to lean. Her family was a mess. The company she'd been raised to run was in trouble.

But she wasn't going to lean.

Donato was sweating like a pig. The terrace doors were wide-open, and the cool air rising off Lake Como swept into the room, but it didn't stop the sweat. Only turned it to ice.

He'd waited until his lover was asleep before he'd crept out of bed and into the adjoining parlour. She'd been thrilled with the trip, with his sweeping her away to the elegant resort on the lake, something he'd promised dozens of times in the past. He'd made a game of it, given her a ridiculous amount of cash so she could charge the room to her credit card.

He thought that had been clever. Very clever. Until he'd seen the news report. Seen his own face. He could only be grateful his mistress had been in the salon.

But they couldn't stay. Someone would recognise him.

He needed help and knew only one source. His hands shook horribly as he dialled the United States. 'It's Donato.'

'I expected it would be.' The man glanced at his watch. Giambelli had the 3.00am sweats, he thought. 'You've been a very busy boy, Don.'

'They think I shot David Cutter.'

'Yes, I know.'

'I didn't. I can prove it,' he whispered desperately.

'Can you? The story I get is you hired a trigger.'

'Hired a . . . What is this? They say I hired someone to shoot him? The damage was done. You said so yourself.'

'Here's how I look at it.' Oh, it was getting better, sweeter than he'd ever imagined. 'You killed two people, probably three with Avano. David Cutter, what's one more?'

'I need help. I have to get out of the country. I have money, but not enough. I need a—a—a passport, a new name.'

'That all sounds very reasonable, Don, but why tell me? You overestimate my reach and my interest in you. Let's consider this conversation a severing of our business association.'

'You can't do this. If they take me, they take you.'

'Oh, I don't think so. There's no way to connect me to you. I've made sure of that. If I were you, I'd hit the road and hit it fast.'

He hung up, poured himself a glass of wine, and lit a cigar for good measure. Then he picked up the phone and called the police.

It irritated her. He'd caught her off guard and when her brain was still mushy from a sleepless night. With indisputable logic he had persuaded her to drive north to spend a day or two working out of the *castello*. With him.

It irked as she recognised how petty it was for her to sulk in silence on the drive. And it added one more layer of temper that he seemed so sublimely unconcerned.

'We're taking separate bedrooms,' she announced. 'It's time we put the brakes on that area of our relationship.'

'OK.'

She'd already opened her mouth to skewer him, and his carelessly agreeable response had it hanging slack. 'Fine,' she managed.

'Fine. You know, we're weeks ahead in the growing season back home. Talked to the operator yesterday. They're seeing the beginnings of new bloom. Keeps up warm, we'll get a normal set. That's the conversion of flower to grape.'

'I know what a set is,' she said between her teeth.

'Just making conversation.'

He turned off the highway and started the drive through the gentle hills. 'It's pretty country. I guess it's been a few years since I made the trip over. Never seen it this early in the spring.'

She had, but had nearly forgotten. The quiet green of the hills, the pretty contrast of colourful houses, the long, sleek rows riding the slopes, fields of sunflowers waiting for summer, and the far-off mountains that were a faint smudge against a blue sky.

The crowds of Venice were miles from this little heart of Italy that pumped steadily, fed by the earth and rain.

She saw the winery—the original stone structure and its various additions. Her great-great-grandfather had placed the first stones. Then his son had added more, then his son's daughter. One day, she thought, she might place her own. On the rise, with the fields spreading out like skirts, the *castello* ruled, gracious and grand with its colonnaded façade, its sweep of balconies, its high arching windows.

Cezare Giambelli had fought, she thought. Not just for the ledgers, not only for the profit. For the land. For the name. It struck her here, more deeply than in the fields at home, more than within the walls of her offices. Here, where one man changed his life and, by doing so, forged hers.

Tyler stopped so the car faced the house, its entrance gardens in young bud. 'Great place,' he said simply, climbing out of the car.

She got out more slowly, breathing in the sight of it as much as she breathed in the lightly scented air. Vines spilt over mosaic walls. An old pear tree bloomed wildly, shedding petals like snow. She remembered suddenly the taste of the fruit, sweet and simple, and how when she'd been a child, the juice had trickled down her throat.

'You wanted me to feel this,' she said, and with the bonnet of the car between them turned to him.

'Sophie'—he leaned on the bonnet, a friendly, companionable stance—'I think you feel all sorts of things. But I know some of them can get lost in the worry and the . . . well, the now. Focus too hard on the now, you lose sight of the big picture.'

'So you badgered me out of Venice so I'd see the big picture?'

'That's part of it. It's blooming time, Sophie. Whatever else is going on, you don't want to miss it.'

He walked back to the boot, popped it open.

'Is that a metaphor?' she asked as she joined him and plucked out her briefcase.

'Me, I'm just a farmer. What do I know about metaphors?' he said.

It was a long flight across an ocean, across a continent. David slept through most of it. He wanted home. And by the time he landed at the Napa airfield, he resented even the short drive that separated him from it.

Then he crossed the tarmac to where his driver was waiting.

'Dad!'

Theo and Maddy sprang from opposite doors of the limo. The rush of emotion had him lunging towards them. He grabbed Maddy with his good arm, then a line of pain spurted through his shoulder as he tried to hug Theo.

'Sorry, bad wing.'

When Theo kissed him, surprise and pleasure flustered him. He couldn't remember the last time this boy, this young man, had done so. 'God, I'm glad to see you.' He pressed his lips to his daughter's hair, leaned into his son. 'So glad to see you.'

'Don't ever do that again.' Maddy kept her face pressed against his chest. 'Not ever again.'

'That's a deal. Don't cry, baby. Everything's OK.'

Afraid he was going to blub, Theo cleared his throat. 'So did you bring us something?'

'You've heard of Ferraris?'

'Wow, Dad! I mean . . .' Theo looked towards the plane as if he expected to see a sleek Italian sports car unloaded.

'Just wondering if you'd heard of them. But I did pick up a couple things that fitted into my suitcases. And if you haul them like a good slave, we'll go car shopping this weekend.'

Theo's jaw dropped. 'No joke?'

'No Ferrari, but no joke. Let's get out of here and . . .' He looked back towards the car.

Pilar stood beside it, her hair blowing in the wind. As their eyes met, she began walking towards him. Then she was running.

Maddy watched her and took her first shaky step towards adulthood by moving aside.

'What's she crying for now?' Theo wanted to know as Pilar clung to his father and sobbed.

'Women wait until it's over before they cry, especially when it's important.' Maddy studied the way her father turned his face into Pilar's hair. 'This is important.'

An hour later he was on the living-room sofa being plied with tea. Maddy sat at his feet, her head resting on his knee while she toyed with the necklace he'd brought her from Venice. Theo was still wearing his new designer sunglasses, occasionally checking the mirror to admire his European cool.

'Well, I've got to get going.' Pilar leaned over the sofa, brushed her lips over David's hair. 'Welcome home.'

He might have been handicapped, but his good arm was quick enough. He grabbed her hand. 'What's your hurry?'

'You've had a long day. We're going to miss you guys over at the main house,' she said to Theo and Maddy. 'I hope you'll keep coming round.'

Maddy rubbed her cheek on David's knee. 'Dad, didn't you bring Ms Giambelli a present from Venice?'

'As a matter of fact.'

'Well, that's a relief.' Pilar gave his uninjured shoulder a squeeze. 'Give it to me tomorrow. You need to rest now.'

'I rested for six thousand miles. I can't handle any more tea. Would you mind taking that into the kitchen, and give me a minute here with the kids?'

'Sure. I'll call tomorrow, see how you're feeling.'

'Don't run off,' he said as she took the tray. 'Just wait.'

He shifted on the couch, tried to put words together. 'Listen, Theo, you want to sit down a minute.'

Obligingly, Theo plopped down on the couch. 'Can we look at convertibles? It'd be so cool to tool around with the top down. Chicks really dig on that.'

'Jeez, Theo. You don't score a convertible by telling him you're going to pick up girls. Anyway, shut up so Dad can tell us how he wants to ask Ms Giambelli to marry him.'

David's grin faded. 'How do you do that?' he asked. 'It's spooky.'

'It's just following logic. That's what you wanted to tell us, right?'

'I wanted to talk to you about it.'

'Dad'—Theo gave him a manly pat—'it's cool.'

'Thank you, Theo. Maddy?'

'When you have a family, you're supposed to stay with them. Sometimes people don't—' She shook her head. 'She'll stay because she wants to. That's better.'

A few minutes later he was walking Pilar home, across the edge of the vineyard. The moon was beginning its slow rise.

'Really, David, I know the way home, and you shouldn't be out in the evening air.'

'I need the exercise and a little time with you.'

'Maddy and Theo are going to need a lot of reassurance.'

'And how about you?'

She laced her fingers together with his. 'I'm feeling considerably steadier. I didn't mean to fall apart at the airport. I swore I wouldn't.'

'You want the truth? I liked it. It's good for the ego for a man to have a woman cry over him.'

He brought their joined hands to his lips. 'Remember that first night? I ran into you out here. Damn, you were gorgeous. And furious. Talking to yourself.'

'Sneaking a temper cigarette,' she remembered. 'And very embarrassed to have been caught at it by the new COO.'

'The new, fatally attractive COO.'

'Oh yes. That, too.'

He stopped, pulled her gently into an embrace. 'I wanted to touch you that night. Now I can.' He skimmed his fingers down her cheek. 'I love you, Pilar.'

'David. I love you, too.'

'I called you from St Mark's, talked to you while the music played and the light faded. Remember that?'

'Of course I do. It was the night you were—'

'Shh.' He laid a finger over her lips. 'I hung up and sat there thinking of you. And I knew.' He took the box out of his pocket.

She stepped back. Pressure dropped onto her chest, leaden weights of panic. 'Oh, David. Wait.'

'Don't put me off. Don't be rational; don't be reasonable. Just marry me.' He struggled a moment, then let out a frustrated laugh. 'Can't open the box. Give me a hand, will you?'

Starlight glittered on his hair, bright silver on deep gold. His eyes were dark, direct, and full of love and amusement. As her breath jerked, she could smell a hint of night jasmine and early roses. All so perfect, she thought. So perfect it terrified her.

'David, we've both been here before, both know it doesn't always work. You have children who've already been hurt.'

'We haven't been here together, and we both know that it takes two people who want to make it work. You won't hurt my kids, because as my odd and wonderful daughter told me, you won't stay because you're supposed to but because you want to. And that's better.'

Some of the weight lifted. 'She said that?'

'Yes. Theo, being a man of few words, told me it was cool.'

Her eyes wanted to blur, but she blinked tears away. It was a time for clear sight. 'You're going to buy him a car. He'd tell you anything you want to hear.'

'See why I love you? You've got him nailed.'

'David, I'm nearly fifty.'

'And?'

'And I . . .' Suddenly it felt foolish. 'I suppose I just had to say it one more time.'

'OK, you're old. Got it.'

'Not that much older than—' She broke off this time, blowing out a breath when he laughed. 'I can't think straight.'

'Good. Pilar, whatever your birth certificate says, I love you. I want to spend my life with you. So help me open this damn box.'

'I'll do it.' The pressure in her chest was gone, and a lightness took its place. 'It's beautiful.' She counted the stones, understood the symbol. 'It's perfect.'

He slid it onto her finger. 'That's what I thought.'

PART FOUR
THE FRUIT

TYLER WAS FILTHY, his back carried a nagging ache dead centre, and he had a nasty scrape across the knuckles of his left hand.

He was in heaven.

The mountains here weren't so different from the jagged outcroppings of his own California ranges. Where his soil was gravelly, this was rocky, but still high in the pH that would produce a soft wine.

Tyler strolled back through the rows towards the great house. He'd helped install new pipelines from the reservoir. It was a good system, well planned, and the hours he'd spent with the crew had given him a chance to casually question the men about Donato.

The language barrier wasn't as much of a problem as he'd anticipated. With the generous assistance of various interpreters, Tyler got a clear enough picture. There wasn't a man in the fields who considered Donato Giambelli more than a joke.

Shadows lengthened towards evening. In the garden, water spewed from a fountain guarded by Poseidon. The Italians, he thought, were big on their gods and their fountains. He passed between mosaic walls with bas-relief figures of well-endowed nymphs and walked down the steps circling a pond swimming with lily pads. From here he couldn't see the fields.

What could be seen, beyond the flowers, the sprawl of terraces, was the swimming pool. And rising out of it, like Venus, was Sophia. She wore a simple black suit that sleeked over her body like the water that streamed from it. Her hair was slicked back, and he could see the glint of something, probably diamonds, fire at her ears. Who but Sophia would swim wearing diamonds?

Watching her, he felt an uncomfortable combination of lust and longing as he walked towards her.

'Water must be cold.'

She went still, the towel she'd picked up concealing her face for an instant. 'It was. I wanted it cold.' Casually, she laid the towel aside and took her time slipping into a towelling robe.

She knew he looked at her, studied her in that thorough and patient way of his. She wanted him to.

'You're filthy, Ty.'

'Yeah. I could use a drink.'

'Honey, you could use a shower.'

'Both. Why don't I clean up? I'll meet you in the centre courtyard in an hour.'

'Why?'

'We'll open a bottle of wine and tell each other all about our day. There's a couple things I want to run by you.'

'All right, that suits me. I have a few things of my own to do.'

'Wear something pretty,' he called after her and grinned when she glanced back over her shoulder. 'Just because I'm not touching doesn't mean I don't like to look.'

He picked up the damp towel when she went into the house, breathed in the scent of her. Beauty, he thought, was rough on a man. No, he didn't want to tame her any more than he wanted to tame the land. But by God, it was time for acceptance, on both sides.

She was going to give him plenty to look at. Plenty to wish for. She was, after all, an expert at packaging. She wore blue, the colour of a lightning strike. The bodice dipped low, to frame the rising swell of her breasts; the skirt rose high to showcase the long, slim length of her thighs. She slipped into ice-pick heels, dabbed scent in all the right places and considered herself ready.

And looked at herself in the mirror.

Why was she so unhappy? The turmoil around her was upsetting, it was challenging, but it wasn't the cause of this gut-deep unhappiness. She was all right when she was working, but the minute she stopped, there it was. This dragging sadness, this flattening of the spirit.

And with it, she admitted, an anger she couldn't identify. She didn't even know whom she was angry with any more. Don, her father, herself. Ty.

She kept him waiting, but he'd expected that. The fact was, it gave him time to put everything in place. Candlelight speared up from the table. He'd chosen the wine—a soft, young white—and had begged some canapés from the kitchen staff.

He heard her footfalls on the tiles but didn't get up. Sophia, he thought, was too used to men springing to attention in her presence. Or falling at her feet.

'What's all this?'

He gestured to the chair beside him. 'Digging ditches put me in a good mood.' He handed her a glass, tapped his to it. '*Salute.*'

'Well, I did some digging of my own. The domestic staff's been very informative. I've learned Don made regular unreported visits.' She sighed. 'Apparently, there's a mistress.'

'They tell you about any other visitors?'

'Yes. My father, and the woman my father came with once—not Rene but Kris. And Jerry DeMorney. Jerry hated my father.'

'Why?'

'You really stay out of the loop, don't you?' she replied. 'A few years back my father had a blistering affair with Jerry's wife. It was fairly common knowledge. She left Jerry, or he kicked her out.'

'You didn't mention this before. What do you think of it now?'

'Now I see a crafty little quartet: Donato, my father, Kris, Jerry. Who was using whom, I can't say, but I think Jerry at least knows about the embezzlement, maybe even the tampering. He would have had access to the winery, and it would have been profitable for Le Coeur for Giambelli to be fighting public scandal. Add Kris in and you have my plans, my campaign, tossed in their lap. Corporate sabotage, spies—that's common enough in business.'

'Murder isn't.'

'No. Murder makes it personal. He could've killed my father. I can more easily see him with a gun in his hand than I can Donato.'

'What do you want to do about it?'

'Tell the police, here and at home. Tomorrow I'm going to Venice to give some interviews. I'll present Don as being a disgrace to the family, play up our shock, sorrow and regret, our unhesitating cooperation with the authorities in the hopes that he will be brought to justice quickly and spare his innocent wife, his young children, his grieving mother any more pain.'

She reached for the bottle to fill her glass again. 'You think that's cold and hard and just a little nasty.'

'No. I think it's hard on you. Hard to be the one saying those things, keeping your head up when you do. You've got your grandmother's spine, Sophie. What time are we leaving?'

'I don't need you for this.'

'Don't be stupid, it doesn't suit you. MacMillan is just as vulnerable as Giambelli. It'll play better in the press if we do this as a team. Family, company, partnership. Solidarity.'

'We leave at seven, sharp.'

'So let's change channels a while, move on to something pleasant.'

'Like wine and candlelight?' She leaned back, looked up at the sky. 'And stars.'

'Like I want to seduce you.'

She choked on her wine.

'I want to make love with you, starting out here, slow, and working our way in, upstairs into that great big bed in your room.'

'When I want you in my bed, you'll know it.'

'Exactly.' Taking his time, he rose, pulled her to her feet. 'You're really stuck on me, aren't you?'

'Stuck? Please. You'll embarrass yourself.'

'Crazy about me.' He slipped his arms round her, chuckling when she pushed against his chest. 'I saw you today, more than once, standing at the window looking at me.'

'I don't know what you're talking about. I might have looked out of the window.'

'Looking at me,' he continued, slowly drawing her against him. 'The way I was looking at you.' He nuzzled gently at her neck. 'The way I was wanting you. And more. There's more than the wanting between us. If it was just the heat, you wouldn't be so scared.'

'I'm not afraid of anything.'

'You don't need to be. I'm not going to hurt you.'

She shook her head, but his lips came down on hers. Unbearably kind and gentle. No, she thought as she softened against him, he wouldn't hurt her, but she was bound to hurt him.

'Ty.' She started to push at him again, and ended by gripping his shirt. She'd missed this, the warmth he brought into her. Those twisted sensations of risk and safety. 'This is a mistake.'

'It doesn't feel like one. You know what?' He lifted her into his arms. 'I think it's stupid to argue, especially when we both know I'm right.'

'Stop it. You're not carrying me into the house. The staff will gossip about it for weeks.'

'I figure they've already laid bets on how this was going to turn out.' He elbowed open a door. 'When we get home, I figure you should move in with me. Then it'll be nobody's business what we do.'

'Move—Move in with you? Have you lost your mind, Ty? Put me down!'

'You don't like it? OK, we'll do it this way.' He shifted, hauling her up and over his shoulder. 'Better?'

He walked into her bedroom, kicked the door shut behind him, and, still carrying her, lit the candles scattered through the room.

'Tyler, I can recommend a good therapist. There's absolutely no shame in seeking help for mental instability.'

'I'll keep it in mind. God knows I haven't been clear in the head since I got tangled up with you. We can make an appointment together, after you move in.'

'I'm not moving in with you.'

'Yes, you are.' He let her slide down until she was back on her feet and facing him. 'Because it's what I want.'

'If you think I give a single damn about what you want—'

'Because I'm as crazy about you as you are about me, and it's time we started dealing with it.'

'I'm sorry.' Her voice shook. 'I don't want this.'

'I'm sorry you don't want it, too. Because it's the way it is. Look at me.' He framed her face with his hands. 'I wasn't looking for this, either. Let's see where it takes us.'

He lowered his mouth to hers again. 'Just us.'

Just him, she thought. She wanted to believe it. To love someone and have it be strong and true. She wanted to believe in miracles.

His mouth was warm and firm on hers, patiently stirring desire. The steady, irresistible rise of passion was a relief. This she could trust, and this she could give.

She went with him willingly when he lowered her to the bed.

He kept the heat banked. This time there would be no mistaking this as anything other than an act of love. Generous, selfless and sweet. He linked his fingers with hers as he deepened the kiss, as he tasted the beginning of surrender on her lips. It was meant to be, here in the old bed in the *castello*, where it had all begun a century before. Another beginning, another dream. As he looked down at her, he knew it.

'Blooming time,' he said quietly. 'Ours.'

He undressed her slowly, watched the candlelight shimmer over her skin, listened to the way her breath caught, released, caught again when he touched her. Did she know the barriers between them were crumbling? He did; he felt them fall. And knew the precise moment her body yielded to her heart.

They seemed to sink into the bed like lovers in a pool. She gave herself to the sensations of those hard palms sliding over her, that persuasive mouth roaming where it pleased.

No one else, he thought as he lost himself in her. No one else had ever unlocked him this way. Once again he linked his hands with hers, holding tight. 'Sophie, I love you.'

Her breath caught. 'Ty, don't.'

He laid his lips on hers, the kiss gentle. Devastating. 'I love you.' He kept his eyes open and on hers. 'Tell me.'

'Ty.' Her heart quaked, seemed to spill over. Then her fingers curled strong to his. 'Ty,' she said, '*ti amo.*'

She met his mouth with hers and let him sweep her away.

Lieutenant DeMarco smoothed a fingertip along his moustache. 'I appreciate your coming in, signorina. The information you and Signore MacMillan bring me is interesting and will be looked into.'

'What exactly does that mean? Looked into. I'm telling you my cousin used the *castello* for assignations with his mistress and for clandestine meetings with a competitor and with an ex-employee.'

'None of which is illegal.' DeMarco spread his hands. 'Interesting, even suspicious, which is why I will look into it. However, the meetings were hardly clandestine, as many employees at the *castello* and at the vineyards were aware of them.'

'They weren't aware of Jeremy DeMorney's identity or his connection with Le Coeur. He is the great-grand-nephew of Le Coeur's current president. He's an ambitious man who had a grudge against my father.'

'And I have no doubt that the proper authorities will want to question this Jeremy DeMorney. My main concern is the apprehension of Donato Giambelli.'

'Who's eluded you for nearly a week,' Sophia pointed out.

'We learned the identity of his travelling companion only yesterday. Her credit card has several extensive charges. I am even now waiting for further information.'

'Of course he used her credit card,' Sophia said. 'He's smart enough to cover his tracks and to get out of Italy. Over the border into Switzerland, I'd imagine. The guards there barely look at a passport.'

'We are aware of this and the Swiss authorities are assisting us. It's only a matter of time.'

'Time is a valuable commodity. My family has suffered personally, emotionally and financially for months. If I have to hunt down Don myself, believe me, that's what I'll do.'

'You're impatient.'

'On the contrary, I've been remarkably patient.' She got to her feet. 'I need results.'

He held up a finger as the phone rang. His expression changed slightly as he listened to the stream of information. When he hung up, he folded his hands. 'You have your results. The Swiss police have just taken your cousin into custody.'

If Tyler knew his woman, and he did, they were going to be spending some time in the Alps.

He'd been taken from a tiny resort nestled in the mountains north of Chur, near the Austrian border. Now Donato was in a Swiss cell, bemoaning his fate. He had no money to hire a lawyer and desperately needed one to fight extradition for as long as possible. For as long as it took for him to think his way clear.

He would throw himself on the mercy of La Signora. He would escape and run to Bulgaria. He would convince the authorities he'd done nothing more than run off with his mistress.

He would rot in prison for the rest of his life.

With his thoughts circling this same loop, round and round, he looked up to see a guard on the other side of the bars. Informed he had a visitor, he got shakily to his feet. At least the Swiss had had the decency to let him dress, though he'd been allowed no tie, no belt, not even the laces in his Guccis.

He smoothed his hair with his hands as he was taken to the visiting area. When he saw Sophia on the other side of the glass, his spirits soared. 'Sophia! *Grazie a Dio.*' He fell into his chair, fumbled with the phone.

She let him ramble—the panic, the pleas, the denials, the despair. And the longer he did so, the thicker the shell grew round her heart.

'*Sta' zitto.*'

He did indeed shut up. He must have seen that she stood for her grandmother now and that her expression was merciless.

'I'm not interested in your pitiful excuses, Donato. I'm here to ask the questions; you'll give the answers.'

'Sophia, you have to listen—'

'I don't have to do anything. I can get up, walk away. You, on the other hand, can't. Did you kill my father?'

'No. *In nome di Dio!* You can't believe that.'

'On the contrary, I find it easy to believe. You stole from the family.'

He started to deny that too, and Sophia set the phone down. Panicked, Don slapped his palm on the glass, shouted. When the guards started forward, she picked the phone up again.

'Yes. Yes, I stole. I was wrong; I was stupid. Gina, she makes me crazy. She nags for more babies, more money, more things. I took money, but please, Sophia, *cara*, you won't let them keep me in prison over money.'

'But it wasn't just money. You tampered with the wine. You killed an old, innocent man.'

'It was an accident. I swear it. It was only supposed to make him a little sick. He knew—He saw . . . I made a mistake.' His hand shook as he rubbed it over his face.

'Knew what, Donato? Saw what?'

'In the vineyard. My lover. He disapproved and might have spoken of it to Zia Tereza.'

'If you play me for a fool, I'll leave you to rot.'

'It was a mistake, I swear it. I was misled.' Desperate, he dragged at his collar. His throat was closing, choking him. 'I was to be paid, you see. If there was bad press, lawsuits, I would be paid more. Baptista, he saw . . . people I spoke with. Sophia, please. I was angry, very angry. I've worked hard my whole life. La Signora never valued me. A man has his pride. I wanted her to value me.'

'And killing an innocent old man, attacking her reputation was the answer?'

'The first, that was an accident. It was the company's reputation—'

'It's one and the same. How could you not know that?'

'I thought, if there's trouble, then I'll help fix it, and she'll see.'

'And you'd get paid from both ends,' Sophia finished. 'It didn't work with Signore Baptista. He didn't get sick, he died. And they buried him believing his heart had just given out at last. How frustrating for you. How annoying. Then Nonna reorganised the company.'

'Yes, yes, and does she reward me for my years of service? No.' Sincerely outraged, he thumped a fist on the counter. 'She brings in an outsider. She promotes an American woman who then can question me.'

'So you killed Margaret and tried to kill David.'

'No, no. Margaret. An accident. I was desperate. She was looking at the invoices. I needed—wanted—only to delay her a short time. How was I to know she would drink so much of the wine? A glass, even two, would only have made her ill.'

'It was inconsiderate of her to spoil things. You sent bottles, poisoned wine, out on the market. You risked lives.'

'I had no choice. No choice. You must believe me.'

'Did my father know? About the wine? The tampering?'

'No. No. He didn't know about the dummy account, because he never took time to look. He didn't know Baptista, because he knew no one who worked in the fields. The business was just a game to Tony, but, Sophia, it was my life.'

She sat back briefly. Her father had been weak, a sad excuse for a husband, even for a man. But he'd had no part in murder, or in sabotage. It was, at least, some small comfort.

'You brought DeMorney to the *castello*, to the winery. You took money from him, didn't you? He paid you to betray your own blood.'

'Listen to me.' His voice dropped to a whisper. 'Stay away from De-Morney. He's a dangerous man. Whatever I've done, I'd never want to hurt you. He'll stop at nothing.'

'Murder? My father?'

'I don't know. I swear on my life, I don't know. He wants to ruin the family. He used me for that. Listen to me,' he repeated, laying his palm on the glass again. 'I took money; I stole. I did what he told me to do to the wine. When I knew Cutter would expose me, I ran. They're saying I hired some thug from the streets to shoot him and steal the papers. It's a lie. Why would I? It was over already for me. I'm begging you to help me. I'm begging you to stay away from him.'

The twists of lies and truths had to be unknotted. It would take a steady hand to do so, she thought. Even now, after all she knew of him, part of her wanted to reach out. She couldn't allow it. 'You want my help, Don? Tell me everything you know about Jerry DeMorney. Everything. If I'm satisfied, I'll see to it Giambelli arranges for your legal needs, and that your children are cared for.'

When Sophia came back, Tyler thought she looked exhausted. Wilted. Before he could speak, she touched a hand to his. 'Don't ask me yet. I'm going to arrange a conference call on the flight so I only have to say it all once.'

'OK. Let's try this instead.' He pulled her in, held her.

'Thanks. Can you do without the things you took to the *castello* for a few days? I'll have them packed up and sent. We need to go home, Ty. I need to go home.'

'**D**o you believe him?'

Tyler waited until she had completed the call, until all had been said. She was pacing the cabin, sipping her third cup of coffee since takeoff.

'Don's a stupid man, weak and selfish. I believe he's convinced himself that Signore Baptista and Margaret were accidents. I don't think he killed my father or tried to kill David.'

'You're looking at DeMorney.'

'Who else, Ty?'

'I'm not sure. I can't figure out why your father'd have a meeting in your apartment with Jerry, or why, after all this time, Jerry would kill him. Would risk that, would bother.'

'The cops will have to question him. Even on the word of someone like Donato. He'll slither and slide, but . . .' She took a breath. 'We'll be stopping in New York to refuel.'

'You won't get anything out of him, Sophie.'

'Just the chance to spit in his face.'

Jerry DeMorney was more amused than annoyed when lobby security announced he had visitors. He turned to his companion. 'We have company. An old friend of yours.'

'Jerry, we've got two solid hours of work to get through.' Kris uncurled her legs from the couch. 'Who is it?'

'Your former boss. Why don't we open a bottle of the Pouilly-Fuissé? The '96.'

'Sophia.' Kris surged to her feet. 'Here? Why?'

The buzzer sounded. 'We're about to find out.'

He strolled to the door. 'Isn't this a lovely surprise. I had no idea you were in town.' He leaned forward to kiss Sophia's cheek. Tyler's hand rammed into Jerry's chest.

'Let's not start out being stupid,' he advised.

'Sorry.' Holding up both hands, Jerry stepped back. 'Didn't realise things had changed between you. Come in. I was just about to open some wine. You both know Kris.'

'Yes. How cosy,' Sophia began. 'You appear to be enjoying all your new employee benefits, Kris.'

'I much prefer the style of my new boss to that of my old one.'

'Ladies, please,' Jerry pleaded as he closed the door. 'We're all pros here. And we know executives switch companies every day. I hope you're not here to scold me for snatching one of yours. After all, Giambelli wooed one of our best. By the way, I heard David had a close call in Venice. And I was shocked to hear about Donato.' He lowered to the arm of a sofa. 'Absolutely shocked.'

'You can save the act, DeMorney,' Tyler said. 'We paid Don a visit before we left Europe. He had some interesting things to say about you. I don't think the police will be far behind us.'

'Really? I have more faith in our system than to believe the police will put much credence in the ravings of a man who'd steal from his own family. This is a difficult time for you, Sophia.' He stood up again. 'If there's anything I can do—'

'You could go to hell, but I'm not sure they'd have you. You should've been more careful,' she continued. 'Both of you,' she added with a nod towards Kris. 'Spending time at the *castello*, the winery. You used Donato.'

'Guilty. But again, nothing illegal about it. He approached me. We discussed the possibility of him coming aboard at Le Coeur.'

'You told him to tamper with the wine. Told him how to do it.'

'That's ridiculous and insulting. Be careful, Sophia. I understand you're upset, but trying to deflect your family's troubles onto me and mine isn't the answer.'

'Here's how it was.' Tyler had spent the hours in the air working it out in his head. Now he sat, made himself comfortable. 'You wanted to cause trouble, serious trouble. Avano'd bounced on your wife. Hard for a man to take that, even if the other guy's busy bouncing on every woman he can find. But trouble just slides right off Avano. Nothing sticks. He keeps his wife just where he wants her, which is out of the way but close enough to lock in his position with her family organisation. Maybe you know Avano's skimming, maybe you don't. But you know enough to look at Don, hint that Le Coeur would love to have him on the team. More money, more power. You find out about the dummy account and now you have something on him.'

'You're fishing, MacMillan, and fishing bores me.'

'It gets better. Avano's snuggling up to Sophia's second-in-command. Isn't that interesting? Dangle a carrot under her nose and you get lots of inside information. Did he offer you money too, Kris? Or just a corner office with a shiny brass plaque?'

'I don't know what you're talking about,' Kris said. 'I had nothing to do with this.'

'Maybe not. Your style's more the backstabbing variety,' Ty commented. 'Meanwhile, DeMorney, you keep playing on Don, nudging him along. Deeper, deeper. He's got some money problems. You lend him a little, just a friendly loan. And you string him along about the move to Le Coeur. What else can he bring to the table? Inside information? Not good enough.'

'My company doesn't require inside information.'

'It's not your company.' Ty inclined his head when he saw the fury spurt out of Jerry's eyes. 'You just want it to be. You talk to Don about the tampering, just a few bottles. Show him what he should do, could do, then how he'd be able to step in and be a hero when the shit hits. But it goes wrong for Don, and an old man dies. No skin off your nose, of course. You've got Don by the short hairs now. He talks, he's up for murder. Meanwhile, Giambelli's moving right along. And one of your own moves to the enemy camp.'

'We've managed to bump along without the help of David Cutter.' He wanted to pour wine, carelessly, but realised his hand was shaking.

'You got your crisis, DeMorney; you spilled your blood. But you want more, and that's what's going to choke you. Going after Cutter was stupid. Legal had copies of the paperwork, and Don knew it. The cops'll work on that angle, and they'll start tying you in.'

'And then . . .' Sophia dug into the leftover lasagne while the family gathered in the kitchen of the Villa Giambelli. 'Ty had his hand—I didn't even see it happen. It was like lightning.' She gulped down some wine. 'Anyway, all of a sudden Jerry's gone white and his eyes are rolling back in his head and he's folding like, I don't know, an accordion towards the floor. And Ty politely suggests that Jerry might want to get his hand X-rayed because he thinks he heard a bone snap.'

'Good Lord.' Pilar helped herself to some wine. 'Really?'

'Mmm.' Sophia swallowed. She was starving. The minute she'd walked in the door, she'd been starving. 'I heard this little sound, like when you step on a twig. Rather horrible, really. Then we just left. And I have to say . . . Here, Eli, your glass is empty. I have to say it was so exciting that when we got back on the plane, I jumped him.'

'Sophie!' Tyler felt heat rise in the back of his neck. 'Shut up and eat.'

'It didn't embarrass you at the time,' she pointed out. 'Now, whatever happens, I'm always going to have that image of Jerry curled up on the floor like a cocktail shrimp. Nobody can take that away from me. Do we have any *gelato*?'

Sophia slept like a log and woke early. At six she was already in her office, refining a press release. By midmorning she stood among the young mustard plants at the MacMillan vineyard.

Tyler walked the rows until he met her. 'You're late.'

'Priorities,' she said. 'Manipulating the press, consulting with legal. Just another quiet day for the wine heiress. How are we doing out here?'

'Nights've been cool and moist. Brings on mildew. We'll do the second sulphur spraying after the grapes have set. I'm not worried.'

'Good. Now, why haven't you kissed me hello?'

'Because I'm working. I want to check the new plantings, run by the old distillery and check on the fermentation vats. And then we've got to move your stuff over to my place.'

'I haven't said I was—'

'But since you're here.' He leaned down and kissed her.

'We're going to have to discuss this,' she began, then pulled her ringing phone out of her pocket. 'Very soon,' she added. 'Sophia Giambelli. *Sì, va bene.*' She angled the phone away. 'It's Lieutenant DeMarco's office. Don was transferred to his custody today.' She shifted the phone back in place. '*Sì, buon giorno. Ma che . . . Scusi? . . . No, no.*'

Gripping Tyler's hand, she shook her head fiercely. '*Come!*' she managed. '*Donato.*' She lifted her stunned gaze to his. '*È morto.*'

He didn't need her to translate the last. He took the phone from her and asked how Donato Giambelli had died.

'**A** heart attack. He wasn't yet forty.' Sophia paced. 'This is my doing. I pushed him, then I went to Jerry and pushed him. I might as well have drawn a target on Don's back.'

'You didn't do it alone,' Tyler reminded her. 'I'm the one who yanked DeMorney's chain.'

'*Basta,*' Tereza ordered. 'If they find Donato died from drugs, if they find he was murdered in the hands of the police, there's no fault here. Donato's choices put him where he was.'

And that, she determined, would end that. She reached out, found Eli's hand, brought it to her lips in a gesture Sophia had never seen her make. 'He was a disappointment to me, but he was once a sweet young boy with a pretty smile. I'll mourn the little boy.'

'Nonna, I'll go to Italy, to the funeral.'

'No. Sophia, you and Tyler have a business to run and vines to tend. And you, Pilar, have a wedding to plan.' She smiled at her daughter. 'Eli and I will go, and that's as it should be. I'll bring Gina and the children back if they want it. God help us if they do,' she finished with spirit, and got to her feet.

Maddy's idea of shopping was hanging around the mall, scoping out the boys who were hanging around the mall scoping out the girls, and spending her allowance on some junk food and new earrings. She expected to be terminally bored spending the day with three adults in fancy dress shops.

But she figured the points she'd earn with her father for agreeing to go would translate into the streaks she wanted to put in her hair. And if she played her cards right, she could cop some pretty cool stuff out of Pilar.

In the end, she wasn't bored. She was surprised to find herself having fun with Pilar, as she was now supposed to call her, and the judge lady. She didn't even mind having the conversation turn absolutely to clothes and fabric and colour and cut.

And when she watched Sophia dash in, wind-blown, flushed, happy, Maddy had a revelation. She wouldn't mind being like her, like Sophia Giambelli, a woman who could do exactly what she wanted in the world and look amazing at the same time.

'Tell me you haven't tried on anything yet.'

'No. I waited for you. What do you think of this blue silk?'

'Hmm. A definite maybe. Hi, Maddy. Aunt Helen.' She let out a quick whoop. 'Oh, Mama! Look at this. The lace is fabulous—romantic, elegant. And the peach colour would be perfect on you.'

'It's lovely, but don't you think it's a little young?'

'No, no. It's for a bride. For you. You have to try it. And this rose linen Helen's picked out.'

When Pilar went off to the changing rooms, Sophia rubbed her hands together. 'All right, your turn.'

Surprised, Maddy blinked. 'This is a grown-up shop.'

'You're probably about the same size as I am.' She studied her target. 'Mama's going for soft colours, so we'll stick with that. Though I'd like to put you in jewel tones.'

'I like black,' Maddy said for the hell of it.

'Mmm, and you wear it well. But we'll expand your horizons for this particular occasion. I like this.' Sophia pulled out a full-length sleeveless gown in smoky blue and held it up in front of Maddy. 'I want to see you in it with your hair up. Show off your neck and shoulders.'

'What if I got it cut? My hair, I mean. Short.'

'Hmm.' Sophia mentally cut and restyled Maddy's straight mop. 'Yes. A little longer in the back. A few highlights.'

'Streaks?' said Maddy, nearly speechless with joy.

'Highlights, subtle. Ask your father, and I'll take you to my guy.'

'Why do I have to ask? It's my hair.'

'Good point. I'll give the salon a call.' She started to hand Maddy the gown, then stopped. 'Oh, Mama.'

'What do you think?' Pilar had started with the peach, the ivory lace romancing the bodice, the skirt sweeping back into a gentle train.

'Helen, come and see. You look beautiful, Mama.'

'Like a bride,' Helen agreed.

'Maddy, what's your vote?'

'You look great. Dad's eyes are going to pop out.'

Pilar beamed. 'We have a winner, first time out.'

It wasn't as simple as that. There were hats, shoes, jewellery, bags, even underwear. It was dark before they headed north, and the back of the four-wheel drive was crammed with shopping bags. Maddy had a pile of new clothes, shoes, and an awesome haircut.

'Mama'—Sophia tapped the steering wheel—'this girl has potential.'

'Agreed. But I'm not taking the rap for those shoes with the two-foot soles. That one's on you.'

'They're great. Funky.'

'Yeah.' Maddy lifted her foot. 'And the soles are only four inches.'

'I don't know why you'd want to clomp around in them.'

Sophia met Maddy's gaze in the rearview mirror. 'It's a mom thing. She has to say that.'

'You bet. But I will say the two of you were right about the hair. It looks great.' Pilar turned to Sophia as the car squealed round a curve. 'At the risk of saying another mom thing, slow down.'

'Tighten your seat belts.' Grimly Sophia's hands viced on the wheel. 'Something's wrong with the brakes.'

Instinctively, Pilar turned back to Maddy. 'Are you strapped in?'

'Yeah. I'm OK. Pull up the emergency brake.'

'Mama, pull it up. I need both hands.' The car squealed again, fish-tailed round the next turn.

'It's up all the way, baby.' And the car didn't slow. 'What if we turned off the engine?'

Maddy swallowed. 'The steering'll lock.'

Gravel spat as Sophia fought to keep the car on the road. 'Use my phone. Call nine-one-one.'

'Downshift!' Maddy shouted. 'Try downshifting.'

'Mama, shove it into third when I tell you. It's going to give us one hell of a jolt. OK. Hold on.' She pushed in the clutch, and the car seemed to gain more speed. 'Now!'

The car jolted hard. 'Into second,' Sophia ordered, wrenching the wheel from the shoulder of the road. 'Now.'

The car threw her forward, back again. She had a moment's panic that the air bags would deploy and leave her helpless.

'We've slowed down some. We're going to head downhill, round more turns. Once we're through them, we go up a slope, and that should do it. Everybody hold on.'

Her eyes were glued to the road now, her mind anticipating each turn. The headlights cut through the dark, slashed across oncoming traffic. She heard the sound of horns blaring as she crossed the centre line.

'Nearly there, nearly there.' She whipped the wheel left, then right. She could feel the ground level. 'Shove it into first, Mama.'

There was a tremendous shudder, as if an enormous fist had punched the bonnet. Something shrieked, then clanged. And as the speed dropped, she pulled to the side of the road.

No one spoke when they stopped. A car whizzed by, then another. Pilar reached for her seat belt. 'Is everyone OK?'

'Yeah.' Maddy dashed tears from her cheeks.

'Yeah,' Sophie said. 'Let's get the hell out.'

She managed to get out of the car before her legs buckled. Bracing her hands on the bonnet, she fought to recover her breath.

'That was really good driving,' Maddy told her.

'Yeah, thanks.'

Pilar held her when the shakes came. And, holding her, reached out for Maddy, who pressed herself into that circle of comfort and let the tears come.

Nearly blind with terror and relief, David bolted out of the house. Even as the police car braked, David scooped Maddy out, held her cradled in his arms.

'You're OK.' He pressed his lips to her cheeks, her hair. 'You're OK.' He said it half a dozen times.

'I'm all right. I'm not hurt.' When she wrapped her arms round his neck, her world came all the way right again. 'Sophie drove like one of those guys on the raceway. It was kinda cool.'

'Bet it was some ride.' Theo awkwardly patted her back. 'I'll haul her in, Dad. You're going to wreck your arm.'

'It's OK, Dad,' Maddy told him. 'I can walk. Theo and I can bring in all the loot.' She wriggled until David set her down.

'What'd you do to your hair?' David ran his hand over it.

'Got rid of most of it. What do you think?'

'I think it makes you look grown up. You're growing up on me, Maddy.' He sighed. 'Go ahead, drag off your loot.'

Theo grabbed some bags, and Maddy clomped off after him in her funky new shoes.

'Oh, David, I'm so sorry,' Pilar said.

'Don't say anything. Just let me look at you.' He cupped her face. Her eyes were huge and full of worry. 'You're OK?'

'I'm fine.'

He drew her close, seemed to fold himself around her. 'Sophia?'

'She's fine. David, I've never been so scared, and all the time it was happening, they were amazing. I didn't like leaving Sophie back there, dealing with the police, but Ty's on his way down.'

'Come inside.' He shifted her, keeping her close to his side, safe in his embrace. 'Tell me everything.'

He dumped half a tube of shower gel that had been around since Christmas into the bath. It smelt like pine, but it bubbled. He figured she'd want bubbles. He stuck candles on the counter. Women went for candlelit baths, for reasons he couldn't fathom. He poured her a glass of wine, set it on the edge of the bath, and was standing back, trying to figure out what else to do, when she came into the bathroom.

Her single huge sigh told him he'd already hit the mark.

'MacMillan, I love you.'

'Yeah, so you said.'

'No, no. At this exact moment no one has ever, will ever love you more. Half an hour in here and I'll feel human again.'

He left her to it and went down to get her things. To his way of thinking, if he dumped her shopping loot in the bedroom, it would take her that much longer to run off again. As far as he was concerned, this was the first stage of her moving in.

At that moment, the doorbell rang. On the doorstep stood Claremont and Maguire.

Deliberate, Sophia thought as she sat in Tyler's living room. The four-wheel had been tampered with as deliberately as the wine had been. Part of her had known it, but having it confirmed now with cold, hard facts brought a fresh chill to her skin.

'Yes. I use that vehicle often. Primarily I drive my car, but it's a two-seater. The three of us were spending the day shopping for my mother's wedding, so we needed the bigger car.'

'Who knew of your plans?' Detective Maguire asked her.

'A number of people, I suppose. Family. We were meeting Judge Moore, so her family.'

'Did you make appointments?'

'Not really. I stopped by to see James Moore, my lawyer, before I met the others for lunch. The rest of the day was free.'

'And the last place you stopped?' Claremont asked.

'We had dinner. Moose's at Washington Square. From around seven to eight thirty. We left for home from there.'

'Any idea, Ms Giambelli, who would want to cause you harm?'

'Yes.' She met Claremont's gaze levelly. 'Jeremy DeMorney.'

'"A dish best served cold",' Claremont mused on the drive back to the city. 'It fits DeMorney's profile. He's cool, sophisticated, erudite. He's got money, position. I can see that type planning things out, but I can't get his type risking losing that position over a cracked marriage. How would you handle it if your man cheated on you?'

'Oh, I'd kick his butt, then scalp him in the divorce and do everything in my power to make the rest of his life a living hell.'

'And people wonder why I'm not married.' Claremont flipped open his notebook. 'Let's go pump up the pressure on DeMorney. The slicker they are, the harder you squeeze.'

He wasn't going to tolerate it. The idiot police.

Of course they could prove nothing. But the muscle in Jerry's cheek twitched as doubts danced in his head. No, he was sure of it. He'd been careful. But that was beside the point.

The Giambellis had publicly humiliated him once before. Avano's affair with his wife had put his name on wagging tongues. It had cost him prestige in the company, in his great-uncle's eyes. Jeremy DeMorney, always considered Le Coeur's heir apparent, had been taken down a painful peg.

The Giambellis hadn't suffered because of it. The talk of Pilar had been respectful sympathy, of Sophia quiet admiration. And there was never talk of the great Signora.

Or hadn't been, until he'd made it happen.

His revenge had cut through to the core of Giambelli. Disgrace, scandal, mistrust, and all brought about by their own. Perfection.

Who'd been taken down a peg now?

But even with all his planning, they were turning it on him, trying to drag him under. His own family had questioned him. *Questioned* him on business practices—his ethics, methods, personal agenda. The idea of it made him shake with black, bitter rage.

The Giambelli women were going to pay dearly for offending him.

Sophia zipped through her interoffice email. She'd have preferred attending to the reports, the memos, the questions in her San Francisco office. But the law had been laid down. She didn't go to the city unaccompanied. Period.

Tyler refused to leave the fields. The weeding wasn't complete, the suckering was just begun, and there was a mild infestation of grape leafhoppers. Nothing very troublesome, as blackberry bushes were planted throughout the vineyard to serve as hosts for the wasps that fed on leafhopper eggs. But Tyler wouldn't budge until it was under control, and by that time she'd be so busy with her mother's wedding she wouldn't be able to spare a day to go into the office.

At least the demands, the tight schedule, helped keep her mind off Jeremy DeMorney and the police investigation. It had been two full weeks since she'd careered round those turns with no brakes.

She brought up another email, clicked to open the attached file. As she watched it scroll onscreen, her heart began to race.

It was a copy of the next ad, set to run in August.

A family picnic, a wash of sunlight, the dapple of shade from a huge old oak tree. A scatter of people at a long wooden table that was loaded with food and bottles of wine.

The image had been altered subtly, slickly. Three of the models' faces had been replaced. Sophia studied her grandmother, her mother, herself. Her eyes were wide with horror. Stabbed into her chest, like a knife, was a bottle of wine.

It read:

THIS IS YOUR MOMENT
IT'LL BE THE DEATH OF YOU
AND YOURS

'You son of a bitch, you son of a bitch.' She jabbed the keyboard, ordering the copy to print, saved the file, then closed it.

He wouldn't shake her, she promised herself. And he wouldn't threaten her family. She would deal with him. She would handle this.

Suckering the vines was a pleasant way to spend a day. Under the brilliant blue sky, the circling mountains were upholstered with green, lush with the promise of summer.

Ty's grapes were protected from the midday sun by a verdant canopy of leaves. Nature's parasol, his grandfather called it. Before long the black grape varieties would begin changing colour, green berries miraculously going blue, then purple as they pushed towards harvest.

When Sophia crouched beside him, he continued his work. 'I thought you were going to hole up in your office all day, waste this sunshine. Hell of a way to make a living, if you ask me.'

'I thought a big, important vintner like yourself would have more to do than suckering vines.' She combed a hand through his hair, lavishly streaked by the sun. 'Where's your hat, pal?'

'Around somewhere. These pinot noir are going to be our earliest to ripen. I've got a hundred down with Paulie. They're our best vintage in five years. His money's on the chenin blanc.'

'I'll take a piece of that. Mine's on the pinot chardonnay.'

'You ought to save your money.' He shifted, their knees bumped before he laid a hand on hers. 'What's the matter, baby?'

'I got this through the interoffice email.' She showed him the doctored advertisement. 'I'm going to send it to the police, call a summit meeting. But . . . I wanted to tell you first.'

Tyler stayed as he was, crouched, his hand dwarfing hers. Overhead a cloud teased the edges of the sun and filtered the light.

'Here's what I want to do. I want to hunt him down and peel the skin off his bones with a dull knife. Until that happy day I want you to promise me something. You don't go anywhere by yourself. Not even for a walk in the gardens. I mean it.'

'I understand how worried you are, but—'

'You can't understand, because it's unreasonable. It's indescribable.' He tripped her heart by bringing her free hand up, pressing his lips to the palm. 'If I wake up in the middle of the night and you're not there, I break out in a cold sweat.'

'Ty.'

'Shut up, just shut up.' In one fast and fluid move he got to his feet. 'I've never loved anyone before. I didn't expect it to be you. But it is and that's it. You're not doing anything to mess this up for me.'

'Ty, I don't intend to mess this up for you, or me, either.'

'Great. Let's go and pack your things.'

'I'm not moving in with you.'

'Why the hell not?' Frustration had him dragging his hands through his hair. 'You're there half the time anyway.'

'I don't want to live with you.'

'Why? Just tell me why.'

'Maybe I'm old-fashioned.'

'Like hell you are.'

'Maybe I'm old-fashioned,' she repeated, 'in this one area. I don't think we should live together. I think we should get married.'

'That's just another . . .' The words sank in, momentarily dulled his brain. 'Whoa.'

'Yes, and with that scintillating response I need to go back home and call the police.'

'You know, one day you're actually going to let me work through a process at my own time and pace. But since that isn't the case on this one, at least you could ask me in a more traditional way.'

'You want me to ask you? Fine. Will you marry me?'

'Sure. November's good for me.' He cupped her elbows, lifted her a couple of inches off the ground. 'Which is when I was going to ask you—but you always have to be first. I figured we could get married, have a nice honeymoon and be back home before pruning time. Kind of a tidy and symbolic cycle, don't you think?'

'I don't know. I have to think about it.'

He gave her a hard kiss. 'Let me finish this vine; then we'll go call the cops. And the family.'

'Ty, just because I did the proposing, doesn't mean I don't want a ring. I'll pick it out.'

'No, you won't.'

On a sigh she tipped her head onto his shoulder as he worked. 'When I came here, I was scared and angry. Now I'm scared, angry and happy. It's better,' she decided. 'A lot better.'

'This is who we are,' Tereza stated, lifting her glass. 'And who we choose to be.'

They were dining alfresco, in a kind of Giambelli reflection of the ad. A purposeful choice, Sophia thought. Her grandmother would always stand straight against a threat.

The evening was warm, the sunlight still brilliant. In the vineyards beyond the lawns and gardens, the grapes were growing fat, and the pinot noir, as Tyler had predicted, was just beginning to turn.

Forty days till harvest, Sophia thought. That was the old rule. When the grapes took colour, forty days. Her mother would be married by then and back from her honeymoon; Maddy and Theo would be her brother and sister; she would be planning her own wedding, though she'd pressured Tyler not to announce their engagement yet.

'When we have trouble,' Tereza continued, 'we band together. This year has brought trouble and grief, but it's also brought joy. In a few weeks Eli and I will have a new son and more grandchildren. In the meantime, we've been threatened. James? Your legal opinion?'

He set down his fork. 'While evidence indicates DeMorney was involved in the embezzlement scheme and the tampering, there's no concrete proof. Donato's claims notwithstanding, there isn't enough to convince the district attorney to file charges on those matters or Tony Avano's death. It's been confirmed that he was in New York when Sophia's car was tampered with. Until the police have evidence, my best advice is to stay above it, let the system work.'

'No offence intended to your system, Uncle James, but it hasn't worked very well to date,' Sophia pointed out.

'Sophia'—Helen reached across the table—'sometimes justice isn't what we want it to be or what we expect.'

'He set out to ruin us.' Tereza spoke calmly. 'He hasn't done so. Damaged, yes. Caused us loss. But he'll pay a price. Today he was asked to resign his position at Le Coeur.' She sipped her wine, enjoyed the bouquet. 'I'm told he didn't take it well. I'll use whatever influence I have to see to it he finds no position at any reputable wine-maker. Professionally, he's finished.'

'It's not enough,' Sophia began.

'It may be too much,' Helen corrected. 'If he's as dangerous as you believe, this sort of interference will push him into a corner, make it only more imperative that he strike back. As a lawyer, as your friend, I'm asking you all to leave it alone.'

'Helen,' Tereza said. 'Could you?'

'Yes.' The single syllable was a fierce declaration. 'Tereza, this is a time for you to celebrate, to move on, not to focus on revenge.'

'We each protect what matters most, Helen. In our own way. The sun's going,' she said. 'Tyler, light the candles. Tell me, do you still pit your pinot noir against my chenin blanc?'

'I do.' He worked his way down the table, setting the candles to flame. 'Of course, it's a win-win situation as we're merged. Speaking of mergers, I'm going to marry Sophia.'

'Damn it, Ty! I told you—'

'Quiet,' he said so casually, Sophia sputtered into silence. 'She asked me, but I thought it was a pretty good idea.'

'Oh, Sophie.' Pilar threw her arms round her daughter.

'I only wanted to wait until after your wedding to tell you, but bigmouth here couldn't keep it shut.'

Ty circled the table. 'The way I see it, you just can't have enough good news. Here.' He grabbed her hand and slipped a simple, spectacular square-cut diamond on her finger. 'That makes it a deal.'

'Why can't you just . . . It's beautiful.'

'It was my grandmother's. MacMillan to Giambelli.' He lifted her hand and kissed it. 'Giambelli to MacMillan. It works for me.'

'I appreciate your seeing me like this. Listening. Hearing me out.' Jerry DeMorney reached for Rene's hand. 'I was afraid you believed those vicious rumours the Giambellis are circulating.'

'I wouldn't believe any of them if they said the sun came up in the east.' Rene settled on the sofa, made herself cosy.

Could she be more perfect? He only wished he'd thought of her months before. 'They've ruined my reputation. I guess I brought part of that on myself. I shouldn't want to win so much.'

'Winning's all there is.' She pursed her lips. 'I'm very attracted to clever businessmen.'

'Really? I used to be one,' he said as he poured the wine.

'Now, Jerry, you still are. You'll land on your feet.'

'I want to believe that. I'm thinking of moving to France. I have some offers there.' Or would have, he thought grimly. 'Luckily I can pick and choose. It might do me good to just travel for a while.'

'I love travelling.' She purred it.

'I don't feel I can leave until I've dealt with the Giambellis face to face. I'll be frank with you, Rene. I want to pay them back for putting this smear on me.'

'I do understand.' In what could be taken for sympathy or otherwise, she laid a hand over his heart. 'They always treated me like something cheap. I hate them.'

'Maybe we can find a way to pay them back. For both of us.'

Rene stretched along the sofa beside Jerry and he topped up her wine-glass. 'Sophia Giambelli is giving her mother a little party on Friday night—wedding eve. All females. She's setting up a damn spa in the villa. Facials, body treatments, the works.'

'And what will the men be doing?'

'Holding their bachelor-night deal at the MacMillan place.'

'We'll know just where everyone is right before the happy event. Rene, you're a jewel.'

'I don't want to be one. I just want to have them.'

'I'll take care of that, too. But first, you and I have a date on Friday night at Villa Giambelli.'

She wanted it to be perfect, the kind of night they'd all remember and laugh about for years. She'd planned it, organised it, fine-tuned the details. In twenty-four hours, Sophia thought, her mother would be dressing for her wedding, but for her last evening as a single woman she was going to bask in a world of females.

'Sophie'—in her long white bathrobe Pilar circled the pool house—'I can't believe you went to all this trouble.'

Stations were set up with lounging sofas and salon chairs. The evening light shimmered towards sunset, while scents from the gardens clung to the air. Tables held platters of fruit, bottles of wine and sparkling water, baskets of flowers.

'I was shooting for a Roman bath thing. Do you like it?'

'It's wonderful. I feel like a queen.'

'When you're finished, you'll feel like a goddess. Where are all the others? We're wasting pampering time.'

'Upstairs. I'll get them.'

'Maddy, pour Mama some wine. She's not to lift a finger except to pick up a chocolate strawberry. I'll get everyone.'

David tried to stare Eli down. 'You're bluffing.'

'Yeah? Put your money up, son, and call me.'

'Go ahead, Dad,' Theo said. 'No guts, no glory.'

David tossed chips into the pot. 'Call. Show 'em.'

'Three little deuces,' Eli began, and watched David's eyes gleam. 'Standing watch over two pretty ladies.'

'Son of a bitch.'

'A Scotsman doesn't bluff over money, son.' Eli, jubilant, raked in his chips.

'The man's scalped me so many times, I wear a helmet when we sit down to cards.' James gestured with his glass.

Ty's head came up at the knock on the door. 'Somebody ordered a stripper, right? I knew you guys wouldn't let me down.'

'It's the pizza.' Theo leapt up.

'More pizza? Theo, you can't possibly want more pizza.'

'He inhaled the last order,' Ty said.

'Sophie, this was a brilliant idea.'

'Thanks, Aunt Helen.' They sat side by side, tipped back with purifying masks, thick and green, covering their faces. 'I wanted Mama to feel relaxed and completely female.'

'This'll do it. Where is she?'

'The lower-level guest bath. Full-body facial.'

'Fabulous. I'm next.'

'Champagne?' Maria asked.

'Maria,' Sophia said, rousing herself enough to sit up, 'you're not to serve. You're a guest.'

'My manicure's dry.' She showed off her nails. 'I have a pedicure next. You can bring me champagne then.'

'That's a deal.'

Maria glanced over as Pilar, looking soft and relaxed, came back in. 'You've made your mama happy tonight. Everything's going to be all right now.'

It had been a long hike from the car to the winery, and the sack he carried seemed to gain weight with every step. Still, there was something to be said for doing the job himself. Personal gratification.

Before the night was over, Giambelli would, one way or another, be in ruins.

'Stay close,' Jerry told Rene. 'Once the winery's on fire, they'll spill out like ants at a picnic.'

'I don't care if you burn the whole damn vineyard to ashes. I just don't want to get caught.'

'Do what I tell you and you won't. Once they're out here, busy trying to put out the fire, we go into the villa, plant the package in Sophia's room, get out. We're in the car five minutes later and back popping champagne before the smoke clears.'

'What's that? It looks like . . . Oh my God. The winery! The winery's on fire. Maria, call nine-one-one! The winery's on fire.'

Sophia rolled off the massage table, snagged her robe on the run.

It was simple, perfect. A matter of minutes. Then, as Jerry had predicted, they poured out of the house. Raised voices, running feet. From the shadows of the garden he counted the figures wrapped in white robes that raced down the path and out across the vineyard.

'In and out,' he whispered to Rene. 'You lead the way.'

She claimed she'd slipped into Sophia's room once. His flashlight would be enough to plant the package at the back of her closet, where the police would find it. He moved up the terrace steps behind Rene, paused to glance over his shoulder. He could see the bright orange and gold of the fire against the night sky. It illuminated the figures rushing like frightened moths towards the flame.

They'd put it out, of course, but it would take time, as precious bottles exploded, as equipment was ruined, as their god of tradition burned to hell.

'Jerry, for God's sake,' Rene hissed. 'This isn't a tourist attraction. You said we had to hurry.'

He stepped up to the terrace door. 'Sure this is her room?'

'Yes, I'm sure.'

'Well then.' He pushed open the door just as Sophia dashed through the opposite door and slapped on the lights.

The sudden glare slashed across his eyes; the shock froze his brain. Before he could recover, she leapt at him, blind fury catapulting her across the room. He struck out, caught her across the cheekbone. She slashed nails like a rake down his cheek.

Maddened, he tossed her aside, into a shrieking Rene. Even as she scrabbled to her feet, the gun was out of the pouch, in his hand.

He nearly ended it with one quick twitch of his nervous finger. Then he saw her eyes filled with fear, and he wanted more.

'You should've run out with the others, Sophia. But maybe it's fate you end up like your worthless father. With a bullet in the heart.'

'Jerry, we have to get out of here.' Rene stared at the gun. 'What're you doing? You can't just shoot her. That's crazy. It's murder. I'm not having any part of murder. I'm getting out. Give me the keys to the car.'

'Shut the hell up.' In an almost absent gesture he smashed the gun into Rene's head. She went down like a stone.

'This is perfect. You'll appreciate the spin on this, Sophia. Rene started the fire. She's had it in for you all along. And she broke into your room to plant evidence against you. You caught her, you struggled, the gun went off. The gun,' he added, 'used to shoot David Cutter. You're dead, and she hangs for it. Very tidy.'

'Why?'

'Nobody screws with me and gets away with it. You Giambellis think you can have it all. Now you'll have nothing.'

'Because of my father?' She could see the bright orange glow from the fire through the open doors behind him. 'All of this because my father embarrassed you?'

'*Embarrassed?* He stole from me—my wife, my pride. He was a user, a liar and a cheat.'

'Yes, he was.' No one would come for her, she thought. There would be no one to race back from the fire to save her. 'You're all that, and so much less.'

'If there was time, we'd debate that. But I'm a little pressed, so . . .' He brought the gun up an inch. '*Ciao, bella.*'

'*Va' a farti fottere.*' She cursed him in a steady voice. When the gun exploded, she stumbled back. And watched blood seep through the tiny hole in his shirt.

Baffled shock crossed his face; then his body jerked and dropped. In the doorway, Helen lowered the gun to her side.

'Oh my God. Aunt Helen. He was going to kill me.'

'I know.' Slowly, Helen came into the room. 'I came back to tell you the men had come. I saw . . .'

'He was going to kill me. Just like he killed my father.'

'No, honey. He didn't kill your father. I did. I did,' she repeated, and dropped the gun to the floor. 'I'm so sorry.'

'No. That's crazy.'

'I used that gun. It was my father's. It was never registered. I don't know why I took it that night. I don't think I planned to kill him. I . . . He wanted money. Again. It was never going to end.'

'What are you talking about?' Sophia took Helen's shoulders. She could smell gunpowder and blood. 'What are you saying?'

'He was using our son against me. Sophia, Linc is Tony's son.'

'They've got it under control. It's—' Pilar rushed in the terrace doors, stopped cold. 'Sophie! What happened here?'

'Wait. Don't come in. Don't touch anything.' Sophia's breath came out in pants, but she was thinking, thinking fast. 'Aunt Helen, we can't stay in here.'

She pulled Helen out onto the terrace. 'Tell us quickly. We can't have much time.'

'I killed Tony. Pilar, I betrayed you. Myself. Everything I believe in.'

'That's not possible. For God's sake, what happened here?'

'She saved my life,' Sophia said. A blast rent the air as bottles exploded in the winery. She barely flinched. 'He was going to kill me with the gun that shot David. Helen, what happened with my father?'

'He wanted money. Over the years he'd contact me when he needed money. He'd just mention Linc—what a fine boy he was, what a bright and promising young man. Then he'd say he needed a bit of a loan. I slept with Tony.' She began to weep then, silently. 'We were all so young. James and I were having problems. We separated for a few weeks.'

'I remember,' Pilar murmured.

'I ran into Tony. He was so charming. He paid attention. There's no excuse. I let it happen. After, I was so ashamed. I found out I was pregnant, and I told Tony. I might as well have told him I'd decided to change my hairstyle. He could hardly be expected to pay for one night's indiscretion, could he? So I paid.' Tears dripped down her cheeks. 'And I paid.'

'Linc is Tony's child.'

'He's James's.' Helen looked pleadingly at Pilar. 'In every way but that one. He doesn't know, neither of them knows. I did everything I could to make up for that night. To James, to Linc—Pilar, to you. I was young and stupid, and I've never forgiven myself. I gave him money every time he asked for it.'

'And you couldn't give any more,' Pilar concurred.

'The night of the party, he told me he had to see me. It was the first time I refused. It made him angry. He said he'd tell James, tell Linc, tell you.

'I couldn't risk it, couldn't bear it. My baby, Pilar. My little boy. When I went home, I got the gun out of the safe. It's been there for years. I don't know why I thought of it. Don't know why I took it. It was like a veil over my mind. He had music on in the apartment, and a good bottle of wine. He sat and told me his financial troubles. Charmingly, as if we were old, dear friends. He needed a quarter of a million this time. He'd be willing, of course, to take half by the end of the week, and give me another month for the rest. It wasn't too much to ask, after all. He'd given me such a fine son.

'I didn't know the gun was in my hand. I didn't know I'd used it until I saw the red against his white tuxedo shirt. He looked at me so surprised, just a little annoyed. I went home and tried to convince myself it never happened. I've carried the gun around with me ever since.'

Cycles, Sophia thought. Sometimes they needed to be stopped. 'You used that gun to save my life tonight.'

'I love you,' Helen said simply.

'I know it. And this is what happened here tonight. Pay attention to me. You came back, saw Jerry holding me at gunpoint. He'd brought both guns to plant in my room. We struggled, and the gun that killed my father was on the floor near the doorway. You picked it up and shot him before he shot me.'

'Sophia.'

'That's what happened. Isn't it, Mama?'

'Yes. That's exactly what happened. You saved my child.'

'I can't.'

'Yes, you can. You want to make it up to me?' Pilar demanded. 'Then you'll do this. I don't care about what happened one night almost thirty years ago, but I care about what happened tonight. If you love me, you'll do exactly what Sophie's asking you to do. Tony was her father. Who has more right to decide than she?'

'Jerry's dead,' Sophia said. 'He killed, threatened, destroyed, all be-cause of one selfish act by my father. And it ends here. I'm going to call the police. Someone should take a look at Rene.' She leaned forward, brushed her lips over Helen's cheek. 'Thank you. For the rest of my life.'

Late, late into the night, Sophia sat in the kitchen sipping tea laced with brandy. She'd given her statement, had sat, her hand holding Helen's, as Helen had given hers.

Justice, she thought, didn't always come as you expected. Helen had said that. And here it was, unexpected justice. It hadn't hurt that Rene had been hysterical, had babbled to Claremont and Maguire that Jerry was a madman, a murderer, and had forced her at gunpoint to come with him.

Life was a messy business.

Now, at last, the police were gone; the house was quiet. She looked up as her mother and grandmother came in. 'Aunt Helen?'

'She's finally sleeping.' Pilar went to the cupboard, got two more cups. 'We've talked. She'll be all right. She's going to resign her judgeship. I suppose she needs to.' Pilar set the cups on the table, poured the tea. 'I've told Mama everything, Sophia. I felt she had a right to know.'

'Nonna.' Sophia reached for Tereza's hand. 'Did I do the right thing?'

'You did the loving thing. That often matters more. It was brave of both of you. It makes me proud.' She sat down, sighed. 'Helen took a life, and gave one back. That closes the circle. We won't speak of it again. Tomorrow my daughter's getting married, and we'll have joy in this house once more. Soon, the harvest—the bounty. And another sea-son ends. The next is yours and Tyler's. Eli and I are retiring the first of the year.'

'Nonna.'

'Torches are meant to be passed. Take what I give you.'

The faint irritation in her grandmother's voice made her smile. 'I will. Thank you, Nonna.'

'Now it's late. The bride needs her sleep, and so do I.' She got to her feet, leaving her tea untouched.

Tyler had set up lights at the winery, and the old building hulked under them. She could see the sparkle of broken glass from the windows, the smears from smoke, the chars from flame. But still, it stood.

Perhaps he sensed her. She liked to think so. He stepped out of the broken doorway as she ran up. And he caught her, held her close and tight.

'There you are, Sophia. I figured you needed a little time.' He pressed his face to her hair. 'When I think—'

'Don't think,' she said, and turned her mouth to his. 'Everything's as it should be. Everything, Ty. We'll rebuild the winery, rebuild our lives. And make them ours. Giambelli-MacMillan is going to come back, bigger and better than ever. That's what I want.'

'That's handy, because that's what I want, too. Let's go home, Sophie.'

She tucked her hand in his and walked away from the damage and the scars. The first hints of dawn lightened the sky in the east. When the sun broke through, she thought, it was going to be a beautiful beginning.

NORA ROBERTS

Perhaps because of her Irish roots, storytelling has always come naturally to Nora Roberts, but the telling didn't turn to writing until she was an adult. She recalls a week in February 1979 when her home in Western Maryland, USA, was hit by a blizzard and it all began. 'I was stuck at home with a two-year-old and a five-year-old,' she explains. 'I had no four-wheel-drive transportation, there was not enough chocolate in the house, and every morning the radio told me kindergarten was cancelled.' In order to keep herself sane, she dragged out a notebook and a pencil and began to write one of the stories stirring in her mind. 'I've always loved to read, and I've always had story ideas running around in my head. But writing as a career never occurred to me until that long week in February.' The result, *Melodies of Love*, was the first of a mind-boggling 140-plus novels which have turned Nora Roberts into a publishing phenomenon around the world. When she was once asked if she ever doubted that she would be successful, the author answered, 'No. I felt successful when I finished my first book, and successful when I sold my first book. Every level has its own joy. It takes tenacity to publish, and drive to write. You just have to keep going, and to remember the pleasure it gives you to tell a story.'

Although her writing has made her a very wealthy woman, Nora Roberts still lives in the same house in Maryland where her career started. But some of her habits have changed—such as the degree to which she can now indulge her passion for shopping. 'I like to shop for anything. I like clothes. I like jewellery. I love shoes—shoes are one of the great things that separate us from the animals. They don't wear shoes or accessorise!'

Nora Roberts loves to communicate personally with her readers through her website *www.noraroberts.com*. After the terrible events of September 11, 2001, the author posted a most poignant letter to her readers on her website about the power of and the need for novels. 'The world is not always what we would wish it to be,' she writes. 'For myself, books are a kind of salvation, a celebration of the human spirit . . . they helped get me through those tumultuous days, taking me into a world where the lines are defined and the good guys win. I need happy endings. To write them and to read them. Within that bubble of fiction, we're assured that good will overcome evil and that love matters most. It's a comfort.'

Jane Eastgate

601-014-1